THE
YEARS
OF
RICE
AND
SALT

BOOKS BY KIM STANLEY ROBINSON

FICTION

The Mars Trilogy
Red Mars
Green Mars
Blue Mars

The California Trilogy
The Wild Shore
The Gold Coast
Pacific Edge

Escape from Kathmandu
A Short Sharp Shock
Green Mars (novella)
The Blind Geometer
The Memory of Whiteness
Icehenge
The Planet on the Table
Remaking History
Antarctica
The Martians

NONFICTION

The Novels of Philip K. Dick

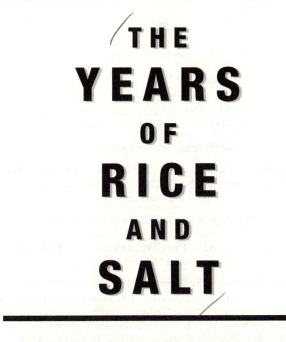

THE
YEARS
OF
RICE
AND
SALT

KIM STANLEY ROBINSON

BANTAM BOOKS

THE YEARS OF RICE AND SALT

A Bantam Book / March 2002

Book design by Virginia Norey

The Sanskrit poems on pages 89 and 646 are adapted from
Sanskrit Love Poetry, translated by W.S. Merwin and
J.M. Masson.

The indented paragraphs on pages 546 and 547 are adapted
from essays by the Mauritanian Zainaba and by the Egyptian
Amina Said, reprinted in *Opening the Gates,* edited by Margot
Badran and Miriam Cooke.

Library of Congress Cataloging-in-Publication Data

Robinson, Kim Stanley.
The years of rice and salt / Kim Stanley Robinson.
p.   cm.
ISBN 0-553-10920-0 (alk. paper)
1. Black death—Fiction.   I. Title.

PS3568.O2893 Y43 2002
813'.54—dc21
2001043492

Published simultaneously in the United States and Canada

PRINTED IN THE UNITED STATES OF AMERICA

BVG   10 9 8 7 6 5 4 3 2

CONTENTS

TRIPITAKA: Monkey, how far is it to the Western Heaven, the abode of Buddha?

WU-KONG: You can walk from the time of your youth till the time you grow old, and after that, till you become young again; and even after going through such a cycle a thousand times, you may still find it difficult to reach the place where you want to go. But when you perceive, by the resoluteness of your will, the Buddha-nature in all things, and when every one of your thoughts goes back to that fountain in your memory, that will be the time you arrive at Spirit Mountain.

—THE JOURNEY TO THE WEST

Chronology

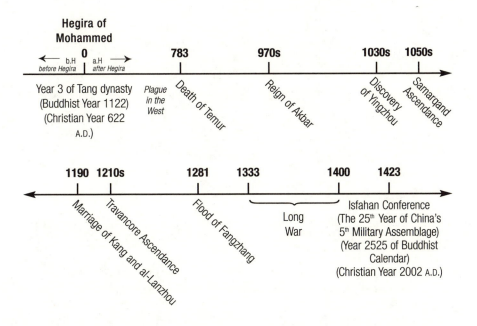

Hegira of
Mohammed

0

b.H a.H
before Hegira after Hegira

783

970s

1030s   **1050s**

Year 3 of Tang dynasty
(Buddhist Year 1122)
(Christian Year 622
A.D.)

Plague
in the
West

Death of Temur

Reign of Akbar

Discovery
of Yingzhou

Samarqand
Ascendance

1190 **1210s**

1281 **1333**

1400 **1423**

Marriage of Kang and al-Lanzhou

Travancore Ascendance

Flood of Fangzhang

Long
War

Isfahan Conference
(The 25th Year of China's
5th Military Assemblage)
(Year 2525 of Buddhist
Calendar)
(Christian Year 2002 A.D.)

NOTE: *Islamic and Chinese calendars are lunar. Christian and Buddhist calendars are solar.*

BOOK 1

◈ A W A K E   T O   E M P T I N E S S ◈

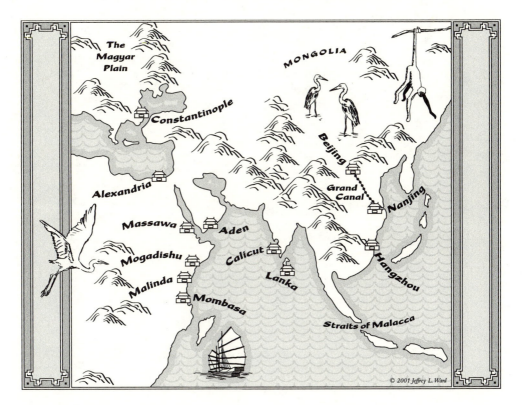

© 2001 Jeffrey L. Ward

1

Another journey west, Bold and Psin find an empty land;
Temur is displeased, and the chapter has a stormy end.

Monkey never dies. He keeps coming back to help us in times of trouble, just as he helped Tripitaka through the dangers of the first journey to the west, to bring Buddhism back from India to China.

Now he had taken on the form of a small Mongol named Bold Bardash, horseman in the army of Temur the Lame. Son of a Tibetan salt trader and a Mongol innkeeper and spirit woman, and thus a traveler from before the day of his birth, up and down and back and forth, over mountains and rivers, across deserts and steppes, crisscrossing always the heartland of the world. At the time of our story he was already old: square face, bent nose, gray plaited hair, four chin whiskers for a beard. He knew this would be Temur's last campaign, and wondered if it would be his too.

One day scouting ahead of the army, a small group of them rode out of dark hills at dusk. Bold was getting skittish at the quiet. Of course it was not truly quiet, forests were always noisy compared to the steppe; there was a big river ahead, spilling its sounds through the wind in the trees; but something was missing. Birdsong perhaps, or some other sound Bold could not quite identify. The horses snickered as the men kneed them on. It did not help that the weather was changing, long mare's tails wisping orange in the highest part of the sky, wind gusting up, air damp—a storm rolling in from the west. Under the big sky of the steppe it would have been obvious. Here in the forested hills there was less sky to be seen, and the winds were fluky, but the signs were still there.

They ride by fields that lay rank with unharvested crops.
Barley fallen over itself,
Apple trees with apples dry in the branches,
Or black on the ground.
No cart tracks or hoofprints or footprints
In the dust of the road. Sun sets,
The gibbous moon misshapen overhead.
Owl dips over field. A sudden gust:
How big the world seems in a wind.
Horses are tense, Monkey too.

They came to an empty bridge and crossed it, hooves thwocking the planks. Now they came on some wooden buildings with thatched roofs. But no fires, no lantern light. They moved on. More buildings appeared through the trees, but still no people. The dark land was empty.

Psin urged them on, and more buildings stood on each side of the widening road. They followed a turn out of the hills onto a plain, and before them lay a black silent city. No lights, no voices; only the wind, rubbing branches together over sheeting surfaces of the big black flowing river. The city was empty.

Of course we are reborn many times. We fill our bodies like air in bubbles, and when the bubbles pop we puff away into the bardo, wandering until we are blown into some new life, somewhere back in the world. This knowledge had often been a comfort to Bold as he stumbled exhausted over battlefields in the aftermath, the ground littered with broken bodies like empty coats.

But it was different to come on a town where there had been no battle, and find everyone there already dead. Long dead; bodies dried; in the dusk and moonlight they could see the gleam of exposed bones, scattered by wolves and crows. Bold repeated the Heart Sutra to himself. "Form is emptiness, emptiness form. Gone, gone, gone beyond, gone altogether beyond. O, what an Awakening! All hail!"

The horses stalled on the outskirts of the town. Aside from the cluck and hiss of the river, all was still. The squinted eye of the moon gleamed on dressed stone, there in the middle of all the wooden buildings. A very big stone building, among smaller stone buildings.

Psin ordered them to put clothes over their faces, to avoid touching anything, to stay on their horses, and to keep the horses from touching anything but the ground with their hooves. Slowly they rode through narrow streets, walled by wooden buildings two or three stories high, leaning together as in Chinese cities. The horses were unhappy but did not refuse outright.

They came into a paved central square near the river, and stopped before the great stone building. It was huge. Many of the local people had come to it to die. Their lamasery, no doubt, but roofless, open to the sky—unfinished business. As if these people had only come to religion in their last days; but too late; the place was a boneyard. Gone, gone, gone beyond, gone altogether beyond. Nothing moved, and it occurred to Bold that the pass in the mountains they had ridden through had perhaps been the wrong one, the one to that other west which is the land of the dead. For an instant he remembered something, a brief glimpse of another life—a town much smaller than this one, a village wiped out by some great rush over their heads, sending them all to the bardo together. Hours in a room, waiting for death; this was why he so often felt he recognized the people he met. Their existences were a shared fate.

"Plague," Psin said. "Let's get out of here."

His eyes glinted as he looked at Bold, his face was hard; he looked like one of the stone officers in the imperial tombs.

Bold shuddered. "I wonder why they didn't leave," he said.

"Maybe there was nowhere to go."

Plague had struck in India a few years before. Mongols rarely caught it, only a baby now and then. Turks and Indians were more susceptible, and of course Temur had all kinds in his army, Persians, Turks, Mongols, Tibetans, Indians, Tajiks, Arabs, Georgians. Plague could kill them, any of them, or all of them. If that was truly what had felled these people. There was no way to be sure.

"Let's get back and tell them," Psin said.

The others nodded, pleased that it was Psin's decision. Temur had told them to scout the Magyar plain and what lay beyond, west for four days' ride. He didn't like it when scouting detachments returned without fulfilling orders, even if they were composed of his oldest qa'uchin. But Psin could face him.

Back through moonlight they rode, camping briefly when the horses got tired. On again at dawn, back through the broad gap in the mountains the earlier scouts had called the Moravian Gate. No smoke from any village or hut they passed. They kicked the horses to their fastest long trot, rode hard all that day.

As they came down the long eastern slope of the range back onto the steppe, an enormous wall of cloud reared up in the western half of the sky.

> Like Kali's black blanket pulling over them,
> The Goddess of Death chasing them out of her land.
> Solid black underside fluted and rippled,
> Black pigs' tails and fishhooks swirling into the air below.
> A portent so bleak the horses bow their heads,
> The men can no longer look at each other.

They approached Temur's great encampment, and the black storm-cloud covered the rest of the day, causing a darkness like night. Hair rose on the back of Bold's neck. A few big raindrops splashed down, and thunder rolled out of the west like giant iron cartwheels overhead. They hunkered down in their saddles and kicked the horses on, reluctant to return in such a storm, with such news. Temur would take it as a portent, just as they did. Temur often said that he owed all his success to an asura that visited him and gave him guidance. Bold had witnessed one of these visitations, had seen Temur engage in conversation with an invisible being, and afterward tell people what they were thinking and what would happen to them. A cloud this black could only be a sign. Evil in the west. Something bad had happened back there, something worse even than plague, maybe, and Temur's plan to conquer the Magyars and the Franks would have to be abandoned; he had been beaten to it by the goddess of skulls herself. It was hard to imagine him accepting any such preemption, but there they were, under a storm like none of them had ever seen, and all the Magyars were dead.

Smoke rose from the vast camp's cooking fires, looking like a great sacrifice, the smell familiar and yet distant, as if from a home they had already left forever. Psin looked at the men around him. "Camp here," he ordered. He thought things over. "Bold."

Bold felt the fear shoot through him.

"Come on."

Bold swallowed and nodded. He was not courageous, but he had the stoic manner of the qa'uchin, Temur's oldest warriors. Psin also would know that Bold was aware they had entered a different realm, that everything that happened from this point onward was freakish, something preordained and being lived through inexorably, a karma they could not escape.

Psin also was no doubt remembering a certain incident from their youth, when the two of them had been captured by a tribe of taiga hunters north of the Kama River. Together they had staged a very successful escape, knifing the hunters' headman and running through a bonfire into the night.

The two men rode by the outer sentries and through the camp to the khan's tent. To the west and north lightning bolts crazed the black air. Neither man had seen such a storm in all their lives. The few little hairs on Bold's forearms stood up like pig bristles, and he felt the air crackling with hungry ghosts, pretas crowding in to witness Temur emerge from his tent. He had killed so many.

The two men dismounted and stood there. Guards came out of the tent, drawing aside the flaps of the doorway and standing at attention, ready with drawn bows. Bold's throat was too dry to swallow, and it seemed to him a blue light glowed from within the great yurt of the khan.

Temur appeared high in the air, seated on a litter his carriers had already hefted on their shoulders. He was pale-faced and sweating, the whites of his eyes visible all the way around. He stared down at Psin.

"Why are you back?"

"Khan, a plague has struck the Magyars. They're all dead."

Temur regarded his unloved general. "Why are you back?"

"To tell you, Khan."

Psin's voice was steady, and he met Temur's fierce gaze without fear. But Temur was not pleased. Bold swallowed; nothing here was the same as that time he and Psin had escaped the hunters, there wasn't a single feature of that effort that could be repeated. Only the idea that they could do it remained.

Something inside Temur snapped, Bold saw it—his asura was speaking through him now, and it looked like it was wreaking great harm in him as it did. Not an asura, perhaps, but his nafs, the spirit animal that lived inside him. He rasped, "They cannot get away as easily as that! They will suffer for this, no matter how they try to escape." He waved an arm weakly. "Go back to your detachment."

Then to his guards he said in a calmer voice, "Take these two back and kill them and their men, and their horses. Make a bonfire and burn everything. Then move our camp two days' ride east."

He raised up his hand.

The world burst asunder.

A bolt of lightning had exploded among them. Bold sat deaf on the ground. Looking around stunned, he saw that all the others there had been flattened as well, that the khan's tent was burning, Temur's litter tipped over, his carriers scrambling, the khan himself on one knee, clutching his chest. Some of his men rushed to him. Again lightning blasted down among them.

Blindly Bold picked himself up and fled. He looked over his shoulder through pulsing green afterimages, and saw Temur's black nafs fly out of his mouth into the night. Temur-i-Lang, Iron the Lame, abandoned by asura and nafs both. The emptied body collapsed to the ground, and rain bucketed onto it. Bold ran into the dark to the west. We do not know which way Psin went, or what happened to him; but as for Bold, you can find out in the next chapter.

2

Through the realm of hungry ghosts
A monkey wanders, lonely as a cloud.

Bold ran or walked west all that night, scrambling through the growing forest in the pouring rain, climbing into the steepest hills he could find, to evade any horsemen who might follow. No one would be too zealous in pursuit of a potential plague carrier, but he could be shot down from a good distance away, and he wanted to disappear from their world as if he had never existed. If it had not been for the uncanny storm he would certainly be dead, already embarked on another existence: now he was anyway. Gone, gone, gone beyond, gone altogether beyond . . .

He walked the next day and all the second night. Dawn of the second day found him hurrying back through the Moravian Gate, feeling that no one would dare follow him there. Once onto the Magyar plain he headed south, into trees. In the morning's wet light he found a fallen tree and slipped deep under its exposed roots, to sleep for the rest of the day in hidden dryness.

That night the rain stopped, and on the third morning he emerged ravenous. In short order he found, pulled, and ate meadow onions, then hunted for more substantial food. It was possible that dried meat still hung in the empty villages' storehouses, or grain in their granaries. He might also be able to find a bow and some arrows. He didn't want to go near the dead settlements, but it seemed the best way to find food, and that took precedence over everything else.

That night he slept poorly, his stomach full and gassy with onions. At dawn he made his way south, following the big river. All the villages and settlements were empty. Any people he saw were dead on the ground. It was disturbing, but there was nothing to be done. He too was in some kind of posthumous existence, a very hungry ghost indeed. Living on from one found bite to the next, with no name or fellows, he began to close in on himself, as during the hardest campaigns on the steppes, becoming more and more an animal, his mind shrinking in like the horns of a touched snail. For many watches at a time he thought little but the Heart Sutra. Form is emptiness, emptiness form. Not for nothing had he been named Sun Wu-kong, Awake to Emptiness, in an earlier incarnation. Monkey in the void.

He came to a village that looked untouched, skirted its edge. In an empty stable he found an unstrung bow and a quiver of arrows, all very primitive and poorly made. Something moved in the pasturage outside, and he went out and whistled up a small black mare. He caught her with onions, and quickly taught her to take him on her back.

He rode her across a stone bridge over the big river, and slowly crossed the grain of the land southward, up and down, up and down. All the villages continued empty, their food rotted or scavenged by animals, but now he had the mare's milk and blood to sustain him, so the matter was not so urgent.

It was autumn here, and he began to live like the bears, eating berries and honey, and rabbits shot with the ridiculous bow. Possibly it had been concocted by a child; he couldn't believe anyone older would make such a thing. It was a single bend of wood, probably ash, partly carved but still misshapen; no arrowrest, no nocking point, its pull like that of a prayer-flag line. His old bow had been a laminate of horn, maplewood, and tendon glue covered by blue leather, with a sweet pull and release, and enough power to pierce body armor from over a li away. Gone now, gone altogether beyond, lost with all the rest of his few possessions, and when he shot these twig arrows with this branch bow and missed, he would shake his head and wonder if it was even worth tracking the arrow down. It was no wonder these people had died.

In one small village, five buildings clustered above a stream ford, the headman's house proved to have a locked larder, still stocked with dried fishcakes that were spiced with something Bold did not recognize, which made his stomach queasy. But with the strange food in him he felt his spirits rise. In a stable he found sidebags for the mare, and stuffed them with more dried food. He rode on, paying more attention than he had been to the land he was passing through.

> White-barked trees hold up black branches,
> Pine and cypress still verdant on the ridge.
> A red bird and a blue bird sit near each other
> In the same tree. Now anything is possible.

Anything but return to his previous life. Not that he harbored any resentment of Temur; Bold would have done the same in his place. Plague was plague, and could not be treated lightly. And this plague was obviously worse than most, having killed everyone in the region. Among the Mongols plague usually killed a few babies, maybe made some adults sick. You killed rats or mice on sight, and if babies got feverish and developed the bumps, their mothers took them out to live or die by the rivers. Indian cities were said to have a worse time with it, with people dying in great crowds. But never anything like this. It was possible something else had killed them.

> Traveling through empty land.
> Clouds hazy, moon waning and chill.
> Sky, frost-colored, cold to look at.
> Wind piercing. Sudden terror.
> A thousand trees roar in the sparse woodland:
> A lonely monkey cries on a barren hill.

But the terror washed through him and then away, like freshets of rain, leaving a mind as empty as the land itself. It was very still. Gone, gone, altogether gone.

For a time he thought he would ride through and out of the region of plague, and find people again. But then he came over a jagged range of black hills, and saw a big town spread below, bigger than any he had ever seen, its rooftops covering a whole valley bottom. But deserted. No smoke, no noise, no movement. In the center of the city another giant stone temple stood open to the sky. Seeing it the terror poured into him again, and he rode into the forest to escape the sight of so many people gone like the autumn leaves.

He knew roughly where he was, of course. South of here, he would eventually come into the Ottoman Turks' holdings in the Balkans. He would be able to speak with them; he would be back in the world, but out of Temur's empire. Something then would start up for him, some way to live.

So he rode south. But still only skeletons occupied the villages. He grew hungrier and hungrier. He drove the mare harder, while drinking more of her blood.

Then one night in the dark of the moon, all of a sudden there were howls and wolves were on them in a snarling rush. Bold just had time to cut the mare's tether and scramble into a tree. Most of the wolves chased the mare, but some sat panting under the tree. Bold got as comfortable as he could and prepared to wait them out. When rain came they slunk away. In the dawn he woke for the tenth time, climbed down. He took off downstream and came on the body of the mare, all skin and gristle and scattered bones. The sidebags were nowhere to be found.

He continued on foot.

One day, too weak to walk, he lay in wait by a stream, and shot a deer with one of the sorry little arrows, and made a fire and ate well, bolting down chunks of cooked haunch. He slept away from the carcass, hoping to return to it. Wolves couldn't climb trees, but bears could. He saw a fox, and as the vixen had been his wife's nafs, long ago, he felt better. In the morning the sun warmed him. The deer had been removed by a bear, it appeared, but he felt stronger with all that fresh meat in him, and pressed on.

He walked south for several days, keeping on ridges when he could, over hills both depopulated and deforested, the ground underfoot sluiced to stone and baked white by the glare of the sun. He watched for the vixen in the valleys at dawn, and drank from springs, and raided dead villages for scraps of food. These grew harder and harder to find, and for a while he was reduced to chewing the leather strap from a harness, an old Mongol trick from the hard campaigns on the steppes. But it seemed to him it had worked better back there, on the endless grass so much easier to cross than these baked tortured white hills.

At the end of one day, after he had long gotten used to living alone in the world, scavenging it like Monkey himself, he came into a little copse of trees to make a fire, and was shocked to see one already there, tended by a living man.

The man was short, like Bold. His hair was as red as maple leaves, his bushy beard the same color, his skin pale and brindled like a dog. At first Bold was sure the man was sick, and he kept his distance. But the man's eyes, blue in color, were clear; and he too was afraid, absolutely on point and ready for anything. Silently they stared at each other, across a small clearing in the middle of the copse.

The man gestured at his fire. Bold nodded and came warily into the glade.

The man was cooking two fish. Bold took a rabbit that he had killed that morning out of his coat, and skinned and cleaned it with his knife. The man watched him hungrily, nodding at each familiar move. He turned his fish on the fire, and made room in the coals for the rabbit. Bold spitted it on a stick and put it in.

After the meat had cooked they ate in silence, sitting on logs on opposite sides of the fire. They both stared into the flames, glancing only occasionally at each other, shy after all their time alone. After all that it was not obvious what one could say to another human.

Finally the man spoke, first brokenly, then at length. Sometimes he used a word that sounded familiar to Bold, but not so familiar as his movements around the fire, and no matter how hard he tried, Bold could make nothing of what the man said.

Bold tried out some simple phrases himself, feeling the strangeness of words in his mouth, like pebbles. The other man listened closely, his blue eyes gleaming in firelight, out of the dirty pale skin of his lean face, but he showed no sign of comprehension, not of Mongolian, Tibetan, Chinese, Turkic, Arabic, Chagatai, or any other of the polyglot greetings Bold had learned through the years crossing the steppe.

At the end of Bold's recitation the man's face spasmed, and he wept. Then, wiping his eyes clear, leaving big streaks on his dirty face, he stood before Bold and said something, gesturing widely. He pointed his finger at Bold, as if angry, then stepped back and sat on his log, and began to imitate rowing a boat, or so Bold surmised. He rowed facing backward, like the fishermen on the Caspian Sea. He made the motions for fishing, then for catching fish, cleaning them, cooking them, and feeding them to little childen. By his gestures he evoked all the people he had fed, his children, his wife, the people he lived with.

Then he turned his face up at the firelit branches over the two men, and cried again. He pulled up the rough shift covering his body, and pointed at his arms—at his underarms, where he made a fist. Bold nodded, felt his stomach shrink as the man mimed the sickness and death of all the children, by lying down on the ground and mewling like a dog. Then the wife, then all the rest. All had died but this man, who walked around the fire pointing at the leaf litter on the ground intoning words, names perhaps. It was all so clear to Bold.

Then the man burned his dead village, all in gestures so clear, and mimed rowing away. He rowed on his log for a long time, so long Bold thought he had forgotten the story; but then he ground to a halt and fell back in his boat. He got out, looking around in feigned surprise. Then he began to walk. He walked around the fire a dozen times, pretend-eating grass and sticks, howling like a wolf, cowering under his log, walking some more, even rowing again. Over and over he said the same things, "Dea, dea, dea, dea," shouting it at the branch-crossed stars quaking over them.

Bold nodded. He knew the story. The man was moaning, with a low growl like an animal, cutting at the ground with a stick. His eyes were as red as any wolf's in the light. Bold ate more of the rabbit, then offered the stick to the man, who snatched it and ate hungrily. They sat there and looked at the fire. Bold felt both companionable and alone. He eyed the other man, who had eaten both his fish, and was now nodding off. The man jerked up, muttered something, lay curled around the fire, fell asleep. Uneasily Bold stoked the fire, took the other side of it, and tried to do the same. When he woke the fire had died and the man was gone. It was a cold dawn, dew-drenched, and the trail of the man led down the meadow to a big bend in a stream, where it disappeared. There was no sign of where the man had gone from there.

Days passed, and Bold continued south. Many watches went by in which he didn't think a thing, only scanning the land for food and the sky for weather, humming a word or two over and over. Awake to emptiness. One day he came on a village surrounding a spring.

Old temples scattered throughout,
Broken round columns pointing at the sky.
All in the midst of a vast silence.
What made these gods so angry
With their people? What might they make
Of a solitary soul wandering by
After the world has ended?
White marble drums fallen this way and that:
One bird cheeps in the empty air.

He did not care to test anything by trespassing, and so circled the temples, chanting "Om mane padme hum, om mane padme hum, hummm," aware suddenly that he often spoke aloud to himself now, or hummed, without ever noticing it, as if ignoring an old companion who always said the same things.

He continued south and east, though he had forgotten why. He scrounged roadside buildings for dried food. He walked on the empty roads. It was an old land. Gnarled olive trees, black and heavy with their inedible fruit, mocked him. No person ate entirely by his own efforts, no one. He got hungrier, and food became his only focus, every day. He passed more marble ruins, foraged in the farmhouses he passed. Once he came on a big clay jar of olive oil, and stayed there four days to drink it all down. Then game became more abundant. He saw the vixen more than once. Good shots with his ridiculous bow kept him away from hunger. He made his fires larger every night, and once or twice wondered what had become of the man he had met. Had meeting Bold made him realize he would be alone no matter what happened or whom he found, so that he had killed himself to rejoin his jati? Or perhaps just slipped while drinking? Or hiked in the stream to keep Bold from tracking him? There was no way of telling, but the encounter kept coming back to Bold, especially the clarity with which he had been able to understand the man.

The valleys ran south and east. He felt the shape of his travels in his mind, and found he could not remember enough of the last few weeks to be sure of his location, relative to the Moravian Gate, or the khanate of the Golden Horde. From the Black Sea they had ridden west about ten days' ride, hadn't they? It was like trying to remember things from a previous life.

It seemed possible, however, that he was nearing the Byzantine empire, coming toward Constantinople from the north and west. Sitting slumped before his nightly bonfire, he wondered if Constantinople would be dead too. He wondered if Mongolia was dead, if perhaps everyone in the world was dead. The wind soughed through the shrubs like ghost's voices, and he fell into an uneasy sleep, waking through the watches of the night to check the stars and throw more branches on his fire. He was cold.

He woke again, and there was Temur's ghost standing across the fire, the light of the flames dancing over his awesome face. His eyes were black as obsidian, and Bold could see stars gleaming in them.

"So," Temur said heavily, "you ran away."

"Yes," Bold whispered.

"What's wrong? Don't want to go out on the hunt again?"

This was a thing he had said to Bold before. At the end he had been so weak he had had to be carried on a litter, but he never thought of stopping. In his last winter he had considered whether to move east in the spring, against China, or west, against the Franks. During a huge feast he weighed the advantages of each, and at one point he looked at Bold, and something on Bold's face caused the khan to jump him with his powerful voice, still strong despite his illness: "What's wrong, Bold? Don't want to go out on the hunt again?"

That earlier time Bold had said, "Always, great khan. I was there when we conquered Ferghana, Khorasan, Sistan, Khrezm, and Moghulistan. One more is fine by me."

Temur had laughed his angry laugh. "But which way this time, Bold? Which way?"

Bold knew enough to shrug. "All the same to me, great khan. Why don't you flip a coin?"

Which got him another laugh, and a warm place in the stable that winter, and a good horse in the campaign. They had moved west in the spring of the year 784.

Now Temur's ghost, as solid as any man, glared reproachfully at Bold from across the fire. "I flipped the coin just like you said, Bold. But it must have come up wrong."

"Maybe China would have been worse," Bold said.

Temur laughed angrily. "How could it have been? Killed by lightning? How could it have been? You did that, Bold, you and Psin. You brought the curse of the west back with you. You never should have come back. And I should have gone to China."

"Maybe so." Bold didn't know how to deal with him. Angry ghosts needed to be defied as often as they needed to be placated. But those jet-black eyes, sparkling with starlight—

Suddenly Temur coughed. He put a hand to his mouth, and gagged out something red. He looked at it, then held it out for Bold to see: a red egg. "This is yours," he said, and tossed it over the flames at Bold.

Bold twisted to catch it, and woke up. He moaned. The ghost of Temur clearly was not happy. Wandering between worlds, visiting his old soldiers like any other preta . . . in a way it was pathetic, but Bold could not shake the fear in him. Temur's spirit was a big power, no matter what realm it was in. His hand could reach into this world and grab Bold's foot at any time.

All that day Bold wandered south in a haze of memories, scarcely seeing the land before him. The last time Temur visited him in the stables had been difficult, as the khan could no longer ride. He had looked at one thick black mare as if at a woman, and smoothed its flank and said to Bold, "The first horse I ever stole looked just like this one. I started poor and life was hard. God put a sign on me. But you would think He would have let me ride to the end." And he had stared at Bold with that vivid gaze of his, one eye slightly higher and larger than the other, just like in the dream. Although in life his eyes had been brown.

Hunger kept Bold hunting. Temur, though a hungry ghost, no longer had to worry about food; but Bold did. All the game ran south, down the valleys. One day, high on a ridge, he saw water, bronze in the distance. A large lake, or sea. Old roads led him over another pass, down into another city.

Again, no one there was alive. All was motionless and silent. Bold wandered down empty streets, between empty buildings, feeling the cold hands of pretas running down his back.

On the central hill of the city stood a copse of white temples, like bones bleaching in the sun. Seeing them, Bold decided that he had found the capital of this dead land. He had walked from peripheral towns of rude stone to capital temples of smooth white marble, and still no one had survived. A white haze filled his vision, and through it he stumbled up the dusty streets, up onto the temple hill, to lay his case before the local gods.

On the sacred plateau three smaller temples flanked a large one, a rectangular beauty with double rows of smooth columns on all four sides, supporting a gleaming roof of marble tiles. Under the eaves carved figures fought, marched, flew, and gestured, in a great stone tableau depicting the absent people, or their gods. Bold sat on a marble drum from a long-toppled column and stared up at the carving in stone, seeing the world that had been lost.

Finally he approached the temple, entered it praying aloud. Unlike the big stone temples in the north, it had been no place of congregation in the end; there were no skeletons inside. Indeed it looked as if it had been abandoned for many years. Bats hung in the rafters, and the darkness was lanced by sunbeams leaking through broken rooftiles. At the far end of the temple it looked as though an altar had been hastily erected. On it a single candlewick burned in a pot of oil. Their last prayer, flickering even after they had died.

Bold had nothing to offer by way of sacrifice, and the great white temple stood silent above him. "Gone, gone, gone beyond, gone altogether beyond! O what an awakening! All hail!" His words echoed hollowly.

He stumbled back outside into the afternoon glare, and saw to the south the blink of the sea. He would go there. There was nothing here to keep him; the people and their gods too had died.

A long bay cut in between hills. A harbor at the head of the bay was empty, except for a few small rowboats slapping against the waves, or upturned on the shingle beach stretching away from the docks. He did not risk the boats, he knew nothing about them. He had seen Issyk Kul and Lake Qinghai, and the Aral, Caspian, and Black seas, but he had never been in a boat in his life, except for ferries crossing rivers. He did not want to start now.

> No traveler seen on this long road,
> No boats from afar return for the night.
> Nothing moves in this dead harbor.

On the beach he scooped a handful of water to drink—spat it out—it was salty, like the Black Sea, or the springs in the Tarim basin. It was strange to see so much wastewater. He had heard there was an ocean surrounding the world. Perhaps he was at the edge of the world, the western edge, or the southern. Possibly the Arabs lived south of this sea. He didn't know; and for the first time in all his wandering, he had the feeling that he had no idea where he was.

He was asleep on the warm sand of a beach, dreaming of the steppes, trying to keep Temur out of the dream by force of will alone, when he was rousted by strong hands, rolling him over and tying his legs together and his arms behind his back. He was hauled to his feet.

A man said "What have we here?" or something to that effect. He spoke something like Turkic, Bold didn't know many of the words, but it was some kind of Turkic, and he could usually catch the drift of what they were saying. They looked like soldiers or perhaps brigands, big hard-handed ruffians, wearing gold earrings and dirty cotton clothes. He wept while grinning foolishly at the sight of them; he felt his face stretch and his eyes burn. They regarded him warily.

"A madman," one ventured.

Bold shook his head at this. "I—I haven't seen anyone," he said in Ulu Turkic. His tongue was big in his mouth, for despite all his babbling to himself and the gods, he had forgotten how to talk to people. "I thought everyone was dead."

He gestured to the north and west.

They did not seem to understand him.

"Kill him," one said, as dismissive as Temur.

"The Christians all died," another said.

"Kill him, let's go. Boats are full."

"Bring him," the other said. "The slavers will pay for him. He won't bring down the boat, thin as he is."

Something like that. They hauled him behind them down the beach. He had to hurry so the rope wouldn't pull him around backward, and the effort made him dizzy. He didn't have much strength. The men smelled of garlic and that made him ravenous, though it was a foul smell. But if they meant to sell him to slavers, they would have to feed him. His mouth was watering so heavily that he slobbered like a dog, and he was weeping as well, nose running, and with his hands tied behind his back he couldn't wipe his face.

"He's foaming at the mouth like a horse."

"He's sick."

"He's not sick. Bring him. Come on," this to Bold, "don't be scared. Where we take you even the slaves live a better life than you barbarian dogs."

Then he was shoved over the side of a beached boat, and with great jerks it was pulled off into the water, where it rocked violently. Immediately he fell sideways into the wooden wall of the thing.

"Up here, slave. On that pile of rope. Sit!"

He sat and watched them work. Whatever happened, it was better than the empty land. Just to see men move, to hear them talk, filled him. It was like watching horses run on the steppe. Hungrily he watched them haul a sail into the air on a mast, and the boat heeled to the side such that he threw himself the other way. They roared with laughter at this. He grinned sheepishly, gesturing at the big lateen.

"It takes more wind than this breath to tip us."

"Allah protect us from it."

"Allah protect us."

Muslims. "Allah protect us," Bold said politely. Then, in Arabic, "In the name of God, the merciful, the compassionate." In his years in Temur's army he had learned to be as much a Muslim as anyone. The Buddha did not mind what you said to be polite. Now it would not keep him from slavery, but it would perhaps earn him a little more food. The men regarded him curiously. He watched the land slide by. They untied his arms and gave him some dried mutton and bread. He tried to chew each bite a hundred times. The familiar tastes called back to him his whole life. He ate what they gave him, drank fresh water from a cup they gave him.

"Praise be to Allah. Thank you in the name of God the compassionate, the merciful."

They sailed down a long bay, into a larger sea. At night they pulled behind headlands and anchored the boat and slept. Bold curled under a coil of rope. Every time he woke in the night he had to remind himself where he was.

In the mornings they sailed south and south again, and one day they passed through a long narrows into an open sea, with big waves. The rocking of the boat was like riding a camel. Bold gestured west. The men named it, but Bold didn't catch the name. "They're all dead," the men said.

The sunset came and they were still on the open sea. For the first time they sailed all night long, always awake when Bold woke, watching the stars without talking to each other. For three days they sailed out of the sight of any land, and Bold wondered how long it would go on. But on the fourth morning the sky to the south grew white, then brown.

> A haze like the one that blew out of the Gobi.
> Sand in the air, sand and fine dust. Land ho!
> Very low land. The sea and sky
> Both turn the same brown
> Before catching sight of a stone tower,
> Then a great stone breakwater, fronting a harbor.

One of the sailors happily named it: "Alexandria!" Bold had heard the name, though he knew nothing about it. Neither do we; but to find out more, you can read the next chapter.

3

In Egypt our pilgrim is sold into slavery;
In Zanj he encounters again the inescapable Chinese.

His captors sailed to a beach, anchored with a stone tied to a rock, tied Bold up securely, and left him in the boat under a blanket while they went ashore.

It was a beach for small boats, near an immense long wooden dock-front behind the seawall, which served much bigger ships. When the men came back they were drunk and arguing. Without untying anything but his legs, and with no more words to him, they pulled Bold out of the boat and marched him down the great seafront of the city, which appeared to Bold dusty and salty and worn down, stinking in the sun like a dead fish, of which there were indeed many scattered about. On the docks before a long building were bales, boxes, great clay jars, netted bolts of cloth; then a fish market, which made his mouth water at the same time that his stomach flopped.

They came to a slave market. A small square with a raised platform in its middle, somewhat like a lama's teaching platform. Three slaves were quickly sold. The women being sold garnered the most attention and comment from the crowd. They were stripped of all but the ropes or chains holding them, if such were necessary, and stood there listlessly, or cowered. Most were black, some brown. They seemed to be at the butt end of auction day, people selling off leftovers. Before Bold an emaciated girl of about ten years was sold to a fat black man in dirty silk robes. The transaction was completed in a kind of Arabic; she sold for some unit of currency Bold had never heard of before, the payment in little gold coins. He helped his captors get his crusted old clothes off. "I don't need tying," he tried to tell them in Arabic, but they ignored him and chained his ankles. He walked onto the platform feeling the baked air settle on him. Even to himself he emitted a powerful smell, and looking down he saw that his time in the empty land had left him about as fleshless as the little girl before him. But what was left was muscle, and he stood up straight, looking into the sun as the bidding went on, thinking the part of the Lapis Lazuli Sutra that went, "The ruffian demons of unkindness roam the earth, begone! begone! The Buddha renounces slavery!"

"Does he speak Arabic?" someone asked.

One of his captors prodded him, and in Arabic he said, "In the name of God the merciful, the compassionate, I speak Arabic, also Turkic, Mongolian, Ulu, Tibetan, and Chinese," and he began to chant the first chapter of the Quran as far as he remembered it, until they pulled his chain and he took this as a sign to stop. He was very thirsty.

A short, slight Arab bought him for twenty somethings. His captors seemed pleased. They handed him his clothes as he stepped down, slapped him on the back and were off. He began to put on his greasy coat, but his new owner stopped him, handing him a length of clean cotton cloth.

"Wrap that around you. Leave the other filth here."

Surprised, Bold looked down at the last vestiges of his previous life. Dirty rags only, but they had accompanied him this far. He pulled his amulet out of them, leaving his knife hidden in a sleeve, but his owner intervened and threw it back onto the clothes.

"Come on. I know a market in Zanj where I can sell a barbarian like you for three times what I just paid. Meanwhile you can help me get ready for the voyage there. Do you understand? Help, and it will go easier for you. I'll feed you more."

"I understand."

"Be sure that you do. Don't think of trying to escape. Alexandria is a very fine city. The Mamluks keep things stricter than sharia here. They are not forgiving of slaves that try to escape. They're orphans brought here from north of the Black Sea, men whose parents were killed by barbarians like you."

In fact Bold himself had killed quite a few of the Golden Horde, so he nodded without comment.

His owner said, "They have been trained by Arabs in the way of Allah, and now they are more than Muslim." He whistled at the thought. "Trained to rule Egypt apart from all lesser influences, to be true only to the sharia. You don't want to cross them."

Bold nodded again. "I understand."

Crossing the Sinai was like traveling with a caravan crossing one of the deserts of the heartland, except this time Bold was walking with the slaves, in the cloud of dust at the back of the camel train. They were part of the year's haj. Enormous numbers of camels and people had tramped over this road through the desert, and now it was a broad dusty smooth swath through rockier hills. Smaller parties going north passed by to their left. Bold had never seen so many camels.

The caravanserai were beaten and ashy. The ropes tying him to his new master's other slaves were never untied, and they slept in circles on the ground at night. The nights were warmer than Bold was used to, and this almost made up for the heat of the days. Their master, whose name was Zeyk, kept them well watered and fed them adequately at night and at dawn, treating them about as well as his camels, Bold observed: a tradesman, taking care of the goods in his possession. Bold approved of the attitude, and did what he could to keep the bedraggled string of slaves in good form. If they all kept the pace it made the walking that much easier. One night he looked up and saw the Archer looking down on him, and he remembered his nights alone in the empty land.

> The ghost of Temur,
> The last survivor of the fisherfolk,
> The empty stone temples open to the sky,
> The days of hunger, the little mare,
> That ridiculous bow and arrow,
> A red bird and blue bird, sitting side by side.

They came to the Red Sea, and boarded a ship three or four times as long as the one that had brought him to Alexandria, a dhow or zambuco, people called it both. The wind always blew from the west, sometimes hard, and they hugged the western shore with their big lateen sail bellied out to the east. They made good time. Zeyk fed his string of slaves more and more, fattening them for the market. Bold happily downed the extra rice and cucumbers, and saw the sores around his ankles begin to heal. For the first time in a long time he was not perpetually hungry, and he felt like he was coming out of a fog or a dream, waking up more each day. Of course now he was a slave, but he wouldn't always be one. Something would happen.

After a stop at a dry brown port called Massawa, one of the hajjira depots, they sailed east across the Red Sea and rounded the low red cape marking the end of Arabia, to Aden, a big seaside oasis, indeed the biggest port Bold had ever seen, a very rich town of green palms waving over ceramic roofs, citrus trees, and numberless minarets. Zeyk did not disembark his goods or slaves here, however; after a day on shore he came back shaking his head.

"Mombasa," he said to the ship's captain, and paid him more, and they sailed south across the strait again, around the horn and Ras Hafun, then down the coast of Zanj, sailing much farther south than Bold had ever been. The sun at noon was nearly directly overhead, and beat on them most cruelly all day, day after day, with never a cloud in the sky. The air baked as if the world were an oven. The coast appeared either dead brown or else vibrant green, nothing in between. They stopped at Mogadishu, Lamu, and Malindi, each a prosperous Arab trading port, but Zeyk only got off briefly at them.

As they sailed into Mombasa, the grandest harbor yet, they came on a fleet of giant ships, ships bigger than Bold had imagined possible. Each one was as big as a small town, with a long line of masts down its center. There were about ten of these gigantic outlandish ships, with another twenty smaller ones anchored among them. "Ah good," said Zeyk to the zambuco's captain and owner. "The Chinese are here."

The Chinese! Bold had had no idea they owned such a great fleet as this one. It made sense, though. Their pagodas, their great wall; they liked to build big.

The fleet was like an archipelago. All on board the zambuco looked at the great ships, abashed and apprehensive, as if faced with seagoing gods. The large Chinese ships were as long as a dozen of the biggest dhows, and Bold counted nine masts on one of them. Zeyk saw him and nodded. "Look well. Those will soon be your home, God willing."

The zambuco's master brought them inshore on a breath of a breeze. The town's waterfront was entirely occupied by the landing boats of the visitors, and after some discussion with Zeyk, the zambuco's owner beached his craft just south of the waterfront. Zeyk and his man rolled up their robes and stepped over the freeboard into the water, and helped the whole string of slaves over the side onto land. The green water was as warm as blood, or even hotter.

Bold spotted some Chinese, wearing their characteristic red felt coats even here, where they were certainly much too warm. They wandered the market, fingering the goods on display and chattering among themselves, trading with the aid of a translator Zeyk knew. Zeyk approached and greeted him effusively, asked about direct trade with the Chinese visitors. The translator introduced him to some of the Chinese, who seemed polite, even affable, in their usual way. Bold found himself trembling slightly, perhaps from heat and hunger, perhaps from the sight of the Chinese, after all these years, on the other side of the world. Still pursuing their business.

Zeyk and his assistant led the slaves through the market. It was a riot of smell, color, and sound. People as black as pitch, their eyeballs and teeth flashing white or yellow against their skin, offered goods and bartered happily. Bold followed the others past

> Great mounds of green and yellow fruit,
> Rice, coffee, dried fish and squid,
> Lengths and bolts of colored cotton cloth,
> Some spotted, others striped white and blue;
> Bales of Chinese silk, piles of Mecca carpets;
> Huge brown nuts, copper pans
> Filled with colored beads or gemstones,
> Or round balls of sweet-smelling opium;
> Pearls, raw copper, carnelian, quicksilver;
> Daggers and swords, turbans, shawls;
> Elephant tusks, rhinoceros horns,
> Yellow sandalwood, ambergris,
> Ingots and coin-strings of gold and silver,

White cloth, red cloth, porcelain,
All the things of this world, solid in the sun.

And then the slave market, again in a square of its own, next to the main market, with a central auction block, so much like a lama's dais when empty.

The locals were gathered around a sale to one side, not a full auction. They were mostly Arabs here, and often dressed in blue cloth robes and red leather shoes. Behind the market a mosque and minaret stood before rows of four- and even five-story buildings. The clamor was great, but surveying the scene, Zeyk shook his head. "We'll wait for a private audience," he said.

He fed the slaves barley cakes and led them to one of the big buildings next to the mosque. There some Chinese arrived with their translator, and they all went inside to an inner courtyard of the building, shaded and full of green broad-leaved plants and a burbling fountain. A room opening onto this courtyard had shelves on all its walls, with bowls and figures placed on them in an elaborate, beautiful display: Bold recognized pottery from Samarqand, and painted figurines from Persia, among Chinese white porcelain bowls painted in blue, gold leaf, and copper.

"Very elegant," Zeyk said.

Then they were to business. The Chinese officers inspected Zeyk's string of slaves. They spoke to the translator, and Zeyk conferred in private with the man, nodding frequently. Bold found he was sweating, though he felt cold. They were being sold to the Chinese as a single lot.

One of the Chinese strolled down the line of slaves. He looked Bold over.

"How did you get here?" he asked Bold in Chinese.

Bold gulped, waved north. "I was a trader." His Chinese was really rusty. "The Golden Horde took me and brought me to Anatolia. Then to Alexandria, then here."

The Chinese nodded, then moved on. Soon after the slaves were led off by Chinese sailors in trousers and short shirts, back to the waterfront. There several other strings and groups of slaves were gathered. They were stripped, washed down with fresh water, an astringent, more fresh water. They were given new robes of plain cotton, led to boats, and rowed out to the huge side of one of the great ships. Bold climbed a lad-der forty-one steps up the wooden wall of the ship's side, following a skinny black slave boy. They were taken together below the main deck, to a room near the rear of the ship. What happened in there we don't want to tell you, but the story won't make sense unless we do, so on to the next chapter. These things happened.

4

After dismal events, a piece of the Buddha appears;
Then the treasure fleet asks Tianfei to calm their fears.

The ship was so big it did not rock on the waves. It was like being on an island. The room they were kept in was low and broad, extending the width of the ship. Gratings on both sides let in air and some light, though it was dim. A hole under one grating overhung the ship's side and served as the place of relief.

The skinny black boy looked down it as if judging whether he could escape through the hole. He spoke Arabic better than Bold, though it was not his native tongue either; he had a guttural accent that Bold had never heard before. "They trot you like derg." He came from the hills behind the sahil, he said, staring down the hole. He stuck one foot through, then another. He wasn't going to get through.

Then the doorlock rattled and he pulled his feet out and sprang away like an animal. Three men came in and had them all stand before them. Ship's petty officers, Bold judged. Checking the cargo. One of them inspected the black boy closely. He nodded to the others, and they put wooden bowls of rice on the floor, and a big bamboo tube bucket of water, and left.

That was the routine for two days. The black boy, whose name was Kyu, spent much of his time looking down the shithole, at the water it seemed, or at nothing. On the third day they were led up and out to help load the ship's cargo. It was hauled aboard on ropes running through pulleys on the masts, then guided down hatches into holds below. The loaders followed instructions from the officer of the watch, usually a big moon-faced Han. Bold learned that the hold was broken by interior walls into nine individual compartments, each several times bigger than the biggest Red Sea dhows. The slaves who had been on ships before said that would make the great ship impossible to sink; if one compartment leaked it could be emptied and repaired, or even left to flood, but the others would keep the ship afloat. It was like being on nine ships tied together.

One morning the deck overhead reverberated with the drumming of sailors' feet, and they could feel the two giant stone anchors being raised. Big sails were hauled up on crossbeams, one for each mast. The ship began a slow stately rocking over the water, heeling slightly.

It was indeed a floating town. Hundreds lived on it; moving bags and boxes from hold to hold, Bold counted five hundred different people, and there were no doubt many more. It was astonishing how many people were aboard. Very Chinese, the slaves all agreed. The Chinese didn't notice it was crowded, to them it was normal, no different from any other Chinese town.

The admiral of the great fleet was on their ship: Zheng He, a giant of a man, a flat-faced western Chinese, a hui as some slaves called him under their breath. Because of his presence the upper deck was crowded with officers, dignitaries, priests, and supernumeraries of every sort. Belowdecks there were a lot of black men, Zanjis and Malays, doing the hardest work.

That night four men came into the slaves' room. One was Hua Man, Zheng's first officer. They stopped before Kyu and grabbed him up. Hua struck him on the head with a short club. The other three pulled off the boy's robe and separated his legs. They tied bandages tightly around his thighs and around his waist. They held the semiconscious boy up, and Hua took a small curved knife from his sleeve. He grasped the boy's penis and pulled it out, and with a single deft slice cut off penis and balls, right next to the body. The boy groaned as Hua squeezed the bleeding wound and slipped a leather thong around it. He leaned down and inserted a slender metal plug into the wound, then pulled the thong tight and tied it off. He went to the shithole and dropped the boy's genitals through it into the sea. Then from one of his assistants he took a wet wad of paper and held it against the wound he had made, while the others bandaged it in place. When it was secured two of them put the boy's arms over their shoulders, and walked him out the door.

They returned with him a watch or so later, and let him lie down. Apparently they had been walking him the whole time. "Don't let him drink," Hua said to the cowed slaves. "If he drinks or eats in the next three days, he'll die."

The boy moaned through the night. The other slaves moved instinctively to the other side of the room, too scared to talk about it yet. Bold, who had gelded quite a few horses in his time, went and sat by him. The boy was perhaps ten or twelve years old. His gray face had some quality that drew Bold, and he stayed by him. For three days the boy moaned for water, but Bold didn't give him any.

On the night of the third day the eunuchs returned. "Now we see whether he will live or die," Hua said. They held up the boy, took off the bandages, and with a swift jerk Hua pulled the plug from the boy's wound. Kyu yelped and groaned as a hard stream of urine sprayed out of him into a porcelain chamber pot held in place by the second eunuch.

"Good," Hua said to the silent slaves. "Keep him clean. Remind him to take out the plug to relieve himself, and to get it back in quick, until he heals."

They left and locked the door.

Now the Abyssinian slaves would talk to the boy. "If you keep it clean it will heal right up. Urine cleans it too, so that's all right, I mean, if you wet yourself when you go."

"Lucky they didn't do it to all of us."

"Who says they won't?"

"They don't do it to men. Too many die of it. Only boys can sustain the loss."

The next morning Bold led the boy to the shithole and helped him to get the bandage off, so he could pull the plug and pee again. Then Bold put it back for him, showing him where it went, trying to be delicate as the boy whimpered. "You have to have the plug, or the tube will close up and you'll die."

The boy lay on his cotton shift, feverish. The others tried not to look at the horrible wound, but it was hard not to see it once in a while.

"How could they do it?" one said in Arabic, when the boy was sleeping.

"They're eunuchs themselves," one of the Abyssinians said. "Hua is a eunuch. The admiral himself is a eunuch."

"You'd think they'd be the ones to know."

"They know and that's why they do it. They hate us all. They rule the Chinese emperor, and they hate everyone else. You can see how it will be," waving around at the immense ship. "They'll castrate all of us. It's the end coming."

"You Christians like to say that, but so far it's only been true for you."

"God took us first to shorten our suffering. Your turn will come."

"It's not God I fear, but Admiral Zheng He, the Three Jewel Eunuch. He and the Yongle Emperor were friends when they were boys, and the emperor ordered him castrated when they were both thirteen. Can you believe it? Now the eunuchs do it to all the boys they take prisoner."

In the days that followed Kyu got hotter and hotter, and was seldom conscious. Bold sat by his side and put wet rags in his mouth, reciting sutras in his mind. The last time he had seen his own son, almost thirty years before, the boy had been about this age. This one's lips were gray and parched, his dark skin dull, and very dry and hot. Bold had never felt anyone that hot who had not died, so it was probably a waste of time for all concerned; best to let the poor sexless creature slip away, no doubt. But he kept giving him water anyway. He recalled the boy looking around the ship as they had loaded it, his gaze intense and searching. Now the body lay there looking like some sad little African girl, sick to death from an infection in her loins.

But the fever passed. Kyu ate more and more. Even when he was active again, however, he spoke little compared to before. His eyes were not the same either; they stared at people like a bird's eyes do, as if they did not quite believe anything they saw. Bold realized that the boy had traveled out of his body, gone into the bardo and come back someone else. All different. That black boy was dead; this one started anew.

"What is your name now?" he asked him.

"Kyu," the boy said, but unsurprised, as if he didn't remember telling Bold before.

"Welcome to this life, Kyu."

Sailing on the open ocean was a strange way to travel. The skies flew by overhead, but it never looked like they had moved anywhere. Bold tried to figure what a day's ride was for the fleet, wondering if it was faster in the long run than horses, but he couldn't do it. He could only watch the weather and wait.

Twenty-three days later the fleet sailed into Calicut, a city much bigger than any of the ports of Zanj, as big as Alexandria, or bigger.

> Sandstone towers bulbed, walls crennellated,
> All overgrown by a riot of greens.
> This close to the sun life fountains into the sky.
> Around the stone of the central districts,
> Light wooden buildings fill the green bush
> Up the coast in both directions,
> Into the hills behind; the city extends
> As far as the eye can see, up the sides
> Of a mountain ringing the town.

Despite the city's great size, all activity stopped at the arrival of the Chinese fleet. Bold and Kyu and the Ethiopians looked through their grating at the shouting crowds, all those people in their colors waving their arms overhead in awe.

"These Chinese will conquer the whole world."

"Then the Mongols will conquer China," Bold said.

He saw Kyu watching the throng on shore. The boy's expression was that of a preta, unburied at death. Certain demon masks had that look, the old Bön look, like Bold's father when enraged, staring into a person's soul and saying I'm taking this along with me, you can't stop me and you'd better not try. Bold shuddered to see such a face on a mere boy.

They were put to work unloading cargo into boats, and taking other loads out of boats onto the ship, but none of the slaves were sold, and only once were they taken ashore, to help break up a mass of cloth bolts and carry them to the long low dugouts being used to transfer goods from the beaches to the treasure fleet.

During this work Zheng He came ashore in his personal barge, which was painted, gilded, and encrusted with jewelry and porcelain mosaics, and had a gold statue facing forward from the bow. Zheng stepped down a walkway from the barge, wearing golden robes embroidered in red and blue. His men had laid a carpet strip on the beach for him to walk on, but he left it to come over and observe the loading of the new cargo. He was truly an immense man, tall, broad, and with a deep draft fore and aft. He had a broad face, not Han; and a eunuch; he was all the Abyssinians had claimed. Bold watched him out of the corner of his eye, and then noticed that Kyu was standing bolt upright staring at him too, work forgotten, eyes fixed like a hawk's on a mouse. Bold grabbed the boy and hauled him back to work. "Come on, Kyu, we're chained together here, move or I'll knock you down and drag you across the ground. I don't want to get in trouble here, Tara knows what happens to a slave in trouble with such people as these."

From Calicut they sailed south to Lanka. Here the slaves were left aboard the ship, while the soldiers went ashore and disappeared for several days. The behavior of the officers left behind made Bold think the detachment was out on a campaign, and he watched them as closely as he could as the days passed and they grew more nervous. Bold could not guess what they might do if Zheng He did not return, but he did not think they would sail away. Indeed the fire officers were hard at work laying out their array of incendiaries, when the admiral's barge and the other boats came flying back out of Lanka's inner harbor, and their men came aboard shouting triumphantly. Not only had they fought their way out of an inland trap, they said, but they had captured the treacherous local usurper who had laid the trap, and taken the rightful king as well—though there seemed to be some confusion in the story as to which was which, and why they should abduct the rightful king as well as the usurper. Most amazing of all, they said that the rightful king had had in his possession the island's holiest relic, a tooth of the Buddha, called the Dalada. Zheng held up the little gold reliquary to show all aboard this prize. An eyetooth, apparently. Crew, passengers, slaves, all spontaneously roared their acclaim, in throat-tearing shouts that went on and on.

"This is a great bit of fortune," Bold told Kyu when the awful noise died down, pressing his hands together and reciting the Descent Into Lanka Sutra. In fact it was so much good fortune it frightened him. And there was no doubt that fright had been a big part of the roar of the crew. The Buddha had blessed Lanka, it was one of his special lands, with a branch of his Bodhi Tree growing in its soil, and his mineralized tears still falling off the sides of the sacred mountain in the island's center, the one that was topped by Adam's footprint. Surely it was not right to take the Dalada away from its rightful place in such a holy land. There was an affront in the act that could not be denied.

As they sailed east, the story circulated through the ship that the Dalada was proof of the deposed king's right to rule; it would be returned to Lanka when the Yongle Emperor determined the rights of the case. The slaves were reassured by this news.

"So the emperor of China will decide who rules that island," Kyu said. Bold nodded. The Yongle Emperor had himself come to the throne in a violent coup, so it was not clear to Bold which of the two Lankan contenders he would favor. Meanwhile, they had the Dalada on board. "It's good," he said to Kyu after thinking it over some more. "Nothing bad can happen to us on this voyage, anyway."

And so it proved. Black squalls, bearing directly down on them, unaccountably evaporated just as they struck. Giant seas rocked all the horizons, great dragon tails visibly whipping up the waves, while they sailed serenely over a moving flat calm at their center. They even sailed through the Malacca Strait without hindrance from Palembanque, or, north of that, from the myriad pirates of Cham, or the Japanese wakou—though, as Kyu pointed out, no pirate in his right mind would challenge a fleet so huge and powerful, tooth of the Buddha or not.

Then as they sailed into the South China Sea, someone saw the Dalada floating about the ship at night, as if, he said, it were a little candle flame. "How does he know it wasn't a candle flame?" Kyu asked. But the next morning the sky dawned red. Black clouds rolled over the horizon in a line from the south, in a way that reminded Bold strongly of the storm that had killed Temur.

Driving rain struck, then a violent wind that turned the sea white. Shooting up and down in their dim little room, Bold realized that such a storm was even more frightening at sea than on land. The ship's astrologer cried out that a great dragon under the sea was angry, and thrashing the water under them. Bold joined the other slaves in holding to the gratings and looking out their little holes to see if they could catch sight of spine or claw or snout of this dragon, but the spume flying over the white water obscured the surface. Bold thought he might have seen part of a dark green tail in the foam.

Wind shrieks through the nine masts,
All bare of sail. The great ship tilts in the wind,

Rolls side to side, and the little ships
Accompanying them bob like corks,
In and out of view through the grating.
In storms like this, nothing to be done but hold on!
Bold and Kyu cling fast to the wall,
Listening through the howl for the officers' shouts
And the thumping feet of the sailors
Doing what they can to secure the sails
And then to tie the tiller securely in place.
They hear the fear in the officers,
And sense it in the sailors' feet.
Even belowdecks they are wet with spray.

Up on the great poop deck the officers and astrologers performed some sort of ceremony of appeasement, and Zheng He himself could be heard calling out to Tianfei, the Chinese goddess of safety at sea.

"Let the dark water dragons go down into the sea, and leave us free from calamity! Humbly, respectfully, piously, we offer up this flagon of wine, offer it once and offer it again, pouring out this fine, fragrant wine! That our sails may meet favorable winds, that the sea-lanes be peaceful, that the all-seeing and all-hearing spirit-soldiers of winds and seasons, the wave-quellers and swell-drinkers, the airborne immortals, the god of the year, and the protectress of our ship, the Celestial Consort, brilliant, divine, marvelous, responsive, mysterious Tianfei might save us!"

Looking up through the dripping cracks in the deck Bold could see a composite vision of sailors watching this ceremony, mouths all open wide shouting against the wind's roar. Their guard yelled at them, "Pray to Tianfei, pray to the Celestial Consort, the sailor's only friend! Pray for her intercession! All of you! Much more of this wind and the ship will be torn apart!"

"Tianfei preserve us," Bold chanted, squeezing Kyu to indicate he should do the same. The black boy said nothing. He pointed up at the forward masts, however, which they could see through the hatchway grating, and Bold looked up and saw red filaments of light dancing between the masts: balls of light, like Chinese lanterns without the paper or the fire, glowing at the top of the mast and over it, illuminating the flying rain and even the black bottoms of the clouds that were peeling by overhead. The otherworldly beauty of the sight tempered the terror of it;

Bold and everyone else moved outside the realm of terror, it was too strange and awesome a sight to worry any longer about life or death. All the men were crying out, praying at the top of their lungs. Tianfei coalesced out of the dancing red light, her figure gleaming brightly over them, and the wind diminished all at once. The seas calmed around them. Tianfei dissipated, ran redly out the rigging and back into the air. Now their grateful voices could be heard above the wind. Whitecaps still toppled and rolled, but all at a distance from them, halfway to the horizon.

"Tianfei!" Bold shouted with the rest. "Tianfei!"

Zheng He stood at the poop rail and raised both hands in a light rain. He shouted "Tianfei! Tianfei has saved us!" and they all bellowed it with him, filled with joy in the same way the air had been filled with the red light of the goddess. Later the wind blew hard again, but they had no fear.

How the rest of the voyage home went is not really material; nothing of note happened, they made it back safely, and what happened after that you can find out by reading the next chapter.

5

In a Hangzhou restaurant, Bold and Kyu rejoin their jati;
In a single moment, end of many months' harmony.

Storm-tossed, Tianfei-protected, the treasure fleet sailed into a big estuary. Ashore, behind a great seawall, stood the rooftops of a vast city. Even the part visible from the ship was bigger than all the cities Bold had ever seen put together—all the bazaars of central Asia, the Indian cities Temur had razed, the ghost towns of Frengistan, the white seaside towns of Zanj, Calicut—all combined would have occupied only a quarter or a third of the land covered by this forest of rooftops, this steppe of rooftops, extending all the way to distant hills visible to the west.

The slaves stood in the waist of the big ship, silent in the midst of the cheering Chinese, who cried out. "Tianfei, Celestial Consort, thank you!" and "Hangzhou, my home, never thought to be seen again!" "Home, wife, new year festival!" "We happy, happy men, to have traveled all the way to the other side of the world and then make it back home!" and so on.

The ships' huge anchor stones were dropped over the side. Where the Chientang River entered the estuary there was a powerful tidal bore, and any ship not securely anchored could be swept far up into the shallows, or flushed out to sea. When the ships were anchored the work of unloading began. This was a massive operation, and once as he ate rice between watches at the hoist, Bold noted that there were no horses, camels, water buffalo, mules, or asses to help with the job, or with any other job in the city: just thousands of laborers, endless lines of them, moving the food and goods in, or taking out the refuse and manure, mostly by canal—in and out, in and out, as if the city were a monstrous imperial body lying on the land, being fed and relieved by all its subjects together.

Many days passed in the labor of unloading, and Bold and Kyu saw a bit of the harbor Kanpu, and Hangzhou itself, when manning barges on trips to state warehouses under the southern hill compound that had once been the imperial palace, hundreds of years before. Now lesser aristocrats and even high-ranking bureaucrats and eunuchs lived in the old palace grounds. North of these extended the walled enclosure of the old city, impossibly crowded with warrens of wooden buildings that were five, six, and even seven stories tall—old buildings that overhung the canals, people's bedding spread out from balconies to dry in the sun, grass growing out of the roofs.

Bold and Kyu gawked up from the canals while unloading the barges. Kyu looked with his bird's gaze, seeming unsurprised, unimpressed, unafraid. "There are a lot of them," he conceded. Constantly he was asking Bold the Chinese words for things, and in the attempt to answer Bold learned many more words himself.

When the unloading was done, the slaves from their ship were gathered together and taken to Phoenix Hill, "the hill of the foreigners," and sold to a local merchant named Shen. No slave market here, no auction, no fuss. They never learned what they had been sold for, or who in particular had owned them during their sea passage. Possibly it had been Zheng He himself.

Chained together at the ankles, Bold and Kyu were led through the narrow crowded streets to a building near the shores of a lake flanking the west edge of the old city. The first floor of the building was a restaurant. It was the fourteenth day of the first moon of the year, Shen told them, the start of the Feast of Lanterns, so they would have to learn fast, because the place was hopping.

> Tables spill out of the restaurant
> Into the broad street bordering the lakefront,
> Every chair filled all day long.
> The lake itself dotted with boats,

Each boat sporting lanterns of all kinds—
Colored glass painted with figures,
Carved white and apple jade,
Roundabouts turning on their candle's hot air,
Paper lanterns burning up in brief blazes.
A dike crowded with lantern bearers
Extends into the lake, the opposite shore is crowded
As well, so at the day's end
The lake and all the city around it
Spark in the dusk of the festival twilight.
Certain moments give us such unexpected beauty.

Shen's eldest wife, I-Li, ran the kitchen very strictly, and Bold and Kyu soon found themselves unloading hundredweight bags of rice from the canal barges tied up behind the restaurant; carrying them in; returning bags of refuse to the compost barges; cleaning the tables; and mopping and sweeping the floor. They ran in and out, also upstairs to the family compound above the restaurant. The pace was relentless, but all the while they were surrounded by the restaurant women, in white robes with paper butterflies in their hair, and by thousands of other women as well, promenading under the globes of colored light, so that even Kyu raced about drunk on the sights and smells, and on drinks salvaged from near-empty cups. They drank lichee, honey and ginger punch, papaw and pear juice, and teas green and black. Shen also served fifteen kinds of rice wine; they tried the dregs of them all. They drank everything but plain water, which they were warned against as dangerous to the health.

As for the food, which again came to them mostly in the form of table scraps—well, it beggared description. They were given a plateful of rice every morning, with some kidneys or other offal thrown in, and after that they were expected to fend for themselves with what customers left behind. Bold ate everything he got his hands on, astonished at the variety. The Feast of Lanterns was a time for Shen and I-Li to offer their fullest menu, and so Bold had the chance to taste roebuck, red deer, rabbit, partridge, quail, clams cooked in rice wine, goose with apricots, lotus-seed soup, pimento soup with mussels, fish cooked with plums, fritters and soufflés, ravioli, pies, and cornflour fruitcakes. Every kind of food, in fact, except for any beef or dairy; strangely, the Chinese had no cattle. But they had eighteen kinds of soy, Shen said, nine of rice, eleven of apricots, eight of pears. It was a feast every day.

After the rush of the Feast of Lanterns was over, I-Li liked to take short breaks from her work in the kitchen, and visit some of the other restaurants of the city, to see what they were offering. She would return to inform Shen and the cooks that they needed to make a sweet soy soup, for instance, like that she had found at the Mixed Wares Market; or pig cooked in ashes, like that at the Longevity-and-Compassion Palace.

She started taking Bold with her on her morning trips to the abbatoir, located right in the heart of the old city. There she chose her pork ribs, and the liver and kidneys for the slaves. Here Bold learned why they were never to drink the city's water; the offal and blood from the slaughter were washed off right into the big canal running down to the river, but often the tides pushed water back up this canal and through the rest of the city's water network.

Returning behind I-Li with his wheelbarrow of pork one day, pausing to let a party of nine intoxicated women in white pass by, Bold felt all of a sudden that he was in a different world. Back at the restaurant he said to Kyu, "We've been reborn without our noticing it."

"Maybe you have. You're like a baby here."

"Both of us! Look about you! It's . . ." He could not express it.

"They are rich," Kyu said, looking about. Then they were back to work.

The lakefront never was an ordinary place. Festival or not—and there were festivals almost every month—the lakefront was one of the main places the people of Hangzhou congregated. Every week there were private parties between the more general festivals, so the promenade was a daily celebration of greater or lesser magnitude, and although there was a great deal of work to be done supplying and maintaining the restaurant, there was also a great deal of food and drink to be scavenged, or poached in the kitchen, and both Bold and Kyu were insatiable. They soon filled out, and Kyu was also still sprouting up, looking tall among the Chinese.

Soon it was as if they had never lived any other life. Well before dawn, resonant wooden fish were struck with mallets, and the weathermen shouted their announcements from the firewatch towers: "It is raining! It is cloudy today!" Bold and Kyu and about twenty other slaves got up and were let out of their room, and most went down to the service canal that ran in from the suburbs, to meet the rice barges. The barge crews had gotten up even earlier—theirs was night work, starting at midnight many li away. All together they heaved the bulging sacks onto wheelbarrows, then the slaves wheeled them back through the alleys to Shen's.

> They sweep up the restaurant,
> Light the stove fires, set the tables,
> Wash bowls and chopsticks, chop vegetables,
> Cook, carry supplies and food
> Out to Shen's two pleasure boats,
> And then as dawn breaks
> And people begin slowly to appear
> On the lakefront for breakfast,
> They help the cooks, wait on tables,
> Bus and clean tables—anything needed,
> Lost in the meditation of labor,

though usually the hardest work in the place was theirs, as they were the newest slaves. But even the hardest work wasn't very hard, and with the constant availability of food, Bold considered their placement a windfall; a chance to put some meat on their bones, and learn better the local dialect and the ways of the Chinese. Kyu pretended never to notice any of these things, indeed pretended not to understand most of the Chinese spoken to him, but Bold saw that he was actually soaking in everything like a dishwasher's sponge, watching sideways so that it seemed he never watched, when he always watched. That was Kyu's way. He already knew more Chinese than Bold.

The eighth day of the fourth moon was another big festival, celebrating a deity who was patron to many of the guilds of the town. The guilds organized a procession, down the broad imperial way that divided the old city north to south, then over to West Lake for dragon-boat jousts, among all the other more usual pleasures of the lakefront. Each guild wore its particular costume and mask, and brandished identical umbrellas, flags or bouquets as they marched in squares together, shouting "Ten thousand years! Ten thousand years!" as they had done ever since the emperors had actually lived in Hangzhou, and heard these shouted hopes for their longevity. Spread out along the lakefront at the end of the parade, they watched a dance of a hundred little eunuchs in a circle, a particular celebration of that festival. Kyu almost looked directly at these children.

Later that day he and Bold were assigned to one of Shen's pleasure boats, which were floating extensions of his restaurant. "We have a wonderful feast for our passengers today," Shen cried as they arrived and filed aboard. "We'll be serving the Eight Dainties today—dragon livers, phoenix marrow, bear paws, lips of apes, rabbit embryo, carp tail, broiled osprey, and kumiss."

Bold smiled to think of kumiss, which was simply fermented mare's milk, included among the Eight Dainties; he had practically grown up on it. "Some of those are easier to obtain than others," he said, and Shen laughed and kicked him into the boat.

Onto the lake they paddled. "How come your lips are still on your face?" Kyu called back at Shen, who was out of hearing.

Bold laughed. "The Eight Dainties," he said. "What these people think of!"

"They do love their numbers," Kyu agreed. "The Three Pure Ones, the Four Emperors, the Nine Luminaries—"

"The Twenty-eight Constellations—"

"The Twelve Horary Branches, the Five Elders of the Five Regions . . ."

"The Fifty Star Spirits."

"The Ten Unforgivable Sins."

"The Six Bad Recipes."

Kyu cackled briefly. "It's not numbers they like, it's lists. Lists of all the things they have."

Out on the lake Bold and Kyu saw up close the magnificent decoration of the day's dragon boats, bedecked with flowers, feathers, colored flags and spinners. Musicians on each boat played madly, trying with drum and horn to drown out the sound of all the others, while pikemen in the bows reached out with padded staves to knock people on other boats into the water.

In the midst of this happy tumult, screams of a different tone caught the attention of those on the water, and they looked ashore and saw that there was a fire. Instantly the games ended and all the boats made a beeline for land, piling up five deep against the docks. People ran right over the boats in their haste, some toward the fire, some toward their own neighborhoods. As they hurried over to the restaurant Bold and Kyu saw for the first time a fire brigade. Each neighborhood had one, with its own equipment, and they would all follow the signal flags from the watch-towers around the city, soaking roofs in districts threatened by the blaze, or putting out flying embers. Hangzhou's buildings were all wood or bamboo, and most districts had gone up in flames at one time or an-other, so the routine was well practiced. Bold and Kyu ran behind Shen up to the burning neighborhood, which was to the north of theirs and upwind, so that they too were in danger.

At the fire's edge thousands of men and women were at work, many in bucket lines that extended to the nearest canals. The buckets were run upstairs into smoky buildings, and tossed down onto the flames. There were also quite a number of men carrying staves, pikes, and even cross-bows, and questioning men hauled out of the fiery alleyways bordering the conflagration. Suddenly these men beat one of those that emerged to a bloody mass, right there amid the firefighting. Looter, someone said. Army detachments would soon arrive to help capture more and kill them on the spot, after public torture, if there was time.

Despite this threat, Bold saw now that there were figures without buckets, darting in and out of the burning buildings. The fight against looters was as intense as that against the fire! Kyu too saw this as he passed wooden or bamboo buckets down the line, openly watching everything.

Days flew by, each busier than the last. Kyu was still nearly mute, head al-ways lowered, a mere beast of burden or kitchen swab—incapable of learning Chinese, or so everyone in the restaurant believed. Only semi-human in fact, which was the usual attitude of the Chinese toward black slaves in the city.

Bold spent more and more time working for I-Li. She appeared to prefer him on her trips out, and he hustled to keep up with her, maneu-vering the wheelbarrow through the crowd. She was always in a tearing hurry, mostly in her quest for new foods; she seemed anxious to try everything. Bold saw that the restaurant's success had resulted from her efforts. Shen himself was more an impediment than a help, as he was bad with his abacus and couldn't remember much, especially about his debts, and he kicked his slaves and his girls for hire.

So Bold was pleased to follow I-Li. They visited Mother Sung's outside the Cash-reserve Gate, to try her white soy soup. They watched Wei Big Knife at the Cat Bridge boil pork, and Chou Number Five in front of the Five-span Pavilion, making his honey fritters. Back in the kitchen I-Li would try to reproduce these foods exactly, shaking her head ominously as she did. Sometimes she would retire to her room to think, and a few times she called Bold up the stairs, to order him out in search of some spice or ingredient she had thought of that might help with a dish.

Her room had a table by the bed, covered with cosmetic bottles, jewelry, perfume sachets, mirrors, and little boxes of lacquered wood, jade, gold, and silver. Gifts from Shen, apparently. Bold glanced at them while she sat there thinking.

> A tub of white foundation powder,
> Still flat and shiny on top.
> A deep rose shade of grease blush,
> For cheeks already chapped dark red.
> A box of pink balsam leaves
> Crushed in alum, for tinted nails,
> Which many women in the restaurant displayed.
> I-Li's nails were bitten to the quick.
> Cosmetics never used, jewelry never worn,
> Mirrors never looked into. The outward gaze.

Once she stained her palms with the pink balsam dye; another time, all the dogs and cats in the kitchen. Just to see what would happen, as far as Bold could tell.

But she was interested in the things of the city. Half her trips out were occupied by talk, by asking questions. Once she came home troubled: "Bold, they say that northerners here go to restaurants that serve human flesh. 'Two-legged mutton,' have you heard that? Different names for old men, women, young girls, children? Are they really such monsters up there?"

"I don't think so," Bold said. "I never met any."

She was not entirely reassured. She often saw hungry ghosts in her sleep, and they had to come from somewhere. And they sometimes complained to her of having had their bodies eaten. It made sense to her that they might cluster around restaurants in search of some kind of retribution. Bold nodded; it made sense to him too, though it was hard to believe the teeming city harbored practicing cannibals when there was so much other food to be had.

As the restaurant prospered, I-Li made Shen improve the place, cutting holes in the side walls and putting in windows, filling them with square trelliswork supporting oiled paper, which blazed or glowed with sunlight, depending on the hour and weather. She opened the front of the building entirely to the lakefront promenade, and paved the downstairs with glazed bricks. She burned pots of mosquito smoke during the summer, when they were at their worst. She built in a number of small wall shrines devoted to various gods—deities of place, animal spirits, demons and hungry ghosts, even, at Bold's humble request, one to Tianfei the Celestial Consort, despite her suspicion that this was only another name for Tara, already much honored in the nooks and crannies of the house. If it annoyed Tara, she said, it would be on Bold's head.

Once she came home retailing a story of a number of people who had died and come back to life shortly thereafter, apparently because of the mistakes of careless celestial scribes, who had written down the wrong names. Bold smiled; the Chinese imagined a complicated bureaucracy for the dead, just like the ones they had established for everything else. "They came back with information for their living relatives, things that turned out to be correct even through the briefly deceased person couldn't have known about it!"

"Marvels," Bold said.

"Marvels happen every day," I-Li replied. It was, as far as she was concerned, a universe peopled by spirits, genies, demons, ghosts—as many kinds of beings as tastes. She had never had the bardo explained to her, and so she didn't understand the six levels of reality that organized cosmic existence; and Bold did not feel that he was in a position to teach her. So it remained at the level of ghosts and demons for her. Malignant ones could be held off by various practices that annoyed them; firecrackers, drums and gongs, these things chased them away. It was also possible to strike them with a stick, or burn artemisia, a Sechuan custom that I-Li practiced. She also bought magic writing on miniature papers or cylinders of silver, and put up white jade square tiles in every doorway; dark demons disliked the light of these. And the restaurant and its household prospered, so she felt she had done the right things.

Following her out several times a week, Bold learned a lot about Hangzhou. He learned that the best rhinoceros skins were found at

Chien's, as you went down from the service canal to little Chinghu Lake; the finest turbans were at Kang Number Eight's, in the Street of the Worn Cash Coin, or at Yang Number Three's, going down the canal after the Three Bridges. The largest display of books was at the bookstalls under the big trees near the summer house of the Orange Tree Garden. Wicker cages for birds and crickets could be found in Ironwire Lane, ivory combs at Fei's, painted fans at the Coal Bridge. I-Li liked to know of these places, even though she only bought what they sold as gifts for her friends or her mother-in-law. A very curious person indeed. Bold could hardly keep up with her. One day in the street, rattling off some story or other, she stopped and looked up at him, surprised, and said "I want to know everything!"

But all the while, Kyu had been watching without watching. And one night, during the tidal bore of the eighth moon, when the Chientang River roared with high waves and there were many visitors in the city, in the hour before the woodblocks and the weathermen's cries, Bold was awakened by a gentle tug on the ear, then the firm pressure of a hand over his mouth.

It was Kyu. He held a key to their room in his hand. "I stole the key."

Bold pulled Kyu's hand away from his mouth. "What are you doing?" he whispered.

"Come on," Kyu said in Arabic, in the phrase used for a balking camel. "We're escaping."

"What? What do you mean?"

"We're escaping, I said."

"But where will we go?"

"Away from this city. North to Nanjing."

"But we have it good here!"

"Come on, none of that. We're finished here. I've already killed Shen."

"You what!"

"Shhhh. We need to set the fires and get out of here before the wake-up."

Stunned, Bold scrambled to his feet, whispering "Why, why, why, why? We had a good thing here, you should have asked me first if I wanted any part of this!"

"I want to escape," Kyu said, "and I need you to do it. I need a master to get around."

"Get around where?"

But now Bold was following Kyu through the silent household, stepping blindly with complete assurance, so well had he come to know this building, the first one he had ever lived in. He liked it. Kyu led him into the kitchen, took a branch sticking out of the smoldering stove fire; he must have put it in before rousing Bold, for the pitchy knot at the end was now blazing. "We're going north to the capital," Kyu said over his shoulder as he led Bold outdoors. "I'm going to kill the emperor."

"What!"

"More about that later," Kyu said, and applied the flaming torch to a bundle of rush and kindling and balls of wax he had put against the walls, in a corner. When it had caught fire he ran outside, and Bold followed him appalled. Kyu lit another bundle of kindling against the house next door, and placed the brand against a third house, and all the while Bold stayed right behind him, too shocked to think properly. He would have stopped the boy if it weren't for the fact that Shen was already murdered. Kyu's and Bold's lives were forfeit; setting the district on fire was probably their only chance, as it might burn the body so that the killing would not show. It also might be assumed that some slaves had been burned up entire, locked in their room as they were. "Hopefully they'll all burn," Kyu said, echoing this thought.

We are as shocked as you are by this development, and don't know what happened next, but no doubt the next chapter will tell us.

6

By way of the Grand Canal our pilgrims escape justice;
In Nanjing they beg the aid of the Three-Jewel Eunuch.

They ran north up the dark alleys paralleling the service canal. Behind them the alarm was being raised already, people screaming, fire bells ringing, a fresh dawn wind blowing in off West Lake.

"Did you take some cash?" Bold thought to ask.

"Many strings," Kyu said. He had a full bag under his arm.

They would need to get as far away as they could, as quickly as possible. With a black like Kyu it would be hard to be inconspicuous. Necessarily he would have to remain a young black eunuch slave, Bold therefore his master. Bold would have to do all the talking; this was why Kyu had brought him along. This was why he had not murdered Bold along with the rest of the household.

"What about I-Li! Did you kill her too?"

"No. Her bedroom has a window. She'll do fine."

Bold wasn't so sure; widows had a hard time of it; she'd end up like Wei Big Knife, on the street cooking meals on a brazier for passersby. Although for her that might be opportunity enough.

Wherever there were a lot of slaves, there were usually quite a few blacks. The canal boats were often moved along through the countryside by slaves, turning capstans or pulling their ropes directly, like mules or camels. Possibly the two of them could take on such a role and hide in it; he could pretend to be a slave himself—but no, they needed a master to account for them. If they could slip onto the end of a rope line . . . He couldn't believe he was thinking about joining a canal boat rope line, when he had been bussing tables in a restaurant! It made him so angry at Kyu that he hissed.

And now Kyu needed him. Bold could abandon the boy and he would stand a much better chance of slipping into obscurity, among the many traders and Buddhist monks and beggars on the roads of China; even their famous bureaucracy of local yamens and district officials could not keep track of all the poor people slipping around in the hills and the backcountry. While with a black boy he stood out like a festival clown with his monkey.

But he was not going to abandon Kyu, not really, so he just hissed. On they ran through the outer city, Kyu pulling Bold by the hand from time to time and urging him in Arabic to hurry. "You know this is what you really wanted, you're a great Mongol warrior, you told me, a barbarian of the steppes, feared by all the peoples, you were only just pretending not to mind being someone's kitchen slave, you're good at not thinking about things, about not seeing things, but it's all an act, of course you always knew, you just pretend not to know, you wanted to escape all the while." Bold was amazed to think anyone could have misunderstood him that completely.

The suburbs of Hangzhou were much greener than the old central quarter, every household compound marked by trees, even small mulberry orchards. Behind them the fire alarm bells were waking the whole city, the day starting in a panic. From a slight rise they could look back between walls and see the lakefront aglow; the entire district appeared to have caught fire as quickly as Kyu's little balls of wax and kindling, fanned by a good stiff west wind. Bold wondered if Kyu had waited for a windy night to make his break. The thought chilled him. He had known the boy was clever, but this ruthlessness he had never suspected, despite the preta look he sometimes had, which reminded Bold of Temur's look—some intensity of focus, some totemic aspect, his raptor nafs looking out no doubt. Each person was in some crucial sense his or her nafs, and Bold had already concluded Kyu's was a falcon, hooded and tied. Temur's had been an eagle on high, stooping to tear at the world.

So he had seen some sign, had had some idea. And there was that closed aspect of Kyu too, the sense that his true thoughts were many rooms away, ever since his castration. Of course that would have had its effects. The original boy was gone, leaving the nafs to negotiate with some new person.

They hurried through the northernmost subprefecture of Hangzhou, and out the gate in the last city wall. The road rose higher into the Su Tung-po Hills, and they got a view back to the lakefront district, the flames less visible in the dawn, more a matter of clouds of black smoke, no doubt throwing sparks east to spread the blaze. "This fire will kill a lot of people!" Bold exclaimed.

"They're Chinese," Kyu said. "There's more than enough to take their place."

Walking hard to the north, paralleling the Grand Canal on its west side, they saw again how crowded China was. Up here a whole country of rice paddies and villages fed the great city on the coast. Farmers were out in the morning light,

> Sticking rice starts into the submerged fields,
> Bending over time after time. A man walks
> Behind a water buffalo. Strange to see
> Such rain-polished black poverty,
> Tiny farms, rundown crossroad villages,
> After all the colorful glories of Hangzhou.

"I don't see why they all don't move to the city," Kyu said. "I would."

"They never think of it," Bold said, marveling that Kyu would suppose other people thought like he did. "Besides, their families are here."

They could just see the Grand Canal through the trees lining it, some two or three li to the east. Mounds of earth and timber stood by it, marking repairs or improvements. They kept their distance, hoping to avoid any army detachments or prefecture posses that might be patrolling the canal on this unfortunate day.

"Do you want a drink of water?" Kyu asked. "Do you think we can drink it here?"

He was very solicitous, Bold saw; but of course now he had to be. Near the Grand Canal the sight of Kyu would probably pass for normal, but Bold had no paperwork, and local prefects or canal officials might very well ask him to produce some. So neither the Grand Canal nor the country away from it would work all the time. They would have to slip on and off it as they went, depending on who was around. They might even have to move by night, which would slow them down and be more dangerous. Then again it seemed unlikely that all the hordes of people moving up and down the canal and its corridor were being checked for papers, or had them either.

So they moved over into the crowd walking the canal road, and Kyu carried his bundle and wore his chains, and fetched water for Bold, and pretended ignorance of any but the simplest commands. He could do a scarily believable imitation of an idiot. Gangs of men hauled barges, or turned the capstans that raised and lowered the lock gates that interrupted the flow of the canal at regular intervals. Pairs of men, master and servant or slave, were common. Bold ordered Kyu about, but was too worried to enjoy it. Who knew what trouble Kyu might cause in the north. Bold didn't know what he felt, it changed minute by minute. He still couldn't believe Kyu had forced this escape on him. He hissed again; he had life-or-death power over the boy, yet he remained afraid of him.

At a new little paved square, next to locks made of new raw timber, a local yamen and his deputies were stopping every fourth or fifth group. Suddenly they waved at Bold, and when he led Kyu over, suddenly hopeless, they asked to see his papers. The yamen was accompanied by a higher official in robes, a prefect wearing a patch with twinned sparrow hawks embroidered on it. The prefects' symbols of rank were easy to read—the lowest rank showed quail pecking the ground, the highest, cranes sporting over the clouds. So this was a fairly senior figure here, possibly on the hunt for the arsonist of Hangzhou, and Bold was trying to think of lies, his body tensing to run, when Kyu reached into his bag and gave Bold a packet of papers tied with a silk ribbon. Bold undid the ribbon's knot and gave the packet to the yamen, wondering what it said. He knew the Tibetan letters for "Om Mani Padme Hum," as who could not with them carved on every rock in the Himalaya, but other than that he was illiterate, and the Chinese alphabet looked like chicken tracks, each letter different from all the rest.

The yamen and the sparrow hawk official read the top two sheets, then handed them back to Bold, who tied them up and gave them to Kyu without looking at him.

"Take care around Nanjing," Sparrow Hawk said. "There are bandits in the hills just south of it."

"We'll stick to the canal," Bold said.

When they were out of sight of the patrol, Bold struck Kyu hard for the first time. "What was that! Why didn't you tell me about the papers! How can you expect me to know what to say to people?"

"I was afraid you would take them and leave me."

"What do you mean? If they say I have a black slave, then I need a black slave, don't I? What do they say?"

"They say you are a horse merchant from the treasure fleet, traveling to Nanjing to complete business in horses. And that I am your slave."

"Where did you get them?"

"A rice boatman who does them wrote one for me."

"So he knows our plans?"

Kyu said nothing, and Bold wondered if the boatman too was dead. The boy seemed capable of anything. Getting a key, getting papers forged, preparing the little fireballs . . . If the time came when he thought he didn't need Bold, Bold would no doubt wake up one morning with a slit throat. He would most certainly be safer on his own.

As they trudged past the barge ropelines, he brooded on this. He could abandon the boy to whatever fate befell him—more enslavement, or quick death as a runaway, or slow death as an arsonist and murderer—and then work his way north and west to the great wall and the steppes beyond, and thence home.

From the way Kyu avoided his gaze and slunk behind him, it was apparent that he knew more or less what Bold was thinking. So for a day or two Bold ordered him about harshly, and Kyu jumped at every word.

But Bold did not leave him, and Kyu did not slit Bold's throat. Thinking it over, Bold had to admit to himself that his karma was somehow tied up with the boy's. He was part of it somehow. Very possibly he was there to help the boy.

"Listen," Bold said one day as they walked. "You can't go to the capital and kill the emperor. It isn't possible. And why would you want to anyway?"

Hunched, sullen, the boy eventually said in Arabic, "To bring them down."

Again the term he used came from camel driving.

"To what?"

"To stop them."

"But killing the emperor, even if you could, wouldn't do that. They'd just replace him with another one, and it would all go on the same as before. That's how it works."

Much trudging, and then: "They wouldn't fight over who got to be the new emperor?"

"Over the succession? Sometimes that happens. It depends on who's in line to succeed. I don't know about that anymore. This emperor, the Yongle, is a usurper himself. He took it away from his nephew, or uncle. But usually the eldest son has a clear right. Or the emperor designates a different successor. In any case the dynasty continues. It isn't often there is a problem."

"But there might be?"

"There might be and there might not. Meanwhile they'd be staying up nights figuring out better ways to torture you. What they did to you on the ship would be nothing compared to it. The Ming emperors have the best torturers in the world, everyone knows that."

More trudging. "They have the best everything in the world," the boy complained. "The best canals, the best cities, the best ships, the best armies. They sail around the seas and everywhere they go people kowtow to them. They land and see the tooth of the Buddha, they take it with them. They install a king who will serve them, and move on and do the same everywhere they go. They'll conquer the whole world, cut all the boys, and all the children will be theirs, and the whole world will end up Chinese."

"Maybe so," Bold said. "It's possible. There certainly are a lot of them. And those treasure ships are impressive, no doubt of that. But you can't sail into the heart of the world, the steppes where I came from. And the people out there are much tougher than the Chinese. They've conquered the Chinese before. So things should be all right. And listen, no matter what happens, you can't do anything about it."

"We'll see about that in Nanjing."

It was crazy, of course. The boy was deluded. Nevertheless there was that look that came into his eye—inhuman, totemic, his nafs looking out at things—the sight of which gave Bold a chill down the chakra nerve right to the first center, behind his balls. Aside from the raptor nafs, which Kyu had been born with, there was something scary in the hatred of a eunuch, something impersonal and uncanny. Bold had no doubt that he was traveling with some kind of power, some African witch child or shaman, a tulku, who had been captured out of the jungles and mutilated, so that his power had been redoubled, and was now turning to revenge. Revenge, against the Chinese! Despite his belief that it was crazy, Bold was curious to see what might come of that.

Nanjing was bigger even than Hangzhou. Bold had to give up being amazed. It was also the home harbor for the great treasure fleet. An entire city of shipbuilders had been established down by the Yangzi River estuary, the shipyards including seven enormous dry docks running perpendicular to the river, behind high dams with guards patrolling their gates so that no one could sabotage them. Thousands of shipwrights, carpenters, and sailmakers lived in quarters behind the dry docks, and this sprawling town of workshops, called Longjiang, included scores of inns for visiting laborers, and sailors ashore. Evening discussions in these inns concerned mainly the fate of the treasure fleet and of Zheng He, who currently was occupied building a temple to Tianfei, while he worked on another great expedition to the west.

It was easy for Bold and Kyu to slip into this scene as small-time trader and slave, and they rented sleeping spaces on the mattresses at the South Sea Inn. Here in the evenings they learned of the construction of a new capital up in Beiping, a project which was absorbing a great deal of the Yongle Emperor's attention and cash. Beiping, a provincial northern outpost except during the Mongol dynasties, had been Zhu Di's first power base before he usurped the Dragon Throne and became the Yongle Emperor, and he was now rewarding it by making it the imperial capital once again, changing its name from Beiping ("northern peace") to Beijing ("northern capital"). Hundreds of thousands of workers had been sent north from Nanjing to build a truly enormous palace, indeed from all accounts the whole city was being made into a kind of palace—the Great Within, it was called, forbidden to any but the emperor and his concubines and eunuchs. Outside this precious ground was to be a larger imperial city, also new.

All this construction was said to be opposed by the Confucian bureaucracy who ruled the country for the emperor. The new capital, like the treasure fleet, was a huge expense, an imperial extravagance that the officials disliked, for it bled the country of its wealth. They must not have seen the treasures being unloaded, or did not believe them equal to what had been spent to gain them. They understood Confucius to say that the wealth of the empire ought to be land-based, a matter of expanded agriculture and assimilation of border people, in the traditional style. All this innovation, this shipbuilding and travel, seemed to them to be manifestations of the growing power of the imperial eunuchs, whom they hated as their rivals in influence. The talk in the sailors' inns supported the eunuchs, for the most part, as the sailors were loyal to sailing, to the fleet and Zheng He, and the other eunuch admirals. But the officials didn't agree.

Bold saw the way Kyu picked up on this talk, and even asked further questions to learn more. After only a few days in Nanjing, he had found out all kinds of gossip Bold had not heard: the emperor had been thrown by a horse given to him by the Temurid emissaries, a horse once owned by Temur himself (Bold wondered which horse it was; strange to think an animal had lived so long, though on reflection he realized it had been less than two years since Temur's death). Then lightning had struck the new palace in Beijing and burned it all down. The emperor had released an edict blaming himself for this disfavor from heaven, causing fear and confusion and criticism. In the wake of these events, certain bureaucrats had openly criticized the monstrous expenditures of the new capital and the treasure fleet, draining the treasury surplus just as famine and rebellion in the south cried out for imperial relief. Very quickly the Yongle Emperor had tired of this criticism, and had had one of the most prominent critics exiled from China, and the rest banished to the provinces.

"That's all bad," one sailor said, a little bit the worse for drink, "but worst of all for the emperor is the fact that he's sixty years old. There's no help for that, even when you're emperor. It may even be worse for him."

Everyone nodded. "Bad, very bad." "He won't be able to keep the eunuchs and officials from fighting." "We could see a civil war before too long."

"To Beijing," Kyu said to Bold.

But before they left, Kyu insisted they go up to Zheng He's house, a rambling mansion with a front door carved to look like the stern of one of his treasure ships. The rooms inside (seventy-two, the sailors said) were each supposed to be decorated to resemble a different Muslim country, and in the courtyard the gardens were planted to resemble Yunnan.

Bold complained all the way up the hill. "He will never see a poor trader and his slave. His servants will kick us away from the door, this is ridiculous!"

It happened just as Bold had predicted. The gatekeeper sized them up and told them to be on their way.

"All right," Kyu said. "Off to the temple for Tianfei."

This was a grand complex of buildings, built by Zheng He to honor the Celestial Consort, and to thank her for her miraculous rescue of them in the storm.

> The centerpiece of the temple
> Is a nine-storied octagonal pagoda,
> Tiled in white porcelain fired with Persian cobalt
> That the treasure fleet brought back with it.
> Each level of the pagoda must be built
> With the same number of tiles, this
> Pleases Tianfei, so the tiles get smaller
> As each story narrows to a graceful peak,
> Far above the treetops. Beautiful offering
> And testament to a goddess of pure mercy.

There in the midst of the construction, conversing with men who looked no better than Bold or Kyu, was Zheng He himself. He looked at Kyu as they approached, and paused to talk to him. Bold shook his head to see this example of the boy's power revealing itself.

Zheng nodded as Kyu explained they had been part of his last expedition. "You looked familiar." He frowned, however, when Kyu went on to explain that they wanted to serve the emperor in Beijing.

"Zhu Di is off campaigning in the west. On horseback, with his rheumatism." He sighed. "He needs to understand that the fleet's way of conquering is best. Arrive with the ships, start trading, install a local ruler who will cooperate, and for the rest, simply let them be. Trade with them. Make sure the man at the top is friendly. There are sixteen countries sending tribute to the emperor as a direct result of the voyages of our fleet. Sixteen!"

"It's hard to get the fleet to Mongolia," Kyu said, frightening Bold. But Zheng He laughed.

"Yes, the Great Without is high and dry. We have to convince the emperor to forget the Mongols, and look to the sea."

"We want to do that," Kyu said earnestly. "In Beijing we will argue the case every chance we get. Will you give us introductions to the eunuch officials at the palace? I could join them, and my master here would be good in the imperial stables."

Zheng looked amused. "It won't make any difference. But I'll help you for old times' sake, and wish you luck."

He shook his head as he wrote a memorial, his brush wielded like a little hand broom. What happened to him afterward is well known: grounded by the emperor, given a landlocked military command, spending his days constructing the nine-storied porcelain pagoda honoring Tianfei; we imagine he missed his voyages over the distant seas of the world, but cannot say for sure. But we do know what happened to Bold and Kyu, and we will tell you in the next chapter.

7

New capital, new emperor, plots reach their ends.
Boy against China; you can guess who wins.

Beijing was raw in every sense, the wind frigid and damp, the wood of the buildings still white and dripping with sap, the smell of pitch and turned earth and wet cement everywhere. It was crowded, too, though not like Hangzhou or Nanjing, so that Bold and Kyu felt cosmopolitan and sophisticated, as if this huge construction site were beneath them somehow. A lot of people here had that attitude.

They made their way to the eunuch clinic named in Zheng He's memorial, located just south of the Meridian Gate, the southern entrance to the Forbidden City. Kyu presented his introduction, and he and Bold were whisked inside to see the clinic's head eunuch. "A reference from Zheng He will take you far in the palace," this eunuch told them, "even if Zheng himself is having troubles with the imperial officials. I know the palace's Director of Ceremonies, Wu Han, very well, and will introduce you. He is an old friend of Zheng's, and needs eunuchs in the Literary Depth Pavilion for rescript writing. But wait, you are not literate, are you. But Wu also administers the eunuch priests maintained to attend to the spiritual welfare of the concubines."

"My master here is a lama," Kyu said, indicating Bold. "He has trained me in all the mysteries of the bardo."

The eunuch regarded Bold skeptically. "Be that as it may, one way or another the memorial from Zheng will get you in. He has recommended you very highly. But you will need your pao, of course."

"Pao?" Kyu said. "My precious?"

"You know." The eunuch gestured at Kyu's groin. "It is necessary to prove your status, even after I have inspected and certified you. Also, more importantly perhaps, when you die you will be buried with it on your chest, to fool the gods. You don't want to come back as a she-mule, after all." He glanced at Kyu curiously. "You don't have yours?"

Kyu shook his head.

"Well, we have many here you can choose from, left over from patients who died. I doubt you can tell black from Chinese after the pickling!" He laughed and led them down a hall.

His name was Jiang, he said; he was an ex-sailor from Fukian, and was puzzled that anyone young and fit would ever leave the coast to come to a place like Beijing. "But as black as you are, you'll be like the quillin that the fleet brought back last time for the emperor, the spotted unicorn with the long neck. I think it also was from Zanj. Do you know it?"

"It was a big fleet," Kyu said.

"I see. Well, Wu and the other palace eunuchs love exotics like you and the quillin, and so does the emperor, so you'll be fine. Keep quiet and don't get mixed up in any conspiracies, and you'll do well."

In a cool storage building they went into a room filled with sealed porcelain and glass jars, and found a black penis for Kyu to take with him. The head eunuch then inspected him personally, to make sure he was what he said he was, and then brushed his certification onto the introduction from Zheng, and put his chop to it in red ink. "Some people try to fake it, of course, but if they're caught they get it handed to them, and then they aren't faking it anymore, are they. You know, I noticed they didn't put in a quill when they cut you. You should have a quill to keep it open, and then the plug goes in the quill. It's much more comfortable that way. They should have done that when you were cut."

"I seem to be all right without it," Kyu said. He held the glass jar up against the light, looking closely at his new pao. Bold shuddered and led the way out of the creepy room.

While further arrangements were made in the palace, Kyu was assigned a bed in the dorm, and Bold was offered a room in the clinic's men's building. "Temporary, you understand. Unless you care to join us in the main building. Great opportunities for advancement . . ."

"No thank you," Bold said politely. But he saw that many men were coming in to request the operation, desperate for a job. When there was famine in the countryside there was no shortage of applicants, they even had to turn people away. As with everything in China, there was a whole bureaucracy at work here, the palace requiring as it did several thousand eunuchs for its operation. This clinic was just a small part of that.

So they were launched in Beijing. Indeed, things had gone so well that Bold wondered if Kyu, no longer needing Bold as he had during their journey north, would now abandon him—move into the Forbidden City and disappear from his life. The idea made him sad, despite all.

But Kyu, after being assigned to the concubines of Zhu Gaozhi, the emperor's eldest legitimate son and the Heir Designate, asked Bold to come with him and apply to be a stabler for the heir. "I still need your help," he said simply, looking like the boy who had boarded the treasure ship so long ago.

"I'll try," Bold said.

Kyu was able to ask the favor of an interview from Zhu Gaozhi's stablemaster, and Bold went in and displayed his expertise with some big beautiful horses, and was given a job. Mongolians had the same kind of advantage in the stable that eunuchs had in the palace.

It was easy work, Bold found; the Heir Designate was an indolent man, his horses seldom ridden, so that the stablers had to exercise them on a track, and in the new parks of the palace grounds. The horses were all very big and white, but slow and weak-winded; Bold saw now why the Chinese could never go north of their Great Wall and attack the Mongols to any great effect, despite their stupendous numbers. Mongols lived on their horses, and lived off them too—made their clothes and shelter from their felt and wool, drank their milk and blood, ate them when they had to. Mongolian horses were the life of the people; whereas these big clodhoppers might as well have been driving millstones in a circle with blinders on, for all the wind and spirit they had.

It turned out Zhu Gaozhi spent a lot of time in Nanjing, where he had been brought up, visiting his mother the Empress Xu. So as the months passed, Bold and Kyu made the trip between the two capitals many times, traveling on barges on the Grand Canal, or on horseback beside it. Zhu Gaozhi preferred Nanjing to Beijing, for obvious reasons of climate and culture; late at night, after drinking vast quantities of rice wine, he could be heard declaring to his intimates that he would move the capital back to Nanjing on the very day of his father's death. This made the enormous labor of building Beijing look odd to them when they were there.

But more and more they were in Nanjing. Kyu helped run the heir's harem, and spent most of his time inside their enclosure. He never told Bold a thing about what he did in there, except one time, when he came out to the stables late at night, a bit drunk. This was almost the only time Bold saw him anymore, and he looked forward to these nocturnal visits, despite the way they made him nervous.

On this occasion Kyu remarked that his main task these days was to find husbands for those of the emperor's concubines who had reached the age of thirty without ever having relations with the emperor. Zhu Di farmed these out to his son, with instructions to marry them off.

"Would you like a wife?" Kyu asked Bold slyly. "A thirty-year-old virgin, expertly trained?"

"No thanks," Bold said uneasily. He already had an arrangement with one of the servant women in the compound in Nanking, and though he supposed Kyu was joking, it made him feel strange.

Usually when Kyu made these midnight visits out to the stables, he was deep in thought. He did not hear things Bold said to him, or answered oddly, as if replying to some other question. Bold had heard that the young eunuch was well liked, knew many people in the palace, and had the favor of Wu, the Director of Ceremonies. But what they all did in the concubines' quarters during the long nights of the Beijing winters, he had no idea. Uusally Kyu came out to the stables reeking of wine and perfume, sometimes urine, once even vomit. "To stink like a eunuch"— the common phrase came back to Bold at those times with unpleasant force. He saw how people made fun of the mincing eunuch walk, the hunched little steps with feet pointing outward, something that was either a physical necessity or a group style, Bold didn't know. They were called crows for their falsetto voices, among other names; but always behind their backs; and everyone agreed that as they fattened and then wizened in their characteristic fashion, they came to look like bent old women.

Kyu was still young and pretty, however, and drunk and disheveled as he was during his night visits to Bold, he seemed very pleased with himself. "Let me know if you ever want women," he said. "We've got more than we need in there."

During one of the heir's visits to Beijing, Bold caught a glimpse of the emperor and his heir together, as he brought their perfectly groomed horses out to the Gate of Heavenly Purity, so that the two could ride together in the parks of the imperial garden. Except the emperor wanted to leave the enclosure and ride well to the north of the city, apparently, and sleep out in tents. Clearly the Heir Designate was unenthusiastic, and the officials accompanying the emperor were as well. Finally he gave in and agreed to make it a day ride, but outside the imperial city, by the river.

As they were mounting the horses he exclaimed to his son, "You have to learn to fit the punishment to the crime! People need to feel the justice of your decision! When the Board of Punishments recommended that Xu Pei-yi be put to the lingering death, and all his male relations over sixteen put to death and all his female relations and children enslaved, I was merciful! I lowered his sentence to beheading, sparing all the relatives. And so they say, 'The emperor has a sense of proportion, he understands things.' "

"Of course they do," the heir agreed blandly.

The emperor glanced sharply at him, and off they rode.

When they returned, late in the day, he was still lecturing his son, sounding even more peeved than he had in the morning. "If you know nothing but the court, you will never be able to rule! The people expect the emperor to understand them, to be a man who rides and shoots as well as the Heavenly Envoy! Why do you think your governors will do what you say if they think you are womanly? They will only obey you to your face, and behind your back they will mock you and do whatever they like."

"Of course they will," said the heir, looking the other way.

The emperor glared at him. "Off the horse," he said in a heavy voice.

The heir sighed and slid from his mount. Bold caught the reins and calmed the horse with a quick hand while leading it toward the emperor's mount, ready when the emperor leaped off and roared, "Obey!"

The heir fell to his knees and kowtowed.

"You think the bureaucrats care about you," the emperor shouted, "but they don't! Your mother is wrong about that, like she is about everything else! They have their own ideas, and they won't support you when there's the least trouble. You need your own men."

"Or eunuchs," the heir said into the gravel.

The Yongle Emperor stared at him. "Yes. My eunuchs know they depend on my goodwill above all else. No one else will back them. So they're the only people in the world you know will back you."

No reply from the prostrated elder son. Bold, facing away and moving to the very edge of earshot, risked a glance back. The emperor, shaking his head heavily, was walking away, leaving his son kneeling on the ground.

"You may be backing the wrong horse," Bold said to Kyu the next time they met, on one of Kyu's increasingly rare night visits to the stables. "The emperor is going out with his second son now. They ride, they hunt, they laugh. One day they killed three hundred deer we had enclosed. While with the Heir Designate, the emperor has to drag him out of doors, can't get him off the palace grounds, and spends the whole time yelling at him. And the heir nearly mocks him to his face. Comes as close as he dares. And the emperor knows it too. I wouldn't be surprised if he changed the Heir Designate."

"He can't," Kyu said. "He wants to, but he can't."

"Whyever not?"

"The eldest is the son of the empress. The second-born is the son of a courtesan. A low-ranking courtesan at that."

"But the emperor can do what he wants, right?"

"Wrong. It only works when they all follow the laws together. If anyone breaks the laws, it can mean civil war, and the end of the dynasty."

Bold had seen this in the Chinggurid wars of succession, which had gone on for generations. Indeed it was said now that Temur's sons had been fighting ever since his death, with the khan's empire divided into four parts, and no sign of it ever coming together again.

But Bold also knew that a strong ruler could get away with things. "You're parroting what you've heard from the empress and the heir and their officials. But it isn't that simple. People make the laws, and sometimes they change them. Or ignore them. And if they've got the swords, that's it."

Kyu considered this in silence. Then he said, "There's talk that the countryside is suffering. Famine in Hunan, piracy on the coast, diseases in the south. The officials don't like it. They think the great treasure fleet brought back disease instead of treasure, and wasted huge sums of money. They don't understand what trade brings back, they don't believe in it. They don't believe in the new capital. They tell the empress and the heir that they should help the people, that we should get back to agriculture, and quit wasting so much cash on extravagant projects."

Bold nodded. "I'm sure they do."

"But the emperor persists. He does what he wants, and he has the army behind him, and his eunuchs. The eunuchs like the foreign trade, as they see it makes them rich. And they like the new capital, and all the rest. Right?"

Bold nodded again. "So it seems."

"The regular officials hate the eunuchs."

Bold glanced at him. "Do you see that yourself?"

"Yes. Although it's the emperor's eunuchs they really hate."

"No doubt. Whoever is closest to power is feared by all the rest."

Again Kyu thought things over. He seemed to Bold to be happy, these days; but then again Bold had thought that in Hangzhou. So it always made Bold nervous to see Kyu's little smile.

Soon after that conversation, when they were all in Beijing, a great storm came.

> Yellow dust makes the first raindrops muddy;
> Lightning cracks down bronze through it,
> Stitching together earth and sky,
> Visible through closed eyelids.
> About an hour later word comes:
> The new palaces have caught fire.
> The whole center of the Forbidden City
> Burning as though drenched in pitch,
> Flames licking the wet clouds,
> Pillar of smoke merging with the storm,
> Rain downwind baked out of the air, replaced by ash.

Running back and forth with terrified horses, then with buckets of water, Bold kept an eye out, and finally, at dawn, when they had given up fighting the blaze, for it was useless, he caught sight of Kyu there among the evacuated imperial concubines. All the Heir Designate's people had a hectic look, but Kyu in particular seemed to Bold elated, the whites of his eyes visible all the way around. Like a shaman after a successful voyage to the spirit world. He started this fire, Bold thought, just like in Hangzhou, this time using the lightning as his cover.

The next time Kyu made one of his midnight visits to the stables, Bold was almost afraid to speak to him.

Nevertheless he said, "Did you set that fire?" Whispering in Arabic, even though they were alone, outside the stables, with no chance of being overheard.

Kyu just stared at him. The look said yes, but he didn't elaborate.

Finally he said calmly, "An exciting night, wasn't it. I saved one of the Script Pavilion's cabinets, and some concubines as well. The redjackets were very grateful for their documents."

He went on about the beauty of the fire, and the panic of the concubines, and the rage, and later the fear, of the emperor, who took the fire to be a sign of heavenly disapproval, the worst bad portent ever to smite him; but Bold could not follow the boy's talk, his mind filled as it was with images of the various forms of the lingering death. To burn down a merchant in Hangzhou was one thing, but the emperor of all China! The Dragon Throne! He glimpsed again that thing inside the boy, the black nafs banging its wings around inside, and felt the distance between them grown vast and unbridgeable.

"Be quiet!" he said sharply in Arabic. "You're a fool. You'll get yourself killed, and me too."

Kyu smiled grimly. "On to a better life, right? Isn't that what you told me? Why should I fear dying?"

Bold had no answer.

After that they saw less of each other than ever. Days passed, festivals, seasons. Kyu grew up. When Bold caught sight of him, he saw a tall slender black eunuch, pretty and perfumed, mincing along with a flash of the eye, and, once, that raptor look as he regarded the people around him. Bejeweled, plump, perfumed, dressed in elaborate silk: a favorite of the empress and the heir, even though they hated the eunuchs of the emperor. Kyu was their pet, and perhaps even a spy in the emperor's harem. Bold feared for him at the same time that he feared him. The boy was wreaking havoc among the concubines of both emperor and heir, many said, even people in the stables who had no way of knowing directly. The way he moved through them was too forward, he was bound to be making enemies. Cliques would be plotting to bring him down. He must know that, he must be courting it; he laughed in their faces, so that they would hate him even more. It all seemed to delight him. But imperial revenge had a long reach. If someone fell, everyone he knew came down too.

So when the news spread that two of the emperor's concubines had hanged themselves, and the furious emperor demanded an accounting, and the whole nest of corruption began to unravel before everyone, fear rippling through the court like the plague itself, lies spreading the blame wider and wider, until fully three thousand concubines and eunuchs were implicated in the scandal, Bold expected to hear any hour of his young friend's torture and lingering death, perhaps from the mouths of guards come to execute him as well.

But it didn't happen. Kyu existed under a spell of protection like that of a sorcerer, it was so obvious that everyone saw it. The emperor executed forty of his concubines with his own hand, swinging the sword furiously, cutting them in half or decapitating them with single strokes, or running them through over and over, until the steps of the rebuilt Hall of Great Harmony ran with their blood; but Kyu stood just to the side, unharmed. One concubine even cried out toward Kyu as she stood naked before them all, a wordless shriek, and then she cursed the emperor to his face, "It's your fault, you're too old, your yang is gone, the eunuchs do it better than you!" Then snick, her head was falling into the puddles of blood like a sacrificed sheep's. All that beauty wasted. And yet no one touched Kyu; the emperor dared not look at him; and the black youth watched it all with a gleam in his eye, enjoying the wastage, and the way the bureaucrats hated him for it. The court was literally a shambles, they were feeding on each other now; and yet none of them had the courage to take on the weird black eunuch.

Bold's last meeting with him happened just before Bold was to accompany the emperor on an expedition to the west, to destroy the Tartars led by Arughtai. It was a hopeless cause; the Tartars were too fast, the emperor not well. Nothing would come of it. They would be back when winter came on, in just a few months. So Bold was suprised when Kyu came by the stables to say farewell.

It was like talking to a stranger now. But the youth clasped Bold by the arm suddenly, affectionate and serious, like a prince talking to a trusted old retainer.

"Do you never want to go home?" he asked.

"Home," Bold said.

"Isn't your family out there?"

"I don't know. It's been years. I'm sure they think I died. They could be anywhere."

"But not just anywhere. You could find them."

"Maybe." He looked at Kyu curiously. "Why do you ask?"

Kyu didn't answer at first. He was still clutching Bold's arm. Finally he said, "Do you know the story of the eunuch Chao Kao, who caused the downfall of the Chin dynasty?"

"No. Surely you're not still talking about that."

Kyu smiled. "No." He pulled a little carving from his sleeve—half of a tiger, carved from black ironwood, its stripes cut into the smooth surface. The amputation across its middle was mortised; it was a tally, like those used by officials to authenticate their communications with the capital when they were in the provinces. "Take this with you when you go. I'll keep the other half. It will help you. We'll meet again."

Bold took it, frightened. It seemed to him like Kyu's nafs, but of course that was something that couldn't be given away.

"We'll meet again. In our lives to come at least, as you always used to tell me. Your prayers for the dead give them instructions on how to proceed in the bardo, right?"

"That's right."

"I must go." And with a kiss to the cheek Kyu was off into the night.

The expedition to conquer the Tartars was a miserable failure, as expected, and one rainy night the Yongle Emperor died. Bold stayed up all through that night, pumping the bellows for a fire the officers used to melt all the tin cups they had, to make a coffin to carry the imperial body back to Beijing. It rained all the way back, the heavens crying. Only when they reached Beijing did the officers let the news be known.

The imperial body lay in state in a proper coffin for a hundred days. Music, weddings, and all religious ceremonies were forbidden during this interval, and all the temples in the land were required to ring their bells thirty thousand times.

For the funeral Bold joined the ten thousand members of the escort.

> Sixty lis' march to the imperial tomb site,
> Northwest of Beijing. Three days zigzagging
> To foil evil spirits, who only travel in straight lines.
> The funeral complex deep underground,
> Filled with the dead emperor's best clothes and goods,
> At the end of a tunnel three li long,
> Lined with stone servants awaiting his next command.
> How many lifetimes will they stand waiting?
> Sixteen of his concubines are hung,
> Their bodies buried around his coffin.

The day the Heir Designate ascended the Dragon Throne, his first edict was read aloud to all in the Great Within and the Great Without. Near the end of the edict, the reader in the palace proclaimed to all assembled there before the Hall of Great Harmony:

"All voyages of the treasure fleet are to be stopped. All the ships moored in Hangzhou are ordered to return to Nanjing, and all goods on the ships are to be turned over to the Department of Internal Affairs, and stored. Officials abroad on business are to return to the capital immediately; and all those called to go on future voyages are ordered back to their homes. The building and repair of all treasure ships is to stop immediately. All official procurement for going abroad must also be stopped, and all those involved in purchasing should return to the capital."

When the reader was done, the new emperor, who had just named himself the Hongxi Emperor, spoke for himself. "We have spent too much on extravagance. The capital will return to Nanjing, and Beijing will be designated an auxiliary capital. There will be no more waste of imperial resources. The people are suffering. Relieving people's poverty ought to be handled as though one were rescuing them from fire, or saving them from drowning. One cannot hesitate."

Bold saw Kyu's face across the great courtyard, a little black figurine with blazing eyes. The new emperor turned to look at his dead father's retinue, so many of them eunuchs. "For years you eunuchs have only been thinking of yourselves, at the expense of China. The Yongle Emperor thought you were on his side. But you were not. You have betrayed all China."

Kyu spoke up before his fellows could stop him. "Your Highness, it's the officials who are betraying China! They are trying to be as regent to you, and make you a boy emperor forever!"

With a roar a gang of the officials rushed at Kyu and some of the other eunuchs, pulling knives from their sleeves as they pounced. The eunuchs struggled or fled, but many were cut down on the spot. Kyu they stabbed a thousand times.

The Hongxi Emperor stood and watched. When it was over he said, "Take the bodies and hang them outside the Meridian Gate. Let all the eunuchs beware."

Later, in the stables, Bold sat holding the half-tiger tally in his hand. He had thought they would kill him too, and was ashamed of how much that thought had dominated him during the slaughter of the eunuchs; but no one had paid the slightest attention to him. It was possible no one else even remembered his connection to Kyu.

He knew he was leaving, but he didn't know where to go. If he went to Nanjing and helped burn the treasure fleet, and all its docks and warehouses, he would certainly be continuing his young friend's project. But all that would be done in any case.

Bold recalled their last conversation. Time to go home, perhaps, to start a new life.

But guards appeared in the doorway. We know what happened next; and so do you; so let's go on to the next chapter.

8

———

In the bardo, Bold explains to Kyu the true nature of reality;
Their jati regathered, they are cast back into the world.

At the moment of death Kyu saw the clear white light. It was everywhere, it bathed the void in itself, and he was part of it, and sang it out into the void.

Some eternity later he thought: this is what you strive for.

And so he fell out of it, into awareness of himself. His thoughts were continuing in their tumbling monologue revelry, even after death. Incredible but true. Perhaps he wasn't dead yet. But there was his body, hacked to pieces on the sand of the Forbidden City.

He heard Bold's voice, there inside his thoughts, speaking a prayer.

> "Kyu, my boy, my beautiful boy,
> The time has come for you to seek the path.
> This life is over. You are now
> Face-to-face with the clear light."

I'm past that, Kyu thought. What happens next? But Bold couldn't know where he was along his way. Prayers for the dead were useless in that regard.

> "You are about to experience reality
> In its pure state. All things are void.
> You will be like a clear sky,

Empty and pure. Your named mind
Will be like clear still water."

I'm past that! Kyu thought. Get to the next part!

"Use the mind to question the mind. Don't sleep at this crucial time. Your soul must leave your body awake, and go out through the Brahma hole."

The dead can't sleep, Kyu thought irritably. And my soul is already out of my body.

His guide was far behind him. But it had always been that way with Bold. Kyu would have to find his own way. Emptiness still surrounded the single thread of his thoughts. Some of the dreams he had had during his life had been of this place.

He blinked, or slept, and then he was in a vast court of judgment. The dais of the judge was on a broad deck, a plateau in a sea of clouds. The judge was a huge black-faced deity, sitting potbellied on the dais. Its hair was fire, burning wildly on its head. Behind it a black man held a pagoda roof that might have come straight out of the palace in Beijing. Above the roof floated a little seated Buddha, radiating calm. To his left and right were peaceful deities, standing with gifts in their arms; but these were all a great distance away, and not for him. The righteous dead were climbing long flying roads up to these gods. On the deck surrounding the dais, less fortunate dead were being hacked to pieces by demons, demons as black as the Lord of Death, but smaller and more agile. Below the deck more demons were torturing yet more souls. It was a busy scene and Kyu was annoyed. This is my judgment, and it's like a morning abbatoir! How am I supposed to concentrate?

A creature like a monkey approached him and raised a hand: "Judgment," it said in a deep voice.

Bold's prayer sounded in his mind, and Kyu realized that Bold and this monkey were related somehow. "Remember, whatever you suffer now is the result of your own karma," Bold was saying. "It's yours and no one else's. Pray for mercy. A little white god and a little black demon will appear, and count out the white and black pebbles of your good and evil deeds."

Indeed it was so. The white imp was pale as an egg, the black imp like onyx; and they were hoeing great piles of white and black stones into heaps, which to Kyu's surprise appeared about equal in size. He could not remember doing any good deeds.

"You will be frightened, awed, terrified."

I will not! These prayers were for a different kind of dead, for people like Bold.

"You will attempt to tell lies, saying I have not committed any evil deed."

I will not say any such ridiculous thing.

Then the Lord of Death, up on its throne, suddenly took notice of Kyu, and despite himself Kyu flinched.

"Bring the mirror of karma," the god said, grinning horribly. Its eyes were burning coals.

"Don't be frightened," Bold's voice said inside him. "Don't tell any lies, don't be terrified, don't fear the Lord of Death. The body you're in now is only a mental body. You can't die in the bardo, even if they hack you to pieces."

Thanks, Kyu thought uneasily. That is such a comfort.

"Now comes the moment of judgment. Hold fast, think good thoughts; remember, all these events are your own hallucinations, and what life comes next depends on your thoughts now. In a single moment of time a great difference is created. Don't be distracted when the six lights appear. Regard them all with compassion. Face the Lord of Death without fear."

The black god held a mirror up with such practiced accuracy that Kyu saw in the glass his own face, dark as the god's. He saw that the face is the naked soul itself, always, and that his was as dark and dire as the Lord of Death's. This was the moment of truth! And he had to concentrate on it, as Bold kept reminding him. And yet all the while the whole antic festival shouted and shrieked and clanged around him, every possible punishment or reward given out at once, and he couldn't help it, he was annoyed.

"Why is black evil and white good?" he demanded of the Lord of Death. "I never saw it that way. If this is all my own thinking, then why is that so? Why is my Lord of Death not a big Arab slave trader, as it would be in my own village? Why are your agents not lions and leopards?"

But the Lord of Death was an Arab slave trader, he saw now, an Arab intaglioed in miniature in the surface of the god's black forehead, looking out at Kyu and waving. The one who had captured him and taken him to the coast. And among the shrieks of the rendered there were lions and leopards, hungrily gnawing the intestines of living victims.

All just my thoughts, Kyu reminded himself, feeling fear rise in his throat. This realm was like the dream world, but more solid; more solid even than the waking world of his just completed life; everything trebly stuffed with itself, so that the leaves on the round ornamental bushes (in ceramic pots!) hung like jade leaves, while the jade throne of the god pulsed with a solidity far beyond that of stone. Of all the worlds the bardo was the one of the utmost reality.

The white Arab face in the black forehead laughed and squeaked, "Condemned!" and the huge black face of the Lord of Death roared, "Condemned to hell!" It threw a rope around Kyu's neck and dragged him off the dais. It cut off Kyu's head, tore out his heart, pulled out his entrails, drank his blood, gnawed his bones; yet Kyu did not die. Body hacked to pieces, yet it revived. And it all began again. Intense pain throughout. Tortured by reality. Life is a thing of extreme reality; death also.

Ideas are planted in the mind of the child like seeds, and may grow to completely dominate the life.

The plea: I have done no evil.

Agony disassembled into anguish, regret, remorse; nausea at his past lives and how little they had gained him. In this terrible hour he sensed them all without actually being able to remember them. But they had happened. Oh, to get off the endless wheel of fire and tears. The sorrow and grief he felt then was worse than the pain of dismemberment. The solidity of the bardo fell apart, and he was bombarded by light exploding in his thoughts, through which the palace of judgment could only be seen as a kind of veil, or a painting on the air.

But there was Bold up there, being judged in his turn. Bold, a cowering monkey, the only person after Kyu's capture who had meant anything at all to him. Kyu wanted to cry out to him for help, but stifled the thought, as he did not want to distract his friend at the very moment, of all the infinity of moments, when he needed not to be distracted. Nevertheless something must have escaped from Kyu, some groan of the mind, some anguished thought or cry for help; for a gang of furious four-armed demons dragged Kyu down and away, out of sight of Bold's judgment.

Then he was indeed in hell, and pain the least of his burdens, as superficial as mosquito bites, compared to the deep, oceanic ache of his loss. The anguish of solitude! Colored explosions, tangerine, lime, quicksilver, each shade more acid than the last, burned his consciousness with an anguish ever deeper. I'm wandering in the bardo, rescue me, rescue me!

And then Bold was there with him.

They stood in their old bodies, looking at each other. The lights grew clearer, less painful to the eyes; a single ray of hope pierced the depth of Kyu's despair, like a lone paper lantern seen across West Lake. You found me, Kyu said.

Yes.

It's a miracle you could find me here.

No. We always meet in the bardo. We will cross paths for as long as the six worlds turn in this cycle of the cosmos. We are part of a karmic jati.

What's that?

Jati, subcaste, family, village. It manifests differently. We all came into the cosmos together. New souls are born out of the void, but infrequently, especially at this point in the cycle, for we are in the Kali-yuga, the Age of Destruction. When new souls do appear it happens like a dandelion pod, souls like seeds, floating away on the dharma wind. We are all seeds of what we could be. But the new seeds float together and never separate by much, that's my point. We have gone through many lives together already. Our jati has been particularly tight since the avalanche. That fate bound us together. We rise or fall together.

But I don't remember any other lives. And I don't remember anyone from this past life but you. I only recognize you! Where are the rest of them?

You didn't recognize me either. We found you. You have been falling away from the jati for many reincarnations now, down and down into yourself alone, in lower and lower lokas. There are six lokas: they are the worlds, the realms, of rebirth and illusion. Heaven, the world of the devas; then the world of the asuras, those giants full of dissension; then the human world; then the animal world; then the world of pretas, or hungry ghosts; then hell. We move between them as our karma changes, life by life.

How many of us are there in this jati?

I don't know. A dozen perhaps, or half a dozen. The group blurs at the boundaries. Some go away and don't come back until much later. We were a village, that time in Tibet. But there were visitors, traders. Fewer every time. People get lost, or fall away. As you have been doing. When the despair strikes.

At the mere sound of the word it washed through Kyu: despair. Bold's figure grew transparent.

Bold, help me! What do I do?

Think good thoughts. Listen, Kyu, listen—as we think, so we are. Both here and hereafter, in all the worlds. For thoughts are things, the parents of all actions, good and bad alike. And as the sowing has been, so the harvest will be.

I'll think good thoughts, or try, but what should I do? What should I look for?

The lights will lead you. Each world has its own color. White light from the devas, green from the asuras, yellow from the human, blue from the beasts, red from ghosts, smoke-colored from hell. Your body will appear the color of the world you are to return to.

But we're yellow! Kyu said, looking at his hand. And Bold was as yellow as a flower.

That means we must try again. We try and try again, life after life, until we achieve Buddha-wisdom, and are released at last. Or some then choose to return to the human world, to help others along their way to release. Those are called bodhisattvas. You could be one of those, Kyu. I can see it inside you. Listen to me now. Soon you'll run for it. Things will chase you, and you'll hide. In a house, a cave, a jungle, a lotus blossom. These are all wombs. You'll want to stay in your hiding place, to escape the terrors of the bardo. That way lies preta, and you will become a ghost. You must emerge again to have any hope. Choose your womb door without any feelings of attraction or repulsion. Looks can be deceiving. Go as you see fit. Follow the heart. Try helping other spirits first, as if you were a bodhisattva already.

I don't know how!

Learn. Pay attention and learn. You must follow, or lose the jati for good.

Then they were attacked by huge male lions, manes already matted with blood, roaring angrily. Bold took off in one direction and Kyu in another. Kyu ran and ran, the lion on his heels. He dodged through two trees and onto a path. The lion ran on and lost him.

To the east he saw a lake, adorned with black-and-white swans. To the west, a lake with horses standing in it; to the south, a scattering of pagodas; to the north a lake with a castle in it. He moved south toward the pagodas, feeling vaguely that this would have been Bold's choice; feeling also that Bold and the rest of his jati were already there, in one of the temples waiting for him.

He reached the pagodas. He wandered from one building to the next, looking in doorways, shocked by visions of crowds in disarray, fighting or fleeing from hyena-headed guards and wardens; a hell of a village, each possible future catastrophic, terrifying. Death's hometown.

A long time passed in this horrible search, and then he was looking through the gates of a temple at his jati, his cohort, Bold and all the rest of them, Shen, I-Li, Dem his mother, Zheng He, all of them immediately known to him—oh, he thought, of course. They were naked and blood-ied, but putting on the gear of war nevertheless. Then hyenas howled, and Kyu fled through the raw yellow light of morning, through trees into the protection of elephant grass. The hyenas prowled between the huge tufts of grass, and he pressed through the knife edges of one broken-down clump to take refuge inside it.

For a long time he cowered in the grass, until the hyenas went away, also the cries of his jati as they looked for him, telling him to stick with them. He hid there through a long night of awful sounds, creatures being killed and eaten; but he was safe; and morning came again. He decided to venture forth, and found the way out was closed. The knife-edged grass blades had grown, and were like long swords caging him, even pressing in on him, cutting him as they grew. Ah, he realized; this is a womb. I've chosen one without trying to, without listening to Bold's ad-vice, separated from my family, unaware and in fear. The worst kind of choosing.

And yet to stay here would be to become a hungry ghost. He would have to submit. He would have to be born again. He groaned at the thought, cursed himself for a fool. Try to have a little more presence of mind next time, he thought, a little more courage! It would not be easy; the bardo was a scary place. But now, when it was too late, he decided he had to try. Next time!

And so he reentered the human realm. What happened to him and to his companions the next time around, it is not our task to tell. Gone, gone, gone altogether beyond! All hail!

BOOK 2

❖ THE HAJ IN THE HEART ❖

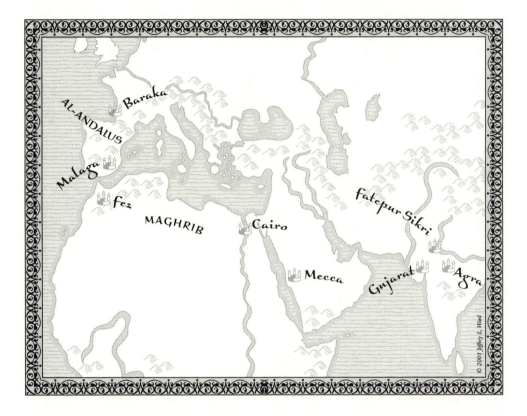

1

The Cuckoo in the Village

What happens is that sometimes there is a confusion, and the reincarnating soul enters into a womb already occupied. Then there are two souls in the same baby, and a fight breaks out. Mothers can feel that kind, the babies that thrash around inside, wrestling themselves. Then they're born and the shock of that ejection stills them for a while, they're fully occupied learning to breathe and otherwise coming to grips with this world. After that the fight between the two souls for the possession of the one body recommences. That's colic.

A baby suffering colic will cry out as if struck, arch its back in pain, even writhe in agony, for many of its waking hours. This should be no surprise, two souls are struggling within it, and so for weeks the baby cries all the time, its guts twisted by the conflict. Nothing can ease its distress. It's not a situation that can last for long, it's too much for any little body to bear. In most cases the cuckoo soul drives out the original, and then the body finally calms down. Or sometimes the first soul successfully drives out the cuckoo and is restored to itself. Or else, in rare cases, neither one is strong enough to drive the other out, and the colic finally subsides but the baby grows up a divided person, confused, erratic, unreliable, prone to insanity.

Kokila was born at midnight, and the dai pulled her out and said "It's a girl, poor thing." Her mother Zaneeta hugged the little creature to her breast, saying, "We will love you anyway."

She was a week old when the colic struck. She spat up her mother's milk and cried inconsolably all through the nights. Very quickly Zaneeta forgot what the cheerful new babe had been like, a kind of placid grub at her breast sucking, gurgling amazedly at the world. Under the assault of the colic she screamed, cried, moaned, writhed. It was painful to see it. Zaneeta could do nothing but hold her, hands under her stomach as it banded with cramping muscles, letting her hang face downward from Zaneeta's hip. Something about this posture, perhaps just the effort of keeping her head upright, quieted Kokila. But it did not always work, and never for long. Then the writhing and screams began again, until Zaneeta was near distraction. She had to keep her husband Rajit fed, and her two older daughters as well, and having borne three daughters in a row she was already out of Rajit's favor, and the babe was intolerable. Zaneeta tried sleeping with her out in the women's ground, but the menstruating women, while sympathetic, did not appreciate the noise. They enjoyed getting out of the home away with the girls, and it was not a place for babies. So Zaneeta was driven to sleeping with Kokila out against the side of their family's house, where they both dozed fitfully between bouts of crying.

This went on for a couple of months, and then it ended. Afterward the baby had a different look in her eye. The dai who had delivered her, Insef, checked her pulse and her irises and her urine, and declared that a different soul had indeed taken over the body, but that this was not really important—it happened to many babies, and could be an improvement, as usually in colic battles the stronger soul won out.

But after all that internal violence, Zaneeta regarded Kokila with trepidation, and all through her infancy and childhood Kokila looked back at her, and at the rest of the world, with a kind of black wild look, as if she were uncertain where she was or what she was doing there. A confused and often angry little girl, in fact, although clever in manipulating others, quick to caress or to yell, and very beautiful. She was strong too, and quick, and by the time she was five she was more help than harm around the home. By then Zaneeta had had two more children, the youngest of them a son, the sun of their lives, all thanks to Ganesh and Kartik, and with all the work there was to be done she appreciated Kokila's self-reliance and quick abilities.

Naturally the new son, Jahan, was the center of the household, and Kokila only the most capable of Zaneeta's daughters, absorbed in the business of her childhood and youth, not particularly well known to Zaneeta compared to Rajit and Jahan, whom naturally she had to study in depth.

So Kokila was free to follow her own thoughts for a few years. Insef often said that childhood was the best time in a woman's life, because as a girl she was somewhat free of men, and mostly just another worker around the house and in the fields. But the dai was old, and cynical about love and marriage, having seen their results so often turn bad, for herself and for others. Kokila was no more inclined to listen to her than to anyone else. To tell the truth she didn't seem to listen much to anybody. She watched everyone with that startled wary look you see on animals you come upon suddenly in the forest, and spoke little. She seemed to enjoy going off to do the daily work. She stayed silent and observant around her father, and the other children of the village didn't interest her, except for one girl, who had been found abandoned as an infant, one morning in the women's ground. This foundling Insef was raising to be the dai after her. Insef had named her Bihari, and often Kokila went by the dai's hut and took Bihari with her on her morning round of chores, not talking to her very much more than she did to anyone else, but pointing things out to her, and most of all, bothering to bring her along in the first place, which surprised Zaneeta. The foundling was nothing unusual, after all, just a little girl like all the rest. It was another of Kokila's mysteries.

In the months before monsoon, the work for Kokila and all the rest of them got harder for several weeks on end. Wake in the morning and stoke the fire. Cross the cool village, the air not yet dusty. Pick up Bihari at the dai's little hut in the woods. Downstream to the defecation grounds, wash up afterward, then back through the village to pick up the water jars and head upstream. Past the laundry pools, where women were already congregating, and on to the watering hole. Fill up and hump the big heavy jars back home, stopping several times to rest. Then off into the forest to forage for firewood. This could take most of the morning. Then back to the fields west of the village, where her father and his brothers had some land, to sow pulse of wheat and barley. They put it in over a few weeks, so that it would ripen through the long harvest month. This week's row was weak, the tops small, but Kokila thrust them in the plowed earth without thought, then in the heat of the day sat with the other women and girls, mixing grain and water to make a pasty dough, throwing chapatis, cooking some of them. After that she went out to their cow. A few rhythmic downward tugs of her finger in its rectum started a spill of dung that she collected warm in her hands, slapped into patties with some straw for drying, and put on the stone-and-turf wall bordering her father's field. After that she took some dried dung cakes by the house, put one on the fire, went out to the stream to wash her hands and the dirty clothes: four saris, dhotis, wraps. Then back to the house in the waning light of the day, the heat and dust making everything golden in the slant air, to the hearth in the central room of their house, to cook chapatis and daal bhat on the little clay stove next to the firepit.

Some time after dark Rajit would come home, and Zaneeta and the girls would surround him with care, and after he had eaten the daal bhat and chapatis he would relax and tell Zaneeta something about his day, as long as it had not gone too badly. If it had, he wouldn't speak of it. But usually he told them something of his juggling of land and cattle deals. The village families used marginal pastures as securities for new animals, or vice versa, and brokering trade in calves and kids and pasture rights was what her father did, mostly between Yelapur and Sivapur. Then also he was always making marriage arrangements for his daughters, a bad business since he had so many of them, but he made up dowries when he could, and had no hesitation in marrying them down. Had no choice, really.

So the evening would end and they slept on rush mattresses unrolled for the night on the floor, by the fire for warmth if it was cool, for the smoke's protection from mosquitoes if it was warm. Another night would pass.

One evening after dinner, a few days before Durga Puja marked the end of the harvest, her father told her mother that he had arranged a possible marriage for Kokila, whose turn it was, to a man from Dharwar, the market village just the other side of Sivapur. The prospective husband was a Lingayat, like Rajit's family and most of Yelapur, and the third son of Dharwar's headman. He had quarreled with his father, however, and this left him unable to ask Rajit for much of a dowry. Probably he was unmarriageable in Dharwar, Kokila guessed, but she was excited anyway. Zaneeta seemed pleased, and said she would look the candidate over during the Durga Puja.

Ordinary life was pegged to whichever festival was coming next, and the festivals all had different natures, coloring the feel of the days leading up to them. Thus the car festival of Krishna takes place in the monsoon, and its color and gaiety stand in contrast to the lowering gray overhead; boys blow their palm-leaf trumpets as if to hold off the rain by the blast of their breath, and everyone would go crazy from the noise if the blowing itself didn't reduce the trumpets quickly to palm leaves again. Then the Swing Festival of Krishna takes place at the end of monsoon, and the fair associated with it is full of stalls selling superfluous things like sitars and drums, or silks, or embroidered caps, or chairs and tables and cabinets. The time for the Id shifts through the year, making it seem a very human event somehow, free of the earth and its gods, and during it all the Muslims come to Sivapur to watch their elephant parade.

Then Durga Puja marks the harvest, the grand climax of the year, honoring the mother goddess and all her works.

So the women gathered on the first day, and mixed a batch of vermilion bindi paste, while drinking some of the dai's fiery chang, and they scattered after that, painted and giggling, following the Muslim drummers in the opening parade, shouting "To the victory of Mother Durga!" The goddess's slant-eyed statue, made of clay and dressed in colored pith and gilding, looked faintly Tibetan. Placed around it were similarly dressed statues of Laksmi and Saraswati, and her sons Ganesh and Kartik. Two goats were tethered in turn to a sacrifical post before these statues and decapitated, the bleeding heads staring up from the dust.

The sacrifice of the buffalo was an even greater matter; a special priest came from Bhadrapur, with a big scimitar sharpened for the occasion. This was important, for if the blade didn't make it all the way through the buffalo's big neck, it meant that the goddess was displeased and had refused the offering. Boys spent the morning rubbing the skin on the top of its neck with ghee, to soften it.

This time the heavy stroke of the priest was successful, and all the shouting celebrants charged the body to make little balls of blood and dust, and throw them at each other, shrieking.

An hour or two later the mood was entirely different. One of the old men started singing, "The world is pain, its load past bearing," and then the women took it up, for it was dangerous for the men to be heard questioning the Great Mother; even the women had to pretend to be wounded demons in the song:

"Who is she that walks the fields as Death, She that fights and swoops as Death? A mother will not destroy her child, Her own flesh, creation's joy, yet we see the Killer looking here then there . . ."

Later, as night fell, the women went home and dressed in their best saris, and came back out and stood in two lines, and the boys and men shouted "Victory to the Great Goddess!" and the music began, wild and carefree, the whole crowd dancing and talking around the bonfire, looking beautiful and dangerous in their firelit finery.

Then people from Dharwar showed up, and the dancing grew wild. Kokila's father took her by the hand out of the line and introduced her to the parents of her intended. Apparently a reconciliation had been patched together for the sake of this formality. The father she had seen before, headman of Dharwar as he was, named Shastri; the mother she had never seen before, as the father had pretensions of purdah, though he was not really wealthy.

The mother looked Kokila over with a sharp, not unfriendly eye, bindi paste running down between her eyebrows, face sweaty in the hot night. Possibly a decent mother-in-law. Then the son was produced; Gopal, third son of Shastri. Kokila nodded stiffly, looking aslant at him, not knowing what she felt. He was a thin-faced, intent-looking youth, perhaps nervous—she couldn't tell. She was taller than he was. But that might change.

They were swept back into their respective parties without exchanging a word. Nothing but that single nervous glance, and she did not see him again for three years. All the while, however, she knew they were destined to marry, and it was a good thing, as her affairs were therefore settled, and her father could stop worrying about her, and treat her without irritation.

Over time she learned from the women's gossip a bit more about the family she was going to join. Shastri was an unpopular headman. His latest offense was to have exiled a Dharwar blacksmith for visiting a brother in the hills without asking his permission first. He had not called the panchayat together to discuss or approve this decision. He had never called the panchayat together, in fact, since inheriting the headman position from his deceased father a few years before. Why, people muttered, he and his eldest son ran Dharwar as if they were the zamindars of the place!

Kokila took all this in without too much concern, and spent as much time as she could with Bihari, who was learning the herbs the dai used as medicines. Thus when they were out collecting firewood, Bihari was also inspecting the forest floor and finding plants to bring back—bittersweet in sunny patches, whiteroot in wet shade, castor bean under saal trees among their roots, and so on. Back at their hut Kokila helped grind the dried plants, or otherwise prepare them, using oils or spirits, for use by Insef in her midwifery, for the most part: to stimulate contractions, relax the womb, reduce pain, open the cervix, slow bleeding, and so on. There were scores of source plants and animal parts that the dai wanted them to learn. "I'm old," she would say, "I'm thirty-six, and my mother died at thirty. Her mother taught her the lore, and the dai who taught my grandmother was from a Dravidian village to the south, where names and even property were reckoned down through the women, and she taught my grandmother all the Dravidians know, and that goes back through all the dais of time to Saraswati, the goddess of learning herself, so we can't let it go forgotten, you must learn it and teach your daughters, so that birthing is made as easy as it can be, poor things, and as many kept alive as possible." People said of Insef that she had a centipede in her head (this was mostly an expression said of eccentrics, although in fact mothers searched your ears for them if you had been lying with your head on the grass, and sometimes rinsed out your ears with oil, for centipedes detest oil), and she often talked as fast as you ever heard anyone talk, rambling on and on, mostly to herself, but Kokila liked to hear her.

And it took very little for Insef to convince Bihari of the importance of these things. She was a lively sweet girl with a good eye in the forest, a good memory for plants, and always a cheerful smile and a kind word for people. She was if anything too cheery and attractive, because in the year Kokila was to be married to Gopal, Shardul, his older brother, the eldest son of Shastri, soon to become Kokila's brother-in-law—one of those in her husband's family who would have the right to tell her what to do—started looking at Bihari in an interested way, and after that, no matter what she did, he watched her. It couldn't lead to any good, as Bihari was perhaps untouchable and therefore unmarriageable, and Insef did what she could to seclude her. But the festivals brought the single men and women together, and the daily life of the village afforded various glimpses and encounters as well. And Bihari was interested, anyway, even though she knew she was unmarriageable. She liked the idea of being normal, no matter how vehemently the dai warned her against it.

The day came when Kokila was married to Gopal and moved to Dharwan. Her new mother-in-law turned out to be withdrawn and irritable, and Gopal himself was no prize. An anxious man with little to say, dominated by his parents, never reconciled with his father, he at first tried to lord it over Kokila the way they did over him, but without much conviction, particularly after she snapped at him a few times. He was used to that, and quickly enough she had the upper hand. She didn't much like him, and looked forward to dropping by to see Bihari and the dai in the forest. Really only the second son, Prithvi, seemed to her at all admirable in the headman's family, and he left early every day and had as little to do with his family as he could, keeping quiet with a distant air.

There was a lot of traffic between the two villages, more than Kokila had ever noticed before it became so important to her, and she made do—secretly taking a preparation that the dai had made for her, to keep from having a baby. She was fourteen years old but she wanted to wait.

Before long things went bad. The dai got so crippled by her swollen joints that Bihari had to take over her work, and she was much more frequently seen in Dharwar. Meanwhile Shastri and Shardul were conspiring to make money by betraying their village, changing the tax assessment with the agent of the zamindar, shifting it to the zamindar's great advantage, with Shastri skimming off some for himself. Basically they were colluding to change Dharwar over to the Muslim form of farm tax rather than the Hindu law. The Hindu law, which was a religious injunction and sacred, allowed a tax of no more than one sixth of all produce, while the Muslim claim was to everything, with whatever the farmers kept being a matter of the pleasure of the zamindar. In practice this often meant little difference, but Muslim allowances varied for crops and circumstance, and this was where Shastri and Shardul were helping the zamindar, by calculating what more could be taken without starving the villagers. Kokila lay there at night with Gopal, and through the open doorway as he slept she heard Shastri and Shardul going over the possibilities.

"Wheat and barley, two fifths when naturally watered, three tenths when watered by wheels."

"That sounds good. Then dates, vines, green crops, and gardens, one third."

"But summer crops one fourth."

Eventually, to aid in this work, the zamindar gave Shardul the post of qanungo, assessor for the village; and he was already an awful man. And he still had an eye for Bihari. The night of the car festival he took her in the forest. From her account afterward it was clear to Kokila that Bihari hadn't completely minded it, she relished telling the details, "I was on my back in the mud, it was raining on my face and he was licking the rain off it, saying 'I love you I love you.' "

"But he won't marry you," Kokila pointed out, worried. "And his brothers won't like it if they hear about this."

"They won't hear. And it was so passionate, Kokila, you have no idea." She knew Kokila was not impressed by Gopal.

"Yes yes. But it could lead to trouble. Is a few minutes' passion worth that?"

"It is, it is. Believe me."

For a while she was happy, and sang all the old love songs, especially one they used to sing together, an old one.

> I like sleeping with somebody different,
> Often.
> It's nicest when my husband is in a far country,
> Far away.
> And there's rain in the streets at night and wind
> And nobody.

But Bihari got pregnant, despite Insef's preparations. She tried to keep to herself, but with the dai crippled there were births that she had to attend, and so she went and her condition was noted, and people put together what they had seen or heard, and said that Shardul had gotten her with child. Then Prithvi's wife was giving birth and Bihari went to help, and the baby, a boy, died a few minutes after it was born, and outside their house Shastri struck Bihari in the face, calling her a witch and a whore.

All this Kokila heard about when she visited Prithvi's house, from Prithvi's wife, who said the birth had gone faster than anyone expected, and that she doubted Bihari had done anything bad. Kokila hurried off to the dai's hut, and found the gnarled old woman puffing with effort between Bihari's legs, trying to get the baby out. "She's miscarrying," she told Kokila. So Kokila took over and did what the dai told her to, forgetting her own family until night fell, when she remembered and exclaimed, "I have to go!" and Bihari whispered, "Go. It will be all right."

Kokila rushed home through the forest to Dharwar, where her mother-in-law slapped her, but perhaps just to preempt Gopal, who punched her hard in the arm and forbade her to return to the forest or Sivapur ever again, a ludicrous command given the realities of their life, and she almost said "How will I fetch your water then?" but bit her lip and rubbed her arm, looking daggers at them, until she judged they were as frightened as they could get without beating her, after which she glared like Kali at the floor instead, and cleaned up after their impromptu dinner, which had been hobbled by her absence. They could not even eat without her. This fury was the thing she would remember forever.

Before dawn next morning she slipped out with the water jugs and hurried through the wet gray forest, leaves scattered at every level from the ground to the high canopy overhead, and arrived at the dai's hut frightened and breathing hard.

Bihari was dead. The baby was dead, Bihari was dead, even the old woman lay stretched on her pallet, gasping with the pain of her exertions, looking like she too might expire and leave this world at any minute. "They went an hour ago," she said. "The baby should have lived, I don't know what happened. Bihari bled too much. I tried to stop it but I couldn't reach."

"Teach me a poison."

"What?"

"Teach me a good poison to use. I know you know them. Teach me the strongest one you know, right now."

The old woman turned her head to the wall, weeping. Kokila pulled her around roughly and shouted, "Teach me!"

The old woman looked over at the two bodies under a spread sari, but there was no one else there to be alarmed. Kokila began to raise a hand to threaten her, then stopped herself. "Please," she begged. "I have to know."

"It's too dangerous."

"Not as dangerous as sticking a knife in Shastri."

"No."

"I'll stab him if you don't tell me, and they'll burn me on a bonfire."

"They'll do that if you poison him."

"No one will know."

"They'll think I did it."

"Everyone knows you can't move."

"That won't matter. Or they'll think you did it."

"I'll do it cleverly, believe me. I'll be at my parents'."

"It won't matter. They'll blame us anyway. And Shardul is as bad as Shastri, or worse."

"Tell me."

The old woman looked into her face for a time. Then she rolled over, opened her sewing basket. She showed Kokila a small dried plant, then some berries. "This is water hemlock. These are castor bean seeds. Grind the hemlock leaves to a paste, add seeds to the paste just before you place it. It's bitter, but you don't need much. A pinch in spicy food will kill without any taste. But it looks like poisoning afterward, I warn you. It's not like being sick."

So Kokila watched and made her plan. Shastri and Shardul continued their work for the zamindar, gaining new enemies every month. And it was rumored Shardul had raped another girl in the forest, the night of Gauri Hunnime, the woman's festival when mud images of Siva and Parvati are worshiped.

Meanwhile Kokila had learned every detail of their routine. Shastri and Shardul ate a leisurely breakfast, and then Shastri heard cases at the pavilion between his house and the well, while Shardul did accounting beside the house. In the heat of midday they napped and received visitors on the verandah facing north into the forest. In the afternoons of most days they ate a small meal while lying on couches, like little zamindars, then walked with Gopal or one or two associates to that day's market, where they "did business" until the sun was low. They returned to the village drunk or drinking, stumbling cheerfully through the dusk to their home and dinner. It was as steady a routine as any in the village.

So Kokila considered her plans while spending some of her firewood walks on the hunt for water hemlock and castor beans. These grew in the dankest parts of the forest, where it shaded into swamp, and hid every manner of dangerous creature, from mosquito to tiger. But at midday all such pests were resting; indeed, in the hot months everything alive seemed sleeping at midday, even the drooping plants. Insects buzzed sleepily in the sleepy silence, and the two poison plants glowed in the dim light like little green lanterns. A prayer to Kali and she plucked them out, while she was bleeding, and pulled apart a bean pod for the seeds, and tucked them in the band of her sari, and hid them for the night in the forest near the defecation grounds, the day before the Durga Puja. That night she did not sleep at all, except for short dreams, in which Bihari came to her and told her not to be sad. "Bad things happen in every life," Bihari said. "No anger." There was more but on waking it all slipped away, and Kokila went to her hiding place and found the plant parts and ground the hemlock leaves furiously together in a gourd with a stone, then cast the stone and gourd away in beds of ferns. With the paste on a leaf in her hand she went to Shastri's house, and waited until their afternoon nap, a day that seemed to last forever; then put the little seeds in the paste, and smeared a tiny dab of the paste inside the doughballs made for Shastri and Shardul's afternoon snack. Then she ran from the house and through the forest, her heart taking flight like a deer ahead of her—too much like a deer, in that she ran wild with the thrill of what she had done, and fell into an unseen deer snare, set by a man from Bhadrapur. By the time he found her, stunned and just starting to struggle in the lines, with some of the paste still on her fingers, and took her to Dharwar, Shastri and Shardul were dead, and Prithvi was the new headman of the village, and Kokila was declared a witch and poisoner and killed on the spot.

2

Back in the Bardo

Back in the bardo Kokila and Bihari sat next to each other on the black floor of the universe, waiting their turn for judgment.

"You're not getting it," said Bihari—also Bold, and Bel, and Borondi, and many, many other incarnations before, back to her original birth in the dawn of this Kali-yuga, this age of destruction, fourth of the four ages, when as a new soul she had spun out of the Void, an eruption of Being out of Nonbeing, a miracle inexplicable by natural law and indicative of the existence of some higher realm, a realm above that even of the deva gods who now sat on the dais looking down at them. The realm that they all sought instinctively to return to.

Bihari continued: "The dharma is a matter that can't be short-changed, you have to work at it step by step, doing what you can in each given situation. You can't leap up to heaven."

"I shit on all that," Kokila said, making a rude gesture at the gods. She was still so mad she could spit, and terrified too, weeping and wiping her nose on the back of her hand, "I'll be damned if I cooperate in such a horrible thing."

"Yes! you will! That's why we keep almost losing you. That's why you never recognize your jati when you're in the world, why you keep doing your own family harm. We rise and fall together."

"I don't see why."

Now Shastri was being judged, kneeling with his hands together in supplication.

"He'd better be sent to hell!" Kokila shouted at the black god. "The lowest, nastiest level of hell!"

Bihari shook her head. "It's step by step, like I said. Little steps up and down. And it's you they're likely to judge down, after what you did."

"It was justice!" Kokila exclaimed with vehement bitterness. "I took justice into my own hands because no one else would do it! And I would do it again too." She shouted up at the black god: "Justice, damn it!"

"Shh!" Bihari said urgently. "You'll get your turn. You don't want to be sent back as an animal."

Kokila glared at her. "We are animals already, and don't you forget it." She took a slap at Bihari's arm and her hand went right through Bihari, which somewhat deflated her point. They were in the realm of souls, there was no denying it. "Forget these gods," she snarled, "it's justice we need! I'll bring the revolt right into the bardo itself if that's what it takes!"

"First things first," Bihari said. "One step at a time. Just try to recognize your jati, and take care of them first. Then on from there."

3

Tiger Mercy

Kya the tiger moved through elephant grass, stomach full and fur warm in the sun. The grass was a green wall around her, pressing in on every side. Above her the grass tips waved in the breeze, crossing the blue of the sky. The grass grew in giant bunches, radiating out from their center and bending over at the tops, and though the clumps were very close, she made her way forward by finding the narrow breaks at the bottom between clumps, pushing through the fallen stalks. Eventually she came to the edge of the grass, bordering a parklike maidan, burned annually by humans to keep it clear. Here grazed great numbers of chital and other deer, wild pig, and antelopes, especially the nilghai.

This morning there stood a lone wapiti doe, nibbling grass. Kya could imitate the sound of a wapiti stag, and when she was in heat, she did it just to do it; but now she simply waited. The doe sensed something and leaped away. But a young gaur wandered into the clearing, dark chestnut in color, white socked. As it approached Kya lifted her left forepaw, straightened her tail back, and swayed slightly forward and back, getting her balance. Then she threw her tail up and leaped across the park in a series of twenty-foot bounds, roaring all the while. She hit the gaur and knocked it down, bit its neck until it died.

She ate.

Ba-loo-ah!

Her kol-bahl, a jackal that had been kicked out of his pack and was now following her around, showed his ugly face at the far end of the maidan, and barked again. She growled at him to leave, and he slunk back into the grass.

When she was full she got up and padded downhill. The kol-bahl and ravens would finish the gaur.

She came to the river that wound its way through this part of the country. The shallow expanse was studded with islands, each a little jungle under its canopy of sal and shisham trees, and several of these held nests of hers, in the matted undergrowth of brake and creepers, under tamarisk trees overhanging the warm sand on the banks of the stream. The tiger padded over pebbles to the water's edge, drank. She stepped in the river and stood, feeling the current push her fur downstream. The water was clear and warmed by the sun. In the sand at the stream's edge were pawprints of a number of animals, and in the grass their scents: wapiti and mouse deer, jackal and hyena, rhinoceros and gaur, pig and pangolin; the whole village, but none in sight. She waded across to one of her islands, lay in the smashed grass of her bed, in the shade. A nap. No cubs this year, no need to hunt for another day or two: Kya yawned hugely in her bed. She fell asleep in the silence that extends out from tigers in the jungle.

She dreamed that she was a little brown village girl. Her tail twitched as she felt again the heat of a cooking fire, the feel of sex face-to-face, the impact of witch-killing stones. A sleeping rumble, big fangs exposed. The fear of it woke her up and she stirred, trying to fall back into a different dream.

Noises pulled her back into the world. Birds and monkeys were talking about the arrival of people, coming in from the west, no doubt to the ford they used downstream. Kya rose quickly and splashed off the island, slipped into thickets of elephant grass backing the curve of the stream. People could be dangerous, especially in groups. Individually they were helpless, it was only a question of picking one's moment and attacking from behind. But groups of them could drive animals into traps or ambushes, and that had been the end of many tigers, left skinned and beheaded. Once she had seen a male tiger try to walk out a pole to some meat, slip on a slippery patch, and fall onto spikes hidden in leaves. People had arranged that.

But today, no drums, no shouts, no bells. And it was too late in the day for humans to hunt. More likely they were travelers. Kya slipped through the elephant grass unobtrusively, testing the air with ear and nose, and moving toward a long glade in the grass that would give her a view of their ford.

She settled down in a broken clump to watch them pass. She lay there with her eyes slitted.

There were other humans there, she saw, hiding as she was, scattered through the sal forest, lying in wait for the humans to arrive at the ford.

As she noticed this, a column of people reached the ford, and the hidden ones leaped out of their hiding places and screamed as they fired arrows at the others. A big hunt, it seemed. Kya settled down and watched more closely, ears flattened. She had come upon such a scene once before, and the number of humans killed had been surprising. It was where she had first tasted their flesh, as she had had twins to feed that summer. They were certainly the most dangerous beast in the jungle, aside from the elephant. They killed wantonly, like kol-bahl sometimes did. There would be meat left here afterward, no matter what else happened. Kya hunkered down and listened more than watched. Screams, cries, roars, shouts, trumpet blasts, death rattles; somewhat like the end of one of her hunts, only multiplied many times.

Eventually it grew quiet. The hunters left the scene. When they had been gone a long time, and the ordinary hush of the jungle had returned, Kya shifted onto her paws and looked around. The air reeked of blood, and her mouth watered. Dead bodies lay on both banks of the river, and were caught on snags against the banks of the stream, or had rolled into shallows. The tiger padded among them cautiously, pulled a large one into the shadows and ate some of it. But she was not very hungry. A noise caused her to slink swiftly back into the shadows, hair erect on her back, looking for the source of the sound, which had been a cracked branch. Now a footfall, over there. Ah. A human, still standing. A survivor.

Kya relaxed. Sated already, she approached the man out of no more than curiosity. He saw her and jumped backward, startling her; his body had done it without his volition. He stood there looking at her in the way hurt animals sometimes did, accepting their fate; only in this one's face there was also a little roll of the eyes, as if to say, What else could go wrong, or, Not this too. It was a gesture so like that of the girls she had watched gathering wood in the forest that she paused, unhungry. The hunters who had ambushed this man's group still occupied the trail to the nearest village. He would soon be caught and killed.

He expected her to do it. Humans were so sure of themselves, so sure they had the world figured out and were lords of it all. And with their monkey numbers and their arrows, so often they were right. This as much as anything was why she killed them when she did. They were a scrawny meal in all truth, which of course was not the main consideration—many a tiger had died trying to reach the tasty flesh of the porcupine—but humans tasted strange. With the things they ate, it was no surprise.

The confounding thing would be to help him; so she padded to his side. His teeth chattered with his trembling. He was no longer stunned, but holding his place on purpose. She nosed up one of his hands, rested it on her head between her ears. She held still until he stroked her head, then moved until he was stroking between her shoulders, and she was standing by his side, facing the same direction. Then very slowly she began to walk, indicating by her speed that he should come along. He did, hand stroking her back with every step.

She led him through the sal forest. Sunlight blinked through trees onto them. There was a sudden noise and clatter, then voices from the trail below, in the trees, and the hand clutched at her fur. She stopped and listened. Voices of the people-hunters. She growled, then coughed deeply, then gave a short roar.

Dead silence from below. In the absence of an organized beat, no human could find her up here. Sounds of them hurrying off came to her on the wind.

The way was now free. The man's hand was clenched in the fur between her shoulder blades. She turned her head and nuzzled his shoulder and he let go. He was more afraid of the other men than of her, which showed sense. He was like a helpless cub in some ways, but quick. Her own mother had held her by biting the same fold of skin between the shoulder blades that he had seized, and at the same pressure—as if he too had once been a tigress mother, and was making an unremembered appeal to her.

She walked the man slowly to the next ford, across it and along one of the deer trails. Wapiti were bigger than humans, and it was an easy trail. She took him to one of her entrances to the big nullah of the region, a steep and narrow ravine, so precipitous and cragbound that its floor was only accessible at a couple of points. This was one, and she led the man down to the ravine floor, then downstream toward a village where the people smelled much like he did. The man had to walk fast to match her gait, but she did not slow down. Only a few pools dotted the ravine floor, as it had been hot for a long time. Springs dripped over ferny rockfalls. As they padded and stumbled along she thought about it, and seemed to recall a hut, near the edge of the village she was headed for, that had smelled almost exactly like him. She led him through a dense grove of date palms filling the floor of the nullah, then still denser clumps of bamboo. Green coverts of jaman fruit bushes covered the sides of the ravine, mixed with the ber thorn bush, dotted with its acid orange fruit.

A gap in this fragrant shrubbery led her up and out of the nullah. She sniffed; a male tiger had been here recently, spraying the exit from the nullah to mark it as his. She growled, and the man clutched the fur between her shoulders again, held on for a help as she climbed the last pitch out.

Back in the forested hills flanking the nullah, angling uphill, she had to nudge him with her shoulder—he wanted to contour the slope, or go directly down to the village, not up and around to it. A few bumps from her and he gave that up, and followed her without resistance. Now he had a male tiger to avoid too, but he did not know that.

She led him through the ruins of an old hill fort, overgrown with bamboo, a place that humans avoided, and that she had made her lair several winters running. She had borne her cubs here, near the human village and among human ruins, to make them safer from male tigers. The man recognized the place, and calmed down. They continued on toward the backside of the village.

At his pace it was a long way. His body hung from his joints, and she saw how hard it must be to walk on two feet. Never a moment's rest, always balancing, falling forward and catching himself, as if always crossing a log over a creek. Shaky as a new cub, blind and wet.

But they reached the village margin, where a barley field rippled in the afternoon light, and stopped in the last elephant grass under the sal trees. The barley field had furrows of dirt into which people poured water, clever monkeys that they were, tiptoeing through life in their perpetual balancing act.

At the sight of the field, the exhausted creature looked up and around. He led the tiger now, around the field, and Kya followed him closer to the village than she would have dared in most situations, though the afternoon's mix of sun and shadow provided her maximum cover, rendering her nearly invisible to others, a mere mind-ripple in the landscape, if she moved quickly. But she had to keep to his faltering pace. It took a bit of boldness; but there were bold tigers and timid tigers, and she was one of the bold ones.

Finally she stopped. A hut lay before them, under a pipal tree. The man pointed it out to her. She sniffed; it was his home, sure enough. He whispered in his language, gave her a final squeeze expressing his gratitude, and then he was stumbling forward through the barley, in the last stages of exhaustion. When he reached the door there were cries from inside, and a woman and two children rushed out and hugged him. But then to the tiger's surprise an older man strode out heavily and beat him across the back, several heavy blows.

The tiger settled down to watch.

The older man refused to allow her refugee into the hut. The woman and children brought out food to him. Finally he curled up outside the door, on the ground, and slept.

Through the following days he remained in disfavor with the old man, though he fed at the house, and worked in the fields around it. Kya watched and saw the pattern of his life, strange as it was. It seemed also that he had forgotten her; or would not risk the jungle to come out and look for her. Or did not imagine she was still there, perhaps.

She was surprised, therefore, when he came out one dusk with his hands held before him, a bird carcass plucked and cooked, it appeared—even boned! He walked right to her, and greeted her very quietly and respectfully, holding out the offering. He was tentative, frightened; he did not know that when her whiskers were down she was feeling relaxed. The offered tidbit smelled of its own hot juices, and some other mix of scents—nutmeg, lavender. She took it gently in her mouth and let it cool, tasting it between her teeth as it dripped hot on her tongue. A very odd perfumed meat. She chewed it, growling a little purr-growl, and swallowed. He said his farewells and backed away, returning to the hut.

After that she came by from time to time in the lancing horizontal light of sunrise, when he was going off to work. After a while he usually came out with a gift for her, some scrap or morsel, nothing like the bird, but tastier than it had been, simple uncooked bits of meat; somehow he knew. He still slept outside the hut, and one cold night she slinked in and slept curled around him, till dawn grayed the skies. The monkeys in the trees were scandalized.

Then the old man beat him again, hard enough to make him bleed from one ear. Kya went off to her hill fort then, growling and making long scratches in the ground. The huge mahua tree on the hill was dropping its great weight of flowers, and she ate some of the fleshy, intoxicating petals. She returned to the village perimeter, and deliberately sniffed out the old man, and found him on the well-traveled road to the village west of theirs. He had met several other men there, and they talked for a long time, drinking fermented drinks and getting drunk. He laughed like her kol-bahl.

On his way home she struck him down and killed him with a bite to the neck. She ate part of his entrails, tasting again all the strange tastes; they ate such odd things that they ended up tasting peculiar themselves, rich and various. Not unlike the first offering her young man had brought out to her. An acquired taste; and perhaps she had acquired it.

Other people were hurrying toward them now, and she slipped away, hearing behind her their cries, shocked and then dismayed, although with that note of triumph or celebration one often heard in monkeys relating bad news—that whatever it was, it hadn't happened to them.

No one would care about that old man, he had left this life as lonely as a male tiger, unregretted even by those in his own hut. It was not his death but the presence of a man-eating tiger that these people lamented. Tigers who learned to like manflesh were dangerous; usually they were mothers who were having trouble feeding their cubs, or old males who had broken their fangs, so that they were likely to do it often. Certainly a campaign to exterminate her would now begin. But she did not regret the killing. On the contrary, she leaped through the trees and shadows like a young tigress just out on her own, licking her chops and growling. Kya, Queen of the Jungle!

But the next time she came to visit her young man, he brought out a morsel of goat meat, and then tapped her gently on the nose, talking very seriously. He was warning her of something, and was worried that the details of the warning were escaping her, which they were. Next time she came by he shouted at her to leave, and even threw rocks at her, but it was too late; she hit a trip line connected to spring-loaded bows, and poisoned arrows pierced her and she died.

4

Akbar

As they carried the body of the tigress into the village, four men working hard, huffing and puffing under its weight as it swung by its tied paws from a stout bamboo bouncing on their shoulders, Bistami understood: God is in all things. And God, may all his ninety-nine names prosper and fall into our souls, did not want any killing. From the doorway of his older brother's hut, Bistami shouted through his tears, "She was my sister, she was my aunt, she saved me from the Hindu rebels, you ought not to have killed her, she was protecting us all!"

But of course no one was listening. No one understands us, not ever.

And it was perhaps just as well, given that this tigress had undoubtedly killed his brother. But he would have given his brother's life ten times over for the sake of that tiger.

Despite himself he followed the procession into the village center. Everyone was drinking rakshi, and the drummers were running out of their homes with their drums, pounding happily. "Kya Kya Kya Kya, leave us alone forevermore!" A tiger holiday was upon them, and the rest of the day and perhaps the next would be devoted to the impromptu festivalizing. They would burn its whiskers to make sure that its soul would not pass into a killer in another world. The whiskers were poisonous: one ground up in tiger meat would kill a man, while a whole one placed inside a tender bamboo shoot would give those who ate it cysts, leading to a slower death. Or so it was said. The hypochondriacal Chinese believed in the efficacious properties of almost everything, including every part of tigers, it seemed. Much of the body of this Kya would be saved and taken north by traders, no doubt. The skin would go to the zamindar.

Bistami sat miserably on the dirt at the edge of the village center. There was no one to explain himself to. He had done everything he could to warn the tigress off, but to no avail. He had addressed her not as Kya but as madame, or Madame Thirty, which was what the villagers called tigers when they were out in the jungle, so as not to offend them. He had given her offerings, and checked to make sure that the markings on her forehead did not form the letter "s," a sign that the beast was a were-tiger, and would change to human form for good at the moment of death. That had not happened, and indeed there had been no "s" on her forehead; the mark was more like a birdwing in flight. He had kept eye contact with her, as one is supposed to do when coming on tigers unexpectedly; he had stayed calm, and been saved by her from death. Indeed all the stories he had heard of helpful tigers—the one that had led two lost children back to the village, the one who had kissed a sleeping hunter on the cheek—all these stories paled in comparison to his, although they had prepared him as well. She had been his sister, and now he was distraught with grief.

The villagers began to dismember her body. Bistami left the village, unable to watch. His brutal older brother was dead; his other relatives, like his brother, had no sympathy for his Sufic interests. "The high look to the high, and so they can see each other from a great distance off." But he was so far away from anyone of wisdom, he could see nothing at all. He remembered what his Sufi master Tustari had told him when he left Allahabad: "Keep the haj in your heart, and make your way to Mecca as Allah wills it. Slow or fast, but always on your tariqat, the path to enlightenment."

He gathered his few possessions in his shoulder bag. The death of the tiger began to take on the cast of a destiny, a message to Bistami, to accept the gift of God and put it to use in his actions, and regret nothing. So that now it was time to say Thank you God, thank you Kya my sister, and leave his home village forever.

Bistami walked to Agra, and there he spent the last of his money to buy a Sufi wanderer's robe. He asked for shelter in the Sufi lodge, a long old building in the southernmost district of the old capital, and he bathed in their pool, purifying himself inside and out.

Then he left the city and walked out to Fatepur Sikri, the new capital of Akbar's empire. He saw that the not-yet-completed city replicated in stone the vast tent camps of Mughal armies, even down to marble pillars standing free of the walls, like tent poles. The city was dusty, or muddy, its white stone already stained. The trees were all short, the gardens raw and new. The long wall of the emperor's palace fronted the great avenue that bisected the city north and south, leading to a big marble mosque, and a dargah Bistami had heard about in Agra, the tomb of the Sufi saint Shaikh Salim Chishti. At the end of his long life Chishti had instructed the young Akbar, and now his memory was said to be Akbar's strongest link to Islam. And this same Chishti in his youth had traveled in Iran, and studied under Shah Esmail, who had also instructed Bistami's master Tustari.

So Bistami approached Chishti's great white tomb walking backward, and reciting from the Quran. "In the name of God, the compassionate, the merciful. Be patient with those who call upon their Lord at morn and even, seeking his face: and let not thine eyes be turned away from them in quest of the pomp of this life; neither obey him whose heart we have made careless of the remembrance of Us, and who followeth his own lusts, and whose ways are unbridled."

At the entry he prostrated himself toward Mecca and said the morning prayer, then entered the walled-in courtyard of the tomb, and made his tribute to Chishti. Others were doing the same, of course, and when he was done paying his respects he spoke to some of them, describing his journey all the way back to his time in Iran, eliding the stops along the way. Eventually he told this tale to one of the ulema of Akbar's own court, and emphasized his master's relation-by-teaching to Chishti, and returned to his prayers. He came back to the tomb day after day, establishing a routine of prayer, purification rites, the answering of questions from pilgrims who spoke only Persian, and socializing with all the people visiting the shrine. This finally led to the grandson of Chishti speaking to him, and this man then spoke well of him to Akbar, or so he heard. He ate his one meal a day at the Sufi lodge, and persevered, hungry but hopeful.

One morning at the very first light, when he was already in the tomb's courtyard at prayers, the emperor Akbar himself came into the shrine, and took up an ordinary broom, and swept the courtyard. It was a cool morning, the night chill still in the air, and yet Bistami was sweating as Akbar finished his devotions, and Chishti's grandson arrived, and asked Bistami to come when he was done with his prayers, to be introduced.

"A great honor," he replied, and returned to his prayers, murmuring them thoughtlessly as the things he might say raced through his head; and he wondered how long he should delay before approaching the emperor, to show that prayer came first. The tomb was still relatively empty and cool, the sun just rising. When it cleared the trees entirely, Bistami stood and walked to the emperor and Chishti's grandson, and bowed deeply. Greeting, obeisances, and then he was obeying a polite request to tell his story to the watchful young man in the imperial finery, whose unblinking gaze never left his face, or indeed his eyes. Study in Iran with Tutsami, pilgrimage to Qom, return home, a year's work as a teacher of the Quran in Gujarat, a journey to visit his family, ambush by Hindu rebels, salvation by tiger: by the end of the story Bistami had been approved, he could see it.

"We welcome you," Akbar said. The whole city of Fatepur Sikri served to show how devout he was, as well as displaying his ability to create devotion in others. Now he had seen Bistami's devotion, exhibited in all the forms of piety, and as they continued their conversation, and the tomb began to fill with the day's visitors, Bistami managed to lead the discussion to the one hadith he knew that had come by way of Chishti to Iran, so that the isnad, or genealogy of the phrase, made a short link between his education and the emperor's.

"I had it from Tutsami, who had it from the Shah Esmail, teacher of Shaikh Chishti, who had it from Bahr ibn Kaniz al-Saqqa, that Uthman ibn Saj related to him, from Said ibn Jubair, God's mercy on him, who said, 'Let him give a general greeting to all the Muslims, including the young boys and the adolescents, and when he has arrived at class, let him restrain whoever was sitting from standing up for him, since neglecting this is one of the banes of the soul.' "

Akbar frowned, trying to follow it. It occurred to Bistami that it could be interpreted as meaning that he had been the one who had refrained from asking for any kind of obeisance from the other. He began to sweat in the chill morning air.

Akbar turned to one of his retainers, standing unobtrusively against the marble wall of the tomb. "Bring this man with us on our return to the palace."

After another hour of prayer for Bistami, and consultations for Akbar, who was relaxed but increasingly terse as the morning wore on and the line of supplicants grew rather than shrank before him, the emperor bade the line to disperse and come back again later. After that he led Bistami and his retinue through the raw worksites of the city to his palace.

The city was being built in the shape of a big square, like any other Mughal military encampment—indeed, in the form of the empire itself, Bistami's guard told him, which was a quadrilateral protected by the four cities of Lahore, Agra, Allahabad, and Ajmer. These were all big compared to the new capital, and Bistami's guard was particularly fond of Agra, where he had worked in the construction of the emperor's great fort, now finished. "Inside it are more than five hundred buildings," he said as he must always have said when speaking of it. He was of the opinion that Akbar had founded Fatepur Sikri because the fort of Agra was mostly complete, and the emperor liked beginning great projects. "He is a builder, that one, he will remake the world itself before he is done, I assure you. Islam has never had such a servant as him."

"It must be so," Bistami said, looking around at the construction, white buildings rising out of cocoons of scaffolding, set in seas of black mud. "Praise be to God."

The guard, whose name was Husain Ali, looked at Bistami suspiciously. Pious pilgrims were no doubt a commonplace. He led Bistami after the emperor and through the gate of the new palace. Inside the outer wall were gardens that looked as if they had been in place for years: big pine trees towering over jasmine bushes, flower beds in all directions. The palace itself was smaller than the mosque, or the tomb of Chishti, but exquisite in every detail. A white marble tent, broad and low, its interior filled by room after cool room, all surrounding a fountain-filled central courtyard and garden. The whole wing at the back of the courtyard consisted of a long gallery walled with paintings: hunting scenes, the skies always turquoise; the dogs and deer and lions rendered to the life; the skirted hunters carrying bow or flintlock. Opposite these scenes were suites of white-walled rooms, finished but empty. Bistami was given one of these to stay in.

That night's meal was a feast, set sumptuously in a long hall opening onto the central courtyard. As it proceeded, Bistami understood that it was simply the ordinary evening meal in the palace. He ate roast quail, yogurt with cucumber, shredded in curry, and tastes of many dishes he didn't recognize.

That began a dreamlike period for him, in which he felt like Manjushri in the tale, fallen upward into the land of milk and honey. Food dominated his days and his thoughts. One day he was visited in his rooms by a team of black slaves dressed better than he was, who quickly brought him up to their level of raiment and beyond, outfitting him in a fine white gown that looked well but hung heavily on him. After that he was given another audience with the emperor.

This meeting, surrounded by sharp-eyed counselors, generals, and imperial retainers of all kinds, felt very different from the dawn meeting at the tomb, when two young men out to smell the morning air and see the sunrise, and sing the glory of Allah's world, had spoken to each other chest to chest. And yet in all these trappings, it was the same face looking at him—curious, serious, interested in what he had to say. Focusing on that face allowed Bistami to relax.

The emperor said, "We invite you to join us and share your knowledge of the law. In return for your wisdom, and the rendering of judgments on certain cases and questions that will be brought before you, you will be made zamindar of the late Shah Muzzafar's estates, may Allah honor his name."

"Praise be to God," Bistami murmured, looking down. "I will ask God's help in fulfilling this great task to your satisfaction."

Even with his gaze steadfast to the ground, or returned to the emperor's face, Bistami could sense that some of the imperial retinue were less than pleased by this decision. But afterward, some who had seemed least pleased came up to him and introduced themselves, spoke kindly, led him around the palace, probed in a most gentle way concerning his background and history, and told him more about the estate he was to administer. This, it appeared, would mostly be overseen by local assistants on-site, and was mainly his title and source of income; and in return he was to outfit and provide one hundred soldiers to the emperor's armies, when required, and teach all he knew of the Quran, and judge various civil disputes given to his charge.

"There are disputes that only the ulema are fit to judge," the emperor's advisor Raja Todor Mal told him. "The emperor has great responsibilities. The empire itself is not yet secure from its enemies. Akbar's grandfather Babur came here from the Punjab, and established a Muslim kingdom only forty years ago, and the infidels still attack us from the south and the east. Every year some campaigns are necessary to drive them back. All the faithful in his empire are under his care, in theory, but the burden of his responsibilities means in practice he simply doesn't have time."

"Of course not."

"Meanwhile, there is no other system of justice for disputes among people. As the law is based on the Quran, the qadis, the ulema, and other holy men such as yourself are the logical choice to take on this burden."

"Of course."

In the weeks following, Bistami did indeed find himself sitting in judgment in disputes brought before him by some of the emperor's slave assistants. Two men claimed the same land; Bistami asked where their fathers had lived, and their fathers' fathers, and determined that one's family had lived in the region longer than the other's. In ways like this he made his judgments.

More new clothes came from the tailors; a new house and complete retinue of servants and slaves were provided; he was given a trunk of gold and silver coins numbering one hundred thousand. And for all this he merely had to consult the Quran and recall the hadith he had learned (really very few, and even fewer relevant), and render judgments that were usually obvious to all. When they were not obvious, he made them as best he could and retired to the mosque and prayed uneasily, then attended the emperor and the evening meal. He went on his own at dawn every day to the tomb of Chishti, and so saw the emperor again in the same informal circumstances as their first meeting, perhaps once or twice a month—enough to keep the very busy emperor aware of his existence. He always had prepared the story he would relate to Akbar that day, when asked what he had been doing; each story was chosen for what it might teach the emperor, about himself, or Bistami, or the empire or the world. Surely a decent and thoughtful lesson was the least he could do for the incredible bounty that Akbar had bestowed on him.

One morning he told him the story from Sura Eighteen, about the men who lived in a city that had forsaken God, and God took them apart to a cave, and made them to sleep as it were a single night, to them; and when they went out they found that three hundred and nine years had passed. "Thus with your work, mighty Akbar, you shoot us into the future."

Another morning he told him the story of El-Khadir, the reputed vizier of Dhoulkarnain, who was said to have drunk of the fountain of life, by virtue of which he still lives, and will live till the day of judgment; and who appeared, clad in green robes, to Muslims in distress, to help them. "Thus your work here, great Akbar, will continue deathless through the years to help Muslims in distress."

The emperor appeared to appreciate these cool dewy conversations. He invited Bistami to join him on several hunts, and Bistami and his retinue occupied a big white tent, and spent the hot days riding horses as they crashed through the jungle after the howling dogs or beaters; or, more to Bistami's taste, sat on the howdah of an elephant, and watched the great falcons leave Akbar's wrist and soar high above, thence to dive in terrific stoops onto hare or fowl. Akbar fixed his attention on you in just the same way the falcons did.

Akbar loved his falcons, in fact, as kin, and always spent the days of the hunt in excellent spirits. He would call Bistami to his side to speak a blessing over the great birds, who looked off to the horizon, unimpressed. Then they were cast into the air, and flapped hard as they made their way quickly up to their hunting height, splaying wide their big wing feathers. When they were settled in their gyres overhead, a few doves were released. These birds flew as fast as they could for cover in trees or bush, but they were not usually fast enough to escape the attack of the hawks. Their broken bodies were returned by the great raptors to the feet of the emperor's retainers, and then the falcons flew back to Akbar's wrist, where they were greeted with a stare as fixed as their own, and bits of raw mutton.

It was just such a happy day that was interrupted by bad news from the south. A messenger arrived saying that Adham Khan's campaign against the Sultan of Malwa, Baz Bahadur, had succeeded, but that the khan's army had gone on to slaughter all of the captured men, women, and children of the town of Malwa, including many Muslim theologians, and even some sayyids, that is to say, direct descendants of the Prophet.

Akbar's fair complexion turned red all over his neck and face, leaving only the mole on the left side of his face untouched, like a white raisin embedded in his skin. "No more," he declared to his falcon, and then he began to give orders, the bird thrown to its falconer and the hunt forgotten. "He thinks I am still underage."

He rode off hard, leaving all his retinue behind except for Pir Muhammad Khan, his most trusted general. Bistami heard later that Akbar had personally relieved Adham Khan of his command.

Bistami had the Chishti tomb to himself for a month. Then he found the emperor there one morning, with a dark look. Adham Khan had been replaced as vakil, the chief minister, by Zein. "It will enrage him but it must be done," Akbar said. "We will have to put him under house arrest."

Bistami nodded and continued to sweep the cool dry floor of the inner chamber. The idea of Adham Khan under permanent guard, usually a prelude to execution, was disturbing to contemplate. He had a lot of friends in Agra. He might be so bold as to try to rebel. As the emperor must very well know.

Indeed, two days later, when Bistami was standing at the edge of Akbar's afternoon group at the palace, he was frightened but not surprised to see Adham Khan appear and stomp to the top of the stairs, armed, bloody, shouting that he had killed Zein not an hour before, in the man's own audience chamber, for usurping what was rightfully his.

Hearing this Akbar went red-faced again, and struck the khan hard on the side of the head with his drinking cup. He grabbed the man by the front of his jacket, and pulled him across the room. The slightest resistance from Adham would have been instant death from the emperor's guards, who stood at each side of them, swords at the ready; and so he allowed himself to be dragged out to the balcony, where Akbar flung him over the railing into space. Then Akbar, redder than ever, raced down the stairs, ran to the half-conscious khan, seized him by the hair and dragged him bodily up the stairs, armored though he was, over the carpet and out to the balcony, where he heaved him over the rail again. Adham Khan hit the patio below with a loose heavy thud.

Indeed he had been killed. The emperor retired into his private quarters in the palace.

The next morning Bistami swept the shrine of Chishti with a tightness all through his body.

Akbar appeared, and Bistami's heart hammered in his chest. Akbar

seemed calm, though distracted. The tomb was a place to give himself
some serenity. But the vigorous brushing he gave the floor that Bistami
had already cleaned belied the calm of his speech. He's the emperor, Bistami thought suddenly, he can do what he wants.

But then again, as a Muslim emperor, he was subservient to God, and
the sharia. All-powerful and yet all-submissive, all at once. No wonder
he seemed thoughtful to the point of distraction, sweeping the shrine in
the early morning. It was hard to imagine him mad with anger, like a bull
elephant in musth, throwing a man bodily to his death. There was within
him a deep well of rage.

Rebellion of ostensibly Muslim subjects struck deepest into this well.
A new rebellion in the Punjab was reported, an army sent to put it down.
The innocents of the region were spared, and even those who had
fought for the rebellion. But its leaders, some forty of them, were
brought to Agra and placed in a circle of war elephants that had long
blades like giant swords attached to their tusks. The elephants were unleashed on the traitors, who screamed as they were mowed down and
trampled underfoot, their bodies then tossed high in the air by the
blood-maddened elephants. Bistami had not realized that elephants
could be driven to such blood lust. Akbar stood high on a throne howdah perched on the biggest elephant of all, an elephant that stood still
before the spectacle, the two of them observing the carnage.

Some days later, when the emperor came to the tomb at dawn, it felt
strange to sweep the shadowed courtyard of the tomb with him. Bistami
swept assiduously, trying not to meet Akbar's gaze.

Finally he had to acknowledge the sovereign's presence. Akbar was
already staring at him.

"You seem troubled," Akbar said.

"No, mighty Akbar—not at all."

"You don't approve of the execution of traitors to Islam?"

"Not at all, yes, of course I do."

Akbar stared at him in the same way one of his falcons would have.

"But didn't Ibn Khaldun say that the caliph has to submit to Allah in
the same way as the humblest slave? Didn't he say that the caliph has a
duty to obey Muslim law? And doesn't Muslim law forbid torture of prisoners? Isn't that Khaldun's point?"

"Khaldun was just a historian," Bistami said.

Akbar laughed. "And what about the hadith that has it from Abu Taiba by way of Murra ibn Hamdan by way of Sufyan al-Thawri, who had it related to him by Ali ibn Abi Talaib, that the Messenger of God, may God bless his name forever, said, 'You shall not torture slaves?' What about the lines of the Quran that command the ruler to imitate Allah and to show compassion and mercy to prisoners? Did I not break the spirit of these commandments, O wise Sufi pilgrim?"

Bistami studied the flagstones of the courtyard. "Perhaps so, great Akbar. Only you know."

Akbar regarded him. "Leave the tomb of Chishti," he said.

Bistami hurried out the gate.

The next time Bistami saw Akbar was at the palace, where he had been commanded to appear; as it turned out, to explain why, as the emperor put it icily, "your friends in Gujarat are rebelling against me?"

Bistami said uneasily, "I left Ahmadabad precisely because there was so much strife. The mirzas were always having trouble. King Muzaffar Shah the Third was no longer in control. You know all this. This is why you took Gujarat under your protection."

Akbar nodded, seeming to remember that campaign. "But now Husain Mirza has come back out of the Deccan, and many of the nobles of Gujarat have joined him in rebellion. If word spreads that I can be defied so easily, who knows what will follow?"

"Surely Gujarat must be retaken," Bistami said uncertainly; perhaps, as last time, this was exactly what Akbar did not want to hear. What was expected of Bistami was not clear to him; he was an official of the court, a qadi, but his advice before had all been religious, or legal. Now, with a previous residence of his in revolt, he was apparently on the spot; not where one wanted to be, when Akbar was angry.

"It may already be too late," Akbar said. "The coast is two months away."

"Must it be?" Bistami asked. "I have made the trip by myself in ten days. Perhaps if you took only your best hundreds, on female camels, you could surprise the rebels."

Akbar favored him with his hawk look. He called for Raja Todor Mal, and soon it was arranged as Bistami had suggested. A cavalry of three thousand soldiers, led by Akbar, with Bistami ordered along, covered the distance between Agra and Ahmadabad in eleven dusty long days, and this cavalry, made strong and bold by the swift march, shattered a gaggle of many thousands of rebels, fifteen thousand by one general's count, most of them killed in the battle.

Bistami spent that day on camelback, following the main charges of the front, trying to stay within sight of Akbar, and when that failed, helping wounded men into the shade. Even without Akbar's great siege guns, the noise of the battle was shocking—most of it created by the screaming of men and camels. Dust blanketing the hot air smelled of blood.

Late in the afternoon, desperately thirsty, Bistami made his way down to the river. Scores of wounded and dying were already there, staining the river red. Even at the upstream edge of the crowd it was impossible to drink a mouthful that did not taste of blood.

Then Raja Todor Mal and a gang of soldiers arrived among them, executing with swords the mirzas and Afghans who had led the rebellion. One of the mirzas caught sight of Bistami and cried out, "Bistami, save me! Save me!"

The next moment he was headless, his body pouring its blood onto the bankside from the open neck. Bistami turned away, Raja Todor Mal staring after him.

Clearly Akbar heard of this later, for all during the leisurely march back to Fatepur Sikri, despite the triumphant nature of the procession, and Akbar's evident high spirits, he did not call Bistami into his presence. This despite the fact that the lightning assault on the rebels had been Bistami's idea. Or perhaps this also was part of it. Raja Todor Mal and his cronies could not be pleased by that.

It looked bad, and nothing in the great victory festival on their return to Fatepur Sikri, only forty-three days after their departure, made Bistami feel any better. On the contrary, he felt more and more apprehensive, as the days passed and Akbar did not come by the tomb of Chishti.

Instead, one morning three guards appeared there. They had been assigned to guard Bistami at the tomb, also back at his own compound. They informed him that he was not allowed to go anywhere else but these two places. He was under house arrest.

This was the usual prelude to the interrogation and execution of traitors. Bistami could see in his guards' eyes that this time was no exception, and that they considered him a dead man. It was hard for him to believe that Akbar had turned on him; he struggled to understand it.

Fear grew daily in him. The image of the mirza's headless body, gushing blood, kept recurring to him, and each time it did the blood in his own body would pound through him as if testing the means of escape, eager for release in a bursting red fountain.

He went to the Chishti tomb on one of these frightful mornings, and decided not to leave it. He sent orders for one of his retainers to bring him food every day at sundown, and after eating outside the gate of the tomb, he slept on a mat in the corner of the courtyard. He fasted through the days as if it were Ramadan, and alternated days reciting from the Quran and from Rumi's "Mathnawi," and other Persian Sufi texts. Some part of him hoped and expected that one of the guards would speak Persian, so that the words of the Mowlana, Rumi the great poet and voice of the Sufis, would be understood as they came pouring out of him.

"Here are the miracle signs you want," he would say in a loud voice, "that you cry through the night and get up at dawn, asking that in the absence of what you ask for, your day gets dark, your neck thin as a spindle, that what you give away is all you own, that you sacrifice belongings, sleep, health, your head, that you often sit down in a fire like aloes wood, and often go out to meet a blade like a battered helmet. When acts of helplessness become habitual, those are the signs. You run back and forth listening for unusual events, peering into the faces of travelers. Why are you looking at me like a madman? I have lost a friend. Please forgive me. Searching like that does not fail. There will come a rider who holds you close. You faint and gibber. The uninitiated say he's faking. How could they know? Water washes over a beached fish.

"Blessed is that intelligence into whose heart's ear from heaven the sound of 'come hither' is coming. The defiled ear hears not that sound— only the deserving gets his desserts. Defile not your eye with human cheek and mole, for that emperor of eternal life is coming; and if it has become defiled, wash it with tears, for the cure comes from those tears. A caravan of sugar has arrived from Egypt; the sound of a footfall and bell is coming. Ha, be silent, for to complete the ode our speaking king is coming."

After many days of that, Bistami began to repeat the Quran sura by sura, returning often to the first sura, the Opening of the Book, the Fatiha, the Healer, which the guards would never fail to recognize:

"Praise be to God, Lord of the worlds! The compassionate, the merciful! King on the day of reckoning! Thee only do we worship, and to Thee do we cry for help. Guide Thou us on the straight path, the path of those to whom Thou has been gracious;—and with whom Thou are not angry, and who go not astray."

This great opening prayer, so appropriate to his situation, Bistami repeated hundreds of times per day. Sometimes he repeated only the prayer "Sufficient for us is God and excellent the Protector"; once he said it thirty-three thousand times in a row. Then he switched to "Allah is merciful, submit to Allah, Allah is merciful, submit to Allah," which he repeated until his mouth was parched, his voice hoarse, and the muscles of his face cramped with exhaustion.

All the while he swept the courtyard clear, and then all the rooms of the shrine, one by one, and he filled the lamps and trimmed the wicks, and swept some more, looking at the skies as they changed through the days, and he said the same things over and over, feeling the wind push through him, watching the leaves of the trees surrounding the shrine pulse, each in their own transparent light. Arabic is learning, but Persian is sugar. He tasted his food at sundown as he had never tasted food before. Nevertheless it became easy to fast, perhaps because it was winter and the days were a bit shorter. Fear still stabbed him frequently, causing his blood to surge in him at enormous pressure, and he prayed aloud in every waking moment, no doubt driving his guards mad with the droning of it.

Eventually the whole world contracted to the tomb, and he began to forget the things that had happened before to him, or the things that presumably were still happening in the world outside the shrine grounds. He forgot them. His mind was becoming clarified; indeed everything in the world seemed to be becoming slightly transparent. He could see into leaves, and sometimes through them, as if they were made of glass; and it was the same with the white marble and alabaster of the tomb, which glowed as if alive in the dusks; and with his own flesh. "All save the face of God doth perish. To Him shall we return." These were the words from the Quran embedded in the Mowlana's beautiful poem of reincarnation:

> I died as mineral and became a plant,
> I died as plant and rose as animal,
> I died as animal and I was Man.
> Why should I fear? When was I less by dying?

Yet once more I shall die as Man, to soar
With angels blessed; but even from angelhood
I must pass on: "All save the face of God doth perish."
When I have sacrificed my angelic soul,
I shall become what no mind has ever conceived,
Oh, let me not exist! for non-existence
Proclaims in organ tones: "To Him shall we return."

He repeated this poem a thousand times, always whispering the last part, for fear the guards would report to Akbar that he was preparing himself for death.

Days passed; weeks passed. He grew hungrier, and hypersensitive to all tastes and smells, then to the air and the light. He could feel the nights that stayed hot and steamy as if they were blankets swaddling him, and in the brief cool of dawn he walked around sweeping and praying, looking at the sky over the leafy trees growing lighter and lighter; and then one morning as dawn grew, everything began to turn into light. "O he, O he who is He, O he who is naught but He!" Over and over he cried these words out into the world of light, and even the words were shards of light bursting out of his mouth. The tomb became a thing of pure white light, glowing in the cool green light of the trees, the trees of green light, and the fountain poured its water of light up into the lit air, and the walls of the courtyard were bricks of light, and everything was light, pulsing lightly. He could see through the earth, and back through time, over a Khyber Pass made of slabs of yellow light, back to the time of his birth, in the tenth day of Moharram, the day when the Imam Hosain, the only living grandson of Muhammad, had died defending the faith, and he saw that whether or not Akbar had him killed he would live on, for he had lived before many times, and was not going to be done when this life ended. "Why should I be afraid? When did I ever lose by dying?" He was a creature of light as everything else was, and had once been a village girl, another time a horseman on the steppes, another time the servant of the Twelfth Imam, so that he knew how and why the Imam had disappeared, and when he would return to save the world. Knowing that, there was no reason to fear anything. "Why should I be afraid? O he, O he who is He, sufficient is God and excellent the Protector, Allah the merciful, the beneficent!" Allah who had sent Muhammad on his isra, his journey into light, just as Bistami was being sent now, toward the ascension of miraj, when all would become a light utterly transparent and invisible.

Understanding this, Bistami looked through the transparent walls and trees and earth to Akbar, across the city in his clear palace, robed in light like an angel, a man surely more than half angel already, an angel spirit that he had known in previous lives, and that he would know again in future lives, until they all came to one place and Allah rang down the universe.

Except this Akbar of light turned his head, and looked through the lit space between them, and Bistami saw then that his eyes were black balls in his head, black as onyx; and he said to Bistami, We have never met before; I am not the one you seek; the one you seek is elsewhere.

Bistami reeled, fell back in the corner formed by the two walls.

When he came to himself, still in a colorful glassine world, Akbar in the flesh stood there before him, sweeping the courtyard with Bistami's broom.

"Master," Bistami said, and began to weep. "Mowlana."

Akbar stopped over him, stared down at him.

Finally he put a hand to Bistami's head. "You are a servant of God," he said.

"Yes, Mowlana."

" 'Now hath God been gracious to us,' " Akbar recited in Arabic. " 'For whoso feareth God and endureth, God verily will not suffer the reward of the righteous to perish.' "

This was from Sura Twelve, the story of Joseph and his brothers. Bistami, encouraged, still seeing through the edges of things, including Akbar and his luminous hand and face, a creature of light pulsing through lives like days, recited verses from the end of the next sura, "Thunder":

" 'Those who lived before them made plots; but all plotting is controlled by God: He knoweth the works of every one.' "

Akbar nodded, looking to Chishti's tomb and thinking his own thoughts.

" 'No blame be on you this day,' " he muttered, speaking the words Joseph spoke as he forgave his brothers. " 'God will forgive you, for He is the most merciful of those who show mercy.' "

"Yes, Mowlana. God gives us all things, God the merciful and compassionate, he who is He. O he who is He, O he who is He, O he who is He . . ." With difficulty he stopped himself.

"Yes." Akbar looked back down at him again. "Now, whatever may have happened in Gujarat, I don't wish to hear any more of it. I don't believe you had anything to do with the rebellion. Stop weeping. But Abul Fazl and Shaikh Abdul Nabi do believe this, and they are among my chief advisors. In most matters I trust them. I am loyal to them, as they are to me. So I can ignore them in this, and instruct them to leave you alone, but even if I do that, your life here will not be as comfortable as it was before. You understand."

"Yes, master."

"So I am going to send you away—"

"No, master!"

"Be silent. I am going to send you on the haj."

Bistami's mouth fell open. After all these days of endless talking, his jaw hung from his face like a broken gate. White light filled everything, and for a moment he swooned.

Then colors returned, and he began to hear again: ". . . you will ride to Surat and sail on my pilgrim ship, Ilahi, across the Arabian Sea to Jidda. The waqf has generated a good donation to Mecca and Medina, and I have appointed Wazir as the mir haj and the party will include my aunt Bulbadan Begam and my wife Salima. I would like to go myself, but Abul Fazl insists that I am needed here."

Bistami nodded. "You are indispensable, master."

Akbar contemplated him. "Unlike you."

He removed his hand from Bistami's head. "But the mir haj can always use another qadi. And I wish to establish a permanent Timurid school in Mecca. You can help with that."

"But—and not come back?"

"Not if you value this existence."

Bistami stared down at the ground, feeling a chill.

"Come now," the emperor said. "For such a devout scholar as you, a life in Mecca should be pure joy."

"Yes, master. Of course." But his voice choked on the words.

Akbar laughed. "It's better than beheading, you must admit! And who knows? Life is long. Perhaps you will come back one day."

They both knew it was not likely. Life was not long.

"Whatever God wills," Bistami murmured, looking around. This courtyard, this tomb, these trees which he knew stone by stone, branch by branch, leaf by leaf—this life, which had filled a hundred years in the last month—it was over. All that he knew so well would pass from him, including this beloved awesome young man. Strange to think that each true life was only a few years long—that one passed through several in each bodily span. He said, "God is great. We will never meet again."

5

The Road to Mecca

From the port of Jidda to Mecca, the pilgrims' camels were continuous from horizon to horizon, looking as if they might continue unbroken all the way across Arabia, or the world. The rocky shallow valleys around Mecca were filled with encampments, and the mutton-greased smoke of cooking fires rose into the clear skies at sunset. Cool nights, warm days, never a cloud in the whitish blue sky, and thousands of pilgrims, enthusiastically making the final rounds of the haj, everyone in the city participating in the same ecstatic ritual, all dressed in white, accented by the green turbans in the crowd, worn by the sayyids, those who claimed direct descent from the Prophet: a big family, if the turbans were to be believed, all reciting verses from the Quran, following the people in front of them, who followed those before them, and those before them, in a line that extended back nine centuries.

On the voyage to Arabia, Bistami had fasted more seriously than ever in his life, even in the tomb of Chishti. Now he flowed through the stone streets of Mecca light as a feather, looking up at the palms dusting the sky with their gently waving green fronds, feeling so airy in God's grace that it sometimes seemed he looked down on the palm tops, or around the corners into the Kaaba, and he would have to stare at his feet for a while to regain his balance and his sense of self, though as he did so his feet began to seem like distant creatures of their own, thrusting forward one after the other, time after time. O he, O he who is He . . .

He had separated himself from the representatives of Fatepur Sikri, as he found Akbar's family an unwelcome reminder of his lost master. With them it was always Akbar this and Akbar that, his wife Salima (a second wife, not the empress) plaintive in a self-satisfied way, his aunt egging her on—no. Women were on their own pilgrimage in any case, but the men in the Mughal retinue were almost as bad. And Wazir the mir haj was an ally of Abul Fazl, and therefore suspicious of Bistami, dismissive of him to the point of contempt. There would be no place for Bistami in the Mughal school, assuming that they established one at all, rather than just disbursing some alms and city funds from an embassy, which was how it looked as though it would come about. Either way Bistami would not be welcome among them, that was clear.

But this was one of those blessed moments when the future was no matter for concern, when past and future both were absent from the world. That was what struck Bistami most, even at the time, even in the act of floating along in the line of belief, one of a million white-robed hajis, pilgrims from all over Dar al-Islam, from the Maghrib to Mindanao, from Siberia to the Seychelles: how they were all there together in this one moment, the sky and the town under it all glowing with their presence, not transparently as at Chishti's tomb, but full of color, stuffed with all the colors of the world. All the people of the world were one.

This holiness radiated outward from the Kaaba. Bistami moved with the line of humanity into the holiest mosque, and passed by the big smooth black stone, blacker than ebony or jet, black as the night sky without stars, like a boulder-shaped hole in reality. He felt his body and soul pulsing in the same rhythm as the line, as the world. Touching the black stone was like touching flesh. It seemed to revolve around him. The dream image of Akbar's black eyes came to him and he shrugged them away, aware they were distractions out of his own mind, aware of Allah's ban on images. The stone was all and it was just a stone, black reality itself, made solid by God. He kept his place in the line and felt the spirits of the people ahead of him lifting as they passed out of the square, as if they were climbing a stairway into heaven.

Dispersal; return to camp; the first sips of soup and coffee at sundown; all occurred in a silent cool evening under the evening star. Everyone at such peace. Washed clean inside. Looking around at all the faces, Bistami thought, Oh why don't we live like this all the time? What is important enough to take us away from this moment? Firelit faces, starry night overhead, ripples of song or soft laughter, peace, peace: no one seemed to want to fall asleep, to end this moment and wake up the next day, back in the sensible world.

Akbar's family and haj left in a caravan back to Jidda. Bistami went to the outskirts of town to see them off; Akbar's wife and aunt said good-bye to him, waving from camelback. The rest were already intent on the long journey to Fatepur Sikri.

After that Bistami was alone in Mecca, a city of strangers. Most were leaving now, in caravan after caravan. It was a lugubrious, uncanny sight: hundreds of caravans, thousands of people, happy but deflated, their white robes packed away or revealed suddenly to be dusty, fringed at the foot with brown dirt. So many were leaving that it seemed the city was being abandoned before some approaching disaster, as perhaps had happened once or twice, in time of war or famine or plague.

But a week or two later the ordinary Mecca was revealed, a white-washed dusty little town of a few thousand people. Many of them were clerics or scholars or Sufis or qadis or ulema, or heterodox refugees of one sort or another, claiming the sanctuary of the holy city. Most, however, were merchants and tradespeople. In the aftermath of the haj they looked exhausted, drained, almost stunned, it seemed, and inclined to disappear into their blank-walled compounds, leaving the remaining outsiders in town to fend for themselves for a month or two. For the remnant ulema and scholars, it was as if they were camping out in the empty heart of Islam, making it full by their own devotions, cooking over fires on the edges of town at dusk, trading for food with passing nomads. Many sang songs through most of the night.

The Persian-speaking group was big, and congregated nightly around fires of its khitta on the eastern edge of town, where the canals came in from the hills. Thus they were the first to experience the spate that burst onto the town after storms to the north, which they heard but never saw. A wall of muddy black water slammed down the canals and spread out through the streets, rolling palm trunks and boulders like weapons into the upper half of the town. Everything flooded after that, until even the Kaaba itself stood in water up to the silver ring that held it in place.

Bistami threw himself with great pleasure into the efforts to drain the waters, and then to clean up the town. After the experience of the light in Chishti's tomb, and the supreme experience of the haj, there was little more he felt he could do in the mystic realm. He lived now in the aftermath of those events, and felt himself utterly changed; but what he wanted to do now was to read Persian poetry for an hour in the brief cool of the mornings, then work outside in the low hot winter sun in the afternoons. With the town broken and waist-deep in mud, there was a lot of work to be done. Pray, read, work, eat, pray, sleep; this was the pattern of a good day. Day after day passed in this satisfying round.

Then as the winter wore on, he began to study at a Sufi madressa established by scholars from the Maghrib, that western end of the world that was becoming more powerful, extending as it was both north into al-Andalus and Firanja, and south into the Sahel. Bistami and the others there read and discussed not just Rumi and Shams, but also the philosophers Ibn Sina and Ibn Rushd, and the ancient Greek Aristotle, and the historian Ibn Khaldun. The Maghribis in the madressa were not as interested in contesting points of doctrine as they were in exchanging new information about the world; they were full of stories of the reoccupation of al-Andalus and Firanja, and tales of the lost Frankish civilization. They were friendly to Bistami; they had no opinion of him one way or another; they thought of him as Persian, and so it was much more pleasant to be among them than with the Mughalis in the Timurid embassy, where he was regarded uneasily at best. Bistami saw that if his being stationed in Mecca was punishment in the form of exile from Akbar and Sind, then the other Mughalis assigned here had to wonder if they too were in disfavor, rather than honored for their religious devotion. Seeing Bistami reminded them of this possibility, and so he was shunned like a leper. He therefore spent more and more of his time at the Maghribi madressa, and out in the Persian-speaking khitta, now set a bit higher in the hills above the canals east of town.

The year in Mecca always oriented itself in time to the haj, in just the same way that Islam oriented itself in space to Mecca. As the months passed, all began to make their preparations, and as Ramadan approached, nothing else in the world mattered but the upcoming haj. Much of the effort involved simply feeding the masses that would descend on the town. A whole system had developed to accomplish this miraculous feat, astonishing in its size and efficiency, here on this out-of-the-way corner of a nearly lifeless desert peninsula. Though of course

Aden and Yemen were rich, to the south below them. No doubt, Bistami thought as he walked by the pastures now filling up with sheep and goats, mulling over his readings in Ibn Khaldun, the system had grown with the growth of the haj itself. Which must have been rapid: Islam had exploded out of Arabia in the first century after the hegira, he was coming to understand. Al-Andalus had been Islamicized by the year 100, the far reaches of the Spice Islands by the year 200; the whole span of the known world had been converted, only two centuries after the Prophet had received the Word and spread it to the people of this little land in the middle. Ever since then people had been coming here in greater and greater numbers.

One day he and a few other young scholars went to Medina, walking all the way, reciting prayers as they went, to see Muhammad's first mosque again. Past endless pens of sheep and goats, past cheese dairies, granaries, date palm groves; then into the outskirts of Medina, a sleepy, sandy, delapidated little settlement when the haj was not there to bring it alive. In one stand of thick ancient palms, the little whitewashed mosque hid in the shade, as polished as a pearl. Here the Prophet had preached during his exile, and taken down most of the verses of the Quran from Allah.

Bistami wandered the garden outside this holy place, trying to imagine how it had happened. Reading Khaldun had made him understand: these things had all happened. In the beginning, the Prophet had stood in this grove, speaking in the open air. Later he had leaned against a palm tree when he spoke, and some of his followers had suggested a chair. He had agreed to it only as long as it was low enough that there was no suggestion he was claiming any sort of privilege for himself. The Prophet, perfect man that he had been, was modest. He had agreed to the construction of a mosque where he taught, but for many years it had gone roofless; Muhammad had declared there was more important business for the faithful to accomplish first. And then they had made their return to Mecca, and the Prophet had led twenty-six military campaigns himself: the jihad. After that, how quickly the word had spread. Khaldun attributed this rapidity to a readiness in people for the next stage in civilization, and to the manifest truth of the Quran.

Bistami, troubled by something he could not pin down, wondered about this explanation. In India, civilizations had come and gone, come and gone. Islam itself had conquered India. But under the Mughals the ancient beliefs of the Indians endured, and Islam itself changed in its constant contact with them. This had become clearer to Bistami as he studied the pure religion in the madressa. Although Sufism itself was perhaps more than a simple return to the pure source. An advance, or (could one say it?) a clarification, even an improvement. An effort to by-pass the ulemas. In any case, change. It did not seem that it could be prevented. Everything changed. As the Sufi Junnaiyd at the madressa said, the word of God came down to man as rain to soil, and the result was mud, not clear water. After the winter's great flood, this image was particularly vivid and troubling. Islam, spreading over the world like a spate of mud, a mix of God and man; it did not seem very much like what had happened to him in the tomb of Chishti, or at the moment of the haj, when it seemed the Kaaba had revolved around him. But even his memory of those events was changing. Everything changed in this world.

Including Medina and Mecca, which grew in population rapidly as the haj approached, and shepherds poured into town with their flocks, tradesmen with their wares—clothing, traveling equipment to replace things broken or lost, religious scripts, mementos of the haj, and so on. In the final month of preparation the early pilgrims began to arrive, long strings of camels carrying dusty, happy travelers, their faces alight with the feeling Bistami remembered from the year before, a year which seemed to have gone so fast—and yet his own haj at the same time seemed as if it were on the far side of a great abyss in his mind. He could not call up in himself the feeling that he saw on their faces. He was no pilgrim this time, but a resident, and he found himself feeling some of the residents' resentment, that his peaceful village, like a big madressa really, was swelling to a ridiculous engorgement, as if a great family of enthusiastic relatives had descended on them all at once. Not a happy way of thinking of it, and Bistami set himself guiltily to a full round of prayers, fasting, and aid of the influx, especially those exhausted or sick: leading them to khittas and finas and caravanserai and hostelries, throwing himself into a routine to make himself feel he was more in the spirit of the haj. But daily exporsure to the ecstatic faces of the pilgrims reminded him how far he was from that. Their faces were alight with God. He saw how clearly faces revealed the soul, they were like windows into a deeper world.

So he hoped that his pleasure at greeting the pilgrims from Akbar's court was obvious on his face. But Akbar himself had not come, nor any of his immediate family, and no one in the group looked at all happy to be there, or to see Bistami. The news from home was ominous. Akbar had become critical of his ulema. He received Hindu rajas, and listened sympathetically to their concerns. He had even begun openly to worship the sun, prostrating himself four times a day before a sacred fire, abstaining from meat, alcohol, and sexual intercourse. These were Hindu practices, and indeed on every Sunday he was initiating twelve of his amirs in his service. The neophytes placed their heads directly on Akbar's feet during this ceremony, an extreme form of prostration known as sijdah, a form of submission to another human being that was blasphemous to Muslims. And he had not been willing to fund much of a pilgrimage; indeed, he had had to be convinced to send any at all. He had sent Shaikh Abdul Nabi and Malauna Abdulla as a way of exiling them, just as he had Bistami the year before. In short, he appeared to be falling away from the faith. Akbar, falling away from Islam!

And, Abdul Nabi told Bistami bluntly, many at the court blamed him, Bistami, for this change in Akbar. It was a matter of convenience only, Abdul Nabi assured him. "Blaming someone who is far away is safest for all, you see. But now they have it that you were sent to Mecca with the idea of reforming you. You were babbling about the light, the light, and you were sent away, and now Akbar is worshiping the sun like a Zoroastrian or some pagan from the ancient times."

"So I can't return," Bistami said.

Abdul Nabi shook his head. "Not only that, but I judge that it isn't even safe for you to stay here. If you do, the ulema may accuse you of heresy, and come and take you back for judgment. Or even judge you here."

"You're saying I should leave here?"

Abdul Nabi nodded, slowly and deeply. "Surely there are more interesting places for you than Mecca. A qadi like you can find good work to do, any place where the ruler is a Muslim. Nothing will happen during the haj, of course. But when it's over . . ."

Bistami nodded and thanked the shaikh for his honesty.

He realized that he wanted to leave anyway. He didn't want to stay in Mecca. He wanted to go back to Akbar, and the timeless hours in Chishti's tomb, and live in that space forever; but if that was not possible, he would have to begin his tariqat again, and wander in search of his real life. He recalled what had happened to Shams when the disciples of Rumi got tired of Rumi's infatuation with his friend. Shams had disappeared, never to be seen again, some said tied to rocks and thrown in a river.

If people in Fatepur Sikri thought that Akbar had found his Shams in Bistami—which struck Bistami as backward—but they had spent a lot of time together, more than seemed explicable; and no one else knew what had gone on between them in those meetings, how much it had been a matter of Akbar teaching the teacher. It is always the teacher who must learn the most, Bistami thought, or else nothing real has happened in the exchange.

The rest of that haj was strange. The crowds seemed huge, inhuman, possessed, a pestilence consuming hundreds of sheep a day, and all the ulema like shepherds, organizing this cannibalism. Of course one could not speak of these things, but only repeat some of the phrases that had burned their way into his soul so deeply, O he who is He, O he who is He, Allah the Merciful, the Compassionate. Why should I be afraid? God sets all in action. No doubt he was supposed to continue his tariqat until he found something more. After the haj one was supposed to move on.

The Maghribi scholars were the friendliest he knew, they exhibited the Sufi hospitality at its finest, as well as a keen curiosity about the world. He could go back up to Isfahan, of course, but something drew him westward. Clarified as he had been in the realm of light, he did not care to go back to the richness of the Iranian gardens. In the Quran the word for Paradise, and all of Muhammad's words for describing Paradise, came out of Persian words; while the word for Hell, in the very same suras, came from Hebrew, a desert language. That was a sign. Bistami did not want Paradise. He wanted something he could not define, a human challenge of some indefinable kind. Say the human was a mix of material and divine, and that the divine soul lived on; there must then be some purpose to this travel through the days, some movement up toward higher realms of being, so that the Khaldunian model of cycling dynasties, moving endlessly from youthful vigor to lethargic bloated old age, had to be altered by the addition of reason to human affairs. Thus the notion of the cycle being in fact a rising gyre, in which the possibility of the next young dynasty beginning at a higher level than the last time around was acknowledged and made a goal. This was what he wanted to teach, this was what he wanted to learn. Westward, following the sun, he would find it, and all would be well.

6

Al-Andalus

Everywhere he went seemed the new center of the world. When he was young, Isfahan had seemed the capital of everywhere; then Gujarat, then Agra and Fatepur Sikri; then Mecca and the black stone of Abraham, the true heart of all. Now Cairo appeared to him the ultimate metropolis, impossibly ancient, dusty, and huge. The Mamluks walked through the crowded streets with their retinues in train, powerful men wearing feathered helmets, confident in their mastery of Cairo, Egypt, and most of the Levant. When Bistami saw them he usually followed for a while, as did many others, and he found himself both reminded of Akbar's pomp, and struck by how different the Mamluks were, how they formed a jati that was brought into being anew with each generation. Nothing could be less imperial; there was no dynasty; and yet their control over the populace was even stronger than a dynasty's. It could be that everything Khaldun had said about dynastic cycling was rendered irrelevant by this new system of governance, which had not existed in his time. Things changed, so that even the greatest historian of all could not speak the last word.

Thus the days in the great old city were exciting. But the Maghribi scholars were anxious to begin their long journey home, and so Bistami helped them prepare their caravan, and when they were ready, he joined them continuing westward on the road to Fez.

This part of the tariqat led them first north, to Alexandria. They led their camels to a caravanserai and went down to have a look at the historic harbor, with its long curving dock against the pale water of the Mediterranean. Looking at it Bistami was struck by the feeling one sometimes gets, that he had seen this place before. He waited for the sensation to pass, and followed the others on.

As the caravan moved through the Libyan desert, the talk at night around the fires was of the Mamluks, and of Suleiman the Magnificent, the Ottoman emperor who had recently died. Among his conquests had been the very coast they were now skirting, though there was no way to tell that, except for an extra measure of respect given to Ottoman officials in the towns and caravanserai they passed through. These people never bothered them, or put a tariff on their passing. Bistami saw that the world of the Sufis was, among many other things, a refuge from worldly power. In each region of the earth there were sultans and emperors, Suleimans and Akbars and Mamluks, all ostensibly Muslim, and yet worldly, powerful, capricious, dangerous. Most of these were in the Khaldunian state of late dynastic corruption. Then there were the Sufis. Bistami watched his fellow scholars around the fire in the evenings, intent on a point of doctrine, or the questionable isnad of a hadith, and what that meant, arguing with exaggerated punctilio and little debater's jokes and flourishes, while a pot of thick hot coffee was poured with solemn attention into little glazed clay cups, all eyes gleaming with firelight and pleasure in the argument; and he thought, these are the Muslims who make Islam good. These are the men who have conquered the world, not the warriors. The armies could have done nothing without the word. Worldly but not powerful, devout but not pedantic (most of them, anyway); men interested in a direct relation to God, without any human authority's intervention; a relation to God, and a fellowship among men.

One night the talk turned to al-Andalus, and Bistami listened with an extra measure of interest.

"It must be strange to reenter an empty land like that."

"Fishermen have been living on the coast for a long time now, and Zott scavengers. The Zott and Armenians have moved inland as well."

"Dangerous, I should think. The plague might return."

"No one appears to be affected."

"Khaldun says that the plague is an effect of overpopulation," said Ibn Ezra, the chief scholar of Khaldun among them. "In his chapter on dynasties in 'The Muqaddimah,' forty-ninth section, he says that plagues result from corruption of the air caused by overpopulation, and the putrefaction and evil moistures that result from so many people living close together. The lungs are affected, and so disease is conveyed. He makes the ironical point that these things result from the early success of a dynasty, so that good government, kindness, safety, and light taxation lead to growth and thence to pestilence. He says 'Therefore, science has made it clear that it is necessary to have empty spaces and waste regions interspersed between urban areas. This makes circulation of the air possible, and removes the corruption and putrefaction affecting the air after contact with living beings, and brings healthy air.' If he is right, well—Firanja has been empty for a long time, and can be expected to be healthy again. No danger of plague should exist, until the time comes when the region is heavily populated once again. But that will be a long time from now."

"It was God's judgment," one of the other scholars said. "The Christians were exterminated by Allah for their persecution of Muslims, and Jews too."

"But al-Andalus was Muslim at the time of the plague," Ibn Ezra pointed out. "Granada was Muslim, the whole south of Iberia was Muslim. And they too died. As did the Muslims in the Balkans, or so says al-Gazzabi in his history of the Greeks. It was a matter of location, it seems. Firanja was stricken, perhaps from overpopulation as Khaldun says, perhaps from its many moist valleys, which held the bad air. No one can say."

"It was Christianity that died. They were people of the Book, but they persecuted Islam. They made war on Islam for centuries, and tortured every Muslim prisoner to death. Allah put an end to them."

"But al-Andalus died too," Ibn Ezra repeated. "And there were Christians in the Maghrib and in Ethiopia that survived, and in Armenia. There are still little pockets of Christians in these places, living in the mountains." He shook his head. "I don't think we know what happened. Allah judges."

"That's what I'm saying."

"So al-Andalus is reinhabited," Bistami said.

"Yes."

"And Sufis are there?"

"Of course. Sufis are everywhere. In al-Andalus they lead the way, I have heard. They go north into still empty land, in Allah's name, exploring and exorcising the past. Proving the way is safe. Al-Andalus was a great garden in its time. Good land, and empty."

Bistami looked in the bottom of his clay cup, feeling the sparks in him of those two words struck together. Good and empty, empty and good. This was how he had felt in Mecca.

Bistami felt that he was now cast loose, a wandering Sufi dervish, homeless and searching. On his tariqat. He kept himself as clean as the dusty, sandy Maghrib would allow, remembering the words of Muhammad concerning holy behavior: one came to prosper after washing hands and face, and eating no garlic. He fasted often, and found himself growing light in the air, his vision altering each day, from the glassy clarity of dawn, to the blurred yellow haze of midday, to the semitransparency of sunset, when glories of gold and bronze haloed every tree and rock and skyline. The towns of the Maghrib were small and handsome, often set out on hillsides, and planted with palms and exotic trees that made each town and rooftop a garden. Houses were square whitewashed blocks in nests of palm, with rooftop patios and interior courtyard gardens, cool and green and watered by fountains. Towns had been set where water leaked out of the hillsides, and the biggest town turned out to have the biggest springs: Fez, the end of their caravan.

Bistami stayed at the Sufi lodge in Fez, and then he and Ibn Ezra traveled by camel north to Ceuta, and paid for a crossing by ship to Málaga. The ships here were rounder than in the Persian Sea, with pronounced high-ended keels, smaller sails, and rudders under their centerposts. The crossing of the narrow strait at the west end of the Mediterranean was rough, but they could see al-Andalus from the moment they left Ceuta, and the strong current pouring into the Mediterranean, combined with a westerly gale, bounced them over the waves at a great rate.

The coast of al-Andalus proved cliffy, and above one indentation towered a huge rock mountain. Beyond it the coast curved to the north, and they took the offshore breezes in their little sails and heeled in toward Málaga. Inland they could see a distant white mountain range. Bistami, exalted by the dramatic sea crossing, was reminded of the view of the Zagros Mountains from Isfahan, and suddenly his heart ached for a home he had almost forgotten. But here and now, bouncing on the wild ocean of this new life, he was about to set foot on a new land.

Al-Andalus was a garden everywhere, green trees foresting the slopes of the hills, snowy mountains to the north, and on the coastal plains great sweeps of grain, and groves of round green trees bearing round orange fruit, lovely to taste. The sky dawned blue every day, and as the sun crossed the sky it was warm in the sun, cool in the shade.

Málaga was a fine little city, with a rough stone fort and a big ancient mosque filling the city center. Wide tree-shaded streets rayed away from the mosque, which was being refurbished, up to the hills, and from their slopes one looked out at the blue Mediterranean, sheeting off to the Maghrib's dry bony mountains, over the water to the south. Al-Andalus!

Bistami and Ibn Ezra found a little lodge like the Persian ribats, in a kind of village at the edge of the town, between fields and orange groves. Sufis grew the oranges, and cultivated grapevines. Bistami went out in the mornings to help them work. Most of their time was spent in the wheat field stretching off to the west. The oranges were easy: "We trim the trees to keep the fruit off the ground," a ribat worker named Zeya told Bistami and Ibn Ezra one morning, "as you see. I've been trying various degrees of thinning, to see what the fruit does, but the trees left alone develop a shape like an olive, and if you keep branches off the ground at the bottom, then the fruit can't pick up any ground-based rots. They are fairly susceptible to diseases, I must say. The fruit gets green or black molds, the leaves go brittle or white or brown. The bark crusts over with orange or white fungi. Ladybugs help, and smoking with smudge pots, which is what we do to save the trees during frosts."

"It gets that cold here?"

"Sometimes, in the late winter, yes. It's not paradise here you know."

"I was thinking it was."

The call of the muezzin came from the house, and they pulled out their prayer mats and knelt to the southeast, a direction Bistami had still not gotten used to. Afterward Zeya led them to a stone stove holding a fire, and brewed them a cup of coffee.

"It does not seem like new land," Bistami noted, sipping blissfully.

"It was Muslim land for many centuries. The Umayyads ruled here from the second century until the Christians took the region, and the plague killed them."

"People of the Book," Bistami murmured.

"Yes, but corrupt. Cruel taskmasters to free men or slave. And always fighting among themselves. It was chaos then."

"As in Arabia before the Prophet."

"Yes, exactly the same, even though the Christians had the idea of one God. They were strange that way, contentious. They even tried to split God Himself in three. So Islam prevailed. But then after a few centuries, life here was so easy that even Muslims grew corrupt. The Umayyads were defeated, and no strong dynasty replaced them. The taifa states numbered more than thirty, and they fought constantly. Then the Almoravids invaded from Africa, in the fifth century, and in the sixth century the Almohads from Morocco ousted the Almoravids, and made Seville their capital. The Christians meanwhile had continued to fight in the north, in Catalonia and over the mountains in Navarre and Firanja, and they came back and retook most of al-Andalus. But never the southernmost part, the Nasrid kingdom, including Málaga and Granada. These lands remained Islam to the very end."

"And yet they too died," Bistami said.

"Yes. Everyone died."

"I don't understand that. They say Allah punished the infidels for their persecution of Islam, but if that were true, why would He kill the Muslims here as well?"

Ibn Ezra shook his head decisively. "Allah did not kill the Christians. People are wrong about that."

Bistami said, "But even if He didn't, He allowed it to happen. He didn't protect them. And yet Allah is all-powerful. I don't understand that."

Ibn Ezra shrugged. "Well, this is another manifestation of the problem of death and evil in the world. This world is not Paradise, and Allah, when he created us, gave us free will. This world is ours to prove ourselves devout or corrupt. This is very clear, because even more than Allah is powerful, He is good. He cannot create evil. And yet evil exists in the world. So clearly we create that ourselves. Therefore our destinies cannot have been fixed or predetermined by Allah. We must work them out for ourselves. And sometimes we create evil, out of fear, or greed, or laziness. That's our fault."

"But the plague," Zeya said.

"That wasn't us or Allah. Look, all living things eat each other, and often the smaller eats the larger. The dynasty ends and the little warriors eat it up. This fungus, for instance, eating this fallen orange. The fungus is like a field of a million small mushrooms. I can show you in a magnifying glass I have. And see the orange—it's a blood orange, see, dark red inside. You people must have bred them for that, right?"

Zeya nodded.

"You get hybrids, like mules. Then with plants you can do it again, and again, until you've bred a new orange. That's just how Allah made us. The two parents mix their stock in the offspring. All traits are mixed, I suspect, though only some show. Some are carried unseen to a later generation. Anyway, say some mold like this, in their bread, or even living in their water, bred with another mold, and made some new creature that was poison. It spread, and being stronger than its parents, supplanted them. And so the people died. Maybe it drifted through the air like pollen in spring, maybe it lived inside the people it poisoned for weeks before it killed them, and passed on their breath, or at the touch. And then it was such a poison that in the end it killed off all its food, in effect, and then died out itself, for lack of sustenance."

Bistami stared at the segments of blood-red orange still in his hand, feeling faintly sick. The red-fleshed segments were like wedges of bright death.

Zeya laughed at him. "Come now, eat up! We can't live like angels! All that happened over a hundred years ago, and people have been coming back and living here without any problems for a long time. Now we are as free from the plague as any other country. I've lived here all my life. So finish your orange."

Bistami did so, thinking it over. "So it was all an accident."

"Yes," Ibn Ezra said. "I think so."

"It doesn't seem like Allah should allow it."

"All living things are free in this world. Besides, it could be that it was not entirely accidental. The Quran teaches us to live cleanly, and it could be that the Christians ignored the laws at their peril. They ate pigs, they kept dogs, they drank wine—"

"We here don't believe that wine was the problem," Zeya said with another laugh.

Ibn Ezra smiled. "But if they lived in their sewage, among the tanneries and shambles, and ate pork and touched dogs, and killed each other like the barbarians of the east, and tortured each other, and had their way with boys, and left the dead bodies of their enemies hanging at the gates—and they did all these things—then perhaps they made their own plague, do you see what I mean? They created the conditions that killed them."

"But were they so different from anyone else?" Bistami asked, thinking of the crowds and filth in Cairo, or Agra.

Ibn Ezra shrugged. "They were cruel."

"More cruel than Temur the Lame?"

"I don't know."

"Did they conquer cities and put every person to the sword?"

"I don't know."

"The Mongols did that, and they became Muslim. Temur was a Muslim."

"So they changed their ways. I don't know. But the Christians were torturers. Maybe it mattered, maybe it didn't. All living things are free. Anyway they're gone now, and we're here."

"And healthy, by and large," said Zeya. "Of course sometimes a child catches a fever and dies. And everyone dies eventually. But it's a sweet life here, while it lasts."

When the orange and grape harvests were done, the days grew short. Bistami had not felt such a chill in the air since his years in Isfahan. And yet in this very season, during the coldest nights, the orange trees blossomed, near the shortest day of the year: little white flowers all over the green round trees, fragrant with a smell reminiscent of their taste but heavier, and very sweet, almost cloying.

Through this giddy air came a cavalry, leading a long caravan of camels and mules, and then, in the evening, slaves on foot.

This was the sultan of Carmona, near Sevilla, someone said; one Mawji Darya, and his traveling party. The sultan was the youngest son of the new caliph, and had suffered a disagreement with his elder brothers in Sevilla and al-Majriti, and had therefore decamped with his retainers with the intent of moving north across the Pyrenees, and establishing a new city. His father and elder brothers ruled in Córdoba, Sevilla, and Toledo, and he planned to lead his group out of al-Andalus, up the Mediterranean coast on the old road to Valencia, then inland to Saragossa, where there was a bridge, he said, over the river Ebro.

At the outset of this "hegira of the heart," as the sultan called it, a dozen or more like-minded nobles and their people had joined him. And it became clear as the motley crowd filed into the ribat yard, that along with the young Sevillan nobles' families, retainers, friends, and dependents, they had been joined by many more followers from the villages and farms that had sprung up in the countryside between Sevilla and Málaga. Sufi dervishes, Armenian traders, Turks, Jews, Zott, Berbers, all were represented; it was like a trade caravan, or some dream haj in which all the wrong people were on their way to Mecca, all the people who would never become hajis. Here there were a pair of dwarves on ponies, behind them a group of one-handed and handless ex-criminals, then some musicians, then two men dressed as women; this caravan had them all.

The sultan spread a broad hand. "They are calling us the 'Caravan of Fools,' like the Ship of Fools. We will sail over the mountains to a land of grace, and be fools for God. God will guide us."

From among them appeared his sultana, riding a horse. She dismounted from it without regard for the big servant there to help her down, and joined the sultan as he was greeted by Zeya and the other members of the ribat. "My wife, the Sultana Katima, originally from al-Majriti."

The Castilian woman was bareheaded, short and slender armed, her riding skirts fringed with gold that swung through the dust, her long black hair swept back in a glossy curve from her forehead, held by a string of pearls. Her face was slender and her eyes a pale blue, making her gaze odd. She smiled at Bistami when they were introduced, and later smiled at the farm, and the waterwheels, and the orange groves. Small things amused her that no one else saw. The men there began to do what they could to accommodate the sultan and stay by his side, so that they could remain in her presence. Bistami did it himself. She looked at him and said something inconsequential, her voice like a Turkish oboe, nasal and low, and hearing it he remembered what the vi-

sion of Akbar had said to him during his immersion in the light: the one
you seek is elsewhere.

Ibn Ezra bowed low when he was introduced. "I am a Sufi pilgrim,
Sultana, and a humble student of the world. I intend to make the haj, but
I like the idea of your hegira very much; I would like to see Firanja for
myself. I study the ancient ruins."

"Of the Christians?" the sultana asked, fixing him with her look.

"Yes, but also of the Romans, who came before them, in the time before the Prophet. Perhaps I can make my haj the wrong way around."

"All are welcome who have the spirit to join us," she said.

Bistami cleared his throat, and Ibn Ezra smoothly brought him forward. "This is my young friend Bistami, a Sufi scholar from Sind, who
has been on the haj and is now continuing his studies in the west."

Sultana Katima looked at him closely for the first time, and stopped
short, visibly startled. Her thick black eyebrows knitted together in con-
centration over her pale eyes, and suddenly Bistami saw that it was the
birdwing mark that had crossed the forehead of his tiger, the mark that
had always made the tigress look faintly surprised or perplexed, as it did
with this woman.

"I am happy to meet you, Bistami. We always look forward to learning from scholars of the Quran."

Later that same day she sent a slave asking him to join her for a private audience, in the garden designated hers for the duration of her stay. Bistami went, plucking helplessly at his robe, grubby beyond all aid.

It was sunset. Clouds shone in the western sky between the black sil-
houettes of cypresses. Lemon blossoms lent the air their fragrance, and
seeing her standing alone by a gurgling fountain, Bistami felt as if he had
entered a place he had been before; but everything here was turned
around. Different in particulars, but more than anything, strangely,
terribly familiar, like the feeling that had come over him briefly in
Alexandria. She was not like Akbar, nor even the tigress, not really. But
this had happened before. He became aware of his breathing.

She saw him standing under the arabesque arches of the entryway,
and beckoned him to her. She smiled at him.

"I hope you do not mind my not wearing the veil. I will never do so.

The Quran says nothing about the veil, except for an injunction to veil the bosom, which is obvious. As for the face, Muhammad's wife Khadijeh never wore the veil, nor did the other wives of the Prophet after Khadijeh died. While she lived he was faithful to her alone, you know. If she had not died he never would have married any other woman, he says so himself. So if she didn't wear the veil, I feel no need to. The veil began when the caliphs in Baghdad wore them, to separate themselves from the masses, and from any khajirites who might be among them. It was a sign of power in danger, a sign of fear. Certainly women are dangerous to men, but not so much that they need hide their faces. Indeed, when you see faces you understand better that we are all the same before God. No veils between us and God, this is what each Muslim has gained by his submission, don't you agree?"

"I do," Bistami said, still shocked by the sense of alreadyness that had overcome him. Even the shapes of the clouds in the west were familiar at this moment.

"And I don't believe there is any sanction given in the Quran for the husband to beat his wife, do you? The only possible suggestion of such a thing is Sura 4:34, 'As to those women on whose part you fear disloyalty and ill-conduct, admonish them, next refuse to share their beds'—how horrible that would be—'last beat them lightly.' Daraba, not darraba, which is really the word 'to beat' after all. Daraba is 'nudge,' or even 'stroke with a feather,' as in the poem, or even to provoke while lovemaking, you know, daraba, daraba. Muhammad made it very clear."

Shocked, Bistami managed to nod. He could feel that there was an astonished look on his face.

She saw it and smiled. "This is what the Quran tells me," she said. "Sura 2:223 says that 'your wife is as your farm to you, so treat her as you would your farm.' The ulema have quoted this as if it meant you could treat women like the dirt under your feet, but these clerics, who stand as unneeded intercessors between us and God, are never farmers, and farmers read the Quran right, and see their wives are their food, their drink, their work, the bed they lie on at night, the very ground under their feet! Yes, of course you treat your wife as the ground under your feet! Give thanks to God for giving us the sacred Quran and all its wisdom."

"Thanks to God," Bistami said.

She looked at him and laughed out loud. "You think I am forward."

"Not at all."

"Oh, but I am forward, believe me. I am very forward. But don't you agree with my reading of the holy Quran? Have I not cleaved to its every phrase, as a good wife cleaves to her husband's every move?"

"So it seems to me, Sultana. I think the Quran . . . insists everywhere that all are equal before God. And thus, men and women. There are hierarchies in all things, but each member of the hierarchy has equal status before God, and this is the only status that really matters. So the high and the low in station here on Earth must have consideration for each other, as fellow members of the faith. Brothers and sisters in belief, no matter caliph or slave. And thus all the Quranic rules concerning treatment of others. Constraints, even of an emperor over his lowest slave, or the enemy he has captured."

"The Christians' holy book had very few rules," she said obliquely, following her own train of thought.

"I didn't know that. You have read it?"

"An emperor over his slave, you said. There are rules even for that. But still, no one would choose to be a slave rather than an emperor. And the ulema have twisted the Quran with all their hadith, always twisting it toward those in power, until the message Muhammad laid out so clearly, straight from God, has been reversed, and good Muslim women are made like slaves again, or worse. Not cattle quite, but not like men either. Wife to husband portrayed as slave to emperor, rather than feminine to masculine, power to power, equal to equal."

By now her cheeks were flushed, and he could see their color even in the dusk's poor light. Her eyes were so pale they seemed like little pools of the twilit sky. When servants brought out torches her blush was enhanced, and now there was a glitter in her pale eyes, the torchfire dancing in those windows to her soul. There was a lot of anger in there, hot anger, but Bistami had never seen such beauty. He stared at her, trying to fix the moment in his memory, thinking You will never forget this, never forget this!

After the silence had gone on a while, Bistami realized that if he did not say something, the conversation might come to an end.

"The Sufis," he said, "speak often of the direct approach to God. It is a matter of illumination; I have . . . I have experienced it myself, in a time of extremity. To the senses it is like being filled with light; for the soul it is the state of baraka, divine grace. And this is available to all equally."

"But do the Sufis mean women when they say 'all'?"

He thought it over. Sufis were men, it was true. They formed brother-hoods, they traveled alone and stayed in ribat or zawiya, the lodges where there were no women, nor women's quarters; if they were married they were Sufis, and their wives were wives of Sufis.

"It depends where you are," he temporized, "and which Sufi teacher you follow."

She looked at him with a small smile, and he realized he had made a move without knowing he had done it, in this game to stay near her.

"But the Sufi teacher could not be a woman," she said.

"Well, no. They sometimes lead the prayers."

"And a woman could never lead prayers."

"Well," Bistami said, shocked. "I have never heard of such a thing happening."

"Just as a man has never given birth."

"Exactly." Feeling relieved.

"But men cannot give birth," she pointed out. "While women could very easily lead prayers. Within the harem I lead them every day."

Bistami didn't know what to say. He was still surprised at the idea.

"And mothers always instruct their children what to pray."

"Yes, that's true."

"The Arabs before Muhammad worshiped goddesses, you know."

"Idols."

"But the idea was there. Women are powers in the realm of the soul."

"Yes."

"And as above, so below. This is true in everything."

And she stepped toward him, suddenly, and put her hand to his bare arm.

"Yes," he said.

"We need scholars of the Quran to come north with us, to help us to clear the Quran of these webs obscuring it, and to teach us about illumi-nation. Will you come with us? Will you do that?"

"Yes."

7

The Caravan of Fools

Sultan Mawji Darya was almost as handsome and gracious as his wife, and just as interested in talking about his ideas, which often returned to the topic of "the convivencia." Ibn Ezra informed Bistami that this was the current enthusiasm among some of the young nobles of al-Andalus: to re-create the golden age of the Umayyad caliphate of the sixth century, when Muslim rulers had allowed the Christians and Jews among them to flourish, and all together had created the beautiful civilization that had been al-Andalus before the Inquisition and the plague.

As the caravan in its ragged glory rode out of Málaga, Ibn Ezra told Bistami more about this period, which Khaldun had treated only very briefly, and the scholars of Mecca and Cairo not at all. The Andalusi Jews in particular had flourished, translating a great many ancient Greek texts into Arabic, with commentaries of their own, and also making original investigations in medicine and astronomy. Andalusi Muslim scholars had then used what they learned of Greek logic, chiefly Aristotle, to defend all the tenets of Islam with the full force of reason, Ibn Sina and Ibn Rashd being the two most important of these. Ibn Ezra was full of praise for the work of these men. "I hope to extend it in my own small way, God willing, with a particular application to nature and to the ruins of the past."

They fell back into the rhythms of caravan, known to them all. Dawn: stoke the campfires, brew the coffee, feed the camels. Pack and load, get the camels moving. Their column stretched out more than a league, with various groups falling behind, catching up, stopping, starting; mostly moving slowly along. Afternoon: into camp or caravanserai, though as they went farther north they seldom found anything but deserted ruins, and even the road was nearly gone, overgrown by fully mature trees, as thick-trunked as barrels.

The beautiful land they crossed was stitched by mountain ridges, between which stood high, broad plateaus. Crossing them, Bistami felt they had traveled up into a higher space, where sunsets threw long shadows over a vast, dark, windy world. Once when a last shard of sunset light shot under dark lowering clouds, Bistami heard from somewhere in their camp a musician playing a Turkish oboe, carving in the air a long plaintive melody that wound on and on, the song of the dusky plateau's own voice or soul, it seemed. The sultana stood at the edge of camp, listening with him, her fine head turned like a hawk's as she watched the sun descend. It dropped at the very speed of time itself. There was no need to speak in this singing world, so huge, so knotted; no human mind could ever comprehend it, even the music only touched the hem of it, and even that strand they failed to understand— they only felt it. The universal whole was beyond them.

And yet; and yet; sometimes, as at this moment, at dusk, in the wind, we catch, with a sixth sense we don't know we have, glimpses of that larger world—vast shapes of cosmic significance, a sense of everything holy to dimensions beyond sense or thought or even feeling—this visible world of ours, lit from within, stuffed vibrant with reality.

The sultana stirred. The stars were shining in the indigo sky. She went to one of the fires. She had chosen him as their qadi, Bistami realized, to give herself more room for her own ideas. A community like theirs needed a Sufi teacher rather than a mere scholar. She had been a studious girl, people said, and had suffered fits about three years before. Now she was changed.

Well, it would become clearer as it happened. Meanwhile, the sultana; the sound of the oboe; this vast plateau. These things only happen once. The force of this sensation struck him just as strongly as the feel of alreadyness had in the ribat garden.

Just as the Andalusi plateaus stood high under the sun, its rivers were likewise deep in ravines, like the wadi of the Maghrib, but always running.

The rivers were also long, and crossing them was no easy matter. The town of Saragossa had grown in the past because of its great stone bridge, which spanned one of the biggest of these rivers, called the Ebro. Now the town was still substantially abandoned, with only some road merchants and vendors and shepherds clustered around the bridge, in stone buildings that looked as if they had been built by the bridge itself, in its sleep. The rest of the town was gone, overgrown by pine trees and shrubbery.

But the bridge remained. It was made of dressed stones, big squarish blocks worn so smooth they appeared beveled, though they eventually met in lines that would not admit a coin or even a fingernail. The foundations on each bank were squat massive stone towers, resting on bedrock, Ibn Ezra said. He studied them with great interest as the backed-up caravan crossed it and set camp on the other side. Bistami looked at his drawing of it. "Beautiful, isn't it? Like an equation. Seven semicircular arches, with a big one in the middle, over the deep part of the stream. Every Roman bridge I've seen is very nicely fitted to the site. Almost always they use semicircular arches, which make for strength, although they don't cover much distance, so they needed a lot of them. And always ashlar, those are the squared stones. So they sit squarely on each other, and nothing ever moves them. There's nothing tricky about it. We could do it ourselves, if we took the time and trouble. The only real problem is protecting the foundations from floods. I've seen some done really well, with iron-tipped piles driven into the river bottom. But if anything's going to go, it's the foundations. When they tried to do those quicker, with a big weight of rock, they dammed the water, and increased its force against what they put in."

"Where I come from bridges are washed out all the time," Bistami said. "People just build another one."

"Yes, but this is so much more elegant. I wonder if they put any of this down on paper. I haven't seen any books of theirs. The libraries left behind here are terrible, all account books, with the occasional bit of pornography. If there was ever anything more it's been burned to start fires. Anyway, the stones tell the story. See, the stones were cut so well there was no need for mortar. The iron pegs you see sticking out were probably used to anchor scaffolding."

"The Mughals build well in Sind," Bistami said, thinking of the perfect joints in Chishti's tomb. "But mostly the temples and forts. The bridges are usually bamboo, set in piles of stone."

Ibn nodded. "You see a lot of that. But maybe this river doesn't flood as much. It seems like dry country."

In the evening Ibn Ezra showed them a little mock-up of the hoists the Romans must have used to move the great stones: stick tripods, string ropes. The sultan and sultana were his principal audience, but many others watched too, while others wandered in and out of the torchlight. These people asked Ibn Ezra questions, they made comments; they stuck around when the sultan's calvary head, Sharif Jalil, came into the circle with two of his horsemen holding between them a third, who had been accused of theft, apparently not for the first time. As the sultan discussed his case with Sharif, Bistami gathered that the accused man had an unsavory reputation, for reasons known to them but left unsaid—an interest in boys perhaps. Apprehension very like dread filled Bistami, recalling scenes from Fatepur Sikri; strict sharia called for thieves' hands to be cut off, and sodomy, the infamous vice of the Christian crusaders, was punishable by death.

But Mawji Darya merely strode up to the man and yanked him down by the ear, as if chastising a child. "You want for nothing with us. You joined us in Málaga, and need only work honestly to be part of our city."

The sultana nodded at this.

"If we wanted to, we would have the right to punish you in ways you would not like at all. Go talk to our handless penitents if you doubt me! Or we could simply leave you behind, and see how you fare with the locals. The Zott don't like anyone but themselves doing things like this. They would dispose of you quickly. I tell you now, this will happen if Sharif brings you before me again. You will be cast out of your family. Believe me"—he glanced significantly toward his wife—"you would regret that."

The man blubbered something submissive (he was drunk, Bistami saw) and was hauled away. The sultan told Ibn Ezra to continue his exposition on Roman bridges.

Later Bistami joined the sultana in the big royal tent, and remarked on the general openness of their court.

"No veils," Katima said sharply. "Not the izar nor the hijab, the veil that kept the caliph from the people. The hijab was the first step on the road to the despotism of the caliph. Muhammad was never like that, never. He made the first mosque an assembly of friends. Everyone had access to him, and everyone spoke their minds. It could have stayed like

that, and the mosque become the place of . . . of a different way. With
women and men both speaking. This was what Muhammad began, and
who are we to change it? Why follow the ways of those who build barriers, who turned into despots? Muhammad wanted group feeling to lead,
and the person in charge to be no more than a hakam, an arbiter. This
was the title he loved the most and was most proud of, did you know
that?"

"Yes."

"But when he was gone to heaven, Muawiya established the caliphate, and put guards in the mosques to protect himself, and it has been
tyranny ever since. Islam changed from submission to subjugation, and
women were banned from the mosques and from their rightful place. It's
a travesty of Islam!"

She was red-cheeked, vibrant with suppressed emotion. Bistami had
never seen such fervor and beauty together in one face, and he could
hardly think; or, he was full of thought on several levels at once, so that
focus on any one stream of ideas left him fluttering in all the others, restless and inclined to stop following that tributary; inclined merely to let
all rivers of thought roll at once.

"Yes," he said.

She stalked away toward the next fire, squatted down all at once in a
fluff of skirts, in the group of handless and one-handed men. They
greeted her cheerfully and offered her one of their cups, and she drank
deeply, then put it down and said, "Come on then, it's time, you're looking ratty again." They pulled out a stool, she sat on it, and one of them
kneeled before her, his broad back to her. She took the offered comb and
a vial of oil, and began to work the comb through the man's long tangled
hair. The motley crew of their ship of fools settled in around her content-
edly.

North of the Ebro the caravan stopped growing. There were fewer towns
on the old road to the north, and they were smaller, composed of recent
Maghribi settlers, Berbers who had sailed straight across from Algiers
and even Tunis. They were growing barley and cucumbers, and pastur-
ing sheep and goats in the long fertile valleys with their rocky ridgelines,
not far inland from the Mediterranean. Catalonia, this had been called,
very fine land, heavily forested on the hills. They had left behind the taifa

kingdoms to the south, and the people here were content; they felt no need to follow a dispossessed Sufi sultan and his motley caravan, over the Pyrenees and into wild Firanja. And in any case, as Ibn Ezra pointed out, the caravan did not boast food enough to feed many more dependents, nor the gold or money to buy more food than they already did from the villages they passed.

So they continued on the old road, and at the head of a long narrowing valley they found themselves on a broad, dry, rocky plateau, leading up to the forested flanks of a range of mountains, formed of rock darker than the rock of the Himalaya. The old road wound up the flattest part of the tilted plateau, by the side of a gravelly streambed almost devoid of water. Farther along it followed a cut in the hills, just above the bed of this small stream, wandering up into mountains that grew rockier and taller. Now when they camped at night they met no one at all, but bedded down in tents or under the stars, sleeping to the sound of the wind in the trees, and the clattering brooks, and the shifting horses against their harness lines. Eventually the road wound up among rocks, a flat way leading through a rockbound pass, then across a mountain meadow among the peaks, then up through another tight pass, flanked by granite battlements; and then down at last. Compared to Khyber Pass it was not much of a struggle, Bistami thought, but many in the caravan were shivering and afraid.

On the other side of the pass, rock slides had buried the old road repeatedly, and each time the road became a mere foot trail, switchbacking at sharp angles across the rock slides. These were hard going, and the sultana often got off her horse and walked, leading her women with no tolerance for ineptitude or complaint. Indeed she had a sharp tongue when she was annoyed, sharp and scornful.

Ibn Ezra inspected the roads every evening when they stopped, and the rock slides too when they passed them, making drawings of any exposed roadbeds, coping stones, or drainage ditches. "It's classic Roman," he said one evening by the fire as they ate roast mutton. "They knitted all the land around the Mediterranean with these roads. I wonder if this was their main route over the Pyrenees. I don't suppose so, it's so far to the west. It will lead us to the western ocean rather than the Mediterranean. But perhaps it's the easiest pass. It's hard to believe this is not the main road, it's so big."

"Perhaps they're all that way," said the sultana.

"Possibly. They may have used things like these carts the people have found, so they needed their roads to be wider than ours. Camels, of course, need no road at all. Or this may be their main road after all. It may be the road Hannibal used on his way to attack Rome, with his army of Carthaginians and their elephants! I have seen those ruins, north of Tunis. It was a very great city. But Hannibal lost and Carthage lost, and the Romans pulled their city down and sowed salt in the fields, and the Maghrib dried up. No more Carthage."

"So elephants may have walked this road," the sultana said. The sultan looked down at the track, shaking his head in wonder. These were the kinds of things the two of them liked to know.

Coming down out of the mountains, they found themselves in a colder land. The midday sun cleared the peaks of the Pyrenees, but only just. The land was flat and gray, and often swathed in ground mist. The ocean lay to the west, gray and cold and wild with high surf.

The caravan came to a river that emptied into this western sea, flanked by the ruins of an ancient city. On the outskirts of the ruins stood some modest new buildings, fishermen's shacks they seemed, on each side of a newly built wooden bridge.

"Look how much less skillful we are than the Romans," Ibn Ezra said, but hurried over to look at the new work anyway.

He came back. "I believe this was a city called Bayonne. There's an inscription on the remaining bridge tower over there. The maps indicate there was a bigger city to the north, called Bordeaux. Water's Edge."

The sultan shook his head. "We've come far enough. This will do. Over the mountains, but yet only a moderate journey back to al-Andalus. That's just what I want. We'll settle here."

Sultana Katima nodded, and the caravan began the long process of settling in.

8

Baraka

In general, they built upstream from the ruins of the ancient town, scavenging stone and beams until very little of the old buildings remained, except for the church, a big stone barn of a structure, stripped of all idols and images. It was not a beautiful structure compared to the mosques of the civilized world, a rude squat rectangular thing, but it was big, and situated on a prominence overlooking a turn in the river. So after discussion among all the members of the caravan, they decided to make it their grand or Friday mosque.

Modifications began immediately. This project became Bistami's responsibility, and he spent a lot of time with Ibn Ezra, describing what he remembered of the Chishti shrine and the other great buildings of Akbar's empire, poring over Ibn Ezra's drawings to see what might be done to make the old church more mosquelike. They settled on a plan to tear the roof off the old structure, which in any case was showing the sky in many places, and to keep the walls as the interior buttressing of a circular or rather egg-shaped mosque, with a dome. The sultana wanted the prayer courtyard to open onto a larger city square, to indicate the all-embracing quality of their version of Islam, and Bistami did what he could to oblige her, despite signs that it would rain often in this region, and snow perhaps in the winter. It wasn't important; the place of worship would continue out from the grand mosque into a plaza and then the city at large, and by extension, the whole world.

Ibn Ezra happily designed scaffolding, hods, carts, braces, buttress-ing, cement, and so on, and he determined by the stars and such maps as they had the direction of Mecca, which would be indicated not only by the usual signs, but also by the orientation of the mosque itself. The rest of the town moved in toward the grand mosque, all the old ruins re-moved and used for new construction as people settled closer and closer. The scattering of Armenians and Zott who had been living in the ruins before their arrival either joined the community, or moved off to the north.

"We should save room near the mosque for a madressa," Ibn Ezra said, "before the town fills this whole district."

Sultan Mawji thought this was a good idea, and he ordered those who had settled next to the mosque while working on it to move. Some of the workers objected to this, and then refused outright. In a meeting the sultan lost his temper and threatened this group with expulsion from the town, though the fact was he commanded only a very small personal bodyguard, barely enough to defend himself, in Bistami's opin-ion. Bistami recalled the giant cavalries of Akbar, the Mamluks' soldiers; nothing like that here for the sultan, who now faced a mere dozen or two sullen recalcitrants, and yet could do nothing with them. And the open tradition of the caravan, the feel of it, was in danger.

But Sultana Katima rode up on her Arabian mare, and slid down from it and went to the sultan's side. She put her hand to his arm, said some-thing just to him. He looked startled, thinking fast. The sultana shot a fierce glance at the uncooperative squatters, such a bitter rebuke that Bistami shuddered; not for the world would he risk such a glance from her. And indeed the miscreants paled and looked down in shame.

She said, "Muhammad told us that learning is God's great hope for humanity. The mosque is the heart of learning, the Quran's home. The madressa is an extension of the mosque. It must be so in any Muslim community, to know God more completely. And so it will be here. Of course."

She then led her husband away from the place, to the palace on the other side of the city's old bridge. In the middle of the night the sultan's guards returned with swords drawn and pikes at the ready, to rouse the squatters and send them off; but the area was already deserted.

Ibn Ezra nodded with relief when he heard the news. "In the future we must plan ahead well enough to avoid such scenes," he said in a low voice to Bistami. "This incident adds to the reputation of the sultana, perhaps, in some ways, but at a cost."

Bistami didn't want to think about it. "At least now we will have mosque and madressa side by side."

"They are two parts of the same thing, as the sultana said. Especially if the study of the sensible world is included in the curriculum of the madressa. I hope so. I can't stand for such a place to be wasted on mere devotionals. God put us in this world to understand it! That is the highest form of devotion to God, as Ibn Sina said."

This small crisis was soon forgotten, and the new town, named by the sultana Baraka, that term for grace that Bistami had mentioned to her, took shape as if there could never have been any other plan. The ruins of the old town disappeared under the new city's streets and plazas, gardens and workshops; the architecture and city plan both resembled Málaga, and the other Andalusi coastal cities, but with higher walls, and smaller windows, for the winters here were cold, and a raw wind blew in from the ocean in the fall and spring. The sultan's palace was the only structure in the town as open and light as a Mediterranean building; this reminded people of their origins, and showed them that the sultan lived above the usual demands of nature. Across the bridge from it, the plazas were small, the streets and alleyways narrow, so that a riverside medina or casbah developed that was, as in any Maghribi or Arabian city, a veritable warren of buildings, mostly three stories tall, with the upper windows facing each other across alleyways so tight that one could, as was said everywhere, pass condiments from window to window across the streets.

The first time snow fell, everyone rushed out to the plaza before the grand mosque, dressed in most of their clothes. A great bonfire was lit, the muezzin made his call, prayers were recited, and the palace musicians played with blue lips and frozen fingers as people danced in the Sufi way around the bonfire. Whirling dervishes in the snow: all laughed to see it, feeling they had brought Islam to a new place, a new climate. They were making a new world! There was plenty of wood in the undisturbed forests to the north, and a constant supply of fish and fowl; they would be warm, they would be fed; in the winters the life of the city would go on, under a thin blanket of wet melting snow, as if they lived in high mountains, and yet the river poured out its long estuary into the gray ocean, which pounded the beach with unrelenting ferocity, eating instantly the snowflakes that fell into the waves. This was their country.

One day in spring another caravan arrived, full of strangers and their possessions; they had heard of the new town Baraka, and wanted to move there. It was another ship of fools, come from the Armenian and Zott settlements in Portugal and Castile, its criminal tendencies made obvious by the high incidence of handlessness and musical instruments, puppeteers and fortune tellers.

"I'm surprised they made it over the mountains," Bistami said to Ibn Ezra.

"Necessity made them inventive, no doubt. Al-Andalus is a dangerous place for people like these. The sultan's brother is proving a very strict caliph, I have heard, almost Almohad in his purity. The form of Islam he enforces is so pure that I don't believe it was ever lived before, even in the time of the Prophet. No, this caravan is made of people on the run. And so was ours."

"Sanctuary," Bistami said. "That's what the Christians called a place of protection. Usually their churches, or else a royal court. Like some of the Sufi ribat in Persia. It's a good thing. The good people come to you when the law elsewhere becomes too harsh."

So they came. Some were apostates or heretics, and Bistami debated these in the mosque itself, trying as he spoke to create an atmosphere in which all these matters could be discussed freely, without a sense of danger hanging overhead—it existed, but far away, back over the Pyrenees—but also without anything blasphemous against God or Muhammad being affirmed. It did not matter whether one was Sunni or Shiite, Arabian or Andalusi, Turk or Zott, man or woman; what mattered was devotion, and the Quran.

It was interesting to Bistami that this religious balancing act got easier to maintain the longer he worked at it, as if he were practicing something physical, on a ledge or high wall. A challenge to the authority of the caliph? See what the Quran said about it. Ignore the hadith that had encrusted the holy book, and so often distorted it: cut through to the source. There the messages might be ambiguous, often they were; but the book had come to Muhammad over a period of many years, and important concepts were usually repeated in it, in slightly different ways each time. They would read all the relevant passages, and discuss the differences. "When I was in Mecca studying, the true scholars would say . . ." This was as much authority as Bistami would claim for himself; that he had heard true authorities speak. It was the method of the hadith, of course, but with a different content: that the hadith could not be trusted, only the Quran.

"I was speaking with the sultana about this matter . . ." This was another common gambit. Indeed, he consulted with her about almost every question that came up, and without fail in all matters having to do with women or child-rearing; concerning family life he always deferred to her judgment, which he learned to trust more and more as the first years passed. She knew the Quran inside out, and had memorized every sura that aided her case against undue hierarchy, and her protectiveness for the weak of the city grew unabated. Above all she commanded the eye and the heart, wherever she went, and never more so than in the mosque. There was no longer any question of her right to be there, and occasionally even to lead the prayers. It would have seemed unnatural to bar such a being, so full of divine grace, from the place of worship in a city named Baraka. As she herself said, "Did God make me? Did He give me a mind and a soul as great as any man's? Did men's children come out of a woman? Would you deny your own mother a place in heaven? Can anyone gain heaven who is not admitted to the sight of God on this earth?"

No one who would answer these questions in the negative stayed long in Baraka. There were other towns being settled upstream and to the north, founded by Armenians and Zott who were less full of Muslim fervor. A fair number of the sultan's subjects moved away as time passed. Nevertheless, the crowds at the grand mosque grew. They built smaller ones on the expanding outskirts of town, the usual neighborhood mosques, but always the Friday mosque remained the meeting place of the city, its plaza and the madressa grounds filled by the whole population on holy days, and during the festivals and Ramadan, and on the first day of snow every year, when the bonfire of winter was lit. Baraka was a single family then, and Sultana Katima its mother and sister.

The madressa grew as fast as the town, or faster. Every spring, after the snows on the mountain roads had melted, new caravans arrived, guided by mountain folk. Some in each group had come to study in the madressa, which grew famous for Ibn Ezra's investigations into plants and animals, the Romans, building technique, and the stars. When they came from al-Andalus they sometimes brought with them newly recovered books by Ibn Rashd or Maimonides, or new Arabic translations of the ancient Greeks, and they brought also the desire to share what they knew, and learn more. The new convivencia had its heart in Baraka's madressa, and word spread.

Then one bad day, late in the sixth year of the Barakan hegira, Sultan Mawji Darya fell gravely ill. He had grown fat in the previous months, and Ibn Ezra had tried to be his doctor, putting him on a strict diet of grain and milk, which seemed to help his complexion and energy; but then one night he took ill. Ibn Ezra woke Bistami from his bed: "Come along. The sultan is so ill he needs the prayers."

This coming from Ibn Ezra was bad indeed, as he was not much of a one for prayer. Bistami hurried after him, and joined the royal family in their part of the big palace. Sultana Katima was white-faced, and Bistami was shocked to see how unhappy his arrival made her. It wasn't anything personal, but she knew why Ibn Ezra had brought him at such an hour, and she bit her lip and looked away, the tears streaming down her cheeks.

Inside their bedroom the sultan writhed, silent but for heavy, choked breathing. His face was a dark red color.

"Has he been poisoned?" Bistami asked Ibn Ezra in a whisper.

"No, I don't think so. Their taster is fine," indicating the big cat sleeping curled in its little bed in the corner. "Unless someone pricked him with a poisoned needle. But I see no sign of that."

Bistami sat by the rolling sultan and took his hot hand. Before a word had escaped him, the sultan gave a weak groan and arched his back. His breathing stopped. Ibn Ezra grabbed his arms and crossed them before his chest and pressed hard, grunting himself. To no avail; the sultan had died, his body still locked in its last paroxysm. The sultana burst weeping into the room, tried to revive him herself, calling to him and to God, and begging Ibn Ezra to keep up his efforts. It took both men some time to convince her that it was all in vain; they had failed; the sultan was dead.

———

Funerals in Islam hearkened back to earlier times. Men and women congregated in different areas during the ceremonies, and only mingled in
the cemetery afterward, during the brief interment.

But of course this was the first funeral for a sultan of Baraka, and the
sultana herself led the whole population into the grand mosque plaza,
where she had ordered the body to lie in state. Bistami could only go
along with the crowd and stand before them, saying the old prayers of
the service as if they were always announced to all together. And why
not? Certain lines of the service only made sense if said to everyone in
the community: and suddenly, looking out at the stripped, desolate
faces of every person in the city, he understood that the tradition had
been wrong, that it was plainly wrong and even cruel to split the community apart at the very moment it needed to see itself all together as
one. He had never felt such a heterodox opinion so strongly before; he
had always agreed with the sultana's ideas out of the unexamined principle that she ought always to be right. Shaken by this sudden conversion
in his ideas, and by the sight of the beloved sultan's body there in its coffin on its dais, he reminded them all that the sun only shone a certain
number of hours on any life. He spoke the words of this impromptu ser-
mon in a hoarse tearing voice, which sounded even to him as if it were
coming from some other throat; it was the same as it had been during
those eternal days long ago, reciting the Quran under the cloud of Akbar's anger. This association was too much, and he began to weep, struggled to speak. All in the plaza wept, the wailing began again, many
striking themselves in the self-flagellation that took some of the pain
away.

The whole town followed the cortege, Sultana Katima leading it on
her bay. The crowd roared in its sorrow like the sea on its pebble beach.
They buried him overlooking the great gray ocean, and after that it was
black cloth and ashes for many months.

Somehow they never came out of that year of mourning. It was more than
the death of the ruler; it was that the sultana continued to rule on alone.

Now Bistami, and everyone else, would have said that Sultana Katima had been the true leader all along, and the sultan merely her gracious and beloved consort. No doubt that was true. But now, when
Sultana Katima of Baraka came into the grand mosque and spoke in the

Friday prayers, Bistami was once again uneasy, and he could see the townspeople were as well. Katima had spoken before many times in this manner, but now all felt the absence of the covering angel provided by the lenient sultan's presence across the river.

This unease communicated itself to Katima, of course, and her talks became more strident and plaintive. "God wants relations in marriage between husband and wife to be between equals. What the husband can be the wife can be also! In the time of the chaos before the year one, in the zero time, you see, men treated women like domestic beasts. God spoke through Muhammad, and made it clear that women were souls equal to men, to be treated as such. They were given by God many specific rights, in inheritance, divorce, power of choice, power to command their children—given their lives, do you understand? Before the first hegira, before the year one, right in the middle of this tribal chaos of murder and theft, this monkey society, God told Muhammad to change it all. He said, Oh yes, of course you can marry more than one wife, if you want to—if you can do it without strife. Then the next verse says 'But it cannot be done without strife!' What is this but a ban on polygamy stated in two parts, in the form of a riddle or a lesson, for men who could not otherwise imagine it?"

But now it was very clear that she was trying to change the way things worked, the way Islam worked. Of course they all had been, all along—but secretly, perhaps, not admitting it to anyone, not even to themselves. Now it faced them with the face of their only ruler, a woman. There were no queens in Islam. None of the hadith applied anymore.

Bistami, desperate to help, made up his own hadith, and either supplied them with plausible but false isnads, attributing them to ancient Sufi authorities made up out of whole cloth; or else he ascribed them to their sultan, Mawji Darya, or to some old Persian Sufi he knew about; or he left them to be understood as wisdom too common to need ascription. The sultana did the same, following his lead, he thought, but took most of her refuge in the Quran itself, returning obsessively to the suras that supported her positions.

But everyone knew how things were done in al-Andalus, and the Maghrib, and in Mecca, and indeed everywhere across Dar al-Islam, from the western ocean to the eastern ocean (which Ibn Ezra now claimed were the two shores of the same ocean, spanning the greater part of the Earth, which was a globe covered mostly by water). Women did not lead prayers. When the sultana did, it remained shocking, and triply so with the sultan gone. Everyone said it; if she wished to continue along this path, she needed to remarry.

But she showed no sign of interest in that. She wore her widow's black, and held herself aloof from everyone in the town, and had no royal communications with anyone in al-Andalus. The man other than Mawji Darya who had spent the most time in her company was Bistami himself; and when he understood the looks some townspeople were giving him, implying that he might conceivably marry the sultana and remove them from their difficulty, it made him feel light-headed, almost nauseous. He loved her so much that he could not imagine himself married to her. It wasn't that kind of love. He didn't think she could imagine it either, so there was no question of testing the idea, which was both attractive and terrifying, and so in the end painful in the extreme. Once she was talking to Ibn Ezra when Bistami was present, asking him about his claims concerning the ocean fronting them.

"You say this is the same ocean as the one seen by the Moluccans and Sumatrans, on the other side of the world? How could this be?"

"The world is most certainly a globe," said Ibn Ezra. "It's round like the moon, or the sun. A spherical ball. And we have come to the western end of the land in the world, and around the globe is the eastern end of the land in the world. And this ocean covers the rest of the world, you see."

"So we could sail to Sumatra?"

"In theory, yes. But I've been trying to calculate the size of the Earth, using some calculations made by the ancient Greeks, and Brahmagupta of south India, and by my studies of the sky, and though I cannot be sure, I believe it must be some ten thousand leagues around. Brahmagupta said five thousand yoganda, which as I understand it is about the same distance. And the land mass of the world, from Morocco to the Moluccas, I reckon to be about five thousand leagues. So this ocean we look out on covers half the world, five thousand leagues or more. No ship could make it across."

"Are you sure it is so big as that?"

Ibn Ezra waggled a hand uncertainly. "Not sure, Sultana. But I think it must be something like that."

"What about islands? Surely this ocean is not completely empty for five thousand leagues! Surely there are islands!"

"Undoubtedly, Sultana. I mean, it seems likely. Andalusi fishermen have reported running into islands when storms or currents carried them far to the west, but they don't describe how far, or in what direction."

The sultana looked hopeful. "So we could perhaps sail away, and find the same islands, or others like them."

Ibn Ezra waggled his hand again.

"Well?" she said sharply. "Do you not think you could build a seaworthy ship?"

"Possibly, Sultana. But supplying it for a voyage that long . . . We don't know how long it would be."

"Well," she said darkly, "we may have to find out. With the sultan dead, and no one for me to remarry"—and she shot a single glance at Bistami—"there will be Andalusi villains thinking to rule us."

It was like a stab to his heart. That night Bistami lay twisting on his bed, seeing that short glance over and over. But what could he do? How could he be expected to help such a situation? He could not sleep, not the entire night long.

Because a husband would have helped. There was no longer a feeling of harmony in Baraka, and word of the situation certainly had made its way over the Pyrenees, for early in the following spring, when the rivers were still running high and the mountains protecting them still stood white and jagged-edged to the south, horsemen came down the road out of the hills, just ahead of a cold spring storm, pouring in from the ocean: a long column of cavalry, in fact, with pennants from Toledo and Granada flying, and swords and pikes at their hips gleaming in the sun. They rode right into the mosque plaza at the center of town, colorful under the lowering clouds, and lowered their pikes until they all pointed forward. Their leader was one of the sultan's elder brothers, Said Darya, and he stood in his silver stirrups so that he towered over the people gathering there, and said,

"We claim this town in the name of the caliph of al-Andalus, to save it from apostasy, and from the witch who threw her spell over my brother and killed him in his bed."

The crowd, growing by the moment, stared stupidly up at the horsemen. Some of the townspeople were red-faced and tight-lipped, some pleased, most confused or sullen. A few of the rabble from the original Ship of Fools were already pulling cobblestones out of the ground.

Bistami saw all this from the avenue leading to the river, and all of a sudden something about the sight struck him like a blow; those pikes and crossbows, pointing inward: it was like the tiger trap, back in India. These people were like the Bagh-mari, the professional tiger-killing clans that went about the country disposing of problem tigers for a fee. He had seen them before! And not only with the tigress, but before that as well, some other time that he couldn't remember but remembered anyway, some ambush for Katima, a death trap, men stabbing her when she was tall and black-skinned—oh, this had all happened before!

In a panic he ran across the bridge to the palace. Sultana Katima was about to get on her horse to go and confront the invaders, and he threw himself between her and the horse; she was furious and tried to brush by him, and he put his arm around her waist, as slender as a girl's, which shocked them both, and he cried, "No, no, no, no, no! No, Sultana, I beg you, I beg you, don't go over there! They'll kill you, it's a trap! I've seen it! They will kill you!"

"I have to go," she said, cheeks flushed. "The people need me—"

"No they don't! They need you alive! We can leave and they can follow! They will follow! We have to let those people have this town, the buildings mean nothing, we can move north and your people will follow! Listen to me, listen!" And he caught her up by the shoulders and held her fast, looked her in the eye: "I have seen all this play out before. I have been given knowledge. We have to escape or we will be killed."

Across the river they could hear screams. The Andalusi horsemen were not used to opposition from a population without any soldiers, without cavalry, and they were charging down the streets after mobs who threw stones as they fled. A lot of Barakis were crazy with rage, certainly the one-handed ones would die to the man to defend her, and the invaders were not going to have as easy a time of it as they had thought. Snow was now twirling down through the dark air, flying sideways on the wind out of gray clouds streaming low overhead, and already there were fires in the city, the district around the grand mosque beginning to burn.

"Come on, Sultana, there's no time to waste! I've seen how this happens, they'll have no mercy, they're on their way here to the palace, we need to leave now! This has happened before! We can make a new city in the north, some of the people will come with us, gather a caravan and start over, defend ourselves properly!"

"All right!" Sultana Katima shouted suddenly, looking across at the burning town. The wind gusted, and they could just hear screaming in the town over the whoosh of the air. "Damn them! Damn them! Get a horse then, come on, all of you come on! We'll need to ride hard."

9

Another Meeting in the Bardo

And so it was that when they all reconvened in the bardo, many years later, after going north and founding the city of Nsara at the mouth of the Lawiyya River, and defending it successfully from the Andalusi taifa sultans coming up to attack them in after years, and building the beginnings of a maritime power, fishing all the way across the sea, and trading farther yet than that, Bistami was well pleased. He and Katima had never married, the matter had never come up again, but he had been Nsara's principal ulema for many years, and had helped to create a religious legitimacy for this new thing, a queen in Islam. And he and Katima had worked together on this project almost every day of those lives.

"I recognized you!" he reminded Katima. "In the midst of life, through the veil of forgetting, when it mattered, I saw who you were, and you—you saw something too. You knew something from a higher reality was going on! We're making progress."

Katima did not reply. They were sitting on the flagstones of a courtyard in a place very like Chishti's shrine in Fatepur Sikri, except that the courtyard was vastly bigger. People waited in a line to go into the shrine and be judged. They looked like hajis in line to see the Kaaba. Bistami could hear Muhammad's voice inside, praising some, admonishing others. "You need to try again," he heard a voice like Muhammad's say to someone. Everything was quiet and subdued. It was the hour before sunrise, cool and damp, the air filled with distant birdsong. Sitting there beside her, Bistami could see very clearly now how Katima was not at all like Akbar. Akbar had no doubt been sent down to a lower realm, and was even now prowling the jungle hunting for his food, as Katima had been in her previous existence, when she had been a tigress, a killer who had nevertheless befriended Bistami. She had saved him from the Hindu rebels, then picked him out of the ribat in al-Andalus: "You recognized me too," he said. "And we both knew Ibn Ezra," who was at this moment inspecting the wall of the courtyard, running his fingernail down the line between two blocks, admiring the stonework of the bardo.

"This is genuine progress," Bistami repeated. "We are finally getting somewhere!"

Katima gave him a skeptical glance. "You call that progress? Chased to a hole at the far corner of the world?"

"But who cares where we were? We recognized each other, you didn't get killed—"

"Wonderful."

"It was wonderful! I saw through time, I felt the touch of the eternal. We made a place where people could love the good. Little steps, life after life; and eventually we will be there for good, in the white light."

Katima gestured; her brother-in-law, Said Darya, was entering the palace of judgment.

"Look at him, a miserable creature, and yet he is not thrown down into hell, nor even become a worm or a jackal, as he deserves. He will return to the human realm, and wreak havoc all over again. He too is part of our jati, did you recognize him? Did you know he was part of our little band, like Ibn Ezra here?"

Ibn Ezra sat beside them. The line moved up and they shifted with it. "The walls are solid," he reported. "Very well built, in fact. I don't think we're going to able to escape."

"Escape!" Bistami cried. "This is God's judgment! No one escapes that!"

Katima and Ibn Ezra looked at each other. Ibn Ezra said, "My impression is that any improvement in the tenor of existence will have to be anthropogenic."

"What?" Bistami cried.

"It's up to us. No one will help us."

"I'm not saying they will. Although God always helps if you ask. But it is up to us, that's what I've been saying all along, and we are doing what we can, we are making progress."

Katima was not at all convinced. "We'll see," she said. "Time will tell. For now, I myself withhold judgment." She faced the white tomb, drew herself up queenlike, spoke with a tigerish curl of the lip: "And no one judges me."

With a wave of the hand she dismissed the tomb. "It's not here that matters. What matters is what happens in the world."

BOOK 3

◈ OCEAN CONTINENTS ◈

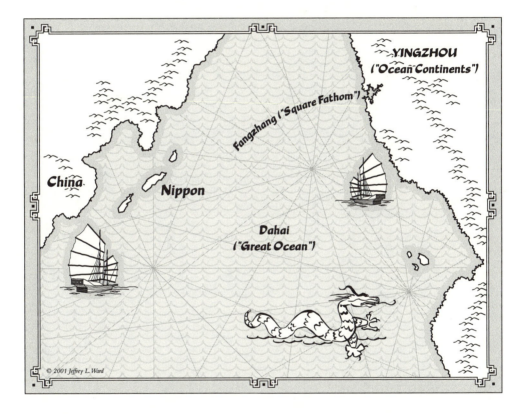

YINGZHOU ("Ocean Continents")

Fangzhang ("Square Fathom")

China

Nippon

Dahai ("Great Ocean")

© 2001 Jeffrey L. Ward

In the thirty-fifth year of his reign, the Wanli Emperor turned his feverish and permanently dissatisfied eye on Nippon. Ten years earlier the Nipponese general Hideyoshi had had the temerity to attempt the conquest of China, and when the Koreans had refused him passage, his army had invaded Korea as the first step in its path. It had taken a large Chinese army three years to drive the invaders off the Korean peninsula, and the twenty-six million ounces of silver it had cost the Wanli Emperor had put his treasury in acute difficulties, difficulties from which it had never recovered. The emperor was inclined to avenge this unprovoked assault (if you did not count the two unsuccessful attacks on Nippon made by Kublai Khan), and to remove the danger of any future problem arising from Nippon, by subjugating it to Chinese suzerainty. Hideyoshi had died, and Ieyasu, the head of a new Tokugawa shogunate, had successfully united all the Nipponese islands under his command, and then closed the country to foreigners. All Nipponese were forbidden to leave, and those who did were forbidden to return. The building of seaworthy ships was also forbidden, although the Wanli noted irritably in his vermilion memoranda that this did not stop hordes of Nipponese pirates from attacking the long Chinese coastline using smaller craft. He thought Ieyasu's retreat from the world signaled weakness, and yet at the same time, a fortress nation of warriors just offshore from the Middle Kingdom was not something to be tolerated either. It pleased the Wanli to think of returning this bastard child of Chinese culture to its rightful place under the Dragon Throne, joining there Korea, Annam, Tibet, Mindanao, and the Spice Islands.

His advisors were not enthusiastic about the plan. For one thing, the treasury was still depleted. For another, the Ming court was already drained by all the previous dramatic events of the Wanli reign, not only the defense of Korea but also the racking dissension caused by the succession problem, still only nominally solved by the Wanli's choice of his elder son, and his younger son's banishment to the provinces; all that could change in a week. And around that highly combustible situation, like a civil war in waiting, constellated all the conflicts and jealous maneuverings of the court powers: the empress mother, the empress, the senior civil servants, the eunuchs, and the generals. Something in the Wanli's combination of intelligence and vacillation, his permanent discontent and his occasional bursts of vengeful fury, made the court of his old age a flayed and exhausted nest of intrigues. To his advisors, particularly the generals and the heads of the treasury, conquering Nippon did not seem even remotely possible.

The emperor, true to form, insisted that it be done.

His senior generals came back with an alternative plan, which they hoped very much would satisfy his desire. They proposed that the emperor's diplomats arrange a treaty with one of the minor Nipponese shoguns, the Tozama Daimyo, who were out of Ieyasu's favor because they had joined him only after his military victory at Sekigahara. The treaty would stipulate that this minor shogun would invite the Chinese to come to one of his ports, and open it permanently to Chinese trade. A Chinese navy would then land at this port in force, and in essence make the port a Chinese port, defended by the full power of the Chinese navy, grown so much bigger during the Wanli's reign in the attempt to defend the coast against pirates. Most of the pirates were from Nippon, so there was a kind of justice there; and a chance to trade with Nippon as well. After that, the treaty port could serve as the staging center of a slower conquest of Nippon, conceived of as happening in stages rather than all at once. That would make it affordable.

The Wanli grumbled about his advisors' meager, partial, eunuchlike enactments of his desires, but patient advocacy by his most trusted advisors of that period finally won him over, and he approved the plan. A secret treaty was arranged with a local lord, Omura, who invited the

Chinese to land and trade at a small fishing village with an excellent harbor, called Nagasaki. Preparations for an expedition that would arrive there with overwhelming force were made in the rebuilt shipyards of Longjiang, near Nanjing, also on the Cantonese coast. The big new ships of the invading fleet were filled with supplies to enable the landing force to withstand a long siege, and they assembled for the first time off the coast of Taiwan, with no one in Nippon except for Omura and his advisors any the wiser.

The fleet was, by the Wanli's direct order, put under the command of one Admiral Kheim, of Annam. This admiral had already led a fleet for the emperor, in the subjugation of Taiwan some years before, but he was still seen by the Chinese bureacracy and military as an outsider, an expert in pirate suppression who had achieved his expertise by spending much of his youth as a pirate himself, plundering the Fujian coast. The Wanli Emperor did not care about this, and even regarded it as a point in Kheim's favor; he wanted someone who could get results, and if he came from outside the military bureaucracy, with its many entanglements at court and in the provinces, so much the better.

The fleet set out in the thirty-eighth year of the Wanli, on the third day of the first month. The spring winds were constant from the northwest for eight days, and the fleet positioned itself in the Kuroshio, the Black River, that great ocean current that runs like a river a hundred li wide, up the long southern shores of the Nipponese islands.

This was as planned, and they were on their way; but then the winds died. Nothing in the air stirred. No bird was seen, and the paper sails of the fleet hung limp, their cross slats ticking the masts only because of the rippling of the Kuroshio itself, which carried them north and east past the main Nipponese islands, past Hokkaido, and out onto the empty expanse of the Dahai, the Great Ocean. This shoreless blue expanse was bisected by their invisible but powerful Black River, flowing relentlessly east.

Admiral Kheim ordered all the captains of the Eight Great Ships and of the Lesser Eighteen Ships to row over to the flagship, where they consulted. Many of the most experienced ocean sailors of Taiwan, Annam, Fujian, and Canton were among these men, and their faces were grave; to be carried off by the Kuroshio was a dangerous business. All of them had heard stories of junks that had been becalmed in the current, or dismasted by squalls, or had had to chop down their masts in order to avoid being capsized, and after that disappeared for years—in one story nine years, in another thirty—after which they had drifted back out of the southeast, bleached and empty, or manned by skeletons. These stories, and the eyewitness evidence of the flagship's doctor, I-Chin, who claimed to have ridden around the Dahai successfully in his youth on a fishing junk disabled by a typhoon, led them to agree that there was probably a big circular current flowing around the vast sea, and that if they could stay alive long enough, they might be able to sail around in it, back to home.

It was not a plan any of them would have chosen to undertake deliberately, but at that point they had no other option but to try it. The captains sat in the admiral's cabin on the flagship and regarded each other unhappily. Many of the Chinese there knew the legend of Hsu Fu, admiral of the Han dynasty of ancient times, who had sailed off with his fleet in search of lands to settle on the other side of the Dahai, and never been heard from again. They knew as well the story of Kublai Khan's two attempts at invading Nippon, both demolished by unseasonable typhoons, which had given the Nipponese the conviction that there was a divine wind that would defend their home islands from foreign attack. Who could disagree? And it seemed all too possible that this divine wind was now doing its work in a kind of joke or ironic reversal, manifesting itself as a divine calm while they were in the Kuroshio, causing their destruction just as effectively as any typhoon. The calm after all was uncannily complete, its timing miraculously good; it could be they had gotten caught up in gods' business. That being the case, they could only give their fate over to their own gods, and hope to ride things out.

This was not Admiral Kheim's favored mode of being. "Enough," he said darkly, ending the meeting. He had no faith in the sea gods' goodwill, and took no stock in old stories, except as they were useful. They were caught in the Kuroshio; they had some knowledge of the currents of the Dahai—that north of the equator they ran east, south of the equator, west. They knew the prevailing winds tended to follow likewise. The doctor I-Chin had successfully ridden the entirety of this great circle, his unprepared ship's crew living off fish and seaweed, drinking rainwater, and stopping for supplies at islands they passed. This was cause for hope. And as the air remained eerily calm, hope was all they had. It was not as if they had any other options; the ships were dead in the water, and the big ones were too big to row anywhere. In truth they had no choice but to make the best of it.

Admiral Kheim therefore ordered most of the men of the fleet to get on board the Eighteen Lesser Ships, and ordered half of these to row north, half south, with the idea they could row at an angle out of the Black Stream, and sail home when the wind returned, to get word to the emperor concerning what had happened. The Eight Great Ships, manned by the smallest crews that could sail them, with as much of the fleet's supplies as could be fitted in their holds, settled in to wait out the ride around the ocean on the currents. If the smaller ones succeeded in sailing back to China, they were to tell the emperor to expect the Great Eight to return at some later date, out of the southeast.

In a couple of days the smaller ships all disappeared over the horizon, and the Eight Great Ships drifted on, roped together in a perfect calm, off the maps to the unknown east. There was nothing else they could do.

Thirty days passed without the slightest breeze. Each day they rode the current farther to the east.

No one had ever seen anything like it. Admiral Kheim rejected all talk of the Divine Calm, however; as he pointed out, the weather had gone strange in recent years, mostly much colder, with lakes freezing over that had never frozen before, and freak winds, such as certain whirlwinds that had stood in place for weeks at a time. Something was wrong in the heavens. This was just part of that.

When the wind returned at last, it was strong from the west, pushing them even farther along. They angled south across the prevailing wind, but cautiously now, hoping to stay within the hypothetical great circle current, as being the fastest way around the ocean and back home. In the middle of the circle there was rumored to be a permanent zone of calm, perhaps the very centerpoint of the Dahai, as it was near the equator, and perhaps equidistant from shores east and west, though no one could say for sure about that. A doldrums that no junk could escape, in any case. They had to go out far enough to the east to get around that, then head south, then, below the equator, back west again.

They saw no islands. Seabirds sometimes flew over, and they shot a few with arrows and ate them for luck. They fished day and night with nets, and caught flying fish in their sails, and pulled in snarls of seaweed that grew increasingly rare, and refilled their water casks when it rained, setting funnels like inverted umbrellas over them. And they were seldom thirsty, and never hungry.

But never a sight of land. The voyage went on, day after day, week after week, month after month. The rattan and the rigging began to wear thin. The sails grew transparent. Their skin began to grow transparent.

The sailors grumbled. They no longer approved of the plan to ride the circle of currents around the great sea; but there was no turning back, as Kheim pointed out to them. So they passed through their grumbling, as through a storm. Kheim was not an admiral anyone wanted to cross.

They rode out storms in the sky, and felt the rocking of storms under the sea. So many days passed that their lives before the voyage grew distant and indistinct; Nippon, Taiwan, even China itself began to seem like dreams of a former existence. Sailing became the whole world: a water world, with its blue plate of waves under an inverted bowl of blue sky, and nothing else. They no longer even looked for land. A mass of seaweed was as astonishing as an island would once have been. Rain was always welcome, as the occasional periods of rationing and thirst had taught them painfully their utter reliance on fresh water. This mostly came from rain, despite the little stills that I-Chin had constructed to clarify saltwater, which gave them a few buckets a day.

All things were reduced to their elemental being. Water was ocean; air was sky; earth, their ships; fire, the sun, and their thoughts. The fires banked down. Some days Kheim woke, and lived, and watched the sun go down again, and realized that he had forgotten to think a single thought that whole day. And he was the admiral.

Once they passed the bleached wreckage of a huge junk, intertwined with seaweed and whitened with bird droppings, barely afloat. Another time they saw a sea serpent out to the east, near the horizon, perhaps leading them on.

Perhaps the fire had left their minds entirely, and was in the sun alone, burning above through rainless days. But something must have remained; gray coals, almost burnt out; for when land poked over the horizon to the east, late one afternoon, they shouted as if it were all they had ever thought of, in every moment of the hundred and sixty days of their unexpected journey. Green mountainsides, falling precipitously into the sea, apparently empty; it didn't matter; it was land. What looked to be a large island.

The next morning it was still there ahead of them. Land ho!

Very steep land, however, so steep that there was no obvious place to make landfall: no bays, no river mouths of any size; just a great wall of green hills, rising wetly out of the sea.

Kheim ordered them to sail south, thinking even now of the return to China. The wind was in their favor for once, and the current also. They sailed south all that day and the next, without a single harbor to be seen. Then, as light fog lifted one morning, they saw they had passed a cape, which protected a sandy southern reach; and farther south there was a gap in the hills, dramatic and obvious. A bay. There was a patch of turbulent white water on the north side of this majestic entrance strait, but beyond that it was clear sailing, and the flood tide helping to usher them in.

So they sailed into a bay like nothing any of them had ever seen in all their travels. An inland sea, really, with three or four rocky islands in it, and hills all around, and marshes bordering most of its shores. The hills were rocky on top but mostly forested, the marshes lime green, yellowed by fall colors. Beautiful land; and empty!

They turned north and anchored in a shallow inlet, protected by a hilly spine that ran down into the water. Then some of them spotted a line of smoke rising up into the evening air.

"People," I-Chin said. "But I don't think this can be the western end of the Muslim lands. We haven't sailed far enough for that, if Hsing Ho is correct. We shouldn't even be close yet."

"Maybe it was a stronger current than you thought."

"Maybe. I can refine our distance-from-equator tonight."

"Good."

But a distance-from-China would have been better, and that was the calculation they could not make. Dead reckoning had been impossible during the long period of their drift, and despite I-Chin's continual guesses, Kheim didn't think they knew to within a thousand li.

As for distance-from-equator, I-Chin reported that night, after measuring the stars, that they were at about the same line as Edo or Beijing—

a little higher than Edo, a little lower than Beijing. I-Chin tapped his astrolabe thoughtfully. "It's the same distance-from-equator as the hui countries in the far west, in Fulan where all the people died. If Hsing Ho's map can be trusted. Fulan, see? A harbor called Lisboa. But there's no Fulan-chi here. I don't think this can be Fulan. We must have come upon an island."

"A big island!"

"Yes, a big island." I-Chin sighed. "If we could only solve the distance-from-China problem."

It was an everlasting complaint with him, causing an obsession with clockmaking; an accurate clock would have made it possible to calculate the distance-from-Beijing, using an almanac to give the star times in China, and timing from there. The emperor had some fine clocks in his palace, it was said, but they had none on their ship. Kheim left him to his muttering.

The next morning they woke to find a group of locals—men, women, and children—dressed in leather skirts, shell necklaces, and feather headdresses, standing on the beach watching them. They had no cloth, it appeared, and no metal except small bits of hammered gold, copper, and silver. Their arrowheads and spear tips were flaked obsidian, their baskets woven of reeds and pine needles. Great mounds of shells lay heaped on the beach above the high-tide mark, and the visitors could see smoke rising from fires set inside wicker hovels, little shelters like those the poor farmers in China used for their pigs in winter.

The sailors laughed and chattered to see such people. They were partly relieved and partly amazed, but it was impossible to be frightened of these folk.

Kheim was not so sure. "They're like the wild people on Taiwan," he said. "We had some terrible fights with them when we went after pirates in the mountains. We have to be careful."

I-Chin said, "Tribes like that exist on some of the Spice Islands too, I've seen them. But even those people have more things than these."

"No brick or wood houses, no iron that I can see, meaning no guns . . ."

"No fields for that matter. They must eat the clams," pointing at the great shell heaps, "and fish. And whatever they can hunt or glean. These are poor people."

"That won't leave much for us."

"No."

The sailors were shouting down at them: "Hello! Hello!"

Kheim ordered them to be quiet. He and I-Chin got in one of the little rowboats they had on the great ship, and had four sailors row them ashore.

From the shallows Kheim stood and greeted the locals, palms up and out, as one did in the Spice Islands with the wild ones. The locals didn't understand anything he said, but his gestures made plain his peaceful intent, and they seemed to recognize it. After a while he stepped ashore, confident of a peaceful welcome, but instructing the sailors to keep their flintlocks and crossbows below the seats at the ready, just in case.

On shore he was surrounded by curious people, babbling in their own tongue. Somewhat distracted by the sight of the women's breasts, he greeted a man who stepped forward, whose elaborate and colorful headdress perhaps confirmed him as their headman. Kheim's silk neck scarf, much salt-damaged and faded, had the image of a phoenix on it, and Kheim untied it and gave it to the man, holding it flat so he could see the image. The silk itself interested the man more than the image on it. "We should have brought more silk," Kheim said to I-Chin.

I-Chin shook his head. "We were invading Nippon. Get their words for things if you can."

I-Chin was pointing to one thing after another, their baskets, spears, dresses, headpieces, shell mounds; repeating what they said, noting it quickly on his slate. "Good, good. Well met, well met. The emperor of China and his humble servants send their greetings."

The thought of the emperor made Kheim smile. What would the Wanli, Heavenly Envoy, make of these poor shell-grubbers?

"We need to teach some of them Mandarin," I-Chin said. "Perhaps a young boy, they are quicker."

"Or a young girl."

"Don't let's get into that," I-Chin said. "We need to spend some time here, to repair the ships and restock. We don't want the men here turning on us."

Kheim mimed their intentions to the headman. Stay for a while— camp onshore—eat, drink—repair ships—go back home, beyond the sunset to the west. It seemed they eventually understood most of this. In return he understood from them that they ate acorns and squash, fish and clams and birds, and larger animals, probably they meant deer.

They hunted in the hills behind. There was lots of food, and the Chinese were welcome to it. They liked Kheim's silk, and would trade fine baskets and food for more of it. Their ornamental gold came from hills to the east, beyond the delta of a big river that entered the bay across from them, almost directly east; they indicated where it flowed through a gap in the hills, somewhat like the gap leading out to the ocean.

As this information about the land obviously interested I-Chin, they conveyed more to him in a most ingenious way; though they had no paper, nor ink, nor writing nor drawing, except for the patterns in their baskets, they did have maps of a particular kind, made in the sand on the beach. The headman and some other notables crouched and shaped damp sand most minutely with their hands, smoothing flat the part meant to represent the bay, then getting into spirited discussions about the true shape of the mountain between them and the ocean, which they called Tamalpi, and which they indicated by gesture was a sleeping maiden, a goddess apparently, though it was hard to be sure. They used grass to represent a broad valley inland of the hills bracketing the bay on the east, and wetted the channels of a delta and two rivers, one draining the north, the other the south part of a great valley. To the east of this big valley were foothills rising to mountains much bigger than the coastal range, snow-capped (indicated by dandelion fluff) and holding in their midst a big lake or two.

All this they marked out with endless disputations concerning the details, and care over fingernail creasings and bits of grass or pine sprays; and all for a map that would be washed away in the next high tide. But when they were done, the Chinese knew that their gold came from people who lived in the foothills; their salt from the shores of the bay; their obsidian from the north and from beyond the high mountains, whence came also their turquoise; and so on. And all without any language in common, merely things displayed in mime, and their sand model of their country.

In the days that followed, however, they exchanged words for a host of daily objects and events, and I-Chin kept lists and started a glossary, and started teaching one of the local children, a girl of about six years who was the child of the headman, and very forward; a constant babbler in her own tongue, whom the Chinese sailors named Butterfly, both for her manner and for the joke that perhaps at this point they were only her dream. She delighted in telling I-Chin what was what, very firmly;

and quicker than Kheim could have believed possible she was using Chinese as well as her own language, mixing them together sometimes, but usually reserving her Chinese for I-Chin, as if it were his private tongue and he some sort of freak, or inveterate joker, always making up fake words for things—neither opinion far from the truth. Certainly her elders agreed that I-Chin was a strange foreigner, feeling their pulse and abdomens, looking in their mouths, asking to inspect their urine (this they refused), and so on. They had a kind of doctor themselves, who led them in ritural purifications in a simple steam bath. This elderly raddled wild-eyed man was no doctor in the sense I-Chin was, but I-Chin took great interest in the man's herbarium and his explanations, as far as I-Chin could make them out, using ever more sophisticated sign language, and Butterfly's growing facility in Chinese. The locals' language was called "Miwok," as the people also called themselves; the word meant "people" or something similar. They made it clear with their maps that their village controlled the watershed of the stream that flowed into the bay. Other Miwok lived in the nearby watersheds of the peninsula, between bay and ocean; other people with different languages lived in other parts of the country, each with their own name and territory, though the Miwok could argue among themselves over the details of these things endlessly. They told the Chinese that the great strait leading out to the ocean had been created by an earthquake, and that the bay had been fresh water before the cataclysm had let the ocean in. This seemed unlikely to I-Chin and Kheim, but then one morning after they had slept on shore, they were awakened by a severe shaking, and the earthquake lasted many heartbeats, and came back twice that morning; so that after that they were not as sure about the strait as they had been before.

They both enjoyed listening to the Miwok speak, but only I-Chin was interested in how the women made the bitter acorns of the jagged-leaved oaks edible, by grinding and leaching the acorn powder in beds of leaves and sand, giving them a sort of flour; I-Chin thought it was most ingenious. This flour, and salmon both fresh and dried, were the staples of their diet, which they offered the Chinese freely. They also ate deer, a kind of giant deer, rabbits, and all manner of waterfowl. Indeed, as the fall descended mildly on them, and the months passed, the Chinese began to understand that food was so plentiful in this place that there was no need for agriculture as practiced in China. Despite which there were very few people living there. That was one of the mysteries of this island.

The Miwok's hunts were big parties in the hills, all-day events that Kheim and his men were allowed to join. The bows used by the Miwok were weak but adequate. Kheim ordered his sailors to leave the cross-bows and guns hidden on the ships, and the cannon were simply left to view but not explained, and none of the locals asked about them.

On one of these hunting trips Kheim and I-Chin followed the head-man, Ta Ma, and some of the Miwok men up the stream that poured through their village, up into hills to a high meadow that had a view of the ocean to the west. To the east they could see across the bay, to range after range of green hills.

The meadow was marshy by the stream, grassy above it, with stands of oak and other trees tufting the air. There was a lake at the lower end of the meadow that was entirely covered with geese—a white blanket of liv-ing birds, all honking now, upset by something, complaining. Then the whole flock thrashed into the air, groups swirling and fragmenting, com-ing together, flying low over the hunters, squawking or silently concen-trating on flight, the distinctive creak of their pumping wing feathers loud in the air. Thousands on thousands.

The men stood and watched the spectacle, eyes bright. When the geese had all departed, they saw the reason they had left; a herd of giant deer had come to the lake to drink. The stags had huge racks of antlers. They stared across the water at the men, vigilant but undeterred.

For a moment, all was still.

In the end the giant deer stepped away. Reality awoke again. "All sen-tient beings," said I-Chin, who had been muttering his Buddhist sutras all along. Kheim normally had no time for such claptrap, but now, as the day continued, and they hiked over the hills on their hunt, seeing great numbers of peaceful beaver, quail, rabbits, foxes, seagulls and crows, or-dinary deer, a bear and two cubs, a slinky long-tailed gray hunting crea-ture, like a fox crossed with a squirrel—on and on—simply a whole country of animals, living together under a silent blue sky—nothing dis-turbed, the land flourishing on its own, the people there just a small part of it—Kheim began to feel odd. He realized that he had taken China for reality itself. Taiwan and the Mindanaos and the other islands he had seen were like scraps of land, leftovers; China had seemed to him the world. And China meant people. Built up, cultivated, parceled off ha by ha, it was so completely a human world that Kheim had never considered that there might once have been a natural world different to it. But here was natural land, right before his eyes, full as could be with animals of every kind, and obviously very much bigger than Taiwan; bigger than China; bigger than the world he had known before.

"Where on Earth are we?" he said to I-Chin.

I-Chin said, "We have found the source of the peach-blossom stream."

Winter arrived, and yet it stayed warm during the days, cool at night. The Miwok gave them cloaks of sea-otter pelts sewn together with leather thread, and nothing could have been more comfortable against the skin, they were as luxurious as the clothes of the Jade Emperor. During storms it rained and was cloudy, but otherwise it was bright and sunny. This was all happening at the same latitude as Beijing, according to I-Chin, and at a time of year when it would have been bitterly cold and windy there, so the climate was much remarked on by the sailors. Kheim could scarcely believe the locals when they said it was like this every winter.

On the winter solstice, a sunny warm day like all the rest, the Miwok invited Kheim and I-Chin into their temple, a little round thing like a dwarves' pagoda, the floor sunken into the earth and the whole thing covered with sod, the weight of which was held up by some tree trunks forking up into a nest of branches. It was like being in a cave, and only the fire's light and the smoky sun shafting down through a smokehole in the roof illuminated the dim interior. The men were dressed in ceremonial feather headdresses and many shell necklaces, which gleamed in the firelight. To a constant drum rhythm they danced round the fire, taking turns as night followed day, going on until it seemed to the stupefied Kheim that they might never stop. He struggled to stay awake, feeling the importance of the event for these men who looked somehow like the animals they fed on. This day marked the return of the sun, after all. But it was hard to stay awake. Eventually he struggled to his feet and joined the younger dancers, and they made room for him as he galumphed about, his sea legs bandying out to the sides. On and on he danced, until it felt right to collapse in a corner, and only emerge at the last part of dawn, the sky fully lit, the sun about to burst over the hills backing the bay. The happy loose-limbed band of dancers and drummers was led by a group of the young unmarried women to their sweat lodge, and in his stupefied state Kheim saw how beautiful the women were, supremely strong, as robust as the men, their feet unbound and their eyes clear and without deference—indeed they appeared to laugh heartily at the weary men as they escorted them into the steam bath, and helped them out of their headdresses and finery, making what sounded like ribald commentary to Kheim, though it was possible he was only making it up out of his own desire. But the burnt air, the sweat pouring out of him, the abrupt clumsy plunge into their little river, blasting him awake in the morning light; all only increased his sense of the women's loveliness, beyond anything he could remember experiencing in China, where a sailor was always being taken by the precious blown flower girls in the restaurants. Wonder and lust and the river's chill battled his exhaustion, and then he slept on the beach in the sun.

He was back on the flagship when I-Chin came to him, mouth tight. "One of them died last night. They brought me to see. It was the pox."

"What! Are you sure?"

I-Chin nodded heavily, as grim as Kheim had ever seen him.

Kheim rocked back. "We will have to stay on board the ships."

"We should leave," I-Chin said. "I think we brought it to them."

"But how? No one had pox on this trip."

"None of the people here have any pox scars at all. I suspect it is new to them. And some of us had it as children, as you can see. Li and Peng are heavily pocked, and Peng has been sleeping with one of the local women, and it was her child died of it. And the woman is sick too."

"No."

"Yes. Alas. You know what happens to wild people when a new sickness arrives. I've seen it in Aozhou. Most of them die. The ones who don't will be balanced against it after that, but they may still be able to tip others of the unexposed off their balance, I don't know. In any case, it's bad."

They could hear little Butterfly squealing up on the deck, playing some game with the sailors. Kheim gestured above. "What about her?"

"We could take her with us, I guess. If we return her to shore, she'll probably die with the rest."

"But if she stays with us she may catch it and die too."

"True. But I could try to nurse her through it."

Kheim frowned. Finally he said, "We're provisioned and watered. Tell the men. We'll sail south, and get in position for a spring crossing back to China."

Before they left, Kheim took Butterfly and rowed up to the village's beach and stopped well offshore. Butterfly's father spotted them and came down quickly, stood knee-deep in the slack tidal water and said something. His voice croaked, and Kheim saw the pox blisters on him. Kheim's hands rowed the boat out a stroke.

"What did he say?" he asked the girl.

"He said people are sick. People are dead."

Kheim swallowed. "Say to him, we brought a sickness with us."

She looked at him, not comprehending.

"Tell him we brought a sickness with us. By accident. Can you say that to him? Say that."

She shivered in the bottom of the boat.

Suddenly angry, Kheim said loudly to the Miwok headman, "We brought a disease with us, by accident!"

Ta Ma stared at him.

"Butterfly, please tell him something. Say something."

She raised her head up and shouted something. Ta Ma took two steps out, going waist-deep in the water. Kheim rowed out a couple of strokes, cursing. He was angry and there was no one to be angry at.

"We have to leave!" he shouted. "We're leaving! Tell him that," he said to Butterfly furiously. "Tell him!"

She called out to Ta Ma, sounding distraught.

Kheim stood up in the boat, rocking it. He pointed at his neck and face, then at Ta Ma. He mimicked distress, vomiting, death. He pointed at the village and swept his hand as if erasing it from a slate. He pointed at Ta Ma and gestured that he should leave, that all of them should leave, should scatter. Not to other villages but into the hills. He pointed at himself, at the girl huddling in the boat. He mimed rowing out, sailing away. He pointed at the girl, indicating her happy, playing, growing up, his teeth clenched all the while.

Ta Ma appeared to understand not a single part of this charade. Looking befuddled, he said something.

"What did he say?"

"He said, what do we do?"

Kheim waved at the hills again, indicating dispersion. "Go!" he said loudly. "Tell him, go away! Scatter!"

She said something to her father, miserably.

Ta Ma said something.

"What did he say, Butterfly? Can you tell me?"

"He said, farewell."

The men regarded each other. Butterfly looked back and forth between them, frightened.

"Scatter for two months!" Kheim said, realizing it was useless but speaking anyway. "Leave the sick ones and scatter. After that you can regather, and the disease won't strike again. Go away. We'll take Butterfly and keep her safe. We'll keep her on a ship without anyone who has ever had smallpox. We'll take care of her. Go!"

He gave up. "Tell him what I said," he told Butterfly. But she only whimpered and sniveled on the bottom of the boat. Kheim rowed them back to the ship and they sailed away, out the great mouth of the bay on the ebb tide, away to the south.

———

Butterfly cried often for the first three days after they sailed, then ate ravenously, and after that began to talk exclusively in Chinese. Kheim felt a stab every time he looked at her, wondering if they had done the right thing to take her. She would probably have died if they had left her, I-Chin reminded him. But Kheim wasn't sure even that was justification enough. And the speed of her adjustment to her new life only made him more uneasy. Was this what they were, then, to begin with? So tough as this, so forgetful? Able to slip into whatever life was offered? It made him feel strange to see such a thing.

One of his officers came to him. "Peng isn't on board any of the ships. We think he must have swum ashore and stayed with them."

Butterfly too fell ill, and I-Chin sequestered her in the bow of the flagship, in an airy nest under the bowsprit and over the figurehead, which was a gold statue of Tianfei. He spent many hours tending the girl through the six stages of the disease, from the high fever and floating pulse of the Greater Yang, through the Lesser Yang and Yang Brightness, with chills and fever coming alternately; then into Greater Yin. He took her pulse every watch, checked all her vital signs, lanced some of the blisters, dosed her from his bags of medicines, mostly an admixture called Gift of the Smallpox God, which contained ground rhinoceros horn, snow worms from Tibet, crushed jade and pearl; but also, when it seemed she was stuck in the Lesser Yin, and in danger of dying, tiny doses of arsenic. The progress of the disease did not seem to Kheim to be like the usual pox, but the sailors made the appropriate sacrifices to the smallpox god nevertheless, burning incense and paper money over a shrine that was copied on all eight of the ships.

Later, I-Chin said that he thought being out on the open sea had proven the key to her recovery. Her body lolled in its bed on the groundswell, and her breathing and pulse fell into a rhythm with it, he noticed, four breaths and six beats per swell, in a fluttering pulse, over and over. This kind of confluence with the elements was extremely helpful. And the salt air filled her lungs with qi, and made her tongue less coated; he even fed her little spoonfuls of ocean water, as well as all she would take of fresh water, just recently removed from her home stream. And so she recovered and got well, only lightly scarred by pox on her back and neck.

They sailed south down the coast of the new island all this while, and every day they became more amazed that they were not reaching the southern end of it. One cape looked as if it would be the turning point, but past it they saw the land curved south again, behind some baked empty islands. Farther south they saw villages on the beaches, and they knew enough now to identify the bath temples. Kheim kept the fleet well offshore, but he did allow one canoe to approach, and he had Butterfly try speaking to them, but they didn't understand her, nor her them. Kheim made his dumb show signifying sickness and danger, and the locals paddled quickly away.

They began to sail against a current from the south, but it was mild, and the winds were constant from the west. The fishing here was excellent, the weather mild. Day followed day in a perfect circle of sameness. The land fell away east again, then ran south, most of the way to the equator, past a big archipelago of low islands, with good anchorages and good water, and seabirds with blue feet.

They came at last to a steeply rising coastline, with great snowy volcanoes in the distance, like Fuji only twice as big, or more, punctuating the sky behind a steep coastal range, which was already tall. This final giganticism finished anyone's ability to think of this place as an island.

"Are you sure this isn't Africa?" Kheim said to I-Chin.

I-Chin was not sure. "Maybe. Maybe the people we left up north are the only survivors of the Fulanchi, reduced to a primitive state. Maybe this is the west coast of the world, and we sailed past the opening to their middle sea in the night, or in a fog. But I don't think so."

"Then where are we?"

I-Chin showed Kheim where he thought they were on the long strips of their map; east of the final markings, out where the map was entirely blank. But first he pointed to the far western strip. "See, Fulan and Africa look like this on their west sides. The Muslim cartographers are very consistent about it. And Hsing Ho calculated that the world is about seventy-five thousand li around. If he's right, we only sailed half as far as we should have, or less, across the Dahai to Africa and Fulan."

"Maybe he's wrong then. Maybe the world occupies more of the globe than he thought. Or maybe the globe is smaller."

"But his method was good. I made the same measurements on our trip to the Moluccas, and did the geometry, and found he was right."

"But look!" Gesturing at the mountainous land before them. "If it isn't Africa, what is it?"

"An island, I suppose. A big island, far out in the Dahai, where no one has ever sailed. Another world, like the real one. An eastern one like the western one."

"An island no one has ever sailed to before? That no one ever knew about?" Kheim couldn't believe it.

"Well?" I-Chin said, stubborn in the face of the idea. "Who else before us could have gotten here, and gotten back to tell about it?"

Kheim took the point. "And we're not back either."

"No. And no guarantee we will be able to do it. Could be that Hsu Fu got here and tried to return, and failed. Maybe we'll find his descendants on this very shore."

"Maybe."

Closing on the immense land, they saw a city on the coast. It was nothing very big compared to back home, but substantial compared to the tiny villages to the north. It was mud-colored for the most part, but several gigantic buildings in the city and behind it were roofed by gleaming expanses of beaten gold. These were no Miwoks!

So they sailed inshore warily, feeling spooked, their ships' cannons loaded and primed. They were startled to see the primitive boats pulled up on the beaches—fishing canoes like those some of them had seen in the Moluccas, mostly two-prowed and made of bundled reeds. There were no guns to be seen; no sails; no wharves or docks, except for one log pier that seemed to float, anchored out away from the beach. It was perplexing to see the terrestrial magnificence of the gold-roofed buildings combined with such maritime poverty. I-Chin said, "It must have been an inland kingdom to start with."

"Lucky for us, the way those buildings look."

"I suppose if the Han dynasty had never fallen, this is what the coast of China would look like."

A strange idea. But even mentioning China was a comfort. After that they pointed at features of the town, saying "That's like in Cham," or "They build like that in Lanka," and so forth; and though it still looked bizarre, it was clear, even before they made out people on the beach gaping at them, that it would be people and not monkeys or birds populating the town.

Though they had no great hope that Butterfly would be understood here, they took her near the shore with them nevertheless, in the biggest landing boat. They kept the flintlocks and crossbows concealed under their seats while Kheim stood in the bow making the peaceful gestures that had won over the Miwok. Then he got Butterfly to greet them kindly in her language, which she did in a high, clear, penetrating voice. The crowd on the beach watched, and some with hats like feathered crowns spoke to them, but it was not Butterfly's language, nor one that any of them had ever heard.

The elaborate headdresses of part of the crowd seemed faintly military to Kheim, and so he had them row offshore a little bit, and keep a lookout for bows or spears or any other weapons. Something in the look of these people suggested the possibility of an ambush.

Nothing of the sort happened. In fact, the next day when they rowed in, a whole contingent of men, wearing checked tunics and feathered headdresses, prostrated themselves on the beach. Uneasily Kheim ordered a landing, on the lookout for trouble.

All went well. Communication by gesture, and quick basic language lessons, was fair, although the locals seemed to take Butterfly to be the visitors' leader, or rather talisman, or priestess, it was impossible to say; certainly they venerated her. Their mimed interchanges were mostly made by an older man in a headdress with a fringe hanging over his forehead to his eyes, and a badge extending high above the feathers. These communications remained cordial, full of curiosity and goodwill. They were offered cakes made of some kind of dense, substantial flower; also huge tubers that could be cooked and eaten; and a weak sour beer, which was all they ever saw the locals drink. Also a stack of finely woven blankets, very warm and soft, made of a wool from sheep that looked like sheep bred with camels, but were clearly some entirely other creature, unknown to the real world.

Eventually Kheim felt comfortable enough to accept an invitation to leave the beach and visit the local king or emperor, in the huge gold-roofed palace or temple on the hilltop behind the city. It was the gold that had done it, Kheim realized as he prepared for the trip, still feeling uneasy. He loaded a short flintlock and put it in a shoulder bag tucked under his arm, hidden by his coat; and he left instructions with I-Chin for a relief operation if one proved necessary. Off they went, Kheim and Butterfly and a dozen of the biggest sailors from the flagship, accompanied by a crowd of local men in checked tunics.

They walked up a track past fields and houses. The women in the fields carried their babies strapped to boards on their backs, and they spun wool as they walked. They hung looms from ropes tied to trees, to get the necessary tension to weave. Checked patterns seemed the only ones they used, usually black and tan, sometimes black and red. Their fields consisted of raised mounds, rectangular in shape, standing out of wetlands by the river. Presumably they grew their tubers in the mounds. They were flooded like rice fields, but not. Everything was similar but different. Gold here seemed as common as iron in China, while on the other hand there was no iron at all to be seen.

The palace above the city was huge, bigger than the Forbidden City in Beijing, with many rectangular buildings arranged in rectangular patterns. Everything was arranged like their cloth. Stone plinths in the courtyard outside the palace were carved into strange figures, birds and animals all mixed up, painted all colors, so that Kheim found it hard to look at them. He wondered if the strange creatures represented on them would be found living in the backcountry, or were their versions of dragon and phoenix. He saw lots of copper, and some bronze or brass, but mostly gold. The guards standing in rows around the palace held long spears tipped with gold, and their shields were gold too; decorative, but not very practical. Their enemies must not have had iron either.

Inside the palace they were led into a vast room with one wall open onto a courtyard, the other three covered in gold filigree. Here blankets were spread, and Kheim and Butterfly and the other Chinese were invited to sit on one.

Into the room came their emperor. All bowed and then sat on the ground. The emperor sat on a checked cloth next to the visitors, and said something politely. He was a man of about forty years, white-toothed and handsome, with a broad forehead, high prominent cheekbones, clear brown eyes, a pointed chin and a strong hawkish nose. His crown was gold, and was decorated with small gold heads, dangling in holes cut into the crown, like pirates' heads at the gates of Hangzhou.

This too made Kheim uneasy, and he shifted his pistol under his coat, looking around surreptitiously. There were no other signs to trouble him. Of course there were hard-looking men there, clearly the emperor's guard, ready to pounce if anything threatened him; but other than that, nothing; and that seemed an ordinary precaution to take when strangers were around.

A priest wearing a cape made of cobalt-blue bird feathers came in, and performed a ceremony for the emperor, and after that they feasted through the day, on a meat like lamb, and vegetables and mashes that Kheim did not recognize. The weak beer was all they drank, except for a truly fiery brandy. Eventually Kheim began to feel drunk, and he could see his men were worse. Butterfly did not like any of the flavors, and ate and drank very little. Out on the courtyard, men danced to drums and reed pipes, sounding very like Korean musicians, which gave Kheim a start; he wondered if these people's ancestors had drifted over from Korea ages ago, carried on the Kuroshio. Perhaps just a few lost ships had populated this whole land, many dynasties before; indeed the music sounded like an echo from a past age. But who could say. He would talk to I-Chin about it when he got back to the ship.

At sundown Kheim indicated their desire to return to their ships. The emperor only looked at him, and gestured to his caped priest, and then rose. Everyone stood and bowed again. He left the room.

When he had gone, Kheim stood and took Butterfly by the hand, and tried to lead her out the way they had come (although he was not sure he could remember it); but the guards blocked them, their gold-tipped spears held crossways, in a position as ceremonial as their dances had been.

Kheim mimed displeasure, very easy to do, and indicated that Butterfly would be sad and angry if she were kept from their ships. But the guards did not move.

So. There they were. Kheim cursed himself for leaving the beach with such strange people. He felt the pistol under his coat. One shot only. He would have to hope that I-Chin could rescue them. It was a good thing he had insisted the doctor stay behind, as he felt I-Chin would do the best job of organizing such an operation.

The captives spent the night huddled together on their blanket, surrounded by standing guards who did not sleep, but spent their time chewing small leaves they took from shoulder bags tucked under their checkered tunics. They watched bright-eyed. Kheim huddled around Butterfly, and she snuggled like a cat against him. It was cold. Kheim got the others to crowd around, all of them together, protecting her by a single touch or at least the proximity of their warmth.

At dawn the emperor returned, dressed like a giant peacock or phoenix, accompanied by women wearing gold breast cones, shaped uncannily like real breasts, with ruby nipples. The sight of these women gave Kheim an absurd hope that they would be all right. Then behind them entered the caped high priest, and a checkered masked figure, whose headdress dangled everywhere with tiny gold skulls. Some form of their death god, there was no mistaking it. He was there to execute them, Kheim thought, and the realization jolted him into a heightened state of awareness, in which all the gold sheeted white in the sun, and the space they walked through had an extra dimension of depth and solidity, the checkered people as solid and vivid as festival demons.

They were led out into the misty horizontal light of dawn, east and uphill. Uphill all that day, and the next day too, until Kheim gasped as he climbed, and looked back amazed from the occasional ridge, down and down to the sea, which was a blue textured surface, extremely flat and very far below. He had never imagined he could get so far above the ocean, it was like flying. And yet there were higher hills still ahead to the east, and on certain crests of the range, massive white volcanoes, like super-Fujis.

They walked up toward these. They were fed well, and given a tea as bitter as alum; and then, in a musical ritual ceremony, given little bags of the tea leaves, the same ragged-edged green leaves their guards had been chewing on the first night. The leaves also were bitter to the taste, but they soon numbed the mouth and throat, and after that Kheim felt better. The leaves were a stimulant, like tea or coffee. He told Butterfly and his men to chew theirs down as well. The thin strength that poured through his nerves gave him the qi energy to think about the problem of escape.

It did not seem likely that I-Chin would be able to get through the mud-and-gold city to follow them, but Kheim could not stop hoping for it, a kind of furious hope, felt every time he looked at Butterfly's face, unblemished yet by doubt or fear; as far as she was concerned this was just the next stage of a journey that was already as strange as it could get. This part was interesting to her, in fact, with its bird-throat colors, its gold and its mountains. She didn't seem affected by the height to which they had climbed.

Kheim began to understand that clouds, which often now lay below them, existed in a colder and less fulfilling air than the precious salty soup they breathed on the sea surface. Once he caught a whiff of that sea air, perhaps just the salt still in his hair, and he longed for it as for food. Hungry for air! He shuddered to think how high they were.

Yet they were not done. They climbed to a ridge covered by snow. The trail was pounded glistening into the hard white stuff. They were given soft wood-soled boots with fur on the inside, and heavier tunics, and blankets with holes for the head and arms, all elaborately checked, with small figures filling small squares. The blanket given to Buttefly was so long it looked as if she were wearing a Buddhist nun's dress, and it was made of such fine cloth that Kheim grew suddenly afraid. There was another child traveling with them, a boy Kheim thought, though he was not sure; and this child too, was dressed as finely as the caped priest.

They came to a campsite made of flat rocks set on the snow. They made a big fire in a sunken pit in this platform, and around it erected a number of yurts. Their captors settled on their blankets and ate a meal, followed by many ritual cups of their hot tea, and beer, and brandy, after which they performed a ceremony to honor the setting sun, which fell into clouds scudding over the ocean. They were well above the clouds now, yet above them to the east a great volcano poked the indigo sky, its snowy flanks glowing a deep pink in the moments after sunset.

That night was frigid. Again Kheim held Butterfly, fear waking him whenever he stirred. The girl even seemed to stop breathing from time to time, but she always started again.

At dawn they were roused, and Kheim was thankful to be given more of the hot tea, then a substantial meal, followed by more of the little green leaves to chew; though these last were handed to them by the executioner god.

They started up the side of the volcano while it was still a gray snow slope under a white dawn sky. The ocean to the west was covered by clouds, but they were breaking up, and the great blue plate lay there far, far below, looking to Kheim like his home village or his childhood.

It got colder as they ascended, and hard to walk. The snow was brittle underfoot, and icy bits of it clinked and glittered. It was extremely bright, but everything else was too dark: the sky blue-black, the row of people dim. Kheim's eyes ran, and the tears were cold on his face and in his thin gray whiskers. On he hiked, placing his feet carefully in the footsteps of the guard ahead of him, reaching back awkwardly to hold Butterfly's hand and pull her along.

Finally, after he had forgotten to look up for a while, no longer expecting anything ever to change, the slope of the snow laid back. Bare black rocks appeared, thrusting out of the snow left and right, and especially ahead, where he could see nothing higher.

Indeed, it was the peak: a broad jumbled wasteland of rock like torn and frozen mud, mixed with ice and snow. At the highest point of the tortured mass a few poles obtruded, cloth streamers and flags flying from them, as in the mountains of Tibet. Perhaps these were Tibetans then.

The caped priest and the executioner god and the guards assembled at the foot of these rocks. The two children were taken to the priest, guards restraining Kheim all the while. He stepped back as if giving up, put his hands under his blanket as if they were cold, which they were; they fumbled like ice for the handle of his flintlock. He cocked the lock and pulled the pistol free of his coat, hidden only under the blanket.

The children were given more hot tea, which they drank willingly. The priest and his minions sang facing the sun, drums pounding like the painful pulse behind Kheim's half-blinded eyes. He had a bad headache, and everything looked like a shadow of itself.

Below them on the snowy ridge, figures were climbing fast. They wore the local blankets, but Kheim thought they looked like I-Chin and his men. Much farther below them, another group straggled up in pursuit.

Kheim's heart was already pounding; now it rolled inside him like the ceremonial drums. The executioner god took a gold knife out of an elaborate carved wooden scabbard, and cut the little boy's throat. The blood he caught in a gold bowl, where it steamed in the sun. To the sound of the drums and pipes and sung prayers, the body was wrapped in a mantle of the soft checkered cloth, and lowered tenderly into the peak, in a crack between two great rocks.

The executioner and the caped priest then turned to Butterfly, who was tugging uselessly to get away. Kheim pulled his pistol free of the blanket and checked the flint, then aimed it with both hands at the executioner god. He shouted something, then held his breath. The guards were moving toward him, the executioner had looked his way. Kheim pulled the trigger and the pistol boomed and blossomed smoke, knocking Kheim two steps back. The executioner god flew backward and skidded over a patch of snow, bleeding copiously from the throat. The gold knife fell from his opened hand.

All the onlookers stared at the executioner god, stunned; they didn't know what had happened.

Kheim kept the pistol pointed at them, while he rooted in his belt bag for charge, plunger, ball, wad. He reloaded the pistol right in front of them, shouting sharply once or twice, which made them jump.

Pistol reloaded, he aimed it at the guards, who fell back. Some kneeled, others stumbled away. He could see I-Chin and his sailors toiling up the snow of the last slope. The caped priest said something, and Kheim aimed his pistol carefully at him and shot.

Again the loud bang of the explosion, like thunder in the ear, and the plume of white smoke jetting out. The caped priest flew back as if struck by a giant invisible fist, tumbled down and lay writhing in the snow, his cape stained with blood.

Kheim strode through the smoke to Butterfly. He lifted her away from her captors, who quivered as if paralyzed. He carried her in his arms down the trail. She was only semiconscious; very possibly the tea had been drugged.

He came to I-Chin, who was huffing and puffing at the head of a gang of their sailors, all armed with flintlocks, a pistol and musket for each. "Back to the ships," Kheim ordered. "Shoot any that get in the way."

Going down the mountain was tremendously easier than going up had been, indeed it was a danger in that it felt so easy, while at the same time they were still light-headed and half-blinded, and so tired that they tended to slip, and more and more as it warmed and the snow softened and smashed under their feet. Carrying Butterfly, Kheim had his view of his footing obscured as well, and he slipped often, sometimes heavily. But two of his men walked at his sides when it was possible, holding him up by the elbows when he slipped, and despite all they made good time.

Crowds of people gathered each time they approached one of the high villages, and Kheim then gave over Butterfly to the men, so that he could hold the pistol aloft for all to see. If the crowds got in their way, he shot the man with the biggest headdress. The boom of the shot appeared to frighten the onlookers even more than the sudden collapse and bloody death of their priests and headmen, and Kheim thought it was probably a system in which local leaders were frequently executed for one thing or another by the guards of the emperor.

In any case, the people they passed seemed paralyzed mostly by the Chinese command of sound. Claps of thunder, accompanied by instant death, as in a lightning strike—that must have happened often enough in these exposed mountains to give them an idea of what the Chinese had mastered. Lightning in a tube.

Eventually Kheim gave Butterfly to his men, and marched down heavily at their head, reloading his gun and firing at any crowd close enough to hit, feeling a strange exultation rise in him, a terrible power over these ignorant primitives who could be awed to paralysis by a gun. He was their executioner god made real, and he passed through them as if they were puppets whose strings had been cut.

He stopped his crew late in the day, to seize food from a village and eat it, then continued down again until nightfall. They took refuge in a storage building, a big stone-walled wooden-roofed barn, stuffed to the rafters with cloth, grain, and gold. The men would have killed themselves carrying gold on their backs, but Kheim restricted them to one item apiece, either jewelry or a single disk ingot. "We'll all come back someday," he told them, "and end up richer than the emperor." He chose for himself a hummingbird moth figured in gold.

Though exhausted, he found it hard to lie down, or even to stop walking. After a nightmare interval, sitting half-asleep by Butterfly's side, he woke them all before dawn and began the march downhill again, their guns all loaded and ready.

As they descended to the coast it became apparent that runners had passed them in the night, and warned the locals below of the disaster on the summit. A fighting force of men held the crossroads just above the great coastal city, shouting to the beat of drums, brandishing clubs, shields, spears, and pikes. The descending Chinese were obviously outnumbered, the fifty men I-Chin had brought approaching some four or five hundred local warriors.

"Spread out," Kheim told his men. "March right down the road at them, singing 'Drunk Again on the Grand Canal.' Get all the guns out front, and when I say stop, stop and aim at their leaders—whoever has the most feathers on their head. All of you shoot together when I say fire, and then reload. Reload as fast as you can, but don't shoot again unless you hear me say so. If I do, fire and reload yet again."

So they marched down the road, roaring the old drinking song at the top of their lungs, then stopped and fired a volley, and their flintlocks might as well have been a row of cannon, they had such an effect: many men knocked down and bleeding, the survivors among them running in a complete panic.

It had only taken one volley, and the coastal city was theirs. They could have burned it to the ground, taken anything in it; but Kheim marched them through the streets as quickly as possible, still singing as loudly as they could, until they were on the beach among the Chinese landing boats, and safe. They never even had to fire a second time.

Kheim went to I-Chin and shook his hand. "Many thanks," he said to him formally before all the others. "You saved us. They would have sacrificed Butterfly like a lamb, and killed the rest of us like flies."

It seemed to Kheim only reasonable that the locals would soon recover from the shock of the guns, after which they would be dangerous in their numbers. Even now crowds were gathering at a safe distance to observe them. So after getting Butterfly and most of the men onto the ships, Kheim consulted with I-Chin and their ships' provision masters, to see what they were still lacking for a voyage back across the Dahai. Then he took a big armed party ashore one last time, and after the ships' cannons were fired at the city, he and his men marched straight for the palace, singing again and stepping to the beat of their drums. At the palace they raced around the wall, and caught a group of priests and women escaping at a gate on the other side, and Kheim shot one priest, and had his men tie the others up.

After that he stood before the priests, and mimed his demands. His head still pounded painfully, he remained floating in the strange exhilaration of killing, and it was remarkable how easy it was to convey by mime alone a fairly elaborate list of demands. He pointed to himself and his men, then to the west, and made one hand sail away on the wind of the other one. He held up samples of food and the bags of tea leaves, indicated that these were wanted. He mimed them being brought to the beach. He went to the chief hostage and imitated untying him and waving farewell. If the goods didn't arrive . . . he pointed the gun at each hostage. But if they did, the Chinese would release everyone and sail away.

He acted out each step of the process, looking the hostages in the eyes and speaking only a little, as he judged it would only be a distraction to their comprehension. Then he had his men release all the women captured, and a few of the men without headdresses, and sent them out with clear instructions to get the required goods. He could tell by their eyes that they understood exactly what they were to do.

After that he marched the hostages to the beach, and they waited. That same afternoon men appeared in one of the main streets, bags slung down their backs from lines hung around their foreheads. They deposited these bags on the beach, bowing, and then retreated, still facing the Chinese. Dried meat; grain cakes; the little green leaves; gold disks and ornaments (though Kheim had not asked for these); blankets and bolts of the soft cloth. Looking at it all spread on the beach, Kheim felt like a tax collector, heavy and cruel; but also relieved; powerful in a tenuous fashion only, as it was by a magic he didn't understand or control. Above all he felt content. They had what they needed to get home.

He untied the hostages himself, gestured for them to go. He gave each of them a pistol ball, curling their unresponsive fingers around

them. "We'll be back someday," he said to them. "Us, or people worse
than us." He wondered briefly if they would catch smallpox, like the Miwok; his sailors had slept on the locals' blankets at the palace.

No way to tell. The locals stumbled away, clutching their pistol balls
or dropping them. Their women stood at a safe distance, happy to see
that Kheim had kept his pantomimed promise, happy to see their men
freed. Kheim ordered his men into the boats. They rowed out to the
ships and sailed away from the big mountain island.

———

After all that, sailing the Great Ocean felt very familiar, very peaceful. The days passed in their rounds. They followed the sun west, always west. Most days were hot and sunny. Then for a month clouds grew every day and broke in the afternoons, in gray thundershowers that quickly dissipated. After that the winds always blew from the southeast, making their way easy. Their memories of the great island behind them began to seem like dreams, or legends they had heard about the realm of the asuras. If it weren't for Butterfly's presence it would have been hard to believe they had done all that.

Butterfly played on the flagship. She swung through the rigging like a little monkey. There were hundreds of men on board, but the presence of one little girl changed everything: they sailed under a blessing. The other ships stayed close to the flagship in the hope of catching sight of her, or being blessed by an occasional visit. Most of the sailors believed she was the goddess Tianfei, traveling with them for their own safety, and that this was why the return voyage was going so much easier than the voyage out had. The weather was kinder, the air warmer, the fish more plentiful. Three times they passed small atolls, uninhabited, and were able to take on coconuts and palm hearts, and once water. Most important, Kheim felt, they were headed west, back home to the known world. It felt so different from the voyage out that it seemed strange it was the same activity. That orientation alone could make such a difference! But it was hard to sail into the morning sun, hard to sail away from the world.

Sailing, day after day. Sun rising at the stern, sinking at the bow, drawing them on. Even the sun was helping them—perhaps too much—it was now the seventh month, and infernally hot; then windless for most of a month. They prayed to Tianfei, ostentatiously not looking at Butterfly as they did so.

She played in the rigging, oblivious to their sidelong glances. She spoke Chinese pretty well now, and had taught I-Chin all the Miwok she could remember. I-Chin had written down every word, in a dictionary that he thought might be useful to subsequent expeditions to the new island. It was interesting, he told Kheim, because usually he was just choosing the ideogram or combination of ideograms that sounded most like the Miwok word as spoken, and writing down as precise a definition of its Miwok meaning as he could, given the source of information; but of course when looking at the ideographs for the sounds it was impossible not to hear the Chinese meanings for them as well, so that the whole Miwok language became yet another set of homonyms to add to the already giant number that existed in Chinese. Many Chinese literary or religious symbols relied on pure accidents of homonymity to make their metaphorical connection, so that one said the tenth day of the month, shi, was the birthday of the stone, shi; or a picture of a heron and lotus, lu and lian, by homynym became the message "may your path (lu) be always upward (lian); or the picture of a monkey on the back of another one could be read in a similar way as "may you rank as a governor from generation to generation." Now to I-Chin the Miwok words for "going home" looked like wu ya, five ducks, while the Miwok for "swim" looked like Peng-zu, the legendary character who had lived for eight hundred years. So he would sing "five ducks swimming home, it will only take eight hundred years," or "I'm going to jump off the side and become Peng-zu," and Butterfly would shriek with laughter. Other similarities in the two languages' maritime words made I-Chin suspect that Hsu Fu's expedition to the east had made it to the ocean continent of Yingzhou after all, and left there some Chinese words if nothing else; if, indeed, the Miwok themselves were not the descendants of his expedition.

Some men already spoke of returning to the new land, usually to the golden kingdom in the south, to subdue it by arms and take its gold back to the real world. They did not say, We will do this, which would be bad luck, obviously, but rather, If one were to do this. Other men listened to this talk from a distance behind their eyes, knowing that if Tianfei allowed them to reach home, nothing ever again would induce them to cross the great ocean.

Then they became entirely becalmed, in a patch of ocean devoid of rain, cloud, wind, or current. It was as if a curse had fallen on them, possibly from the loose talk of return for gold. They began to bake. There were sharks in the water, so they could not swim freely to cool off, but had to set a sail in the water between two of the ships, and let it sink until they could jump off into a pool, very warm, about chest deep. Kheim had Butterly wear a shift and let her jump in. To refuse her wish would have been to astound and infuriate the crew. It turned out she could swim like an otter. The men treated her like the goddess she was, and she laughed to see them sporting like boys. It was a relief to do something different, but the sail couldn't sustain the wetness and bouncing on it, and gradually came apart. So they only did it once.

The doldrums began to endanger them. They would run out of water, then food. Possibly subtle currents continued to carry them west, but I-Chin was not optimistic. "It's more likely we've wandered into the center of the big circular current, like a whirlpool's center." He advised sailing south when possible, to get back into both wind and current, and Kheim agreed, but there was no wind to sail. It was much like the first month of their expedition, only without the Kuroshio. Again they discussed putting out the boats and rowing the ships, but the vast junks were too big to move by oar power alone, and I-Chin judged it dangerous to tear the skin off the palms of the men when they were already so dried out. There was no recourse but to clean their stills, and keep them in the sun and primed all day long, and ration what water remained in the casks. And keep Butterfly fully watered, no matter what she said about doing like all the rest. They would have given her the last cask in the fleet.

It had gotten to the point where I-Chin was proposing that they save their dark yellow urine and mix it with their remaining water supplies, when black clouds appeared from the south, and it quickly became clear that their problem was going to change very swiftly from having too little water to having too much. Wind struck hard, clouds rolled over them, water fell in sheets, and the funnels were deployed over the casks, which refilled almost instantly. Then it was a matter of riding out the storm.

Only junks as big as theirs were high enough and flexible enough to survive such an onslaught for long; and even the Eight Great Ships, desiccated above the water as they had been in the doldrums, now swelled in the rain, snapping many of the ropes and pins holding them together, so that riding out the storm became a continuous drenched frantic stemming of leaks, and fixing of broken spars and staves and ropes.

All this time the waves were growing bigger, until eventually the ships were rising and falling as over enormous smoking hills, rolling south to north at a harried but inexorable, even majestic pace. In the flagship they shot up the face of these and crested in a smear of white foam over the deck, after which they had a brief moment's view of the chaos from horizon to horizon, with perhaps two or three of the other ships visible, bobbing in different rhythms and being blown away into the watery murk. For the most part there was nothing to do but hunker down in the cabins, drenched and apprehensive, unable to hear each other over the roar of wind and wave.

At the height of the storm they entered the fish's eye, that strange and ominous calm in which disordered waves sloshed about in all directions, crashing into each other and launching solid bolts of white water into the dark air, while all around them low black clouds obscured the horizon. A typhoon, therefore, and none were surprised. As in the yin-yang symbol, there were dots of calm at the center of the wind. It would soon return from the opposite direction.

So they worked on repairs in great haste, feeling as one always did, that having gotten halfway through it they should be able to reach the end. Kheim peered through the murk at the nearest ship to them, which appeared to be in difficulty. The men crowded its railing, staring longingly at Butterfly, some even crying out to her. No doubt they thought their trouble resulted from the fact they did not have her on board with them. Its captain shouted to Kheim that they might have to cut down their masts in the second half of the storm to keep from being rolled over, and that the others should hunt for them if necessary, after it had passed.

But when the other side of the typhoon struck, things went badly on the flagship as well. An odd wave threw Butterfly into a wall awkwardly, and after that the fear in the men was palpable. They lost sight of the other ships. The huge waves again were torn to foam by the wind, and their crests crashed over the ship as if trying to sink it. The rudder snapped off at the rudder post, and after that, though they tried to get a yard over the side to replace the rudder, they were in effect a hulk, struck in the side by every passing wave. While men fought to get steerage and save the ship, and some were swept overboard, or drowned in the lines, I-Chin attended to Butterfly. He shouted to Kheim that she had broken an arm and apparently some ribs. She was gasping for breath, Kheim saw. He returned to the struggle for steerage, and finally they got a sea anchor over the side, which quickly brought their bow around into the wind. This saved them for the moment, but even coming over the bow the waves were heavy blows, and it took every effort they could make to keep the hatches from tearing off and the ship's compartments from filling. All done in an agony of apprehension about Butterfly; men shouted angrily that she should have been cared for better, that it was inexcusable that something like this should happen. Kheim knew that was his responsibility.

When he could spare a moment he went to her side, in the highest cabin on the rear deck, and looked beseechingly at I-Chin, who would not reassure him. She was coughing up a foamy blood, very red, and I-Chin was sucking her throat clear of it from time to time with a tube he stuck down her mouth. "A rib has punctured a lung," he said shortly, keeping his eyes on her. She meanwhile was conscious, wide-eyed, in pain but quiet. She said only, "What's happening to me?" After I-Chin cleared her throat of another mass of blood, he told her what he had told Kheim. She panted like a dog, shallow and fast.

Kheim went back into the watery chaos abovedecks. The wind and waves were no worse than before, perhaps a bit better. There were scores of problems large and small to attend to, and he threw himself at them in a fury, muttering to himself, or shouting at the gods; it didn't matter, no one could hear anything abovedecks, unless it was shouted directly in their ears. "Please, Tianfei, stay with us! Don't leave us! Let us go home. Let us return to tell the emperor what we have found for him. Let the girl live."

They survived the storm: but Butterfly died the next day.

Only three ships found each other and regathered on the quiet blank of the sea. They sewed Butterfly's body in a man's robe and tied two of the gold disks from the mountain empire into it, and let it slide over the side into the waves. All the men were weeping, even I-Chin, and Kheim could barely speak the words of the funeral prayer. Who was there to pray to? It seemed impossible that after all they had gone through, a mere storm could kill the sea goddess; but there she was, slipping under the waves, sacrificed to the sea just as that island boy had been sacrificed to the mountain. Sun or seafloor, it was all the same.

"She died to save us," he told the men shortly. "She gave that avatar of herself to the storm god, so he would let us be. Now we have to carry on to honor her. We have to get back home."

So they repaired the ship as best they could, and endured another month of desiccated life. This was the longest month of the trip, of their lives. Everything was breaking down, on the ships, in their bodies. There wasn't enough food and water. Sores broke out in their mouths and on their skin. They had very little qi, and could hardly eat what food was left.

Kheim's thoughts left him. He found that when thoughts left, things just did themselves. Doing did not need thinking.

One day he thought: sail too big cannot be lifted. Another day he thought: more than enough is too much. Too much is less. Therefore least is most. Finally he saw what the Daoists meant by that.

Go with the way. Breathe in and out. Move with the swells. Sea doesn't know ship, ship doesn't know sea. Floating does itself. A balance in balance. Sit without thinking.

The sea and sky melded. All blue. There was no one doing, nothing being done. Sailing just happened.

Thus, when a great sea was crossed, there was no one doing it.

Someone looked up and noticed an island. It turned out to be Mindanao, and after the rest of its archipelago, Taiwan, and all the familiar landfalls of the Inland Sea.

The three remaining Great Ships sailed into Nanjing almost exactly twenty months after their departure, surprising all the inhabitants of the city, who thought they had joined Hsu Fu at the bottom of the sea. And they were happy to be home, no doubt about it, and bursting with stories to tell of the amazing giant island to the east.

But any time Kheim met the eye of any of his men, he saw the pain there. He saw also that they blamed him for her death. So he was happy to leave Nanjing and travel with a gang of officials up the Grand Canal to Beijing. He knew that his sailors would scatter up and down the coast, go their ways so they wouldn't have to see each other and remember; only after years had passed would they want to meet, so that they could remember the pain when it had become so distant and faint that they actually wanted it back, just to feel again they had done all those things, that life had held all those things.

But for now it was impossible not to feel they had failed. And so when Kheim was led into the Forbidden City, and brought before the Wanli Emperor to accept the acclaim of all the officials there, and the interested and gracious thanks of the emperor himself, he said only, "When a great sea has been crossed, there is no one to take credit."

The Wanli Emperor nodded, fingering one of the gold disk ingots they had brought back, and then the big hummingbird moth of beaten gold, its feathers and antennae perfectly delineated with the utmost delicacy and skill. Kheim stared at the Heavenly Envoy, trying to see in to the hidden emperor, the Jade Emperor inside him. Kheim said to him, "That far country is lost in time, its streets paved with gold, its palaces roofed with gold. You could conquer it in a month, and rule over all its immensity, and bring back all the treasure that it has, endless forest and furs, turquoise and gold, more gold than there is yet now in the world; and yet still the greatest treasure in that land is already lost."

———

Snowy peaks, towering over a dark land. The first blinding crack of sunlight flooding all. He could have made it then—everything was so bright, he could have launched himself into pure whiteness at that moment and never come back, flowed out forever into the All. Release, release. You have to have seen a lot to want release that much.

But the moment passed and he was on the black stage floor of the bardo's hall of judgment, on its Chinese side, a nightmare warren of numbered levels and legal chambers and bureaucrats wielding lists of souls to be remanded to the care of meticulous torturers. Above this hellish bureaucracy loomed the usual Tibet of a dais, occupied by its menagerie of demonic gods, chopping up condemned souls and chasing the pieces off to hell or a new life in the realm of preta or beast. The lurid glow, the giant dais like the side of a mesa towering above, the hallucinatorily colorful gods roaring and dancing, their swords flashing in the black air; it was judgment—an inhuman activity—not the pot calling the kettle black, but true judgment, by higher authorities, the makers of this universe. Who were the ones, after all, that had made humans as weak and craven and cruel as they so often were—so that there was a sense of doom enforced, of loaded dice, karma lashing out at whatever little pleasures and beauties the miserable subdivine sentiences might have concocted out of the mud of their existence. A brave life, fought against the odds? Go back as a dog! A dogged life, persisting despite all? Go back as a mule, go back as a worm. That's the way things work.

Thus Kheim reflected as he strode up through the mists in a growing rage, as he banged through the bureaucrats, smashing them with their own slates, their lists and tallies, until he caught sight of Kali and her court, standing in a semicircle taunting Butterfly, judging her—as if that poor simple soul had anything to answer for, compared to these butcher gods and their eons of evil—evil insinuated right into the heart of the cosmos they themselves had made!

Kheim roared in wordless fury, and charged up and seized a sword from one of the death goddess's six arms, and cut off a brace of them with a single stroke; the blade was very sharp. The arms lay scattered and bleeding on the floor, flopping about—then, to Kheim's unutterable consternation, they were grasping the floorboards and moving themselves crabwise by the clenching of the fingers. Worse yet, new shoulders were growing back behind the wounds, which still bled copiously. Kheim screamed and kicked them off the dais, then turned and chopped Kali in half at the waist, ignoring the other members of his jati who stood up there with Butterfly, all of them jumping up and down and shouting "Oh no, don't do that Kheim, don't do that, you don't understand, you have to follow protocol," even I-Chin, who was shouting loudly over the rest of them, "At least we might direct our efforts at the dais struts, or the vials of forgetting, something a little more technical, a little less direct!" Meanwhile Kali's upper body fisted itself around the stage, while her legs and waist staggered, but continued to stand; and the missing halves grew out of the cut parts like snail horns. And then there were two Kalis advancing on him, a dozen arms flailing swords.

He jumped off the dais, thumped down on the bare boards of the cosmos. The rest of his jati crashed down beside him, crying out in pain at the impact. "You got us in trouble," Shen whined.

"It doesn't work like that," Butterfly informed him as they panted off together into the mists. "I've seen a lot of people try. They lash out in fury and cut the hideous gods down, and how they deserve it—and yet the gods spring back up, redoubled in other people. A karmic law of this universe, my friend. Like conservation of yin and yang, or gravity. We live in a universe ruled by very few laws, but the redoubling of violence by violence is one of the main ones."

"I don't believe it," Kheim said, and stopped to fend off the two Kalis now pursuing them. He took a hard swing and decapitated one of the new Kalis. Swiftly another head grew back, swelling atop the gusher on the neck of the black body, and the new white teeth of her new head laughed at him, while her bloody red eyes blazed. He was in trouble, he saw; he was going to be hacked to pieces. For resisting these evil unjust absurd and horrible deities he was going to be hacked to pieces and returned to the world as a mule or a monkey or a maimed old geezer—

BOOK 4

❋ THE ALCHEMIST ❋

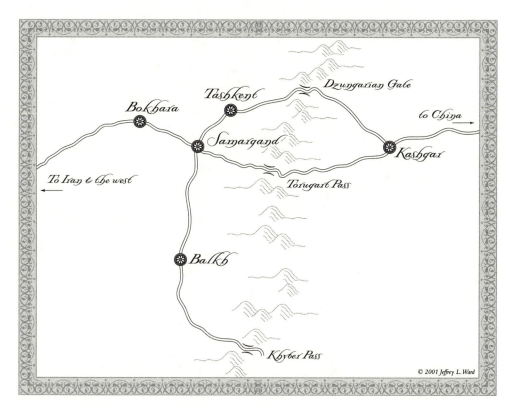

Transmutation

Now it so happened that as the time approached for the great alchemist's red work to reach its culmination, in the final multiplication, the projection of the sophic hydrolith into the ferment, causing tincture—that is to say, the transmuting of base metals into gold—the son-in-law of the alchemist, one Bahram al-Bokhara, ran and jostled through the bazaar of Samarqand on last-minute errands, ignoring the calls of his various friends and creditors. "I can't stop," he called to them, "I'm late!"

"Late paying your debts!" said Divendi, whose coffee stall was wedged into a slot next to Iwang's workshop.

"True," Bahram said, but stopped for a coffee. "Always late but never bored."

"Khalid keeps you hopping."

"Literally so, yesterday. The big pelican cracked during a descension, and it all spilled right next to me—vitriol of Cyprus mixed with sal ammoniac."

"Dangerous?"

"Oh my God. Where it splashed on my trousers the cloth was eaten away, and the smoke was worse. I had to run for my life!"

"As always."

"So true. I coughed my guts out, my eyes ran all night. It was like drinking your coffee."

"I always make yours from the dregs."

"I know," tossing down the last gritty shot. "So are you coming to-morrow?"

"To see lead turned into gold? I'll be there."

Iwang's workshop was dominated by its brick furnace. Familiar sizzle and smell of bellowed fire, tink of hammer, glowing molten glass, Iwang twirling the rod attentively: Bahram greeted the glassblower and silver-smith, "Khalid wants more of the wolf."

"Khalid always wants more of the wolf." Iwang continued turning his blob of hot glass. Tall and broad and big-faced, a Tibetan by birth, but long a resident of Samarqand, he was one of Khalid's closest associates. "Did he send payment this time?"

"Of course not. He said to put it on his tab."

Iwang pursed his lips. "He's got too many tabs these days."

"All paid after tomorrow. He finished the seven hundred and seventy-seventh distillation."

Iwang put down his work and went to a wall stacked with boxes. He handed Bahram a small leather pouch, heavy with small beads of lead. "Gold grows in the earth," he said. "Al-Razi himself couldn't grow it in a crucible."

"Khalid would debate that. And Al-Razi lived a long time ago. He couldn't get the heat we can now."

"Maybe." Iwang was skeptical. "Tell him to be careful."

"Of burning himself?"

"Of the khan burning him."

"You'll be there to see it?"

Iwang nodded reluctantly.

The day of the demonstration came, and for a wonder the great Khalid Ali Abu al-Samarqandi seemed nervous; and Bahram could understand why. If Sayyed Abdul Aziz Khan, ruler of the khanate of Bokhara, immensely rich and powerful, chose to support Khalid's enterprises, all would be well; but he was not a man you wanted to disappoint. Even his closest advisor, his treasury secretary Nadir Divanbegi, avoided distressing him at all costs. Recently, for instance, Nadir had caused a new caravanserai to be built on the east side of Bokhara, and the khan had been brought out for its opening ceremony, and being a bit inattentive by nature, he had congratulated them for building such a fine madressa; and rather than correct him on the point, Nadir had ordered the complex turned into a madressa. That was the kind of khan

Sayyed Abdul Aziz was, and he was the khan to whom Khalid was going to demonstrate the tincture. It was enough to make Bahram's stomach tight and his pulse fast, and while Khalid sounded as he always did, sharp and impatient and sure of himself, Bahram could see that his face was unusually pale.

But he had worked on the projection for years, and studied all the alchemical texts he could obtain, including many bought by Bahram in the Hindu caravanserai, including "The Book of the End of the Search" by Jildaki, and Jabir's "Book of Balances," as well as "The Secret of Secrets," once thought to be lost, and the Chinese text "Reference Book for the Penetration of Reality"; and Khalid had in his extensive workshops the mechanical capacity to repeat the required distillations at high heat and very good clarities, all seven hundred and seventy-seven times. Two weeks earlier he had declared that his final efforts had borne fruit, and now all was ready for a public demonstration, which of course had to include regal witnesses to matter.

So Bahram hurried around in Khalid's compound on the northern edge of Samarqand, sprawling by the banks of the Zeravshan River, which provided power to the foundries and the various workshops. The walls of the establishment were ringed by great heaps of charcoal waiting to be burned, and inside there were a number of buildings, loosely grouped around the central work area, a yard dotted with vats and discolored chemical baths. Several different stinks combined to form the single harsh smell that was particular to Khalid's place. He was the khanate's principal gunpowder producer and metallurgist, among other things, and these practical enterprises supported the alchemy that was his ruling passion.

Bahram wove through the clutter, making sure the demonstration area was ready. The long tables in the open-walled shops were crowded with an orderly array of equipment; the walls of the shops were neatly hung with tools. The main athanor was roaring with heat.

But Khalid was not to be found. The puffers had not seen him; Bahram's wife Esmerine, Khalid's daughter, had not seen him. The house at the back of the compound seemed empty, and no one answered Bahram's calls. He began to wonder if Khalid had run away in fear.

Then Khalid appeared out of the library next to his study, the only room in the compound with a door that locked.

"There you are," Bahram said. "Come on, Father, Al-Razi and Mary the Jewess will be no help to you now. It's time to show the world the thing itself, the projection."

Khalid, startled to see him, nodded curtly. "I was making the last preparations," he said. He led Bahram into the furnace shed, where the geared bellows, powered by the waterwheel on the river, pumped air into the roaring fires.

The khan and his party arrived quite late, when much of the afternoon was spent. Twenty horsemen thundered in, their finery gleaming, and then a camel train fifty beasts long, all foaming at the gallop. The khan dismounted from his white bay and walked across the yard with Nadir Divanbegi at his side, and several court officials at their heels.

Khalid's attempt at a formal greeting, including the presentation of a gift of one of his most cherished alchemical books, was cut short by Sayyed Adbul Aziz. "Show us," the khan commanded, taking the book without looking at it.

Khalid bowed. "The alembic I used is this one here, called a pelican. The base matter is mostly calcinated lead, with some mercurials. They have been projected by continuous distillation and redistillation, until all the matter has passed through the pelican seven hundred and seventy-seven times. At that point the spirit in the lion—well, to put it in more worldly terms, the gold condenses out at the highest athanor heat. So, we pour the wolf into this vessel, and put that in the athanor, and wait for an hour, stirring meanwhile seven times."

"Show us." The khan was clearly bored by the details.

Without further ado Khalid led them into the furnace shed, and his assistants opened the heavy thick door of the athanor, and after allowing the visitors to handle and inspect the ceramic bowl, Kahlid grabbed up tongs and poured the gray distillate into the bowl, and placed the tray in the athanor and slid it into the intense heat. The air over the furnace shimmered as Sayyed Abdul Aziz's mullah said prayers, and Khalid watched the second hand of his best clock. Every five minutes he gestured to the puffers, who opened the door and pulled out the tray, at which point Khalid stirred the liquid metal, now glowing orange, with his ladle, seven times seven circles, and then back into the heat of the fire. In the last minutes of the operation, the crackle of the charcoal was the only sound in the yard. The sweating observers, including many acquaintances from the town, watched the clock tick out the last minute of the hour in a silence like that of Sufis in a trance of speechlessness, or, Bahram thought uneasily, like hawks inspecting the ground far below.

Finally Khalid nodded to the puffers, and he himself hefted the bowl off the tray with big tongs, and carried it to a table in the yard, cleared for this demonstration. "Now we pour off the dross, great Khan," paddling the molten lead out of the bowl into a stone tub on the table. "And at the bottom we see—ah . . ."

He smiled and wiped his forehead with his sleeve, gestured at the bowl. "Even when molten it gleams to the eye."

At the bottom of the bowl the liquid was a darker red. With a spatula Khalid carefully skimmed off the remaining dross, and there at the bottom of the bowl lay a cooling mass of liquid gold.

"We can pour it into a bar mold while it is still soft," Khalid said with quiet satisfaction. "It looks to be perhaps ten ounces. That would be one seventh of the stock, as predicted."

Sayyed Abdul Aziz's face shone like the gold. He turned to his secretary Nadir Divanbegi, who was regarding the ceramic bowl closely.

Without expression, Nadir gestured for one of the khan's guards to come forward. The rest of them rustled behind the alchemist's crew. Their pikes were still upright, but they were now at attention.

"Seize the instruments," Nadir told the head guard.

Three soldiers helped him take possession of all the tools used in the operation, including the great pelican itself. When they were all in hand, Nadir went to one guard and took up the ladle Khalid had used to stir the liquid metals. In a sudden move he smashed it down on the table. It rang like a bell. He looked over at Sayyed Abdul Aziz, who stared at his secretary, puzzled. Nadir gestured with his head to one of the pikemen, then put the ladle on the table.

"Cut it."

The pike came down hard, and the ladle was sliced just above its scoop. Nadir picked up the handle and the scoop and inspected them. He showed them to the khan.

"You see—the shaft is hollow. The gold was in the tube inside the handle, and when he stirred, the heat melted the gold, and it slid out and into the lead in the bowl. Then as he continued to stir, it moved to the bottom of the bowl."

Bahram looked at Khalid, shocked, and saw that it was true. His father-in-law's face was white, and he was no longer sweating. Already a dead man.

The khan roared wordlessly, then leaped at Khalid and struck him down with the book he had been given. He beat him with the book, and Khalid did not resist.

"Take him!" Sayyed Abdul Aziz shouted at his soldiers. They picked up Khalid by the arms and dragged him through the dust, not allowing him to get to his feet, and threw him over a camel. In a minute they were all gone from the compound, leaving the air filled with smoke and dust and echoing shouts.

The Mercy of the Khan

No one expected Khalid to be spared after this debacle. His wife Fedwa was in a state of mourning already, and Esmerine was inconsolable. All the work of the yard stopped. Bahram fretted in the strange silence of the empty workshops, waiting to be given the word that they could collect Khalid's body. He realized he didn't know enough to run the compound properly.

Eventually the call came; they were ordered to attend the execution. Iwang joined Bahram for the trip to Bokhara and the palace there. Iwang was both sad and irritated. "He should have asked me, if he was so short of cash. I could have helped him."

Bahram was a little surprised at this, as Iwang's shop was a mere hole in the wall of the bazaar, and did not seem so very prosperous. But he said nothing. When all was said and done he had loved his father-in-law, and the black grief he felt left little room for thinking about Iwang's finances. The impending violent death of someone that close to him, his wife's father—she would be distraught for months, perhaps for years—a man so full of energy: the prospect emptied him of other thought, and left him sick with apprehension.

The next day they reached Bokhara, shimmering in the summer heat, its array of brown and sandy tones capped by its deep blue and turquoise mosque domes. Iwang pointed at one minaret. "The Tower of Death," he noted. "They'll probably throw him off that."

The sickness grew in Bahram. They entered the east gate of the city and made their way to the palace. Iwang explained their business. Bahram wondered if they, too, would be taken and killed as accomplices. This had not occurred to him before, and he was shaking as they were led into a room that opened onto the palace grounds.

Nadir Divanbegi arrived shortly thereafter. He looked at them with his usual steady gaze: a short elegant man, black goatee, pale blue eyes; a sayyed himself, and very wealthy.

"You are said to be as great an alchemist as Khalid," Nadir said abruptly to Iwang. "Do you believe in the philosopher's stone, in projection, in all the so-called red work? Can base metals be transmuted to gold?"

Iwang cleared his throat. "Hard to say, Effendi. I cannot do it, and the adepts who claimed they could, never said precisely how in their writing. Not in ways that I can use."

"Use," Nadir repeated. "That's a word I want to emphasize. People like you and Khalid have knowledge that the khan might use. Practical things, like gunpowder that is more predictable in power. Or stronger metallurgy, or more effective medicine. These could be real advantages in the world. To waste such abilities on fraud . . . Naturally the khan is very angry."

Iwang nodded, looking down.

"I have spoken with him at length about this matter, reminding him of Khalid's distinction as an armorer and alchemist. His past contributions as master of arms. His many other services to the khan. And the khan in his wisdom has decided to show a mercy that Muhammad himself must have approved."

Iwang looked up.

"He will be allowed to live, if he promises to work for the khanate on things that are real."

"I am sure he will agree to that," Iwang said. "That is merciful indeed."

"Yes. He will of course have his right hand chopped off for thievery, as the law requires. But considering the effrontery of his crime, this is a very light punishment indeed. As he himself has admitted."

The punishment was administered later that day, a Friday, after the market and before prayers, in the great plaza of Bokhara, by the side of the central pool. A big crowd gathered to witness it. They were in high spirits as Khalid was led out by guards from the palace, dressed in white robes as if celebrating Ramadan. Many of the Bokharis shouted abuse at Khalid, as a Samarqandi as well as a thief.

He knelt before Sayyed Abdul Aziz, who proclaimed the mercy of Allah, and of he himself, and of Nadir Divanbegi for arguing to spare the miscreant's life for his heinous fraud. Khalid's arm, looking from a distance like a bird's scrawny leg and claw, was lashed to the executioner's block. Then a soldier hefted a big axe overhead and dropped it on Khalid's wrist. Khalid's hand fell from the block and blood spurted onto the sand. The crowd roared. Khalid toppled onto his side, and the soldiers held him while one applied hot pitch from a pot on a brazier, using a short stick to plaster the black stuff to the end of the stump.

Bahram and Iwang took him back to Samarqand, laid out in the back of Iwang's bullock cart, which Iwang had had built in order to move weights of metal and glass that camels couldn't carry. It bumped horribly over the road, which was a broad dusty track worn in the earth by centuries of camel traffic between the two cities. The big wooden wheels jounced in every dip and over every hump, and Khalid groaned in the back, semiconscious and breathing stentorously, his left hand holding his pallid, burned right wrist. Iwang had forced an opium-laced potion down him, and if it weren't for his groans it would have seemed he was asleep.

Bahram regarded the new stump with a sickened fascination. Seeing the left hand clutching the wrist, he said to Iwang, "He'll have to eat with his left hand. Do everything with his left hand. He'll be unclean forever."

"That kind of cleanliness doesn't matter."

They had to sleep by the road, as darkness caught them out. Bahram sat by Khalid, and tried to get him to eat some of Iwang's soup. "Come on, Father. Come on, old man. Eat something and you'll feel better. When you feel better it'll be all right." But Khalid only groaned and rolled from side to side. In the darkness, under the great net of stars, it seemed to Bahram that everything in their lives had been ruined.

Effect of the Punishment

But as Khalid recovered, it seemed that he didn't see it that way. He boasted to Bahram and Iwang about his behavior during his punishment: "I never said a word to any of them, and I had tested my limits in jail, to see how long I could hold my breath without fainting, so when I saw the time was near I simply held my breath, and I timed it so well that I was fainting anyway when the stroke fell. I never felt a thing. I don't even remember it."

"We do," said Iwang, frowning.

"Well it was happening to me," Khalid said sharply.

"Fine. You can use the method again when they chop off your head. You can teach it to us for when they throw us off the Tower of Death."

Khalid stared at him. "You're angry with me, I see." Truculent and hurt in his feelings.

Iwang said, "You could have gotten us all killed. Sayyed Abdul would command it without a second thought. If it weren't for Nadir Divanbegi, it might have happened. You should have talked to me. To Bahram here, and to me. We could have helped you."

"Why were you in such trouble, anyway?" asked Bahram, emboldened by Iwang's reproaches. "Surely the works here make a lot of money for you."

Khalid sighed, ran his stump over his balding head. He got up and went to a locked cabinet, unlocked it and drew out a book and a box.

"This came from the Hindu caravanserai two years ago," he told them, showing them the book's old pages. "It's the work of Mary the Jewess, a very great alchemist. Very ancient. Her formula for projection was very convincing, I thought. I needed only the right furnaces, and a lot of sulphur and mercury. So I paid a lot for the book, and for the preparations. And once in debt to the Armenians, it only got worse. After that, I needed the gold to pay for the gold." He shrugged with disgust.

"You should have said so," Iwang repeated, glancing through the old book.

"You should always let me do the trading at the caravanserai," Bahram added. "They know you really want things, while I am ignorant, and so trade from the strength of indifference."

Khalid frowned.

Iwang tapped the book. "This is just warmed-over Aristotle. You can't trust him to tell you anything useful. I've read the translations out of Baghdad and Seville, and I judge he's wrong more often than he's right."

"What do you mean?" Khalid cried indignantly. Even Bahram knew Aristotle was the wisest of the ancients, the supreme authority for all alchemists.

"Where is he not wrong," Iwang said dismissively. "The least country doctor in China can do more for you than Aristotle can. He thought the heart did the thinking, he didn't know it pumped the blood—he has no idea of the spleen or the meridian lines, and he never says a word about the pulse or the tongue. He did some fair dissections of animals, but never dissected a human as far as I can tell. Come with me to the bazaar and I can show you five things he got wrong, any Friday you like."

Khalid was frowning. "Have you read Al-Farudi's 'Harmony Between Aristotle and Plato'?"

"Yes, but that is a harmony that can't be made. Al-Farudi only made the attempt because he didn't have Aristotle's 'Biology.' If he had known that work, he would have seen that for Aristotle it all remains material. His four elements all try to reach their levels, and as they try, our world results. Obviously it's not that simple." He gestured around at the bright dusty day and the clangor of Khalid's shop, the mills, the waterworks powering the big blast furnaces, the noise and movement. "The Platonists know that. They know it is all mathematical. Things happen by number. They should be called Pythagoreans, to be accurate. They are like Buddhists, in that for them the world is alive. As is obviously the case. A great creature of creatures. For Aristotle and Ibn Rashd, it's more like a broken clock."

Khalid grumbled at this, but he was not in a good position to argue. His philosophy had been cut off with his hand.

He was often in some pain, and smoked hashish and drank Iwang's opiated potions to dull the pain, which also dulled his wits, which dulled his spirits. He could not leap in to teach the boys the proper uses of the machinery; he could not shake people's hands, or eat with others, having only his unclean hand left to him; he was permanently unclean. That was part of the punishment.

The realization of this, and the shattering of all his philosophical and alchemical inquiries, finally caught up with him, and cast him into a melancholia. He left his sleeping quarters late in the mornings, and moped around the works watching all the activity like a ghost of himself. There everything continued much as it had before. The great mills wheeled on the river's current, powering the ore stamps and the bellows of the blast furnaces. The crews of workers came in directly after the morning prayers, making their marks on the sheets that kept record of their work hours, then scattering through the compound to shovel salt or sift saltpeter, or perform any other of the hundred activities that Khalid's enterprises demanded, under the supervision of the group of old artisans who had helped Khalid to organize the various works.

But all this was known, accomplished, routinized, and meant nothing to Khalid anymore. Wandering around aimlessly or sitting in his study, surrounded by his collections like a magpie in its nest with a broken wing, he would stare at nothing for hours, or else page through his manuscripts, Al-Razid and Jalduki and Jami, looking at who knew what. He would flick a finger against the objects of wonder that used to fascinate him so—a chunk of pitted coral, a unicorn horn, ancient Indian coins, nested polygons of ivory and horn, a goblet made of a rhinoceros horn chased with gold leaf, stone shells, a tiger leg bone, a gold tiger statue, a laughing Buddha made of some unidentified black material, Nipponese netsuke, forks and crucifixes from the lost civilization of Frengistan—all these objects, which used to give him such delight, and which he would discuss for hours in a manner that grew tedious to his regulars, now only seemed to irritate him. He sat amid his treasures and

he was no longer on the hunt, as Bahram used to think of it, seeking re-
semblances, making conjectures and speculations. Bahram had not understood before how important this was to him.

As his mood grew blacker, Bahram went to the Sufi ribat in the Registan, and asked Ali, the Sufi master in charge of the place, about it.
"Mowlana, he has been punished worse than he thought at first. He's no
longer the same man."

"He is the same soul," said Ali. "You are simply seeing another aspect
of him. There is a secret core in everyone that not even Gabriel can know
by trying to know. Listen now. The intellect derives from the senses,
which are limited, and come from the body. The intellect therefore is also
limited, and it can never truly know reality, which is infinite and eternal.
Khalid wanted to know reality with his intellect, and he can't. Now he
knows that, and is downcast. Intellect has no real mettle, you see, and
at the first threat, into a hole it scuttles. But love is divine. It comes from
the realm of the infinite, and is entrusted to the heart as a gift from God.
Love has no calculation in it. 'God loves you' is the only possible sentence! So it's love you must follow to the heart of your father-in-law. Love
is the pearl of an oyster living in the ocean, and intellect lives on the shore
and cannot swim. Bring up the oyster, sew the pearl onto your sleeve for
all to see. It will bring courage to the intellect. Love is the king that must
rescue his coward slave. Do you understand?"

"I think so."

"You must be sincere and open, your love must be bright as the lightning flash itself! Then his inner consciousness might see it, and be
snatched from itself in a twinkling. Go, feel the love course through you,
and out to him."

Bahram tried this strategy. Waking in his bed with Esmerine, he felt
the love rising in him, for his wife and her beautiful body, the child after
all of the mutilated old man he regarded so fondly. Full of love, he would
make his way through the workshops or into town, feeling the cool of
the springtime air on his skin, and the trees around the pools would
gleam dustily, like great living jewels, and the intense white clouds
would accentuate the deep blue of the sky, echoed underneath by the
turquoise and cobalt tiles of the mosque domes. Beautiful town on a
beautiful morning, at the very center of the world, and the bazaar its
usual massed chaos of noise and color, all human intercourse there to

be seen at once, and yet pointless as an anthill, unless it was infused with love. Everyone did what they did for love of the people in their lives, day after day—or so it seemed to Bahram on those mornings, as he took on more and more of Khalid's old assignments at the compound—and in the nights too, as Esmerine enfolded him.

But he could not seem to convey this apprehension to Khalid. The old man snarled at any expression of high spirits, much less love, and became irritated at any gesture of affection, not just from Bahram but from his wife Fedwa, or Esmerine, or Bahram and Esmerine's children, Fazi and Laila, or anyone else. The bustle of the workshops would surround them in the sunlight with their clangor and stink, all the protocols of metalworking and gunpowder-making that Khalid had formulated going on before them as if in a giant loud dance, and Bahram would make a gesture encompassing it all and say, "Love fills all this so full!" and Khalid would snarl, "Shut up! Don't be a fool!"

One day he slammed out of his study with his single hand holding two of his old alchemical texts, and threw them into the door of a blazing athanor. "Complete nonsense," he replied bitterly when Bahram cried out for him to stop. "Get out of my way, I'm burning them all."

"But why?" Bahram cried. "Those are your books! Why, why, why?"

Khalid took a lump of dusty cinnabar in his one hand, and shook it before Bahram. "Why? I'll tell you why! Look at this! All the great alchemists, from Jabir to Al-Razi to Ibn Sina, all agree that all the metals are various combinations of sulphur and mercury. Iwang says the Chinese and Hindu alchemists agree on this matter. But when we combine sulphur and mercury, as pure as we can make them, we get exactly this: cinnabar! What does that mean? The alchemists who actually speak to this problem, who are very few I might add, say that when they talk about sulphur and mercury, they don't really mean the substances we usually call sulphur and mercury, but rather purer elements of dryness and moisture, that are like sulphur and mercury, but finer! Well!" He threw the chunk of cinnabar across the yard at the river. "What use is that? Why even call them that? Why believe anything they say?" He waved his stump at his study and alchemical workshop, and all the apparatus littering the yard outside. "It's all so much junk. We don't know anything. They never knew what they were talking about."

"All right, Father, maybe so, but don't burn the books! There may be something useful in some of them, you need to make distinctions. And besides, they were expensive."

Khalid only snarled and made the sound of spitting.

Bahram told Iwang about this incident the next time he was in town. "He burned a lot of books. I couldn't talk him out of it. I try to get him to see the love filling everything, but he doesn't see it."

The big Tibetan blew air through his lips like a camel. "That approach will never work with Khalid," he said. "It's easy for you to be full of love, being young and whole. Khalid is old and one-handed. He is out of balance, yin and yang are disarranged. Love has nothing to do with it." Iwang was no Sufi.

Bahram sighed. "Well, I don't know what to do then. You need to help me, Iwang. He's going to burn all his books and destroy all his apparatus, and then who knows what will happen to him."

Iwang grumbled something inaudible.

"What?"

"I'll think it over. Give me some time."

"There isn't much time. He'll break all the apparatus next."

Aristotle Was Wrong

The very next day Khalid ordered the blacksmith apprentices to move everything in the alchemical shops out into the yard to be destroyed. He had a black and wild look as he watched it all shed dust in the sunlight. Sand baths, water baths, descensory furnaces, stills, cucurbits, flasks, alumbixes, alembics with double or even triple spouts, all stood in a haze of antique dust. The largest battery alembic had last been used for distilling rose water, and seeing it Khalid snorted. "That's the only thing we could make work. All this stuff, and we made rose water."

Mortars and pestles, phials, flasks, basins and beakers, glass crystallizing dishes, jugs, casseroles, candle lamps, naphtha lamps, braziers, spatulas, tongs, ladles, shears, hammers, aludels, funnels, miscellaneous lenses, filters of hair, cloth, and linen: finally everything was out in the sun. Khalid waved it all away. "Burn it all, or if it won't burn, break it up and throw it in the river."

But just then Iwang arrived, carrying a small glass-and-silver mechanism. He frowned when he saw the display. "Some of this you could at least sell," he said to Khalid. "Don't you still have debts?"

"I don't care," Khalid said. "I won't sell lies."

"It's not the apparatus that lies," Iwang said. "Some of this stuff could prove very useful."

Khalid glared at him blackly. Iwang decided to change the subject, and raised his device to Khalid's attention. "I brought you a toy that refutes all Aristotle."

Surprised, Khalid examined the thing. Two iron balls sat in an armature that looked to Bahram like one of the waterwheel trip-hammers in miniature.

"Water poured here will weight the rocker, here, and the two doors are one, and open at the same time. One side can't open before the other, see?"

"Of course."

"Yes, obvious, but consider, Aristotle says that a heavier mass will fall faster than a lighter mass, because it has more of the prediliction to join the Earth. But look. Here are the two iron balls, one big and one small, heavy and light. Place them on the doors, set the device level, using a bubble level, high on your outside wall, where there is a good distance to fall. A minaret would be better, the Tower of Death would be better yet, but even from your wall it will work."

They did as he suggested, Khalid climbing the ladder slowly to inspect the arrangement.

"Now, pour water in the funnel, and watch."

The water filled the lower basin until the doors suddenly fell open. The two balls fell. They hit the ground at the same time.

"Ho," Khalid said, and clambered down the ladder to retrieve the balls and try it again, after hefting them, and even weighing them precisely on one of his scales.

"You see?" Iwang said. "You can do it with balls of unequal size or the same size, it doesn't matter. Everything falls at the same rate, except if it is so light and broad, like a feather, that it floats down on the air."

Khalid tried it again.

Iwang said, "So much for Aristotle."

"Well," said Khalid, looking at the balls, then lofting them in his left hand. "He could be wrong about this and right about other things."

"No doubt. But everything he says has to be tested, if you ask me, and also compared with what Hsing Ho and Al-Razi say, and the Hindus. Demonstrated to be true or false, in the full light of day."

Khalid was nodding. "I would have some questions, I admit."

Iwang gestured at the alchemical equipment in the yard. "It's the same for all this—you could test them, see what's useful and what's not."

Khalid frowned. Iwang returned his attention to the falling balls. The two men dropped a number of different items from the device, chattering away all the while.

"Look, something has to be bringing them down," Khalid said at one point. "Bringing them, forcing them, drawing them, what have you."

"Of course," said Iwang. "Things happen by causes. An attraction must be caused by an agent, acting according to certain laws. What the agent might be, however . . ."

"But this is true of everything," Khalid said, muttering. "We know nothing, that's what it comes down to. We live in darkness."

"Too many conjoined factors," Iwang said.

Khalid nodded, hefting a carved block of ironwood in his hand. "I'm tired of it, though."

"So we try things. You do something, you get something else. It looks like a causal chain. Describable as a logical sequence, even as a mathematical operation. So that you might say, reality manifests itself thus. Without worrying too much about defining what force it is."

"Perhaps love is the force," Bahram offered. "The same attraction as of persons to persons, extended between things in a general way."

"It would explain how one's member rises away from the Earth," Iwang said with a smile.

Bahram laughed, but Khalid said only, "A joke. What I am speaking of could not be less like love. It is as constant as the stars in their places, a physical force."

"The Sufis say that love is a force, filling everything, impelling everything."

"The Sufis," Khalid said scornfully. "Those are the last people on Earth I would consult if I wanted to know how the world works. They moon about love and drink lots of wine and spin themselves. Bah! Islam was an intellectual discipline before the Sufis came along, studying the world as it is, we had Ibn Sina and Ibn Rashd and Ibn Khaldun and all the rest, and then the Sufis appeared and there hasn't been a single Muslim philosopher or scholar since then who has advanced our understanding of things by a single whit."

"They have too," Bahram said. "They've made it clear how important love is in the world."

"Love, oh yes, all is love, God is love, but if everything is love and all is one with Allah, then why do they have to get so drunk every day?"

Iwang laughed. Bahram said, "They don't really, you know."

"They do! And the good fellowship halls fill up with good fellows looking for a good time, and the madressas grow emptier, and the khans give them less, and here we are in the year 1020 arguing over the ideas of the ancient Frengis, without a single idea why things act the way they do. We know nothing! Nothing!"

"We have to start small," Iwang said.

"We can't start small! Everything is all tied together!"

"Well, then we need to isolate one set of actions that we can see and control, and then study that, and see if we can understand it. Then work onward from there. Something like this falling, just the simplest movement. If we understood movement, we could study its manifestations in other things."

Khalid thought about that. He had finally stopped dropping things through the device.

"Come here with me," Iwang said. "Let me show you something that makes me curious."

They followed him toward the shop containing the big furnaces. "See how you obtain such hot fires now. Your waterworks drive the bellows faster than any number of puffers ever could, and the heat of the fire is accordingly higher. Now, Aristotle says fire is trapped in wood, and released by heat. Fair enough, but why does more air make the fire burn hotter? Why does wind drive a wildfire so? Does it mean air is essential to fire? Could we find out? If we built a chamber in which the air was pulled out by the bellows rather than pushed in, would the fire burn less?"

"Suck air out of a chamber?" Khalid said.

"Yes. Arrange a valve that lets air out but won't let it back in. Pump out what's there, and then hold any replacement air out."

"Interesting! But what would remain in the chamber then?"

Iwang shrugged. "I don't know. A void? A piece of the original void, perhaps? Ask the lamas about that, or your Sufis. Or Aristotle. Or just make a glass chamber, and look in it."

"I will," Khalid said.

"And motion is easiest of all to study," Iwang said. "We can try all manner of things with motion. We can time this attraction of things to the Earth. We can see if the speed is the same up in the hills and down in the valleys. Things speed up as they fall, and this might be measurable too. Light itself might be measurable. Certainly the angles of refraction are constant, I've measured those already."

Khalid was nodding. "First this reverse bellows, to empty a chamber. Although surely it cannot be a true void that results. Nothingness is not possible in this world, I think. There will be something in there, thinner than air."

"That is more Aristotle," Iwang said. " 'Nature abhors the void.' But what if it doesn't? We will only know when we try."

Khalid nodded. If he had had two hands he would have been rubbing them together.

The three of them walked out to the waterworks. Here a canal brought a hard flow from the river, its gliding surface gleaming in the morning light. The water powered a mill, which geared out to axles turning a bank of heavy metalworking hammers and stamps, and finally the rotating bellows handles that powered the blast furnaces. It was a noisy place, filled with sounds of falling water, smashed rock, roaring fire, singed air; all the elements raging with transmutation, hurting their ears and leaving a burnt smell in the air. Khalid stood watching the waterworks for a while. This was his achievement, he was the one who had organized all the artisans' skills into this enormous articulated machine, so much more powerful than people or horses had ever been. They were the most powerful people in all the history of the world, Bahram thought, because of Khalid's enterprise; but with a wave Khalid dismissed it all. He wanted to understand why it worked.

He led the other two back to the shop. "We'll need your glassblowing, and my leather and iron workers," he said. "The valve you mention could perhaps be made of sheep intestines."

"It might have to be stronger than that," said Iwang. "A metal gate of some sort, pressed into a leather gasket by the suck of the void."

"Yes."

No Jinn in This Bottle

Khalid set his artisans to the task, and Iwang did the glassblowing, and after a few weeks they had a two-parted mechanism: a thick glass globe to be emptied, and a powerful pump to empty it. There were any number of collapses, leaks, and valve failures, but the old mechanists of the compound were ingenious, and attacking the points of failure, they ended up with five very similar versions of the device, all very heavy. The pump was massive and lathed to newly precise fits of plunger, tube, and valves; the glass globes were thick flasks, with necks even thicker, and knobs on the inside surfaces from which objects could be hung, to see what would happen to them when the air in the globe was evacuated. When they solved the leakage problems, they had to build a rack-and-pinion device to exert enough force on the pump to evacuate the final traces of air from the globe. Iwang advised them not to create such a perfect void that they ended up sucking in the pump, the compound, or perchance the whole world, like jinn returning to their confinement; and as always, Iwang's stone face did not give them any clue as to whether he was joking or serious.

When they had the mechanisms working fairly reliably (occasionally one would still crack its glass, or break a valve), they set one on a wooden frame, and Khalid began a sequence of trials, inserting things in the glass globes, pumping out the air, and seeing what resulted. All philosophical questions on the nature of what remained inside the globe after the air was removed, he now refused to address. "Let's just see what happens," he said. "It is what it is." He kept big blank-paged books on the table beside the apparatus, and he or his clerks recorded every detail of the trials, timing them on his best clock.

After a few weeks of learning the apparatus and trying things, he asked Iwang and Bahram to arrange a small party, inviting several of the qadi and teachers from the madressas in the Registan, particularly the mathematicians and astronomers of Sher Dor Madressa, who were already involved in discussions of ancient Greek and classical caliphate notions of physical reality. On the appointed day, when all those invited had gathered in the open-walled workshop next to Khalid's study, Khalid introduced the apparatus to them, describing how it worked and indicating what they could all see, that he had hung an alarm clock from a knob inside the glass globe, so that it swung freely at the end of a short length of silk thread. Khalid cranked the piston of the rack-and-pinion down twenty times, working hard with his left arm. He explained that the alarm clock was set to go off at the sixth hour of the afternoon, shortly after the evening prayers would be sung from Samarqand's northernmost minaret.

"To be sure the alarm is truly sounding," Khalid said, "we have exposed the clapper, so that you can see it hitting the bells. I will also introduce air back into the globe little by little, after we have seen the first results, so you can hear for yourself the effect."

He was gruff and direct. Bahram saw that he wanted to distance himself from the portentous, magical style he had affected during his alchemical transmutations. He made no claims, spoke no incantations. The memory of his last disastrous demonstration—his fraud—must have been in his mind, as it was in everyone else's. But he merely gestured with his hand at the clock, which advanced steadily toward six.

Then the clock began to spin on its thread, and the clapper was visibly smashing back and forth between the little brass bells. But there was no sound coming from the glass. Khalid gestured: "You might think that the glass itself is stopping the sound, but when the air is let back into the flask, you will see that it isn't so. First I invite you to put your ear to the glass, so you can confirm that there is no sound at all."

They did so one by one. Then Khalid unscrewed a stopcock that released a valve set in the side of the flask, and a brief penetrating hiss was joined by the muted banging of the alarm, which grew louder quickly, until it sounded much like an alarm heard from an adjoining room.

"It seems there is no sound without air to convey it," Khalid commented.

The visitors from the madressa were eager to inspect the apparatus, and to discuss its uses in trials of various sorts, and to speculate about what, if anything, remained in the globe when the air was pumped out. Khalid was adamant in his refusal to discuss this question, preferring to talk about what the demonstration seemed to be indicating about the nature of sound and its transmission.

"Echoes might elucidate this matter in another way," one of the qadis said. He and all the other visiting witnesses were bright-eyed, pleased, intrigued. "Something strikes air, pushes it, and the sound is a shock moving through the air, like waves across water. They bounce back, like waves in water bounce when they strike a wall. It takes time for this movement to cross the intervening space, and thus echoes."

Bahram said, "With the aid of an echoing cliff we could perhaps time the speed of sound."

"The speed of sound!" Iwang said. "Very nice!"

"A capital idea, Bahram," Khalid said. He checked to make sure his clerk was noting all done or said. He unscrewed the stopcock all the way and removed it, so that they all heard the noisy clanging of the alarm as he reached into the flask to turn off the device. It was strange that the clapper should have been so silent before. He rubbed his scalp with his right wrist. "I wonder," he said, "if we could establish a speed for light too, using the same principle."

"How would it echo?" Bahram asked.

"Well, if it were aimed at a distant mirror, say . . . a lantern unveiled, a distant mirror, a clock that one could read very precisely, or start and stop, even better . . ."

Iwang was shaking his head. "The mirror might have to be very far away to give the recorder time to determine an interval, and then the lantern flash would not be visible unless the mirror were perfectly angled."

"Make a person the mirror," Bahram suggested. "When the person on the far hill sees the first lantern light, he reveals his, and a person next to the first person times the appearance of the second light."

"Very good," several people said at once. Iwang added, "It may still be too fast."

"It remains to be seen," Khalid said cheerfully. "A demonstration will clarify the issue."

With that Esmerine and Fedwa wheeled in the ice tray and its "demonstration of sherbets" as Iwang termed it, and the crowd fell to, talking happily, Iwang speaking of the thin sound of goraks in the high Himalaya where the air itself was thin, and so on.

The Khan Confronts the Void

So Iwang brought Khalid back out of his black melancholy, and Bahram saw the wisdom of Iwang's approach to the matter. Every day now, Khalid woke up in a hurry to get things done. The businesses of the compound were given over to Bahram and Fedwa and the old hands heading each of the shops, and Khalid was distracted and uninterested if they came to him with matters of that sort. All his time was taken by conceiving, planning, executing, and recording his demonstrations with the void pump, and later with other equipment and phenomena. They went to the great western city wall at dawn when all was quiet, and timed the sound of wood blocks slapped together and their returning echoes, measuring their distance from the wall with a length of string one third of a li long. Iwang did the calculations, and soon declared that the speed of sound was something like two thousand li an hour, a speed that everyone marveled at. "About fifty times faster than the fastest horse," Khalid said, regarding Iwang's figures happily.

"And yet light will be much faster," Iwang predicted.

"We will find out."

Meanwhile Iwang was puzzling over the figures. "There remains the question of whether sound slows down as it moves along. Or speeds up for that matter. But presumably it would slow, if it did anything, as the air resisted the shock."

"Noise gets quieter the farther away it is," Bahram pointed out. "Maybe it gets quieter rather than slower."

"But why would that be?" Khalid asked, and then he and Iwang were into a deep discussion of sound, movement, causation, and action at a distance. Quickly Bahram was out of his depth, being no philosopher, and indeed Khalid did not like the metaphysical aspect of the discussion, and concluded as he always did these days: "We will test it."

Iwang was agreeable. Ruminating over his figures, he said, "We need a mathematics that could deal not only with fixed speeds, but with the speed of the change of a speed. I wonder if the Hindus have considered this." He often said that the Hindu mathematicians were the most advanced in the world, very far ahead of the Chinese. Khalid had long ago given him access to all the books of mathematics in his study, and Iwang spent many hours in there reading, or making obscure calculations and drawings, on slates with chalk.

The news of their void pump spread, and they frequently met with the interested parties in the madressas, usually the masters teaching mathematics and natural philosophy. These meetings were often contentious, but everyone kept to the ostentatiously formal disputation style of the madressa's theological debates.

Meanwhile the Hindu caravanserai frequently sheltered booksellers, and these men called Bahram over to have a look at old scrolls, leather- or wood-bound books, or boxes of loose-leaved pages. "Old One-Hand will be interested in what this Brahmagupta has to say about the size of the Earth, I assure you," they would say, grinning, knowing that Bahram could not judge.

"This one here is the wisdom of a hundred generations of Buddhist monks, all killed by the Mughals."

"This one is the compiled knowledge of the lost Frengis, of Archimedes and Euclid."

Bahram would look through the pages as if he could tell, buying for the most part by bulk and antiquity, and the frequent appearance of numbers, especially Hindi numbers, or the Tibetan ticks that only Iwang could decipher. If he thought Khalid and Iwang would be interested, he haggled with a firmness based on ignorance, "Look this isn't even in Arabic or Hindi or Persian or Sanskrit, I don't even recognize this alphabet! How is Khalid to make anything of this?"

"Oh, but this is from the Deccan, Buddhists everywhere can read it, your Iwang will be very happy to learn this!"

Or, "This is the alphabet of the Sikhs, their last guru invented an alphabet for them, it's a lot like Sanskrit, and the language is a form of Punjabi," and so on. Bahram came home with his finds, nervous at having spent good money on dusty tomes incomprehensible to him, and Khalid and Iwang would inspect them, and either page through them like vultures, congratulating Bahram on his judgment and haggling skills, or else Khalid would curse him for a fool while Iwang stared at him, marveling that he could not identify a Travancori accounting book full of shipping invoices (this was the Deccan volume that any Buddhist could read).

Other attention drawn by their new device was not so welcome. One morning Nadir Divanbegi appeared at the gate with some of the khan's guards. Khalid's servant Paxtakor ushered them across the compound, and Khalid, carefully impassive and hospitable, ordered coffee brought to his study.

Nadir was as friendly as could be, but soon came to the point. "I argued to the khan that your life be spared because you are a great scholar, philosopher, and alchemist, an asset to the khanate, a jewel of Samarqand's great glory."

Khalid nodded uncomfortably, looking at his coffee cup. He lifted a finger briefly, as if to say, Enough, and then muttered, "I am grateful, Effendi."

"Yes. Now it is clear that I was right to argue for your life, as word comes to us of your many activities, and wonderful investigations."

Khalid looked up at him to see if he were being mocked, and Nadir lifted a palm to show his sincerity. Khalid looked down again.

"But I came here to remind you that all these fascinating trials take place in a dangerous world. The khanate lies at the center of all the trade routes in the world, with armies in all directions. The khan is concerned to protect his subjects from attack, and yet we hear of cannon that would reduce our cities' walls in a week or less. The khan wishes you to help him with this problem. He is sure you will be happy to bring him some small part of the fruits of your learning, to help him to defend the khanate."

"All my trials are the khan's," Khalid said seriously. "My every breath is the khan's."

Nadir nodded his acknowledgment of this truth. "And yet you did not invite him to your demonstration with this pump that creates a void in the air."

"I did not think he would be interested in such a small matter."

"The khan is interested in everything."

None of them could tell by Nadir's face whether he was joking or not.

"We would be happy to display the void pump to him."

"Good. That would be appreciated. But remember also that he wishes specific help with cannonry, and with defense against cannonry."

Khalid nodded. "We will honor his wish, Effendi."

After Nadir was gone, Khalid grumbled unhappily. "Interested in everything! How can he say that and not laugh!" Nevertheless he sent a servant with a formal invitation to the khan, to witness the new apparatus. And before the visit occurred he had the whole compound at work, developing a new demonstration of the pump that he hoped would impress the khan.

When Sayyed Abdul Aziz and his retinue made their visit, the globe that was to hold the void this time was made of two half-globes, one edge mortised to fit the other precisely, with a thin oiled leather gasket placed between the two before the air was pumped out of the space between them, and thick steel braces for each globe, to which ropes could be tied.

Sayyed Abdul sat on his cushions and inspected the two halves of the globe closely. Khalid explained to him: "When the air is removed, the two halves of the globe will adhere together with great strength." He placed the halves together, pulled them apart; placed them together again, screwed the pump into the one that had the hole for it, and gestured for Paxtakor to wind the pump out and in and out again, ten times. Then he brought the device over to the khan, and invited him to try to pull the two halves of the globe apart.

It could not be done. The khan looked bored. Khalid took the device out to the central yard of the compound, where two teams of three horses each were held waiting. Their draft harnesses were hooked to the two sides of the globe, and the horses led apart until the globe hung in the air between them. When the horses were steadied, still facing away from each other, the horseboys cracked their whips, and the two teams of horses snorted and shoved and skipped as they attempted to pull away; they skittered sideways, shifted, struggled, and all the while the globe hung from the quivering horizontal ropes. The globe could not be pulled apart; even little charges made by the horse teams only brought them up short, staggering.

The khan watched the horses with interest, but the globe he seemed to disregard. After a few minutes of straining, Khalid had the horses stopped, and he unhooked the apparatus and brought it over to the khan and Nadir and their group. When he unscrewed the stopcock, the air hissed back into the globe, and the two halves came apart as easily as slices of an orange. Khalid stripped out the smashed leather gasket. "You see," he said, "it was the force of the air, or rather the pull of the void, that kept the halves together so strongly."

The khan got up to leave, and his retainers rose with him. It seemed he was almost falling asleep. "So?" he said. "I want to blow my enemies apart, not hold them together." With a wave of his hand he left.

Inside the Night, Inside the Light

This unenthusiastic response on the part of the khan worried Bahram. No interest in an apparatus that had fascinated the scholars of the madressa; instead, a command to discover some new weapon or fortification that had eluded the hard search of all the armorers of all the ages. And if they failed, the possible punishments were only too easy to imagine. Khalid's absent hand mocked them from its own kind of void. Khalid would stare at the end of his wrist and say, "Someday all of me will look like you."

Now he merely looked around the compound. "Tell Paxtakor to obtain new cannon from Nadir for testing. Three at each weight, and all manner of powder and shot."

"We have powder here."

"Of course." A withering glare: "I want to see what they have that is not ours."

In the days that followed, he revisited all the old buildings of the compounds, the ones he and his old ironmongers had built when they were first making guns and gunpowder for the khan. In those days, before he and his men had followed the Chinese system and connected the power of their waterwheel to the furnaces, making their first river-powered blast furnaces and freeing up their crew of young puffers for other work, everything had been small and primitive, the iron more brittle, everything they made rougher, bulkier. The buildings themselves showed it. Now the gears of the waterwheels whirred with all the power of the river, pouring into the bellows and roaring as fire. The chemical pits steamed lemon and lime in the sun, and the puffers packed boxes and ran camels and moved immense mounds of charcoal around the yards. Khalid shook his head at the sight of it all, and made a new gesture, a kind of sweep and punch with his ghost hand. "We need better clocks. We can only make progress if our measurement of time is more exact."

Iwang puffed his lips when he heard this. "We need more understanding."

"Yes, yes, of course. Who could dispute that in this miserable world. But all the wisdom of the ages cannot tell us how long it takes flashpowder to ignite a charge."

When the days ended the great compound fell silent, except for the grinding of the watermill on the canal. After the resident workers had washed and eaten and said their last prayers of the day, they went to their apartments at the river end of the compound, and fell asleep. The town workers went home.

Bahram dropped onto his bed beside Esmerine, across the room from their two small children, Fazi and Laila. Most nights he was out as soon his head hit the silk of his pillow, exhausted. Blessed slumber.

But often he and Esmerine woke sometime after midnight, and sometimes they lay there breathing, touching, whispering conversations that were usually brief and disjointed, other times the longest and deepest conversations they ever had; and if ever they were to make love, now that the children were there to exhaust Esmerine, it would be in the blessed cool and quiet of these midnight hours.

Afterward Bahram might get up and walk around the compound, to see it in moonlight and check that all was well, feeling the afterglow of love pulse in him; and usually on these occasions he would see the lamplight in Khalid's study, and pad by to find Khalid slumped over a book, or scribbling left-handed at his writing stand, or recumbent on his couch, in murmured conversation with Iwang, both of them holding tubes of a narghile wreathed by the sweet smell of hashish. If Iwang was there and the men seemed awake, Bahram would sometimes join them for a while, before he got sleepy again and returned to Esmerine. Khalid and Iwang might be speaking of the nature of motion, or the nature of vision, sometimes holding up one of Iwang's lenses to look through as they talked. Khalid held the position that the eye received small impressions or images of things, sent through the air to it. He had found many an old philosopher, from China to Frengistan, who held the same view, calling the little images "eidola" or "simulacra" or "species" or "image" or "idol" or "phantasm" or "form" or "intention" or "passion" or "similitude of the agent," or "shadow of the philosophers," a name that made Iwang smile. He himself believed the eye sent out projections of a fluid as quick as light itself, which returned to the eye like an echo, with the contours of objects and their colors intact.

Bahram always maintained that none of these explanations was adequate. Vision could not be explained by optics, he would say; sight was a matter of spirit. The two men would hear him out, then Khalid would shake his head. "Perhaps optics are not sufficient to explain it, but they are necessary to begin an explanation. It's the part of the phenomenon that can be tested, you see, and described mathematically, if we are clever enough."

The cannon arrived from the khan, and Khalid spent part of every day out on the bluff over the curve in the river, shooting them off with old Jalil and Paxtakor; but by far the bulk of his time was spent thinking about optics and proposing tests to Iwang. Iwang returned to his shop, blowing thick glass balls with cut sides, mirrors concave and convex, and big, perfectly polished triangular rods, which were for him objects of almost religious reverence. He and Khalid spent afternoon hours in the old man's study with the door closed, having made a little hole in the south wall letting in a chink of light. They put the prism over the hole, and its straight rainbow shone on the walls or a screen they set up. Iwang said there were seven colors, Khalid six, as he called Iwang's purple and lavender two parts of the same color. They argued endlessly about everything they saw, at least at first. Iwang made diagrams of their arrangement that gave the precise angles each band of color bent as it went through the prism. They held up glass balls and wondered why the light did not fractionate in these balls as it did in the prism, when everyone could see that a sky full of minuscule clear balls, that is to say, raindrops, hit by low afternoon sunlight, created the towering rainbows that hung east of Samarqand after a rainshower had passed. Many a time when black storms had passed over the city, Bahram stood outside with the two older men observing some truly beautiful rainbows, often double rainbows, a lighter one arched over the brighter one—and sometimes even a third very faint one above that. Eventually Iwang worked up a law of refraction which he assured Khalid would account for all the colors. "The primary rainbow is produced by a refraction as the light enters the raindrop, an internal reflection at the back surfaces, and a second refraction out of the raindrop. The secondary bow is created by light reflected two or three times inside the raindrops. Now look you, each color has its own index of refraction, and so to bounce around inside the raindrop is to separate each color out from the others, with them appearing to the eye always in their correct sequence, reversed in the secondary because there is an extra bounce making it upside down, as in my drawing here, see?"

"So if raindrops were crystalline, there would be no rainbows."

"That's right, yes. That's snow. If there was only reflection, the sky might sparkle everywhere with white light, as if filled with mirrors. Sometimes you see that in a snowstorm too. But the roundness of raindrops means there is a steady change in the angle of incidence between zero and ninety degrees, and that spreads the different rays to an observer here, who must always stand at an angle from forty to forty-two degrees off from the incoming sunlight. The secondary one appears when the angle is between fifty and a half degrees and fifty-four and a half. See, the geometry predicts the angles, and out here we measure, using this wonderful sky viewer Bahram found for you at the Chinese caravanserai, and it confirms, as precisely as hand can hold, the mathematical prediction!"

"Well, of course," Khalid said, "but that's circular reasoning. You get your angles of incidence by observation of a prism, then confirm the angles in the sky by more observation."

"But one was colors on the wall, the other rainbows in the sky!"

"As above, so below." This of course was a truism of the alchemists, so there was a dark edge to Khalid's comment.

The current rainbow was waning as a cloud in the west blocked the sun. The two old men did not notice, however, absorbed as they were in their discussion. Bahram alone was left to enjoy the vibrant colors arcing across the sky, Allah's gift to show that he would never again drown the world. The two men jabbed fingers at Iwang's chalkboard and Khalid's sky device.

"It's leaving," Bahram said, and they looked up, slightly annoyed to be interrupted. While the rainbow had been bright, the sky under it had been distinctly lighter than the sky over it; now the inside and outside were the same shade of slate blue again.

The rainbow left the world, and they squelched back to the compound, Khalid cheering up with every step, many of them landing right in puddles, as he was still staring at Iwang's chalkboard.

"So—so—well. I must admit, it is as neat as a proof of Euclid. Two refractions, two or three reflections—rain and sun, an observer to see—and there you have it! The rainbow!"

"And light itself, divisible into a banding of colors," Iwang mused, "traveling all together out of the sun. So bright it is! And when it strikes anything at all, it bounces off and into an eye, if there be an eye to see it, and whatever part of the band, hmm, how would that work . . . are the surfaces of the world all variously rounded, if you could but look at them close enough . . ."

"It's a wonder things don't change color when you move," Bahram said, and the other two went silent, until Khalid started laughing.

"Another mystery! Allah preserve us! They will just keep coming forever, until we are one with God."

This thought appeared to please him immensely.

He set up a permanent dark room in the compound, all boarded and draped until it was much darker than his study had been, with shuttered chinks in the east wall that could let in small shafts of light, and many a morning he was in there with assistants, running in and out, arranging demonstrations one way or another. With one he was pleased enough to invite the scholars of the Sher Dor Madressa to witness it, because it so neatly refuted Ibn Rashd's contention that white light was whole, and the colors created by a prism an effect of the glass. If this were so, Khalid argued, then light twice bent would change color twice. To test this, his assistants allowed sunlight in through the wall, and a first prism's array was spread across a screen in the center of the room. Khalid himself opened an aperture in the screen small enough only to allow the red part of the little rainbow through it, into a draped closet where it immediately encountered another prism, directing it onto another screen inside the closet.

"Now, if the bend of refraction caused by itself the change in color, surely the red band would change at this second refraction. But look: it remains red. Each of the colors holds when put through a second prism." He moved the aperture slowly from color to color, to demonstrate. His guests crowded around the door of the closet, examining the results closely.

"What does this mean?" one asked.

"Well, this you must help me with, or ask Iwang. I am no philosopher, myself. But I think it proves the change in color is not just a matter of bending per se. I think it shows sunlight, white light if you will, or full light, or simply sunlight, is composed of all the individual colors traveling together."

The witnesses nodded. Khalid ordered the room opened up, and they retired blinking into the sun to have coffee and cakes.

"This is wonderful," Zahhar, one of Sher Dor's senior mathematicians said, "very illuminating, so to speak. But what does it tell us about light, do you think? What is light?"

Khalid shrugged. "God knows, but not men. I think only that we have clarified, so to speak, some of light's behavior. And that behavior has a geometrical aspect. It seems regulated by number, you see. As do so many things in this world. Allah appears to like mathematics, as you yourself have often said, Zahhar. As for the substance of light, what a mystery! It moves quickly, how quickly we do not know; it would be good to find out. And it is hot, as we know by the sun. And it will cross a void, if indeed there is any such thing as a void in this world, in a way that sound will not. It could be that the Hindus are right and there is another element besides earth, fire, air and water, an ether so fine we do not see it, that fills the universe to a plenum and is the medium of movement. Perhaps little corpuscles, bouncing off whatever they strike, as in a mirror, but usually less directly. Depending on what it strikes, a particular color band is reflected into the eye. Perhaps." He shrugged. "It is a mystery."

The Madressas Weigh In

The color demonstrations caused a great deal of discussion and debate in the madressas, and Khalid learned during this period never to speak of causes in any opinionated way, or to impinge on the realm of the madressa scholars by speaking of Allah's will, or any other aspect of the nature of reality. He would only say, "Allah gave us our intelligence to better understand the glory of his work," or, "The world often works mathematically. Allah loves numbers, and mosquitoes in springtime, and beauty."

The scholars went away amused, or irritated, but in any case in a ferment of philosophy. The madressas of Registan Square and elsewhere in the city, and out at Ulug Bek's old observatory, were buzzing with the new fashion of making demonstrations of various physical phenomena, and Khalid's was not the only mechanical workshop that could build an ever more complex array of new machines and devices. The mathematicians of Sher Dor Madressa, for instance, interested everyone with a surprising new mercury scale, simple to construct—a bowl containing a pool of mercury, with a narrow tube of mercury, sealed at the top but not the bottom, set upright in the liquid in the bowl. The mercury in the tube dropped a certain distance, creating another mysterious void in the gap left at the top of the tube; but the remainder of the tube stayed filled with a column of mercury. The Sher Dor mathematicians asserted that it was the weight of the world's air on the mercury in the bowl that pushed down on it enough to keep the mercury in the cylinder from falling all the way down into the bowl. Others maintained it was the disinclination of the void in the top of the tube to grow. Following a suggestion of Iwang's, they took their device to the top of Snow Mountain, in the Zeravshan Range, and all there saw that the level of mercury in the tube had dropped, presumably because there was less weight of air on it up there, two or three thousand hands higher than the city. This was a great support for Khalid's previous contention that air weighed on them, and a refutation of Aristotle, and al-Farabi and the rest of the Aristotelian Arabs, who claimed that the four elements want to be in their proper places, high or low. This claim Khalid openly ridiculed, at least in private. "As if stones or the wind could want to be someplace or other, as a man does. It's really nothing but circular definition again. 'Things fall because they want to fall,' as if they could want. Things fall because they fall, that's all it means. Which is fine, no one knows why things fall, certainly not me, it is a very great mystery. All the seeming cases of action at a distance are a mystery. But first we must say so, we must distinguish the mysteries as mysteries, and proceed from there, demonstrating what happens, and then seeing if that leads us to any thoughts concerning the how or the why."

The Sufi scholars were still inclined to extrapolate from any given demonstration to the ultimate nature of the cosmos, while the mathematically inclined were fascinated by the purely numerical aspects of the results, the geometry of the world as it was revealed. These and other approaches combined in a burst of activity, consisting of demonstrations and talk, and private work on slates over mathematical formulations, and artisanal labor on new or improved devices. On some days it seemed to Bahram that these investigations had filled all Samarqand: Khalid's compound and the others, the madressas, the ribat, the bazaars, the coffee stalls, the caravanserai, where the traders would take the news out to all the world . . . it was beautiful.

The Chest of Wisdom

Out beyond the western wall of the city, where the old Silk Road ran toward
Bokhara, the Armenians were quiet in their little caravanserai, tucked
beside the large and raucous Hindu one. The Armenians were cooking
in the dusk over their braziers. Their women were bareheaded and bold-
eyed, laughing among themselves in their own language. Armenians
were good traders, and yet reclusive for all that. They trafficked only in
the most expensive goods, and knew everything about everywhere, it
seemed. Of all the trading peoples, they were the most rich and powerful. Unlike the Jews and Nestorians and Zott, they had a little homeland
in the Caucasus to which most of them regularly returned, and they
were Muslim, most of them, which gave them a tremendous advantage
across Dar al-Islam—which was to say all the world, except for China,
and India below the Deccan. Rumors that they only pretended to be
Muslim, and were secretly Christians all the while, struck Bahram as envious backstabbing by other traders, probably the tricky Zott, who had
been cast out of India long before (some said Egypt), and now wandered
the world homeless, and did not like the Armenians' inside position in
so many of the most lucrative markets and products.

Bahram wandered among their fires and lamplight, stopping to chat
and accept a swallow of wine with familiars of his, until an old man
pointed out the bookseller Mantuni, even older, a wizened hunch-
backed little man who wore spectacles that made his eyes appear the

size of lemons. His Turkic was basic and heavily accented, and Bahram switched to Persian, which Mantuni acknowledged with a grateful dip of the head. The old man indicated a wooden box on the ground, filled entirely with books he had obtained for Khalid in Frengistan. "Will you be able to carry it?" he asked Bahram anxiously.

"Sure," Bahram said, but he had his own worry: "How much is this going to cost?"

"Oh no, it's already paid for. Khalid sent me off with the funds, otherwise I would not have been able to afford to buy these. They're from an estate sale in Damascus, a very old alchemical family that came to an end with a hermit who had no issue. See here, Zosimos' 'Treatise on Instruments and Furnaces,' printed just two years ago, that's for you. I've got the rest arranged chronologically by date of composition, as you can see, here is Jabir's 'Sum of Perfection,' and his 'Ten Books of Rectification,' and look, 'The Secret of Creation.' "

This was a huge sheepskin-bound volume. "Written by the Greek Apollonius. One of its chapters is the fabled 'Emerald Table,' " tapping its cover delicately. "That chapter alone is worth twice what I paid for this whole collection, but they didn't know. The original of 'The Emerald Table' was found by Sara the wife of Abraham, in a cave near Hebron, sometime after the Great Flood. It was inscribed on a plate of emerald, which Sara found clasped in the hands of the mummified corpse of Thrice-greatest Hermes, the father of all alchemy. The writing was in Phoenician characters. Although I must admit I have read other accounts that have it discovered by Alexander the Great. In any case here it is, in an Arabic translation from the time of the Baghdad caliphate."

"Fine," Bahram said. He wasn't sure Khalid would still be interested in this stuff.

"You will also find 'The Complete Biographies of the Immortals,' a rather slender volume, considering, and 'The Chest of Wisdom,' and a book by a Frengi, Bartholomew the Englishman, 'On the Properties of Things,' also 'The Epistle of the Sun to the Crescent Moon,' and 'The Book of Poisons,' perhaps useful, and 'The Great Treasure,' and 'The Document Concerning the Three Similars,' in Chinese—"

"Iwang will be able to read that," Bahram said. "Thank you." He tried to pick up the box. It was as if filled with rocks, and he staggered.

"Are you sure you'll be able to get it back to the city, and safely?"

"I'll be fine. I'm going to take them to Khalid's, where Iwang has a room for his work. Thanks again. I'm sure Iwang will want to call on you to talk about these, and perhaps Khalid too. How long will you be in Samarqand?"

"Another month, no more."

"They'll be out to talk to you about these."

Bahram hiked along with the box balanced on his head. He took breaks from time to time to give his head a break, and fortify himself with more wine. By the time he got back to the compound it was late and his head was swimming, but the lamps were lit in Khalid's study, and Bahram found the old man in there reading and dropped the box triumphantly before him.

"More to read," he said, and collapsed on a chair.

The End of Alchemy

Shaking his head at Bahram's drunkenness, Khalid began going through the box, whistling and chirping. "Same old crap," he said at one point. Then he pulled one out and opened it. "Ah," he said, "a Frengi text, translated from Latin to Arabic by an Ibn Rabi of Nsara. Original by one Bartholomew the Englishman, written sometime in the sixth century. Let's see what he has to say, hmm, hmm . . ." He read with the forefinger of his left hand leading his eyes on a rapid chase over the pages. "What! That's Ibn Sina direct! . . . And this too!" He looked up at Bahram. "The alchemical sections are taken right out of Ibn Sina!"

He read on, laughed his brief unamused laugh. "Listen to this! 'Quicksilver,' that's mercury, 'is of so great virtue and strength, that though thou do a stone of an hundred pound weigh upon quicksilver of the weight of two pounds, the quicksilver anon withstandeth the weight.' "

"What?"

"Have you ever heard such nonsense. If he was going to speak of measures of weight at all, you'd think he would have the sense to understand them."

He read on. "Ah," he said after a while. "Here he quotes Ibn Sina directly. 'Glass, as Avicenna saith, is among stones as a fool among men, for it taketh all manner of color and painting.' Spoken by a very mirror glass of a man . . . Ha . . . Look, here is a story that could be about our Sayyed

Abdul Aziz. 'Long time past, there was one that made glass pliant, which might be amended and wrought with an hammer, and brought a vial made of such glass before Tiberius the Emperor, and threw it down on the ground, and it was not broken, but bent and folded. And he made it right and amended it with a hammer,' We must demand this glass from Iwang! 'Then the Emperor commanded to smite off his head anon, lest that this craft were known. For then gold should be no better than clay, and all other metal should be of little worth, for certain if glass vessels were not brittle, they should be accounted of more value than vessels of gold,' that's a curious proposition. I suppose glass was rare in his time." He stood up, stretched, sighed. "Tiberiuses, on the other hand, will always be common."

Most of the other books he paged through quickly and dropped back in the box. He did go through "The Emerald Table" page by page, enlisting Iwang, and later some of the Sher Dor mathematicians, to help him test every sentence in it that contained any tangible suggestion for action in the shops, or out in the world at large. They agreed in the end that it was mostly false information, and that what was true in it was the most trivial of commonplace observations in metallurgy or natural behavior.

Bahram thought this might be a disappointment to Khalid, but in fact, after all that had passed, he actually seemed pleased at these results, even reassured. Suddenly Bahram understood: Khalid would have been shocked if something magical had occurred, shocked and disappointed, for that would have rendered irregular and unfathomable the very order that he now assumed must exist in nature. So he watched all the tests fail with grim satisfaction, and put the old book containing the wisdom of Hermes Trimestigus high on a shelf with all its brethren, and ignored them from then on. After that it was only his blank books that he cared about, filling them immediately after his demonstrations, and later through the long nights; they lay open everywhere, mostly on the tables and floors of his study. One cold night when Bahram was out for a walk around the compound, he went into Khalid's study and found the old man asleep on his couch, and he pulled a blanket over him and snuffed most of the lamps, but by the light of the one left burning, he looked at the big books open on the floor. Khalid's left-handed writing was jagged to the point of illegibility, a private code, but the little sketched drawings were rather fine in their abrupt way: a cross section of an eyeball, a big cart, bands of light, cannonball flights, bird's wings, gearing systems, lists of many varieties of damasked steel, athanor interiors, thermometers, altimeters, clockworks of all kinds, little stick figures fighting with swords or hanging from giant spirals like linden seeds, leering nightmare faces, tigers couchant or rampant, roaring at the scribbles from the margins.

Too cold to look at any more pages, Bahram stared at the sleeping old man, his father-in-law whose brain was so crowded. Strange the people who surround us in this life. He stumbled back to bed and the warmth of Esmerine.

The Speed of Light

The many tests of light in a prism brought back to Khalid the question of how fast it moved, and despite the frequent visits from Nadir or his minions, he could only speak of making a demonstration to determine this speed. Finally he made his arrangements for a test of the matter: they were to divide into two parties, with lanterns in hand, and Khalid's party would bring along his most accurate timing clock, which now could be stopped instantly with the push of a lever that blocked its movement. A preliminary trial had determined that during the dark of the moon, the biggest lanterns' light could be seen from the top of Afrasiab Hill to the Shamiana Ridge, across the river valley, about ten li as the crow flies. Using small bonfires blocked and unblocked by rugs would no doubt have extended the maximum distance visible, but Khalid did not think it would be necessary.

They therefore went out at midnight during the next dark of the moon, Bahram with Khalid and Paxtakor and several other servants to Afrasiab Hill, Iwang and Jalil and other servants to the Shamiana Ridge. Their lanterns had doors that would drop open in an oiled groove at a speed they had timed, and was as close to an instantaneous reply as they could devise. Khalid's team would reveal a light and start the clock; when Iwang's team saw the light, they would open their lantern, and when Khalid's team saw its light, they would stop the clock. A very straightforward test.

It was a long walk to Afrasiab Hill, over the old east bridge, up a track through the ruins of the ancient city of Afrasiab, dim but visible in the starlight. The dry night air was lightly scented with verbena and rosemary and mint. Khalid was in good spirits, as always before a demonstration. He saw Paxtakor and the servants taking pulls from a bag of wine and said, "You suck harder than our void pump, be careful or you'll suck the Buddhist void into existence, and we will all pop into your bag."

Up on the flat treeless top of the hill, they stood and waited for Iwang's crew to reach Shamiana Ridge, black against the stars. The peak of Afrasiab Hill, when seen from Shamiana, had the mountains of the Dzhizak Range behind it, so that Iwang would see no stars on top of Afrasiab to confuse him, but merely the black mass of the empty Dzhizaks.

They had left marker sticks on the hill's top pointing to the opposite station, and now Khalid grunted impatiently and said, "Let's see if they're there yet."

Bahram faced Shamiana Ridge and dropped open the box lantern's door, then waved it back and forth. In a moment they saw the yellow gleam of Iwang's lantern, perfectly visible just below the black line of the ridge. "Good," Khalid said. "Now cover." Bahram pulled up his door, and Iwang's lantern went dark as well.

Bahram stood on Khalid's left. The clock and lantern were set on a folding table, and fixed together in an armature that would open the door of the lantern and start the finger of the clock in one motion. Khalid's forefinger was on the tab that would stop the clock short. Khalid muttered. "Now," and Bahram, his heart pounding absurdly, flicked the armature tab down, and the light on Iwang's lantern appeared on the Shamiana Ridge in that very same moment. Surprised, Khalid swore and stopped the clock. "Allah preserve us!" he exclaimed. "I was not ready. Let's do it again."

They had arranged to make twenty trials, so Bahram merely nodded while Khalid checked the clock by a shielded second lantern, and had Paxtakor mark down the time, which was two beats and a third.

They tried it again, and again the light appeared from Iwang the same moment Bahram opened their lantern. Once Khalid became used to the speed of the exchange, the trials all took less than a beat. For Bahram it was as if he were opening the door on the lantern across the valley; it was shocking how fast Iwang was, not to mention the light. Once he even pretended to open the door, pushing lightly then stopping, to see if the Tibetan was perhaps reading his mind.

"All right," Khalid said after the twentieth trial. "It's a good thing we're only doing twenty. We would get so good we would begin to see theirs before we opened ours."

Everyone laughed. Khalid had gotten snappish during the trials themselves, but now he seemed content, and they were relieved. They made their way down the hill to town talking loudly and drinking from the wine bag, even Khalid, who very seldom drank anymore, though it had once been one of his chief pleasures. They had tested their reflexes back in the compound, and so knew that most of their trials had been timed at that very same speed, or faster. "If we throw out the first trial, and average the rest, it's going to be about the same speed as our procedure itself."

Bahram said, "Light must be instantaneous."

"Instantaneous motion? Infinite speed? I don't think Iwang will ever agree to that notion, certainly not as a result of this demonstration alone."

"What do you think?"

"Me? I think we need to be farther apart. But we have demonstrated that light is fast, no doubt of that."

They traversed the empty ruins of Afrasiab by taking the ancient city's main north-south road to the bridge. The servants began to hurry ahead, leaving Khalid and Bahram behind.

Khalid was humming unmusically, and hearing it, remembering the full pages of the old man's notebooks, Bahram said, "How is it you are so happy these days, Father?"

Khalid looked at him, surprised. "Me? I'm not happy."

"But you are!"

Khalid laughed. "My Bahram, you are a simple soul."

Suddenly he waved his right wrist with its stump under Bahram's nose. "Look at this, boy. Look at this! How could I be happy with this? Of course I couldn't. It's dishonor, it's all my stupidity and greed, right there for everyone to see and remember, every day. Allah is wise, even in his punishments. I am dishonored forever in this life, and will never be able to recover from it. Never eat cleanly, never clean myself cleanly, never stroke Fedwa's hair at night. That life is over. And all because of fear, and pride. Of course I'm ashamed, of course I'm angry—at Nadir, the khan, at myself, at Allah, yes Him too! At all of you! I'll never stop being angry, never!"

"Ah," Bahram said, shocked.

They walked along a while in silence, through the starlit ruins.

Khalid sighed. "But look you, youth—given all that—what am I supposed to do? I'm only fifty years old, I have some time left before Allah takes me, and I have to fill that time. And I have my pride, despite all. And people are watching me, of course. I was a prominent man, and people enjoyed watching my fall, of course they did, and they watch still! So what kind of story am I going to give them next? Because that's what we are to other people, boy, we are their gossip. That's all civilization is, a giant mill grinding out gossip. And so I could be the story of the man who rode high and fell hard, and had his spirit broken and crawled off into a hole like a dog, to die as soon as he could manage it. Or I could be the story of a man who rode high and fell hard, and then got up defiant, and walked away in a new direction. Someone who never looked back, someone who never gave the mob any satisfaction. And that's the story I'm going to make them all eat. They can fuck themselves if they want any other kind of a story out of me. I'm a tiger, boy, I was a tiger in a previous existence, I must have been, I dream about it all the time, stalking through trees and hunting things. Now I have my tiger hitched to my chariot, and off we go!" He skimmed his left hand off toward the city ahead of them. "This is the key, youth, you must learn to hitch your tiger to your chariot."

Bahram nodded. "Demonstrations to make."

"Yes! Yes!" Khalid stopped and gestured up at the spangle of stars. "And this is the best part, boy, the most marvelous thing, because it is all so very damned interesting! It isn't just something to while away the time, or to get away from this," waving his stump again, "it's the only thing that matters! I mean, why are we here, youth? Why are we here?"

"To make more love."

"All right, fair enough. But how do we best love this world Allah gave us? We do it by learning it! It's here, all of a piece, beautiful every morning, and we go and rub it in the dust, making our khans and our caliphates and such. It's absurd. But if you try to understand things, if you look at the world and say, why does that happen, why do things fall, why does the sun come up every morning and shine on us, and warm the air and fill the leaves with green—how does all this happen? What rules has Allah used to make this beautiful world?—Then it is all transformed. God sees that you appreciate it. And even if He doesn't, even if you never know anything in the end, even if it's impossible to know, you can still try."

"And you're learning a lot," Bahram said.

"Not really. Not at all. But with a mathematician like Iwang on hand, we can maybe figure out a few simple things, or make little beginnings to pass on to others. This is God's real work, Bahram. God didn't give us this world for us to stand around in it chewing our food like camels. Muhammad himself said, 'Pursue learning even if it take you to China!' And now with Iwang, we have brought China to us. It makes it all the more interesting."

"So you are happy, you see? Just like I said."

"Happy and angry. Happily angry. Everything, all at once. That's life, boy. You just keep getting fuller, until you burst and Allah takes you and casts your soul into another life later on. And so everything just keeps getting fuller."

An early cock crowed on the edge of the town. In the sky to the east the stars were winking out. The servants reached Khalid's compound ahead of them and opened up, but Khalid stopped outside among the great piles of charcoal, looking around with evident satisfaction. "There's Iwang now," he said quietly.

The big Tibetan slouched up to them like a bear, body weary but a grin on his face.

"Well?" he said.

"Too fast to measure," Khalid admitted.

Iwang grunted.

Khalid handed him the wine bag, and he took a long swig.

"Light," he said. "What can you say?"

The eastern sky was filling with this mysterious substance or quality. Iwang swayed side to side like a bear dancing to music, as obviously happy as Bahram had ever seen him. The two old men had enjoyed their night's work. Iwang's party had had a night of mishaps, drinking wine, getting lost, falling in ditches, singing songs, mistaking other lights for Khalid's lantern, and then, during the tests, having no idea what kind of times were being registered back on Afrasiab Hill, an ignorance which had struck them funny. They had gotten silly.

But these adventures were not the source of Iwang's good humor—rather it was some train of thought of his own, which had put him under a description, as the Sufis said, murmuring things in his own language, hummed deep in his chest. The servants were singing a song for the coming of dawn.

He said to Khalid and Bahram, "Coming down the ridge I was falling asleep on my feet, and thinking about your demonstration cast me into a vision. Thinking of your light, winking in the darkness across the valley, I thought, If I could see all moments at once, each distinct and alone as the world sailed through the stars, each that little bit different . . . if I moved through each moment as if through different rooms in space, I could map the world's own travel. Every step I took down the ridge was as it were a separate world, a slice of infinity made up of that step's world. So I stepped from world to world, step by step, never seeing the ground in the dark, and it seemed to me that if there was a number that would bespeak the location of each footfall, then the whole ridge would be revealed thereby, by drawing a line from one footfall to the next. Our blind feet do it instinctively in the dark, and we are equally blind to the ultimate reality, but we could nevertheless grasp the whole by regular touches. Then we could say, This is what is there, or that, trusting that there were no great boulders or potholes between steps, and so the whole shape of the ridge would be known. With every step I walked from world to world."

He looked at Khalid. "Do you see what I mean?"

"Maybe," Khalid said. "You propose to chart movement with numbers."

"Yes, and also the movement within movement, changes in speed, you know, which must always be occurring in this world, as there is resistance or encouragement."

"Resistance of air," Khalid said luxuriously. "We live at the bottom of an ocean of air. It has weight, as the mercury scales have shown. It bears down on us. It carries the beams of the sun to us."

"Which warm us," Bahram added.

The sun cracked the distant mountains to the east, and Bahram said, "All praise and thanks to Allah for the glorious sun, sign in this world of his infinite love."

"And so," Khalid said, yawning hugely, "to bed."

A Demonstration of Flight

Inevitably, however, all their various activities brought them another visit from Nadir Divanbegi. This time Bahram was in the bazaar, sack over his shoulder, buying melons, oranges, chickens, and rope, when Nadir suddenly appeared before him with his personal bodyguard. It was an event Bahram could not regard as a coincidence.

"Well met, Bahram. I hear you are busy these days."

"Always, Effendi," Bahram said, ducking his head. The two bodyguards were eyeing him like falcons, wearing armor and carrying long-barreled muskets.

"And these many fine activities must include many undertaken for the sake of Sayyed Abdul Aziz Khan, and the glory of Samarqand?"

"Of course, Effendi."

"Tell me about them," Nadir said. "List them for me, and tell me how each one is progressing."

Bahram gulped apprehensively. Of course Nadir had nabbed him in a public place like this because he thought he would learn more from Bahram than from Khalid or Iwang, and more in a public space, where Bahram might be too flustered to prevaricate.

So he frowned and tried to look serious but foolish, not really much of a stretch at this moment. "They do much that I don't understand, Effendi. But the work seems to fall roughly into the camps of weapons and of fortifications."

Nadir nodded, and Bahram gestured at the melon market they were standing beside. "Do you mind?"

"Not at all," Nadir said, following him in.

So Bahram went to the honey and muskmelon trays, and began to lift some onto the scale. He was certainly going to get a good deal for them with Nadir Divanbegi and his bodyguards in the shop!

"In weapons," Bahram improvised as he pointed out the red melons to a sullen seller, "we are working on strengthening the metal of cannon barrels, so they can be both lighter and stronger. Then again, we have been conducting demonstrations of the flight of cannonballs in different conditions, with different gunpowders and guns, you know, and recording them and studying the results, so that one would be able to determine where precisely one's shots would land."

Nadir said, "That would be useful indeed. Have they done that?"

"They are working on it, Effendi."

"And fortifications?"

"Strengthening walls," Bahram said simply. Khalid would be furious to hear of all these promises Bahram was so rashly making, but Bahram did not see any good way out of it, except to make his descriptions as vague as possible, and hope for the best.

"Of course," Nadir said. "Please do me the courtesy of arranging one of these famous demonstrations for the court's edification." He caught Bahram's eye to emphasize this was not a casual invitation. "Soon."

"Of course, Effendi."

"Something that will get the khan's attention as well. Something exciting to him."

"Of course."

Nadir gestured with a finger to his men, and they moved off through the bazaar, leaving behind a swirling wake in the press of the crowd.

Bahram heaved a deep breath, wiped his brow. "Hey, there," he said sternly to the seller, who was slipping a melon off the scale.

"Not fair," the seller said.

"True," Bahram said, "but a deal's a deal."

The seller couldn't deny it; in fact he grinned under his moustache as Bahram sighed again.

———

Bahram went back to the compound and reported the exchange to Khalid, who growled to hear it, as Bahram knew he would. Khalid finished eating his evening meal in silence, stabbing chunks of rabbit out of a bowl with a small silver prong held in his left hand. He put the prong down and wiped his face with a cloth, rose heavily. "Come to my study and tell me exactly what you said to him."

Bahram repeated the conversation as closely as he could, while Khalid spun a leather globe on which he had tried to map the world. Most of it he had left blank, dismissing the claims of the Chinese cartographers he had studied, their golden islands swimming about in the ocean to the east of Nippon, located differently on every map. He sighed when Bahram finished. "You did well," he said. "Your promises were vague, and they follow good lines. We can pursue them more or less directly, and they may even tell us some things we wanted to know anyway."

"More demonstrations," Bahram said.

"Yes." Khalid brightened at the thought.

In the weeks that followed, the furor of activity in the compound took a new turn. Khalid took out all the cannon he had obtained from Nadir, and the loud booms of the guns filled their days. Khalid and Iwang and Bahram and the gunpowder artisans from the shop fired the big things west of the city on the plain, where they could relocate the cannonballs, after shots aimed at targets that were very seldom struck.

Khalid growled, picking up one of the ropes they used to pull the gun back up to the mark. "I wonder if we could stake the gun to the ground," he said. "Strong ropes, thick stakes . . . it might make the balls fly farther."

"We can try it."

They tried all manner of things. At the end of the days their ears rang with reverberations, and Khalid took to stuffing them with cotton balls to protect them some little bit.

Iwang became more and more absorbed in the flights of the cannonballs. He and Khalid conferred over mathematical formulas and diagrams that Bahram did not understand. It seemed to Bahram they were losing sight of the goal of the exercise, and treating the gun merely as a mechanism for making demonstrations of motion, of speed and the change of speed.

But then Nadir came calling with news. The khan and his retinue were to visit the next day, to witness improvements and discoveries.

Khalid spent the entire night awake in his study, making lists of demonstrations to be considered. The next day at noon everyone congregated on the sunny plain beside the Zeravshan River. A big pavilion was set up for the khan to rest under while he observed events.

He did so lying on a couch covered with silks, spooning sherbet and talking with a young courtesan more than watching the demonstrations. But Nadir stood by the guns and watched everything very closely, taking the cotton out of his ears to ask questions after every shot.

"As to fortifications," Khalid replied to him at one point, "this is an old matter, solved by the Frengis before they died. A cannonball will break anything hard." He had his men shoot the gun at a wall of dressed stone that they had cemented together. The ball shattered the wall very nicely, and the khan and his party cheered, although as a matter of fact both Samarqand and Bokhara were protected by sandstone walls much like the one that had just fallen.

"Now," Khalid said. "See what happens when a ball of the same size, from the same gun loaded with the same charge, strikes the next target."

This was an earthen mound, dug at great effort by Khalid's expuffers. The gun was fired, the acrid smoke cleared; the earthen mound stood unchanged, except for a barely visible scar at its center.

"The cannonball can do nothing. It merely sinks into the dirt and is swallowed up. A hundred balls would make no difference to such a wall. They would merely become part of it."

The khan heard this and was not amused. "You're suggesting we pile dirt all around Samarqand? Impossible! It would be too ugly! The other khans and emirs would laugh at us. We cannot live like ants in an anthill!"

Khalid turned to Nadir, his face a polite blank.

"Next?" Nadir said.

"Of course. Now see, we have determined that at the distances a gun can cast a ball, it cannot shoot straight. The balls are tumbling through the air, and they can spin off in any direction, and they do."

"Surely air cannot offer any significant resistance to iron," Nadir said, sweeping a hand in illustration.

"Only a little resistance, it is true, but consider that the ball passes through more than two lis of air. Think of air as a kind of thinned water. It certainly has an effect. We can see this better with light wooden balls of the same size, thrown by hand so you can still see their movement. We will throw into the wind, and you can see how the balls dart this way and that."

Bahram and Paxtakor palmed the light wooden balls off, and they veered into the wind like bats.

"But this is absurd!" the khan said. "Cannonballs are much heavier, they cut through the wind like knives through butter!"

Khalid nodded. "Very true, great Khan. We only use these wooden balls to exaggerate an effect that must act on any object, be it heavy as lead."

"Or gold," Sayyed Abdul Aziz joked.

"Or gold. In that case the cannonballs veer only slightly, but over the great distances they are cast, it becomes significant. And so one can never say exactly what the balls will hit."

"This must ever be true," Nadir said.

Khalid waved his stump, oblivious for the moment of how it looked. "We can reduce the effect quite a great deal. See how the wooden balls fly if they are cast with a spin to them."

Bahram and Paxtakor threw the balsam balls with a final pull of the fingertips to impart a spin to them. Though some of these balls curved in flight, they went farther and faster than the palmed balls had. Bahram hit an archery target with five throws in a row, which pleased him greatly.

"The spin stabilizes their flight through the wind," Khalid explained. "They are still pushed by the wind, of course. That cannot be avoided. But they no longer dart unexpectedly when they are caught on the face by a wind. It is the same effect you get by fletching arrows to spin."

"So you propose to fletch cannonballs?" the khan inquired with a guffaw.

"Not exactly, Your Highness, but yes, in effect. To try to get the same kind of spin. We have tried two different methods to achieve this. One is to cut grooves into the balls. But this means the balls fly much less far. Another is to cut the grooves into the inside of the gun barrel, making a long spiral down the barrel, only a turn or a bit less down the whole barrel's length. This makes the balls leave the gun with a spin."

Khalid had his men drag out a smaller cannon. A ball was fired from it, and the ball tracked down by the helpers standing by, then marked with a red flag. It was farther away than the bigger gun's ball, though not by much.

"It is not distance so much as accuracy that would be improved," Khalid explained. "The balls would always fly straight. We are working up tables that would enable one to choose the gunpowder by type and weight, and weigh the balls, and thus, with the same cannons, of course, always send the balls precisely where one wanted to."

"Interesting," Nadir said.

Sayyed Abdul Aziz Khan called Nadir to his side. "We're going back to the palace," he said, and led his retinue to the horses.

"But not that interesting," Nadir said to Khalid. "Try again."

Better Gifts for the Khan

"I suppose I should make the khan a new suit of damasked armor," Khalid said afterward. "Something pretty."

Iwang grinned. "Do you know how to do it?"

"Of course. It's watered steel. Not very mysterious. The crucible charge is an iron sponge called a wootz, forged into an iron plate together with wood, which yields its ash into the mix, and some water too. Some crucibles are placed in the furnace, and when they are melted their contents are poured into molten cast iron, at a temperature below that of complete fusion of the two elements. The resulting steel is then etched with a mineral sulfate of one kind or another. You get different patterns and colors depending on which sulfate you use, and what kind of wootz, and what kind of temperatures. This blade here"—he rose and took down a thick curved dagger with an ivory handle, and a blade covered with a dense pattern of cross-hatchings in white and dark gray—"is a good example of the etching called 'Muhammad's Ladder.' Persian work, reputed to be from the forge of the alchemist Jundi-Shapur. They say there is alchemy in it." He paused, shrugged.

"And you think the khan . . ."

"If we systematically played with the composition of the wootz, the structure of the cakes, the temperatures, the etching liquid, then we would certainly find some new patterns. I like some of the swirls I've gotten with very woody steel."

The silence stretched out. Khalid was unhappy, that was clear.

Bahram said, "You could treat it as a series of tests."

"As always," Khalid said, irritated. "But in this case you can only do things in ignorance of their causes. There are too many materials, too many substances and actions, all mixed together. I suppose it is all happening at a level too small to see. The breaks you see after the casting look like crystalline structures when they are broken. It's interesting, what happens, but there's no way to tell why, or predict it ahead of time. This is the thing about a useful demonstration, you see. It tells you something distinct. It answers a question."

"We can try to ask questions that steelwork can answer," Bahram suggested.

Khalid nodded, still dissatisfied. But he glanced at Iwang to see what he thought of this.

Iwang thought it was a good idea in theory, but in practice, he too had a hard time coming up with questions to ask about the process. They knew how hot to make the furnace, what ores and wood and water to introduce, how long to mix it, how hard it would turn out. All questions on the matter of practice were long since answered, ever since damasking had been done in Damascus. More basic questions of cause, which yet could be answered, were hard to formulate. Bahram himself tried mightily, without a single idea coming to him. And good ideas were his strength, or so they always told him.

While Khalid worked on this problem, Iwang was getting terrifically absorbed in his mathematical labors, to the exclusion even of his glassblowing and silversmithing, which he left mostly to his new apprentices, huge gaunt Tibetan youths who had appeared without explanation some time before. He pored over his Hindi books and old Tibetan scrolls, marking up his chalk slates and then adding to the notes he saved on paper: inked diagrams, patterns of Hindi numerals, Chinese or Tibetan or Sanskrit symbols or letters; a private alphabet for a private language, or so Bahram thought. A rather useless enterprise, disturbing to contemplate, as the paper sheets seemed to radiate a palpable power, magical or perhaps just mad. All those foreign ideas, arranged in hexagonal patterns of number and ideogram; to Bahram the shop in the bazaar began to seem the dim cave of a magus, fingering the hems of reality . . .

Iwang himself brushed all these cobwebs aside. Out in the sun of Khalid's compound he sat down with Khalid, and Zahhar and Tazi from Sher Dor, and with Bahram shading them and looking over their shoulders, he outlined a mathematics of motion, what he called the speed-of-the-speed.

"Everything is moving," he said. "That is karma. The Earth revolves around the Sun, the Sun travels through the stars, the stars too travel. But for the sake of study here, for demonstrations, we postulate a realm of nonmovement. Perhaps some such motionless void contains the universe, but it doesn't matter; for our purposes these are purely mathematical dimensions, which can be marked by vertical and horizontal, thusly, or by length, breadth, and height, if you want the three dimensions of the world. But start with two dimensions, for simplicity's sake. And moving objects, say a cannonball, can be measured against these two dimensions. How high or low, how left or right. Placed as if on a map. Then again, the horizontal dimension can mark time passed, and the vertical movement in a single direction. That will make for curved lines, representing the passage of objects through the air. Then, lines drawn tangent to the curve indicate the speed of the speed. So you measure what you can, mark those measurements, and it's like passing through rooms of a house. Each room has a different volume, like flasks, depending on how wide and how tall. That is to say, how far, in how much time. Quantities of movement, do you see? A bushel of movement, a dram."

"Cannonball flights could be described precisely," Khalid said.

"Yes. More easily than most things, because a cannonball pursues a single line. A curved line, but not something like an eagle's flight, say, or a person in his daily rounds. The mathematics for that would be . . ." Iwang became lost, jerked, came back to them. "What was I saying?"

"Cannonballs."

"Ah. Very possible to measure them, yes."

"Meaning if you knew the speed of departure from the gun, and the angle of the gun . . ."

"You could say pretty closely where it was going to land, yes."

"We should tell Nadir about this privately."

Khalid worked up a set of tables for calculating cannonfire, with artful drawings of the curves describing the flight of shot, and a little Tibetan book filled with Iwang's careful numerics. These items were placed in an ornate carved ironwood box, encrusted with silver, turquoise, and lapis, and brought to the Khanaka in Bokhara, along with a gorgeous damasked breastplate for the khan. The steel rectangle at the center of this breastplate was a dramatic swirl of white and gray steel, with iron flecks very lightly etched by a treatment of sulphuric acids and other caustics. The pattern was called by Khalid the "Zeravshan Eddies," and indeed the swirl resembled a standing eddy in the river, spinning off the foundation of the Dagbit Bridge whenever the water was high. It was one of the handsomest pieces of metalwork Bahram had ever seen, and it seemed to him that it, and the decorated box filled with Iwang's mathematics, made for a very impressive set of gifts for Sayyed Abdul Aziz.

He and Khalid dressed in their best finery for their audience, and Iwang joined them in the dark red robes and conical winged hat of a Tibetan monk, indeed a lama of the highest distinction. So the presenters were as impressive as their presents, Bahram thought; although once in the Registan, under the vast arch of the gold-covered Tilla Kari Madressa, he felt less imposing. And once in the company of the court he felt slightly plain, even shabby, as if they were children pretending to be courtiers, or, simply, bumpkins.

The khan, however, was delighted by the breastplate, and praised Khalid's art highly, even putting the piece on over his finery and leaving it there. The box he also admired, while handing the papers inside to Nadir.

After a few moments more they were dismissed, and Nadir guided them to the Tilla Kari garden. The diagrams were very interesting, he said as he looked them over; he wanted to inquire more closely into them; meanwhile, the khan had been informed by his armorers that cutting a spiral into the insides of their cannon barrels had caused one to explode on firing, the rest to lose range. So Nadir wanted Khalid to visit the armorers and speak to them about it.

Khalid nodded easily, though Bahram could see the thought in his eyes; once again he would be taken away from what he wanted to be doing. Nadir did not see this, though he watched Khalid's face closely. In fact, he went on cheerfully to say how much the khan appreciated Khalid's great wisdom and craft, and how much all the people of the khanate and in Dar al-Islam generally would owe to Khalid if, as seemed likely, his efforts helped them to stave off any further encroachments of the Chinese, reputed to be on the march in the west borders of their empire. Khalid nodded politely, and the men were dismissed.

Walking back out the river road, Khalid was irritated. "This trip accomplished nothing."

"We don't know yet," Iwang said, and Bahram nodded.

"We do. The khan is a . . ." He sighed. "And Nadir clearly thinks of us as his servants."

"We are all servants of the khan," Iwang reminded him.

That silenced him.

As they came back toward Samarqand, they passed by the ruins of old Afrasiab. "If only we had the Sogdian kings again," Bahram said.

Khalid shook his head. "Those are not the ruins of the Sogdian kings, but of Markanda, which stood here before Afrasiab. Alexander the Great called it the most beautiful city he ever conquered."

"And look at it now," Bahram said. Dusty old foundations, broken walls . . .

Iwang said, "Samarqand too will come to this."

"So it doesn't matter if we are at Nadir's beck and call?" Khalid snapped.

"Well, it too will pass," Iwang said.

Jewels in the Sky

Nadir asked for more and more of Khalid's time, and Khalid grew very restive. One time he went to Divanbegi with a proposal to build a complete system of drains underneath both Bokhara and Samarqand, to move the water of the scores of stagnant pools that dotted both cities, especially Bokhara. This would keep the water from becoming foul, and decrease the number of mosquitoes and the incidence of disease, including the plague, which the Hindu caravans reported to be devastating parts of Sind. Khalid suggested sequestering all travelers outside the city whenever they heard such news, and causing delays in caravans that came from affected areas, to be sure of cleanliness. A purification delay, analogous to the spiritual purifications of Ramadan.

But Nadir ignored all these ideas. An underground system of pipes, though common in Persia from before the invasions of the Mongols, was too expensive now to contemplate. Khalid was being asked for military aid, not physic. Nadir did not believe he knew anything about physic.

So Khalid returned to his compound and put the whole place to work on the khan's artillery, making every aspect of the cannons a matter for demonstrations, but without trying to learn anything of primary causes, as he called them, except occasionally in motion. He worked on metal strength with Iwang, and made use of Iwang's mathematics to do cannonflight studies, and tried a number of methods to cause the cannonballs to spiral reliably in flight.

All this was done with reluctance and ill-humor; and only in the afternoon, after a nap and a meal of yogurt, or late in the evening, after smoking from one of his narghiles, did he recover his equanimity, and pursue his studies with soap bubbles and prisms, air pumps and mercury scales. "If you can measure the weight of air you should be able to measure heat, up to temperatures far beyond what we can distinguish with our blisters and ouches."

Nadir sent his men by on a monthly basis to receive the latest news of Khalid's studies, and from time to time dropped by himself unannounced, throwing the compound into a flurry, like an anthill hit by water. Khalid was polite at all times, but complained to Bahram bitterly about the monthly request for news, particularly since they had very little. "I thought I escaped the moon curse when Fedwa went through menopause," he groused.

Ironically, these unwelcome visits were also losing him allies in the madressas, as he was thought to be favored by the treasurer, and he could not risk telling them the real situation. So there were cold looks, and slights in the bazaar and the mosque; also, many examples of grasping obsequiousness. It made him irritable, indeed sometimes he rose to a veritable fury of irritability. "A little power and you see how awful people are."

To keep him from plunging back into black melancholy, Bahram scoured the caravanserai for things that might please him, visiting the Hindus and the Armenians in particular, also the Chinese, and coming back with books, compasses, clocks, and a curious nested astrolabe, which purported to show that the six planets occupied orbits that filled polygons that were progressively simpler by one side, so that Mercury circled inside a decagon, Venus a nonagon just large enough to hold the decagon, Earth an octagon outside the nonagon, and so on up to Saturn, circling in a big square. This object astonished Khalid, and caused night-long discussions with Iwang and Zahhar about the disposition of the planets around the sun.

This new interest in astronomy quickly superseded all others in Khalid, and grew to a passion after Iwang brought by a curious device he had made in his shop, a long silver tube, hollow except for glass lenses placed in both ends. Looking through the tube, things appeared closer than they really were, with their detail more fine.

"How can that work?" Khalid demanded when he looked through it. The look of suprise on his face was that of the puppets in the bazaar, pure and hilarious. It made Bahram happy to see it.

"Like the prism?" Iwang suggested uncertainly.

Khalid shook his head. "Not that you can see things as bigger, or closer, but that you can see so much more detail! How can that be?"

"The detail must always be there in the light," Iwang said. "And the eye only powerful enough to discern part of it. I admit I am surprised, but consider, most people's eyes weaken as they age, especially for things close by. I know mine have. I made my first set of lenses to use as spectacles, you know, one for each eye, in a frame. But while I was assembling one I looked through the two lenses lined up together." He grinned, miming the action. "I was really very anxious to confirm that you two saw the same things I saw, to tell the truth. I couldn't quite believe my own eyes."

Khalid was looking through the thing again.

So now they looked at things. Distant ridges, birds in flight, approaching caravans. Nadir was shown the glass, and its military uses were immediately obvious to him. He took one they had made for him, encrusted with garnets, to the khan, and word came back that the khan was pleased. That did not ease the presence of the khanate in Khalid's compound, of course; on the contrary, Nadir mentioned casually that they were looking forward to the next remarkable development out of Khalid's shop, as the Chinese were said to be in a turmoil. Who knew where that kind of thing might end.

"It will never end," Khalid said bitterly when Nadir had gone. "It's like a noose that tightens with our every move."

"Feed him your discoveries in little pieces," Iwang suggested. "It will seem like there are more of them."

Khalid followed this advice, which gave him a little more time, and they worked on all manner of things that it seemed would help the khan's troops in battle. Khalid indulged his interest in primary causes mostly at night, when they trained the new spyglass on the stars, and later that month on the moon, which proved to be a very rocky, mountainous, desolate world, ringed by innumerable craters, as if fired upon by the cannon of some superemperor. Then on one memorable night they looked through the spyglass at Jupiter, and Khalid said, "By God it's a world too, clearly. Banded by latitude—and look, those three stars near it, they're brighter than stars. Could they be moons of Jupiter's?"

They could. They moved fast, around Jupiter, and the ones closer to Jupiter moved faster, just like the planets around the sun. Soon Khalid and Iwang had seen a fourth one, and mapped all four orbits, so that they could prepare new viewers to comprehend the sight, by looking at the diagrams first. They made it all into a book, another gift to the khan—a gift with no military use, but they named the moons after the khan's four oldest wives, and he liked that, it was clear. He was reported to have said, "Jewels in the sky! For me!"

Who Is the Stranger

There were factions in town who did not like them. When Bahram walked through the Registan, and saw the eyes watching him, the conversations begun or ended by his passage, he saw that he was part of a coterie or a faction, no matter how innocuous his behavior had been. He was related to Khalid, who was allied with Iwang and Zahhar, and together they formed part of Nadir Divanbegi's power. They were therefore Nadir's allies, even if he had forced them to it like wet pulp in a paper press; even if they hated him. Many other people in Samarqand hated Nadir, no doubt even more than Khalid did, as Khalid was under his protection, while these other people were his enemies: relatives of his dead or imprisoned or exiled foes, perhaps, or the losers of many earlier palace struggles. The khan had other advisors—courtiers, generals, relatives at court—all jealous of their own share of his regard, and envious of Nadir's great influence. Bahram had heard rumors from time to time of palace intrigues against Nadir, but he remained unaware of the details. The fact that their involuntary association with Nadir could cause them trouble elsewhere struck him as grossly unfair; the association itself was already trouble enough.

One day this sense of hidden enemies became more material: Bahram was visiting Iwang, and two qadis Bahram had never seen before appeared in the door of the Tibetan's shop, backed by two of the khan's soldiers, and a small gaggle of ulema from the Tilla Kari Madressa, demanding that Iwang produce his tax receipts.

"I am not a dhimmi," Iwang said with his customary calm.

The dhimmi, or people of the pact, were those nonbelievers who were born and lived their lives in the khanate, who had to pay a special tax. Islam was the religion of justice, and all Muslims were equal before God and the law; but of the lesser ones, women, slaves and the dhimmi, the dhimmi were the ones who could change their status by a simple decision to convert to true belief. Indeed there had been times in the past when it had been "the book or the sword" for all pagans, and only people of the book—Jews, Zoroastrians, Christians, and Sabians—had been allowed to keep their faith, if they insisted on it. Nowadays pagans of all sort were allowed to keep their various religions, as long as they were registered with the qadis, and paid the annual dhimma tax.

This was clear, and ordinary. Ever since the Shiite Safavids had come to the throne in Iran, however, the legal position of dhimmi had worsened—markedly in Iran, where the Shiite mullahs were so concerned with purity, but also in the khanates to the east, at least sometimes. It was a matter for discretion, really. As Iwang had once remarked, the uncertainty itself was a part of the tax.

"You are not a dhimmi?" one of the qadis said, surprised.

"No, I come from Tibet. I am mustamin."

The mustamin were foreign visitors, permitted to live in Muslim lands for specified periods of time.

"Do you have an aman?"

"Yes."

This was the safe-conduct pass issued to mustamin, renewed by the Khanaka on an annual basis. Now Iwang brought a sheet of parchment out of his back room, and showed it to the qadis. There were a number of wax seals at the bottom of the document, and the qadis inspected these closely.

"He's been here eight years!" one of them complained. "That's longer than allowed by the law."

Iwang shrugged impassively. "Renewal was granted this spring."

A heavy silence ruled as the men checked the document's seals again.

"A mustamin cannot own property," someone noted.

"Do you own this shop?" the chief qadi asked, surprised again.

"No," Iwang said. "Naturally not. Rental only."

"Monthly?"

"Lease by year. After my aman is renewed."

"Where are you from?"

"Tibet."

"You have a house there?"

"Yes. In Iwang."

"A family?"

"Brothers and sisters. No wives or children."

"So who's in your house?"

"Sister."

"When are you going back?"

A short pause. "I don't know."

"You mean you have no plans to return to Tibet."

"No, I plan to return. But—business has been good. Sister sends raw silver, I make it into things. This is Samarqand."

"And so business will always be good! Why would you ever leave? You should be dhimmi, you are a permanent resident here, a nonbelieving subject of the khan."

Iwang shrugged, gestured at the document. That was something Nadir had brought to the khanate, it occurred to Bahram, something from deep in the heart of Islam: the law was the law. Dhimmi and mustamin were both protected by contract, each in their way.

"He is not even one of the people of the book," one of the qadis said indignantly.

"We have many books in Tibet," Iwang said calmly, as if he had misunderstood.

The qadis were offended. "What is your religion?"

"I am Buddhist."

"So you don't believe in Allah, you don't pray to Allah."

Iwang did not reply.

"Buddhists are polytheists," one of them said. "Like the pagans Muhammad converted in Arabia."

Bahram stepped before them. " 'There is no compulsion in religion,' " he recited hotly. " 'To you your religion, to me my religion.' That's what the Quran tells us!"

The visitors stared at him coldly.

"Are you not Muslim?" one said.

"I certainly am! You would know it if you knew the Sher Dor mosque! I've never seen you there—where do you pray on Friday?"

"Tilla Kari Mosque," the qadi said, angry now.

This was interesting, as the Tilla Kari Madressa was the center for the Shiite study group, which was opposed to Nadir.

" 'Al-kufou millatun wahida,' " one of them said; a counterquote, as theologians called it. Unbelief is one religion.

"Only digaraz can make complaint to the law," Bahram snapped back. Digaraz were those who spoke without grudge or malice, disinterested Muslims. "You don't qualify."

"Neither do you, young man."

"You come here! Who sent you? You challenge the law of the aman, who gives you the right? Get out of here! You have no idea what this man does for Samarqand! You attack Sayyed Abdul himself here, you attack Islam itself! Get out!"

The qadis did not move, but something in their gazes had grown more guarded. Their leader said, "Next spring we will talk again," with a glance at Iwang's aman. With a wave of his hand that was just like the khan's, he led the others out and down the narrow passage of the bazaar.

For a long while the two friends stood silently in the shop, awkward with each other.

Finally Iwang sighed. "Did not Muhammad set laws concerning the way men should be treated in Dar al-Islam?"

"God set them. Muhammad only transmitted them."

"All free men equal before the law. Women, children, slaves, and unbelievers less under the law."

"Equal beings, but they all have their particular rights, protected by law."

"But not as many rights as those of Muslim free men."

"They are not as strong, so their rights are not so burdensome. They are all people to be protected by Muslim free men, upholding God's laws."

Iwang pursed his lips. Finally he said, "God is the force moving in everything. The shapes things take when they move."

"God is love moving through all," Bahram agreed. "The Sufis say this."

Iwang nodded. "God is a mathematician. A very great and subtle mathematician. As our bodies are to the crude furnaces and stills of your compound, so God's mathematics is to our mathematics."

"So you agree there is a God? I thought Buddha denied there was any God."

"I don't know. I suppose some Buddhists might say not. Being springs out of the Void. I don't know, myself. If there is only the Void enveloping all we see, where did the mathematics come from? It seems to me it could be the result of something thinking."

Bahram was surprised to hear Iwang say this. And he could not be quite sure how sincere Iwang was, given what had just happened with the qadis from Tilla Kari. Although it made sense, in that it was obviously impossible that such an intricate and glorious thing as the world could have come to pass without some very great and loving God to make it.

"You should come to the Sufi fellowship, and listen to what my teacher there says," Bahram finally said, smiling at the thought of the big Tibetan in their group. Although their teacher would probably like it.

Bahram returned to the compound by way of the western caravanserai, where the Hindu traders were camped in their smell of incense and milktea. Bahram completed the other business he had there, buying scents and bags of calcinated minerals for Khalid, and then when he saw Dol, an acquaintance from Ladakh, he joined him and sat with him and drank tea for a while, then rakshi, looking over the trader's pallets of spices and small bronze figurines. Bahram gestured at the detailed little statues. "Are these your gods?"

Dol looked at him, surprised and amused. "Some are gods, yes. This is Shiva—this Kali, the destroyer—this Ganesh."

"An elephant god?"

"This is how we picture him. They have other forms."

"But an elephant?"

"Have you ever seen an elephant?"

"No."

"They're impressive."

"I know they're big."

"It's more than that."

Bahram sipped his tea. "I think Iwang might convert to Islam."

"Trouble with his aman?"

Dol laughed at Bahram's expression, urged him to drink from the jar of rakshi.

Bahram obliged him, then persisted. "Do you think it's possible to change religions?"

"Many people have."

"Could you? Could you say, There is only one God?" Gesturing at the figurines.

Dol smiled. "They are all aspects of Brahman, you know. Behind all, the great God Brahman, all one in him."

"So Iwang could be like that too. He might already believe in the one great God, the God of Gods."

"He could. God manifests in different ways to different people."

Bahram sighed.

Bad Air

Bahram had just gone inside the compound gate, and was on his way to tell Khalid about the incident at Iwang's, when the door of the chemical shed burst open and men crashed out, chased by a shouting Khalid and a dense cloud of yellow smoke. Bahram turned and ran for the house, intending to grab Esmerine and the children, but they were out and running already, and he followed them through the main gate, everyone shrieking, and then, as the cloud descended on them, dropping to the ground and crawling away like rats, coughing and hacking and spitting and crying. They rolled down the hill, throats and eyes burning, lungs aching with the caustic stink of the poisonous yellow cloud. Most of them followed Khalid's lead and plunged their heads into the river, emerging only to puff shallow breaths, and then dunk themselves again.

When the cloud had dispersed and he had recovered a little, Khalid began to curse.

"What was it?" Bahram said, coughing still.

"A crucible of acid exploded. We were testing it."

"For what?"

Khalid didn't answer. Slowly the caustic burn of their delicate membranes cooled. The wet and unhappy crew straggled back into the compound. Khalid set some of the men to clean up the shed, and Bahram went with him into his study, where he changed his clothes and washed, then wrote notes in his big book, presumably about the failed demon-stration.

Except it had not been completely a failure, or so Bahram began to gather from Khalid's muttering.

"What were you trying to do?"

Khalid did not answer directly. "It seems certain to me that there are different kinds of air," he said instead. "Different constituents, perhaps, as in metals. Only all invisible to the eye. We smell the differences, some-times. And some can kill, as at the bottom of wells. It isn't an absence of air, in those cases, but a bad kind of air, or part of air. The heaviest no doubt. And different distillations, different burnings . . . you can sup-press or stoke a fire . . . Anyway, I thought that sal ammoniac and salt-peter and sulphur mixed, would make a different air. And it did, too, but too much of it, too fast. Like an explosion. And clearly a poison." He coughed uncomfortably. "It is like the Chinese alchemists' recipe for wan-jen-ti, which Iwang says means 'killer of myriads.' I supposed I could show Nadir this reaction, and propose it as a weapon. You could perhaps kill a whole army with it."

They regarded the thought silently.

"Well," Bahram said, "it might help him keep his own position more secure with the khan."

He explained what he had witnessed at Iwang's.

"And so you think Nadir is in trouble at the court?"

"Yes."

"And you think Iwang might convert to Islam?"

"He seemed to be asking about it."

Khalid laughed, then coughed painfully. "That would be odd."

"People don't like to be laughed at."

"Somehow I don't think Iwang would mind."

"Did you know that's the name of his town, Iwang?"

"No. Is it?"

"Yes. So he seemed to say."

Khalid shrugged.

"It means we don't know his real name."

Another shrug. "None of us know our real names."

Love the Size of the World

The fall harvests came and passed, and the caravanserai emptied for the winter, when the passes to the east would close. Bahram's days were enriched by Iwang's presence at the Sufi ribat, where Iwang sat at the back and listened closely to all that the old master Ali said, very seldom speaking, and then only to ask the simplest questions, usually the meaning of one word or another. There were lots of Arabic and Persian words in the Sufi terminology, and though Iwang's Sogdi-Turkic was good, the religious language was opaque to him. Eventually the master gave Iwang a lexicon of Sufi technical terms, or istilahat, by Ansari, titled "One Hundred Fields and Resting Places," which had an introduction that ended with the sentence "The real essence of the spiritual states of the Sufis is such that expressions are not adequate to describe it: nevertheless, these expressions are fully understood by those who have experienced these states."

This, Bahram felt, was the main source of Iwang's problem: he had not experienced the states being described.

"Very possibly," Iwang would agree when Bahram said this to him. "But how am I to reach them?"

"With love," Bahram would say. "You must love everything that is, especially people. You will see, it is love that moves everything."

Iwang would purse his lips. "With love comes hate," he would say. "They are two sides of an excess of feeling. Compassion rather than love, that seems to me the best way. There is no bad obverse side to compassion."

"Indifference," Bahram suggested.

Iwang would nod, thinking things over. But Bahram wondered if he could ever come to the right view. The fount of Bahram's own love, like a powerful artesian spring in the hills, was his feeling for his wife and children, then for Allah, who had allowed him the privilege of living his life among such beautiful souls—not only the three of them, but Khalid and Fedwa and all their relatives, and the community of the compound, the mosque, the ribat, Sher Dor, and indeed all of Samarqand and the wide world, when he was feeling it. Iwang had no such starting point, being single and childless, as far as Bahram knew, and an infidel to boot. How was he to begin to feel the more generalized and diffuse loves, if the specific ones were not there for him?

"The heart which is greater than the intellect is not that which beats in the chest." So Ali would say. It was a matter of opening his heart to God, and letting the love appear from there first. Iwang was already good at calming himself, at paying attention to the world in its quiet moments, sitting out at the compound some dawns after he had spent the night on a couch in the shops. Bahram once or twice joined him in these sittings, and once he was inspired by a windless pure gold sky to recite from Rumi.

> How silent it has become in the house of the heart!
> The heart as hearth and home
> Has encompassed the world.

When Iwang finally responded, after the sun had broken over the eastern ridges and flooded the valley with buttered light, it was only to say, "I wonder if the world is as big as Brahmagupta said it was."

"He said it was a sphere, right?"

"Yes, of course. You can see that out on the steppes, when a caravan comes over the horizon heads first. We are on the surface of a great ball."

"The heart of God."

No reply but the swaying head, which meant that Iwang did not agree but did not want to disagree. Bahram desisted, and asked about the Hindu's estimate of the size of the earth, which was clearly what interested Iwang now.

"Brahmagupta noticed that the sun shone straight down a well in the Deccan on a certain day, and the next year he arranged to be a thousand yoganda north of there, and he measured the angle of the shadows, and used spherical geometry to calculate what percentage of the circle that arc of a thousand yoganda was. Very simple, very interesting."

Bahram nodded; no doubt true; but they would only ever see a small fraction of those yoganda, and here, now, Iwang was in need of spiritual illumination. Or—in need of love. Bahram invited him to eat with his family, to observe Esmerine serve the meals, and instruct the children in their manners. The children were a pleasure all their own, their liquid eyes huge in their faces as they stopped in their racing about to listen impatiently to Esmerine's lectures. Their racing about the compound was a pleasure as well. Iwang nodded at all this. "You're a lucky man," he told Bahram.

"We are all lucky men," Bahram replied. And Iwang agreed.

The Goddess and the Law

Parallel to his new religious studies, Iwang continued his investigations and demonstrations with Khalid. They devoted the greater portion of these efforts to their projects for Nadir and the khan. They worked out a long-range signaling system for the army that used mirrors and small telescopes; they also cast bigger and bigger cannons, with giant wagons to haul them by horse or camel train from one battlefield to the next.

"We will need cart roads for these, if we are ever to move them," Iwang noted. Even the great Silk Road itself was nothing but a camel track for most of its length.

Their latest private investigation into causes concerned a little telescope which magnified objects too small to be seen by the eye alone. The astronomers from the Ulug Bek Madressa had devised the thing, which could only be focused on a very narrow slice of air, so that translucent items caught between two plates of glass were best, lit by mirrored sunlight from below. Then new little worlds appeared, right under their fingers.

The three men spent hours looking through this telescope at pond water, which proved to be full of strangely articulated creatures, all swimming about. They looked at translucently thin slabs of stone, wood, and bone; and at their own blood, which was filled with blobs that were frighteningly like the animals in the pond water.

"The world just keeps getting smaller," Khalid marveled. "If we could draw the blood of those little creatures in our blood, and put it under a lens even more powerful than this one, I have no doubt that their blood would contain animalcules just like ours does; and so on for those animals as well, and down to . . ." He trailed off, awe giving him a dazed look. Bahram had never seen him so happy.

"There is probably some smallest possible size of things," Iwang said practically. "So the ancient Greeks postulated. The ultimate particulates, out of which all else is constructed. No doubt smaller than we will ever see."

Khalid frowned. "This is just a start. Surely stronger lenses will be made. And then who knows what will be seen. Maybe it will allow us to understand the composition of metals at last, and work the transmutations."

"Maybe," Iwang allowed. He stared into the eye of the lens, humming to himself. "Certainly the little crystals in granite are made clear."

Khalid nodded, wrote notes in one of his notebooks. He returned to the glass, then drew the shapes he saw on the page. "The very small and the very large," he said.

"These lenses are a great gift from God," Bahram said, "reminding us that it is all one world. One substance, all interpenetrated with structure, but still one, big to small."

Khalid nodded. "Thus the stars may have their sway over us after all. Maybe the stars are animals too, like these creatures, could we only see them better."

Iwang shook his head. "All one, yes. It seems more and more obvious. But not all animal, surely. Perhaps the stars are more like rocks than these fine creatures."

"The stars are fire."

"Rocks, fire—but not animals."

"But all one," Bahram insisted.

And both of the older men nodded, Khalid emphatically, Iwang reluctantly, and with a low humming in his throat.

After that day it seemed to Bahram that Iwang was always humming. He came to the compound and joined Khalid in his demonstrations, and went with Bahram to the ribat and listened to Ali's lectures, and whenever Bahram visited him in his shop he was playing with numbers, or clicking a Chinese abacus back and forth, and always distracted, always humming. On Fridays he came to the mosque and stood outside the door, listening to the prayers and the readings, facing Mecca and blinking at the sun, but never kneeling or prostrating or praying; and always humming.

Bahram did not think he should convert. Even if he had to move back to Tibet for a time and then return, it seemed clear to Bahram that he was no Muslim. And so it would not be right.

Indeed, as the weeks passed he began to seem more strange and foreign, rather than less; even more an unbeliever; performing little demonstrations for himself, that were like sacrifices to light, or magnetism, or the void, or gravity. An alchemist, precisely, but in an eastern tradition stranger than any Sufi's, as if he were not only reverting to Buddhism but going beyond it, back to Tibet's older religion, Bön as Iwang called it.

That winter he sat in his shop with Bahram, before the open fire of his furnace, hands extended to keep the fingers warm as they poked out of the glove ends like his little babies, smoking hashish from a long-stemmed pipe and handling it to Bahram occasionally, until the two men sat there watching the coals' film dance over the hot orange underneath. One night, deep in a snowstorm, Iwang went out to get more wood for the fire, and Bahram looked over at a movement and saw an old Chinese woman sitting by the stove, dressed in a red dress, with her hair pulled up in a knot on top of her head. Bahram jerked; the old woman turned her head and looked at him, and he saw her black eyes were filled with stars. He promptly fell off his stool, and groped to his feet to find her no longer there. When Iwang came back in the room and Bahram described her, Iwang shrugged, smiled slyly:

"There's lots of old women in this quarter of the city. This is where the poor people live, among them the widows, who have to sleep in their dead husband's shops on the floor, on the sufferance of the new owners, and do what they can to keep hunger from the door."

"But the red dress—her face—her eyes!"

"That all sounds like the goddess of the stove, actually. She appears next to the hearth, if you're lucky."

"I'm not smoking any more of your hashish."

Iwang laughed. "If only that was all it took!"

Another frosty night, a few weeks later, Iwang knocked on the gate of the compound, and came in greatly excited—drunk, one would have said of another man—a man possessed.

"Look!" he said to Khalid, taking him by his shortened arm and pulling him into the old man's study. "Look, I've figured it out at last."

"The philosopher's stone?"

"No no! Nothing so trivial! It's the one law, the law above all the others. An equation. See here."

He got out a slate and chalked on it rapidly, using the alchemical symbols Khalid and he had decided on to mark quantities that were different in different situations.

"Same above, same below, just as Bahram is always saying. Everything is attracted to everything else by precisely this level of attraction. Multiply the two masses attracting each other, divide that by the square of the distance they are apart from each other—multiply by whatever speed away from the central body there might be, and the force of the attraction results. Here—try it with the planets' orbits around the sun, they all work. And they travel in ellipses around the sun, because they all attract each other as well as being pulled down to the sun, so the sun sits at one focus of the ellipse, while the sum of all other attractions make the other focus." He was sketching furiously as he spoke, as agitated as Bahram had ever seen him. "It explains the discrepancies in the observations out at Ulug Bek. It works for the planets, the stars in their constellations no doubt, and the flight of a cannonball over the Earth, and the movement of those little animalcules in pond water or in our blood!"

Khalid was nodding. "This is the power of gravity itself, portrayed mathematically."

"Yes."

"The attraction is in inverse proportion to the square of the distance away."

"Yes."

"And it acts on everything."

"I think so."

"What about light?"

"I don't know. Light itself must have so little mass. If any. But what mass it has, is being attracted to all other masses. Mass attracts mass."

"But this," Khalid said, "is again action at a distance."

"Yes." Iwang grinned. "Your universal spirit, perhaps. Acting through some agency we don't know. Thus gravity, magnetism, lightning."

"A kind of invisible fire."

"Or perhaps to fire as the tiniest animals are to us. Some subtle force. And yet nothing escapes it. Everything has it. We all live within it."

"An active spirit in all things."

"Like love," Bahram put in.

"Yes, like love," Iwang agreed for once. "In that without it, all would be dead on Earth. Nothing would attract or repel, or circulate, or change form, or live in any way, but merely lie there, dead and cold."

And then he smiled, he grinned outright, his smooth shiny Tibetan cheeks dimpled by deep creases, his big horsey teeth gleaming: "And here we are! So it must be, do you see? It all moves—it all lives. And the force acts exactly in inverse proportion to the distance between things."

Khalid began, "I wonder if this could help us to transmute—"

But the other two men cut him off: "Lead into gold! Lead into gold!" Laughing at him.

"It's all gold already," Bahram said, and Iwang's eyes suddenly gleamed, it was as if the goddess of the stove had filled him, he pulled Bahram to him and gave him a rough wet woolly hug, humming again.

"You're a good man, Bahram. A very good man you are. Listen, if I believe in your love, can I stay here? Will it be blasphemy to you, if I believe in gravity and love, and the oneness of all things?"

Theories Without Application Make Trouble

Bahram's days became busier than ever, as was true for everyone in the compound. Khalid and Iwang continued to debate the ramifications of Iwang's great figure, and to run demonstrations of all kinds, either testing it or investigating matters related to it. But their investigations did little to help Bahram in his work at the forge, it being difficult or impossible to apply the two explorers' esoteric and highly mathematical arguments to the daily effort to make stronger steel or more powerful cannons. To the khan, bigger was better, and he had heard of new cannons of the Chinese emperor that dwarfed even the old giants left stranded in Byzantium by the great plagues of the seventh century. Bahram was trying to match these rumored guns, and finding it hard to cast them, hard to move them, and hard to fire them without causing them to crack. Khalid and Iwang both had suggestions, but these did not work out, and Bahram was left with the same old trial-and-error that metallurgists had used for centuries, always coming back to the idea that if he could only get the molten iron hot enough, and the right mix of feed stocks, then the resulting metal of the cannon would be stronger. So it was a matter of increasing the amount of the river's force applied to the blast furnaces, to create temperatures that turned the melts incandescent white, so brilliant it hurt to look at them. Khalid and Iwang observed the scene at dusk, and argued till dawn about the origins of such vivid light, released out of iron by heat.

All well and good, but no matter how much air they blasted into the charcoal fire, causing the iron to run white as the sun and liquid as water, or even thinner, the cannons that resulted were just as prone to cracks as before. And Nadir would appear, unannounced, aware of even the latest results. Clearly he had his spies in the compound, and did not care if Bahram knew it. Or wanted him to know it. And so he would show up, not pleased. His look would say, More, and quickly!—even as his words reassured them that he was confident they were doing the best they could, that the khan was pleased with the flight tables. He would say, "The khan is impressed by the power of mathematics to stave off Chinese invaders," and Bahram would nod unhappily, to indicate he had gotten the message even if Khalid had studiously avoided seeing it, and he would hold back from asking after the assurance of an aman for Iwang the following spring, thinking it might be best to trust to Nadir's goodwill at a better time, and go back to the shop to try something else.

A New Metal,
A New Dynasty, A New Religion

Just as a practical matter, then, Bahram was getting interested in a dull gray metal that looked like lead on the outside and tin on its interior. There was obviously very much sulphur in the mercury—if that whole description of metals could be credited—and it was, at first, so nondescript as to pass notice. But it was proving in various little demonstrations and trials to be less brittle than iron, more ductile than gold, and, in short, a different metal than those mentioned by al-Razi and Ibn Sina, strange though that was to contemplate. A new metal! And it mixed with iron to form a kind of steel that seemed as if it would work well as cannon barrel material.

"How could there be a new metal?" Bahram asked Khalid and Iwang. "And what should it be called? I can't just keep calling it 'the gray stuff.' "

"It's not new," Iwang said. "It was always there among the rest, but we're achieving heats never before reached, and so it expresses out."

Khalid called it "leadgold" as a joke, but the name stuck for lack of another. And the metal, found now every time they smelted certain bluish copper ores, became part of their armory.

Days passed in a fever of work. Rumors of war to the east increased. In China, it was said, barbarians were again crashing over the Great Wall, bringing down the rotten Ming dynasty and setting that whole giant off in a ferment of violence that was now rippling outward from it. This time the barbarians came not from Mongolia but Manchuria, northeast of China, and they were the most accomplished warriors ever yet seen in the world, it was said, and very likely to conquer and destroy everything in their path, including Islamic civilization, unless something was done to make a defense against them possible.

So people said in the bazaar, and Nadir too, in his more circuitous way, confirmed that something was happening; and the feeling of danger grew as the winter passed, and the time for military campaigns came around again. Spring, the time for war and for plague, the two biggest arms of six-armed death, as Iwang put it.

Bahram worked through these months as if a great thunderstorm were always visible, just topping the horizon to the east, moving backward against the prevailing winds, portending catastrophe. Such a painful edge this added to the pleasure he took in his little family, and in the larger familial existence of the compound: his son and daughter racing about or fidgeting at prayers, dressed impeccably by Esmerine, and the very politest of children, except when enraged, which both of them had a tendency to become to a degree that astonished both their parents. It was one of their chief topics of conversation, in the depths of the night, when they would stir and Esmerine go out briefly to relieve herself, then return and pull off her shift again, her breasts silvery raindrops spilling down her ribs in the moonlight, over Bahram's hands as he warmed them, in that somnolent world of second-watch sex that was one of the beautiful spaces of daily life, the salvation of sleep, the body's dream, so much warmer and more loving than any other part of the day that it was sometimes hard in the mornings to believe it had really happened, that he and Esmerine, so severe in dress and manner, Esmerine who ran the women at their work as hard as Khalid had at his most tryrannical, and who never spoke to Bahram or looked at him except in the most businesslike way, as was only fitting and proper, had in fact been transported together with him to whole other worlds of rapture, in the depths of the night in their bed. As he watched her work in the afternoons, Bahram thought: love changed everything. They were all just animals after all, creatures God had made not much different from monkeys, and there was no real reason why a woman's breasts should not be like the udders on a cow, swinging together inelegantly as she leaned forward to work at one labor or another; but love made them orbs of the utmost beauty, and the same was true of the whole world. Love put all things under a description, and only love could save them.

In searching for a provenance for this new "leadgold," Khalid read through some of the more informative of his old tomes, and he was interested when he came on a passage in Jabir Ibn Hayyam's ancient classic "The Book of Properties," penned in the first years of the jihad, in which Jabir listed seven metals, namely gold, silver, lead, tin, copper, iron, and kharsini, meaning "Chinese iron"—dull gray, silver when polished, known to the Chinese themselves as paitung, or "white copper." The Chinese, Jabir wrote, had made mirrors of it capable of curing the eye diseases of those who looked into them. Khalid, whose eyes got weaker every year, immediately set to the manufacture of a little mirror of their own lead-gold, just to see. Jabir also suggested kharsini made bells of a particularly melodious tone, and so Khalid had the rest of the quantity they had on hand cast into bells, to see if their tone was especially pretty, which might help secure the identification of the metal. All agreed that the bells tinkled very prettily; but Khalid's eyes did not improve after looking into a mirror of the metal.

"Call it kharsini," Khalid said. He sighed. "Who knows what it is. We don't know anything."

But he continued to try various demonstrations, writing voluminous commentaries on each test, through the nights and on to many a sleep-less dawn. He and Iwang pursued their studies. Khalid directed Bahram and Paxtakor and Jalil and the rest of his old artisans in the shops to build new telescopes, and microsopes, and pressure gauges, and pumps. The compound had become a place where their skills in metallurgy and me-chanical artisanry combined to give them great power to make new things; if they could imagine something, they could make some rude first approximation of it. Every time the old artisans were able to make their molds and tools more exactly, it allowed them to set their tolerances finer still, and thus as they progressed, anything from the intricacies of clock-work to the massive strength of waterwheels or cannon barrels could be improved. Khalid took apart a Persian carpet-making device to study all its little metal pieces, and remarked to Iwang that combined with a rack-and-pinion, the device might be fitted with stamps shaped like letters, instead of threaders, in arrays that could be inked and then pressed against paper, and a whole page thus written all at once, and repeated as many times as one liked, so that books became as common as cannon-balls. And Iwang had laughed, and said that in Tibet the monks had carved just such inkblocks, but that Khalid's idea was better.

Meanwhile Iwang worked on his mathematical concerns. Once he said to Bahram, "Only a god could have thought these things in the first place. And then to have used them to embody a world! If we trace even a millionth part of it, we may find out more than any sentient beings have ever known through all the ages, and see plainly the divine mind."

Bahram nodded uncertainly. By now he knew that he did not want Iwang to convert to Islam. It seemed false to God and to Iwang. He knew it was selfishness to feel so, and that God would take care of it. As indeed it seemed He already had, as Iwang no longer was coming to the mosque on Fridays, or to the religious studies at the ribat. God or Iwang, or both, had taken Bahram's point. Religion could not be faked or used for worldly purposes.

Dragon Bites World

Now when Bahram visited the caravanserai, he heard many disquieting stories from the east. Things were in turmoil, China's new Manchu dynasty was in an expansive temper; the new Manchu emperor, usurper that he was, was not content with the old and fading empire he had conquered, but was determined to reinvigorate it by war, extending his conquests into the rich rice kingdoms to the south, Annam and Siam and Burma, as well as the parched wastelands in the middle of the world, the deserts and mountains separating China from the Dar, crossed by the threads of the Silk Road. After crossing that waste they would run into India, the Islamic khanates, and the Savafid empire. In the caravanserai it was said that Yarkand and Kashgar were already taken—perfectly believable, as they had been defended for decades by the merest remnants of the Ming garrisons, and by bandit warlords. Nothing lay between the khanate of Bokhara and these wastelands but the Tarim basin and the Ferghana mountains, and the Silk Road crossed those in two or three places. Where caravans went, banners could certainly follow.

And soon after that, they did. News came that Manchu banners had taken Torugart Pass, which was the high point of one of the silk routes, between Tashkent and the Takla Makan. Caravan travel from the east would be disrupted for a little while at least, which meant that Samarqand and Bokhara would go from being the centerpoint of the great world exchange, to a largely useless end point. It was a catastrophe for trade.

A final group of caravan people, Armenian, Zott, Jewish, and Hindu, showed up with this news. They had been forced to run for their lives and leave their goods behind. Apparently the Dzungarian Gate, between Xinjiang and the Khazakh steppe, was also about to be taken. As the news raced through the caravanserai ringing Samarqand, most of the caravans resting in them changed their plans. Many decided to return to Frengistan, which though full of petty taifa conflict was at least Muslim entire, its little khanates and emirates and sultanates trading between themselves most of the time, even when fighting.

Such decisions as these would soon cripple Samarqand. As an end point in itself it was nothing, the mere edge of Dar al-Islam. Nadir was worried, and the khan in a rage. Sayyed Abdul Aziz ordered the Dzungarian Gate retaken, and an expedition sent to help defend Khyber Pass, so that trade relations with India at the least would remain secure.

Nadir, accompanied by a heavy guard, described these orders very briefly to Khalid and Iwang. He presented the problem as if it were somehow Khalid's fault. At the end of his visit, he informed them that Bahram and his wife and children were to return with Nadir to the Khanaka in Bokhara. They would be allowed to return to Samarqand only when Khalid and Iwang devised a weapon capable of defeating the Chinese.

"They will be allowed to receive guests at the palace. You are welcome to visit them, or indeed join them there, though I believe your work is best pursued here with all your men and machines. If I thought you would work faster in the palace, I would move you there too, believe me."

Khalid glared at him, too angry to speak without endangering them all.

"Iwang will move out here with you, as I judge him most useful here. He will be given an extension on his aman in advance, in recognition of his importance to matters of state. Indeed he is forbidden to leave. Not that he could. The wakened dragon to the east has already eaten Tibet. So you are taking on a godly task, one that you can be proud to have been yoked to."

He spared one glance for Bahram. "We will take good care of your family, and you will take good care of things here. You can live in the palace with them, or here helping the work, whichever you please."

Bahram nodded, speechless with dismay and fear. "I will do both," he managed to say, looking at Esmerine and the children.

Nothing was ever normal again.

Many lives change like that—all of a sudden, and forever.

A Weapon from God

In deference to Bahram's feelings, Khalid and Iwang organized the whole
compound as an armory, and all their tests and demonstrations were
devoted to increasing the powers of the khan's army. Stronger cannon,
more explosive gunpowder, spinning shot, killer-of-myriads; also firing
tables, logistical protocols, mirror alphabets to talk over great distances;
all this and more they produced, while Bahram lived half in the Khanaka
with Esmerine and the kids, and half out at the compound, until the
Bokhara Road became like the courtyard path to him, traversed at all
hours of the day and night, sometimes asleep on horses that knew the
way blind.

The increases they made in the khan's war-making powers were
prodigious; or would have been, if the commanders of Sayyed Abdul's
army could have been made to submit to Khalid's instruction, and if
Khalid had had the patience to teach them. But both sides were too
proud for accommodation, and though it seemed to Bahram a critical
failure on Nadir's part not to force the issue and command the generals
to obey Khalid, also not to spend more of the khan's treasury on hiring
more soldiers with more experience, nothing was done. Even the great
Nadir Divanbegi had limits to his power, which came down in the end to
the sway of his advice over the khan. Other advisors had different advice,
and it was possible Nadir's power was in fact waning just at the moment
it was most needed, and despite Khalid and Iwang's innovations—or,

who knew, perhaps even because of them. It was not as if the khan had distinguished himself for good judgment. And possibly his pocket was not as bottomless as it had seemed back in the days when the bazaars and caravanserai and building sites were all bustling like beehives, and paying taxes.

So Esmerine seemed to suggest, though Bahram had mostly to deduce this from her looks and silences. She seemed to believe they were spied upon at all times, even during their sleepless hours in the dead of night, which was a rather terrible thought. The children had taken to life in the palace as if falling into some dream out of the Arabian Nights, and Esmerine did nothing to disabuse them of this notion, although she of course knew that they were prisoners, and their lives forfeit if the khan should happen to experience a fit of bad temper at the way things were going at Khalid's, or to the east, or anywhere else. So naturally she avoided saying anything objectionable, and mentioned only how well fed and kindly treated they were, how much the children and she were thriving. Only the look in her eye when they were alone told Bahram how afraid she was, and how much she wished to encourage him to fulfill the khan's desires.

Khalid of course knew all this without his daughter's glances to tell him. Bahram could see him putting more and more effort into improving the military capacity of the khan, not only by exerting himself in the armory, but by trying to ingratiate himself with the most amenable of the generals, and by making suggestions discreet or direct on all manner of subjects, from the renovation of the walls of the city, in keeping with his demonstrations of the strength of raw earthworks, to plans for well-digging and drainage of stale water in Bokhara and Samarqand. All purely theoretical demonstrations went by the board in this effort, with no time spent grumbling about it either. But progress was uneven.

Rumors began to fly about the city like bats, sucking the light out of the day. The Manchurian barbarians had conquered Yunnan, Mongolia, Cham, Tibet, Annam, and the eastern extensions of the Mughal empire; every day it was somewhere different, somewhere closer. There was no way to confirm any of these assertions, and indeed they were often denied, either by direct contradiction, or simply by the fact that caravans kept coming from some of those regions, and the traders had seen nothing unusual, though they too had heard rumors. Nothing was certain but that there was turmoil to the east. The caravans certainly came less often, and included not only traders but whole families, Muslim or Jewish or Hindu, driven out by fear of the new dynasty, called the Qing. Centuries-old foreign settlements dissipated like frost in the sun, and the exiles streamed west with the idea things would be better in Dar al-Islam, under the Mughals or the Ottomans or in the taifa sultanates of Frengistan. No doubt true, as Islam was lawful; but Bahram saw the misery on their faces, the destitution and fear, the need for their men to angle and beg for provisions, their goods for trade already depleted, and all the wide western half of the world still before them to be traversed.

At least it would be the Muslim half of the world. But visits to the caravanserai, once one of Bahram's favorite parts of the day, now left him anxious and fearful, as intent as Nadir to see Khalid and Iwang come up with ways to defend the khanate from invasion.

"It's not us slowing things down," Khalid said bitterly, late one night in his study. "Nadir himself is no great general, and his influence over the khan is shaky, and getting shakier. And the khan himself—" He blew through his lips.

Bahram sighed. No one could contradict it. Sayyed Abdul Aziz was not a wise man.

"We need something both deadly and spectacular," Khalid said. "Something both for the khan and for the Manchu." Bahram left him looking at various recipes for explosives, and made the long cold ride back to the palace in Bokhara.

Khalid arranged a meeting with Nadir, and came back muttering that if all went well with the demonstration he had proposed, Nadir would release Esmerine and the children back to the compound. Bahram was elated, but Khalid warned him: "It depends on the khan being pleased, and who knows what will impress such a man."

"What demonstration do you have in mind?"

"We must manufacture shells containing the Chinese wan-jen-ti formula, shells that won't break on firing, but will when they hit the ground."

They tried out several different designs, and even the demonstrations proved quite dangerous; more than once people had to run for their lives. It would be a terrible weapon if it could be made to work. Bahram hurried around all day every day, imagining his family returned,

Samarqand saved from infidels; surely if Allah meant these things to be, then the weapon was a gift from Him. It was not hard to overlook the terror of it.

Eventually they manufactured hollow flat-backed shells, pumped full of the liquid constituents of the killer-of-myriads, in two chambers separated by a tin wall. A packet of flashpowder in the nose of the shell exploded on contact, blowing the interior wall apart and mixing the constituents of the gas.

They got them to work about eight times out of ten. Another kind of shell, entirely filled with gunpowder and an igniter, exploded on impact most deafeningly, scattering the shell like fragmented bullets.

They made fifty of each, and arranged a demonstration out on their test grounds by the river. Khalid bought a small herd of broken nags from the gluemaker, with the promise of selling them back ready for rendering. The ostlers staked these poor beasts out at the extreme range of the test cannon, and when the khan and his courtiers arrived in their finery, looking somewhat bored by now with this routine, Khalid kept his face turned away in as close to a gesture of contempt as he could risk, pretending to attend busily to the gun. Bahram saw that this would not do, and went to Nadir and Sayyed Abdul Aziz and made obeisances and pleasantries, explaining the mechanism of the weapon, and introducing Khalid with a little flourish as the old man approached, sweating and puffing.

Khalid declared the demonstration ready. The khan flicked a hand casually, his characteristic gesture, and Khalid gave the sign to the men at the gun, who applied the match. The cannon boomed and expelled white smoke, rolled back. Its barrel had been set at a fairly high angle, so that the shell would come down hard on its tip. The smoke swirled, all stared down the plain at the staked horses; nothing happened; Bahram held his breath—

A puff of yellow smoke exploded among the horses, and they leaped away from it, two pulling out of their stakes and galloping off, a few falling over when the ropes pulled them back. All the while the smoke spread outward as from an invisible brushfire, a thick mustard-yellow smoke, obscuring the horses as it passed over them. It covered one that had burst its tether but charged by accident back into a tendril of the cloud; this was the one they could see rear up in the mist, fall and struggle wildly to get back on its feet, then collapse, twitching.

The yellow cloud cleared slowly, drifting away downvalley on the prevailing wind, seeming heavy and clinging long in the hollows of the ground. There lay two dozen dead horses, scattered in a circle that encompassed two hundred paces at least.

"If there was an army in that circle," Khalid said, "then, most excellent servant of the one true God, Supreme Khan, they would be just as dead as those horses. And you could have a score of cannon loaded with such shells, or a hundred. And no army ever born could conquer Samarqand."

Nadir, looking faintly shocked, said, "What if the wind changed its course and blew our way?"

Khalid shrugged. "Then we too would die. It is important to make small shells, that can be fired a long distance, and always downwind, if possible. The gas does disperse, so if the wind was mildly toward you, it might not matter much."

The khan himself looked startled at the demonstration, but more and more pleased, as at a new form of fireworks; it was hard to be sure with him. Bahram suspected that he sometimes pretended to be oblivious to things, in order to make a veil between himself and his advisors.

Now he nodded to Nadir, and led his court off on the road to Bokhara.

"You have to understand," Khalid reminded Bahram on the way back to the compound, "there are men in that very group around the khan who want to bring Nadir down. For them it doesn't matter how good our weapon is. The better the worse, in fact. So it's not just a matter of them being utter simpletons."

These Things Happened

The next day Nadir was out with his full guard, and they had with them Esmerine and the children. Nadir nodded brusquely at Bahram's fulsome thanks and then said to Khalid, "The poison air shells may become necessary, and I want you to compile as many as you can, five hundred at least, and the khan will reward you accordingly on his return, and he makes promise of that reward in advance, by the return of your family."

"He's going away?"

"The plague has appeared in Bokhara. The caravanserai and the bazaars, the mosques and madressas and the Khanaka are all closed. The crucial members of the court will accompany the khan to his summer residence. I will be making all his arrangements for him from there. Look to yourselves. If you can leave the city and still do your work, the khan does not forbid it, but he hopes you can close yourself up here in your compound, and carry on. When the plague passes we can reconvene."

"And the Manchu?" Khalid asked.

"We have word that they too have been struck. As you might expect. It may be they have brought it with them. They may even have sent their sick among us to pass along the infection. It would be little different than casting poisoned air on an enemy."

Khalid colored at that but said nothing. Nadir left, clearly on his way to other tasks necessary before his flight from Samarqand. Khalid slammed the gate shut after him, cursed him under his breath. Bahram, ecstatic at the unexpected return of Esmerine and the children, hugged them until Esmerine cried out that he would crush them. They wept with joy, and only later, in the midst of shutting the compound off from the city, something they had done successfully ten years before when a plague of distemper had passed through the city, losing only one servant who had slipped into town to see his girlfriend and never come back—only later did Bahram see that his daughter Laila was red-cheeked, with a hectic flush, and lying listlessly on a chest of drawers.

They put her in a room with a bed. Esmerine's face was pinched with fear. Khalid decreed that Laila be sequestered there, and fed and kept in drink from the door, by poles and net bags and plates and gourds that were not to be returned to the rest of them. But Esmerine hugged the little girl, of course, before all this regime was introduced, and the next day in their bedroom Bahram saw her red cheeks, and how she groaned awake and lifted her arms, and there were the tokens in her armpits, hard yellow protuberances emerging from the skin, even (he seemed to see as she put down her arm) faceted as if they were carbuncles, or as if she were turning to jewels from the inside.

After that they were a sickhouse, and Bahram spent his days nursing the others, running about all hours of the day and night, in a fever of a different kind than that of the sick ones, urged by Khalid never to touch or come within the breath of his stricken family. Sometimes Bahram tried, sometimes he didn't, holding them as if he could clasp them to this world. Or drag them back into it, when the children died.

Then the adults started dying too, and they were locked out of the town as a sickhouse rather than a safe house. Fedwa died but Esmerine held on; Khalid and Bahram took turns caring for her, and Iwang joined them in the compound.

One night Iwang and Khalid had Esmerine breathe on a glass, and they looked at the moisture through their small-lens, and said little. Bahram looked briefly and glimpsed the host of little dragons, gargoyles, bats, and other creatures. He could not look again, but knew they were doomed.

Esmerine died and Khalid showed the tokens that same hour. Iwang could not rise from his couch in Khalid's workshop, but studied his own breath and blood and bile through the smallscope, trying to make a clear record of the disease's progress through him. One night as he lay there gasping he said in his low voice, "I'm glad I did not convert. I know you did not want it. And now I would be a blasphemer, for if there is a God I would want to rebuke Him for this."

Bahram said nothing. It was a judgment, but of what? What had they done? Were the gas shells an affront to God?

"Old men live to be seventy," Iwang said. "I'm just over thirty. What will I do with those years?"

Bahram couldn't think. "You said we return," he said dully.

"Yes. But I liked this life. I had plans for this life."

He lingered on his couch but could take no food, and his skin was very hot. Bahram did not tell him that Khalid had died already, very swiftly, felled by grief or anger at the loss of Fedwa and Esmerine and the children—as if by apoplexy rather than plague. Bahram only sat with the Tibetan in the silent compound.

At one point Iwang croaked, "I wonder if Nadir knew they were infected, and gave them back to kill us."

"But why?"

"Perhaps he feared the killer-of-myriads. Or some faction of the court. He had other considerations than us. Or it might have been someone else. Or no one."

"We'll never know."

"No. The court itself might be gone by now. Nadir, the khan, all of them."

"I hope so," Bahram's mouth said.

Iwang nodded. He died at dawn, wordless and struggling.

Bahram got all the compound's survivors to put cloths over their faces and move the bodies into a closed workshop beyond the chemical pits. He was so far outside himself that the movements of his numb limbs surprised him, and he spoke as if he were someone else. Do this— do that. Let's eat. Then, carrying a big pot to the kitchen, he felt the lump in his armpit, and sat down as if the tendons in the back of his knees had been cut, thinking I guess it's my turn now.

Back in the Bardo

Well, it was, as might be imagined after an end like that, a very discouraged and dispirited little jati that huddled together on the black floor of the bardo this time around. Who could blame them? Why should they have had any will to continue? It was hard to discern any reward for virtue, any forward progress—any dharmic justice of any kind. Even Bahram could not find the good in it, and no one else even tried. Looking back down the vale of the ages at the endless recurrence of their reincarnations, before they were forced to drink their vials of forgetting and all became obscure to them again, they could see no pattern at all to their efforts; if the gods had a plan, or even a set of procedures, if the long train of transmigrations was supposed to add up to anything, if it was not just mindless repetition, time itself nothing but a succession of chaoses, no one could discern it; and the story of their transmigrations, rather than being a narrative without death, as the first experiences of reincarnation perhaps seemed to suggest, had become instead a veritable charnel house. Why read on? Why pick up their book from the far wall where it has been thrown away in disgust and pain, and read on? Why submit to such cruelty, such bad karma, such bad plotting?

The reason is simple: these things happened. They happened countless times, just like this. The oceans are salt with our tears. No one can deny that these things happened.

And so there is no choice in the matter. They cannot escape the wheel of birth and death, not in the experience of it, or in the contemplation of it afterward; and their anthologist, Old Red Ink himself, must tell their stories honestly, must deal in reality, or else the stories mean nothing. And it is crucial that the stories mean something.

So. No escape from reality: they sat there, a dozen sad souls, huddled together at a far corner of the great stage of the hall of judgment. It was dim, and cold. The perfect white light had lasted this time for only the briefest of moments, a flash like the eyeball exploding; after that, here they were again. Up on the dais the dogs and demons and black gods capered, in a hazy mist that shrouded all, that damped all sound.

Bahram tried, but could think of nothing to say. He was still stunned by the events of their last days in the world; he was still ready to get up and go out and start another day, on another morning just like all the rest. Deal with the crisis of an invasion from the east, the taking of his family, if that was what it meant—whatever problems the day happened to bring, trouble, crisis, sure, that was life. But not this. Not this already. Salt tears of timely death, alum tears of untimely death: bitterness filled the air like smoke. I liked that life! I had plans for that life!

Khalid sat there just as Khalid always had, as if esconced in his study thinking over some problem. The sight gave Bahram a deep pang of regret and sorrow. All that life, gone. Gone, gone, gone altogether beyond . . . The past is gone. Even if you can remember it, it's gone. And even at the time it was happening Bahram had known how he had loved it, he had lived in a state of nostalgia-for-the-present, every day of it.

Now gone.

The rest of the jati sat or sprawled on the cheap wooden floor around Khalid. Even Sayyed Abdul looked distraught, not just sorry for himself, but distraught for them all, sad to have left that turbulent but oh-so-interesting world.

An interval passed; a moment, a year, an age, the kalpa itself, who could tell in such a terrible place?

Bahram took a deep breath, exerted himself, sat up.

"We're making progress," he announced firmly.

Khalid snorted. "We are like mice to the cats." He gestured up at the stage, where the grotesqueries continued to unfold. "They are petty assholes, I say. They kill us for sport. They don't die and they don't understand."

"Forget them," Iwang advised. "We're going to have to do this on our own."

"God judges, and sends us out again," Bahram said. "Man proposes, God disposes."

Khalid shook his head. "Look at them. They're a bunch of vicious children playing. No one leads them, there is no god of gods."

Bahram looked at him, surprised. "Do you not see the one enfolding all the rest, the one we rest within? Allah, or Brahman, or what have you, the one only true God of Gods?"

"No. I see no sign of him at all."

"You aren't looking! You've never looked yet! When you look, you will see it. When you see it, everything will change for you. Then it will be all right."

Khalid scowled. "Don't insult us with that fatuous nonsense. Good Lord, Allah, if you are there, why have you inflicted me with this fool of a boy!" He kicked at Bahram. "It's easier without you around! You and your damned all right! It's not all right! It's a fucking mess! You only make it worse with that nonsense of yours! Did you not see what just happened to us, to your wife and children, to my daughter and grandchildren? It's not all right! Start from that, if you will! We may be in a hallucination here, but that's no excuse for being delusional!"

Bahram was hurt by this. "It's you who give up on things," he protested. "Every time. That's what your cynicism is—you don't even try. You don't have the courage to carry on."

"The hell I don't. I've never given up yet. I'm just not willing to go at it babbling lies. No, it's you who are the one who never tries. Always waiting for me and Iwang to do the hard things. You do it for once! Quit babbling about love and try it yourself one time, damn it! Try it yourself, and see how hard it is to keep a sunny face when you're looking the truth of the situation eye to eye."

"Ho!" said Bahram, stung. "I do my part. I have always done my part. Without me none of you would be able to carry on. It takes courage to keep love at the center when you know just as well as anyone else the real state of things! It's easy to get angry, anyone can do that. It's making good that's the hard part, it's staying hopeful that's the hard part! It's staying in love that's the hard part."

Khalid waggled his left hand. "All very well, but it only matters if the truth is faced and fought. I'm sick of love and happiness—I want justice."

"So do I!"

"All right, then show me. Show me what you can do this next time out in the miserable world, something more than happy happy."

"I will then!"

"Good."

Heavily Khalid pulled himself up, and limped over to Sayyed Abdul Aziz, and without any warning kicked him sprawling across the stage. "And you!" he roared. "What is your EXCUSE! Why are you always so bad? Consistency is no excuse, your CHARACTER is NO EXCUSE!"

Sayyed glared up at him from the floor, sucking on a torn knuckle. Daggers in his stare: "Leave me alone."

Khalid made as if to kick him again, then gave up on it. "You'll get yours," he promised. "One of these days, you'll get yours."

"Forget about him," Iwang advised. "He's not the real problem, and he'll always be part of us. Forget about him, forget about the gods. Let's concentrate on doing it ourselves. We can make our own world."

BOOK 5

❋ WARP AND WEFT ❋

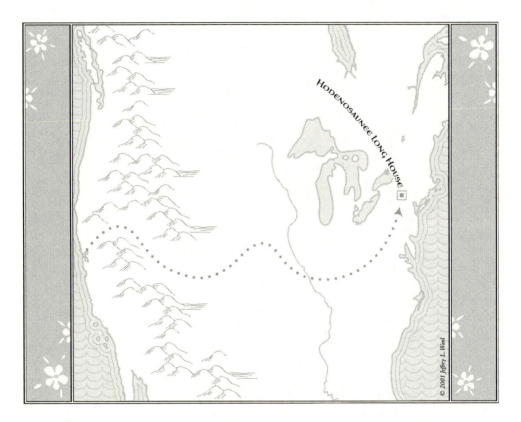

HODENOSAUNEE LONG HOUSE

© 2001 Jeffrey L. Ward

One night can change the world.

The Doorkeepers sent runners out with strings of wampum, announcing a council meeting at Floating Bridge. They wanted to raise to chiefdom the foreigner they called Fromwest. The fifty sachems had agreed to the meeting, as there was nothing unusual about it. There were many more chiefs than sachems, and the title died with the man, and each nation was free to choose its own, depending on what happened on the warpath and in the villages. The only unusual feature of this raising-up was the foreign birth of the candidate, but he had been living with the Doorkeepers for some time, and word had spread through the nine nations and the eight tribes that he was interesting.

He had been rescued by a war party of Doorkeepers who had run far to the west to inflict another shock on the Sioux, the western people bordering the Hodenosaunee. The warriors had come on a Sioux torture, the victim hung by his chest from hooks, and a fire building under him. While waiting for their ambush to set, the warriors had been impressed by the victim's speech, which was in a comprehensible version of the Doorkeeper dialect, as if he had seen them out there.

The usual behavior while being tortured was a passionate laughter in the faces of one's enemies, to show that no pain inflicted by man can triumph over the spirit. This foreigner hadn't been like that. Calmly he remarked to his captors, in Doorkeeper rather than Sioux: "You are very incompetent torturers. What wounds the spirit is not passion, for all passion is encouragement. As you hate me you help me. What really hurts is to be ground like acorns in a grinding hole. Where I come from they have a thousand devices to tear the flesh, but what hurts is their indifference. Here you remind me I am human and full of passion, a target of passion. I am happy to be here. And I am about to be rescued by warriors much greater than you."

The Senecans lying in ambush had taken this as an undeniable sign to attack, and with war whoops they had descended on the Sioux and scalped as many as they could catch, while taking particular care to rescue the captive who had spoken so eloquently, and in their own tongue.

How did you know we were there? they asked him.

Suspended as high as he was, he said, he had seen their eyes out in the trees.

And how do you know our language?

There is a tribe of your kinsmen on the west coast of this island, who moved there long ago. I learned your language from them.

And so they had nursed him and brought him home, and he lived with the Doorkeepers and the Great Hill People, near Niagara, for several moons. He went on the hunt and the warpath, and word of his accomplishments had spread through the nine nations, and many people had met him and been impressed. No one was surprised at his nomination to chief.

The council was set for the hill at the head of Canandaigua Lake, where the Hodenosaunee had first appeared in the world, out of the ground like moles.

Hill People, Granite People, Flint Owners, and Shirt Weavers, who came up out of the south two generations before, having had bad dealings with the people who had come over the sea from the east, all walked west on the Longhouse Trail, which extends across the league's land from east to west. They encamped at some distance from the Doorkeepers' council house, sending runners to announce their arrival, according to the old ways. The Senecan sachems confirmed the day of the council, and repeated their invitation.

On the appointed morning before dawn, people rose and gathered their rolls, and hunched around fires and a quick meal of burnt corn cakes and maple water. It was a clear sky at dawn, with only a trace of receding gray cloud to the east, like the finely embroidered hems of the coats the women were donning. The mist on the lake swirled as if twisted by sprites skating over the lake, to join a sprite council matching the human one, as often occurred. The air was cool and damp, with no hint of the oppressive heat that was likely to arrive in the afternoon.

The visiting nations trooped onto the water meadows at the lakeshore and gathered in their accustomed places. By the time the sky lightened from gray to blue there were already a few hundred people there to listen to the Salute to the Sun, sung by one of the old Senecan sachems.

The Onandaga nations keep the council brand, and also the wampum into which the laws of the league have been talked, and now their powerful old sachem, Keeper of the Wampum, rose and displayed in his outstretched hands the belts of wampum, heavy and white. The Onondagas are the central nation, their council fire the seat of the league's councils. Keeper of the Wampum trod a pedestrian dance around the meadow, chanting something most of them heard only as a faint cry.

A fire was kindled at the center point, and pipes passed around. The Mohawks, Onondagas, and Senecans, brother to each other and father to the other six, settled west of the fire; the Oneidas, Cayugas, and Tuscaroras sat to the east; the new nations, Cherokee, Shawnee, and Choctaw, sat to the south. The sun cracked the horizon; its light flooded the valley like maple water, poured over everything and making it summer yellow. Smoke curled, gray and brown turned to one. A morning without wind, and the wisps on the lake burned away. Birds sang from the forest canopy to the east of the meadow.

Out of the arrows of shadow and light walked a short, broadshouldered man, barefoot and dressed only in a runner's waist belt. He had a round face, very flat. A foreigner. He walked with his hands together, looking down humbly, and came through the junior nations to the central fire, there offering his open palms to Honowenato, Keeper of the Wampum.

Keeper said to him, "Today you become a chief of the Hodenosaunee. At these occasions it is customary for me to read the history of the league as recalled by the wampum here, and to reiterate the laws of the league that have given us peace for many generations, and new nations joining us from the sea to the Mississippi, from the Great Lakes to the Tennessee."

Fromwest nodded. His chest was marked deeply by the puckered scars of the Sioux hooking ceremony. He was as solemn as an owl. "I am more than honored. You are the most generous of nations."

"We are the greatest league of nations under heaven," Keeper said. "We live here on the highest land of Longer House, with good routes down in all directions.

"In each nation there are the eight tribes, divided in two groups. Wolf, Bear, Beaver, and Turtle; then Deer, Snipe, Heron, and Hawk. Each member of the Wolf tribe is brother and sister to all other Wolves, no matter what nation they come from. The relationship with other Wolves is almost stronger than the relation with those of one's nation. It is a cross-relation, like warp and weft in basket-weaving and cloth-making. And so we are one garment. We cannot disagree as nations, or it would tear the fabric of the tribes. Brother cannot fight brother, sister cannot fight sister.

"Now, Wolf, Bear, Beaver, and Turtle, being brother and sister, cannot intermarry. They must marry out of Hawk, Heron, Deer, or Snipe."

Fromwest nodded at each pronouncement of Keeper, made in the heavy, ponderous tones of a man who had labored all his life to make this system work, and to extend it far and wide. Fromwest had been declared a member of the Hawk tribe, and would play with the Hawks in the morning's lacrosse match. Now he watched Keeper with a hawk's intensity, taking in the irascible old man's every word, oblivious to the growing crowd at lakeside. The crowd in turn went about its own affairs, the women at their fires preparing the feast, some of the men setting out the lacrosse pitch on the biggest water meadow.

Finally Keeper was done with his recital, and Fromwest addressed all in earshot.

"This is the great honor of my life," he said loudly and slowly, his accent strange but comprehensible. "To be taken in by the finest people of the Earth is more than any poor wanderer could hope for. Although I did hope for it. I spent many years crossing this great island, hoping for it."

He bowed his head, hands together.

"A very unassuming man," remarked Iagogeh, the One Who Hears, wife of Keeper of the Wampum. "And not so young either. It will be interesting to hear what he says tonight."

"And to see how he does in the games," said Tecarnos, or Dropping Oil, one of Iagogeh's nieces.

"Tend the soup," said Iagogeh.

"Yes, mother."

The lacrosse field was being inspected by the field judges for rocks and rabbit holes, and the tall poles of the gates were set up at either end of the field. As always, the games set the Wolf, Bear, Beaver, and Turtle tribes against Deer, Snipe, Hawk, and Heron. The betting was active, and wagered goods were laid out by the managers in neat rows, mostly personal items of ornamentation, but also flints, flutes, drums, bags of tobacco and pipes, needles and arrows, two flintlock pistols, and four muskets.

The two teams and the referees gathered at midfield, and the crowd bordered the green field and stood on the hill overlooking it. The day's match was to be a ten-on-ten, so five passes through the gate would win. The head referee listed the main rules, as always: no touching the ball with hand, foot, limb, body, or head; no deliberate hitting of opponents with the ball bats. He held up the round ball, made of deerskin filled with sand, about the size of his fist. The twenty players stood ten to a side, defending their goals, and one from each side came forward to contest the dropped ball that would start the match. To a great roar from the crowd the referee dropped the ball and retreated to the side of the field, where he and the others would watch for any infraction of the rules.

The two team leaders fenced madly for the ball, the hooped nets at the end of their bats scraping the ground and knocking together. Though hitting another person was forbidden, striking another player's bat with yours was allowed; it was a chancy play, however, as a mistaken strike on flesh would give the hit player a free shot at the gate. So the two players whacked away until the Heron scooped the ball up and flicked it back to one of his teammates, and the running began.

Opponents ran at the ball carrier, who twisted through them as long as he could, then passed the ball with a flick of his bat, into the net of one of his teammates. If the ball fell to the ground then most of the players nearby converged on it, bats clattering violently as they struggled for possession. Two players from each team stood back from this scrum, on defense in case an opponent caught up the ball and made a dash for the gate.

Soon enough it became clear that Fromwest had played lacrosse before, presumably among the Doorkeepers. He was not as young as most of the other players, nor as fleet as the fastest runners on each side, but the fastest were set guarding each other, and Fromwest had only to face the biggest of the Bear-Wolf-Beaver-Turtle team, who could counter his low and solid mass with body checks, but did not have Fromwest's quickness. The foreigner held his bat in both hands like a scythe, out low to the side or before him, as if inviting a slash that would knock the ball free. But his opponents soon learned that such a slash would never land, and if they tried it, Fromwest would spin awkwardly and be gone, stumbling forward quite quickly for a big short man. When other opponents blocked him, his passes to open teammates were like shots from a bow; they were if anything perhaps too hard, as his teammates had some trouble catching his throws. But if they did, off to the gate they scampered, waving their bats to confuse the final gate guard, and screaming along with the excited crowd. Fromwest never shouted or said a word, but played in an uncanny silence, never taunting the other team or even meeting their eyes, but watching either the ball or, it seemed, the sky. He played as if in a trance, as if confused; and yet when his teammates were tracked down and blocked, he was always somehow open for a pass, no matter how hard his guard, or soon guards, ran to cover him. Surrounded teammates, desperately keeping their bat free to throw the ball out, would find Fromwest there in the only direction the ball could be thrown, stumbling but miraculously open, and they would flip it out to him and he would snare the ball dexterously and be off on one of his uncertain runs, cutting behind people and across the field at odd angles, wrong-headed angles, until he was blocked and an opportunity to pass opened, and one of his hard throws would flick over the grass as if on a string. It was a pleasure to watch, comical in its awkward look, and the crowd roared as the Deer-Snipe-Hawk-Heron team threw the ball past the diving guardian and through the gate. Seldom had a first score happened faster.

After that the Bear-Wolf-Beaver-Turtle team did what it could to stop Fromwest, but they were puzzled by his strange responses, and could not defend well against him. If they ganged up on him, he passed out to his fast young teammates, who were growing bolder with their success. If they tried to cover him singly, he weaved and bobbed and stumbled in seeming confusion past his guard, until he was within striking distance of the gate, when he would spin, suddenly balanced, his bat at knee height, and with a turn of the wrist launch the ball through the gate like an arrow. No one there had ever seen such hard throws.

Between scores they gathered on the sidelines to drink water and maple water. The Bear-Wolf-Beaver-Turtle team conferred grimly, made substitutions. After that an "accidental" bat blow to Fromwest's head gashed his scalp and left him covered with his own red blood, but the foul gave him a free shot, which he converted from near midfield, to a great roar. And it did not stop his weird but effective play, nor gain his opponents even a glance from him. Iagogeh said to her niece, "He plays as if the other team were ghosts. He plays as if he were out there by himself, trying to learn how to run more gracefully." She was a connoisseur of the game, and it made her happy to see it.

Much more quickly than was normal, the match was four to one in favor of the junior side, and the senior tribes gathered to discuss strategy. The women gave out gourds of water and maple water, and Iagogeh, a Hawk herself, sidled next to Fromwest and offered him a water gourd, as she had seen earlier that that was all he was taking.

"You need a good partner now," she murmured as she crouched beside him. "No one can finish alone."

He looked at her, surprised. She pointed with a gesture of her head at her nephew Doshoweh, Split the Fork. "He's your man," she said, and was off.

The players regathered at midfield for the drop, and the Bear-Wolf-Beaver-Turtle team left behind only a single man to defend. They got the ball, and pressed west with a fury born of desperation. Play went on for a long time, with neither side gaining advantage, both running madly up and down the field. Then one of the Deer-Snipe-Hawk-Herons hurt his ankle, and Fromwest called on Doshoweh to come out.

The Bear-Wolf-Beaver-Turtle team pressed forward again, pushing at the new player. But one of their passes came too near Fromwest, who snagged it out of the air while leaping over a fallen man. He flipped it to Doshoweh and all converged on the youngster, who looked frightened and vulnerable; but he had the presence of mind to make a long toss downfield, back to Fromwest, already running full speed. Fromwest caught the toss and everyone took off in pursuit of him. But it seemed he had an extra turn of speed he had never yet revealed, for no one could catch up to him before he reached the eastern gate, and after a feint with body and bat he spun and fired the ball past the guardian and far into the woods, to end the match.

The crowd erupted with cheers. Hats and bags of tobacco filled the air and rained down on the field. The contestants lay flat on their backs, then rose and gathered in a great hug, overseen by the referees.

Afterward Fromwest sat on the lakeshore with the others. "What a relief," he said. "I was getting tired." He allowed some of the women to wrap his head wound in an embroidered cloth, and thanked them, face lowered.

In the afternoon the younger ones played the game of throwing javelins through a rolling hoop. Fromwest was invited to try it, and he agreed to make one attempt. He stood very still, and threw with a gentle motion, and the javelin flew through the hoop, leaving it rolling on. Fromwest bowed and gave up his place. "I played that game when I was a boy," he said. "It was part of the training to become a warrior, what we called a samurai. What the body learns it never forgets."

Iagogeh witnessed this exhibit, amd went to her husband, Keeper of the Wampum. "We should invite Fromwest to tell us more about his country," she said to him. He nodded, frowning a little at her interference as he always did, even though they had discussed every aspect of the league's affairs, every day for forty years. That was the way Keeper was, irritable and glowering; but all because the league meant so much to him, so that Iagogeh ignored his demeanor. Usually.

The feast was readied and they set to. As the sun dropped into the forest the fires roared bright in the shadows, and the ceremonial ground between the four cardinal fires became the scene of hundreds of people filing past the food, filling their bowls with spiced hominy and corn cakes, bean soup, cooked squash, and roasted meat of deer, elk, duck, and quail. Things grew quiet as people ate. After the main course came popcorn and strawberry jelly sprinkled with maple sugar, usually taken more slowly, and a great favorite of the children.

During this sunset feast Fromwest wandered the grounds, a goose drumstick in hand, introducing himself to strangers and listening to their stories, or answering their questions. He sat with his teammates' families and recalled the triumphs of the day on the lacrosse field. "That game is like my old job," he said. "In my country warriors fight with weapons like giant needles. I see you have needles, and some guns. These must have come from one of my old brothers, or the people who come here from over your eastern sea."

They nodded. Foreigners from across the sea had established a forti-fied village down on the coast, near the entrance of the big bay at the mouth of East River. The needles had come from them, as well as toma-hawk blades of the same substance, and guns.

"Needles are very valuable," Iagogeh said. "Just ask Needle-breaker."

People laughed at Needle-breaker, who grinned with embarrass-ment.

Fromwest said, "The metal is melted out of certain rocks, red rocks that have the metal mixed in them. If you make a fire hot enough, in a big clay oven, you could make your own metal. The right kind of rocks are just south of your league's land, down in the narrow curved valleys." He drew a rough map on the ground with a stick.

Two or three of the sachems were listening along with Iagogeh. Fromwest bowed to them. "I mean to speak to the council of sachems about these matters."

"Can a clay oven hold fires hot enough?" Iagogeh asked, inspecting the big leather-punch needle she kept on one of her necklaces.

"Yes. And the black rock that burns, burns as hot as charcoal. I used to make swords myself. They're like scythes, but longer. Like blades of grass, or lacrosse bats. As long as the bats, but edged like a tomahawk or a blade of grass, and heavy, sturdy. You learn to swing them right"—he swished a hand backhanded before them—"and off with your head. No one can stop you."

Everyone in earshot was interested in this. They could still see him whipping his bat around him, like an elm seed spinning down on the wind.

"Except a man with a gun," the Mohawk sachem Sadagawadeh, Even-tempered, pointed out.

"True. But the important part of the guns are tubes of the same metal."

Sadagawadeh nodded, very interested now. Fromwest bowed.

Keeper of the Wampum had some Neutral youths round up the other sachems, and they wandered around the grounds until they found all fifty. When they returned, Fromwest was sitting in a group, holding out a lacrosse ball between thumb and forefinger. He had big square hands, very scarred.

"Here, let me mark the world on this. The world is covered by water, mostly. There are two big islands in the world lake. Biggest island is on opposite side of world from here. This island we are on is big, but not as big as big island. Half as big, or less. How big the world lakes, not so sure."

He marked the ball with charcoal to indicate the islands in the great world sea. He gave Keeper the lacrosse ball. "A kind of wampum."

Keeper nodded. "Like a picture."

"Yes, a picture. Of the whole world, on a ball, because the world is a big ball. And you can mark it with the names of the islands and lakes."

Keeper didn't look convinced, but what he was put off by, Iagogeh couldn't tell. He instructed the sachems to get ready for the council.

Iagogeh went off to help with the cleanup. Fromwest brought bowls over to the lakeside to be washed.

"Please," Iagogeh said, embarrassed. "We do that."

"I am no one's servant," Fromwest said, and continued to bring bowls to the girls for a while, asking them about their embroidery. When he saw Iagogeh had drawn back to sit down on a bit of raised bank, he sat on the bank beside her.

As they watched the girls, he said, "I know that Hodenosaunee wisdom is such that the women decide who marries whom."

Iagogeh considered this. "I suppose you could say that."

"I am a Doorkeeper now, and a Hawk. I will live the rest of my days here among you. I too hope to marry someday."

"I see." She regarded him, looked at the girls. "Do you have someone in mind?"

"Oh no!" he said. "I would not be so bold. That is for you to decide. After your advice concerning lacrosse players, I am sure you will know best."

She smiled. She looked at the festive dress of the girls, aware or unaware of their elders' presence. She said, "How many summers have you seen?"

"Thirty-five or so, in this life."

"You have had other lives?"

"We all have. Don't you remember?"

She regarded him, unsure if he was serious. "No."

"The memories come in dreams, mostly, but sometimes when something happens that you recognize."

"I've had that feeling."

"That's what it is."

She shivered. It was cooling down. Time to get to the fire. Through the net of leafy branches overhead a star or two winked. "Are you sure you don't have a preference?"

"None. Hodenosaunee women are the most powerful women in this world. Not just the inheritance and the family lines, but choosing the marriage partnerships. That means you are deciding who comes back into the world."

She scoffed at that: "If children were like their parents." The offspring she and Keeper had had were all very alarming people.

"The one who comes into the world was there waiting. But many were waiting. Which one comes depends on which parents."

"Do you think so? Sometimes, when I watched mine—they were only strangers, invited into the longhouse."

"Like me."

"Yes. Like you."

Then the sachems found them, and took Fromwest to his raising-up.

Iagogeh made sure the cleaning was near its finish, then went after the sachems, and joined them to help prepare the new chief. She combed his straight black hair, much the same as hers, and helped him tie it up the way he wanted, in a topknot. She watched his cheery face. An unusual man.

He was given appropriate waist and shoulder belts, each a winter's work for some skillful woman, and in these he suddenly looked very fine, a warrior and a chief, despite his flat round face and hooded eyes. He did not look like anyone she had ever met, certainly not like the one glimpse she had had of the foreigners who had come over the eastern sea to their shores. But she was beginning to feel he was familiar anyhow, in a way that made her feel peculiar.

He looked up at her, thanking her for her help. When she met his gaze she felt some odd sense of recognition.

Some branches and several great logs were thrown on the central fire, and the drums and turtleshell rattles grew loud as the fifty sachems of the Hodenosaunee gathered in their great circle for the raising-up. The crowd drew in behind them, maneuvering and then sitting down so all could see, forming a kind of broad valley of faces.

The raising-up ceremony for a chief was not long compared to that of the fifty sachems. The sponsoring sachem stepped forward and announced the nomination of the chief. In this case it was Big Forehead, of the Hawk tribe, who stood forth and told them all again the story of Fromwest, how they had come across him being tortured by the Sioux, how he had been instructing the Sioux in the superior methods of torture found in his own country; how he already spoke an unfamiliar version of the Doorkeeper dialect, and how it had been his hope to come visit the People of the Longhouse before his capture by the Sioux. How he had lived among the Doorkeepers and learned their ways, and led a band of warriors far down the Ohio River to rescue many Senecan people enslaved by the Lakotas, guiding them so that they were able to effect the rescue and bring them home. How this and other actions had made him a candidate for chiefdom, with the support of all who knew him.

Big Forehead went on to say that the sachems had conferred that morning, and approved the choice of the Doorkeepers, even before Fromwest's display of skill in lacrosse. Then with a roar of acclamation Fromwest was led into the circle of sachems, his flat face shiny in the firelight, his grin so broad that his eyes disappeared in their folds of flesh.

He held out a hand, indicating he was ready to make his speech. The sachems sat on the beaten ground so that the whole congregation could see him. He said, "This is the greatest day of my life. Never as long as I live will I forget any moment of this beautiful day. Let me tell you now how I came to this day. You have heard only part of the story. I was born on the island Hokkaido, in the island nation Nippon, and grew up there as a young monk and then a samurai, a warrior. My name was Busho.

"In Nippon people arranged their affairs differently. We had a group of sachems with a single ruler, called the emperor, and a tribe of warriors were trained to fight for the rulers, and make the farmers give part of their crops to them. I left the service of my first ruler because of his cruelty to his farmers, and became a ronin, a warrior without tribe.

"I lived like that for years, wandering the mountains of Hokkaido and Honshu as beggar, monk, singer, warrior. Then all Nippon was invaded by people from farther west, on the great island of the world. These people, the Chinese, rule half the other side of the world, or more. When they invaded Nippon no great kamikaze storm wind came to sink their canoes, as always had happened before. The old gods abandoned Nippon, perhaps because of the Allah worshipers who had taken over its southernmost islands. In any case, with the water passable at last, they were unstoppable. We used banks of guns, chains in the water, fire, ambush in the night, swimming attacks over the inner sea, and we killed a great many of them, fleet after fleet, but they kept coming. They established a fort on the coast we could not eject them from, a fort protecting a long peninsula, and in a month they had filled that peninsula. Then they attacked the whole island at once, landing on every west beach with thousands of men. All the people of the Hodenosaunee league would have been but a handful in that host. And though we fought and fought, back up into the hills and mountains where only we knew the caves and ravines, they conquered the flatlands, and Nippon, my nation and my tribe, was no more.

"By then I should have died a hundred times over, but in every battle some fluke or other would save me, and I would prevail over the enemy at hand, or slip away and live to fight another time. Finally there were only scores of us left in all Honshu, and we made a plan, and joined together one night and stole three of the Chinese transport canoes, huge vessels like many floating longhouses tied together. We sailed them east under the command of those among us who had been to Gold Mountain before.

"These ships had cloth wings held up on poles to catch the wind, like those you may have seen the foreigners from the east use, and most winds come from the west, there as here. So we sailed east for a few moons, and when the winds were bad drifted on a great current in the sea.

"When we reached Gold Mountain we found other Nipponese had gotten there before us, either by months, or years, or scores of years. There were great-grandchildren of settlers there, speaking an older form of Nipponese. They were happy to see a band of samurai land; they said we were like the legendary fifty-three ronin, because Chinese ships had already arrived, and sailed into the harbor and shelled the villages with their great guns, before leaving to return to China to tell their emperor that we were there to be put to the needle." He poked to show how death from a giant needle would take place, his mimicry horribly suggestive.

"We resolved to help our tribes there to defend the place and make it a new Nippon, with the idea of eventually returning to our true home. But a few years later the Chinese appeared again, not on ships coming in through the Gold Gate, but on foot from the north, with a great army, building roads and bridges as they went, and speaking of gold in the hills. Once again the Nipponese were exterminated like rats in a granary, sent reeling south or east, into a waste of steep mountains where only one in ten survived.

"When the remnants were safely hidden away in caves and ravines, I resolved that I would not see the Chinese overrun Turtle Island as they are overrunning the great world island to the west, if I could help it. I lived with tribes and learned some language, and over the years I made my way east, over deserts and great mountains, a bare waste of rock and sand held so high up to the sun that it is cooked everywhere and the ground is like burned corn, it crunches underfoot. The mountains are enormous rock peaks with narrow canyons leading through them. On the broad eastern slope of these mountains are the grasslands beyond your rivers, covered with great herds of buffalo, and tribes of people who live off them in encampments. They move north or south with the buffalo, wherever they go. These are dangerous people, always fighting each other despite their plenty, and I took care to hide myself when I traveled among them. I walked east until I came on some slave farmers who were from the Hodenosaunee, and from what they told me, in a language that to my surprise I could already understand, the Hodenosaunee were the first people I had heard of who might be able to defeat the invasion of the Chinese.

"So I sought the Hodenosaunee, and came here, sleeping inside logs, and creeping about like a snake to see what I could of you. I came up the Ohio and explored all around this land, and rescued a Senecan slave girl and learned more words from her, and then one day we were captured by a Sioux war party. It was the girl's mistake, and she fought so hard they killed her. And they were killing me too, when you arrived and saved me. As they were testing me, I thought, A Senecan war party will rescue you—there is one out there even now. There are their eyes, reflecting the firelight. And then you were there."

He threw out his arms, and cried, "Thank you, people of the Longhouse!" He took tobacco leaves from his waist belt and tossed them gracefully into the fire. "Thank you, Great Spirit, One Mind holding us all."

"Great Spirit," murmured all the people together in response, feeling their concourse.

Fromwest took a long ceremonial pipe from Big Forehead, and filled it with tobacco very carefully. As he crumbled the leaves into the bowl he continued his speech.

"What I saw of your people astonished me. Everywhere else in the world, guns rule. Emperors put the gun to the heads of sachems, who put it to warriors, who put it to farmers, and they all together put it to the women, and only the emperor and some sachems have any say in their affairs. They own the land like you own your clothes, and the rest of the people are slaves of one kind or another. In all the world there are perhaps five or ten of these empires, but fewer and fewer as they run into each other, and fight until one wins. They rule the world, but no one likes them, and when the guns aren't pointed at them, people go away or rebel, and all is violence of one against another, of man against man, and men against women. And despite all that, their numbers grow, for they herd cattle, like elk, who provide meat and milk and leather. They herd pigs, like boars, and sheep and goats, and horses that they ride on, like little buffalo. And so their numbers are grown huge, more than the stars in the sky. Between their tame animals and their vegetables, like your three sisters, squash and beans and corn, and a corn they call rice, which grows in water, they can feed so many that in each of your valleys, they might have living as many people as all the Hodenosaunee together. This is true, I have seen it with my own eyes. On your own island it is already beginning, on the far western coast, and perhaps on the eastern coast as well."

He nodded at them all, paused to pluck a brand from the fire and light the filled pipe. He handed the smoking instrument to Keeper of the Wampum, and continued as the sachems each took one great puff from the pipe.

"Now, I have watched the Hodenosaunee as closely as a child watches its mother. I see how sons are brought up through their mother-line, and cannnot inherit anything from their fathers, so that there can be no accumulation of power in any one man. There can be no emperors here. I have seen how the women choose the marriages and advise all aspects of life, how the elderly and orphans are cared for. How the nations are divided into the tribes, woven so that you are all brothers and sisters through the league, warp and weft. How the sachems are chosen by the people, including the women. How if a sachem were to do something bad they would be cast out. How their sons are nothing special, but men like any other men, soon to marry out and have sons of their own who will leave, and daughters who will stay, until all have their say. I have seen how this system of affairs brings peace to your league. It is, in all this world, the best system of rule ever invented by human beings."

He raised his hands in thanksgiving. He refilled the pipe and got it burning again, and shot a plume of smoke into the greater smoke rising from the fire. He cast more leaves on the fire, and gave the pipe to the another sachem in the circle, Man Frightened, who indeed at this moment appeared a little awed. But the Hodenosaunee reward skills in oratory as well as skills in war, and now all listened happily as Fromwest continued.

"The best government, yes. But look you—your island is so bountiful in food that you do not have to make tools to feed yourselves. You live in peace and plenty, but you have few tools, and your numbers have not grown. Nor have you metals, or weapons made of metal. This is how it has happened; you can dig deep in the earth and find water, but why should you when there are streams and lakes everywhere? This is the way you live.

"But the big island's people have fought each other for many generations, and made many tools and weapons, and now they can sail across the great seas on all sides of this island, and land here. And so they are coming, driven as the deer by crowds of wolves behind. You see it on your east coast, beyond Beyond the Opening. These are people from the other side of the same great island I escaped, stretching halfway around the world.

"They will keep coming! And I will tell you what will happen, if you do not defend yourselves in this island of yours. They will come, and they will build more forts on the coast, as they have begun to do already. They will trade with you, cloth for furs—cloth!—cloth for the right to own this land as if it were their clothing. When your warriors object, they will shoot you with guns, and bring more and more warriors with guns, and you will not be able to oppose them for long, no matter how many of them you kill, for they have as many people as grains of sand on the long beaches. They will pour over you like Niagara."

He paused to let that potent image sink in.

He raised his hands. "It does not have to happen that way. A people as great as the Hodenosaunee, with its wise women and its wily warriors, a nation that every single person would gladly die for, as if for family—a people like this can learn to prevail over empires, empires in which only the emperors truly believe.

"How can we? you ask. How can we stop Niagara's water from falling?"

He made another pause, refilling the pipe and casting more tobacco on the fire. He passed the pipe out beyond the ring of sachems.

"Here is how. Your league is expandable, as you have shown already by the inclusion of the Shirtweavers, the Shawnee, the Choctaw and the Chickasaw. You should invite all the neighboring nations to join you, then teach them your ways, and tell them of the danger from the big island. Each nation can bring its own skill and devotion to the defense of this island. If you work together, the invaders will never be able to make headway into the depths of the great forest, which is nearly impenetrable even without opposition.

"Also, and most importantly, you need to be able to make your own guns."

Now the attention of the crowd was fixed very closely. One of the sachems held up for all to regard the musket he had obtained from the coast. Wooden stock, metal barrel, metal trigger and sparking apparatus, holding a flint. It looked sleek and unearthly in the orange firelight, gleaming like their faces, something born not made.

But Fromwest pointed at it. "Yes. Like that. Fewer parts than any basket. The metal comes from crushed rocks put in a fire. The pots and molds to hold the melted metal are made of yet harder metal, that doesn't melt anymore. Or in clay. Same with the rod you wrap a sheet of hot metal around, to make the barrel of the gun. The fire is made hot enough by using charcoal and coal for fuel, and blowing on the fire with bellows. Also, you can stick a wheel spinning in the river's flow, that will squeeze a bellows open and closed with the force of a thousand men."

He went into a description of this process that appeared to be mostly in his own language. The something did something to the something. But he illustrated by blowing on a glowing branch end held before his mouth, till it burst back into yellow flame.

"Bellows are like deerskin bags, squeezed over and over in wooden hands, wooden walls on a hinge," flapping his hands vigorously. "The devices can be pushed by the river. All work can be linked to the power of the rivers flowing by, and greatly increased. Thus the river's power becomes yours. Niagara's power becomes yours to command. You can make metal disks with toothed edges, connect them to the river, and cut through trees like sticks, cut trees longways into planks for houses and boats." He gestured around them. "A forest covers the whole eastern half of Turtle Island. Numberless trees. You could make anything. Great ships to cross the great seas, to bring the fight to their shores. Anything. You could sail there and ask their people if they want to be slaves of an empire, or a tribe woven into the league. Anything!"

Fromwest paused for another toke on the pipe. Keeper of the Wampum took the opportunity to say, "You speak always of struggle and fighting. But the foreigners on the coast have been most friendly and solicitous. They trade, they give us guns for furs, they do not shoot us, or fear us. They speak of their god as if it is none of our concern."

Fromwest nodded. "So it will be, until you look around you, and find there are foreigners all around you, in your valleys, in forts on your hilltops, and insisting that they own the land of their farm as if it were their tobacco pouch, and willing to shoot anyone who kills an animal there, or cuts a tree. And at that point they will say their law rules your law, because there are more of them and they have more guns. And they will have permanently armed warriors, ready to go on the warpath for them anywhere in the whole world. And then you will be running north to try to escape them, leaving this land here, the highest land on Earth."

He wiggled upward to show how high. Many laughed despite their consternation. They had watched him take three or four giant pulls on the pipe, and they had all taken a puff themselves by now, so they knew how high he must be feeling. He was leaving them now, they could see it. He began to speak as from a great distance away, from inside his spirit, or out among the stars.

"They will bring disease. Many of you will die of fevers, and infections coming as if from nowhere, spreading from person to person. The diseases eat you from within, like mistletoe, growing everywhere inside you. Tiny parasites inside you, big parasites outside you, people living from your work even though they stay on the other side of the world, making you do it by the force of laws and guns. Laws like mistletoe! There to support the luxuries of an emperor around the world. So many of them that they will be able to cut down all the trees in the forest."

He took a deep breath, and shook his head like a dog to get out of that dark place.

"Well!" he cried. "So! You must live as if you are already dead! Live as if you are warriors already captured, do you understand? The foreigners on the coast must be resisted, and confined to a harbor town, if you can do it. War will come eventually, no matter what you do. But the later it comes the more you can prepare for it, and hope to win it. Defending a home is easier than conquering the other side of the world, after all. So we might succeed! Certainly we must try, for all the generations that come after us!"

Another long inhalation on the pipe.

"Therefore, guns! Guns big and small! Gunpowder. Sawmills. Horses. With these things alone, we could do it. And messages on birchbark. A particular mark for each sound in the languages. Make the mark, make the sound. Easy. So talk like this can go on all the time, at great distances in space and time, between speakers and listeners. These things are being done all over the other side of the world. Listen, your island is isolated from the other by such great seas, that you have been as on another world, all the ages since the Great Spirit made people. But now the others are coming here! To resist them you have only your understanding, your spirit, your courage, and the arrangement of your nation, like the warp and weft of your baskets, so much stronger than any mere gathering of reeds. Stronger than guns!"

Suddenly he looked up and shouted it to the eastern stars. "Stronger than guns!" To the western stars: "Stronger than guns!" To the northern stars: "Stronger than guns!" To the southern stars: "Stronger than guns!"

Many cried out with him.

He waited for silence again.

"Each new chief is allowed to ask the council of sachems, gathered to honor his raising-up, consideration of some point of policy. I now ask the sachems to look at the matter of the foreigners on the east coast, and at opposing them, by harnessing river power, and making guns, and pursuing a general campaign against them. I ask the sachems to pursue our own power over our affairs."

He put his hands together and bowed.

The sachems stood.

Keeper said, "That is more than one proposal. But we will take the first one into consideration, and that will cover the rest."

The sachems gathered in small bunches and began to confer, Pounds the Rock talking fast as always, making a case for Fromwest, Iagogeh could tell.

All of them are required to be of one mind in decisions like this. The sachems of each nation divide into classes of two or three men each, and these talk in low voices to each other, very concentrated on each other. When they decide the view their class will take, one of them joins representatives from the other classes in their nation—four for the Doorkeepers and the Swampers. These also confer for a while, while the sachems finished with their work consult with the pipe. Soon one sachem from each nation expresses that view to the other eight, and they see where they stand.

On this night, the conference of the eight representatives went on for a long time, so long that people began to look at them curiously. A few years before, when conferring over how to deal with the foreigners on the east coast, they had not been able to come to a unanimous view, and nothing then had been done. By accident or design, Fromwest had brought up again one of the most important and unresolved problems of their time.

Now it was somewhat similar. Keeper called a halt to the conference, and announced to the people, "The sachems will meet again in the morning. The matter before them is too large to conclude tonight, and we don't want to delay the dancing any longer."

This met with general approval. Fromwest bowed deeply to the sachems, and joined the first knot of dancers, who led with the turtleshell rattles. He took a rattle and shook it vigorously side to side, as oddly as he had swung his lacrosse bat. There was a fluid quality to his moves, very unlike the Hodenosaunee warriors' dancing, which looked something like attacks with tomahawks, extremely agile and energetic, leaping up into the air over and over, singing all the while. A sheen of sweat quickly covered their bodies, and their singing was punctuated by hard sucks for air. Fromwest regarded these gyrations with an admiring grin, shaking his head to indicate how beyond his abilities these dancers were; and the crowd, pleased that there was something he was not good at, laughed and joined in the dance. Fromwest shuffled to the back, dancing with the women, like the women, and the string of dancers went around the fire, around the lacrosse field, and back to the fire. Fromwest stepped out of the snake, and took ground tobacco leaves from his pouch and placed a small amount on the tongue of each passerby, including Iagogeh and all the dancing women, whose graceful shuffling would long outlast the leaping warriors. "Shaman's tobacco," he explained to each person.

"Shaman gift, for dancing." It had a bitter taste, and many ate some maple water afterward to dispel it. The young men and women continued dancing, their limbs blurring in the bonfire's light, more robust and burnished than before. The rest of the crowd, younger or older, danced slightly in place as they wandered, talking over the events of the day. Many gathered around those who were inspecting Fromwest's lacrosse-ball map of the world, which seemed to glow in the firelit night as if burning a little at its heart.

"Fromwest," Iagogeh said after a while, "what was in that shaman tobacco?"

Fromwest said, "I lived with a nation to the west who gave it to me. Tonight of all nights the Hodenosaunee need to take a vision quest together. A spirit voyage, as it always is. This time all out of the longhouse together."

He took up a flute given to him, and put his fingers carefully on the stops, then played a sequence of notes, then a scale. "Ha!" he said, and looked closely at it. "Our holes are set in different places! I'll try anyway."

He played a song so piercing they were all dancing on the sound of it together, like birds. Fromwest winced as he played, until at last his face grew peaceful, and he played reconciled to the new scale.

When he was done he looked again at the flute. "That was 'Sakura,' " he said. "The holes for 'Sakura,' but it came out something else. No doubt everything I say to you comes out changed in a similar fashion. And your children will take what you do and change it yet again. So it will not matter much what I say tonight, or you do tomorrow."

One of the girls danced by holding an egg painted red, one of their toys, and Fromwest stared after her, startled by something. He looked around, and they saw that the cut on his head had started to bleed again. His eyes rolled, and he slumped as if struck, and dropped the flute. He shouted something in another language. The crowd grew quiet, and those nearest him sat on the ground.

"This has happened before," he declared in a stranger's voice, slow and grinding. "Oh yes—now it all comes back!" A faint cry, or moan. "Not this night, repeated exactly, but a previous visit. Listen—we live many lives. We die and then come back in another life, until we have lived well enough to be done. Once before I was a warrior from Nippon—no, from China!—" He paused, thinking that over. "Yes. Chinese. And it was my brother, Peng. He crossed Turtle Island, rock by rock, sleeping in logs,

fighting a bear in her den, all the way here to the top, to this very encampment, this council house, this lake. He told me about it after we
died." He howled briefly, looked around as if searching for something,
then ran off to the bone house.

Here the bones of the ancestors are stored after the individual burials
have exposed them long enough to the birds and gods to have cleansed
them white. They are stacked neatly in the bone house under the hill,
and it is not a place people visit during dances, and rarely ever.

But shamans are notoriously bold in these matters, and the crowd
watched the bone house needling light through the chinks in its bark
walls, sparking as Fromwest moved his torch here and there. A huge
groaning shout from him, rising to a scream, "Ahhhhhh!" and he
emerged holding his torch up to illuminate a white skull, which he was
jabbering at in his language.

He stopped by the fire and held up the skull to them. "You see—it's
my brother! It's me!" He moved the broken skull beside his face, and it
looked out at them from its empty eye sockets, and indeed it seemed a
good match for his head. This caused everyone to stop still and listen to
him again.

"I left our ship on the west coast, and wandered inland with a girl.
East always, to the rising sun. I arrived here just as you were meeting in
council like this, to decide on the laws you live by now. The five nations
had quarreled, and then been called together by Daganoweda for a
council to decide how to end the fighting in these fair valleys."

This was true; this was the story of how the Hodenosaunee had begun.

"Daganoweda, I saw him do it! He called them together and proposed a league of nations, ruled by sachems, and by the tribes cutting
across the nations, and by the old women. And all the nations agreed to
it, and your league of peace was born in that meeting, in the first year,
and has stayed as designed by the first council. No doubt many of you
were there too, in your previous lives, or perhaps you were on the other
side of the world, witnessing the monastery that I grew up in being built.
Strange the ways of rebirth. Strange the ways. I was here to protect your
nations from the diseases we were certain to bring. I did not bring you
your marvelous government, Daganoweda did that with all the rest of
you together, I knew nothing of that. But I taught you about scabbing.

He brought the scabs, and taught you to make a shallow scratch and put some scab in the cut, and save some of the scab that formed, and to go through the smallpox rituals, the diet and the prayers to the smallpox god. Oh that we can heal ourselves on this Earth! And thus in the sky."

He turned the skull to him and looked inside it. "He did this and no one knew," he said. "No one knew who he was, no one remembers this act of mine, no record of it exists, except in my mind, intermittently, and in the existence of all the people here who would have died if I had not done it. This is what the human story is, not the emperors and the generals and their wars, but the nameless actions of people who are never written down, the good they do for others passed on like a blessing, just doing for strangers what your mother did for you, or not doing what she always spoke against. And all that carries forward and makes us what we are."

The next part of his address was in his own language, and went on for some time. Everyone watched attentively as he spoke to the skull in his hand, and caressed it. The sight held all in its spell, and when he stopped to listen so raptly to the skull speaking back to him, they seemed to hear it too, more words in his own birdlike speech. Back and forth they spoke, and briefly Fromwest wept. It was a shock when he turned to speak to them again, in his weird Senecan:

"The past reproaches us! So many lives. Slowly we change, oh so slowly. You think it doesn't happen, but it does. You"—he used the skull to point at Keeper of the Wampum—"you could never have become sachem when I knew you last, O my brother. You were too angry, but now you are not. And you—"

Pointing the skull at Iagogeh, who felt her heart skip within her—

"You would never have known before what to do with your great power, O my sister. You would never have been able to teach Keeper so much.

"We grow together, as the Buddha told us would happen. Only now can we understand and take on our burden. You have the finest government on this Earth, no one else has understood that all are noble, all are part of the One Mind. But this is a burden too, do you see? You have to carry it—all the unborn lives to come depend on you! Without you the world would become a nightmare. The judgment of the ancestors," swinging the skull around like a pipe to be smoked, gesturing wildly at the bone house. His head wound was bleeding freely now and he was weeping, sobbing, the crowd watching him openmouthed, traveling out now with him into the sacred space of the shaman.

"All the nations on this island are your will-be brothers, your will-be sisters. This is how you should greet them. Hello, will-be brother! How fare you? They will recognize your soul as theirs. They will join you if you are their elder brother, showing them the way forward. Struggle between brothers and sisters will cease, and the league of the Hodenosaunee will be joined by nation after nation, tribe after tribe. When the foreigners arrive in their canoes to take your land, you can face them as one, resist their attacks, take from them what is useful and reject what is harmful, and stand up to them as equals on this Earth. I see now what will happen in the time to come, I see it! I see it! I see it! I see it! The people I will become dream now and speak back to me, through me, they tell me all the world's people will stand before the Hodenosaunee in wonder at the justice of its government. The story will move from longhouse to longhouse, to everywhere people are enslaved by their rulers, they will speak to each other of the Hodenosaunee, and of a way things could be, all things shared, all people given the right to be a part of the running of things, no slaves and no emperors, no conquest and no submission, people like birds in the sky. Like eagles in the sky! Oh bring it, oh come the day, oh ooohhhhhhhhhhhh . . ."

Fromwest paused then, sucking in air. Iagogeh approached him and tied a cloth around his head, to stanch the bleeding from his wound. He reeked of sweat and blood. He stared right through her, then looked up at the night sky and said "Ah," as if the stars were birds, or the twinkling of unborn souls. He stared at the skull as if wondering how it got there in his hand. He gave it to Iagogeh, and she took it. He stepped toward the young warriors, sang feebly the first part of one of the dance songs. This released the men from the spell cast over them, and they leaped to their feet, and the drumming and rattling picked up again. Quickly the dancers surrounded the fire.

Fromwest took the skull back from Iagogeh. She felt as if she were giving him his head. He walked slowly back to the bone house, weaving like a drunk, looking smaller with every weary step. He went inside without a torch. When he came out his hands were free, and he took a flute given him, and returned to the edge of the dance. There he swayed feebly in place and played with the other musicians, tootling rhythmically with no particular melody. Iagogeh shuffled in the dance, and when she passed him she pulled him back into the line, and he followed her.

"That was good," she said. "That was a good story you told."

"Was it?" he said. "I don't remember."

She was not surprised. "You were gone. Another Fromwest spoke through you. It was a good story."

"Did the sachems think so?"

"We'll tell them to think so."

She led him through the crowd, testing the look of him against one maid or another who had occurred to her as possibilities. He did not react to any of these pairings, but only danced and breathed through his flute, looking down or into the fire. He appeared drained and small, and after more dancing Iagogeh led him away from the fire. He sat down cross-legged, playing the flute with his eyes closed, adding wild trills to the music.

In the time before dawn the fire crumbled to a great mound of gray coals, glowing orangely here and there. Many people had gone into the Onondagas' longhouse to sleep, and many others were curled like dogs in their blankets on the grass under the trees. Those still awake sat in circles by the fire, singing songs or telling stories while they waited for dawn, tossing a branch on the fire to watch it catch and blaze.

Iagogeh wandered the lacrosse field, tired but buzzing in her limbs from the dance and the tobacco. She looked for Fromwest, but he was not to be found, in longhouse, on meadow, in the forest, in the bone house. She found herself wondering if the whole marvelous visitation had been only a dream they had shared.

The sky to the east was turning gray. Iagogeh went down to the lakeshore, to the women's area, beyond a small forested spit of land, thinking to wash before anyone else was around. She took off her clothes, all but her shift, and walked out into the lake until she was thigh deep, then washed herself.

Across the lake she saw a disturbance. A black head in the water, like a beaver. It was Fromwest, she decided, swimming like a beaver or an otter in the lake. Perhaps he had become an animal again. His head was preceded by a series of ripples in the water. He breathed like a bear.

She had been still for some time, and when he put his feet on the bottom, down by the spit where it was muddy, she turned and stood facing him. He saw her and froze. He was wearing only his waist belt, as in the game. He put his hands together, bowed deeply. She sloshed slowly toward him, off the sand bottom and onto soft mud.

"Come," she said quietly. "I have chosen for you."

He regarded her calmly. He looked much older than he had the day before. "Thank you," he said, and added something from his tongue. A name, she thought. Her name.

They walked onshore. Her foot hit a snag and she put a hand on his offered forearm, decorously, to balance herself. On the bank she dried herself with her fingers and dressed, while he retrieved his clothes and did likewise. Side by side they walked back to the fire, past the humming dawn watchers, through the knots of sleeping bodies. Iagogeh stopped before one. Tecarnos, a young woman, not a girl, but unmarried. Sharp tongued and funny, intelligent and full of spirit. In sleep she did not reveal much of this, but one leg was stretched out gracefully, and under her blanket she looked strong.

"Tecarnos," Iagogeh said softly. "My daughter. Daughter of my eldest sister. Wolf tribe. A good woman. People rely on her."

Fromwest nodded, hands again pressed together before him, watching her. "I thank you."

"I'll talk to the other women about it. We'll tell Tecarnos, and the men."

He smiled, looked around him as if seeing through everything. The wound on his forehead looked raw and was still seeping watery blood. The sun blinked through the trees to the east, and the singing back by the fires was louder.

She said, "You two will bring more good souls into the world."

"We can hope."

She put her hand on his arm, as she had when they emerged from the lake. "Anything can happen. But we"—meaning the two of them, or the women, or the Hodenosaunee—"we will make the best chance we can. That's all you can do."

"I know." He looked at her hand on his arm, at the sun in the trees. "Maybe it will be all right."

Iagogeh, the teller of this tale, saw all these things herself.

———

Thus it was that many years later, when the jati had again convened in the bardo, after years of work fighting off the foreigners living at the mouth of the East River, fighting to hold together their peoples in the face of all the devastating new diseases that struck them, making alliances with Fromwest's people embattled in like fashion on the west coast of their island, doing all they could to knit together the nations and to enjoy life in the forest with their kin and their tribes, Fromwest approached Keeper of the Wampum and said to him proudly, "You have to admit it, I did what you demanded of me, I went out in the world and fought for what was right! And we did some good again!"

Keeper put a hand to the shoulder of his young brother as he approached the great edifice of the bardo's dais of judgment, and said, "Yes, you performed well, youth. We did what we could."

But already he was looking ahead at the bardo's enormous towers and battlements, wary and unsatisfied, focused on the tasks ahead. Things in the bardo seemed to have gotten even more Chinese since their last time there, like all the rest of the realms, perhaps, or perhaps it was just a coincidence having to do with their angle of approach, but the great wall of the dais was broken up into scores of levels, leading into hundreds of chambers, so that it looked somewhat like the side of a beehive.

The bureaucrat god at the entryway to this warren, one Biancheng by name, handed out guidebooks to the process facing them above, thick tomes all entitled "The Jade Record," each hundreds of pages long, filled with detailed instructions, and with descriptions, illustrated copiously, of the various punishments they could expect to suffer for the crimes and affronteries they had committed in their most recent lives.

Keeper took one of these thick books and without hesitation swung it like a tomahawk, knocking Biancheng over his paper-laden desk. Keeper looked around at the long lines of souls waiting their turn to be judged, and saw them staring at him amazed, and he shouted at them, "Riot! Revolt! Rebel! Revolution!", and without waiting to see what they did, he led his little jati into a chamber of mirrors, the first room on their passage through the process of judgment, where souls were to look at themselves and see what they really were.

"A good idea," Keeper admitted, after stopping in the middle and staring at himself, seeing what no one else could see. "I am a monster," he announced. "My apologies to you all. And especially to you, Iagogeh, for putting up with me this last time, and all the previous times. And to you, youth," nodding at Busho, whom he had known as Fromwest. "But nevertheless, we have work to do. I intend to tear this whole place down." And he began looking around the room for something to throw at the mirrors.

"Wait," Iagogeh said. She was reading her copy of "The Jade Record," skimming pages rapidly, "Frontal assaults are ineffective, as I recall. I'm remembering things. We have to go at the system itself. We need a technical solution . . . Here. Here's just the thing: just before we're sent back into the world, the Goddess Meng administers to us a vial of forgetting."

"I don't remember that," Keeper said.

"That's the point. We go into each life ignorant of our pasts, and so we struggle on each time without learning anything from the times before. We have to avoid that if we can. So listen, and remember: when you are in the hundred and eight rooms of this Meng, don't drink anything! If they force you to, then only pretend to drink it, and spit it out when you are released." She read on. "We emerge in the Final River, a river of blood, between this realm and the world. If we can get there with our minds intact, then we might be able to act more effectively."

"Fine," Keeper said. "But I intend to destroy this place itself."

"Remember what happened last time you tried that," Busho warned him, getting into the corner of the chamber so he could see the reflection of the reflections. Some things were coming back to him as Iagogeh had spoken. "When you took a sword to the Goddess of Death, and she redoubled on you with each stroke."

Keeper frowned, trying to recall. Outside there was a roaring, shouts, sounds of gunfire, boots running. Irritated, distracted, he said, "You can't be cautious at times like this, you have to fight evil whenever the chance comes."

"True, but cleverly. Little steps."

Keeper regarded him skeptically. He held his thumb and forefinger together in the air. "That small?" He grabbed up Iagogeh's book and threw it at one wall of the mirrors. One of them cracked, and a shriek came from behind the wall.

"Quit arguing," Iagogeh said. "Pay attention now."

Keeper picked the book back up and they hurried through close little rooms, moving higher and higher, then lower again, then higher, always up or down stairs in multiples of seven or nine. Keeper abused several more functionaries with the big book. Pounds the Rock kept slipping into side rooms and getting lost.

Finally they reached the hundred and eight chambers of Meng, the Goddess of Forgetting. Everyone had to pass through a different one of the chambers, and drink the cup of the wine-that-was-not-wine set out for them. Guards who did not look as if they would notice the slap of a book, be it ever so thick, stood at every exit to enforce this requirement; souls were not to return to life too burdened or advantaged by their pasts.

"I refuse," Keeper shouted, they could all hear it from the nearby rooms. "I don't remember this ever being required before!"

"That's because we're making progress," Busho tried to call to him. "Remember the plan, remember the plan."

He himself took up his vial, happily fairly small, and faked swallowing its sweet contents with an exaggerated gulp, tucking the liquid under his tongue. It tasted so good he was sorely tempted to swallow it down, but resisted and only let a little seep to the back of his tongue.

Thus when his guard tossed him out into the Final River with the rest, he spat out what he could of the not-wine, but he was disoriented nevertheless. The other members of the jati thrashed likewise in the shallows, choking and spitting, Straight Arrow giggling drunkenly, totally oblivious. Iagogeh rounded them up, and Keeper, no matter what he had forgotten, had not lost his main purpose, which was to wreak havoc however he could. They half swam, half floated across the red stream to the far shore.

There, at the foot of a tall red wall, they were hauled out of the river by two demon gods of the bardo, Life-Is-Short and Death-by-Gradations. Overhead a banner hanging down the side of the wall displayed the message "To be a human is easy, to live a human life is hard; to desire to be human a second time is even harder. If you want release from the wheel, persevere."

Keeper read the message and snorted. "A second time—what about the tenth? What about the fiftieth?" And with a roar he shoved Death-by-Gradations into the river of blood. They had spit enough of Meng's not-wine of forgetting in the stream that the god guard quickly forgot who had shoved him, and what his job was, and how to swim.

But the others of the jati saw what Keeper had done, and their purpose came back ever more clearly to their consciousness. Busho shoved the other guard into the stream: "Justice!" he shouted after the suddenly absentminded swimmer. "Life is short indeed!"

Other guards appeared upstream on the bank of the Final River, hurrying toward them. The members of the jati acted quickly, and for once like a team; by twisting and tangling the banner hanging down the wall, they made it into a kind of rope they could use to pull themselves up the Red Wall. Busho and Keeper and Iagogeh and Pounds the Rock and Straight Arrow and Zigzag and all the rest hauled themselves up to the top of the wall, which was broad enough to sprawl onto. There they could catch their breath, and have a look around: back down into the dark and smoky bardo, where a struggle even more chaotic than usual had broken out; it looked like they had started a general revolt; and then forward, down onto the world, swathed in clouds.

"It looks like that time when they took Butterfly up that mountain to sacrifice her," Keeper said. "I remember that now."

"Down there we can make something new," Iagogeh said. "It's up to us. Remember!"

And they dove off the wall like drops of rain.

BOOK 6

❋ WIDOW KANG ❋

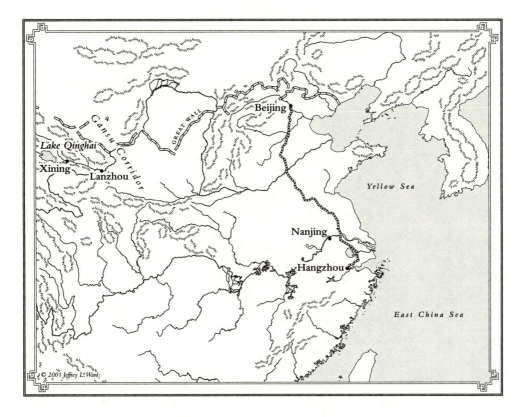

1

A Case of Soul Theft

The Widow Kang was extremely punctilious about the ceremonial aspects of her widowhood. She referred to herself always as wei-wang-ren, "the person who has not yet died." When her sons wanted to celebrate her fortieth birthday she demurred, saying "This is not appropriate for one who has not yet died." Widowed at the age of thirty-five, just after the birth of her third son, she had been cast into the depths of despair; she had loved her husband Kung Xin very much. She had dismissed the idea of suicide, however, as a Ming affectation. A truer interpretation of Confucian duty made it clear that to commit suicide was to abandon one's responsibilities to one's children and parents-in-law, which was obviously out of the question. Widow Kang Tongbi was instead determined to remain celibate past the age of fifty, writing poetry and studying the classics and running the family compound. At fifty she would be eligible for certification as a chaste widow, and would receive a commendation in the Qianlong Emperor's elegant calligraphy, which she planned to frame and place in the entrance to her home. Her three sons might even build a stone arch in her honor.

Her two older sons moved around the country in the service of the imperial bureaucracy, and she raised the youngest while continuing to run the family household left in Hangzhou, now reduced in number to her son Shih, and the servants left behind by her older sons. She oversaw the sericulture that was the principal support for the household, as her older sons were not yet in a position to send much money home, and the whole process of silk production, filature, and embroidery was under her command. No house under a district magistrate was ruled with any more iron hand. This too honored Han learning, as women's work in the better households, usually hemp and silk manufacture, was considered a virtue long before Qing policies revived official support for it.

Widow Kang lived in the women's quarters of the small compound, which was located near the banks of the Chu River. The outer walls were stuccoed, the inner walls wood shingle, and the women's quarters, in the innermost reach of the property, were contained in a beautiful white square building with a tile roof, filled with light and flowers. In that building, and the workshops adjacent to it, Widow Kang and her women would weave and embroider for at least a few hours every day, and often several more, if the light was good. Here too Widow Kang had her youngest son recite the parts of the classics he had memorized at her command. She would work at the loom, flicking the shuttle back and forth, or in the evening simply spin thread, or work at the larger patterns of embroidery, all the while running Shih through the "Analects," or Mencius, insisting on perfect memorization, just as the examiners would when the time came. Little Shih was not very good at it, even compared to his older brothers, who had been only minimally acceptable, and often he was reduced to tears by the end of the evening; but Kang Tongbi was relentless, and when he was done crying, they would get back to it. Over time he improved. But he was a nervous and unhappy boy.

So no one was happier than Shih when the ordinary routine of the household was interrupted by festivals. All three of the Bodhisattva Guanyin's birthdays were important holidays for his mother, especially the main one, on the nineteenth day of the sixth month. As this great festival approached, the widow would relent in her strict lessons, and make her preparations: proper reading, writing of poetry, collection of incense and food for the indigent women of the neighborhood; these activities were added to her already busy days. As the festival approached she fasted and abstained from any polluting actions, including becoming angry, so that she stopped Shih's lessons for the time, and offered sacrifices in the compound's little shrine.

> The old man in the moon tied red threads
> Around our legs when we were babies.

We met and married; now you are gone.
Ephemeral life is like water flowing;
Suddenly we have been separated by death all these years.
Tears well up as an early autumn begins.
The one who has not yet died is dreamed of
By a distant ghost. A crane flies, a flower falls;
Lonely and desolate, I set aside my needlework
And stand in the courtyard to count the geese
Who have lost their flocks. May Bodhisattva Guanyin
Help me get through these chill final years.

When the day itself came they all fasted, and in the evening joined a big procession up the local hill, carrying sandalwood in a cloth sack, and twirling banners, umbrellas, and paper lanterns, following their temple group's flag, and the big pitchy torch leading the way and warding off demons. For Shih the excitement of the night march, added to the cessation of his studies, made for a grand holiday, and he walked behind his mother swinging a paper lantern, singing songs, and feeling happy in a way usually impossible for him.

"Miao Shan was a young girl who refused her father's order to marry," his mother told the young women walking ahead of them, although they had all heard the story before. "In a rage he committed her to a monastery, then he burned the monastery down. A bodhisattva, Dizang Wang, took her spirit to the Forest of Corpses, where she helped the unsettled ghosts. After that she went down through the levels of hell, teaching the spirits there to rise above their suffering, and she was so successful that Lord Yama returned her as the Bodhisattva Guanyin, to help the living learn these good things while they are still alive, before it's too late for them."

Shih did not listen to this oft-heard tale, which he could not make sense of. It did not seem like anything in his mother's life, and he didn't understand her attraction to it. Singing, firelight, and the strong smoky smells of incense all converged at the shrine on the top of the hill. Up there the Buddhist abbot led prayers, and people sang and ate small sweets.

Long after moonset they trooped back down the hill and along the river path home, still singing songs in the windy darkness. Everyone from the household moved slowly along, not only because they were tired, but to accommodate Widow Kang's mincing stride. She had very small beautiful feet, but got around almost as well as the big flat-footed servant girls, by using a quick step and a characteristic swivel of the hips, a gait that no one ever commented on.

Shih wandered ahead, still nursing his last candle's guttering, and by its light he glimpsed movement against their compound wall: a big dark figure, stepping awkwardly in just the way his mother did, so that he thought for a moment it was her shadow on the wall.

But then it made a sound like a dog whimpering, and Shih jumped back and shouted a warning. The others rushed forward, Kang Tongbi at their fore, and by torchlight they saw a man in ragged robes, dirty, hunched over, staring up at them, his frightened eyes big in the torch-light.

"Thief!" someone shouted.

"No," he said in a hoarse voice. "I am Bao Ssu. I'm a Buddhist monk from Suzhou. I'm just trying to get water from the river. I can hear it." He gestured, then tried to limp away toward the river sound.

"A beggar," someone else said.

But sorcerers had been reported west of Hangzhou, and now Widow Kang held her lantern so close to his face that he had to squint.

"Are you a real monk, or just one of the hairy ones that hide in their temples!"

"A true monk, I swear. I had a certificate, but it was taken from me by the magistrate. I studied with Master Yu of the Purple Bamboo Grove Temple." And he began to recite the Diamond Sutra, a favorite of women past a certain age.

Kang inspected his face carefully in the lamplight. She shuddered palpably, stepped back. "Do I know you?" she said to herself. Then to him: "I know you!"

The monk bowed his head. "I don't know how, lady. I come from Suzhou. Perhaps you've visited there?"

She shook her head, still disturbed, peering intently into his eyes. "I know you," she whispered.

Then to the servants she said, "Let him sleep by the back gate. Guard him, and we'll find out more in the morning. It's too dark now to see a man's nature."

In the morning the man had been joined by a boy just a few years younger than Shih. Both were filthy, and were busy sifting the compost for the freshest scraps of food, which they wolfed down. They regarded the members of the household at the gate as warily as foxes. But they could not run away; the man's ankles were both swollen and bruised.

"What were you questioned for?" Kang asked sharply.

The man hesitated, looking down at the boy. "My son and I were traveling through on our way back to the Temple of the Purple Bamboo Grove, and apparently some young boy had his queue clipped about that time."

Kang hissed, and the man looked her in the eye, one hand up. "We're no sorcerers. That's why they let us go. But my name is Bao Ssu, fourth son of Bao Ju, and a beggar they had in hand for cursing a village headmaster was questioned, and he named a sorcerer he said he had met, called Bao Ssu-ju. They thought I might be that man. But I'm no soulstealer. Just a poor monk and his son. In the end they brought the beggar back in, and he confessed he had made it all up, to stop his questioning. So they let us go."

Kang regarded them with undiminished suspicion. It was a cardinal rule to stay out of trouble with the magistrates; so they were guilty of that, at the least.

"Did they torture you too?" Shih asked the boy.

"They were going to," the boy replied, "but they gave me a pear instead, and I told them Father's name was Bao Ssu-ju. I thought it was right."

Bao kept watching the widow. "You don't mind if we get water from the river?"

"No. Of course not. Go." And she watched him while the man limped down the path to the river.

"We can't let them inside," she decided. "And Shih, don't you go near them. But they can keep the gate shrine. Until winter comes that will be better than the road for them, I suppose."

This did not surprise Shih. His mother was always adopting stray cats and castaway concubines; she helped to maintain the town orphanage, and stretched their finances by supporting the Buddhist nuns. She often spoke of becoming one herself. She wrote poetry: "These flowers I walk on hurt my heart," she would recite from one of her day poems. "When my days of rice and salt are over," she would say, "I'll copy out the sutras and pray all day. But until then we had all better get to the day's work!"

So, after that the monk Bao and his boy became fixtures at the gate, and around that part of the river, in the bamboo groves and the shrine hidden in the thinning forest there. Bao never regained a normal walk, but he was not quite as hobbled as on the night of Guanyin's enlightenment day, and what he could not do his son Xinwu, who was strong for his size, did for both of them. On the next New Year's Day they joined the festivities, and Bao had managed to obtain a few eggs and color them red, so that he could give them out to Kang and Shih and other members of the household.

This was a south China custom, called "sending happiness for the new year." Possibly the author means to suggest the monk Bao had lied about his place of origin.

Bao presented the eggs with great seriousness: "Ge Hong related that the Buddha said the cosmos is egg-shaped, and the Earth like the yolk inside it." As he gave one to Shih he said, "Here, put it longways in your hand, and try to crush it."

Shih looked startled, and Kang objected: "It's too pretty."

"Don't worry, it's strong. Go ahead, try to crush it. I'll clean it up if you can."

Shih squeezed gingerly, turning his head aside, then harder. He squeezed until his forearm was taut. The egg held. Widow Kang took it from him and tried it herself. Her arms were very strong from embroidery, but the egg stood fast.

"You see," Bao said. "Eggshell is weak stuff, but the curve is strong. People are like that too. Each person weak, but together strong."

After that, on religious festival days Kang would often join Bao outside the gate, and discuss the Buddhist scriptures with him. The rest of the time she ignored the two, concentrating on the world inside the walls.

Shih's studies continued to go badly. He did not seem to be able to understand arithmetic beyond addition, and could not memorize the classics beyond a few words at the start of each passage. His mother found his study sessions intensely frustrating. "Shih, I know you are not a stupid boy. Your father was a brilliant man, your brothers are solid thinkers, and you have always been quick to find reasons why nothing is ever your fault, and why everything has to be your way. Think of equations as excuses, and you'll be fine! But all you do is think of ways not to think of things!"

Before this kind of scorn, poured on in sharp tones, no one could stand. It was not just Kang's words, but the way she said them, with a cutting edge and a crow's voice; and the curl of her lip, and the blazing, self-righteous glare—the way she looked right into you as she flailed you with her words—no one could face it. Wailing miserably as always, Shih retreated from this latest withering blast.

Not long after that scolding, he came running back from the market, wailing in earnest. Shrieking, in fact, in a full fit of hysterics. "My queue, my queue, my queue!"

It had been cut off. The servants shouted in consternation, all was an uproar for a moment, but the commotion was cut as short as Shih's little pigtail stub by his mother's grating voice:

"Shut up all of you!"

She seized Shih by the arms and put him down on the window seat where she had so often examined him. Roughly she brushed away his tears and petted him.

"Calm yourself, calm down. Calm down! Tell me what happened."

Through convulsive sobs and hiccoughs he got the story out. He had stopped on the way home from the market to watch a juggler, when hands had seized him across the eyes, and a cloth had been put across his face, covering both mouth and eyes. He had felt dizzy then and had collapsed, and when he picked himself off the ground, there was no one there, and his queue was gone.

Kang watched him intently through the course of his tale, and when he had finished and was staring at the floor, she pursed her lips and went to the window. She looked out at the chrysanthemums under the old gnarled juniper for a long time. Finally her head servant, Pao, approached her. Shih was led off to have his face washed and get some food.

The Qing dynasty forced all Han Chinese men to shave their foreheads and wear a queue, in the Manchurian manner, to show submission of the Hans to their Manchu emperors. In the years before the White Lotus conspiracy, Han bandits began to cut their queues off as a mark of rebellion.

"What shall we do?" Pao asked in a low voice.

Kang heaved a heavy sigh. "We'll have to report it," she said darkly. "If we didn't, it would surely become known anyway, from the servants talking at the market. And then it would look like we were encouraging rebellion."

"Of course," Pao said, relieved. "Shall I go inform the magistrate now?"

For the longest time there was no reply. Pao stared at Widow Kang, more and more frightened. Kang seemed under a malignant enchantment, as if she were even at that moment fighting soul-stealers for the soul of her son.

"Yes. Go with Zunli. We will follow with Shih."

Pao left. Kang wandered the household, looking at one object after another, as if inspecting the rooms. Finally she went out the compound front gate, slowly down the river path.

On the bank under the great oak tree she found Bao and his boy Xinwu, just where they always were.

She said, "Shih has had his queue cut."

Bao's face went gray. Sweat sprang on his brow.

Kang said, "We take him to the magistrate presently."

Bao nodded, swallowing. He glanced at Xinwu.

"If you want to go on a pilgrimage to some far shrine," Kang said harshly, "we could watch your son."

Bao nodded again, face stricken. Kang looked at the river flowing by in the afternoon light. The band of sun on water made her squint.

"If you go," she added, "they will be sure you did it."

The river flowed by. Down the bank Xinwu threw stones in the water and yelled at the splashes.

"Same if I stay," Bao said finally.

Kang did not reply.

After a time Bao called Xinwu over, and told him that because he had to go on a long pilgrimage, Xinwu was to stay with Kang and Shih and their household.

"When will you be back?" Xinwu asked.

"Soon."

Xinwu was satisfied, or unwilling to think about it.

Bao reached out and touched Kang's sleeve. "Thank you."

"Go. Be careful not to get caught."

"I will. If I can I'll send word to the Temple of the Purple Bamboo Grove."

"No. If we don't hear from you, we will know you are well."

He nodded. As he was about to take his leave, he hesitated. "You know, lady, all beings have lived many lives. You say we have met before, but before the festival of Guanyin, I never came near here."

"I know."

"So it must be that we knew each other in some other life."

"I know." She glanced at him briefly. "Go."

He limped off upstream on the bank path, glancing around to see if there were any witnesses. Indeed, there were fisherfolk on the other bank, their straw hats bright in the sun.

Kang took Xinwu back to the house, then got in a sedan chair to take the sniveling Shih to town and the magistrate's offices.

The magistrate looked as displeased as the Widow Kang had been to have this kind of matter thrown in his lap. But like her, he could not afford to ignore it, and so he interviewed Shih, angrily, and had him lead them all to the spot in town where it had happened. Shih indicated a place on the path next to a copse of bamboo, and just out of sight of the first stalls of the market in that district. No one habitually there had seen Shih or any unusual strangers that morning. It was a complete dead end.

So Kang and Shih went home, and Shih cried and complained that he felt sick and could not study. Kang stared at him and gave him the day off, plus a healthy dose of powdered gypsum mixed with the gallstones of a cow. They heard nothing from Bao or the magistrate, and Xinwu fit in well with the household's servants. Kang let Shih be for a time, until one day she got angry at him and seized what was left of his queue and yanked him into his examination seat, saying, "Stolen soul or not, you are going to pass your exams!", and stared down at his catlike face, until he muttered the lesson for the day before his queue had been cut, looking sorry for himself, and implacable before his mother's disdain. But she was more implacable still. If he wanted dinner he had to learn.

Then news came that Bao had been apprehended in the mountains to the west, and brought back to be interrogated by the magistrate and the district prefect. The soldiers who brought the news wanted Kang and Shih down at the prefecture immediately; they had brought a palanquin to carry them in.

Kang hissed at this news, and returned to her rooms to dress properly for the trip. The servants saw that her hands were shaking, indeed, her whole body trembled, and her lips were white beyond the power of gloss to color them. Before she left her room she sat down before the loom and wept bitterly. Then she stood and redid her eyes, and went out to join the guards.

At the prefecture Kang descended from the chair and dragged Shih with her into the prefect's examination chamber. There the guards would have stopped her, but the magistrate called her in, adding ominously, "This is the woman who was giving him shelter."

Shih cringed at this, and looked at the officials from behind Kang's embroidered silk gown. Along with the magistrate and prefect were several other officials, wearing robes striped with armbands and decorated with the insignia squares of very high-ranking officials: bear, deer, even an eagle.

They did not speak, however, but only sat in chairs watching the magistrate and prefect, who stood by the unfortunate Bao. Bao was clamped in a wooden device that held his arms up by his head. His legs were tied into an ankle press.

The ankle press was a simple thing. Three posts rose from a wooden base; the central one, between Bao's ankles, was fixed to the base. The other two were linked to the middle one at about waist height by an iron dowel rod that ran through all three, leaving the outer two loose, though big bolts meant they could only move outward so far. Bao's ankles were secured to either side of the middle post; the lower ends of the outer posts were pressing against the outsides of Bao's ankles. The upper ends had been pressed apart from the middle post by wooden wedges. All was already as tight as could be; any further taps on top of the wedges by the magistrate with his big mallet would press on Bao's ankles with enormous leverage.

"Answer the question!" the magistrate roared, leaning down to shout in Bao's face. He straightened up, walked back slowly, and gave the nearest wedge a sharp tap with his mallet.

Bao howled. Then: "I'm a monk! I've been living with my boy by the river! I can't walk any farther! I don't go anywhere!"

"Why are there scissors in your bag?" the prefect demanded quietly. "Scissors, powders, books. And a bit of a queue."

"That's not hair! That's my talisman from the temple, see how it's braided! Those are scriptures from the temple—ah!"

"It is hair," the prefect said, looking at it in the light.

The magistrate tapped again with his mallet.

"It isn't my son's hair," the Widow Kang interjected, surprising everyone. "This monk lives near our house. He doesn't go anywhere but to the river for water."

"How do you know?" the prefect asked, boring into Kang with his gaze. "How could you know?"

"I see him there at all hours. He brings our water, and some wood. He has a boy. He watches our shrine. He's just a poor monk, a beggar. Crippled by this thing of yours," she said, gesturing at the ankle press.

"What is this woman doing here?" the prefect asked the magistrate.

The magistrate shrugged, looking angry. "She's a witness like any other."

"I didn't call for witnesses."

"We did," said one of the officials from the governor. "Ask her more."

The magistrate turned to her. "Can you vouch for the presence of this man on the nineteenth day of last month?"

"He was at my property, as I said."

"On that day in particular? How can you know that?"

"Guanyin's annunciation festival was the next day, and Bao Ssu here helped us in our preparations for it. We worked all day at preparing for the sacrifices."

Silence in the room. Then the visiting dignitary said sharply, "So you are a Buddhist?"

Widow Kang regarded him calmly. "I am the widow of Kung Xin, who was a local yamen before his death. My sons Kung Yen and Kung Yi have both passed their examinations, and are serving the emperor at Nanjing and—"

"Yes yes. But are you Buddhist, I asked."

"I follow the Han ways," Kang said coldly.

The official questioning her was a Manchu, one of the Qianlong Emperor's high officers. He reddened slightly now. "What does this have to do with your religion?"

"Everything. Of course. I follow the old ways, to honor my husband and parents and ancestors. What I do to occupy the hours before I rejoin my husband is of no importance to anyone else, of course. It is only the spiritual work of an old woman, one who has not yet died. But I saw what I saw."

"How old are you?"

"Forty-one sui."

"And you spent all day on the nineteenth day of the ninth month with this beggar here."

"Enough of it to know he could not have gone to the town market and back. Naturally I worked at the loom in the afternoon."

Age in Chinese reckoning was calculated by taking the lunar year of one's birth as year one, and adding a year at each lunar New Year's Day.

Another silence in the chamber. Then the Manchu official gestured to the magistrate irritably.

"Question the man further."

With a vicious glance at Kang, the magistrate leaned over to shout down at Bao, "Why do you have scissors in your bag!"

"For making talismans."

The magistrate tapped the wedge harder than before, and Bao howled again.

"Tell me what they were really for! Why was there a queue in your bag?" With hard taps at each question.

Then the prefect asked the questions, each accompanied by a tap of the mallet from the angry magistrate, and continuous gasping groans from Bao.

Finally, scarlet and sweating, Bao cried, "Stop! Please stop. I confess. I'll tell you what happened."

The magistrate rested his mallet on the top of one wedge. "Tell us."

"I was tricked by a sorcerer into helping them. I didn't know at first what they were. They said if I didn't help them then they would steal my boy's soul."

"What was his name, this sorcerer?"

"Bao Ssu-nen, almost like mine. He came from Suzhou, and he had lots of confederates working for him. He would fly all over China in a night. He gave me some of the stupefying powder and told me what to do. Please, release the press, please. I'm telling you everything now. I couldn't help doing it. I had to do it for the soul of my boy."

"So you did cut queues on the nineteenth day of last month."

"Only one! Only one, please. When they made me. Please, release the press a little."

The Manchu official lifted his eyebrows at Widow Kang. "So you were not with him as much as you claimed. Perhaps it's better for you that way."

Someone tittered.

Kang said in her sharp hoarse bray, "Obviously this is one of those confessions we have heard about, coerced by the ankle press. The whole soul-stealing scare is based on such forced confessions, and all it does is cause panic among the servants and the workers. Nothing could be worse service of the emperor—"

"Silence!"

"You send up these reports and cause the emperor endless worry and then when a more competent investigation is made the string of forced lies is revealed—"

"Silence!"

"You are transparent from above and below! The emperor will see it!"

The Manchu official stood and pointed at Kang. "Perhaps you would like to take this sorcerer's place in the press."

Kang was silent. Shih trembled beside her. She leaned on him and pushed forward one foot until it stood outside her gown, shod in a little silk slipper. She stared the Manchu in the eye.

"I have already withstood it."

"Remove this demented creature from the examination," the Manchu said tightly, his face a dark red. A woman's foot, exposed during the examination of a crime as serious as soul-stealing: it was beyond all regulation.

No woman of breeding ever referred to her feet or revealed them in public. This was a bold person!

"I am a witness," Kang said, not moving.

"Please," Bao called out to her. "Leave, lady. Do what the magistrate says." He could barely twist far enough to look at her. "It will be all right."

So they left. On the way home in the guard's palanquin Kang wept, knocking aside Shih's comforting hands.

"What's wrong, Mother? What's wrong?"

"I have shamed your family. I have destroyed my husband's fondest hopes."

Shih looked frightened. "He's just a beggar."

"Be quiet!" she hissed. Then she cursed like one of the servants. "That Manchu! Miserable foreigners! They're not even Chinese. Not true Chinese. Every dynasty begins well, cleansing the decay of the fallen one before it. But then their turn for corruption comes. And the Qing are there. That's why they're so concerned with queue-clipping. That's their mark on us, their mark on every Chinese man."

"But that's the way it is, Mother. You can't change dynasties!"

"No. Oh, I am ashamed! I have lost my temper. I never should have gone there. I only added to the blows against poor Bao's ankles."

At home she went to the women's quarters. She fasted, worked at her weaving all the hours she was awake, and would not talk with anyone.

Then news came that Bao had died in prison, of a fever that had nothing to do with his interrogation, or so said the jailers. Kang threw herself into her room, weeping, and would not come out. When she did, days later, she spent all her waking hours weaving or writing poems, and she ate at the loom and her writing desk. She refused to teach Shih, or even to speak to him, which upset him, indeed frightened him more than anything she might have said. But he enjoyed playing down by the river. Xinwu was required to stay away from him, and was cared for by the servants.

> My poor monkey dropped its peach
> The new moon forgot to shine.
> No more climbing in the pine tree
> No little monkey on its back.
> Come back as a butterfly
> And I will be your dream.

One day not long after that, Pao brought Kang a small black queue, found buried in the mulberry compost by a servant who had been turning the muck. It was cut at an angle that matched the remnant at the back of Shih's head.

Kang hissed at the sight, and went into Shih's room and slapped him hard on the ear. He howled, crying, "What? What?" Ignoring him Kang went back to the women's quarters, groaning, and took up a pair of scissors and slashed through all the silk cloth stretched over the frames for embroidering. The servant girls cried out in alarm, no one could believe their eyes. The mistress of the house had gone crazy at last. Never had they seen her weep so hard, not even when her husband died.

Later she ordered Pao to say nothing about what had been found. Eventually all the servants found out about the discovery anyway, and Shih lived shunned in his own house. He did not seem to care.

But from that time, Widow Kang stopped sleeping at night. Often she called to Pao for wine. "I've seen him again," she would say. "He was a young monk this time, in different robes. A hui-hui. And I was a young queen. He saved me then, we ran off together. Now his ghost is hungry, and he wanders between the worlds."

They put offerings for him outside the gate, and at the windows. Still Kang woke the house with her sleeping cries, like a peacock's, and sometimes they would find her sleepwalking in between the buildings of the compound, speaking in strange tongues and even in voices not her own.

It was established practice never to wake someone walking in their sleep, to avoid startling the spirit and causing it to become confused and not find its way back to its body. So they went in front of her, moving furniture so she would not hurt herself, and they pinched the rooster to make it crow early. Pao tried to get Shih to write to his older brothers and tell them what was happening, or at least to write down what his mother was saying at night, but Shih wouldn't do it.

Eventually Pao told Shih's eldest brother's head servant's sister about it, at the market when she was visiting Hangzhou, and after that word eventually got to the eldest brother, in Nanjing. He did not come; he could not get away from his duties.

> Note that if it had been his father sick at home, or beset by ghosts, he would certainly have been given leave to go.

He did, however, have a Muslim scholar visiting him, a doctor from the frontier, and as this man had a professional interest in possessions such as Widow Kang's, he came by a few months later to visit her.

2

The Remembering

Kang Tongbi received the visitor in the rooms off the front courtyard devoted to entertaining guests, and sat watching him closely as he explained who he was, in a clear if strangely accented Chinese. His name was Ibrahim ibn Hasam. He was a small, slight man, about Kang's height and build, white-haired. He wore reading glasses all the time, and his eyes swam behind the lenses like pond fish. He was a true hui, originally from Iran, though he had lived in China for most of the Qianlong Emperor's reign, and like most long-term foreigners in China, had made a lifelong commitment to stay there.

"China is my home," he said, which sounded odd with his accent. He nodded observantly at her expression. "Not a pure Han, obviously, but I like it here. Actually, I am soon moving back to Lanzhou, to live among people of my faith. I think I have learned enough studying with Liu Zhi to be of service to those wishing for a better understanding between Muslim Chinese and Han Chinese. That is my hope, anyway."

Kang nodded politely at this unlikely quest. "And you have come here to . . . ?"

He bowed. "I have been assisting the governor of the province in these reported cases of—"

"Soul-stealing?" Kang said sharply.

"Well. Yes. Queue-cuttings, in any case. Whether they are a matter of sorcery, or merely of rebellion against the dynasty, is not so very easy to determine. I am a scholar for the most part, a religious scholar, but I have also been a student of the medical arts, and so I was summoned to see if I could bring any light to bear on the matter. I have also studied cases of—possession of the soul. And other things like that."

Kang regarded him coldly. He hesitated before continuing. "Your eldest son informs me that you have suffered some incidents of this kind."

"I know nothing about them," she said sharply. "My youngest son's queue was cut, that I am aware of. It has been investigated with no particular result. As for the rest, I am ignorant. I sleep, and have woken up a few times cold, and not in my bed. Elsewhere in the household, in fact. My servants tell me that I have been saying things they don't understand. Speaking something that is not Chinese."

His eyes swam. "Do you speak any other languages, madam?"

"Of course not."

"Excuse me. Your son said you were extremely well educated."

"My father was pleased to educate me in the classics along with his sons."

"You have the reputation of being a fine poet."

Kang did not reply, but colored slightly.

"I hope I shall have the privilege of reading some of your poems. They could help me in my work here."

"Which is?"

"Well—to cure you of these visitations, if such is possible. And to aid the emperor in his inquiry into the queue-clippings."

Kang frowned and looked away.

Ibrahim sipped his tea and waited. He seemed to have the ability to wait more or less indefinitely.

Kang gestured to Pao to refill his teacup. "Proceed, then."

Ibrahim bowed from his seat. "Thank you. Perhaps we can start by discussing this monk who died, Bao Ssu."

Kang stiffened in her wall seat.

"I know it is difficult," Ibrahim murmured. "You care still for his son."

"Yes."

"And I am told that when he arrived you were convinced that you knew him from somewhere else."

"Yes, that's right. But he said he came from Suzhou, and had never been here before. And I have never been to Suzhou. But I felt that I knew him."

"And did you feel the same way about his boy?"

"No. But I feel the same about you."

She clapped her hand over her mouth.

"You do?" Ibrahim watched her.

Kang shook her head. "I don't know why I said that! It just came out."

"Such things sometimes do." He waved it off. "But this Bao, who did not recognize you. Shortly after he arrived, there were incidents reported. Queue-chopping, people's names written on pieces of paper and placed under wharf pilings about to be driven in—that sort of thing. Soul-stealing activities."

Kang shook her head. "He had nothing to do with that. He spent every day by the river, fishing with his son. He was a simple monk, that's all. They tortured him to no purpose."

"He confessed to queue-clipping."

"On the ankle press he did! He would have said anything, and so would anyone else! It's a stupid way to investigate such crimes. It makes them spring up everywhere, like a ring of poison mushrooms."

"True," the man said. He took a sip of tea. "I have often said so myself. And in fact it's becoming clear that that is what has happened here, in the present situation."

Kang looked at him grimly. "Tell me."

"Well." Ibrahim looked down. "Monk Bao and his boy were first brought in for questioning in Anchi, as he may have told you. They had been begging by singing songs outside the village headsman's house. The headman gave them a single piece of steamed bread, and Bao and Xinwu were apparently so hungry that Bao cursed the headman, who decided they were bad characters, and repeated his order for them to be off. Bao cursed him again before leaving, and the headman was so angry he had them arrested and their bags searched. They found some writings and medicines, and scissors—"

"Same as they found here."

"Yes. And so the headman had them tied to a tree and beaten with chains. Nothing more was learned, however, and yet the two were pretty badly hurt. So the headman took part of a false queue worn by a bald guard in his employ, and put it in Bao's bag and sent him along to the prefecture for examination with the ankle press."

"Poor man," Kang exclaimed, biting her lip. "Poor soul."

"Yes." Ibrahim took another sip. "So, recently the governor-general began looking into these incidents by order of the emperor, who is very concerned. I've helped somewhat in the investigation—not with any questionings—examining physical evidence, like the false queue, which I showed was made of several different kinds of hair. So the headman was questioned, and told the whole story."

"So it was all a lie."

"Indeed. And in fact all the incidents can be traced back to an origin in a case similar to Bao's, in Suzhou—"

"Monstrous."

"—except for the case of your son Shih."

Kang said nothing. She gestured, and Pao refilled the teacups.

After a very long silence, Ibrahim said, "No doubt hooligans in town took advantage of the scare to frighten your boy."

Kang nodded.

"And also," he went on, "if you have been experiencing—possessions by spirits—possibly he also . . ."

She said nothing.

"Do you know of any oddities . . . ?"

For a long time they sat together in silence, sipping tea. Finally Kang said, "Fear itself is a kind of possession."

"Indeed."

They sipped tea for a while more.

"I will tell the governor-general that there is nothing to worry about here."

"Thank you."

Another silence.

"But I am interested in any subsequent manifestations of . . . anything out of the ordinary."

"Of course."

"I hope we can discuss them. I know of ways to investigate such things."

"Possibly."

Soon after the hui doctor ended his visit.

After he was gone, Kang wandered the compound from room to room, trailed by the worried Pao. She looked into Shih's room, now empty, his books on their shelves unopened. Shih had gone down to the riverside, no doubt to be with his friend Xinwu.

Kang looked in the women's quarters, at the loom on which so much

of their fortune resided; and the writing stand, ink block, brushes, stacks
of paper.

> Geese fly north against the moon.
> Sons grow up and leave.
> In the garden, my old bench.
> Some days I'd rather have rice and salt.
> Sit like a plant, neck outstretched:
> Honk, honk! Fly away!

Then on to the kitchens, and the garden under the old juniper. Not a
word did she say, but retired to her bedroom in silence.

That night, however, cries again woke the household. Pao rushed out
ahead of the other servants, and found Widow Kang slumped against the
garden bench, under the tree. Pao pulled her mistress's open night shift
over her breast and hauled her up onto the bench, crying "Mistress
Kang!" because her eyes were open wide; yet they saw nothing of this
world. The whites were visible all the way around, and she stared
through Pao and the others, seeing other people and muttering in
tongues. "In challa, in challa"—a babble of sounds, cries, squeaks—"um
mana pada hum"; and all in voices not hers.

"Ghosts!" squealed Shih, who had been wakened by the fuss. "She's
possessed!"

"Quiet please," hissed Pao. "We must return her to her bed still
asleep."

She took one arm, Zunli took the other, and as gently as they could,
they lifted her. She was as light as a cat, lighter than she ought to have
been. "Gently," Pao said as they bumped her over the sill and laid her
down. Even as she lay there she popped back up like a puppet, and said,
in something like her own voice, "The little goddess died despite all."

Pao sent word to the hui doctor of what had occurred, and a note
came back with their servant, requesting another interview. Kang
snorted and dropped the note on the table and said nothing. But a week
later the servants were told to prepare lunch for a visitor, and it was
Ibrahim ibn Hasam who appeared at the gate, blinking behind his spectacles.

Kang greeted him with the utmost formality, and led him into the
parlor, where the best porcelain was laid out for a meal.

After they had eaten and were sipping tea, Ibrahim nodded and said, "I am told that you suffered another attack of sleepwalking."

Kang colored. "My servants are indiscreet."

"I'm sorry. It's just that this may pertain to my investigation."

"I recall nothing of the incident, alas. I woke to a very disturbed household."

"Yes. Perhaps I could ask your servants what you said while under the . . . under the spell?"

"Certainly."

"Thank you." Another seated bow, another sip. "Also . . . I was wondering if you might agree to help me attempt to reach this . . . this other voice inside you."

"How do you propose to do this?"

"It is a method developed by the doctors of al-Andalus. It involves a kind of meditation on an object, as in a Buddhist temple. An examiner helps to put the meditating subject under a description, as they call it, and then the inner voices sometimes will speak with the examiner."

"Like soul-stealing, then?"

He smiled. "No stealing is involved. It is mainly conversation, you see. Like calling the spirit of someone absent, even to themselves. Like the soul-calling done in your southern cities. Then when the meditation ends, all returns to normal."

"Do you believe in the soul, Doctor?"

"Of course."

"And in soul-stealing?"

"Well." Long pause. "This concept has to do with a Chinese understanding of the soul, I think. Perhaps you can clarify it for me. Do you make a distinction between the hun, the spiritual soul, and the po, or bodily soul?"

"Yes, of course," Kang said. "It is an aspect of yin-yang. The hun soul belongs to the yang, the po soul to the yin."

Ibrahim nodded. "And the hun soul, being light and active, volatile, is the one that can separate from the living person. Indeed it does separate, every night in sleep, and returns on waking. Normally."

"Yes."

"And if by chance, or design, it does not return, this is a cause of illness, especially in children's illnesses, like colic, and in various forms of sleeplessness, madness, and the like."

"Yes." Now the Window Kang was not looking at him.

"And the hun is the soul that the soul-stealers supposedly roaming the countryside are after. Chiao-hun."

"Yes. Obviously you don't believe this."

"No no, not at all. I reserve judgment for what is shown. I can see the distinction being made, no doubt of that. I myself travel in dreams—believe me, I travel. And I have treated unconscious patients, whose bodies continue to function well, in the pink of health you might say, while they lie there on their bed and never move, no, not for years. I cleaned her face—I was washing her eyelashes, and all of a sudden she said, 'Don't do that.' After sixteen years. No, I have seen the hun soul go and return, I think. I think it is like most matters. The Chinese have certain words, certain concepts and categories, while Islam has other words, naturally, and slightly different categories, but on closer inspection these can all be correlated and shown to be one. Because reality is one."

Kang frowned, as if perhaps she did not agree.

"Do you know the poem by Rumi Balkhi, 'I Died As Mineral'? No? It is by the founder of the dervishes, the most spiritual of Muslims." He recited:

> I died as mineral and came back as plant,
> Died as plant and came back as animal,
> Died as animal and came back a man.
> Why should I fear? When have I ever lost by dying?
> Yet once more I shall die human,
> To soar with angels blessed above.
> And when I sacrifice my angel soul
> I shall become what no mind ever conceived.

"That last death I think refers to the hun soul, moving away from the po soul to some transcendence."

Kang was thinking it over. "So, in Islam you believe that souls come back? That we live many lives, and are reincarnated?"

Ibrahim sipped his green tea. "The Quran says, 'God generates beings, and sends them back over and over again, till they return to Him.' "

"Really!" Now Kang regarded Ibrahim with interest. "This is what we Buddhists believe."

Ibrahim nodded. "A Sufi teacher I have followed, Sharif Din Maneri, said to us, 'Know for certain that this work has been before thee and me in bygone ages, and that each person has already reached a certain stage. No one has begun this work for the first time.' "

Kang stared at Ibrahim, leaning from her wall seat toward him. She cleared her throat delicately. "I remember bits of these sleepwalking spells," she admitted. "I often seem to be some other person. Usually a young woman, a—a queen, of some far country, in trouble. I have the impression it was long ago, but it is all confused. Sometimes I wake with the sense of a year or more having passed. Then I come fully into this world again, and it all falls apart, and I can recall nothing but an image or two, like a dream, or an illustration in a book, but less whole, less . . . I'm sorry. I can't make it clear."

"But you can," Ibrahim said. "Very clear."

"I think I knew you," she whispered. "You and Bao, and my son Shih, and Pao, and certain others. I . . . it's like that moment one sometimes feels, when it seems that whatever is happening has already happened before, in just the same way."

Ibrahim nodded. "I have felt that. Elsewhere in the Quran, it says, 'I tell you of a truth, that the spirits which now have affinity will be kindred together, although they all meet in new persons and names.' "

"Truly?" Kang exclaimed.

"Yes. And elsewhere again, it says, 'His body falls off like the shell of a crab, and he forms a new one. The person is only a mask which the soul puts on for a season, wears for its proper time, and then casts off, and another is worn in its stead.' "

Kang stared at him, mouth open. "I can scarcely believe what I am hearing," she whispered. "There has been no one I can tell these things. They think me mad. I am known now as a . . ."

Ibrahim nodded and sipped his tea. "I understand. But I am interested in these things. I have had certain—intimations, myself. Perhaps then we can try the process of putting you under a description, and see what we can learn?"

Kang nodded decisively. "Yes."

Because he wanted darkness, they settled on a window seat in the reception hall, with its window shuttered and the doors closed. A single candle burned on a low table. The lenses of his glasses reflected the flame. The house had been ordered to be silent, and faintly they could hear dog barks, cart wheels, the general hum of the city in the distance, all very faint.

Ibrahim took Widow Kang by the wrist, very loosely, fingers cool and light against her pulse, at which sensation her pulse quickened; surely he could feel it. But he had her look into the candle flame, and he spoke in Persian, Arabic, and Chinese: low chanting, with no emphasis of tone, a gentle murmur. She had never heard such a voice.

"You are walking in the cool dew of the morning, all is peaceful, all is well. In the heart of the flame the world unfolds like a flower. You breathe in the flower, slowly in, slowly out. All the sutras speak through you into this flower of light. All is centered, flowing up and down your spine like the tide. Sun, moon, stars, in their places, wheeling around us, holding us."

In like manner he murmured on and on, until Kang's pulse was steady at all three levels, a floating, hollow pulse, her breathing deep and relaxed. She truly appeared to Ibrahim to have left the room, through the portal of the candle flame. He had never had anyone leave him so quickly.

"Now," he suggested, "you travel in the spirit world, and see all your lives. Tell me what you see."

Her voice was high and sweet, unlike her usual voice. "I see an old bridge, very ancient, across a dry stream. Bao is young, and wears a white robe. People follow me over the bridge to a . . . a place. Old and new."

"What are you wearing?"

"A long . . . shift. Like night garments. It's warm. People call out as we pass."

"What are they saying?"

"I don't understand it."

"Just make the sounds they make."

"In sha ar am. In sha ar am. There are people on horses. Oh—there you are. You too are young. They want something. People cry out. Men on horses approach. They're coming fast. Bao warns me—"

She shuddered. "Ah!" she said, in her usual voice. Her pulse became leathery, almost a spinning-bean pulse. She shook her head hard, looked up at Ibrahim. "What was that? What happened?"

"You were gone. Seeing something else. Do you remember?"

She shook her head.

"Horses?"

She closed her eyes. "Horses. A rider. Cavalry. I was in trouble!"

"Hmm." He released her wrist. "Possibly so."

"What was it?"

He shrugged. "Perhaps some . . . Do you speak any—no. You said already that you did not. But in this hun travel, you seemed to be hearing Arabic."

"Arabic?"

"Yes. A common prayer. Many Muslims would recite it in Arabic, even if that was not their language. But . . ."

She shuddered. "I have to rest."

"Of course."

She looked at him, her eyes filling with tears. "I . . . can it be—why me, though—" She shook her head and her tears fell. "I don't understand why this is happening!"

He nodded. "We so seldom understand why things happen."

She laughed shortly, a single "Ho!" Then: "But I like to understand."

"So do I. Believe me; it is my chief delight. Rare as it is." A small smile, or grimace of chagrin, offered for her to share. A shared understanding, of their solitary frustration at understanding so little.

Kang took a deep breath and stood. "I appreciate your assistance. You will come again, I trust?"

"Of course." He stood as well. "Anything, madam. I feel that we have just begun."

She was suddenly startled, looking through him. "Banners flew, do you remember?"

"What?"

"You were there." She smiled apologetically, shrugged. "You too were there."

He was frowning, trying to understand her. "Banners . . ." He seemed lost himself for a while. "I . . ." He shook his head. "Maybe. I recall—it used to be, when I saw banners, as a child in Iran, it would mean so much to me. More than could be explained. Like I was flying."

"Come again, please. Perhaps your hun soul too can be called forth."

He nodded, frowning, as if still in pursuit of a receding thought, a banner in memory. Even as he said his farewells and left, he was still distracted.

He returned within the week, and they had another session "inside the candle" as Kang called it. From the depths of her trance she burst into speech that neither of them understood—not Ibrahim as it happened, nor Kang when he read back to her what he had written down.

He shrugged, looking shaken. "I will ask some colleagues. Of course, it may be some language totally lost to us now. We must concentrate on what you see."

"But I remember nothing! Or very little. As you recall dreams, that slip away on waking."

"When you are actually inside the candle, then, I must be clever, ask the right questions."

"But if I don't understand you? Or if I answer in this other tongue?"

He nodded. "But you seem to understand me, at least partly. There must be translation in more than one realm. Or there may be more to the hun soul than has been suspected. Or the tendril that keeps you in contact with the traveling hun soul conveys other parts of what you know. Or it is the po soul that understands." He threw up his hands: who could say?

Then something struck her, and she put her hand to his arm. "There was a landslide!"

They stood together in silence. Faintly the air quivered.

He went away puzzled, distracted. At every departure he left bemused, and at every return he was fairly humming with ideas, with anticipation of their next voyage into the candle.

"A colleague in Beijing thinks it may be a form of Berber that you are speaking. At other times, Tibetan. Do you know these places? Morocco is at the other end of the world, the west end of Africa, in the north. It was Moroccans who repopulated al-Andalus when the Christians died."

"Ah," she said, but shook her head. "I was always Chinese, I am sure. It must be an old Chinese dialect."

He smiled, a rare and pleasant sight. "Chinese in your heart, perhaps. But I think our souls wander the whole world, life to life."

"In groups?"

"People's destinies intertwine, as the Quran says. Like threads in your embroideries. Moving together like the traveling races on Earth—the Jews, the Christians, the Zott. Remnants of older ways, left without a home."

"Or the new islands across the Eastern Sea, yes? So we might have lived there too, in the empires of gold?"

"Those may be Egyptians of ancient times, fled west from Noah's flood. Opinion is divided."

"Whatever they are, I am certainly Chinese through and through. And always have been."

He regarded her with a trace of his smile in his eye. "It does not sound like Chinese that you speak when inside the candle. And if life is inextinguishable, as it seems it might be, you may be older than China itself."

She took a deep breath, sighed. "Easy to believe."

The next time he came to put her under a description, it was night, so they could work in silence and darkness; so that the candle flame, the dim room, and the sound of his voice would be all that seemed to exist. It was the fifth day of the fifth month, an unlucky day, the day of the festival of hungry ghosts, when those poor preta who had no living descendants were honored and given some peace. Kang had said the Surangama Sutra, which expounded the rulai-zang, a state of empty mind, tranquil mind, true mind.

Spuriously Sanskrit, originally written in Chinese and titled "Lengyan jing." The awareness it describes, changzhi, is sometimes called "Buddha-nature," or tathagatagarbha, or "mind ground." The sutra claims that devotees can be "suddenly awakened" to this state of high awareness.

She made the purification of the house rituals, and fasted, and she asked Ibrahim to do the same. So when the preparations were finally finished, they sat alone in the stuffy dark chamber, watching a candle burn. Kang entered into the flame almost the moment Ibrahim touched her wrist, her pulse flooding, a yin-in-yang pulse. Ibrahim watched her closely. She muttered in the language he could not understand, or perhaps another language yet. There was a sheen on her forehead, and she seemed distraught.

The flame of the candle shrank down to the size of a bean. Ibrahim swallowed hard, holding off fear, squinting with the effort.

She stirred, her voice grew more agitated.

"Tell me in Chinese," he said gently. "Speak Chinese."

She groaned, muttered. Then she said, very clearly, "My husband died. They wouldn't—they poisoned him, and they wouldn't accept a queen among them. They wanted what we had. Ah!" And she began again to speak in the other language. Ibrahim fixed her clearest words in mind, then saw that the candle's flame had grown again, but past its normal height, rising so high that the room grew hot and stifling, and he feared for the paper ceiling. "Please be calm, O spirits of the dead," he said in Arabic, and Kang cried out in the voice not hers:

"No! No! We're trapped!" And then she was sobbing, crying her heart out. Ibrahim held her by the arms, gently squeezing her, and suddenly she looked up at him, seeming awake, and her eyes grew round. "You were there! You were with us, we were trapped by an avalanche, we were stuck there to die!"

He shook his head: "I don't remember—"

She struggled free and slapped him hard on the face. His spectacles flew across the room, she jumped on him and held him by the throat as if to strangle him, eyes locked on his, suddenly so much smaller. "You were there!" she shouted. "Remember! Remember!"

In her eyes he seemed to see it happen. "Oh!" he said, shocked, looking through her now. "Oh, my God. Oh . . ."

She released him, and he sank to the floor. He patted it as if searching for his glasses. "Inshallah, inshallah." He groped about, looked up at her. "You were just a girl . . ."

"Ah," she said, and collapsed onto the floor beside him. She was weeping now, eyes running, nose running. "It's been so long. I've been so alone." She sniffed hard, wiped her eyes. "They keep killing us. We keep getting killed."

"That's life," he said, wiping his own eyes once. He collected himself. "That's what happens. Those are the ones you remember. You were a black boy, once, a beautiful black boy, I can see you now. And you were my friend once, old men together. We studied the world, we were friends. Such a spirit."

The candle flame slowly dropped back to its normal height. They sat beside each other on the floor, too drained to move.

Eventually Pao knocked hesitantly on the door, and they started guiltily, though they had both been lost in their own thoughts. They got up and sat in the window seats, and Kang called out to Pao to bring some peach juice. By the time she came with it they were both composed; Ibrahim had relocated his spectacles, and Kang had opened the window shutter to the night air. The light of a clouded half-moon added to the glow of the candle flame.

Hands still shaking, Kang sipped some peach juice, nibbled on a plum. Her body too was trembling. "I'm not sure I can do that anymore," she said, looking away. "It's too much."

He nodded. They went into the compound garden, and sat in the cool of the night under the clouds, eating and drinking. They were hungry. The scent of jasmine filled the dark air. Though they did not speak, they seemed companionable.

> I am older than China itself
> I walked in the jungle hunting for food
> Sailed the seas across the world
> Fought in the long war of the asuras.
> They cut me and I bled. Of course. Of course.
> No wonder my dreams are so wild,
> No wonder I feel so tired. No wonder I am always
> Angry.
> Clouds mass, concealing a thousand peaks;
> Winds sweep, coloring ten thousand trees.
> Come to me husband and let us live
> The next ten lives together.

The next time Ibrahim visited, his face was solemn, and he was dressed more finely than they had seen before, in the garb of a Muslim cleric, it seemed.

After the usual greetings, when they were alone again in the garden, he stood and faced her.

"I must return to Gansu," he said. "I have family matters I must attend to. And my Sufi master has need of me in his madressa. I've put it off as long as I could, but I have to go."

Kang looked aside. "I will be sorry."

"Yes. I also. There is much still to discuss."

Silence.

Then Ibrahim stirred and spoke again. "I have thought of a way to solve this problem, this separation between us, so unwished for, which is that you should marry me—accept my proposal of marriage and marry me, and bring you and your people with you out with me, to Gansu."

The Widow Kang looked utterly astonished. Her mouth hung open.

"Why—I cannot marry. I am a widow."

Ibrahim said, "But widows may remarry. I know the Qing try to discourage it, but Confucius says nothing at all against it. I have looked, and checked with the best experts. People do it."

"Not respectable people!"

He narrowed his eyes, looking suddenly Chinese. "Respect from whom?"

She looked away. "I cannot marry you. You are hui, and I am one who has not yet died."

"The Ming emperors ordered all hui to marry good Chinese women, so that their children would be Chinese. My mother was a Chinese woman."

She looked up, surprised again. Her face was flushed.

"Please," he said, hand out. "I know it's a new idea. A shock. I'm sorry. Please think about it, before you make your final reply. Consider it."

She straightened up and faced him formally. "I will consider it."

A flick of the hand indicated her desire to be left alone, and with a truncated farewell, ended by a phrase in another language, spoken most intently, he made his way out of the compound.

After that, the Widow Kang wandered through her household. Pao was out in the kitchen, ordering the girls about, and Kang asked her to come speak to her in the garden. Pao followed her out, and Kang told her what had happened, and Pao laughed.

"Why do you laugh!" Kang snapped. "Do you think I care so much for a testimonial from a Qing emperor! That I should lock myself in this box for the rest of my life, for the sake of a paper covered with vermilion ink?"

Pao froze, first startled, then frightened. "But, Mistress Kang— Gansu . . ."

"You know nothing about it. Leave me."

After that no one dared to speak to her. She wandered the house like a hungry ghost, acknowledging no one. She scarcely spoke. She visited the shrine at the Temple of the Purple Bamboo Grove, and recited the Diamond Sutra five times, and went home with her knees hurting. Li Anzi's poem "Sudden View of Years" came to her mind:

> The mother of two successful officials, who reared them alone as a widow.

> Sometimes all the threads on the loom
> Suggest the carpet to come.

Then we know that our children-to-be
Hope for us in the bardo.
For them we weave until our arms grow tired.

She had the servants carry her to the magistrate's building, where she had them set down the sedan chair, and did not move for an hour. The men could just see her face behind the gauze of the window curtain. They took her home without her ever having emerged.

The next day she had them carry her to the cemetery, though it was not a festival day, and under the empty sky she shuffled about with her peculiar gait, sweeping the graves of all the family ancestors, then sitting at the foot of her husband's grave, head in her hands.

The next day she went down to the river on her own, walking the entire way, crimping along, looking at trees, ducks, the clouds in the sky. She sat on the riverbank, as still as if she were in one of the temples.

Xinwu was down there as he almost always was, trailing his fishing pole and bamboo basket. He brightened at the sight of her, showed her the fish he had caught. He sat by her, and they watched the great brown river flow past, glossy and compact. He fished, she sat and watched.

"You're good at that," she said, watching him flick the line out into the stream.

"My father taught me." After a time: "I miss him."

"I do too." Then: "Do you think . . . I wonder what he would think."

After another pause: "If we move west, you must come with us."

She invited Ibrahim to return, and when he came, Pao led him into the reception hall, which Kang had ordered filled with flowers.

He stood before her, head bowed.

"I am old," she told him. "I have passed through all the life stages. I am one who has not yet died. I cannot go backward. I cannot give you any sons."

"I understand," he murmured. "I too am old. Still—I ask your hand in marriage. Not for sons, but for me."

She regarded him, her color rising.

"Then I accept your offer of marriage."

He smiled.

> "all the life stages": milk teeth, hair-pinned-up, marriage, children, rice and salt, widowhood.

After that the household was as if caught in a whirlwind. The servants, though highly critical of the match, nevertheless had to work all day every day to make the place ready in time for the fifteenth day of the sixth month, the midsummer time traditionally favored for starting travel. Kang's elder sons disapproved of the match, of course, but made plans to attend the wedding anyway. The neighbors were scandalized, shocked beyond telling, but as they were not invited, there was no way for them to express this to the Kang household. The widow's sisters at the temple congratulated her and wished her well. "You can bring the wisdom of the Buddha to the hui," they told her. "It will be very useful for all."

So they were married in a small ceremony attended by all Kang's sons, and only Shih was less than congratulatory, pouting most of the morning in his room, a fact Pao did not even report to Kang. After the ceremony, held in the garden, the party spread down to the river, and though small, it was determinedly cheery. After that the household was packed up, its furniture and goods loaded in carts either destined for their new home in the west, or else for the orphanage that Kang had helped establish in town, or for her elder sons.

When all was ready, Kang took a last walk through the household, stopping to stare into the bare rooms, oddly small now.

> This square fathom has held my life.
> Now the goose flies away,
> Chased by a Phoenix from the west.
> How could one life encompass such change.
> Truly we live more lives than one.

Soon she came out and climbed into the sedan chair. "It is already gone," she said to Ibrahim. He handed her a gift, an egg painted red: happiness in the new year. She bowed her head. He nodded, and directed their little train to begin the journey west.

3

Waves Slap Together

The trip took over a month. The roads and tracks they followed were dry, and they made good time. Partly this was because Kang asked to ride in a cart rather than be carried in a palanquin or smaller chair. At first the servants were convinced this decision had caused some discord in the new couple, for Ibrahim took to riding in the covered cart with Kang, and they heard the arguing between them go on sometimes for whole days on end. But Pao walked close enough one afternoon to catch the drift of what they were saying, and she came back to the others relieved. "It's only religion they're debating. A real pair of intellectuals, those two."

So the servants traveled on, reassured. They went up to Kaifeng, stayed with some of Ibrahim's Muslim colleagues there, then followed the roads paralleling the Wei River, west to Xi'an in Shaanxi, then over hard passes in dry hills, to Lanzhou.

By the time they arrived, Kang was amazed beyond amazement. "I can't believe there is so much world," she would say to Ibrahim. "So much China! So many fields of rice and barley, so many mountains, so empty and wild. Surely we should have crossed the world by now."

"Scarcely a hundredth part of it, according to the sailors."

"This outlandish country is so cold and dry, so dusty and barren. How will we keep a house clean here, or warm? It's like trying to live in hell."

"Not that bad, surely."

"Is this really Lanzhou, the renowned city of the west? This little brown windblown mud-brick village?"

"Yes. It's growing quite rapidly, actually."

"And we are to live here?"

"Well, I have connections here, and in Xining, a bit farther to the west. We could settle in either place."

"Let me see Xining before we decide. It must be better than this."

Ibrahim said nothing, but ordered their little caravan on. More days of travel, as the seventh month passed, and storm clouds rolled overhead almost every day, never quite breaking on them. Under these low ceilings the sere broken hills looked even more inhospitable than before, and except in the irrigated, terraced central flats of the long narrow valleys, there was no more agriculture to be seen. "How do people live here?" Kang asked. "How do they eat?"

"They herd sheep and goats," Ibrahim said. "Sometimes cattle. It's like this all over, west of here, all the way across the dry heart of the world."

"Astonishing. It's like traveling back in time."

Finally they came to Xining, another little walled mud-brick town, huddling under shattered mountainsides, in a high valley. A garrison of imperial soldiers manned the gates, and some new wooden barracks had been thrown up under the town walls. A big caravanserai stood empty, as it was too late in the year to start traveling. Beyond it several walled ironworks used what little power the river provided to run their stamps and forges.

"Ugh!" Kang said. "I did not think Lanzhou could be beaten for dust, but I was wrong."

"Wait for your decision," Ibrahim requested. "I want you to see Qinghai Lake. It's just a short journey farther."

"Surely we will fall off the edge of the world."

"Come see."

Kang agreed without argument; indeed, it seemed to Pao that she was actually enjoying these insanely dry and barbarous regions, or at least enjoying her complaining about them. The dustier the better, her face seemed to say, no matter what words she spoke.

A few more days west on a bad road brought them through a draw to the shores of Qinghai Lake, the sight of which took speech away from all of them. By chance they had arrived on a day of wild, windy weather, with great white clouds floored by blue-gray embroidery charging overhead, and these clouds were reflected in the lake's water, which in sunlight was just as blue-green as the name of the lake would suggest. To the west the lake extended right off to the horizon; the curve of its visible shores was a bank of green hills. Out here in this brown desolation, it was like a miracle.

Kang got out of the cart and walked slowly down to the pebbled shore, reciting the Lotus Sutra, and holding up her hands to feel the hard rush of the wind on her palms. Ibrahim gave her some time to herself, then joined her.

"Why do you weep?" he inquired.

" 'So this is the great lake,' " she recited.

> "Now I can at last comprehend
> The immensity of the universe;
> My life has gained new meaning!
> But think of all the women
> Who never leave their own courtyards,
> Who must spend their whole lives
> Without once enjoying a sight like this."

Ibrahim bowed. "Indeed. Whose poem is this?"

She shook her head, dashing the tears away. "That was Yuen, the wife of Shen Fu, on seeing the T'ai Hu. The Great Lake! What would she have thought if she saw this one! It is part of 'Six Chapters from a Floating Life.' Do you know it? No. Well. What can one say?"

"Nothing."

"Indeed." She turned to him, put her hands together. "Thank you, husband, for showing me this great lake. It is truly magnificent. Now I can settle, let us live wherever you please. Xining, Lanzhou, the other side of the world, where once we met in a previous life—wherever you like. It is all the same to me." And she leaned weeping against his side.

For the time being, Ibrahim decided to settle the household in Lanzhou. This gave him better access to the Gansu Corridor, and therefore the routes to the west, as well as the return routes to the Chinese interior. Also, the madressa he had had the closest contact with in his youth had moved to Lanzhou, forced there from Xining by pressure from newly arrived western Muslims.

They set up their household in a new mud-brick compound by the banks of the Tao River, close to where it joined the Yellow River. The Yellow River's water was indeed yellow, a completely opaque sandy roiling yellow, precisely the color of the hills to the west out of which it sprang. The Tao River was a bit clearer and more brown.

The household was bigger than Kang's old place in Hangzhou, and she quickly set up the women's quarters in a back building, staking out a garden in the ground around it, and demanding potted trees to begin the process of landscaping. She also wanted a loom, but Ibrahim pointed out that silk thread would be unavailable here, as there were neither mulberry groves nor filatures. If she wanted to continue weaving, she would have to learn to work wool. With a sigh she agreed, and began the process on hand looms. Embroidering silk cloth that was already made also occupied them.

Ibrahim meanwhile went to work meeting with his old associates in the Muslim schools and fellowships, and with the new Qing officials of the town, thereby beginning the process of sorting out and assisting the new political and religious situations in the area, which had changed, apparently, since he had last been home. In the evenings he would sit with Kang on the verandah overlooking the muddy yellow river and explain it to her, answering her endless questions.

"To simplify slightly, ever since Ma Laichi came back from Yemen, bearing texts of religious renewal and rectification, there has been conflict within the Muslims of this part of the world. Understand that Muslims have lived here for centuries, almost since the beginning of Islam, and at this distance from Mecca and the other centers of Islamic learning, various heterodoxies and error were introduced. Ma Laichi wanted to reform these, but the old umma here brought suit against him in the Qing civil court, accusing him of huozhong."

Deluding the people, a serious offense anywhere in China.

Kang looked severe, no doubt remembering the effects of such delusion back in the interior.

"Eventually the governor-general out here, Paohang Guangsi, dismissed the suit. But that did not end matters. Ma Laichi proceeded to convert the Salars to Islam—they are a people out here who speak a Turkic language, and live on the roads. They are the ones you see in the white caps, who do not look Chinese."

"Who look like you."

Ibrahim frowned. "A little, perhaps. Anyway, this made people nervous, as the Salars are considered dangerous people."

"I can see why—they look like it."

"These people who look like me. But no matter. Anyway, there are many other forces in Islam, sometimes in conflict. A new sect called the Naqshabandis are trying to purify Islam by a return to more orthodox older ways, and in China they are led by Aziz Ma Mingxin, who, like Ma Laichi, spent many years in Yemen and Mecca, studying with Ibrahim ibn Hasa al-Kurani, a very great shaikh whose teachings are spread now all over the Islamic world.

"Now, these two great shaikhs came back here from Arabia with reforms in mind, after studying with the same people, but alas, they are different reforms. Ma Laichi believed in the silent recital of prayer, called dhikri, while Ma Mingxin, being younger, studied with teachers who believed prayers could be chanted aloud as well."

"This seems a minor difference to me."

"Yes." When Ibrahim looked Chinese it meant he was amused by his wife.

"In Buddhism we allow both."

"True. But they mark deeper divisions, as often happens. Anyway, Ma Mingxin practices jahr prayer, meaning 'spoken aloud.' This Ma Laichi and his followers dislike, as it represents a new and even purer religious revival coming to this area. But they can't stop them coming. Ma Mingxin has the support of the Black Mountain Sufis who control both sides of the Pamirs, so more of them are coming in here all the time, escaping the battles between Iran and the Ottomans, and between the Ottomans and the Fulanis."

"It sounds like such a trouble."

"Yes, well, Islam is not so well organized as Buddhism," which made Kang laugh. Ibrahim continued:

"But it is a trouble, you are right. The split between Ma Laichi and Ma Mingxin could be fatal to any hope of unity in our time. Ma Laichi's Khafiya cooperate with the Qing, you see, and they call the Jahriya practices superstitious, and even immoral."

"Immoral?"

"Dancing and suchlike. Rhythmic motion during prayers—even the praying aloud."

"It sounds fairly ordinary to me. Celebrations are celebrations, after all."

"Yes. So the Jahriya counter by accusing the Khafiya of being a cult of personality around Ma Laichi. And they accuse him of excessive tithing, implying his whole movement is simply a ploy for power and wealth. And in collaboration with the emperor against other Muslims as well."

"Trouble."

"Yes. And everyone out here has weapons, you see, usually guns, because as you noted on our journey out, hunting is still an important source of food here. So each little mosque has its militia ready to join a scrape, and the Qing have bolstered their garrisons to try to deal with all this. The Qing so far have backed the Khafiya, which they translate as 'Old Teaching,' and the Jahriya they call the 'New Teaching,' which makes them bad by definition, of course. But what is bad for the Qing dynasty is precisely what appeals to the young Muslim men. There is a lot that is new out there. West of the Black Mountains things are changing fast."

"As always."

"Yes, but faster."

Kang said slowly, "China is a country of slow change."

"Or, depending on the temperament of the emperor, no change at all. In any case, neither Khafiya or Jahriya can challenge the strength of the emperor."

"Of course."

"As a result, they fight each other a lot. And because the Qing armies now control the land all the way to the Pamirs, land that once was composed of independent Muslim emirates, the Jahriya are convinced that Islam must be returned to its roots, in order to retake what was once a part of Dar al-Islam."

"Unlikely, if the emperor wants it."

"Yes. But most of those who say these things have never even visited the interior, much less lived there like you and me. So they cannot know the power of China. They only see these little garrisons, the soldiers spread out by the tens and scores over this immense land."

In this case "malign energy," sometimes translated as "vital essence" or "psychophysical stuff," or "bad vibrations."

Kang said, "That would make a difference. Well. You seem to have brought me out to a land filled with qi."

"I hope it will not be too bad. What is needed, if you ask me, is a comprehensive history and analysis that will show the basic underlying identity of the teachings of Islam and Confucius."

Kang's eyebrows shot up. "You think so?"

"I am sure of it. It is my task. It has been for twenty years now."

Kang composed her face. "You will have to show me this labor."

"I would like that very much. And perhaps you can help me with the Chinese version of it. I intend to publish it in Chinese, Persian, Turkic, Arabic, Hindi, and other languages, if I can find translators."

Kang nodded. "I will help you happily, if my ignorance does not prevent it."

The household became settled, with everyone's routine established much as it had been before. The same celebrations and festivals were held by the small crowd of Han Chinese exiled to this remote region, who worked on festival days to build temples on the bluffs overlooking the river. To these festivals were added the Muslim holy days, major events for most of the town's occupants.

Every month more Muslims came in from the west. Muslims; Confucians; a few Buddhists, these usually Tibetan or Mongolian; almost no Daoists. Mainly Lanzhou was a town of Muslims and Han Chinese, coexisting uneasily, though they had been doing it for centuries, only mixing in the occasional cross marriage.

This twofold nature of the region was an immediate problem for Kang's arrangements concerning Shih. If he was going to continue his studies for the government examinations, it was time to start him with a tutor. He did not want to do this. One alternative was to study in one of the local madressas, thus in effect converting to Islam. This of course was unthinkable—to Widow Kang. Shih and Ibrahim seemed to consider it within the realm of possibility. Shih tried to extend the time given him to make up his mind. I'm only seven, he said. Turn east or west, Ibrahim said. Both said to the boy, You can't just do nothing.

Kang insisted he continue his studies for the imperial service examinations. "This is what his father would have wanted." Ibrahim agreed with the plan, as he considered it likely they would return someday to the interior, where passing the exams was crucial to one's hopes of advancement.

Shih, however, did not want to study anything. He claimed an interest in Islam, which Ibrahim could not help but approve, if warily. But Shih's childish interest was in the Jahriya mosques, filled with chanting, song, dancing, sometimes drinking and self-flagellation. These direct expressions of faith trumped any possible intellectualism, and not only that, they often led to exciting fights with Khafiya youth.

"The truth is he likes whatever course allows him the least work," Kang said darkly. "He must study for the examination, no matter if he turns Muslim or not."

Ibrahim agreed to this, and Shih was forced by both of them to attend to his studies. He grew less interested in Islam as it became clear that if he chose that path, he would merely add another course of study to his workload.

It should not have been so hard for him to devote himself to books and scholarship, for certainly it was the dominant activity in the household. Kang had taken advantage of the move west to gather all the poems in her possession into a single trunk, and now she was leaving most of the wool work and embroidery to the servant girls, and spending her days going through these thick sheaves of paper, rereading her own voluminous bundles of poems, and also those of the friends, family, and strangers she had collected over the years. The well-off respectable women of south China had writen poems compulsively for the whole of the Ming and Qing dynasties, and now, going through her small sample of them, numbering twenty-six thousand or so, Kang spoke to Ibrahim of the patterns she was beginning to see in the choice of topics: the pain of concubinage, of physical enclosure and restriction (she was too discreet to mention the actual forms this sometimes took, and Ibrahim studiously avoiding looking at her feet, staring her hard in the eye); the grinding repetitive work of the years of rice and salt; the pain and danger and exaltation of childbirth; the huge primal shock of being brought up as the precious pet of her family, only to be forced to marry, and in that very instant become something like a slave to a family of strangers. Kang spoke feelingly of the permanent sense of rupture and dislocation caused by this basic event of women's lives: "It is like living through a reincarnation with one's mind intact, a death and rebirth into a lower world, as hungry ghost and beast of burden both, while still holding full memory of the time when you were queen of the world! And for the concubines it's even worse, descent down through the realms of beast and preta, into hell itself. And there are more concubines than wives."

Ibrahim would nod, and encourage her to write on these matters, and also to collect the best of the poems she had in her possession, into an anthology like Yun Zhu's "Correct Beginnings," recently published in Nanjing. "As she says herself in her introduction," Ibrahim pointed out, " 'For each one I have recorded, there must be ten thousand I have omitted.' And how many of those ten thousand were more revealing than hers, more dangerous than hers?"

"Nine thousand and nine hundred," Kang replied, though she loved Yun Zhu's anthology very much.

So she began to organize an anthology, and Ibrahim helped by asking his colleagues back in the interior, and to the west and south, to send any women's poems they could obtain. Over time this process grew, like rice in the pot, until whole rooms of their new compound were filled with stacks of paper, carefully marked by Kang as to author, province, dynasty, and the like. She spent most of her time on this work, and appeared completely absorbed in it.

Once she came to Ibrahim with a sheet of paper. "Listen," she said, voice low and serious. "It's by a Kang Lanying, and called 'On the Night Before Giving Birth to My First Child.' " She read:

> On the night before I first gave birth
> The ghost of the old monk Bai
> Appeared before me. He said,
> With your permission, Lady, I will come back
> As your child. In that moment
> I knew reincarnation was real. I said,
> What have you been, what kind of person are you
> Thus to replace the soul already in me?
> He said, I have been yours before.
> I've followed you through all the ages
> Trying to make you happy. Let me in
> And I will try again.

Kang looked at Ibrahim, who nodded. "It must have happened to her as it happened to us," he said. "Those are the moments that teach us something greater is going on."

When she took breaks from her labors as an anthologist, Kang Tongbi also spent a fair number of her afternoons out in the streets of Lanzhou. This was something new. She took a servant girl, and two of the biggest servant men in their employ, heavy-bearded Muslim men who wore short curved swords in their belts, and she walked the streets, the riverbank strand, the pathetic city square and the dusty markets around it, and the promenade on top of the city wall that surrounded the old part of town, giving a good view over the south shore of the river. She bought several different kinds of "butterfly shoes" as they were called, which fit her delicate little feet and yet extended out beyond them, to make the appearance of normal feet, and—depending on their design and materials—provide her with some extra support and balance. She would buy any butterfly shoes she found in the market that had a different design than those she already owned. None of them seemed to Pao to help her walking very much—she was still slow, with her usual short and crimping gait. But she preferred walking to being carried, even though the town was bare and dusty, and either too hot or too cold, and always windy. She walked observing everything very closely as she made her slow way along.

"Why have you given up sedan chairs?" Pao complained one day as they trudged home.

Kang only said, "I read this morning, 'Great principles are as weighty as a thousand years. This floating life is as light as a grain of rice.' "

"Not to me."

"At least you have good feet."

"It's not true. They're big but they hurt anyway. I can't believe you won't take the chair."

"You have to have dreams, Pao."

"Well, I don't know. As my mother used to say, a painted rice cake doesn't satisfy hunger."

"The monk Dogen heard that expression, and replied by saying, 'Without painted hunger you never become a true person.' "

Every year for the spring equinoctial festivals of Buddhism and Islam, they made a trip out to Qinghai Lake, and stood on the shore of the great blue-green sea to renew their commitment to life, burning incense and paper money, and praying each in their own way. Exhilarated by the sights of the journey, Kang would return to Lanzhou and throw herself into her various projects with tremendous intensity. Before, in Hangzhou, her ceaseless activity had been a wonder to the servants; now it was a terror. Every day she filled with what normal people would do in a week.

Ibrahim meanwhile continued to work away at his great reconciliation of the two religions, colliding now in Gansu right before their eyes. The Gansu Corridor was the great pass between the east and west halves of the world, and the long caravans of camels that had headed east to Shaanxi or west to the Pamirs since time immemorial were now joined by immense trains of oxen-hauled wagons, coming mostly from the west, but also from the east. Muslim and Chinese alike settled in the region, and Ibrahim talked to the leaders of the various factions, and collected texts and read them, and sent letters to scholars all over the world, and wrote his books for many hours every day. Kang helped him in this work, as he helped her in hers, but as the months passed, and they saw the increasing conflict in the region, her help more and more took the form of criticism, of pressure on his ideas—as he sometimes pointed out, when he felt a little tired or defensive.

Kang was remorseless, in her usual way. "Look," she would say, "you can't just talk your way out of these problems. Differences are differences! Look here, your Wang Daiyu, a most inventive thinker, takes great trouble to equate the Five Pillars of the Islamic faith with the Five Virtues of Confucianism."

"That's right," Ibrahim said. "They combine to make the Five Constants, as he calls them, true everywhere and for everyone, unchanging. Creed in Islam is Confucius's benevolence, or ren. Charity is yi, or righteousness. Prayer is li, propriety, fasting is shi, knowledge. And pilgrimage is xin, faith in humankind."

Kang threw her hands up. "Listen to what you are saying! These concepts have almost nothing to do with each other! Charity is not righteousness, not at all! Fasting is not knowledge! And so it is no surprise to find that your teacher from the interior, Liu Zhi, identifies the same Five Pillars of Islam not with the Five Virtues, but with the Five Relationships, the wugang not the wuchang! And he too has to twist the words, the concepts, beyond all recognition to make the correspondences between the two groups fit. Two different sets of bad results! If you pursue the same course they did, then anything can be matched to anything."

Ibrahim pursed his lips, looking displeased, but he did not contradict her. Instead he said, "Liu Zhi made a distinction between the two ways, as well as finding their similarities. For him, the Way of Heaven, tiando, is best expressed by Islam, the Way of Humanity, rendao, by Confucianism. Thus the Quran is the sacred book, but the "Analects" express the principles fundamental to all humans."

Kang shook her head again. "Maybe so, but the Mandarins of the interior will never believe that the sacred Book of Heaven came from Tiangfang. How could they, when only China matters to them? The Middle Kingdom, halfway between heaven and earth; the Dragon Throne, home of the Jade Emperor—the rest of the world is simply the place of barbarians, and could not possibly be the origin of something as important as the sacred Book of Heaven. Meanwhile, turning to your shaikhs and caliphs in the west, how can they ever accept the Chinese, who do not believe at all in their one god? This is the most important aspect of their faith!" And she muttered, "As if there could ever only be one god."

Again Ibrahim looked troubled. But he insisted: "The fundamental way is the same. And with the empire extending westward, and more Muslims coming east, there simply must be some kind of synthesis. We will not be able to get along without it."

Kang shrugged. "Maybe so. But you cannot mix oil and vinegar."

"Ideas are not chemicals. Or they are like the Daoists' mercury and sulphur, combining to make every kind of thing."

"Please don't tell me you plan to become an alchemist."

"No. Only in the realm of ideas, where the great transmutation remains to be made. After all, look at what the alchemists have accomplished in the world of matter. All the new machines, the new things . . ."

"Rock is much more malleable than ideas."

"I hope not. You must admit, there have been other great collisions of civilizations before, making a synthetic culture. In India, for instance, Islam invaders conquered a very ancient Hindu civilization, and the two have often been at war since, but the prophet Nanak brought the values of the two together, and that is the Sikhs, who believe in Allah and karma, in reincarnation and in divine judgment. He found the harmony beneath the discord, and now the Sikhs are among the most powerful groups in India. Indeed, India's best hope, given all its wars and troubles. We need something like that here."

Kang nodded. "But maybe we have it already. Maybe it has been here all along, before Muhammad or Confucius, in the form of Buddhism."

Ibrahim frowned, and Kang laughed her short unhumorous laugh. She was teasing him while at the same time she was serious, a combination very common in her dealings with her husband.

"You must admit, the material is at hand. There are more Buddhists out here in these wastelands than anywhere else."

He muttered something about Lanka and Burma.

"Yes, yes," she said. "Also Tibet, Mongolia, the Annamese, the Thais and Malays. Always they are there, you notice, in the border zone between China and Islam. Already there. And the teachings are very fundamental. The most fundamental of all."

Ibrahim sighed. "You will have to teach me."

She nodded, pleased.

In that year, the forty-third year of the reign of the Qianlong Emperor, an influx of Muslim families greater than ever before came in from the west on the old Silk Road, speaking all manner of languages and including women and children, and even animals. Whole villages and towns had emptied and their occupants headed east, apparently, driven by intensifying wars between the Iranians, Afghans, and Kazakhs, and the civil wars of Fulan. Most of the new arrivals were Shiites, Ibrahim said, but there were many other kinds of Muslims as well, Naqshabandis, Wahhabis, different kinds of Sufis . . . As Ibrahim tried to explain it to Kang, she pursed her lips in disapproval. "Islam is as broken as a vase dropped on the floor."

Later, seeing the violent reaction to the newcomers from the Muslims already esconced in Gansu, she said, "It's like throwing oil on a fire. They will end up all killing each other."

She did not sound particularly distressed. Shih was again asking to study in a Jahriya qong, claiming that his desire to convert to Islam had returned, which she was sure represented only laziness at his studies, and an urge to rebellion that was troubling in one so young. Meanwhile she had had ample opportunity to observe Muslim women in Lanzhou, and while before she had often complained that Chinese women were oppressed by men, she now declared that Muslim women had it far worse. "Look at that," she said to Ibrahim one day on their riverside verandah. "They are hidden like goddesses behind their veils, but treated like cows. You can marry as many as you like of them, and so none of them have any family protection. And there's not a single one of them who can read. It's disgraceful."

"Chinese men take concubines," Ibrahim pointed out.

"Nowhere is it a good thing to be a woman," Kang replied irritably. "But concubines are not wives, they don't have the same family rights."

"So things are only better in China if you are married."

"This is true everywhere. But not to be able to read, even the daughters of the rich and educated men! To be cut off from literature, to be unable to write letters to your birth family . . ."

This was something Kang never did, but Ibrahim did not mention that. He only shook his head.

"It was far worse for women before Muhammad brought Islam to the world."

"That says very little. How bad it must have been before, and that was over a thousand years ago, correct? What barbarians they must have been. By then Chinese women had enjoyed two thousand years of secure privileges."

Ibrahim was frowning at this, looking down. He did not reply.

All over Lanzhou they saw signs of change. The iron mines of Xinjiang fueled the foundries being built upstream and down from the town, and the new influx of potential foundry workers made possible many more expansions, in ironworks and construction more generally. One of the main products of these foundries was cannon, and so the town garrison was beefed up, the Green Standard Chinese guards supplemented by Manchu horsemen. The foundries were under permanent orders to sell all their guns to the Qianlong, so that the weaponry flowed only east toward the interior. As most of the workers were Muslim—and dirty work it was—quite a few guns made their way west in defiance of the imperial edict. This caused more military surveillance, larger garrisons of Chinese, more Manchu banners, and increased friction between local workers and the Qing garrison. It was not a situation that could last.

The residents who had been there longest could only watch things degenerate. There was nothing any one individual could do. Ibrahim continued to work for a good relationship between the hui and the emperor, but this made him enemies among the new arrivals, intent on revival and jihad.

In the midst of all this trouble, Kang told Pao one day that she found herself to be pregnant. Pao was shocked, and Kang herself appeared to be stunned.

"An abortion might be arranged," Pao whispered, looking the other way.

Kang politely declined. "I will have to be an old mother. You must help me."

"Oh we will, I will."

Ibrahim too was surprised by the news, but he adjusted quickly. "It will be good to see a child come of our union. Like our books, but alive."

"It might be a daughter."

"If Allah wills it, who am I to object?"

Kang studied his face closely, then nodded and went away.

Now she seldom went out into the streets, and then only by day, and in a chair. After dark it would be too dangerous in any case. No respectable people remained out after dark now, only gangs of young men, often drunk, Jahriya or Khafiya or neither, though usually it was the Jahriyas spoiling for a fight. The babblers versus the deaf-mutes, as Kang said contemptuously.

Indeed, it was intra-Muslim battling that caused the first great disaster of the troubles, or so Ibrahim judged. Hearing of the fighting between Jahriya and Khafiya, a banner arrived with a high Qing official, Xinzhu, who joined Yang Shiji, the town's prefect. Ibrahim came back from a meeting with these men deeply troubled.

"They don't understand," he said. "They talk about insurrection, but no one out here is thinking of the Great Enterprise, how could they be? We are so far from the interior that people out here barely know what China is. It is only local quarreling, but they come out here thinking they are bound for real war."

dynastic replacement

Despite Ibrahim's reassurances, the new officials had Ma Mingxin arrested. Ibrahim shook his head gloomily. Then the new banners marched out into the countryside to the west. They met with the Salar

Jahriya chief, Su Forty-three, at Baizhuangzi. The Salars had concealed their weapons, and they claimed to be adherents of the Old Teaching. Hearing this, Xinzhu announced to them he intended to eliminate the New Teaching, and Su's men promptly attacked the company and stabbed both Xinzhu and Yang Shiji to death.

When the news of this violence got back to Lanzhou with the Manchu horsemen who had managed to escape the assault, Ibrahim groaned with frustration and anger. "Now it really is insurrection," he said. "Under Qing law, it will go very bad for all concerned. How could they be so stupid?"

A large force arrived soon thereafter, and was attacked by Su Forty-three's band; and after that, more imperial troops arrived. In response Su Forty-three and an army of two thousand men attacked Hezhou, then crossed the river on pifaci and camped right outside Lanzhou itself. All of a sudden they were indeed in a war.

Inflated hide rafts that for centuries had allowed people to cross the Yellow, Wei, and Tao rivers.

The Qing authorities who had survived the Jahriya ambush had Ma Mingxin shown on the town walls, and his followers cried out to see his chains, and prostrated themselves, crying "Shaikh! Shaikh!" audibly from across the river and from the hilltops overlooking the town. Having thus identified the rebels' leader definitively, the authorities had him hauled down off the wall and beheaded.

When the Jahriya learned what had happened they were frantic for revenge. They had no equipment for a proper siege of Lanzhou, so they built a fort on a nearby hill, and began systematically to attack any movement into or out of the city walls. The Qing officials in Beijing were informed of the harrassment, and they reacted angrily to this assault on a provincal capital, and sent out imperial commissioner Agui, one of the Qianlong's senior military governors, to pacify the region.

This he failed to do, and life in Lanzhou grew lean and cold. Finally Agui sent Hushen, his chief military officer, back to Beijing, and when he came back out with new imperial orders, he called up a very large armed militia of Gansu Tibetans, also Alashan Mongols, and all the men from the other Green Standard garrisons in the region. Such ferocious huge men now walked the streets of the town that it seemed it was only a big barracks. "It's an old Han technique," Ibrahim said with some bitterness.

"Pit the non-Hans against each other out on the frontier, and let them kill each other."

Thus reinforced, Agui was able to cut off the water supply from the Jahriyas' hilltop fort across the river, and the tables were turned; besieger became besieged, as in a game of go. At the end of three months, word came into town that the final battle had occurred, and Su Forty-three and every single one of his thousands of men had been killed.

Ibrahim was gloomy at this news. "That won't be the end of it. They'll want revenge for Ma Mingxin, and for those men. The more the Jahriya are put down, the more young Muslim men will turn to them. The oppression itself makes the rebellion!"

"It's like the soul-stealing craze," Kang noted.

Ibrahim nodded, and redoubled his efforts on his books. It was as though if he could only reconcile the two civilizations on paper, the bloody battles happening all around them would come to an end. So he wrote many hours each day, ignoring the meals set on his table by the servants. His conversations with Kang were extensions of his day's thought; and conversely, what his wife said to him in these conversations was often quickly incorporated into his books. No one else's opinions were so important to him. Kang would curse the young Muslim fighters, and say, "You Muslims are too religious, to kill and die as they are doing, and all for such puny differences in dogma, it's crazy!"

Presumably the work in five volumes published in the sixtieth year of the Qianlong as "Reconciliation of the Philosophies of Lu Zhi and Ma Mingxin."

And soon thereafter Ibrahim's writing in the immensely long study that Kang had nicknamed "Muhammad Meets Confucius" included the following passage:

> When observing the tendency toward physical extremism in Islam, ranging from fasting, whirling, and self-flagellation, all the way up to jihad itself, one wonders at its causes, which may be several, including the words of Muhammad sanctioning jihad, the early history of Islamic expansion, the harsh and otherworldly desert landscapes that have been the home of so many Muslim societies, and, perhaps most importantly, the fact that for Islamic peoples the religious language is by definition Arabic, and therefore a second language to the great majority of them. This has fateful

consequences, because one's native tongue is always
grounded in a physical reality by vocabularly, grammar, logic,
and metaphors, images and symbols of all kinds, many of
them buried and forgotten in names themselves; but in the
case of Islam, instead of having a physical reality attached to
it linguistically, its sacred language is detached from all that,
for most believers, by its secondary and translated quality, its
only partly learned nature, so that it conveys only abstract
concepts, removed from the world, conveying the devout
into a world of ideas abstracted and detached from the life of
the senses and the physical realities of life, creating the
possibility and even the likelihood of extremism resulting
from a lack of perspective, a lack of grounding, to give a good
example of the kind of linguistic process I mean; Muslims
who have Arabic as a second language do not "have their feet
on the ground"; their behavior is all too often directed by
abstract thought, floating alone in the empty space of
language. We need the world. Each situation must be placed
in its setting to be understood. Possibly, therefore, our
religion should be taught mostly in the vernacular tongues,
the Quran translated into all the languages of Earth; or else
better instruction in Arabic be given to all; although taking
this road might entail requiring Arabic to become the first
language of all the world, not a practical project and likely to
be regarded as another aspect of jihad.

Another time, when Ibrahim was writing about the theory of dynastic cycles, which was held in common by both Chinese and Islamic historians and philosophers, his wife had brushed it all aside like a piece of
botched embroidery: "That's just thinking of history as if it were the seasons of a year. It's a most simpleminded metaphor. What if they are
nothing at all alike, what if history meanders like a river forever, what
then?"

And soon afterward Ibrahim wrote in his "Commentary on the Doctrine of the Great Cycle in History":

Ibn Khaldun, the most influential of Muslim historians,
speaks of the great cycle of dynasties in his "Muqaddimah,"

and most of the Chinese historians identify a cyclic pattern in history as well, beginning with the Han historian Dong Zhongshu, in his "Luxuriant Dew of the Spring and Autumn Annals," a system that indeed was an elaboration of Confucius himself, and which was elaborated in its turn by Kang Yuwei, who in his "Commentary on the Evolution of Rites" speaks of the Three Ages, each of which—Disorder, Small Peace, and Great Peace—go through internal rotations of disorder, small peace, and great peace, so that the three become nine, and then eighty-one when these are recombined, and so on. And Hindu religious cosmology, which so far is that civilization's only statement on history as such, speaks also of great cycles, first the kalpa, which is a day of Brahma, said to be 4,320,000,000 years long, divided into fourteen manvantaras, each of which is divided into seventy-one maha-yugas, length 3,320,000 years. Each maha-yuga or Great Age is divided into four ages, Satya-yuga, the age of peace, Treta-yuga, Dvapara-yuga, and Kali-yuga, said to be our current age, an age of decline and despair, awaiting renewal. These spans of time, so vastly greater than those of the other civilizations, seemed to many earlier commentators excessive, but it must be said that, the more we learn of the antiquity of the Earth, with stone seashells found on mountaintops, and layers of rock deposits enjambed perpendicularly to each other, and so on, the more the introspections of India seem to have pierced through the veil of the past most accurately to the true scale of things.

But in all of them, in any case, the cycles are only observed by ignoring most of what has been recorded as actually happening in the past, and are very probably theories based on the turning of the year and the return of the seasons, with civilizations seen as leaves on a tree, going through a cycle of growth and decay and new growth. It may be that history itself has no such pattern to it, and that civilizations each create a unique fate that cannot be read into a cyclic pattern without doing damage to what really happened in the world.

Thus the extremely rapid spread of Islam seems to

support no particular cyclic pattern, while its success
perhaps resulted from it proposing not a cycle but a progress
toward God, a very simple message—resisting the great urge
to elaboration that fills most of the world's philosophies, in
favor of comprehensibility by the masses.

Kang Tongbi was also writing a great deal at this time, compiling her anthologies of women's poetry, arranging them into groups and writing
commentaries on what they meant in the aggregate. She also began,
with her husband's help, a "Treatise on the History of the Women of Hunan," in which her thoughts very often reflected, or commented on,
those of her husband, just as his did hers; so that later scholars were able
to collate the writings of the two during their Lanzhou years, and construct of them a kind of ongoing dialogue or duet.

Kang's opinions were her own, however, and often would not
have been agreed with by Ibrahim. Later that year, for instance, frustrated by the irrational nature of the conflict now tearing the region
apart, and fearful of greater conflict to come, feeling as if they were living under a great storm cloud about to burst on them, Kang wrote in her
"Treatise":

> So you see systems of thought and religion coming out of the
> kinds of societies that invented them. The means by which
> people feed themselves determine how they think and what
> they believe. Agricultural societies believe in rain gods and
> seed gods and gods for every manner of thing that might
> affect the harvest (China). People who herd animals believe
> in a single shepherd god (Islam). In both these kinds of
> cultures you see a primitive notion of gods as helpers, as big
> people watching from above, like parents who nevertheless
> act like bad children, deciding capriciously whom to reward
> and whom not to, on the basis of craven sacrifices made to
> them by the humans dependent on their whim. The religions
> that say you should sacrifice or even pray to a god like that,
> to ask them to do something material for you, are the
> religions of desperate and ignorant people. It is only when
> you get to the more advanced and secure societies that you

get a religion ready to face the universe honestly, to announce there is no clear sign of divinity, except for the existence of the cosmos in and of itself, which means that everything is holy, whether or not there be a god looking down on it.

Ibrahim read this in manuscript and shook his head, sighing. "I have married one wiser than myself," he said to his empty room. "I am a lucky man. But sometimes I wish that I had chosen to study not ideas, but things. Somehow I have drifted outside the range of my talent."

Every day news of more Qing suppression of Muslims came to them. Supposedly the Old Teaching was favored over the New Teaching, but ignorant and ambitious officials arrived from the interior, and mistakes were made more than once. Ma Wuyi, for instance, the successor to Ma Laichi, not to Ma Mingxin, was ordered to move with his adherents to Tibet. Old Teaching to new territory, people said, shaking their heads at the bureaucratic mistake, which was sure to get people killed. It became the third of the Five Great Errors of the suppression campaign. And the disorder grew.

Eventually a Chinese Muslim named Tian Wu rallied the Jahriyas openly, to revolt and free themselves from Beijing. This happened just north of Gansu, and so everyone in Lanzhou stockpiled again for war.

Soon the banners came, and like everything else the war had to move through the Gansu Corridor to get from east to west. So though much of the fighting took place far away in eastern Gansu, the news of it in Lanzhou was constant, as was the movement of troops through town.

Kang Tongbi found it unnerving to have the major battles of this revolt happening east of them, between them and the interior. It was several weeks before the Qing army managed to put down Tian Wu's force, even though Tian Wu had been killed almost immediately. Soon after that, news came that Qing general Li Shiyao had ordered the slaughter of over a thousand Jahriya women and children in east Gansu.

Ibrahim was in despair. "Now all the Muslims in China are Jahriya in their hearts."

"Maybe so," Kang said cynically, "but I see it doesn't keep them from accepting Jahriya lands confiscated by the government."

But it was also true that Jahriya orders were springing up everywhere now, in Tibet, Turkestan, Mongolia, Manchuria, and all the way south to distant Yunnan. No other Muslim sect had ever attracted so many adherents, and many of the refugees streaming in from the wars to the far west became Jahriya the moment they arrived, happy after the confusions of Muslim civil war to join a straightforward jihad against infidels.

Even during all this trouble, in the evenings Ibrahim and the heavily pregnant Kang would retire to their verandah and watch the Tao River flow into the Yellow River. They talked over the news and their day's work, comparing poems or religious texts, as if these were the only things that really mattered. Kang tried to learn the Arabic alphabet, which she found difficult, but instructive.

"Look," she would say, "there is no way to mark the sounds of Chinese in this alphabet, not really. And no doubt the same is true the other way around!"

She gestured at the rivers' confluence. "You have said the two peoples can mix like the waters of these two rivers. Maybe so. But see the ripple line where the two meet. See the clear water, still there in the yellow."

"But a hundred li downstream," Ibrahim suggested.

"Maybe. But I wonder. Truly, you must become like these Sikhs you talk about, who combine what is best from the old religions, and make something new."

"What about Buddhism?" Ibrahim asked. "You say it has already changed Chinese religion completely. How can we apply it to Islam as well?"

She thought about it. "I'm not sure it's possible. The Buddha said there are no gods, rather that there are sentient beings in everything, even clouds and rocks. Everything holy."

Ibrahim sighed. "There has to be a god. The universe could not arise from nothing."

"We don't know that."

"I believe Allah made it. But now, it may be that it is up to us. He gave us free will to see what we would do. Again, Islam and China may have two parts of the whole truth. Perhaps Buddhism has another part. And we must find whole sight. Or all will be desolation."

Darkness fell on the river.

"You must raise Islam to the next level," Kang said.

Ibrahim shuddered. "Sufism has been trying to do that for centuries. The Sufis try to rise up, the Wahhabis drag them back down, claiming there can be no improvement, no progress. And here the emperor crushes both!"

"Not so. The Old Teaching has standing in imperial law, the books by your Liu Zhu are in the imperial collection of sacred texts. It's not like with the Daoists. Even Buddhism finds no favor with the emperor, compared to Islam."

"So it used to be," Ibrahim said. "As long as it stayed quiet, out here in the west. Now these young hotheads are inflaming the situation, wrecking all chance of coexistence."

There was nothing Kang could say to that. It was what she had been saying all along.

Now it was fully dark. No prudent citizen would be out in the streets of the rude little town, walled though it was. It was too dangerous.

News arrived with a new influx of refugees from the west. The Ottoman sultan had apparently made alliances with the steppes emirates north of the Black Sea, descendant states of the Golden Horde that had only recently come out of anarchic conditions, and together they had defeated the armies of the Safavid empire, shattering the Shiite stronghold in Iran and continuing east into the disorganized emirates of central Asia and the Silk Roads. The result was chaos all across the middle of the world, more war in Iraq and Syria, widespread famine and destruction; although it was said that with the Ottoman victory, peace might come to the western half of the world. Meanwhile, thousands of Shiite Muslims were headed east over the Pamirs, where they thought sympathetic reformist states were in power. They did not seem to know that China was there.

"Tell me more about what the Buddha said," Ibrahim would say in the evenings on the verandah. "I have the impression it is all very primitive and self-concerned. You know: things are the way they are, one adapts to that, focuses on oneself. All is well. But obviously things in this world are not well. Can Buddhism speak to that? Is there an 'ought to' in it, as well as an 'is'?"

" 'If you want to help others, practice compassion. If you want to help yourself, practice compassion.' This the Tibetans' Dalai Lama said. And Buddha himself said to Sigala, who worshiped the six directions, that the noble discipline would interpret the six directions as parents, teachers, spouse and children, friends, servants and employees, and religious people. All these should be worshiped, he said. Worshiped, do you understand? As holy things. The people in your life! Thus daily life becomes a form of worship, do you see? It's not a matter of praying on Friday and then the rest of the week terrorizing the world."

"This is not what Allah calls for, I assure you."

"No. But you have your jihads, yes? And now it seems the whole of Dar al-Islam is at war, conquering each other or strangers. Buddhists never conquer anything. In the Buddha's ten directives to the Good King, nonviolence, compassion, and kindness are the matter of more than half of them. Asoka was laying waste to India when he was young, and then he became Buddhist, and never killed another man. He was the good king personified."

"But not often imitated."

"No. But we live in barbarous times. Buddhism spreads by people converting out of their own wish for peace and right action. But power condenses around those willing to use force. Islam will use force, the emperor will use force. They will rule the world. Or fight over it, until it is all destroyed."

Another time she said, "What I find interesting is that of all these religious figures of ancient times, only the Buddha did not claim to be a god, or to be talking to God. The others all claim to be God, or God's son, or to be taking dictation from God. Whereas the Buddha simply said, there is no God. The universe itself is holy, human beings are sacred, all the sentient beings are sacred and can work to be enlightened, and one must only pay attention to daily life, the middle way, and give thanks and worship in daily action. It is the most unassuming of religions. Not even a religion, but more a way to live."

"What about these statues of Buddha I see everywhere, and the worship in the Buddhist temples? You yourself spend a great deal of time at prayer."

"Partly the Buddha is revered as the exemplary man. Simple minds might have it otherwise, no doubt. But these are mostly people who worship everything that moves, and Buddha is just one god among many others. They miss the point. In India they made him an avatar of Vishnu, an avatar who is deliberately trying to mislead people away from the proper worship of Brahman, isn't that right? No, many people miss the point. But it is there for all to see, if they would."

"And your prayers?"

"I pray to see things better."

Quickly enough the Jahriya insurrection was crushed, and the western part of the empire apparently at peace. But now there were deep-seated forces, driven underground, that were working all the while for a Muslim rebellion. Ibrahim feared that even the Great Enterprise was no longer out of the question. People spoke of trouble in the interior, of Han secret societies and brotherhoods, dedicated to the eventual overthrow of the Manchu rulers and a return to the Ming dynasty. So even Han Chinese could not be trusted by the imperial government; the dynasty was Manchu after all, outsiders, and even the extremely punctilious Confucianism of the Qianlong Emperor could not obscure this basic fact of the situation. If the Muslims in the western part of the empire revolted, there would be Chinese in the interior and the south coast who would regard it as an opportunity to pursue their own rebellion; and the empire might be shattered. Certainly it seemed that the sheng shi, the peak of this particular dynastic cycle (if there were any such thing), had passed.

This danger Ibrahim memorialized to the emperor repeatedly, urging him to infold the Old Teaching even more firmly into imperial favor, making Islam one of the imperial religions in law as well as fact, as China in the past had infolded Buddhism and Daoism.

No reply ever came to these memoranda, and judging by the contents of the beautiful vermilion calligraphy brushed at the bottom of other petitions returned from the emperor to Lanzhou, it seemed unlikely that Ibrahim's would be received any more favorably. "Why am I surrounded by knaves and fools?" one imperial commentary read. "The coffers have been filling with gold and silver from Yingzhou for every year of our rule, and we have never been more prosperous."

He had a point, no doubt; and knew more about the empire than anyone else. Still, Ibrahim persevered. Meanwhile more refugees came pouring east, until the Gansu Corridor, Shaanxi, and Xining were all crowded with new arrivals—all Muslim, but not necessarily friendly toward each other, and oblivious of their Chinese hosts. Lanzhou appeared to be prospering; the markets were jammed, the mines and foundries and smithies and factories were all pouring out armaments, and new machinery of all kinds, threshers, power looms, carts; but the ramshackle west end of town now extended along the bank of the Yellow River for many li, and both banks of the Tao River were slums, where people lived in tents, or in the open air. No one in town recognized the place anymore, and everyone stayed behind locked doors at night, if they were prudent.

> Child of mine coming into this world
> Be careful where you take yourself.
> So many ways for things to go wrong;
> Sometimes I grow afraid.
> If only we lived in the Age of Great Peace
> I could be happy to see your innocent face
> Watching the geese fly south in the fall.

Once Kang was helping Ibrahim clean up the clutter of books and paper, inkstones and brushes, in his study, and she stopped to read one of his pages.

"History can be seen as a series of collisions of civilizations, and it is these collisions that create progress and new things. It may not happen at the actual point of contact, which is often racked by disruption and war, but behind the lines of conflict, where the two cultures are most trying to define themselves and prevail, great progress is often made very swiftly, with works of permanent distinction in arts and technique. Ideas flourish as people try to cope, and over time the competition yields to the stronger ideas, the more flexible, more generous ideas. Thus Fulan, India, and Yingzhou are prospering in their disarray, while China grows weak from its monolithic nature, despite the enormous infusion of gold from across the Dahai. No single civilization could ever progress; it is always a matter of two or more colliding. Thus the waves on the shore never rise higher than when the backwash of some earlier wave falls back into the next one incoming, and a white line of water jets up to a startling height. History may not resemble so much the seasons of a year, as waves in the sea, running this way and that, crossing, making patterns, sometimes a triple peak, a very Diamond Mountain of cultural energy, for a time."

Kang put the sheet down, looked at her husband fondly. "If only it were true," she said to herself.

"What?" He looked up.

"You are a good man, husband. But it may be you have taken on an impossible task, out of your goodness."

Then, in the forty-fourth year of the Qianlong Emperor's reign, rain fell for all of the third month. Everywhere the land was flooded, just at the time when Kang Tongbi was nearing her confinement. Whether general rebellion across the west broke out because of the misery caused by the floods, or was calculatedly initiated to take advantage of the disaster's confusion, no one could say. But Muslim insurgents attacked town after town, and while Shiite and Wahhabi and Jahriya and Khafiya factions murdered each other in mosque and alleyway, Qing banners too went down before the furious attacks of the rebels. It became so serious that the bulk of the imperial army was rumored to be heading west; but meanwhile the devastation was widespread, and in Gansu the food began to run out.

Lanzhou was again besieged, this time by a coalition of immigrant Muslim rebels of all sects and national origins. Ibrahim's household did everything it could to protect the mistress of the house in her late pregnancy. But even this high in its watershed, the Yellow River had risen dangerously with the rains, and being located at the confluence of the Yellow and the Tao made things worse for their compound. The town's high bluff began to look not so high. It was a frightening sight to see the rivers risen so startlingly, brown and foaming at the very tops of their banks. Finally, on the fifteenth day of the tenth month, when an imperial army was a day's march downstream, and relief from the siege therefore almost in sight, the rain fell harder than ever, and the rivers rose and spilled over their banks.

Someone, rebels everyone assumed, chose this worst of all moments to break the dam upstream on the Tao River, sending an immense muddy flow of water ripping down the watershed, over the Tao's already overtopped banks, rushing into the Yellow River and even backing up the larger stream, so that all was brown water, spreading up into the hills on each side of the narrow river valley. By the time the imperial army arrived the whole of Lanzhou was covered with a sheet of dirty brown water, to knee height, and rising still.

Ibrahim had already gone out to meet the imperial army, taken there by the governor of Lanzhou to consult with the new command, and to help them find rebel authorities to negotiate with. So as the water rose inexorably around the walls of Ibrahim's compound, there were only the women of the household and a few servants to deal with the flood.

The compound wall and sandbags at the gates appeared to be adequate to protect them, but then word of the broken dam and its surge of water was shouted into the compound by people departing for higher ground.

"Come quickly," Zunli cried. "We must get to higher ground too. We must leave now!"

Kang Tongbi ignored him. She was busy stuffing trunks with her papers and with Ibrahim's. There were rooms and rooms full of books and papers, as Zunli exclaimed when he saw what she was doing. There wasn't time to save them all.

"Then help me," Kang grated, working at a furious clip.

"How will we move it all?"

"Put the boxes in the sedan chair, quickly."

"But how will you go?"

"I will walk! Go! Go! Go!"

They stuffed boxes. "This isn't right," Zunli protested, looking at Kang's rounded form. "Ibrahim would want you to leave. He wouldn't worry about these books!"

"Yes he would!" she shouted. "Pack! Get the rest in here and pack!"

Zunli did what he could. A wild hour of racing around in a pure panic had him and the other servants exhausted, but Kang Tongbi was just getting started.

Finally she relented, and they hurried out the front gate of the compound, sloshing immediately into knee-high brown water that poured into the compound until they closed the gate against it. It was a strange sight indeed to see the whole town become a shallow foamy brown lake. The sedan chair was piled so full with books and papers that it took all the servants jammed together under the hoist bars to lift and move it. A low, hair-raising boom of moving water shook the air. The foaming brown lake that covered both rivers and the town extended into the hills on all sides, and Lanzhou itself was completely awash. The servant girls were crying, filling the air with shrieks, shouts, screams. Pao was nowhere to be seen. Thus it was that only a mother's ears heard a single boy crying out.

Kang realized: she had forgotten her own son. She turned and hopped back inside the gate that had been pushed open by water, unnoticed by the servants staggering under the loaded sedan chair.

She splashed through rushing water to Shih's room. The compound itself was already flooded.

Shih had apparently been hiding under his bed, and the water had flushed him out and onto it, where he curled up terrified. "Help! Mother, help me!"

"Come quickly then!"

"I can't! I can't!"

"I can't carry you, Shih. Come on! The servants are all gone, it's just you and me now!"

"I can't!" And he began to wail, balled up on his bed like a three-year-old.

Kang stared at him. Her right hand even jerked toward the gate, as if leaving ahead of the rest of her. She snarled then, grabbed the boy by the ear and jerked him howling to his feet.

"Walk or I'll tear your ear off, you hui!"

"I'm not the hui! Ibrahim is the hui! Everyone out here is hui! Ow!" And he howled as she twisted his ear almost off his head. She dragged him like that through the flooding household to the gate.

As they passed out the gate a surge of water, a low wave, washed into them—waist high on her, chest high on him. When it passed, the level of the flood stayed higher. They were now thigh-deep in water. The roar was much greater than before. They couldn't hear each other. No servants were in sight.

Higher ground stood at the end of the lane leading south, and the city wall was there as well, so Kang sloshed that way, looking for her servants. She stumbled and cursed; one of her butterfly shoes had been sucked away in the tow of water. She kicked the other one off, proceeded barefoot. Shih seemed to have fainted, or gone catatonic, and she had to put an arm under his knees, and lift him up and carry him, resting him on the top shelf of her pregnant belly. She shouted angrily for her servants, but could not even hear herself. She slipped once and cried out to Guanyin, She Who Hears Cries.

Then she saw Xinwu, swimming toward her like an otter with arms, serious and determined. Behind him Pao was wading toward her, and Zunli. Xinwu pulled Shih away from Kang and whacked him on his reddened ear. "That way!" Xinwu shouted loudly at Shih, pointing out the city wall. Kang was surprised to see Shih almost run toward it, leaping out of the water time after time. Xinwu stayed at her side and helped her slosh up the lane. She was like a canal barge being towed upstream, bow waves lapping at her distended waist. Pao and Zunli joined them and helped her, Pao crying and shouting, "I went ahead to check the depth, I came back and thought you were in the chair!" while Zunli was saying something to the effect that they thought she had gone ahead with Pao. The usual confusion.

On the city wall the other servants were urging them on, staring upstream white-eyed with fright. Hurry! their mouths mouthed. Hurry!

At the foot of the wall the brown water was streaming hard by. Kang struggled against the flow awkwardly, slipping on her little feet. People lowered a wooden ladder from the top of the city wall, and Shih scampered up it. Kang started to climb. She had never climbed a ladder before, and Xinwu and Pao and Zunli pushing her from below did not really help. It was hard getting her feet to curl over the submerged rungs; indeed her feet were not as long as the rungs were wide. She could get no purchase. Now she could see out of the corner of her eye a big brown wave, filled with things, smashing along the wall, sweeping it clean of ladders and everything else that had been leaned against it. She pulled herself up by the arms and pegged her foot down onto a dry rung.

Pao and Zunli shoved her up from below, and she was lifted bodily onto the top of the city wall. Pao and Zunli and Xinwu shot up beside her. The ladder was pulled up after them just as the big wave swept by.

Many people had taken refuge up on the wall, as it now formed a sort of long island in the flood. People on a pagoda rooftop nearby waved to them. Everyone on the wall was staring at Kang, who rearranged her gown and pulled her hair out of her face with her fingers, checking to see that everyone from her compound was there. Briefly she smiled. It was the first time any of them had ever seen her smile.

By the time they were reunited with Ibrahim, late that same day, having been rowed to a hill to the south and above the flooded town, Kang was done with smiling. She pulled Ibrahim down next to her, and they sat there in the chaos of people. "Listen to me," she said, hand on her belly, "if this is a daughter we have here—"

"I know," Ibrahim said.

"—if this is a daughter we have been given—there will be no more footbinding."

4

The Afterlife

Many years later, an age later, two old people sat on their verandah watching the river flow. In their time together they had discussed all things, they had even written a history of the world together, but now they seldom spoke, except to note some feature of the waning day. Very rarely did they talk about the past, and they never spoke at all of that time they had sat together in a dark room, diving into the light of the candle, and seeing there strange glimpses of former lives. It was too disturbing to recall the awe and terror of those hours. And besides, the point had been made, the knowledge gained. That they had known each other ten thousand years: of course. They were an old married couple. They knew, and that was enough. There was no need to delve deeper into it.

This, too, is the bardo; or nirvana itself. This is the touch of the eternal.

One day, then, before going out to the verandah to enjoy the sunset hour with his partner, the old man sat before his blank page all the long afternoon, thinking, looking at the stacks of books and manuscripts that walled his study. Finally he took up his brush and wrote, performing the strokes very slowly.

This is what his wife had taught him to see.

"Wealth and the Four Great Inequalities"

The scattered records and broken ruins of the Old World tell us that the earliest civilizations arose in China, India, Persia, Egypt, the Middle West, and Anatolia. The first farmers in these fertile regions taught themselves farming and storage methods that created harvests beyond the needs of the day. Very quickly soldiers, supported by priests, took power in each region, and their own numbers grew, gathering these new abundant harvests largely into their own hands, by means of taxes and direct seizures. Labor divided into the groups described by Confucius and the Hindu caste system: the warriors, priests, artisans, and farmers. With this division of labor the subjugation of farmers by warriors and priests was institutionalized, a subjugation that has never ended. This was the first inequality.

In this division of civilized labor, if it had not happened earlier, men established a general domination over women. It may have happened during the earlier ages of bare subsistence, but there is no way to tell; what we can see with our own eyes is that in farming cultures women labor both at home and in the fields. In truth the farming life requires work from all. But from early on, women did as men required. And in each family, the control of legal power resembled the situation at large: the king and his heir dominated the rest. These were the second and the third inequalities, of men over women and children.

The next small age saw the beginning of trade between the first civilizations, and the silk roads connecting China, Bactria, India, Persia, the Middle West, Rome, and Africa moved the surplus harvests around the Old World. Agriculture responded to the new chances to trade, and there was a great rise in the production of bulk cereals and meats, and specialized crops like olives, wine, and mulberry trees. The artisans also made new tools, and with them more powerful farming implements and ships. Trading groups and peoples began to undermine the monopoly on power of the first military-priest empires, and money began to replace land as the source of ultimate power. All this happened much earlier than Ibn Khaldun and the Maghribi historians recognized. By the time of the classical period—around 1200 b.H.—the changes brought by trade had unsettled the old ways and spread and deepened the first three inequalities, raising many questions about human nature. The great classical religions came into being precisely to attempt to answer these questions—Zoroastrianism in Persia, Buddhism in India, and the rationalist philosophers in Greece. But no matter their metaphysical details, each civilization was part of a world transferring wealth back and forth, back and forth, eventually to the elite groups; these movements of wealth became the driving force of change in human affairs—in other words, of history. Gathered wealth gathered more wealth.

From the classical period to the discovery of the New World (say 1200 b.H. to 1000 a.H.), trade made the Middle West the focal point of the Old World, and much wealth ended up there. At about the midpoint of this period, as the dates indicate, Islam appeared, and very quickly it came to dominate the world. Very likely there were some underlying economic reasons for this phenomenon; Islam, perhaps by chance but perhaps not, appeared in the "center of the world," the area sometimes called the Isthmus Region, bounded by the Persian Gulf, the Red Sea, the Mediterranean, the Black Sea, and the Caspian Sea. All the trade routes necessarily knotted here, like dragon arteries in a feng shui analysis. So it is not particularly surprising that for a time Islam provided the world with a general currency—the dinar—and a generally used language—Arabic. But it was also a religion, indeed it became almost the universal religion, and we must understand that its appeal as a religion arose partly from the fact that in a world of growing inequalities, Islam spoke of a realm in which all were equal—all equal before God no matter their age, gender, occupation, race, or nationality. Islam's appeal lay in this: that inequality could be neutralized and done away with in the most important realm, the eternal realm of the spirit.

Meanwhile, however, trade in food and in luxury goods continued all across the Old World, from al-Andalus to China, in animals, timber and metals, cloth, glass, writing materials, opium, medicines, and, more and more as the centuries passed, in slaves. The slaves came chiefly from Africa and they became more important because there was more labor to be done, while at the same time the mechanical improvements allowing for more powerful tools had not yet been made, so that all this new work had to be accomplished by animal and human effort alone. So added to the subjugation of farmers, women, and the family was this fourth inequality, of race or group, leading to the subjugation of the most powerless peoples to slavery. And the unequal accumulation of wealth by the elites continued.

The discovery of the New World has only accelerated these processes, providing both more wealth and more slaves. The trade routes themselves have moved substantially from land to sea, and Islam no longer controls the crossroads as it did for a thousand years. The main center of accumulation has shifted to China; indeed, China may have been the center all along. It has always had the most people; and from ancient times people everywhere else have traded for Chinese goods. Rome's trade balance with China was so poor that it lost a million ounces of silver a year to China. Silk, porcelain, sandalwood, pepper—Rome and all the rest of the world sent their gold to China for these products, and China grew rich. And now that China has taken control of the west coasts of the New World, it has also begun to enjoy a direct infusion of huge amounts of gold and silver, and slaves. This doubled gathering of wealth, both by trade of manufactured goods and by direct extraction, is something new, a kind of cumulation of accumulations.

So it seems apparent that the Chinese are clearly the rising dominant power in the world, in competition with the previous dominant power, Dar al-Islam, which still exerts a powerful attraction to people hoping for justice before God, if no longer much expecting it on Earth. India then exists as a third culture between the other two, a go-between and influence on both, while also, of course, influenced by both. Meanwhile the primitive New World cultures, newly connected to the bulk of humanity and immediately subjugated by them, struggle to survive.

So. To a very great extent human history has been the story of the unequal accumulation of harvested wealth, shifting from one center of power to another, while always expanding the four great inequalities. This is history. Nowhere, as far as I know, has there ever been a civilization or moment when the wealth of the harvests created by all has been equitably distributed. Power has been exerted wherever it can be, and each successful coercion has done its part to add to the general inequality, which has risen in direct proportion to the wealth gathered; for wealth and power are much the same. The possessors of the wealth in effect buy the armed power they need to enforce the growing inequality. And so the cycle continues.

The result has been that while a small percentage of human beings have lived in a wealth of food, material comfort, and learning, those not so lucky have been the functional equivalent of domestic beasts, in harness to the powerful and well-off, creating their wealth for them but not benefiting from it themselves. If you happen to be a young black farm girl, what can you say to the world, or the world to you? You exist under all four of the great inequalities, and will live a shortened life of ignorance, hunger, and fear. Indeed it only takes one of the great inequalities to create such conditions.

So it must be said that the majority of humans ever to have lived, have existed in conditions of immiseration and servitude to a small minority of wealthy and powerful people. For every emperor and bureacrat, for every caliph and qadi, for every full rich life, there have been ten thousand of these stunted, wasted lives. Even if you grant a minimal definition of a full life, and say that the strength of spirit in people, and the solidarity among people, have given many of the world's poor and powerless a measure of happiness and achievement amidst their struggle, still, there are so many who have lived lives destroyed by immiseration that it seems impossible to avoid concluding that there have been more lives wasted than fully lived.

All the world's various religions have attempted to explain or mitigate these inequalities, including Islam, which originated in the effort to create a realm in which all are equal; they have tried to justify the inequalities in this world. They all have failed; even Islam has failed; the Dar al-Islam is as damaged by inequality as anywhere else. Indeed I now think that the Indian and Chinese description of the afterlife, the system of the six lokas or realms of reality—the devas, asuras, humans, beasts, pretas, and inhabitants of hell—is in fact a metaphorical but precise description of this world and the inequalities that exist in it, with the devas sitting in luxury and judgment on the rest, the asuras fighting to keep the devas in their high position, the humans getting by as humans do, the beasts laboring as beasts do, the homeless preta suffering in fear at the edge of hell, and the inhabitants of hell enslaved to pure immiseration.

My feeling is that until the number of whole lives is greater than the number of shattered lives, we remain stuck in some kind of prehistory, unworthy of humanity's great spirit. History as a story worth telling will only begin when the whole lives outnumber the wasted ones. That means we have many generations to go before history begins. All the inequalities must end; all the surplus wealth must be equitably distributed. Until then we are still only some kind of gibbering monkey, and humanity, as we usually like to think of it, does not yet exist.

To put it in religious terms, we are still indeed in the bardo, waiting to be born.

The old woman read the pages her husband had given her, walking up and down their long verandah, full of agitation. When she had finished, she put her hand on his shoulder. The day was coming to its end; the sky in the west was indigo, a new moon resting in it like a scythe. The

black river flowed below them. She went to her own writing stand, at the
far end of the verandah, and took up her brush, and in quick blind
strokes filled a page.

> Two wild geese fly north in the twilight.
> One bent lotus droops in the shallows.
> Near the end of this existence
> Something like anger fills my breast;
> A tiger: next time I will hitch it
> To my chariot. Then watch me fly.
> No more hobbling on these bad feet.
> Now there is nothing left to do
> But scribble in the dusk and watch with the beloved
> Peach blossoms float downstream.
> Looking back at all the long years
> All that happened this way and that
> I think I liked most the rice and the salt.

BOOK 7

✦ THE AGE OF GREAT PROGRESS ✦

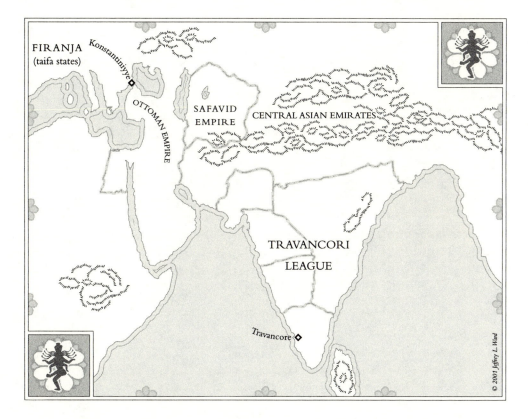

1

The Fall of Konstantiniyye

The Ottoman Sultan Caliph Selim the Third's doctor, Ismail ibn Mani al-Dir, began as an Armenian qadi who studied law and medicine in Konstantiniyye. He rose quickly through the ranks of the Ottoman bureaucracy by the efficacy of his ministrations, until eventually the sultan required him to tend one of the women of his seraglio. The harem girl recovered under Ismail's care, and shortly thereafter Sultan Selim too was cured by Ismail, of a complaint of the skin. After that the sultan made Ismail the chief doctor of the Sublime Porte and its seraglio.

Ismail then spent his time slipping about unobtrusively from patient to patient, continuing his medical education as doctors do, by practicing. He did not attend court functions. He filled thick books with case studies, recording symptoms, medicines, treatments and results. He attended the janissaries' inquisitions as required, and kept notes there as well.

The sultan, impressed by his doctor's dedication and skill, took an interest in his case studies. The bodies of all the janissaries he had executed in the countercoup of the year 1202 were put at Ismail's disposal, and the religious ban on autopsy and dissection declared invalid for this case of executed criminals. A lot of work had to be completed quickly, even with the bodies on ice, and indeed the sultan participated in several of the dissections himself, asking questions at every cut. He was quick to see and suggest the advantages of vivisection.

One night in the year 1207, the sultan called his doctor to the palace in the Sublime Porte. One of his old stablehands was dying, and Selim had had him made comfortable on a bed placed on one balance of a large scale, with weights of gold piled on the other balance, so that the two big pans hung level in the middle of the room.

As the old man lay on his bed wheezing, the sultan ate a midnight meal and watched. He told the doctor that he was sure this method would allow them to determine the presence of the soul, if one existed, and its weight.

Ismail stood at the side of the stablehand's elevated bed, fingering the old man's wrist gently. The old man's breaths weakened, became gasps. The sultan stood and pulled Ismail back, pointing to the scale's extremely fine fulcrum. Nothing was to be disturbed.

The old man stopped breathing. "Wait," the sultan whispered. "Watch."

They watched. There were perhaps ten people in the room. It was perfectly silent and still, as if all the world had stopped to witness the test.

Slowly, very slowly, the balance tray holding the dead man and his bed began to rise. Somebody gasped. The bed rose and hung in the air overhead. The old man had lightened.

"Take away the very smallest weight from the other tray," the sultan whispered. One of his bodyguards did so, removing a few flakes of gold leaf. Then some more. Finally the tray holding the dead man in the air began to descend, until it drifted below the height of the other one. The bodyguard put the smallest flake back on. Skillfully he rebalanced the scale. The man at dying had lost a quarter grain of weight.

"Interesting!" the sultan declared in his normal voice. He returned to his repast, gesturing to Ismail. "Come, eat. Then tell me what you think of these rabble from the east, whom we hear are attacking us."

The doctor indicated that he did not have an opinion.

"Surely you have heard things," the sultan encouraged him. "Tell me what you have heard."

"Like everyone else, I have heard they come from the south of India," Ismail said obediently. "The Mughals have been defeated by them. They have an effective army, and a navy that moves them around and shells coastal cities. Their leader styles himself the Kerala of Travancore. They have conquered the Safavids, and attacked Syria and Yemen—"

"This is all old news," the sultan interrupted. "What I require of you,

Ismail, is explanation. How have they managed to accomplish these things?"

Ismail said, "I do not know, Excellency. The few letters I have received from medical colleagues to the east do not discuss military matters. I gather their army moves quickly, I have heard a hundred leagues a day."

"A hundred leagues! How is that possible?"

"I do not know. One of my colleagues wrote of treating burn wounds. I hear their armies spare those they capture, and set them to farm in areas they have conquered."

"Curious. They are Hindu?"

"Hindu, Buddhist, Sikh—I get the impression they practice some mix of these three faiths, or some kind of new religion, made up by this sultan of Travancore. Indian gurus often do this, and he is apparently that kind of leader."

Sultan Selim shook his head. "Eat," he commanded, and Ismail took up a cup of sherbet. "Do they attack with Greek fire, or the black alchemy of Samarqand?"

"I don't know. Samarqand itself has been abandoned, I understand, after years of plague, and then earthquakes. But its alchemy may have been developed further in India."

"So we are being attacked by black magic," reflected the sultan, looking intrigued.

"I cannot say."

"What about this navy of theirs?"

"You know more than I, Excellency. I have heard they sail into the eye of the wind."

"More black magic!"

"Machine power, Excellency. I have a Sikh correspondent who told me that they boil water in sealed pots, and force the steam through tubes, like bullets out of guns, and the steam pushes against paddles like a river pushing a waterwheel, and thus the ships are rowed forward."

"Surely that would only move them backward in the water."

"They could call that forward, Excellency."

The sultan stared suspiciously at his doctor. "Do any of these ships blow up?"

"It seems as if they might, if something goes wrong."

Selim considered it. "Well, this should be most interesting! If a cannonball hits one of their boiler pots, it should blow up the whole ship!"

"Very possibly."

The sultan was pleased. "It will make for good target practice. Come with me."

He led his usual train of retainers out of the room: bodyguard of six, cook and waiters, astonomer, valet, and the Chief Black Eunuch of the seraglio, all trailing him and the doctor, whom the sultan held by the shoulder. He brought Ismail through the Gate of Felicity into his harem without a word to its guards, leaving his retainers behind to figure out yet again who was intended to follow him into the seraglio. In the end only a waiter and the Chief Black Eunuch entered.

In the seraglio all was gold and marble, silk and velvet, the walls of the outer rooms covered with religious paintings and icons from the age of Byzantium. The sultan gestured to the Black Eunuch, who nodded to a guard at the far door.

One of the harem concubines emerged, trailed by four maids: a white-skinned redheaded young woman, her naked body glowing in the gaslight jets. She was not an albino, but rather a naturally pale-skinned person, one of the famous white slaves of the seraglio, among the only known survivors of the vanished Firanjis. They had been bred for several generations by the Ottoman sultans, who kept the line pure. No one outside the seraglio ever saw the women, and no one outside the sultan's palace ever saw the men used for breeding.

This young woman's hair was a gold-burnished red, her nipples pink, her skin a translucent white that revealed blue veins under it, especially in her breasts, which were slightly engorged. The doctor reckoned her three months pregnant. The sultan did not appear to notice; she was his favorite, and he still had her every day.

The familiar routine unfolded. The odalisque walked to the draped area of her bed, and the sultan followed, not bothering to pull the drapes. The ladies-in-waiting helped the woman to cushion herself properly, held her arms out, her legs spread and pulled up. Selim said "Ah yes," and went to the bed. He pulled his erect member from his pantaloons and covered her. They rocked together in the usual fashion, until with a shudder and a grunt the sultan finished and sat beside her, stroking her belly and legs.

He looked over at Ismail as a thought occurred to him. "What is it like now where she came from?" he asked.

The doctor cleared his throat. "I don't know, Excellency."

"Tell me what you have heard."

"I have heard that Firanja west of Vienna is mainly divided between Andalusis and the Golden Horde. The Andalusis occupy the old Frankish lands and the islands north of it. They are Sunni, with the usual Sufi and Wahhabi elements fighting for the patronage of the emirs. The east is a mix of Golden Horde and Safavid client princes, many of them Shiites. Many Sufi orders. They also have occupied the offshore islands, and the Roman peninsula, though it is mostly Berber and Maltese."

The sultan nodded. "So they prosper."

"I don't know. It rains there more than on the steppes, but there are mountains everywhere, or hills. There is a plain on the north coast where they grow grapes and the like. Al-Andalus and the Roman peninsula do well, I gather. North of the mountains it is harder. It's said the lowlands are still pestilential."

"Why is that? What happened there?"

"It's damp and cold all the time. So it is said." The doctor shrugged. "No one knows. It could be that the pale skin of the people there made them more susceptible to plague. That's what Al-Ferghana said."

"But now good Muslims live there, with no ill effects."

"Yes. Balkan Ottomans, Andalusis, Safavids, the Golden Horde. All Muslim, except perhaps for some Jews and Zotts."

"But Islam is fractured." The sultan thought it over, brushing the odalisque's red pubic hair with his palm. "Tell me again, where did this girl's ancestors come from?"

"The islands off the north coast of Frankland," the doctor ventured. "England. They were very pale there, and some of the outermost islands escaped the plague, and their people were discovered and enslaved a century or two later. It is said they didn't even know anything had changed."

"Good land?"

"Not at all. Forest or rock. They lived on sheep or fish. Very primitive, almost like the New World."

"Where they have found much gold."

"England was known more for tin than gold, as I understand it."

"How many of these survivors were taken?"

"I have read a few thousand. Most died, or were bred into the general populace. You may have the only purebreds left."

"Yes. And this one is pregnant by one of their men, I'll have you know.

We care for the men as carefully as we do the women, to keep the line going."

"Very wise."

The sultan looked at his Black Eunuch. "I'm ready for Jasmina now."

In came another girl, very black, her body almost twin to that of the white girl, though this one was not pregnant. Together they looked like chess pieces. The black girl replaced the white one on the bed. The sultan stood and went to her.

"Well, the Balkans are a sorry place," he mused, "but farther west may be better. We could move the capital of the empire to Rome, just as they moved theirs here."

"Yes. But the Roman peninsula is fully repopulated."

"Venice too?"

"No. Still abandoned, Excellency. It is often flooded, and the plague was particularly bad there."

Sultan Selim pursed his lips. "I don't—ah—I don't like the damp."

"No, Excellency."

"Well, we will have to fight them here. I will tell the troops that their souls, the most precious quarter grain of them, will rise up to the Paradise of Ten Thousand Years if they die in defense of the Sublime Porte. There they will live as I do here. We will meet these invaders down at the straits."

"Yes, Excellency."

"Leave me now."

But when the Indian navy appeared it was not in the Aegean, but in the Black Sea, the Ottoman Sea. Little black ships crowding the Black Sea, ships with waterwheels on their sides, and no sails, only white plumes of smoke pouring out of chimneys topping black deckhouses. They looked like the furnaces of an ironworks, and it seemed they should sink like stones. But they didn't. They puffed down the relatively unguarded Bosporus, blasting shore batteries to pieces, and anchored offshore the Sublime Porte. From there they fired explosive shells into Topkapi Palace, also into the mostly ceremonial batteries defending that side of the city, long neglected as there had been no one to attack Konstantiniyye for centuries. To have appeared in the Black Sea—no one could explain it.

In any case there they were, shelling the defenses until they were pounded into silence, then firing shot after shot into the walls of the palace, and the remaining batteries across the Golden Horn, in Pera. The populace of the city huddled indoors, or took refuge in the mosques, or left the city for the countryside outside the Theodosian Wall; soon the city seemed deserted, except for some young men out to watch the assault. More of these appeared in the streets as it began to seem that the iron ships were not going to bombard the city, but only Topkapi, which was taking a terrific beating despite its enormous impregnable walls.

Ismail was called into this great artillery target by the sultan. He boxed up the mass of papers that had accumulated in the last few years, all the notes and records, sketches and samples and specimens. He wished he could make arrangements to send it all out to the medical madressa in Nsara, where many of his most faithful correspondents lived and worked; or even to the hospital in Travancore, home of their assailants, but also of his other most faithful group of medical correspondents.

There was no way now to arrange such a transfer, so he left them in his rooms with a note on top describing the contents, and walked through the deserted streets to the Sublime Porte. It was a sunny day; voices came from the big blue mosque, but other than that only dogs were to be seen, as if Judgment Day had come and Ismail been left behind.

Judgment Day had certainly come for the palace; shells struck it every few minutes. Ismail ducked inside the outer gate and was taken to the sultan, whom he found seemingly exhilarated by events, as if at a fair: Selim the Third stood on Topkapi's highest bartizan, in full view of the fleet bombarding them, watching the action through a long silver telescope.

"Why doesn't the iron sink the ships?" he asked Ismail. "They must be as heavy as treasure chests."

"There must be enough air in the hulls to make them float," the doctor said, apologetic at the inadequacy of this explanation. "If their hulls were punctured, they would surely sink faster than wooden ships."

One of the ships fired, erupting smoke and seemingly sliding backward in the water. Their guns shot forward, one per ship. Fairly little things, like big bay dhows, or giant water bugs.

The shot exploded down the palace wall to their left. Ismail felt the jolt in his feet. He sighed.

The sultan glanced at him. "Frightened?"

"Somewhat, Excellency."

The sultan grinned. "Come, I want you to help me decide what to take. I need the most valuable of the jewels." But then he spotted something in the sky. "What's that?" He clapped the telescope to his eye. Ismail looked up; there was a dot of red in the sky. It drifted on the breeze over the city, looking like a red egg. "There's a basket hanging under it!" the sultan exclaimed, "and people in the basket!" He laughed. "They know how to make things fly in the sky!"

Ismail shaded his eyes. "May I use the spyglass, Excellency?"

Under white, puffy clouds, the red dot floated toward them. "Hot air rises," Ismail said, shocked as it became clear to him. "They must have a brazier in the basket with them, and the hot air from its fire rises up into the bag and is caught there, and so the whole thing rises up and flies."

The sultan laughed again. "Wonderful!" He took the glass back from Ismail. "I don't see any flames, though."

"It must be a small fire, or they would burn the bag. A brazier using charcoal, you wouldn't see that. Then when they want to come down, they damp the fire."

"I want to do that," the sultan declared. "Why didn't you make one of these for me?"

"I didn't think of it."

Now the sultan was in especially high spirits. The red floating bag was drifting their way.

"We can hope the winds carry it elsewhere," Ismail remarked as he watched it.

"No!" the sultan cried. "I want to see what it can do."

He got his wish. The floating bag drifted over the palace, just under the clouds, or between them, or even disappearing inside one, which gave Ismail the strongest sense yet that it was flying in the air like a bird. People in the air like birds!

"Shoot them down!" the sultan was shouting enthusiastically. "Shoot the bag!"

The palace guards tried, but the cannon that were left standing on the broken walls could not be elevated high enough to fire at it. The musketeers shot at it, the flat cracks of their muskets followed by shouts from the sultan. The acrid smoke of gunpowder filled the grounds, mixing with the smells of citrus and jasmine and pulverized dust. But as far as any of them could tell, no one hit bag or basket. Judging by the minute faces looking down from the basket's edge, wrapped in heavy woolen scarves it appeared, Ismail thought they were perhaps out of range, too high to be hit. "The bullets probably won't go that far up," he said.

And yet they would never be too high to drop things on whatever lay below. The people in the basket appeared to wave at them, and then a black dot dropped like a stooping hawk, a hawk of incredible compaction and speed, crashing right into the roof of one of the inner buildings, exploding and sending shards of tile clattering all over the courtyard and garden.

The sultan was shouting ecstatically. Three more gunpowder bombs dropped onto the palace, one on a wall where soldiers surrounded one of the big guns, killing them with much damage.

Ismail's ears hurt more from the sultan's roars than the explosions. He pointed to the iron ships. "They're coming in."

The ships were close onshore, launching boats filled with men. The bombardment from other ships continued during the disembarking, more intense than ever; their boats were going to land uncontested at a section of the city walls they had blasted down. "They'll be here soon," Ismail ventured. Meanwhile the floating bag and basket had drifted west, past the palace and over the open fields beyond the city wall.

"Come on," Selim said suddenly, grabbing Ismail by the arm. "I need to hurry."

Down broken marble stairs they ran, followed by the sultan's immediate retinue. The sultan led the way into the warren of rooms and passageways deep beneath the palace.

Down here oil lamps barely illuminated chambers filled with the loot of four Ottoman centuries, and perhaps Byzantine treasure as well, if not Roman or Greek, or Hittite or Sumerian; all the riches of the world, stacked in room after room. One was filled entirely with gold, mostly in the form of coins and bars; another with Byzantine devotional art; another with old weapons; another with furniture of rare woods and furs; another with chunks of colored rock, worthless as far as Ismail could tell. "There won't be time to go through all this," he pointed out, trotting behind the sultan.

Selim just laughed. He swept through a long gallery or warehouse of paintings and statues to a small side room, empty except for a line of bags on a bench. "Bring these," he ordered his servants as they caught up; then he was off again, sure of his course.

They came to staircases descending through the rock underlying the palace: a strange sight, smooth marble stairs dropping through a craggy rock hole into the bowels of the Earth. The city's great cistern-cavern lay some way to the south and east, as far as Ismail knew; but when they came down into a low natural cave, floored by water, they found a stone dock, and moored to it, a long narrow barge manned by imperial guards. Torches on the dock and lanterns on the barge illuminated the scene. Apparently they were in a side passage of the cistern-cavern, and could row into it.

Selim indicated to Ismail the roof around the stairwell, and Ismail saw that explosives were packed into crevices and drilled holes; when they were off and some distance away, this entrance would presumably be demolished, and some part of the palace grounds might fall onto it; in any case their escape route would be obscured, and pursuit made impossible.

Men busied themselves with loading the barge, while the sultan inspected the charges. When they were ready to leave he himself lit their fuses, grinning happily. Ismail stared at the sight, which had the lamplit quality of some of the Byzantine icons they had passed in the treasure hoards. "We'll join the Balkan army, and cross the Adriatic into Rome," the sultan announced. "We'll conquer the west, then come back to smite these infidels for their impudence!"

The bargemen cheered on cue from their officers, sounding like thousands in the echoing confinement of the underground lake and its sky of rock. The sultan took the acclaim with open arms, then stepped onto the barge, balanced by three or four of his men. No one saw Ismail turn and dash up the doomed stairs to a different destiny.

2

Travancore

More bombs had been rigged by the sultan's bodyguards to blow up the cages in the palace zoo, and when Ismail climbed back up the stairs and reemerged into the air, he found the grounds in chaos, invaders and defendants alike running around chasing or fleeing from elephants, lions, cameleopards, and giraffes. A pair of black rhinoceroses, looking like boars out of a nightmare, charged about bleeding through crowds of shouting, shooting men. Ismail raised his hands, fully expecting to be shot, and thinking escape with Selim might have been all right after all.

But no one was being shot except the animals. Some of the palace guard lay dead on the ground, or wounded, and the rest had surrendered and were under guard, and much less trouble than the animals. For now it looked as if massacre of the defeated was not part of the invaders' routine, just as rumor had had it. In fact they were hustling their captives out of the palace, as booms were shaking the ground, and plumes of smoke shooting out of windows and stairwells, walls and roofs collapsing: the rigged explosions and the maddened beasts made it prudent to vacate Topkapi for a while.

They were regathered to the west of the Sublime Porte, just inside the Theodosian Wall, on a parade ground where the sultan had surveyed his troops and done some riding. The women of the seraglio, in full chador, were surrounded by their eunuchs and a wall of guards. Ismail sat with the household retinue that remained: the astronomer, the ministers of various administrative departments, cooks, servants, and so on.

The day passed and they got hungry. Late in the afternoon a group of the Indian army came among them with bags of flatbread. They were small dark-skinned men.

"Your name, please?" one of them asked Ismail.

"Ismail ibn Mani al-Dir."

The man drew his finger down a sheet of paper, stopped, showed another of them what he had found.

The other one, now looking like an officer, inspected Ismail. "Are you the doctor, Ismail of Konstantiniyye, who has writen letters to Bhakta, the abbess of the hospital of Travancore?"

"Yes," Ismail said.

"Come with me, please."

Ismail stood and followed, devouring the bread he had been given as he went. Doomed or not, he was famished; and there was no sign that he was being taken out to be shot. Indeed, the mention of Bhakta's name seemed to indicate otherwise.

In a plain but capacious tent a man at a desk was interviewing prisoners, none of whom Ismail recognized. He was led to the front, and the interviewing officer looked at him curiously, and said in Persian, "You are high on the list of people required to report to the Kerala of Travancore."

"I am surprised to hear it."

"You are to be congratulated. This appears to be at the request of Bhakta, abbess of the Travancori hospital."

"A correspondent of many years standing, yes."

"All is explained. Please allow the captain here to lead you to the ship departing for Travancore. But first, one question; you are reported to be an intimate of the sultan's. Is this true?"

"It was true."

"Can you tell us where the sultan has gone?"

"He and his bodyguards have absconded," Ismail said. "I believe they are headed for the Balkans, with the intention of reestablishing the sultanate in the west."

"Do you know how they escaped the palace?"

"No. I was left behind, as you see."

Their machine ships ran by the heat of fires, as Ismail had heard, burning in furnaces that boiled water, the steam then forced by pipes to push paddlewheels, encased by big wooden housings on each side of the hull. Valves controlled the amount of steam going to each wheel, and the ship could turn on a single spot. Into the wind it thumped along, bouncing awkwardly over and through waves, throwing spray high over the ship. When the winds came from behind, the crew raised small sails, and the ship was pushed forward in the usual way, but with an extra impulse provided by the two wheels. They burned coal in the furnaces, and spoke of coal deposits in the mountains of Iran that would supply their ships till the end of time.

"Who made the ships?" Ismail asked.

"The Kerala of Travancore ordered them built. Ironmongers in Anatolia were taught to make the furnaces, boilers, and paddlewheels. Shipbuilders in the ports at the east end of the Black Sea did the rest."

They landed at a tiny harbor near old Trebizond, and Ismail was included in a group that rode south and east through Iran, over range after range of dry hills and snowy mountains, into India. Everywhere there were short dark-skinned troops wearing white, on horseback, with many wheeled cannon prominently placed in every town and at every crossroads. All the towns looked undamaged, busy, prosperous. They changed horses at big fortified changing stations run by the army, and slept at these places as well. Many stations were placed under hills where bonfires burned through the night; intermittently blocking the light from these fires transmitted messages over great distances, all over the new empire. The Kerala was in Delhi, he would be back in Travancore in a few weeks; the abbess Bhakta was in Benares, but due back in Travancore in days. It was conveyed to Ismail that she was looking forward to meeting him.

Ismail, meanwhile, was finding out just how big the world was. And yet it was not infinite. Ten days of steady riding brought them across the Indus. On the green west coast of India, another surprise: they boarded iron carts like their iron ships, with iron wheels, and rode them on causeways that held two parallel iron rails, over which the carts rolled as smoothly as if they were flying, right through the old cities so long ruled by the Mughals. The causeway of the iron rails crossed the broken edge of the Deccan, south into a region of endless groves of coconut palms, and they rolled by the power of steam as fast as the wind, to Travancore, on the southwesternmost shore of India.

Many people had moved to this city following the recent imperial successes. After rolling slowly through a zone of orchards and fields filled with crops Ismail did not recognize, they came to the edges of the city. The outskirts were crowded with new buildings, encampments, lumber yards, holding facilities: indeed for many leagues in all directions it seemed nothing but construction sites.

Meanwhile the inner core of the city was also being transformed. Their train of linked iron carts stopped in a big yard of paired rails, and they walked out a gate into the city center. A white marble palace, very small by the standards of the Sublime Porte, had been erected there in the middle of a park that must have replaced much of the old city center. The harbor this park overlooked was filled with all manner of ships. To the south could be seen a shipyard building new vessels; a mole was being extended out into the shallow green seas; and the enclosed water, in the shelter of a long low island, was as crowded with ships as the inner harbor, with many small boats sailing or being rowed between them. Compared to the dusty torpor of Konstantiniyye's harbors, it was a tumultuous scene.

Ismail was taken on horseback through the bustling city and down the coast farther, to a grove of palm trees behind a broad yellow beach. Here walls surrounded an extensive Buddhist monastery, and new buildings could be seen a long way through the grove. A pier extended out from the seaside buildings, and several fire-powered ships were docked there. This was apparently the home of the famous hospital of Travancore.

Inside the monastery grounds it was windless and calm. Ismail was led to a dining room and given a meal, then invited to wash off the grime of his travel. The baths were tiled, the water either warm or cool, depending on which pool he preferred, and the last ones were under the sky.

Beyond the baths stood a small pavilion on a green lawn, surrounded by flowers. Ismail donned a clean brown robe he was offered, and padded barefoot across the cut grass to the pavilion, where an old woman was in conversation with a number of others.

She stopped when she saw them, and Ismail's guide introduced him.

"Ah. A great pleasure," the woman said in Persian. "I am Bhakta, the abbess here, and your humble correspondent." She stood and bowed to Ismail, hands together. Her fingers were twisted, her walk stiff; it looked to Ismail like arthritis. "Welcome to our home. Let me pour you some tea, or coffee if you prefer."

"Tea will be fine," Ismail said.

"Bodhisattva," a messenger said to the abbess, "we will be visited by the Kerala on the next new moon."

"A great honor," the abbess said. "The moon will be in close conjunction with the morning star. Will we have time to complete the mandalas?"

"They think so."

"Very good."

The abbess continued to sip her tea.

"He called you bodhisattva?" Ismail ventured.

The abbess grinned like a girl. "A sign of affection, with no basis in reality. I am simply a poor nun, given the honor of guiding this hospital for a time, by our Kerala."

Ismail said, "When we corresponded, you did not mention this. I thought you were simply a nun, in something like a madressa and hospital."

"For a long time that was the case."

"When did you become the abbess?"

"In your year, what would it be, 1194. The previous abbot was a Japanese lama. He practiced a Japanese form of Buddhism, which was brought here by his predecessor, with many more monks and nuns, after the Chinese conquered Japan. The Chinese persecute even the Buddhists of their own country, and in Japan it was worse. So they came here, or first to Lanka, then here."

"And they made studies in medicine, I take it."

"Yes. My predecessor in particular had very clear sight, and a great curiosity. Generally we see as if it were night, but he stood in the light of morning, because he tested the truth of what we say we know, in regularized trials. He could sense the strengths of things, the force of movement, and devise tests of them in trials of various kinds. We are still walking through the doors he opened for us."

"Yet I think you have been following him into new places."

"Yes, more is always revealed, and we have been working hard since he left that body. The great increase in shipping has brought us many useful and remarkable documents, including some from Firanja. It's becoming clear to me that the island England was a sort of Japan-about-to-happen, on the other side of the world. Now they have a forest uncut for centuries, regrown over the ruins, and so they have wood to trade, and they build ships themselves. They bring us books and manuscripts found in the ruins, and scholars here and all around Travancore have learned the languages and translated the books, and they are very interesting. People like the Master of Henly were more advanced than you might think. They advocated efficient organization, good accounting, auditing, the use of trial and record to determine yields—in general, to run their farms on a rational basis, as we do here. They had water-powered bellows, and could get their furnaces white hot, or high yellow at least. They were even concerned with the loss of forest in their time. Henly calculated that one furnace could burn all the tress within a yoganda's radius, in only forty days."

"Presumably that will be happening again," Ismail said.

"No doubt even faster. But meanwhile, it's making them rich."

"And here?"

"Here we are rich in a different fashion. We help the Kerala, and he extends the reach of the kingdom every month, and within its bounds, all tends to improvement. More food is grown, more cloth made. Less war and brigandage."

After tea Bhakta showed him around the grounds. A lively river ran through the center of the monastery, and its water ran through four big wooden mills and their wheels, and a big sluice gate at the bottom end of a catchment pond. All around this rushing stream was green lawn and palm trees, but the big wooden halls built next to the mills on both banks hummed and clanked and roared, and smoke billowed out of tall brick chimneys rising out of them.

"The foundry, ironworks, sawmill, and manufactory."

"You wrote of an armory," Ismail said, "and a gunpowder facility."

"Yes. But the Kerala did not want to impose that burden on us, as Buddhism is generally against violence. We taught his army some things about guns, because they protect Travancore. We asked the Kerala about this—we told him it was important to Buddhists to work for good, and he promised that in all the lands that came under his control, he would impose a rule of laws that would keep the people from violence or evil dealing. In effect, we help him to protect people. Of course one is suspicious of that, seeing what rulers do, but this one is very interested in law. In the end he does what he likes, of course. But he likes laws."

Ismail thought of the nearly bloodless aftermath of the conquest of Konstantiniyye. "There must be some truth in it, or I would not be alive."

"Yes, tell me about that. It sounded as if the Ottoman capital was not so vigorously defended."

"No. But that is partly because of the vigor of the assault. People were unnerved by the fireships, and the flying bags overhead."

Bhakta looked interested. "Those were our doing, I must admit. And yet the ships do not seem that formidable."

"Consider each ship to be a mobile artillery battery."

The abbess nodded. "Mobility is one of the Kerala's watchwords."

"As well it might be. In the end mobility prevails, and all within shot of the sea can be destroyed. And Konstantiniyye is all within shot of the sea."

"I see what you mean."

After tea the abbess took Ismail through the monastery and workshops, down to the docks and shipworks, which were loud. Late in the day they walked over to the hospital, and Bhakta led Ismail to the rooms used for teaching monks to become doctors. The teachers gathered to greet him, and they showed him the shelf on one wall of books and papers that they had devoted to the letters and drawings he had sent to Bhakta over the years, all catalogued according to a system he did not understand. "Every page has been copied many times," one of the men said.

"Your work seems very different from Chinese medicine," one of the others said. "We were hoping you might speak to us about the differences between their theory and yours."

Ismail shook his head, fingering through these vestiges of his former existence. He would not have said he had written so much. Perhaps there were multiple copies even on this shelf.

"I have no theories," he said. "I have only noted what I have seen." His face tightened. "I will be happy to speak with you about whatever you like, of course."

The abbess said, "It would be very good if you would speak to a gathering about these things; there are many who would like to hear you, and to ask questions."

"My pleasure, of course."

"Thank you. We will convene tomorrow for that, then."

A clock somewhere struck the bells that marked every hour and watch.

"What kind of clock do you employ?"

"A version of Bhaskara's mercury wheel," Bhakta said, and led Ismail by the tall building that housed it. "It does very well for the astronomical calculations, and the Kerala has decreed a new year using it, more accurate than any before. But to tell the truth, we are now trying horologues with weight-driven mechanical escapements. We are also trying clocks with spring drives, which would be useful at sea, where accurate time-keeping is essential for determining longitude."

"I know nothing of that."

"No. You have been attending to medicine."

"Yes."

The next day they returned to the hospital, and in a large room where surgeries were performed, a great number of monks and nuns in brown and maroon and yellow robes sat on the floor to hear him. Bhakta had assistants bring several thick wide books to the table where Ismail was to speak, all of them filled with anatomical drawings, most Chinese.

They seemed to be waiting for him to speak, so he said, "I am pleased to tell you what I have observed. Perhaps it will help you, I don't know. I know little of any formal medical system. I studied some of the ancient Greek knowledge as it was translated by Ibn Sina and others, but I never could profit much from it. Very little from Aristotle, somewhat more from Galen. Ottoman medicine itself was no very impressive thing. In truth, nowhere have I found a general explanation that fits what I have seen with my own eyes, and so, long ago I gave up on all hypothesis, and decided to try to draw and to write down only what I saw. So you must tell me about these Chinese ideas, if you can express them in Persian, and I will see if I can tell you how my observations match with them." He shrugged. "That's all I can do."

They stared at him, and he continued nervously: "So useful, Persian. The language that bridges Islam and India." He waggled a hand. "Any questions?"

Bhakta herself broke the silence. "What about the meridian lines that the Chinese speak of, running through the body from the skin inward and back again?"

Ismail looked at the drawings of the body she turned to in one of the books. "Could they be nerves?" he said. "Some of these lines follow the paths of major nerves. But then they diverge. I have not seen nerves crisscrossing like this, cheek to neck, down spine to thigh, up into back. Nerves generally branch like an almond tree's branches, while the blood vessels branch like a birch tree. Neither tangle like these are shown to."

"We don't think meridian lines refer to the nerves."

"To what, then? Do you see anything there when you do autopsies?"

"We do not do autopsies. When opportunity has allowed us to inspect torn bodies, their parts look as you have described them in your letters to us. But the Chinese understanding is of great antiquity and elaboration, and they get good results by sticking pins in the right meridian points, among other methods. They very often get good results."

"How do you know?"

"Well—some of us have seen it. Mostly we understand it from what they have said. We wonder if they are finding systems too small to be seen. Can we be sure that the nerves are the only messengers of motion to the musculature?"

"I think so," Ismail said. "Cut the right nerve and the muscles beyond it will not move. Prick a nerve and the appropriate muscle will jump."

His audience stared at him. One of the older men said, "Perhaps some other kind of energy transference is happening, not necessarily through the nerves, but through the lines, and this is needed as much as the nerves."

"Perhaps. But look here," pointing at one diagram, "they show no pancreas. No adrenal glands either. These both perform necessary functions."

Bhakta said, "For them the crucial organs are eleven, five yin and six yang. Heart, lungs, spleen, liver, and kidneys, they are yin."

"A spleen is not essential."

". . . Then the six yang organs are gall bladder, stomach, small intestine, large intestine, bladder, and triple burner."

"Triple burner? What is that?"

She read from the Chinese notations by the drawing: "They say, 'It has a name but no shape. It combines the effects of the organs that regulate water, as a fire must control water. The upper burner is a mist, the middle burner a foam, the lower burner a swamp. Thus top to bottom, corresponding to head and upper body, middle from nipples to navel, lower the abdomen below the navel."

Ismail shook his head. "Do they find it in dissections?"

"Like us, they rarely do dissections. There are similar religious barriers. Once in their Sung dynasty, about year 390 in Islam, they dissected forty-six rebels."

"I doubt that would have helped. You have to see a lot of dissections, and vivisections, with no preconceptions in mind, before it begins to come clear."

Now the monks and nuns were staring at him with an odd expression, but he forged on as he examined the drawings. "This flow through the body and all its parts, do they not mean blood?"

"A harmonious balance of fluids, some material, like blood, some spiritual, like jing and shen and qi, the so-called Three Treasures—"

"What are they, please?"

"Jing is the source of change," one nun said hesitantly, "supportive and nutritive, like a fluid. 'Essence' is another Persian word we could use to translate it. In Sanskrit, 'semen,' or the generative possibility."

"And shen?"

"Shen is awareness, consciousness. Like our spirit, but a part of the body too."

Ismail was interested in this. "Have they weighed it?"

Bhakta led the laughter. "Their doctors do not weigh things. With them it is not things, but forces and relationships."

"Well, I am just an anatomist. What animates the parts is beyond me. Three treasures, one, a myriad—I cannot tell. It does seem there is some animating vitality, that comes and goes, waxes and wanes. Dissection cannot find it. Our souls, perhaps. You believe that the soul returns, do you not?"

"We do."

"The Chinese also?"

"Yes, for the most part. For their Daoists there is no pure spirit, it is always mixed with material things. So their immortality requires movement from one body to another. And all Chinese medicine is strongly influenced by Daoism. Their Buddhism is mostly like ours, although again, more materialist. It is chiefly what the women do in their older years, to help the community, and prepare for their next life. The official Confucian culture does not speak much of the soul, even though they acknowledge its existence. In most Chinese writing the line drawn between spirit and matter is vague, sometimes nonexistent."

"Evidently," Ismail said, looking at the meridian-line drawing again. He sighed. "Well. They have studied long, and helped living people, while I have only drawn dissections."

They continued. The questions came from more and more of them, with comments and observations. Ismail answered every question as best he could. The movement of the blood in the chambers of the heart; the function of the spleen, if there was one; location of the ovaries; shock reactions to amputation of the legs; flooding of punctured lungs; movement of the various limbs when parts of the exposed brain were prodded with needles: he described what he had seen in each case, and as the day wore on, the crowd sitting on the floor looked up at him with expressions more and more guarded, or odd. A pair of nuns left quietly. As Ismail was describing the coagulation of the blood after extraction of teeth, the room went completely silent. Few of them met his eye, and noticing that, he faltered. "As I said, I am a mere anatomist . . . We will have to see if we can reconcile what I have seen with your theoretical texts . . ." He looked hot, as if he had a fever, but only in his face.

Finally the abbess Bhakta rose to her feet, stepped stiffly to him, and held his shaking hands in hers. "No more," she said gently. All the monks and nuns rose to their feet, their hands placed together before them, as in prayer, and bowed toward him. "You have made good from bad," Bhakta said. "Rest now, and let us take care of you."

So Ismail settled into a small room in the monastery provided for him, and studied Chinese texts freshly translated into the Persian by the monks and nuns, and taught anatomy.

One afternoon he and Bhakta walked from the hospital to the dining hall, through hot and muggy air, the premonsoon air, like a warm wet blanket. The abbess pointed to a little girl running through the rows of melons in the big garden. "There is the new incarnation of the previous lama. She just came to us last year, but she was born the very hour the old lama died, which is very unusual. It took a while for us to find her, of course. We did not start the search until last year, and immediately she showed up."

"His soul moved from man to woman?"

"Apparently. The search certainly looked among the little boys, as is traditional. That was one of the things that made identifying her so easy. She insisted on being tested, despite her sex. At four years of age. And she identified all of Peng Roshi's things, many more than the new incarnation usually can do, and told me the contents of my final conversation with Peng, almost word for word."

"Really!" Ismail stared at Bhakta.

Bhakta met his gaze. "It was like looking into his eyes again. So, we say that Peng has come back to us as a Tara bodhisattva, and we started paying more attention to the girls and the nuns, something of course that I have always encouraged. We have emulated the Chinese habit of inviting the old women of Travancore to come to the monastery and give their lives over to studying the sutras, but also to studying medicine, and going back out to care for those in their villages, and to teach their grandchildren and great-grandchildren."

The little girl disappeared into the palm trees at the end of the garden. The new moon sickled the sky, pendant under a bright evening star. The sound of drumming came on a breeze. "The Kerala has been delayed," Bhakta said as she listened to the drums. "He will be here tomorrow."

The drumming became audible again at dawn, just after the clock bells had clonged the coming of day. Distant drums, like thunder or gunfire, but more rhythmic than either, announced his arrival. As the sun rose it seemed the ground shook. Monks and nuns and their families living in the monastery poured out of the dormitories to witness the arrival, and the great yard inside the gate was hastily cleared.

The first soldiers danced in a rapid walk, all stepping together, taking a skip forward at every fifth step, and shouting as they reversed their rifles from one shoulder to the other. The drummers followed, skipping in step as their hands beat their tablas. A few snapped hand cymbals. They wore uniform shirts with red patches sewn to the shoulders, and came circling in a column around the great yard, until perhaps five hundred men stood in curved ranks facing the gate. When the Kerala and his officers rode in on horseback, the soldiers presented their arms and shouted three times. The Kerala raised a hand, and his detachment commander shouted orders: the tabla players rolled out the surging beat, and the soldiers danced into the dining hall.

"They are fast, just as everyone said," Ismail said to Bhakta. "And everything is so together."

"Yes, they live in unison. In battle they are the same. The reloading of their rifles has been broken down into ten movements, and there are ten command drumbeats, and different groups of them are coordinated to different points of the cycle, so they fire in rotating mass, to very devastating effect, I am told. No army can stand up to them. Or at least, that was true for many years. Now it seems the Golden Horde are beginning to train their armies in similar ways. But even with that, and with modern weapons, they won't be able to withstand the Kerala."

Now the man himself dismounted, and Bhakta approached him, bringing Ismail along. The Kerala waved aside their bows, and Bhakta said without preamble, "This is Ismail of Konstantiniyye, the famous Ottoman doctor."

The Kerala stared at him intently, and Ismail gulped, feeling the heat of that impatient eye. The Kerala was short and compact, black haired, narrow faced, quick of movement. His torso seemed just a touch too long for his legs. His face was very handsome, chiseled like a Greek statue.

"I hope you are impressed by the hospital here," he said in clear Persian.

"It is the best I have ever seen."

"What was the state of Ottoman medicine when you left it?"

Ismail said, "We were making progress in understanding a little of the parts of the body. But much remained mysterious."

Bhakta added, "Ismail has examined the medical theories of the ancient Egyptians and Greeks, and brought what was useful in them to us, as well as making very many new discoveries of his own, correcting the ancients or adding to their knowledge. His letters to us have formed one of the main bases of our work in the hospital."

"Indeed." Now the Kerala's gaze was even more piercing. His eyes were protuberant, their irises a jumble of colors, like circles of jasper. "Interesting! We must speak more of these things. But first I want to discuss recent developments with you alone, Mother Bodhisattva."

The abbess nodded, and walked hand-in-hand with the Kerala to a pavilion overlooking the dwarf orchard. No bodyguard accompanied them, but only settled back and watched from the yard, rifles at the ready, with guards posted on the monastery wall.

Ismail went with some monks to the streamside, where they were arranging a ceremony of sand mandalas. Monks and nuns in maroon and saffron robes flowed everywhere about the bankside, setting out rugs and flower baskets, happily chattering and in no great hurry, as the Kerala often conferred with their abbess for half the day, or longer. They were famous friends.

Today, however, they were done earlier, and the pace quickened considerably as word came back that the two were leaving the pavilion. Flower baskets were cast on the stream, and the soldiers reappeared to the sound of the pulse-quickening tablas. They skipped to the banksides without their rifles and sat, cleaving an aisle for their leader's approach. He came among them, stopping to put a hand to one shoulder or another, greeting men by name, asking after their wounds, and so on. The monks who had led the mandala effort came out of their studio, chanting to a gong and the blast of bass trumpets, carrying two mandalas— wooden disks as big as millstones, each held level by two men, with the vibrantly colored mandalas laid in unfixed sand on their tops. One was a complex geometrical figure in bold red, green, yellow, blue, white, and black. The other was a map of the world, with Travancore a red dot like a bindi, and India occupying the center of the circle, and the rest of the mandala depicting almost the whole width of the world, from Firanja to Korea and Japan, with Africa and the Indies curved around the bottom. All was colored naturally, the oceans dark blue, inland seas lighter blue, land green or brown, as the case might be, with the mountain ranges marked by dark green and snowy white. Rivers ran in blue threads, and a vivid red line enclosed what Ismail took to be the border of the Kerala's conquests, now including the Ottoman empire up through Anatolia and Konstantiniyye, though not the Balkans or the Crimea. A most beautiful object, like looking down on the world from the vantage of the sun.

The Kerala of Travancore walked with the abbess, helping her with her footing down the path. At the riverside they stopped, and the Kerala inspected the mandalas closely, slowly, pointing and asking the abbess and her monks questions about one feature or another. Other monks chanted in low voices, and the soldiers helped to sing a song. Bhakta faced them and sang over their sound in a high thin voice. The Kerala took the mandala in his hands and lifted it up carefully; it was almost too large for one man to hold. He stepped down into the river with it, and bouquets of hydrangea and azalea floated into his legs. He held the geometrical mandala over his head, offering it to the sky, and then, at a shift in the song, and the growling entry of trumpets, he lowered the disk in front of him, and very slowly tilted it up on its side. The sand slid off all at once, the colors pouring into the water and blurring together, staining the Kerala's silken leggings. He dipped the disk into the water and washed the rest of the sand away in a multicolored cloud that dissipated in the flow. He cleared the surface with his bare hand, then strode out of the water. His shoes were muddy, his wet leggings stained green and red and blue and yellow. He took the other mandala from its makers, bowed over it to them, turned, and took it into the river. This time the soldiers shifted and bowed forehead to ground, chanting a prayer together. The Kerala lowered the disk slowly, and like a god offering a world to a higher god, rested it on the water and let it float, spinning slowly round and round under his fingers, a floating world that at the height of the song he plunged down into the stream as far as it would go, releasing all the sand into the water to float up over his arms and legs. As he walked to shore, spangled with color, his soldiers stood and shouted three times, then three again.

Later, over tea scented with delicate perfumes, the Kerala sat in repose and spoke with Ismail. He heard all Ismail could tell him of Sultan Selim the Third, and then he told Ismail the history of Travancore, his eyes never leaving Ismail's face.

"Our struggle to throw off the yoke of the Mughals began long ago with Shivaji, who called himself Lord of the Universe, and invented modern warfare. Shivaji used every method possible to free India. Once he called the aid of a giant Deccan lizard to help him climb the cliffs guarding the Fortress of the Lion. Another time he was surrounded by the Bijapuri army, commanded by the great Mughal general Afzal Khan, and after a siege Shivaji offered to surrender to Afzal Khan in person, and appeared before that man clad only in a cloth shirt, that nevertheless concealed a scorpion-tail dagger; and the fingers of his hidden left hand were sheathed in razor-edged tiger claws. When he embraced Afzul Khan he slashed him to death before all, and on that signal his army set on the Mughals and defeated them.

"After that Alamgir attacked in earnest, and spent the last quarter century of his life reconquering the Deccan, at a cost of a hundred thousand lives per year. By the time he subdued the Deccan his empire was hollowed. Meanwhile there were other revolts against the Mughals to the northwest, among Sikhs, Afghans, and the Safavid empire's eastern subjects, as well as Rajputs, Bengalis, Tamils, and so forth, all over India. They all had some success, and the Mughals, who had overtaxed for years, suffered a revolt of their own zamindars, and a general breakdown of their finances. Once Marathas and Rajputs and Sikhs were successfully established, they all instituted tax systems of their own, you see, and the Mughals got no more money from them, even if they still swore alliegance to Delhi.

"So things went poorly for the Mughals, especially here in the south. But even though the Marathas and Rajputs were both Hindu, they spoke different languages, and hardly knew each other, so they developed as rivals, and this lengthened the Mughals' hold on mother India. In these end days the Nazim became premier to a khan completely lost to his harem and hookah, and this nazim went south to form the principality that inspired our development of Travancore on a similar system.

"Then Nadir Shah crossed the Indus at the same ford used by Alexander the Great, and sacked Delhi, slaughtering thirty thousand and taking home a billion rupees of gold and jewels, and the Peacock Throne. With that the Mughals were finished.

"Marathas have been expanding their territory ever since, all the way into Bengal. But the Afghans freed themselves from the Safavids, and surged east all the way to Delhi, which they sacked also. When they withdrew the Sikhs were given control of the Punjab, for a tax of one-fifth of the harvests. After that the Pathans sacked Delhi yet once more, rampaging for an entire month in a city become nightmare. The last emperor with a Mughal title was blinded by a minor Afghan chieftain.

"After that a Marathan cavalry of thirty thousand marched on Delhi, picking up two hundred thousand Rajput volunteers as they moved north, and on the fateful field of Panipat, where India's fate has so often been decided, they met an army of Afghan and ex-Mughal troops, in full jihad against the Hindus. The Muslims had the support of the local populace, and the great general Shah Abdali at their head, and in the battle a hundred thousand Marathas died, and thirty thousand were captured for ransom. But afterward the Afghan soldiers tired of Delhi, and forced their khan to return to Kabul.

"The Marathas, however, were likewise broken. The Nazim's successors secured the south, and the Sikhs took the Punjab, and the Bengalese Bengal and Assam. Down here we found the Sikhs to be our best allies. Their final guru declared their sacred writings to be the embodiment of the guru from that point on, and after that they prospered greatly, creating in effect a mighty wall between us and Islam. And the Sikhs taught us as well. They are a kind of mix of Hindu and Muslim, unusual in Indian history, and instructive. So they prospered, and learning from them, coordinating our efforts with them, we have prospered too.

"Then in my grandfather's time a number of refugees from the Chinese conquest of Japan arrived in this region, Buddhists drawn to Lanka, the heart of Buddhism. Samurai, monks, and sailors, very good sailors— they had sailed the great eastern ocean that they call the 'Dahai,' in fact they sailed to us both by heading east and by heading west."

"Around the world?"

"Around. And they taught our shipbuilders much, and the Buddhist monasteries here were already centers of metalworking and mechanics, and ceramics. The local mathematicians brought calculation to full flower for use in navigation, gunnery, and mechanics. All came together here in the great shipyards, and our merchant and naval fleets were soon greater even than China's. Which is a good thing, as the Chinese empire subdues more and more of the world—Korea, Japan, Mongolia, Turkestan, Annam and Siam, the islands in the Malay chain—the region we used to called Greater India, in fact. So we need our ships to protect us from that power. By sea we are safe, and down here, below the gnarled wildlands of the Deccan, we are not easily conquered by land. And Islam seems to have had its day in India, if not the whole of the West."

"You have conquered its most powerful city," Ismail observed.

"Yes. I will always smite Muslims, so that they will never be able to attack India again. There have been enough rapes of Delhi. So I had a small navy built on the Black Sea to attack Konstantiniyye, breaking the Ottomans like the Nazim broke the Mughals. We will establish small states across Anatolia, taking their land under our influence, as we have done in Iran and Afghanistan. Meanwhile we continue to work

with the Sikhs, treating them as chief allies and partners in what is becoming a larger Indian confederation of principalities and states. The
unification of India on that basis is not something many people resist,
because when it succeeds, it means peace. Peace for the first time since
the Mughals invaded more than four centuries ago. So India has
emerged from its long night. And now we will spread the day everywhere."

The following day Bhakta took Ismail to a garden party at the Kerala's
palace in Travancore. The big park containing the little marble building
overlooked the northern end of the harbor, away from the great noise
and smoke of the shipworks, visible at the south side of the shallow bay,
but innocuous at that distance. Outside the park, more elaborate white
palaces belonged not to the Kerala, but to the local merchant leaders,
who had become rich in shipbuilding, trade expeditions, and most of all,
the financing of other such expeditions. Among the Kerala's guests were
many men of this sort, all richly dressed in silks and jewelry. Especially
prized in this society, it seemed to Ismail, were semiprecious stones—
turquoise, jade, lapis, malachite, onyx, jasper, and the like—polished
into big round buttons and necklace beads. The wives and daughters of
the men wore brilliant saris, and some walked with tamed cheetahs on
leashes.

People circulated in the shade of the garden's arbors and palm trees,
eating at long tables of delicacies, or sipping from glass goblets. Buddhist monks stood out in their maroon or saffron, and Bhakta was approached by quite a few of these. The abbess introduced some of them
to Ismail. She pointed out to him the Sikhs in attendance, men who wore
turbans and were bearded; and Marathas; and Bengalis; also Africans,
Malaysians, Burmese, Sumatrans, Japanese, and Hodenosaunee from
the New World. The abbess either knew all these people personally, or
could identify them by some characteristic of dress or figure.

"So very many different peoples here," Ismail observed.

"Shipping brings them."

Many of them seemed to crave a word with Bhakta, and she introduced Ismail to one of the Kerala's "most trusted assistants," in the person of one Pyidaungsu, a short dark man who, he said, had grown up in
Burma and on the eastern side of India's tip. His Persian was excellent,

which was no doubt why the abbess had introduced Ismail to him, as she dealt with her own press of conversants.

"The Kerala was most pleased to meet you," Pyidaungsu said immediately, drawing Ismail off to one side. "He is very desirous of making progress in certain medical matters, especially infectious diseases. We lose more soldiers to disease or infection than to our enemies in battle, and this grieves him."

"I know only a little of that," Ismail said. "I am an anatomist, attempting to learn the structures of the body."

"But all advances in understanding of the body help us in what the Kerala wants to know."

"In theory, anyway. Over time."

"But could you not examine the army's procedures, in search of some aspects of them that contribute perhaps to diseases spreading?"

"Perhaps," Ismail said. "Although some aspects cannot be changed, like traveling together, sleeping together."

"Yes, but the way those things are done . . ."

"Possibly. There seems to be a likelihood that some diseases are transmitted by creatures smaller than the eye can see—"

"The creatures in microscopes?"

"Yes, or smaller. Exposure to a very small amount of these, or to some that are killed beforehand, seems to give people a resistance to later exposures, as happens with survivors of pox."

"Yes, variolation. The troops are already scabbed for pox."

Ismail was surprised to hear this, and the officer saw it.

"We are trying everything," he said with a laugh. "The Kerala believes all habits must be reexamined with an eye to changing them, improving them as much as possible. Eating habits, bathing, evacuation—he began as an artillery officer when he was very young, and he learned the value of regular procedure. He proposed that the barrels of cannons be bored out rather than cast, as the casting could never be done with any true smoothness. With uniform bores cannons become more powerful and lighter at once, and ever so much more accurate. He tested all these things, and reduced gunnery to a set of settled motions, like a dance, much the same for cannon of all sizes, making them capable of deployment as quickly as infantry, almost as quick as cavalry. And easily carried on ships. Results have been prodigious, as you see." Waving around complacently at the party.

"You have been an artillery officer, I suppose."

The man laughed. "Yes, I was."

"So now you enjoy a celebration here."

"Yes, and there are other reasons for this gathering. The bankers, the shippers. But they all ride on the back of the artillery, if you will."

"And not the doctors."

"No. But I wish it were so! Tell me again if you see any part of military life that might be made more healthy."

"No contact with prostitutes?"

The man laughed again. "Well, it is a religious duty for many of them, you must understand. The temple dancers are important for many ceremonies."

"Ah. Well. Cleanliness, then. The animalcules move from body to body in dirt, by touch, in food or water, and breath. Boiled surgical instruments reduce infections. Masks on doctors and nurses and patients, to reduce spread of infection."

The officer looked pleased. "Cleanliness is a virtue of caste purity. The Kerala does not approve of caste, but it should be possible to make cleanliness more of a priority."

"Boiling kills the animalcules, it seems. Cooking implements, pots and pans, drinking water—all might be boiled to advantage. Not very practical, I suppose."

"No, but possible. What other methods could be applied?"

"Certain herbs, perhaps, and things poisonous to the animalcules but not to people. But no one knows whether such things exist."

"But trials could be made."

"Possibly."

"On poisoners, for instance."

"It's been done."

"Oh, the Kerala will be pleased. How he loves trials, records, numbers laid out by his mathematicians to show whether the impressions of one doctor are true when applied to the army as a whole body. He will want to speak to you again."

"I will tell him all I can," Ismail said.

The officer shook his hand, holding it in both of his. "I will bring you back to the Kerala presently. For now, the musicians are here, I see. I like to listen to them from up on the terraces."

Ismail followed him for a while, as if in an eddy, and then one of the abbess's assistants snagged him and brought him back to the party gathered by the Kerala to watch the concert.

The singers were dressed in beautiful saris, the musicians in silk jackets cut from bolts of different color and weave, mostly of brilliant sky blue and blood-orange red. The musicians began to play; the drummers set a pattern on tablas, and others played tall stringed instruments, like long-necked ouds, making Ismail recall Konstantiniyye, the whole city called up by these twangy things so like an oud.

A singer stepped forward and sang in some foreign tongue, the notes gliding through tones without a stop anywhere, always curving through tonalities unfamiliar to Ismail, no tones or quarter tones that did not bend up or down rapidly, like certain birdcalls. The singer's companions danced slowly behind her, coming as close to still positions as she came close to steady tones, but always moving, hands extended palm outward, speaking in dance languages.

Now the two drummers shifted into a complex but steady rhythm, woven together in a braid with the singing. Ismail closed his eyes; he had never heard such music. Melodies overlapped and went on without end. The audience swayed in time with them, the soldiers dancing in place, all moving around the still center of the Kerala, and even he shimmied in place, moved by sound. When the drummers went into a final mad flurry to mark the end of the piece, the soldiers cheered and shouted and leaped in the air. The singers and musicians bowed deeply, smiling, and came forward to receive the Kerala's congratulations. He conferred for a time with the lead singer, talking to her as to an old friend. Ismail found himself in something like a reception line gathered by the abbess, and he nodded to the sweaty performers one by one as they passed. They were young. Many different perfumes filled Ismail's nostrils, jasmine, orange, sea spray, and his breathing swelled his chest. The sea smell came in stronger on a breeze, from the sea itself this time, though there had been a perfume like it. The sea lay green and blue out there, like the road to everywhere.

The party began to swirl about the garden again, in patterns determined by the Kerala's slow progress. Ismail was introduced to a quartet of bankers, two Sikhs and two Travancori, and he listened to them discuss, in Persian to be polite to him, the complicated situation in India and around the Indian Ocean and the world more generally. Towns and harbors fought over, new towns built in hitherto empty river mouths, loyalties of local populations shifting, Muslim slavers in west Africa, gold in south Africa, gold in Inka, the island west of Africa—all these things had been going on for years, but somehow it was different now. Collapse of the old Muslim empires, the mushrooming of new machines, new states, new religions, new continents, and all emanating from here, as if the violent struggle within India were vibrating change outward in waves all the way around the world, meeting again coming the other way.

Bhakta introduced another man to Ismail, and the two men nodded to each other, bowing slightly. The man's name was Wasco, and he was from the New World, the big island west of Firanja, which the Chinese called Yingzhou. Wasco indentified it as Hodenosauneega, "meaning territories of the peoples of the Longhouse," he said in passable Persian. He represented the Hodenosaunee League, Bhakta explained. He looked like a Siberian or Mongolian, or a Manchu who did not shave his forehead. Tall, hawk nosed, striking to the eye, even there in the intense sunlight of the Kerala himself; he looked as if those isolated islands on the other side of the world might have produced a more healthy and vigorous race. No doubt sent by his people for that very reason.

Bhakta left them, and Ismail said politely, "I come from Konstantiniyye. Do your people have music like what we heard?"

Wasco thought about it. "We do sing and dance, but they are done by all together, informally and by chance, if you see what I am driving at. The drumming here was much more fluid and complicated. Thick sound. I found it fascinating. I would like to hear more of it, to see if I heard what I heard." He waggled a hand in a way Ismail didn't understand—amazement, perhaps, at the drummers' virtuosity.

"They play beautifully," Ismail said. "We have drummers too, but these have taken drumming to a higher level."

"Truly."

"What about cities, ships, all that? Does your land have a harbor like this one?" Ismail asked.

Wasco's expression of surprise looked just like anyone else's, which, Ismail thought, made perfect sense, as one saw the same look on the faces of babies just birthed. In fact, with his fluent Persian, it was impressive to Ismail how immediately comprehensible he was, despite his exotic home.

"No. Where I come from we do not gather in such numbers. More people live around this bay than in all my country, I think."

Now Ismail was the surprised one. "So few as that?"

"Yes. Although there are a lot of people here, I think. But we live in a great forest, extremely thick and dense. The rivers make the best ways. Until you people arrived, we hunted and grew some crops, we made only what we needed, with no metal or ships. The Muslims brought those to our east coast, and set up forts in a few harbors, in particular at the mouth of the East River, and on Long Island. There were not so many of them, at first, and we learned a lot from them that we put to use for ourselves. But we have been stricken by sicknesses we never knew before, and many have died, at the same time that many more Muslims have come, bringing slaves from Africa to help them. But our land is very big, and the coast itself, where the Muslims cluster, is not very good land. So we trade with them, and even better, with ships from here, when the Travancoris arrived. We were very happy to see these ships, truly, because we were worried about the Firanji Muslims. We still are. They have lots of cannon, and they go where they want, and tell us we do not know Allah, and that we should pray to him, and so on. So we liked to see the coming of other people, in good ships. People who were not Muslim."

"Did the Travancoris attack the Muslims already there?"

"Not yet. They landed at the mouth of the Mississippi, a big river. It may be they will come to blows eventually. They both are very well armed, and we are not, not yet." He looked Ismail in the eye and smiled cheerfully. "I must remember you are Muslim yourself, no doubt."

Ismail said, "I do not insist on it for others. Islam allows you to choose."

"Yes, they said that. But here in Travancore you see it really happening. Sikh, Hindu, Africans, Japanese, you see them all here. The Kerala does not seem to care. Or he likes it."

"Hindus absorb all that touch them, they say."

"That sounds all right to me," said Wasco. "Or in any case, preferable to Allah at gunpoint. We're making our own ships now in our great lakes, and soon we can come around Africa to you. Or, now the Kerala is proposing to dig a canal through the desert of Sinai, connecting the Mediterranean to the Red Sea, and giving us more direct access to you.

He proposes to conquer all Egypt to make this possible. No, there is much talk to be made, many decisions to be made. My league is very fond of leagues."

Then Bhakta came by and took Ismail off again. "You have been honored with an invitation to join the Kerala in one of the sky chariots."

"The floating bags?"

Bhakta smiled. "Yes."

"Oh joy."

Following the hobbling abbess, Ismail passed through terraces each with its own perfume scenting it, through nutmeg, lime, cinnamon, mint, rose, rising level by level in short stone staircases, feeling as he went something like a step into some higher realm, where both senses and emotions were keener: a faint terror of the body, as the odors cast him farther and farther into a higher state. His head whirled. He did not fear death, but his body did not like the idea of what would happen to take him to that final moment. He caught up to the abbess and walked by her, to stabilize himself by her calm. By the way she went up the stairs he saw that she was always in pain. And yet she never spoke of it. Now she looked back down at the ocean, catching her breath, and put one gnarled hand to Ismail's arm, and told him how glad she was that he was there among them, how much they might accomplish together working under the guidance of the Kerala, who was creating the space for greatness to occur. They were going to change the world. As she spoke Ismail reeled again on the scents in the air, he seemed to catch sight of things to come, of the Kerala sending back people and things from all over the world as he conquered one place after another, sending back to the monastery books, maps, instruments, medicines, tools, people with unusual diseases or new skills, from west of the Urals and east of the Pamirs, from Burma and Siam and the Malay Peninsula and Sumatra and Java, from the east coast of Africa, Ismail saw a witch doctor from Madagascar showing him the nearly transparent wings of a kind of bat, which allowed for a full examination of living veins and arteries, at which point he would give the Kerala a complete description of the circulation of the blood, and the Kerala would be very pleased at this, and then Ismail saw a Chinese Sumatran doctor showing him what the Chinese meant by qi and shen, which turned out to be what Ismail had always called lymph, produced by small glands under the arms, which might be affected by poultices of steamed herbs and drugs, as the Chinese had always claimed, and then he saw a group of Buddhist monks arranging charts of different elements in different families, depending on chemical and physical properties, all laid out in a very beautiful mandala, the subject of endless discussions in reading rooms, workshops, foundries and hospitals, everyone exploring even if they did not sail around the world, even if they never left Travancore, all of them anxious to have something interesting to tell the Kerala the next time he came by—not so the Kerala would reward them, though he would, but because he would be so happy at the new information. There was a look on his face everyone craved to see, and that was the whole story of Travancore, right there.

They came to a broad terrace where the flying basket was tethered. Already its huge silken bag was full of heated air, and straining up in jerks against its anchor ropes. The bamboo wicker basket was as big as a large carriage or a small pavilion; the rigging connecting it to the bottom of the silk bag was a network of lines, each slender, but clearly strong in the aggregate. The silk of the bag was diaphanous. A coal-fired enclosed brazier, with a hand bellows affixed to its side, was bolted to a bamboo frame affixed beneath the bag, just over head level when they stepped through a carriage door up into the basket.

The Kerala, the singer, Bhakta, and Ismail crowded in and stood at the corners. Pyidaungsu looked in and said, "Alas, it does not look as if there is room for me, I will crowd you uncomfortably; I will go up next time, regretful though I am to have lost the opportunity."

The ropes were cast off by the pilot and his passengers, except for a single line; it was a nearly windless day, and this, Ismail was told, was to be a controlled flight. They were to ascend like a kite, the pilot explained, and then when they were near the full extension of the line, they would shut the stove down, and stabilize in that one spot like any other kite, hanging some thousand hands over the landscape. The usual slight onshore afternoon breeze would insure that they would float inland, if the line happened to part.

Up they rose. "It is like Arjuna's chariot," the Kerala said to them, and they all nodded, eyes shining with excitement. The singer was beautiful, the memory of her singing like a song in the air around them; and the Kerala more beautiful still; and Bhakta the most beautiful of all. The pilot pumped the bellows once or twice. The wind whistled in the rigging.

From the air the world proved to be flat-looking. It extended a tremendous distance to the horizon—green hills to the northeast and south, and to the west the flat blue plate of the sea, the sunlight on it gleaming like gold on blue ceramic. Things down there were small but distinct. The trees were like green tufts of wool. It looked like the landscapes painted in Persian miniatures, spread out and laid in space below them, gorgeously articulated. Fields of rice were banked and bordered by sinuous lines of palm trees, and beyond them were orchards of small trees, planted in rows and lines, looking like a tight weave of cloth, all the way out to the dark green hills in the east. "What kind of trees are those?" Ismail asked.

The Kerala answered, for as became clear, he had directed the establishment of most of the orchards they could see. "They are part of the city lands, and used to grow the sources of essential oils that we trade for the goods that come in. You smelled some of them on our walk to the basket. Vetiver, costus, valerian, and angelica, shrubs like keruda, lotes, kadam, parijat, and night queen. Grasses like citronella, lemon grass and ginger grass and palmarosa. Flowers, as you see, including tuberose, champac, roses, jasmine, frangipani. Herbs including peppermint, spearmint, patchouli, artemisia. Then there, back in the woods, those are orchards of sandalwood and agarwood. All these are bred, planted, grown, harvested, processed, and bottled or bagged for trade with Africa and Firanja and China and the New World, where formerly they had no scents and no healing substances anything near as powerful, and so are much amazed, and desire them very much. And now I have people out scouring the world to find more stock of various kind, to see what will grow here. Those that prosper are cultivated, and their oils sold round the world. Demand for them is so high it is hard to match it, and gold comes flowing into Travancore as its wondrous scents perfume the whole Earth."

The basket turned as it came to the top of its anchor rope, and below them the heart of the kingdom was revealed, the city of Travancore as seen by the birds, or God. The land beside the bay was covered with roofs, trees, roads, docks, all as small as the toys of a princess, extending not as far as Konstantiniyye would have, but big enough, and sprinkled by a veritable arboretum of green trees, hardly displaced by the buildings and roads. Only the docks area was more roof than tree.

Just above them floated a tapestry of crosshatched cloud, moving inland on the wind. Off to sea a great line of tall white marbled clouds sailed toward them. "We'll have to get down before too long," the Kerala said to the pilot, who nodded and checked his stove.

A flock of vultures pinioned about them curiously, and the pilot shouted once at them, pulling a fowling gun out of a bag on the inside of the basket. He had never seen it happen, he said, but he had heard of a flock of birds pecking a bag right out of the sky. Hawks, jealous of their territory, apparently; probably vultures would not be so bold; but it would be a bad thing by which to be surprised.

The Kerala laughed, looked at Ismail and gestured at the colorful and fragrant fields. "This is the world we want you to help us make," he said. "We will go out into the world and plant gardens and orchards to the horizons, we will build roads through the mountains and across the deserts, and terrace the mountains and irrigate the deserts until there will be garden everywhere, and plenty for all, and there will be no more empires or kingdoms, no more caliphs, sultans, emirs, khans, or zamindars, no more kings or queens or princes, no more qadis or mullahs or ulema, no more slavery and no more usury, no more property and no more taxes, no more rich and no more poor, no killing or maiming or torture or execution, no more jailers and no more prisoners, no more generals, soldiers, armies or navies, no more patriarchy, no more clans, no more caste, no more hunger, no more suffering than what life brings us for being born and having to die, and then we will see for the first time what kind of creatures we really are."

3

Gold Mountain

In the twelfth year of the Xianfeng Emperor, rain inundated Gold Mountain. It started raining in the third month of the autumn, the usual start of the rainy season on this part of the coast of Yingzhou, but then it never stopped raining until the second month of the following spring. It rained every day for half a year, and often a pounding, drenching rain, as if it were the tropics. Before that winter was halfway over the great central valley of Gold Mountain had flooded up and down its entire length, forming a shallow lake 1500 li long and 300 li wide. The water poured brownly between the green hills flanking the delta, into the great bay and out the Gold Gate, staining the ocean the color of mud all the way out to the Peng-lai Islands. The outflow ran hard both ebb and flood, but still this was not enough to empty the great valley. The Chinese towns and villages and farms on the flat valley floor were drowned to the rooftops, and the entire population of the valley had to leave for higher ground, in the coastal range or the foothills of the Gold Mountains, or, for the most part, down to the city, fabled Fangzhang. Those who lived on the eastern side of the central valley tended to move up into the foothills, ascending the rail and stage roads that ran up through apple orchards and vine-yards overlooking the deep canyons that cut between the tablelands. Here they ran into the large foothill population of Japanese.

Many of these Japanese had come in the diaspora, after the Chinese armies had conquered Japan, in the Yung Cheng dynasty, a hundred and twenty years before. They were the ones who had first begun to grow rice in the central valley; but after only a generation or two, Chinese immigration filled the valley like the rains were now filling it, and most of the Japanese nisei and sansei moved up into the foothills, looking for gold, or growing grapes and apples. There they encountered a fair number of the old ones, hidden in the foothills and struggling to survive a malaria epidemic that recently had killed most of them off. The Japanese got along with the survivors, and the other old ones that came from the east, and together they resisted Chinese incursions into the foothills in every way they could, short of insurrection; for over the Gold Mountains lay high desolate alkaline deserts, where nothing could live. Their backs were to the wall.

So the arrival of so many Chinese refugee farming families was no very happy event for those already there. The foothills were composed of plateaus tilted up toward the high mountains, and cut by very deep, rugged, heavily forested river canyons. These manzanita-choked canyons were impenetrable to the Chinese authorities, and hidden in them were many Japanese families, most of them panning for gold or working small diggings. Chinese road-building campaigns stuck to the plateaus for the most part, and the canyons had remained substantially Japanese, despite the presence of Chinese prospectors: a Hokkaido-in-exile, tucked between the Chinese valley and the great desert of the natives. Now this world was filling with soaked Chinese rice farmers.

Neither side liked it. By now bad relations between Chinese and Japanese were as natural as dog and cat. The foothill Japanese tried to ignore the Chinese setting up refugee camps by all the stage and railroad stations; the Chinese tried to ignore the Japanese homesteads they were intruding on. Rice ran low, tempers got short, and the Chinese authorities sent troops into the area to keep order. The rain kept falling.

One group of Chinese walked out of the flooding on the stage road that followed the course of Rainbow Trout River. Overlooking the river's north bank were apple orchards and cattle pasturage, mostly owned by Chinese in Fangzhang, but worked by Japanese. This group of Chinese camped in one of the orchards, and did what they could to construct shelter from the rain, which continued to fall, day after day after day. They built a pole-framed barnlike building with a shingle roof, an open fire at one end, and mere sheets for walls; meager protection, but better than none. By day the men scrambled down the canyon walls to fish in the roaring river, and others went into the forest to hunt deer, shooting great numbers of them and drying their meat.

The matriarch of one of these families, Yao Je by name, was frantic that her silkworms had been left behind on their farm, in boxes tucked in the rafters of her filature. Her husband did not think there was anything that could be done about it, but the family employed a Japanese servant boy named Kiyoaki, who volunteered to go back down to the valley and take their rowboat out on the first calm day, and recover the silkworms. His master did not like the proposal, but his mistress approved of it, as she wanted the silkworms. So one rainy morning Kiyoaki left to try to return to their flooded farm, if he could.

He found the Yao family's rowboat still tied to the valley oak where they had left it. He untied it and rowed out over what had been the eastern rice paddies of their farm, toward their compound. A west wind churned up high waves, and both pushed him back east. His palms were blistered by the time he coasted up to the Yaos' inundated compound, scraped the flat bottom of the boat over the outer wall, and tied it to the roof of the filature, the tallest building on the farm. He climbed through a side window into the rafters, and found the sheets of damp paper covered with silkworm eggs, in their boxes filled with rocks and mulberry mulch. He gathered all the sheets into an oilcloth bag and lowered them out the window into the rowboat, feeling pleased.

Now rain was violently thrashing the surface of the flood, and Kiyoaki considered spending the night in the attic of the Yaos' house. But the emptiness of it frightened him, and for no better reason than that, he decided to row back. The oilcloth would protect the eggs, and he had been wet for so long that he was used to it. He was like a frog hopping in and out of its pond, it was all the same to him. So he got in the boat and began to row.

But now, perversely, the wind was from the east, blowing up waves of surprising weight and power. His hands hurt, and the boat occasionally brushed over drowned things: treetops, wiregraph poles, perhaps other things, he was too jumpy to look. Dead men's fingers! He could not see far in the growing gloom, and as night fell he lost his feeling for what direction he was headed. The rowboat had a oiled canvas decking bunched in its bow, and he pulled it back over the gunwales, tied it in place, got under it and floated over the flood, lying in the bottom of the boat and occasionally bailing with a can. It was wet, but it would not founder. He let it bounce over the waves, and eventually fell asleep.

He woke several times in the night, but after bailing he always forced himself to sleep again. The rowboat swirled and rocked, but the waves never broke over it. If they did the boat would founder and he would drown, but he avoided thinking about that.

Dawn made it clear he had drifted west rather than east. He was far out on the inland sea that the central valley had become. A knot of valley oaks marked a small island of higher ground that still stood above the flood, and he rowed toward it.

As he was facing away from the new little island, he did not see it well until he had thumped the bow onto it. Immediately he discovered it was coated with a host of spiders, bugs, snakes, squirrels, moles, rats, mice, raccoons, and foxes, all leaping onto the rowboat at once, as representing the new highest ground. He himself was the highest ground of all, and he was shouting in dismay and slapping desperate snakes and squirrels and spiders off him, when a young woman and baby leaped onto the boat like the rest of the crowd of animals, except the girl pushed off from the tree Kiyoaki had rowed against, weeping and crying loudly, "They're trying to eat her, they're trying to eat my baby!"

Kiyoaki was preoccupied by the scores of creatures still crawling on him, to the point of nearly losing an oar over the side. Eventually he had squished or brushed or thrown overboard all the interlopers, and he replaced the oars in the oarlocks and rowed swiftly away. The girl and her baby sat on the boat deck, the girl still whacking insects and spiders and shouting, "Ugh! Ugh! Ugh!" She was Chinese.

The lowering gray clouds began to leak rain yet again. They could see nothing but water in all directions, except for the trees of the little island they had so hastily vacated.

Kiyoaki rowed east. "You're going the wrong way," the girl complained.

"This is the way I came," Kiyoaki said. "The family that employs me is there."

The girl did not reply.

"How did you get on that island?"

Again she said nothing.

Having passengers made rowing harder, and the waves came closer to breaking over the boat. Crickets and spiders continued to leap around underfoot, and an opossum had wedged itself in the bow under the decking. Kiyoaki rowed until his hands were bleeding, but they never caught sight of land; it was raining so hard now that it formed a kind of thick falling fog.

The girl complained, nursed her baby, killed bugs. "Row west," she kept saying. "The current will help you."

Kiyoaki rowed east. The boat jounced over the waves, and from time to time they bailed it out. The whole world seemed to have become a sea. Once Kiyoaki glimpsed a sight of the coastal range through a rent in the low clouds to the west, much closer than he would have expected or hoped. A current in the floodwaters must have been carrying them west.

Near dark they came on another tiny tree island.

"It's the same one!" the young woman said.

"It just looks that way."

The wind was rising again, like the evening delta breeze they enjoyed so much during the hot dry summers. The waves were getting higher and higher, slapping hard into the bow and splashing over the canvas and in on their feet. Now they had to land, or they would sink and drown.

So Kiyoaki landed the boat. Again a tide of animal and insect life overran them. The Chinese girl cursed with surprising fluency, beating the larger creatures away from her baby. The smaller ones you just had to get used to. Up in the vast branches of the valley oaks sat a miserable troop of snow monkeys, staring down on them. Kiyoaki tied the boat to a branch and got off, arranged a wet blanket on the squirming mud between two roots, pulled the rowboat's decking off, and draped it over the girl and her baby, weighing it down as best he could with broken branches. He crawled underneath the canvas with her, and they and an entire menagerie of bugs and snakes and rodents settled in for the long night. It was hard to sleep.

The next morning was as rainy as ever. The young woman had put her baby between the two of them to protect her from the rats. Now she nursed her. Under the canvas it was warmer than outside. Kiyoaki wished he could start a fire to cook some snakes or squirrels, but nothing was dry. "We might as well get going," he said.

They went out into the chill drizzle and got back in the boat. As

Kiyoaki cast off about ten of the snow monkeys leaped down through the branches and climbed into the boat with them. The girl shrieked and pulled her shirt over her baby, huddling over it and staring at the monkeys. They sat there like passengers, looking down or off into the rain, pretending to be thinking about something else. She threatened one and it shrank back.

"Leave them alone," Kiyoaki said. The monkeys were Japanese; the Chinese didn't like them, and complained about their presence on Yingzhou.

They spun over the great inland sea. The young woman and her baby were dotted with spiders and fleas, as if they were dead bodies. The monkeys began to groom them, eating some insects and throwing others overboard.

"My name is Kiyoaki."

"I am Peng-ti," the young Chinese woman said, brushing things off the babe and ignoring the monkeys.

Rowing hurt the blisters on Kiyoaki's hands, but after a while the pain would subside. He headed west, giving in to the current that had already taken them so far that way.

Out of the drizzle appeared a small sailboat. Kiyoaki shouted, waking the girl and baby, but the men on the sailboat had already spotted them, and they sailed over.

There were two sailors on board, two Japanese men. Peng-ti watched them with narrowed eyes.

One told the castaways to climb into their boat. "But tell the monkeys to stay there," he said with a laugh.

Peng-ti passed her baby up to them, then hauled herself over the gunwale.

"You're lucky they're just monkeys," the other one said. "Up north valley, Black Fort is high ground for a lot of country that hadn't been cleared, and the animals that swam onto it were more than you see here in your rice paddies. They closed the gates, but walls are nothing much to bears, brown bears and gold bears, and they were shooting them when the magistrate ordered them to stop, because it was just going to use up all their ammunition and then they'd still have a whole town of bears. And the giant gold bears opened the gates and in came wolves, elk, the whole damn Hsu Fu walking the streets of Black Fort, and the people all locked up in their attics waiting it out." The men laughed with pleasure at the thought.

"We're hungry," Peng-ti said.

"You look it," they said.

"We were going east," Kiyoaki mentioned.

"We're going west."

"Good," Peng-ti said.

It continued to rain. They passed another knot of trees on an embankment just covered by water, and sitting in the branches like the monkeys were a dozen soaked and miserable Chinese men, very happy to leap on the sailboat. They had been there six days, they said. The fact that Japanese had rescued them did not seem to register with them one way or the other.

Now the sailboat and rowboat were carried on a current of brown water, between misted green hills.

"We're going over to the city," their tillerman said. "It's the only place where the docks are still secure. Besides, we want to get dry and have a big dinner in Japantown."

Across the rain-spattered brown water they sailed. The delta and its diked islands were all under the flood, it was all a big brown lake with occasional lines of treetops sticking out of it, giving the sailors a fix on their position, apparently. They pointed at certain lines and discussed them with great animation, their fluid Japanese a great contrast to their rough Chinese.

Eventually they came into a narrow strait between tall hillsides, and as the wind was shooting up this strait—the Inner Gate, Kiyoaki presumed—they let down the sail and rode the current, shifting their rudder to keep in the fast part of it, which curved with the bend around the tall hills to the south, beyond which they were through the narrows and thrust out onto the broad expanse of Golden Bay, now a rocking foam-streaked brown bay, ringed by green hills that disappeared into a ceiling of low gray cloud. As they tacked across to the city the clouds thinned in a few bands over the tall ridge of the northern peninsula, and weak light fell onto the hive of buildings and streets covering the peninsula, all the way up to the peak of Mount Tamalpi, turning certain neighborhoods white or silver or pewter, amid the general gray. It was an awesome sight.

The western side of the bay just north of the Gold Gate was broken by several peninsulas extending into the bay, and these peninsulas were covered with buildings too, indeed among the city's busiest districts, as they formed the capes of three little harbor bays. The middle of these three was the largest, the commercial harbor, and the peninsula on its south side also served the Japantown, tucked among the warehouses and a working neighborhood behind them. Here, as their sailors had said, the floating docks and the wharves were intact and functioning normally, as if the central valley were not completely flooded. Only the dirt-brown water of the bay revealed that anything was different.

As they approached the docks, the monkeys on the rowboat began to look agitated. It was a case of going from flood to frying pan for them, and eventually one slipped overboard and struck out swimming for an island to the south, and all the others immediately followed with a splash, picking up their conversation among themselves where they had left off.

"That's why they call it Monkey Island," their pilot said.

He brought them into the middle harbor. The men on the dock included a Chinese magistrate, who looked down and said, "Still flooded out there I see."

"Still flooded and still raining."

"People must be getting hungry."

"Yes."

The Chinese men climbed onto the dock, and thanked the sailors, who got out with Kiyoaki and Peng-ti and the baby. The tillerman joined them as they followed the magistrate to the "Great Valley Refugee Office," set up in the customs building at the back of the dock. There they were registered—their names, place of residence before the flood, and the whereabouts of their families and neighbors, if known, all recorded. The clerks gave them chits that would allow them to claim beds in the immigration-control buildings, located on the steep-sided big island out in the bay.

The tillerman shook his head. These big buildings had been built to quarantine non-Chinese immigrants to Gold Mountain, about fifty years before. They were surrounded by fences tipped with barbed wire, and contained big dormitories with men's and women's sides. Now they housed some of the stream of refugees flowing down into the bay on the flood, mostly displaced valley Chinese, but the keepers of the place had retained the prison attitude they had had with the immigrants, and the valley refugees there were complaining bitterly and doing their best to get cleared to move in with local relatives, or to relocate up or down the coast, or even to return to the flooded valley and wait around the edges until the water receded. But there had been outbreaks of cholera reported, and the governor of the province had declared a state of emergency that allowed him to act directly in the emperor's interests: martial law was in effect, enforced by army and navy.

The tillerman, having explained this, said to Kiyoaki and Peng-ti, "You can stay with us if you want. We stay at a boardinghouse in Japantown, it's clean and cheap. They'll put you up on credit if we say you're good for it."

Kiyoaki regarded Peng-ti, who looked down. Snake or spider: refugee housing or Japantown.

"We'll come with you," she said. "Many thanks."

The street leading inland from the docks to the high central district of the city was lined on both sides by restaurants and hotels and small shops, the fluid calligraphy of Japanese as common as the blockier Chinese ideograms. Side streets were tight alleyways, the peaked rooftops curving up into the rain until the buildings almost met overhead. People wore oilcloth ponchos or jackets, and carried black or colorful print umbrellas, many very tattered by now. Everyone was wet, heads lowered and shoulders hunched, and the middle of the street was like an open stream, bouncing brownly to the bay. The green hills rising to the west of this quarter of the city were bright with tile roofs, red and green and a vivid blue: a prosperous quarter, despite the Japantown at its foot. Or, perhaps, because of it. Kiyoaki had been taught to call the blue of those tiles Kyoto blue.

They walked through alleys to a big merchant house and chandlery in the warren of Japantown, and the two Japanese men—the older named Gen, they learned—introduced the young castaways to the proprietress of a boardinghouse next door. She was a toothless old Japanese woman, in a simple brown kimono, with a shrine in her hallway and reception room. They stepped in her door and began to shed their wet raingear, and she regarded them with a critical eye. "Everyone so wet these days," she complained. "You look like they pulled you off the bottom of the bay. Chewed by crabs."

She gave them dry clothes, and had theirs sent to a laundry. There were women and men's wings to her establishment, and Kiyoaki and

Peng-ti were assigned mats, then fed a hot meal of rice and soup, followed by cups of warm sake. Gen was paying for them, and he waved off their thanks in the usual brusque Japanese manner. "Payment on return home," Gen said. "Your families will be happy to repay me."

Neither of the castaways had much to say to that. Fed, dry; there was nothing left but to go to their rooms and sleep as if felled.

Next day Kiyoaki woke to the sound of the chandler next door, shouting at an assistant. Kiyoaki looked out the window of his room into a window of the chandlery, and saw the angry chandler hit the unfortunate youth on the side of the head with an abacus, the beads rattling back and forth.

Gen had come in the room, and he regarded the scene in the next building impassively. "Come on," he said to Kiyoaki. "I've got some errands to do, it'll be a way to show you some of the city."

Off they went, south on the big coastal street fronting the bay, connecting all of the smaller harbors facing the big bay and the islands in it. The southernmost harbor was tighter than the one fronting Japantown, its bay a forest of masts and smokestacks, the city behind and above it jammed together in a great mass of three- and four-story buildings, all wooden with tile roofs, crammed together in what Gen said was the usual Chinese city style, and running right down to the high-tide line, in places even built out over the water. This compact mass of buildings covered the whole end of the peninsula, its streets running straight east and west from the bay to the ocean, and north and south until they ended in parks and promenades high over the Gold Gate. The strait was obscured by a fog that floated in over the yellow spill of floodwater pouring out to sea; the yellow-brown plume was so extensive that there was no blue ocean to be seen. On the ocean side of the point lay the long batteries of the city defenses, concrete fortresses that Gen said commanded the strait and the waters outside it for up to fifty li offshore.

Gen sat on the low wall of one of the promenades overlooking the strait. He waved a hand to the north, where streets and rooftops covered everything they could see.

"The greatest harbor on Earth. The greatest city in the world, some say."

"It's big, that's for sure. I didn't know it would be so—" ·

"A million people here now, they say. And more coming all the time. They just keep building north, on up the peninsula."

Across the strait, on the other hand, the southern peninsula was a waste of marshes and bare steep hills. It looked very empty compared to the city, and Kiyoaki remarked on it.

Gen shrugged: "Too marshy, I guess, and too steep for streets. I suppose they'll get to it eventually, but it's better over here."

The islands dotting the bay were occupied by the compounds of the imperial bureaucrats. Out on the biggest island the governor's mansion was roofed with gold. The brown foam-streaked surface of the water was dotted with little bay boats, mostly sail, some smoking two-strokes. Little marinas of square houseboats were tucked against the islands. Kiyoaki surveyed the scene happily. "Maybe I'll move here. There must be jobs."

"Oh yeah. Down at the docks, unloading the freighters—get a room at the boardinghouse—there's lots of work. In the chandlery too."

Kiyoaki recalled his awakening. "Why was that man so angry?"

Gen frowned. "That was unfortunate. Tagomi-san is a good man, he doesn't usually beat his help, I assure you. But he's frustrated. We can't get the authorities to release supplies of rice to feed the people stranded in the valley. The chandler is very high in the Japanese community here, and he's been trying for months now. He thinks the Chinese bureaucrats, over on the island there"—gesturing—"are hoping that most of the people inland will starve."

"But that's crazy! Most of them are Chinese."

"Yeah sure, a lot are Chinese, but it would mean even more Japanese."

"How so?"

Gen regarded him. "There are more of us in the central valley than there are Chinese. Think about it. It may not be so obvious, because the Chinese are the only ones allowed to own land, and so they run the rice paddies, especially where you came from, over east side. But upvalley, downvalley—it's mostly Japanese at the ends, and in the foothills, the coastal range, even more so. We were here first, you understand? Now comes this big flood, people are driven away, flooded out, starving. The bureaucrats are thinking, when it's over and the land reemerges, assuming it will someday, if most of the Japanese and natives have died of hunger, then new immigrants can be sent in to take over the valley. And they'll all be Chinese."

Kiyoaki didn't know what to say to this.

Gen stared at him curiously. He seemed to like what he saw. "So, you know, Tagomi has been trying to organize private relief, and we've been taking it inland on the flood. But it isn't going well, and it's been expensive, and so the old man is getting testy. His poor workers are paying for it." Gen laughed.

"But you rescued those Chinese stuck in the trees."

"Yeah, yeah. Our job. Our duty. Good must result from good, eh? That's what the old woman boarding you says. Of course she's always getting taken."

They regarded a new tongue of fog licking into the strait. Rain clouds on the horizon looked like a great treasure fleet arriving. A black broom of rain already swept the desolate southern peninsula.

Gen clapped him on the shoulder in a friendly way. "Come on, I have to get her some stuff at the store."

He led Kiyoaki up to a tram station, and they got on the next tram that ran up the western side of the city, overlooking the ocean. Up streets and down, past shady residential districts, then another government district, high on the slopes overlooking the stained ocean, wide esplanades lined with cherry trees; then another fortress. The hilly neighborhoods north of these guns held many of the city's richest mansions, Gen said. They gazed at some of them from the tram as it squeaked past. From the tops of the precipitous streets they could see the temples on the summit of Mount Tamalpi. Then down into a valley, off that tram, and east on another one, across the peninsula and back to Japantown, with bags of food from a market for the proprietress of the boardinghouse.

Kiyoaki looked in the women's wing to see how Peng-ti and her baby were doing. She was sitting in a window embrasure holding the child, looking blank and desolate. She had not gone to find any Chinese relatives, or to seek help from the Chinese authorities, not that there appeared to be much help from that direction; but she seemed not at all interested. Staying with the Japanese, as if in hiding. But she spoke no Japanese, and that was all they used here, unless they thought to speak to her directly in Chinese.

"Come out with me," he said to her in Chinese. "I have some money from Gen for the tram, we can see the Gold Gate."

She hesitated, then agreed. Kiyoaki led her onto the tram system he had just learned, and they went down to the park overlooking the strait. The fog had almost burned off, and the next line of storm clouds were not yet arrived, and the spectacle of the city and the bay shone in wet blinking sunlight. The brown flood continued to pour out to sea, the scraps and lines of foam showing how fast the current was; it must have been ebb tide. That was every rice paddy in the central valley, scoured away and flushed out into the big ocean. Inland everything would have to be built anew. Kiyoaki said something to this effect, and a flash of anger crossed Peng-ti's face, quickly suppressed.

"Good," she said. "I never want to see that place again."

Kiyoaki regarded her, shocked. She could not have been more than about sixteen. What about her parents, her family? She wasn't saying, and he was too polite to ask.

Instead they sat in the rare sun, watching the bay. The babe whimpered, and unobtrusively Peng-ti nursed it. Kiyoaki watched her face and the tidal race in the Gold Gate, thinking about the Chinese, their implacable bureaucracy, their huge cities, their rule of Japan, Korea, Mindanao, Aozhou, Yingzhou, and Inka.

"What's your baby's name?" Kiyoaki said.

"Hu Die," the girl said. "It means—"

"Butterfly," Kiyoaki said, in Japanese. "I know." He fluttered with a hand, and she smiled and nodded.

Clouds obscured the sun again, and it cooled rapidly in the onshore breeze. They took the tram back to Japantown.

At the boardinghouse Peng-ti went to the women's wing, and as the men's wing was empty, Kiyoaki entered the chandlery next door, thinking to inquire about a job. The shop on the first floor was deserted, and he heard voices on the second floor, so he went up the stairs.

Here were the accounting rooms and the offices. The chandler's big office door was closed, but voices came through it. Kiyoaki approached, heard men speaking Japanese:

". . . don't see how we could coordinate our efforts, how we could be sure it was all going off at once—"

The door flew open and Kioyaki was seized by the neck and dragged into the room. Eight or nine Japanese men glared at him, all seated around one elderly bald foreigner, in the chair of the honored guest. The chandler roared, "Who let him in here!"

"There's no one downstairs," Kiyoaki said. "I was just looking for someone to ask for a—"

"How long were you listening!" The old man looked as if he were ready to hit Kiyoaki with his abacus, or worse. "How dare you eavesdrop on us, you could get rocks tied to your ankles and thrown in the bay for that!"

"He's just one of the folks we plucked out of the valley," Gen said from a corner. "I've been getting to know him. Might as well enlist him, since he's here. I've already vetted him. He hasn't got anything better to do. In fact, he'll be good."

While the old man spluttered some objection, Gen got up and grabbed Kiyoaki by the shirtfront.

"Get someone to lock the front door," he told one of the younger men there, who left quickly. Gen turned to Kiyoaki:

"Listen, youth. We're trying to help the Japanese here, like I told you down at the gate."

"That's good."

"We're working to free the Japanese, actually. Not only here, but in Japan itself."

Kiyoaki gulped, and Gen shook him. "That's right, Japan itself! A war of independence for the old country, and here too. You can work for us, and join one of the greatest things possible for a Japanese. Are you in or are you out?"

"In!" Kiyoaki said. "I'm in, of course! Just tell me what I can do!"

"You can sit down and shut up," Gen said. "First of all. Listen and then you'll be told more."

The elderly foreigner asked a question in his language.

Another of the men waved Kiyoaki aside, answered in the same language. In Japanese he said to Kiyoaki, "This is Doctor Ismail, visiting us from Travancore, the capital of the Indian League. He's here to help us organize our resistance to the Chinese. If you are to stay in this meeting, you must swear never to tell anyone what you see and hear. It means you are committed to the cause without a chance of backing out. If we find out you've ever told anyone about this, you'll be killed, do you understand?"

"I understand," Kiyoaki said. "I'm in, I said. You can proceed with no fear of me. I've worked like a slave for the Chinese in the valley, all my life."

The men in the room stared at him; only Gen grinned at the spectacle of such a youth using the phrase "all my life." Kiyoaki saw that and blushed hotly. But it was true no matter how old he was. He set his jaw and sat on the floor in the corner by the door.

The men resumed their conversation. They were asking questions of the foreigner, who watched them with a birdlike blank expression, fingering a white moustache, until the man translating spoke to him, in a fluid language that did not seem to have enough sounds to create all the words; but the old foreigner understood him, and replied to the questions carefully and at length, taking pauses every few sentences to let the young interpreter speak in Japanese. He was obviously very used to working with a translator.

"He says his country was under the yoke of the Mughals for many centuries, and finally they freed themselves in a military campaign run by their Kerala. The methods used have been systematized, and can be taught. The Kerala himself was assassinated, about twenty years ago. Doctor Ismail says this was a, a disaster beyond telling, you can see it still upsets him to talk about it. But the only cure is to go on and do what the Kerala would have wanted them to do. And he wanted everyone everywhere free of all empires. So Travancore itself is now part of an Indian League, which has its disagreements, even violent disagreements, but mostly they work out their differences as equals. He says this kind of league was first developed here in Yingzhou, out in the east, among the Hodenosaunee natives. The Firanjis have taken most of the east coast of Yingzhou, as we have the west, and many of the old ones out there have died of disease, as here, but the Hodenosaunee still hold the area around the great lakes, and the Travancoris have helped them to fight the Muslims. He says that is the key to success; those fighting the great empires have to help each other. He says they have helped some Africans as well, down in the south, a King Moshesh of the Basutho tribe. The doctor here traveled there himself, and arranged for aid to the Basuthos that allowed them to defend themselves from Muslim slave traders and the Zulu tribe as well. Without their help the Basuthos probably wouldn't have survived."

"Ask him what he means when he says help."

The foreign doctor nodded when the question was put to him. He used fingers to enumerate his answer.

"He says, first they help by teaching the system their Kerala worked out, for organizing a fighting force, and fighting armies when the opposing armies are much bigger. Then second, they can in some instances help with weapons. They will smuggle them in for us, if they think we are serious. And third, rare but possible, they can join the fight, if they think it will turn the tide."

"They fought Muslims, and so do the Chinese. Why should they help us?"

"He says, good question. He says, it's a matter of keeping a balance, and of setting the two great powers against each other. The Chinese and the Muslims are fighting each other everywhere, even in China itself, where there are Muslim rebellions. But right now the Muslims in Firanja and Asia are splintered and weak, they are always fighting each other, even here in Yingzhou. Meanwhile China continues to fatten on its colonies here and around the Dahai. Even though the Qing bureaucracy is corrupt and inefficient, their manufacturers are always busy, and gold keeps coming, from here and from Inka. So no matter how inefficient they are, they keep getting richer. At this point, he says, the Travancoris are interested in keeping China from becoming so strong they take over the whole world."

One of the Japanese men snorted. "No one can take over the world," he said. "It's too big."

The foreigner inquired what had been said, and the translator translated for him. Doctor Ismail raised a finger as he heard it, and replied.

"He says, that may have been true before, but now, with steamships, and communication by qi, and trade and travel everywhere by ocean, and machines exerting several thousandcamels of power, it could be that some dominant country could get an advantage and keep growing. There is a kind of, what, multiplying power to power. So that it's best to try to keep any one country from getting powerful enough to start that process. It was Islam that looked to be taking over the world for a while, he says, before their Kerala went at the heart of the old Muslim empires and broke them. It could be that China needs a similar treatment, and then there will be no empires, and people can do as they choose, and form leagues with whoever helps them."

"But how can we stay in contact with them, on the other side of the world?"

"He agrees it is not easy. But steamships are fast. It can be done. They have done it in Africa, and in Inka. Qi wires can be strung very quickly between groups."

They went on, the questions becoming more practical and detailed, losing Kiyoaki, as he didn't know where many of the places mentioned were: Basutho, Nsara, Seminole, and so on. Eventually Doctor Ismail appeared to tire, and they ended the meeting with tea. Kiyoaki helped Gen pour cups and pass them around, and then Gen took him downstairs and reopened the chandlery.

"You almost got me in trouble there," he told Kiyoaki, "and yourself too. You'll have to work hard for us to make up for scaring me that bad."

"Sorry—I will. Thanks for helping me."

"Oh that poisonous feeling. No thanks. You do your job, I do mine."

"Right."

"Now, the old man will take you in at the chandlery here, and you can live next door. He'll hit you with his abacus, as you saw. But your main job will be running messages for us and the like. If the Chinese get wind of what we're doing, it will get ugly, I warn you. It will be war, do you understand? It may be a secret war, at night, in the alleyways and out on the bay. Do you understand?"

"I understand."

Gen regarded him. "We'll see. First thing, we'll go back into the valley and get the word into the foothills, to some friends of mine. Then back to the city, to work here."

"Whatever you say."

An assistant gave Kiyoaki a tour of the chandlery, which he was soon to know so well. After that he went back to the boardinghouse next door. Peng-ti was helping the old woman chop vegetables; Hu Die was sunning in a laundry basket. Kiyoaki sat next to the baby, entertaining it with a finger and thinking things over. He watched Peng-ti, learning the Japanese words for the vegetables. She didn't want to go back to the valley either. The old woman spoke pretty good Chinese, and the two women were talking, but Peng-ti wasn't telling her any more about her past than she had told Kiyoaki. It was warm in the kitchen. Rain was coming down again outside. The baby smiled at him, as if to reassure him. As if telling him that it would be all right.

The next time they were down at Gold Gate Park, looking at the brown flood still pouring, he sat by Peng-ti on a bench. "Listen," he said, "I'm going to stay here in the city. I'll go back out to the valley on a trip, and get Madame Yao's silkworms to her, but I'm going to live here."

She nodded. "Me too." She waved at the bay. "How could you not." She picked up Hu Die and held her up in the air, face out toward the bay, and turned her around to face the four winds. "This is your new home, Hu Die! This is where you are going to grow up!" Hu Die goggled at the view.

Kiyoaki laughed. "Yes. She will like it here. But listen, Peng-ti, I'm going to be . . ." He considered how to say it. "I'm going to work for Japan. Do you understand?"

"No."

"I'm going to work for Japan, against China."

"I see."

"I'm going to be working against China."

Her jaw clenched. She said harshly, "Do you think I care?" She looked across the bay to the Inner Gate, where brown water split the green hills. "I'm so glad to be out of there." She looked him in the eye, and he felt his heart jump. "I'll help you."

4

Black Clouds

Because China's emerging empire was now chiefly maritime, its shipping again became the biggest in the world. The emphasis was on carrying capacity, and so the typical Chinese fleet of the early modern period was very big, and slow. Speed was not a consideration. This made difficulties for them later, in naval disputes with the Indians and with the Muslims of Africa, the Mediterranean, and Firanja. In the Mediterranean, the Islamic Sea, Muslims developed ships that were smaller but much faster and nimbler than their Chinese contemporaries, and in several decisive naval encounters of the tenth and eleventh centuries, Muslim fleets defeated larger Chinese fleets, preserving the balance of power and preventing Qing China from achieving world hegemony. Indeed Muslim privateering in the Dahai became a major source of revenue to Islamic governments, and a source of friction between Islamic and Chinese, one of the many factors leading to war. With the sea far surpassing land as a means of commercial and military travel, the superior speed and maneuverability of Muslim ships was one of the advantages they held that allowed them to challenge Chinese sea power.

The development of steam power and metal hulls in Travancore was quickly taken up by both of the other major Old World hegemons, but the lead in this technology and others allowed the Indian League also to compete with the larger rivals on both sides of it.

Thus the twelfth and thirteenth Muslim centuries, or the Qing dynasty in China, was a period of rising competition between the three major Old World cultures, to dominate and extract the wealth of the New World, Aozhou, and the hinterlands of the Old World, now being fully occupied and exploited.

The problem was that the stakes became too high. The two biggest empires were both the strongest and the weakest at the same time. The Qing dynasty continued to grow to the south, north, in the New World, and inside itself. Meanwhile Islam controlled a huge part of the Old World, and the eastern coasts of the New as well. Yingzhou had a Muslim east coast, the League of Tribes in the middle, Chinese settlements in the west, and new Travancori trading ports. Inka was a battleground between Chinese, Travancori, and the Muslims of west Africa.

So the world was fractured into the two big old hegemons, China and Islam, and the two new and smaller leagues, the Indian and the Yingzhou. Chinese ocean trade and conquest slowly extended their hegemony over the Dahai, settling Aozhou, the west coasts of Yingzhou and Inka, and making inroads by sea in many other places; becoming the Middle Kingdom in fact as well as by name, the center of the world by sheer numbers alone, as well as by the new power of its navies. A danger to all the other peoples on Earth, in fact, despite the various problems in the Qing bureaucracy.

At the same time Dar al-Islam kept spreading, through all Africa, the east coasts of the New World, across central Asia, and even into India, where it had never really left, and into southeast Asia as well, even onto the isolated west coast of Aozhou.

And in the middle, caught between these two expansions, so to speak, was India. Travancore took the lead here, but the Punjab, Bengal, Rajistan, and all the other states of the subcontinent were active and prospering at home and abroad, in turmoil and conflict, always at odds, and yet free of emperors and caliphs, and in their ferment the scientific leaders of the world, with trading posts on every continent, constantly in opposition against the hegemons, the ally of anyone against Islam, and often against the Chinese, with whom they kept a most uneasy relationship, both fearing them and needing them; but as the decades went by, and the old Muslim empires showed more and more aggression to the east, across Transoxiana and into all north Asia, more and more inclined to court China, as a counterweight, trusting the Himalaya and the great jungles of Burma to keep them out from under the big umbrella of Chinese patronage.

Thus it was that the Indian states were often uneasily allied with China in hope of aid against their ancient foe Islam. So that when Islam and Chinese finally fell into active war, first in central Asia, then all over the world, Travancore and the Indian League were pulled into it, and Muslim-Hindu violence began yet another deadly round.

It began in the twenty-first year of the Kuang Hsu emperor, the last of the Qing dynasty, when south China's Muslim enclaves all revolted at once. The Manchu banners were sent south and the rebellion put down, more or less, over the course of the next several years. But the suppression may have worked too well, for the Muslims of west China had been chafing under Qing military rule for many generations, and with their fellow believers to the east being exterminated, it became a matter of jihad or death. So they revolted, out in the vast empty deserts and mountains of central Asia, and the brown towns in their green valleys quickly turned red.

The Qing government, corrupt but massively entrenched, massively wealthy, made its move against its Muslim rebellions by initiating another campaign of conquest, west across Asia. This succeeded for a time, because there was no strong state in the abandoned center of the world to oppose them. But eventually it triggered a defensive jihad from the Muslims of west Asia, whom nothing would have united at that point except for the threat of Chinese conquest.

This unintended consolidation of Islam was quite an accomplishment. Wars between the remnants of the Safavid and Ottoman empires, between Shiite and Sunni, Sufi and Wahhabi, the Firanji states and the Maghrib, had been continuous throughout the period of consolidation of states and boundaries, and even with sovereign borders more or less fixed, except for ongoing struggles here and there, they were not initially in a position to respond as a civilization to the threat from China.

But when threatened by a Chinese expansion across all Asia, the fractured Islamic states pulled together, and began to fight back as a united force. A collision that had been building for centuries now came to a head: for both of the big old civilizations, global hegemony or complete annihilation were thinkable possibilities. The stakes could not be higher.

The Indian League tried at first to remain neutral, as did the Hodenosaunee. But the war drew them in too, when Islamic invaders crossed into north India, as they had so many times before, and conquered it south to the Deccan, across Bengal and down into Burma. Similarly, Muslim armies began to conquer Yingzhou east to west, attacking both the Hodenosaunee League and the Chinese in the west. All the world descended into this realm of conflict together.

And so the long war came.

BOOK 8

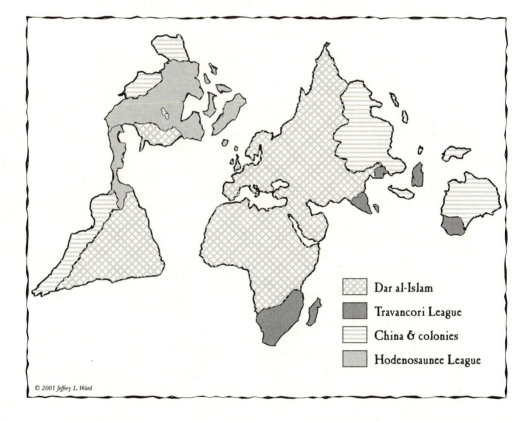

Dar al-Islam

Travancori League

China & colonies

Hodenosaunee League

© 2001 Jeffrey L. Ward

———————

"China is indestructible, there are too many of us. Fire, flood, famine, war—they're like pruning a tree. Branches cut to stimulate new life. The tree keeps growing."

Major Kuo was feeling expansive. It was dawn, the Chinese hour. Early light illuminated the Muslim outposts and put the sun in their eyes, so that they were wary of snipers, and bad at it themselves. Sunset was their hour. Call to prayer, sniper fire, sometimes a rain of artillery shells. Best stay in the trenches at sunset, or in the caves below them.

But now they had the sun on their side. Sky frost-blue, standing around rubbing gloved hands together, tea and cigarettes, the low whump of cannon to the north. Rumbling for two weeks now. Preparation for another big assault, possibly, perhaps even the breakout spoken of for so many years—so many that it had become a catchword for something that would never happen—"when the breakout comes" as "when pigs fly" or the like. So perhaps not.

Nothing they could see would tell them one way or another. Out in the middle of the Gansu Corridor, the vast mountains to the south and the endless deserts to the north were not visible. It looked like the steppes, or it had, before the war. Now the whole width of the corridor, from mountains to desert, and the whole length, from Ningxia to Ji-ayuguan, was torn to mud. The trenches had moved back and forth, li by li, for over sixty years. In that time every blade of grass and clod of dirt had been blasted into the sky more than once. What remained was a kind of disordered black ocean, ringed and ridged and cratered. As if someone had tried to replicate in mud the surface of the moon. Every spring weeds made brave efforts to return, and failed. The town of Ganzhou had once stood near this very spot, paralleling the Jo River; now there was no sign of either. Land pulverized to bedrock. Ganzhou had been home to a thriving Sino-Muslim culture, so this wasteland they observed, stark in dawn light, was a perfect ideograph of the long war.

The sound of the big guns began behind them. The shells from the latest guns were cast into space, and fell two hundred li away. The sun rose higher. They retreated into the subterranean realm of black mud and wet planks that was their home. Trenches, tunnels, caves. Many caves held Buddhas, usually in his adamant posture, hand out like a traffic cop. Water at the bottom of the lowest trenches, after the night's heavy rain.

Down in the communications cave the wiregraph operator had received orders. General attack to commence in two days. Assault all the way across the corridor. An attempt to end the stalemate, or so Iwa speculated. Cork bunged out of its hole. Onto the steppes and westward ho! Of course the lead point of the breakout was the worst place to be, he noted, but with only his usual academic interest. Once at the front it could not really get any worse. It would be parsing degrees of the absolute, for they were already in hell and dead men, as Major Kuo reminded them with every toast of their rakshi: "We are dead men! A toast to Lord Death-by-gradations!"

So now Bai and Kuo merely nodded: worst place, yes, that was where they were always sent, where they had spent the last five years, or, seen in a larger temporal perspective, their whole lives. Finishing his tea, Iwa said, "It is bound to be very interesting."

He liked to read the wiregrams and newspapers and try to figure out what was going on. "Look at this," he would say, scanning papers as they lay in their bunks. "The Muslims have been kicked off Yingzhou. Twenty-year campaign." Or: "Big battle at sea, two hundred ships sunk! Only twenty of them ours, but ours are bigger, admittedly. North Dahai, water zero degrees, ouch that's cold, glad I'm not a sailor!" He kept notes and drew maps; he was a scholar of the war. The appearance of the wireless had pleased him greatly, he had spent hours in the comm cave talking with other enthusiasts around the globe. "Big bounce in the qisphere tonight, I heard from a guy in South Africa! Bad news, though," marking up his maps, "he said the Muslims have retaken all the Sahel and have conscripted everyone in west Africa as slave soldiers." He considered the voices wafting out of the darklight to be unreliable informants, but no more so than the official communiqués from headquarters, which were mostly propaganda, or lies designed to deceive enemy spies. "Look at this," he would scoff as he lay reading in his bunk. "It says they're rounding up all the Jews and Zotts and Christians and Armenians and killing them. Subjected to medical experimentation . . . blood replaced by mules' blood to see how long they will live . . . who thinks up these things?"

"Maybe it's true," Kuo suggested. "Kill off the undesirables, the ones that might betray them on the home front . . ."

Iwa turned the page. "Unlikely. Why waste all that labor?"

Now he was on the wireless trying to find out more about the upcoming assault. But you did not have to be a scholar of the war to know about breakouts. They had all been part of past attempts, and this knowledge tended to put a damper on the rest of their day. The front had moved ten li in three years, and eastward at that. Three consecutive Ramadan campaigns, at tremendous cost to the Muslims, a million men per campaign, Iwa calculated, so that they now fought with boys and batallions of women: as did the Chinese. So many had died that those who had survived the past three years were like the Eight Immortals, walking under a description, surviving day after day at a great distance from a world that they only heard about, only saw wrong way through the telescope. Tea in cup was all to them now. Another general assault, masses of men moving west into mud, barbed wire, machine guns, artillery shells coming down from space: so be it. They drank their tea. But it had a bitter taste.

Bai was ready to get it over with. He had lost his heart for this life. Kuo was irritated at the Fourth Assemblage of Military Talent, for ordering the assault during the brief rainy season. "Of course what can you expect of any body named 'The Fourth Assemblage of Military Talent'!" This wasn't entirely fair, as Kuo's usual analysis of them made plain: the First Assemblage had been old men trying to fight the previous war; the Second Assemblage, overambitious arrivistes ready to use men like bullets; the Third Assemblage, a bad mix of cautious corporals and desperate fuckwits; and the Fourth had come only after the coup that had overthrown the Qing dynasty and replaced it with a military government, so that in principle it was possible that the Fourth Assemblage was an improvement and the one that might finally get things right. Results so far, however, had not supported the notion.

Iwa felt they had discussed this matter too many times already, and confined his remarks to the quality of the day's rice. When it was ready and they had eaten it, they went out to tell their men to get prepared. Bai's squads were mostly conscripts from Sichuan, including three women's squads who kept trenches four through six, considered the lucky ones. When Bai was young and the only women he knew were those from the brothels of Lanzhou, he had felt uncomfortable in their presence, as if dealing with members of another species, worn creatures who regarded him as from across a gaping abyss, looking, as far as he could determine, guardedly appalled and accusatory, as if thinking to themselves, You idiots have destroyed the whole world. But now that they were in the trenches they were just soldiers like any others, different only in that they gave Bai an occasional sense of how bad things had gotten: there was no one in the world left now to reproach them.

That evening the three officers gathered again for a brief visit from the general of their part of the line, a new luminary of the Fourth Assemblage, a man they had never seen before. They stood at loose attention while he spoke briefly, emphasizing the importance of their attack on the morrow.

"We're a diversion," Kuo declared when General Shen had boarded his personal train and headed back toward the interior. "There are spies among us, and he wanted to fool them. If this was the real point of attack there would be a million more soldiers stacking up behind us, and you can hear the trains, they're on their usual schedule."

In fact there had been extra trains, Iwa said. Thousands of conscripts brought in, and no shelter for them. They wouldn't be able to stay here long.

That night it rained. Fleets of Muslim fliers buzzed overhead, dropping bombs that damaged the railroad tracks. Repair began as soon as the raid was over. Arc lamps turned the night brilliant silver streaked by white, like a ruined photo negative, and in that chemical glare men scurried about with picks and shovels and hammers and wheelbarrows, as after any other disaster, but speeded up, as film sometimes was. No more trains arrived, and when dawn came there were not very many reinforcements after all. Extra ammunition for the attack was missing as well.

"They won't care," Kuo predicted.

The plan was to release poison gas first, to precede them downslope on the daily morning east wind. At the first watch a wiregram came from the general: attack.

Today, however, there was no morning breeze. Kuo wiregraphed this news to the Fourth Assemblage command post thirty li down the corridor, asking for further orders. Soon he got them: proceed with the attack. Gas as ordered.

"We'll all be killed," Kuo promised.

They put on their masks, turned the valves on the steel tanks that released the gas. It shot out and spread, heavy, almost viscous, in color virulent yellow, seeping forward and down a slight slope, where it lay in the death zone, obscuring their way. Fine in that regard, although its effect on those with defective gas masks would be disastrous. No doubt it was an awful sight for the Muslims, to see yellow fog flowing heavily toward them, and then, emerging out of it, wave after wave of insect-faced monsters firing guns and launchers. Nevertheless they stuck to their machine guns and mowed them down.

Bai was quickly absorbed in the task of moving from crater to crater, using mounds of earth or dead bodies as a shield, and urging groups of soldiers who had taken refuge in holes to keep going. "Safer if you get out of holes now, the gas settles. We need to overrun their lines and stop the machine guns," and so on, in the deafening clatter, which meant none of them could hear him. A gust of the usual steady morning breeze moved the gas cloud over the devastation onto the Muslim lines, and less machine-gun fire struck at them. Their attack picked up speed, cutters busy everywhere at the barbed wire, men filing through. Then they were in the Muslim trenches, and they turned the big Iranian machine guns on the retreating enemy, until their ammunition was drained.

After that, if there had been any reinforcements available, it might have gotten interesting. But with the trains stuck fifty li behind the lines, and the breeze now pushing the gas back to the east, and the Muslim big guns now beginning to pulverize their own front lines, the breakout's position became untenable. Bai directed his troops down into the Muslim tunnels for protection. The day passed in a confusion of shouts and mobile wiregraph and wireless miscommunication. It was Kuo who shouted down to him that the order had finally come to retreat, and they rounded up their survivors and made their way back across the poisoned, shattered, body-strewn mud that had been the day's gain. An hour after nightfall they were back in their own trenches, less than half as numerous as they had been in the morning.

Well after midnight the officers convened in their little cave and got the stove burning and started cooking rice, each trapped in his own ears' roaring; they could barely hear each other talk. It would be like that for a day or two. Kuo was still fizzing with irritation, one did not have to be able to hear what he was saying to see that. He seemed to be trying to decide whether he should revise the Five Great Errors of the Gansu campaign by dropping the least of the previous great errors, or by turning it into the Six Great Errors. Assemblage of talent indeed, he shouted as he held their rice pot over the burning coals of their little stove, his bare blackened hands shaking. A bunch of fucking idiots. Up the hole the sounds of the hospital trains chugged and clanked. Their ears rang. Too much had happened for them to be able to speak anyway. They ate in the silence of a great roaring. Unfortunately Bai began vomiting, and then could not catch his breath. He had to submit to being carried up and back to one of the hospital trains. Put on with the host of wounded, gassed, and dying men. It took all the next day to move twenty li to the east, and then another day waiting to be processed by the overwhelmed medical crews. Bai almost died of thirst, but was saved by a girl in a mask, given sips of water while a doctor diagnosed gas-burned lungs, and stuck him with acupuncture needles in the neck and face, after which he could breathe much easier. This gave him the strength to drink more, then eat some rice, then talk his way out of the hospital before he died there of hunger or someone else's infection. He walked back to the front, hitching a ride at the end on a mule-drawn cart. It was night when he passed one of the immense batteries of artillery, and the garish sight of the huge black mortars and cannons pointed at the night sky, the tiny figures scurrying about under the arc lamps servicing them, holding hands to their ears (Bai did too) before they went off, made it clear to him yet again that they must all have been dragged into the next realm and gotten caught in a war of asuras, a titanic conflict in which humans were as ants, crushed under the wheels of the asuras' superhuman machines.

Back in their cave Kuo laughed at him for returning so quickly—

You're like a pet monkey, can't get rid of you—but Bai in his relief only said, It's safer here than in the hospital, which made Kuo laugh again. Iwa came back from the comm cave full of news: apparently their assault had been a diversion after all, just as Kuo had said. The Gansu plug had been pushed at in order to tie up Muslim armies, while a Japanese force had finally honored their agreement to help the cause, given in exchange for their liberty, which was already accomplished anyway but which could have been challenged, and the Japanese, being fresh, had made a hard push in the far north, and broken through the line there and started a big breakout, rolling west and south like a bunch of crazed ronin out on a murderous lark. Hopefully they would fold down the back side of the Muslim line and force a retreat from Gansu, leaving the shattered Chinese alone and at peace in the field.

Iwa said, "I guess the Japanese hatred for us was superseded by a disinclination to have Islam conquer the world."

"They'll pick off Korea and Manchuria," Kuo predicted. "They'll never give those back. A few port cities too. Now that we're bled white they can take whatever they please."

"Fine," Bai said. "Give them Beijing if they want it, if it only ends this war."

Kuo glanced at him. "I'm not sure which would be a worse master, Muslims or Japanese. Those Japanese are tough, and they don't like us. And after the earthquake demolished Edo they think they've got the gods on their side. They already killed every Chinese in Japan."

"In the end we won't serve either side," Bai said. "The Chinese are indestructible, remember?"

The previous two days had not proved the proverb very well. "Except by the Chinese," Kuo said. "By Chinese talent."

"They may have turned the north flank this time," Iwa noted. "That would be something."

"It could be the end game," Bai said, and coughed.

Kuo laughed at him. "Caught between mortar and pestle," he said. He went to their locked cabinet, inserted into the mud wall of the cave, and unlocked it and brought out a jug of rakshi and took a drink. He drank a jug of these strong spirits every day, when he could get a supply, starting with his first waking moment and ending with his last. "Here's to the Tenth Great Success! Or is it the Eleventh? And we've survived all of them." For the moment he had passed beyond the ordinary precaution of not speaking of these matters. "Survived them, and the Six Great Errors, and the Three Incredible Fuckups, and the Nine Greatest Incidents of Bad Luck. A miracle! There must be hungry ghosts holding big umbrellas over us, brothers."

Bai nodded uneasily; he did not like to talk of such things. He tried to hear only the roaring. He tried to forget all he had seen the last three days.

"How can we have possibly survived for so long?" Kuo asked recklessly. "Everyone else we began with is dead. In fact the three of us have outlasted five or six generations of officers. How long has it been? Five years? How can it be?"

"I am Peng-zu," Iwa said. "I am the Unfortunate Immortal, I can never be killed. I could dive right into the gas and it still wouldn't work." He looked up from his rice mournfully.

Even Kuo was spooked by this. "Well, you'll get more chances, don't worry. Don't think it's going to end any time soon. The Japanese could take the north because no one cares about it. When they try to come off the taiga onto the steppes, that's when it'll get interesting. I don't think they'll be able to turn the hinge very far. It would mean a lot more if the breakout was in the south. We need to connect up with the Indians."

Iwa shook his head. "That won't happen." This kind of analysis was more like him, and the other two asked him to explain. For the Chinese the southern front consisted of the great wall of the Himalaya and Pamirs, and the jungles of Annam and Burma and Bengal and Assam. There were only a few passes over the mountains that were even thinkable, and the defenses of these were impregnable. As for the jungles, the rivers offered the only passage through them, and they were too exposed. The fortifications of their south front were therefore geographical and immovable, but the same could be said for the Muslims on the other side of them. Meanwhile the Indians were trapped below the Deccan. The steppes were the only way; but the armies of both sides were concentrated there. Thus the deadlock.

"It has to end someday," Bai pointed out. "Otherwise it will never end."

Kuo spat out a mouthful of rakshi in a burst of laughter. "Very deep logic, friend Bai! But this is not a logical war. This is the end that will never end. We will live our lives in this war, and so will the next generation, and the next, until everyone is dead and we can start the world all over, or not, as the case may be."

"No," Iwa disagreed mildly. "It can't go on that long. The end will come somewhere else, that's all. The war at sea, or in Africa or Yingzhou. The break will come somewhere else, and then this region will just be a, a what, a feature of the long war, an anomaly or whatnot. The front that could not be moved. The frozen aspect of the long war at its most frozen. They will tell our story forever, because there will never be anything like it again."

"You're such a comfort," Kuo said. "To think we're in the worst fix any soldiers have ever been in!"

"We might as well be something," Iwa said.

"Exactly! It's a distinction! An honor, if you think about it."

Bai preferred not to. An explosion above shook dirt out of their ceiling onto them. They bustled about covering cups and plates.

A few days later and they were back in the usual routine. If there was still a Japanese breakout to the north there was no way to tell it here, where the daily barrage and sniping from the Muslims was the same as always, as if the Sixth Great Error, with its loss of perhaps fifty thousand men and women, had never happened.

Soon after that the Muslims too started using poison gas, spreading over the death zone on the wind just as the Chinese had done, but also sending it over contained in explosive shells that came down with a loud whistle, scattering the usual shrapnel (including anything that would cut, as they too were running low on metal, so that they found sticks, cat bones, hooves, a set of false teeth) and now with the shrapnel a thick yellow geyser of the gas, apparently not just mustard gas but a variety of poisons and caustics, which forced the Chinese to keep both gas mask and hood and gloves always by them. Dressed or not, when one of these shells came down it was hard not to get burned around the wrists and ankles and neck.

The other new inconvenience was a shell so huge, cast so high by such big cannons, that when it came down out of the sky it was falling faster than its sound, so there was no warning. These shells were bigger around than a man, and taller, designed to penetrate the mud some distance and then go off, in stupendous explosions that often would bury many more men in trenches and tunnels and caves than were killed by the blasts themselves. Duds of these shells were dug out and removed, very cautiously, each one occupying an entire train car. The explosive used in them was a new one that looked like fish paste, and smelled like jasmine.

One evening after dusk they were standing around drinking rakshi and discussing news that Iwa had gotten from the comm cave. The southern army was being punished for some failure on that front, and each squad commander had to send back one percent of his command, to be executed as encouragement to those that remained.

"What a good idea!" Kuo said. "I know just who I'd send."

Iwa shook his head. "A lottery would create better solidarity."

Kuo scoffed: "Solidarity. Might as well get rid of the malingerers while you can, before they shoot you in the back some night."

"It's a terrible idea," Bai said. "They're all Chinese, how can we kill Chinese when they haven't done anything wrong? It's crazy. The Fourth Assemblage of Military Talent has gone insane."

"They were never sane to begin with," Kuo said. "It's been forty years since anyone on Earth has been sane."

Suddenly they were all knocked to their feet by a violent blast of air. Bai struggled to his feet, banged into Iwa doing the same. He couldn't hear a thing. There was no sight of Kuo, he was gone and there was a big hole in the ground where he had been standing, a hole perfectly round and some twelve feet wide, thirty feet deep, and floored by the back end of one of the big Muslim supershells. Another dud.

A right hand lay on the ground beside the hole like a white cane spider. "Oh damn," Iwa said through the roar. "We've lost Kuo."

The Muslim shell had landed directly on him. Possibly, Iwa said later, his presence had kept it from exploding somehow. It had squished him into the earth like a worm. Only his poor hand remained.

Bai stared at the hand, too stunned to move. Kuo's laugh seemed still to ring in his ears. Kuo certainly would have laughed if he had been able to see this turn of events. His hand was completely recognizable as his, Bai found that he knew it intimately without ever being aware of the fact until now, so many hours sitting together in their little cave, Kuo holding the rice pot or the tea kettle over the stove, or offering a cup of tea or rakshi, his hand, like all the rest of him, a part of Bai's life, callused and scarred, clean palmed and dirty backed, looking still just like itself, even without the rest of him around. Bai sat back down on the mud.

Iwa gently picked up the severed hand, and they gave it the same funeral ceremony given to more complete corpses, before taking it back to one of the death trains for disposal in the crematoriums. Afterward they drank Kuo's remaining rakshi. Bai could not speak, and Iwa didn't try to make him. Bai's own hands displayed the quivering of ordinary trench fatigue. What had happened to their magic umbrella? What would he do now, without Kuo's acid laughter to cut through the deathly miasmas?

Then the Muslims took their turn to attack, and the Chinese were busy for a week with the defense of their trenches, living in their gas masks, firing belt after belt at the ghostly fellahin and assassins emerging from the yellow fog. Bai's lungs gave out again briefly, he had to be evacuated; but at the end of the week he and Iwa were back in the same trenches they had started in, with a new squad composed almost entirely of conscripts from Aozhou, land of the turtle who held up the world, green southerners thrown into the conflict like so many rounds of machine-gun ammunition. They had been so busy that already it seemed a long time since the incident of the dud shell. "Once I had a brother named Kuo," Bai explained to Iwa.

Iwa nodded, patted Bai on the shoulder. "Go see if we have new orders." His face was black with cordite, except around mouth and nose where his mask had been, and under his eyes, white with deltas of tear streaks. He looked like a puppet in a play, his face the mask of asura suffering. He had been at his machine gun for over forty straight hours, and in that time had killed perhaps three thousand men. His eyes looked sightlessly through Bai, through the world.

Bai staggered away, down the tunnel to the comm cave. He ducked in and fell into a chair, trying to catch his breath, feeling himself continuing to fall, through the floor, through the earth, on the airy drop to oblivion. A creak pulled him up; he looked to see who was already in the chair at the wireless table.

It was Kuo, sitting there grinning at him.

Bai straightened up. "Kuo!" he said. "We thought you were dead!"

Kuo nodded. "I am dead," he said. "And so are you."

His right hand was there at the end of his wrist.

"The shell went off," he said, "and killed us all. Since then you've been in the bardo. All of us have. You've gone at it by pretending you weren't there yet. Although why you would want to hang on to that hell world we were living in, I can't imagine. You are so damned obstinate,

Bai. You need to see you're in the bardo to be able to understand what's happening to you. It's the war in the bardo that matters, after all. The battle for our souls."

Bai tried to say yes; then no; then he found himself on the floor of the cave, having fallen off the chair, apparently, which had woken him up. Kuo was gone, his chair empty. Bai groaned. "Kuo! Come back!" But the room stayed empty.

Later Bai told Iwa what had happened, his voice shaking, and the Tibetan had given him a sharp glance, then shrugged. "Maybe he was right," he said, gesturing around. "What is there to prove him wrong?"

Another assault struck and suddenly they were ordered to retreat, to get to the back lines and then on the trains. At the depot yard it was chaotic, of course; but men with guns trained on them boarded them on the cars like cattle, and off the trains squealed and clanked.

Iwa and Bai sat at one end of a car as they trained south. From time to time they used their officers' privilege and went out onto the car's coupling base to smoke cigarettes and regard the steel sky lowering overhead. Higher and higher they rose, colder and colder. Thin air hurt Bai's lungs. "So," he said, gesturing at the rock and ice rolling past. "Maybe it is the bardo."

"It's just Tibet," Iwa said.

But Bai could see very well that it was more desolate than that. Cirrus clouds hung like sickles just overhead, as on a stage set, the sky black and flat. It didn't look the slightest bit real.

In any case, whatever the realm, Tibet or the bardo, in life or out of it, the war continued. At night winged roaring fliers, their blimp components dispensed with, buzzed overhead dropping bombs on them. Arc-lamp searchlights lanced the darkness, pinning fliers to the stars and sometimes blowing them up in gouts of falling flame. Images from Bai's dreams fell right out of the thin air. Black snow glittered in the white light of a low sun.

They stopped before an impossibly huge mountain range, another stage set from the dream theater. A pass so deep that from their distance it dipped under the sere tabletop of the steppe. That pass was their goal. Their task now was to blast the defenses away and go south through that pass, down to some level below this floor of the universe. The pass to India, supposedly. Gate to a lower realm. Very well defended, of course.

The "Muslims" defending it remained invisible, always over the great snowy mass of granite peaks, greater than any mountains on Earth could be, asura mountains, and the big guns brought to bear on them, asura guns. Never had it been so clear to Bai that they had gotten caught up in some bigger war, dying by the millions for some cause not their own. Ice and black rock fangs touched the ceiling of stars, snow banners streamed on the monsoon wind away from the peaks, merging with the Milky Way, at sunset becoming asura flames blowing horizontally, as if the realm of the asuras stood perpendicularly to their own, another reason perhaps that their puny imitation battles were always so hopelessly askew.

The Muslims' big guns were on the south side of the range, they never even heard them. Their shells whistled over the stars, leaving white rainbow frost trails on the black sky. The majority of these shells landed on the massive white mountain to the east of the huge pass, blasting it with one stupendous explosion after another, as if the Muslims had gone crazy and declared war on the rocks of the Earth. "Why do they hate that mountain so much?" Bai asked.

"That's Chomolungma," Iwa said. "That was the tallest mountain in the world, but the Muslims have knocked the summit pyramid down until it's lower than the second tallest, which is a peak in Afghanistan. So now the tallest peak in the world is Muslim."

His face was its usual blank, but he sounded sad, as though the mountain mattered to him. This worried Bai: if Iwa had gone mad, everyone on Earth had gone mad. Iwa would be the last to go. But maybe it had happened. A soldier in their squad had begun to weep helplessly at the sight of dead horses and mules; he was fine at the sight of dead men scattered about, but the bloated bodies of their poor beasts broke his heart. It made sense in a strange way, but for mountains Bai could conjure up no sympathy. At the most it was one god less. Part of the struggle in the bardo.

Nights the cold approached pure stasis. Starlight gleaming on the empty plateau, smoking a cigarette by the latrines, Bai considered what it might mean that there was war in the bardo. That was the place souls were sorted out, reconciled to reality, sent back down into the world. Judgment rendered, karma assessed; souls sent back to try again, or released to nirvana. Bai had been reading Iwa's copy of the "Book of the Dead," looking around him seeing each sentence shape the plateau. Alive or dead, they walked in a room of the bardo, working on their fate.

It was always so! This room as bleak as any empty stage. They camped on gravel and sand at the butt end of a gray glacier. Their big guns hunkered, barrels tilted to the sky. Smaller guns on the valley walls guarded against air attack; these emplacements looked like the old dzong-style monasteries that still lined some buttresses in these mountains.

Word came they were going to try to break through Nangpa La, the deep pass interrupting the range. One of the old salt trading passes, the best pass for many li in both directions. Sherpas would guide, Tibetans who had moved south of the pass. On its other side extended a canyon to their capital, tiny Namche Bazaar, now in ruins like everything else. From Namche trails ran directly south to the plains of Bengal. A very good passage across the Himalaya, in fact. Rail could replace trail in a matter of days, and then they could ship the massed armies of China, what was left of them, onto the Gangetic Plain. Rumors swirled, replaced daily by new rumors. Iwa spent all night at the wireless.

It looked to Bai like a change in the bardo itself. Shift to the next room, a tropical hellworld clogged with ancient history. The battle for the pass would therefore be particularly violent, as is any passage between worlds. The artilleries of the two civilizations massed on both sides. Triggered avalanches in the granite escarpments were frequent. Meanwhile explosions on the peak of Chomolungma continued to lower it. The Tibetans fought like pretas as they saw this. Iwa seemed to have reconciled himself to it: "They have a saying about the mountain coming to Muhammad. But I don't think it matters to the mother goddess."

Still, it brought home to them yet again how insane their opponents were. Ignorant fanatical disciples of a cruel desert cult, promised eternity in a paradise where sexual orgasm with beautiful houris lasted ten thousand years, no surprise they were so often suicidally brave, happy to die, reckless in frenzied opiated ways that were hard to counter. Indeed they were known to be prodigious benzedrine eaters and opium smokers, pursuing the entire war in a jerky drugged dream state that could include bestial rage. Most of the Chinese would have been happy to join them there, and opium had made its way into the Chinese army, of course, but supplies were short. Iwa had local contacts, however, and as they prepared for the assault on Nangpa La he obtained some from some military policemen. He and Bai smoked it in cigarettes and drank it as a tincture of alcohol, along with cloves and a pill of Travancori medicines said to sharpen sight while dulling the emotions. It worked pretty well.

Eventually there were so many banners and divisions and big guns collected on this high plane of the bardo that Bai became convinced that the rumors were right, and a general assault on Kali or Shiva or Brahma was about to begin. As confirming evidence he noted that many divisions were composed of experienced soldiers, rather than raw boys or peasants or women—divisions with extensive battle experience in the islands or the New World, where the fighting had been particularly intense, and where they claimed to have won. In other words, they were precisely those soldiers most likely to have been killed already. And they looked dead. They smoked cigarettes like dead men. A whole army of the dead, gathered and poised to invade the rich south of the living.

The moon waxed and waned and the bombardment of the invisible foe across the range continued. Fleets of fliers shaped like sickles shot through the pass and never came back. On the eighth day of the fourth month, the date of the conception of the Buddha, the assault began.

The pass itself had been rigged, and when its immediate defenders were all killed or had retreated south, the ridges guarding the pass erupted in massive explosions and poured down onto the broad saddle. Cho Oyu itself lost some of its mass to this explosion. That was the end for several banners securing the pass. Bai watched from below and wondered, When one died in the bardo where did one go? It was only a matter of chance that Bai's squad had not been in the first wave.

The defenses as well as the Chinese first wave were buried. After that the pass was theirs, and they could begin the descent of the giant glacier-cut canyon south to the Gangetic Plain. They were attacked every step of the way, chiefly by distant bombardment, and with booby traps and enormous mines buried in the trails at crucial points. They defused or set these off as often as they could, suffered the occasional missed ones, rebuilt a road and rail bed as they descended. It was mostly road work at great speed, as the Muslims gave ground and retreated to the plain, and only their most distant aerial bombardment remained, shots fired from around Delhi, erratic and hilarious unless they happened to make a lucky strike.

In the deep southern canyon they found themselves in a different world. Indeed Bai had to reconsider the idea that he was in the bardo at all. If he was, this was certainly a different level of it: hot, wet, lush, the green trees and bushes and grasses exploding out of the black soil and overrunning everything. The granite itself seemed living down here. Perhaps Kuo had lied to him, and he and Iwa and the rest here had been alive all the while, in a real world become deathly with death. What an awful thought! The real world become the bardo, the two the same . . . Bai hustled through his hectic days feeling appalled. After all that suffering he had only been reborn into his own life, still ongoing, now regained as if there had been no break, only a moment of cruel irony, a few days' derangement, and now moved on into a new karmic existence while trapped in the same miserable biological cycle that for some reason had turned into a fine simulacrum of hell itself, as if the karmic wheel had broken and the gears between karmic life and biological life become detached, gone so that one fluctuated without warning, lived sometimes in the physical world, other times in the bardo, sometimes in dream sometimes awake, and very often all at once, without cause or explanation. Already the years in the Gansu Corridor, the whole of his life he would have said before, had become a dream mostly forgotten, and even the mystic high strangeness of the Tibetan plain was fast becoming an unreal memory, hard to recall though it was etched on his eyeballs and he was still looking right through it.

One evening the wiregraph officer came rushing out and ordered them all to get uphill fast. A glacial lake upstream had had its ice dam bombed by the Muslims, and now a huge bolus of water was headed downstream, filling the canyon to a depth of five hundred feet or more, depending on the narrowness of the gorge.

The scramble began. How they climbed. Here they were, dead men already, dead for years, and yet they climbed like monkeys, frantic to move up the slope of a canyon. They had been camped in a narrow steep defile, the better to avoid bombs from the air, and as they hauled themselves up through brush they heard ever more clearly a distant roar like continuous thunder, possibly a falls in the ordinarily loud Dudh Kosi, but probably not, probably the approaching flood, until finally they came to a layback in the slope, and after an hour they were all a good thousand feet above the Dudh Kosi, looking down at the white thread of it that seemed so harmless from the broad nose of a promontory where the officers had regathered them, looking down into the gorge but also around them at the stupendous icy walls and peaks of the range, hearing a roar come out of the higher ones to the north, a healthy booming roar, like a tiger god roaring. Up here they were in a good position to witness the flood, which arrived just as night was falling: the roar grew to something almost as loud as a bombardment on the front, but all below, almost subterranean, coming through the soles of their feet as much as their ears, and then a dirty white wall of water appeared, carrying trees and rocks on its chaotic tumbling front wall, tearing the walls of the canyon right down to bedrock and causing slides down into it, some of which were large enough to dam the whole stream for a few minutes, before water poured over it and ripped it away, causing a smaller surge in the general flood. After the front of it had passed out of sight down the canyon, it left behind torn walls white in the dusk, and a brown foaming river that roared and clunked at just above its usual level.

"We should build the roads higher," Iwa noted.

Bai could only laugh at Iwa's cool. The opium was making everything pulse. A sudden realization: "Why, it just occurred to me—I've been drowned in floods before! I've felt the water come over me. Water and snow and ice. You were there too! I wonder if that was meant for us, and we've escaped by accident. I don't really think we're supposed to be here."

Iwa regarded him. "In what sense?"

"In the sense that that flood down there was supposed to kill us!"

"Well," Iwa said slowly, looking concerned, "I guess we got out of its way."

Bai could only laugh. Iwa: what a mind. "Yes. To hell with the flood. That was a different life."

The routemakers however had learned a good lesson without much loss of life (equipment was another matter). Now they built high on the canyon walls where they sloped back, cutting grades and traverses, going far up tributary canyons and then building bridges over their streams, also antiaircraft emplacements, even a small airstrip on one nearly level bench near Lukla. Becoming a construction batallion was much better than fighting, which was what others were doing down in the mouth of the canyon, to keep it open long enough to get the train down there. They could not believe their luck, or the warm days, or the reality of life behind the front, so luxurious, the silence, the lessening of muscle tension, lots of rice, and strange but fresh vegetables . . .

Then in a blur of happy days the roadbeds and tracks were complete and they took some of the first trains down and encamped on a great dusty green plain, no monsoon yet, division after division making their way to the front, some fluctuating distance to the west of them. That was where it was all happening now.

Then one morning they were on their way too, trained all day to the west and then off and marching over one pontoon bridge after another, until they were somewhere near Bihar. Here another army was already encamped, an army on their side. Allies, what a concept. The Indians themselves, here in their own country, moving north after four decades of holding out against the Islamic horde, down in the south of the continent. Now they too were breaking out, crossing the Indus, and the Muslims therefore in danger of being cut off by a pincer attack as large as Asia, some of them already trapped in Burma, the bulk of them still together in the west and beginning a slow, stubborn retreat.

So Iwa gathered in an hour's conversation with some Travancori officers who spoke Nepali, which he had known as a child. The Indian officers and their soldiers were dark skinned and small, both men and women, very fast and nimble, clean, well dressed, well armed—proud, even arrogant, assuming that they had taken the brunt of the war against Islam, that they had saved China from conquest by holding on as a second front. Iwa came away unsure whether it was a good idea to discuss the war with them.

But Bai was impressed. Perhaps the world would be saved from slavery after all. The breakout across north Asia was apparently stalled, the Urals being a kind of natural Great Wall of China for the Golden Horde and the Firanjis. Although maps seemed to indicate that it was nicely to the west. And to have crossed the Himalaya in force against such resistance, to have met up with the Indian armies, to be cutting the world of Islam in two . . .

"Well, sea power could make the whole land war in Asia irrelevant," Iwa said as they sat one evening on the ground eating rice that had been spiced to newly incendiary heights. Between choking swallows, sweating profusely, he said, "In the time of this war we've seen three or four generations of weaponry, of technology generally, the big guns, sea power, now air power—I don't doubt that a time is coming when fleets of airships and fliers will be all that matter. The fight will go on up there, to see who can control the skies and drop bombs bigger than anything you could ever shoot out of a cannon, right onto the capitals of the enemy. Their factories, their palaces, their government buildings."

"Good," Bai said. "Less messy that way. Go for the head and get it over with. That's what Kuo would say."

Iwa nodded, grinning at the thought of just how Kuo would say it. The rice here was nothing compared to their Kuo.

The generals from the Fourth Assemblage of Military Talent met with the Indian generals, and as they conferred more railways were built out to the new front west of them. A combined offensive was clearly in the works, and everyone was full of speculation about it. That they would be kept behind to defend their rear from the Muslims still in the Malay Peninsula; that they would be boarded on ships in the mouth of the sacred Ganges and deposited on the Arabian coast to attack Mecca itself; that they were destined for a beachhead attack on the peninsulas of northwest Firanja; and so on. Never an end to the stories they told themselves of how their travail would continue.

In the end, though, they marched forward in the usual fashion, westward, holding the right flank against the foothills of Nepal, hills that shot abrupt and green out of the Gangetic Plain—as though, Iwa remarked idly one day, India were a ramming ship that had slammed into Asia and plowed under it, pushing all the way under Tibet, and doubling the height of that land but dipping down here almost to sea level.

Bai shook his head at this geomorphic fancy, not wanting to think of the ground as moving like big ships, wanting to understand the ground as solid, because he was trying to convince himself now that Kuo had been wrong and that he was still alive and not in the bardo, where of course lands could slip about like the stage sets they were. Kuo had probably been disoriented by his own abrupt death, and confused as to his own whereabouts; not a good sign concerning his reappearance in his next incarnation. Or perhaps he had just been playing a joke on Bai—Kuo would mock you harder than anyone, though he seldom played jokes. Perhaps he had even been doing Bai a favor, getting him through the worst part of the war by convincing him that he was already dead and had nothing to lose—indeed, was fighting the war on a level where it might actually mean something, might have some use, might be a matter of changing people's souls in their pure existence outside the world, where they might be capable of change, where they might learn what was important and return to life next time with new capacities in their hearts, with new goals in mind.

What might those be? What were they fighting for? It was clear what they were fighting against—against fanatical slaveholding reactionaries, who wanted the world to stand still in the equivalent of the Tang or Sung dynasties—absurdly backward and bloody religious zealots—assassins with no scruples, who fought crazed on opium and ancient blind beliefs. Against all that, certainly, but for what? What the Chinese were fighting for, Bai decided, was . . . clarity, or whatever else it was that was the opposite of religion. For humanity. For compassion. For Buddhism, Daoism and Confucianism, the triple strand that did so well in describing a relationship to the world: the religion with no God, with only this world, also several other potential realms of reality, mental realms, and the void itself, but no God, no shepherd ruling with the drooling strictures of a demented old patriarch, but rather innumerable immortal spirits in a vast panoply of realms and being, including humans and many other sentient beings besides, everything living, everything holy, sacred, part of the Godhead—for yes, there was a GOD if by that you meant only a transcendent universal self-aware entity that was reality itself, the cosmos, including everything, including human ideas and mathematical forms and relationships. That idea itself was God, and evoked a kind of worship that was attention to the real world, a kind of natural study. Chinese Buddhism was the natural study of reality, and led to feelings of devotion just from noting the daily leaves, the colors of the sky, the animals seen from the corner of the eye. The movements of chopping wood and carrying water. This initial study of devotion led to deeper understanding as they pursued the mathematical underpinnings of the ways of things, just out of curiosity and because it seemed to help them see even more clearly, and so they made instruments to see farther in and farther out, higher yang, deeper yin.

What followed was a kind of understanding of human reality that placed the greatest value on compassion, created by enlightened understanding, created by study of what was there in the world. This was what Iwa was always saying, while Bai preferred to think of the emotions created by all that proper attention and focused effort: the peace, the sharp curiosity and enraptured interest, the compassion.

But now: all a nightmare. A nightmare speeding up, however, breaking apart and full of non sequiturs, as if the dreamer felt the rapid-eyed stirrings of the end of sleep and the waking of a new day. Every day we wake up into a new world, each sleep causes yet another reincarnation. Some of the local gurus spoke of it as happening with every breath.

They took off out of the bardo into the real world, into battle, with their left wing made up of India's crack regiments, little bearded black men, taller hook-nosed white men, bearded turbaned Sikhs, deep-chested women, Gurkhas come out of the mountains, a banner of Nepali women each of whom was the beauty of her district, or so it appeared; all of them together like a circus crew, but so fast, so well armed, in train and truck divisions, the Chinese could not keep up with them, but got more train lines established and tried to catch up, running vast numbers of men forward with all their supplies. Beyond the forward ends of the train lines the Indians continued to race forward on foot, and in engined cars on rubber wheels, hundreds of them that ran freely over the village paths in this dry season, throwing dust everywhere, and also over a more limited network of asphalted roads, the only ones that would still be passable when the monsoon hit.

They advanced toward Delhi all at once, more or less, and they fell on the Muslim army retreating up the Ganges on both sides of the river, as soon as the Chinese were in position at the foot of the Nepali hills.

Of course the right flank extended up into the hills, each army trying to outflank the other. Bai and Iwa's squad was counted among the mountain troops now because of their experiences in the Dudh Kosi, and so orders came to seize and hold the hills up to the first ridge at least, which entailed taking some higher points on ridges even farther north. They moved by night, learning to climb in the dark along trails found and marked by Gurkha scouts. Bai also became a day scout, and as he crawled up brush-choked ravines he worried not that he would be discovered by any Muslims, for they stuck to their trails and encampments without fail, but whether or not a mass of hundreds of men could follow the tortuous monkey routes he was forced to use in some places. "That's why they send you, Bai," Iwa explained. "If you can do it, anyone can." He smiled and added, "That's what Kuo would say."

Each night Bai went up and down the line guiding and checking to see if routes went as he had expected, learning and studying, and only going to sleep after observing the sunrise from some new hideaway.

They were still doing that when the Indians broke through on the south flank. They heard the distant artillery and then saw smoke pluming into the white skies of a hazy morning, the haze a possible mark of the monsoon's arrival. To make a full breakout assault with the monsoon coming passed all understanding; it seemed possible it would go right to the head of the list of the recently augmented Seven Great Errors, and as the afternoon's clouds bloomed, and built, and dropped black on them, blasting foothills and plain with volleys of thick lightning that struck the metal in several gun emplacements on ridges, it was amazing to hear that the Indians were pressing on unimpeded. They had, among all their other accomplishments, perfected war in the rain. These were not Chinese Daoist Buddhist rationalists, Bai and Iwa agreed, not the Fourth Assemblage of Military Talent, but wild men of all manner of religion, even more spiritual than the Muslims, as the Muslims' religion seemed all bluster and wish fulfillment and support of tyranny with its Father God. The Indians had a myriad of gods, some elephant headed or six armed, even death was a god, both female and male—life, nobility, there were gods for each, each human quality deified. Which made for a motley, godly people, very ferocious in war, among many other things—great cooks, very sensual people, scents, tastes, music, color in their uniforms, detailed art, it was all right there in their camps to be seen, men and women standing around a drummer singing, the women tall and big breasted, big eyed and thick eyebrowed, awesome women really, arms like a woodsman's and filling all the sharpshooter regiments of the Indians, "Yes," one Indian adjutant had said in Tibetan, "women are better shots, women from Travancore especially. They start when they are five, that may be all there is to it. Start boys at five and they would do as well."

Now the rains were full of black ash, falling in a watery mud. Black rain. The call came for Bai and Iwa's squad to hurry down to the plain and join the general assault as soon as they could. They ran down the trails and assembled some twenty li behind the front line of the battle, and started marching. They were to hit at the very end of the flank, on the plain itself but right at the foot of the foothills, ready to scale the first rise of the hills if there was any resistance to their charge.

That was the plan, but as they came up to the front word came that the Muslims had broken and were in full retreat, and they joined the chase.

But the Muslims were in full flight, the Indians close on their heels, and the Chinese could only follow the two faster armies across the fields and forests, over canals and through the breaks in bamboo fences and

walls, and groups of houses too small even to be called villages, all still
and silent, usually burned, and yet slowing them down somehow nevertheless. Dead bodies on the ground in knots, already bloating. The full
meaning of embodiment made manifest here by its opposite, disem-
bodiment, death—departure of the soul, leaving behind so little: a pu-
trefying mass, stuff like what one found in a sausage. Nothing human
about it. Except for here or there, a face undestroyed, even sometimes
undisturbed; an Indian man lying there on the ground for instance, staring sideways but utterly still, not moving, not breathing; the statue of
what must have been a very impressive man, well built, strong shoulders, capable—a commanding, high-foreheaded, moustached face, eyes
like fish in the market, round and surprised, but still—impressive. Bai
had to say a charm to be able to walk by him, and then they were in a
zone where the land itself was smoking like the dead zone of Gansu,
pools of silvery gassed water reeking in water holes and the air full of
smoke and dust, cordite, blood haze. The bardo itself would be looking
much like this, crowded now with new arrivals all angry and confused,
in agony, the worst possible way to enter the bardo. Here the empty mirror of it, blasted and still. The Chinese army marched through in silence.

Bai found Iwa, and they made their way into the burned ruins of
Bodh-Gaya, to a park on the west bank of the Phalgu River. This was
where the Bodhi Tree had stood, they were told, the old assattha tree, pipal tree, under which the Buddha had received enlightenment so many
centuries before. The area had taken as many hits as the peak of
Chomolungma, and no trace of tree or park or village or stream remained, only black rendered mud for as far as the eye could see.

A group of Indian officers discussed root fragments someone had
found in the mud near what some thought had been the location of the
tree. Bai didn't recognize the language. He sat down with a small frag-
ment of bark in his hands. Iwa went over to see what the officers were
saying.

Then Kuo stood before Bai. "Cut is the branch," he said, offering a
small twig from the Bodhi Tree.

Bai took it from him. From his left hand; Kuo's right hand was still
missing. "Kuo," Bai said, and swallowed. "I'm surprised to see you."

Kuo gave him a look.

"So we are in the bardo after all," Bai said.

Kuo nodded. "You didn't always believe me, did you, but it's true.

Here you see it—" waving his hand at the black smoking plain. "The floor of the universe. Again."

"But why?" Bai said. "I just don't get it."

"Get what?"

"Get what I'm supposed to be doing. Life after life—I remember them now!" He thought about it, seeing back through the years. "I remember them now, and I've tried in every one. I keep trying!" Out across the black plain it seemed they could see together the faint afterimages of their previous lives, dancing in the infinite silk of lightly falling rain. "It doesn't seem to be making any difference. What I do makes no difference."

"Yes, Bai. Perhaps so. But after all you are a fool. A good-natured fucking idiot."

"Don't, Kuo, I'm not in the mood," though his face was attempting painfully to smile, pleased to be ribbed again. Iwa and he had tried to do this for each other, but no one could bring it off like Kuo. "I may not be a great leader like you but I've done some good things, and they haven't made a bit of difference. There seem to be no rules of dharma that actually pertain."

Kuo sat down next to him, crossed his legs and made himself comfortable. "Well, who knows. I've been thinking these things over myself, this time out in the bardo. There's been a lot of time, believe me—so many have been tossed out here at once that there's quite a waiting line, it's just like the rest of the war, a logistical nightmare, and I've been watching you all struggle on, bashing against things like moths in a bottle, and I know I did it too, and I've wondered. I've thought sometimes that maybe it went wrong back when I was Kheim and you were Butterfly, a little girl we all loved. Do you remember that one?"

Bai shook his head. "Tell me."

"As Kheim I was Annamese. I continued the proud tradition of the great Chinese admirals being foreigners and disreputable, I had been a pirate king for years on the long coast of Annam, and the Chinese made a treaty with me as they would with any great potentate. Struck a deal in which I agreed to lead an invasion of Nippon, at least the sea aspect of it and perhaps more.

"Anyway we missed all that for lack of a wind, and went on and discovered the ocean continents, and found you, and then we took you, and lost you, and saved you from the executioner god of the southern people; and that's when I felt it, coming back down the mountain after we had saved you. I aimed my pistol at people and pulled the trigger, and felt the power of life and death in my hands. I could kill them, and they deserved it, bloody cannibals that they were, killers of children. I could do it merely by pointing at them. And it seemed to me then that my so much greater power had a meaning to it. That our superiority in weapons came out of a general superiority of thought that included a superiority of morals. That we were better than they were. I strode back down to the ships and sailed west still feeling that we were superior beings, like gods to those horrid savages. And that's why Butterfly died. You died to teach me that I was wrong—that though we had saved her we had killed her too, that that feeling we had had, striding through them as if through worthless dogs, was a poison that would never stop spreading in men who had guns. Until all the people like Butterfly, who lived in peace without guns, were dead, murdered by us. And then only men with guns would be left, and they would murder each other too, as fast as they could in the hope that it wouldn't happen to them, until the human world died, and we all fell into this preta realm and then to hell.

"So our little jati is stuck here with everyone else, no matter what you do, not that you have been notably effectual, I must say again, Bai, speaking of your tendency toward credulous simplicity, gullibility, and general soft-hearted namby-pamby ineffectiveness—"

"Hey," Bai said. "Not fair. I've been helping you. I've just been going along with you."

"Well, all right. Granted. In any case we're all in the bardo together now, and headed for the lower realms again, at best the realm of the human, but possibly spinning down the death spiral into the hellworlds always underfoot, we may have done it and are in the spin you can't pull out of, humanity lost to us for a time even as a possibility, so much harm have we done. Stupid fucking bastards! Damn it, do you think I haven't been trying too?" Kuo popped to his feet, agitated. "Do you think you're the only one who has tried to make some good in this world?" He shook his solitary fist at Bai, and then at the lowering gray clouds. "But we failed! We killed reality itself, do you understand me! Do you understand me?"

"Yes," Bai said, hugging his knees and shivering miserably. "I understand."

"So. Now we are in this lower realm. We must make do. Our dharma still commands right action, even here. In the hope of small advances upward. Until reality itself be reestablished, by many millions of lives of effort. The whole world will have to be rebuilt. That's where we are now," and with a farewell tap to Bai's arm he walked away, sinking into the black mud deeper with every step, until he had disappeared.

"Hey," Bai said. "Kuo! Don't leave!"

After a while Iwa returned and stood before him, looked down quizzically at him.

"Well?" Bai said, lifting his head from his knees, collecting himself. "What is it? Will they save the Bodhi Tree?"

"Don't worry about the tree," Iwa said. "They'll get a shoot from a daughter tree in Lanka. It's happened before. Best worry about the people."

"More shoots there too. On to the next life. To a better time." Bai shouted it after Kuo: "To a better time!"

Iwa sighed. He sat down where Kuo had been sitting. Rain fell on them. A long time passed in exhausted silence.

"The thing is," Iwa said, "what if there is no next life? That's what I think. This is it. Fan Chen said the soul and body are just two aspects of the same thing. He speaks of sharpness and the knife, soul and body. Without knife, no sharpness."

"Without sharpness, no knife."

"Yes . . ."

"And sharpness goes on, sharpness never dies."

"But look at those dead bodies over there. Who they were won't come back. When death comes, we don't come back."

Bai thought of the Indian man, lying so still on the ground. He said, "You're just distraught. Of course we come back. I was talking to Kuo this very minute."

Iwa gazed at him. "You shouldn't try to hold on, Bai. This is what the Buddha learned, right here. Don't try to stop time. No one can do it."

"Sharpness remains. I tell you, he was cutting me up same as always!"

"We have to try to accept change. And change leads to death."

"And then through death." Bai said this as cheerfully as he could, but his voice was desolate. He missed Kuo.

Iwa considered what Bai had said, with a look that seemed to say he had been hoping that a Buddhist at the Bodhi Tree would perhaps have had something more helpful to say. But what could you say? The Buddha himself had said it: suffering is real. You have to face it, live with it. There is no escape.

After a while longer Bai got up and went over to see what the officers were doing. They were chanting a sutra, in Sanskrit perhaps, Bai thought, and he joined in softly with the "Lengyan jing," in Chinese. And as the day wore on many Buddhists in both armies gathered around the site, hundreds of them, the mud was covered with people, and they said prayers in all the languages of Buddhism, standing there on the burnt land that smoked in the rain for as far as the eye could see, black gray and silver. Finally they fell silent. Peace in the heart, compassion, peace. Sharpness remained in them.

BOOK 9

✸ N S A R A ✸

1 ❋ On sunny mornings the parks on the lakefront were filled with families out walking. In the early spring, before the plants had done more than create the tight green buds soon to blossom in their profusion of colors, the hungry swans would congregate in the gleaming black water beside the promenade to fight over the loaves of stale bread thrown at them by children. This had been one of Budur's favorite activities as a young girl, it had cast her into gales of laughter to see the swans flop and tussle for the scraps; now she watched the new kids convulsed by the same hilarity, with a stab of grief for her lost childhood, and for the awareness that the swans, though beautiful and comical, were also desperate and starving. She wished she had the boldness to join the children and throw more bread to the poor things. But if she did it now she would look odd, like one of the mentally deficient ones on their trip out from their school. And in any case there was not a great deal of bread left in their house anyway.

Sunlight bounced on the water, and the buildings lining the back of the lakeshore promenade glowed lemon, peach, and apricot, as if lit from within by some light trapped in their stone. Budur walked back through the old town toward home, through the gray granite and black wood of the ancient buildings. Turi had begun as a Roman town, a way station on their main route through the Alps; Father had once driven them up to an obscure alpine pass called the Keyhole, where a stretch of the Roman road was still there, switchbacking through the grass like a petrified dragon's back, looking lonely for the feet of soldiers and traders. Now after centuries of obscurity Turi was a way station again, this time for trains, and the greatest city in all of central Firanja, the capital of the united Alpine emirates.

The city center was bustling and squeaky with trams, but Budur liked to walk. She ignored Ahab, her chaperone; though she liked him personally, a simple man with few pretensions, she did not like his job, which included accompanying her on her excursions. She shunned him on principle as an affront to her dignity. She knew also that he would report her behavior to Father, and when he reported her refusal to acknowledge his presence, yet another small protest of harem would reach Father, if only indirectly.

She led Ahab up through the apartments studding the hillside overlooking the city, to High Street. The wall around their house was beautiful, a tall patterned weave of green and gray dressed stones. The wooden gate was topped by a stone arch seemingly held in a network of wisteria vines; you could pull out the keystone and it would still stand. Ahmet, their gatekeeper, was in his seat in the cozy little wooden closet on the inside of the gateway, where he held forth to all who wanted to pass, his tea tray ready to serve those who had time to tarry.

Inside the house Aunt Idelba was talking on the telephone, which was set on a table in the inner courtyard under the eaves, where anyone could hear you. This was Father's way of trying to keep anything untoward from ever being said, but the truth was that Aunt Idelba was usually talking about microscopic nature and the mathematics of the interiors of atoms, and so no one could have any idea what she was talking about. Budur liked to listen to her anyway, because it reminded her of the fairy tales Aunt Idelba had told in the past when Budur was younger, or her cooking talk with Mother in the kitchen—cooking was one of her passions, and she would rattle off recipes, procedures, and tools, all mysterious and suggestive just like this talk on the telephone, as if she were cooking up a new world. And sometimes she would get off the phone looking worried, and absentmindedly accept Budur's hugs and admit that this was precisely the case: the ilmi, the scientists, were indeed cooking up a new world. Or they could be. Once she rang off flushed pink, and danced a little minuet around the courtyard, singing nonsense syllables, and their laundry ditty, "God is great, great is God, clean our clothes, clean our souls."

This time she rang off and did not even see Budur, but stared up at the bit of sky visible from the courtyard.

"What is it, Idelba? Are you feeling hem?" Hem was the women's term for a kind of mild depression that had no obvious cause.

Idelba shook her head. "No, this is a mushkil," which was a specific problem.

"What is it?"

"Well . . . Simply put, the investigators at the laboratory are getting some very strange results. That's what it comes down to. No one can say what they mean."

This laboratory Idelba talked to over the phone was currently her main contact with the world outside their home. She had been a mathematics teacher and researcher in Nsara, and, with her husband, an investigator of microscopic nature. But her husband's untimely death had revealed some irregularities in his affairs, and Idelba had been left destitute; and the job they had shared had turned out to be his in the end, so that she had nowhere to work, and nowhere to live. Or so Yasmina had said; Idelba herself never spoke about it. She had shown up one day with a single suitcase, weeping, to confer with Budur's father, her half brother. He had agreed to put her up for a time. This, Father explained later, was one of the things harems were for; they protected women who had nowhere else to go. "Your mother and you girls complain about the system, but really, what is the alternative? The suffering of women left alone would be enormous."

Mother and Budur's older cousin, Yasmina, would snort or snarl at this, cheeks turning red. Rema and Aisha and Fatima would look at them curiously, trying to understand what they should feel about what to them was after all the natural order of things. Aunt Idelba never said anything about it one way or the other, neither thanks nor complaint. Old acquaintances still called her on the phone, especially a nephew of hers, who apparently had a problem he thought she could help him with; he called regularly. Once Idelba tried to explain why to Budur and her sisters, with the aid of a blackboard and chalk.

"Atoms have shells around them, like the spheres in the heavens in the old drawings, all surrounding the heartknot of the atom, which is small but heavy. Three kinds of particles clump together in the heart-knot, some with yang, some with yin, some neuter, in different amounts for each substance, and they're held bound together there by a strong force, which is very strong, but also very local, in that you don't have to get far away from the heartknot for the force to reduce a great deal."

"Like a harem," Yasmina said.

"Yes, well. That may be more like gravity, I'm afraid. But anyway, there is a qi repulsion between all particles, that the strong force counteracts, and the two compete, more or less, along with other forces. Now, certain very heavy metals have so many particles that a certain number leak away from them one by one, and the single particles that leak leave distinctive traces at distinct rates of speed. And down in Nsara they've been getting strange results from a particular heavy metal, an elemental that is heavier than gold, the heaviest elemental found so far, called alactin. They're bombarding it with neuter particles, and getting very strange results, all over the plates, in a way hard to explain. The heavy heart of this elemental appears to be unstable."

"Like Yasmina!"

"Yes, well, interesting that you say so, in that it is not true but it suggests the way we keep trying to think of ways to visualize these things that are always too small for us to see." She paused, looking at the blackboard, then at her uncomprehending students. A spasm of some emotion marred her features, disappeared. "Well. It is yet another phenomenon that needs explaining, let's leave it at that. It will take more investigation in a lab."

After that she scribbled in silence for a while. Numbers, letters, Chinese ideograms, equations, dots, diagrams—like something out of the illustrations for the books about the Alchemist of Samarqand.

After a time she slowed down, shrugged. "I'll have to talk to Piali about it."

"But isn't he in Nsara?" Budur asked.

"Yes." This too was part of her mishkul, Budur saw. "We will talk by the telephone, of course."

"Tell us about Nsara," Budur asked for the thousandth time.

Idelba shrugged; she was not in the mood. She never was, to begin with; it took a while to break through the barrier of regrets to get her to that time. Her first husband, divorcing her near the end of her fertility, with no children; her second husband, dying young; she had a lot of regrets to get through. But if Budur was patient and merely followed her around the terrace, and in and out of rooms, she often would make the passage, helped perhaps by her shifts from room to room, matching the way each place on Earth we have lived in is like a room in our mind, with its sky for a roof, hills for walls, and buildings for furniture, so that our lives have moved from one room to the next in some larger structure; and the old rooms still exist and yet at the same time are gone, or emptied, so that in reality one could only move on to some new room, or stay locked in the one you were in, as in a jail; and yet, in the mind . . .

First Idelba would speak of the weather there, the storm-tossed Atlantic rolling in with water, wind, cloud, rain, fog, sleet, mist, sometimes snow, all broken by sunny days with their low shards of light emblazoning the seafront and the rivermouth, the docks of the giant city filling the valley on both banks all the way upstream to Anjou, all the states of Asia and Firanja come west to this westernmost town, to meet the other great influx by sea, people from all over the world, including the handsome Hodenosaunee, and the shivering exiles from Inka, with their serapes and gold jewelry splashing the dark gray afternoons of the storm-thrashed winters with little bits of metallic color. These exotics all together made Nsara fascinating, Idelba said, as did the unwelcome embassies of the Chinese and Tranvancoris, enforcing the terms of the postwar settlement, standing there like monuments to the Islamic defeat in the war, long windowless blocks at the back of the harbor district. As she described all this, Idelba's eyes would begin to gleam and her voice grow animated, and she almost always, if she did not cut herself short, ended by exclaiming Nsara! Nsara! Ohhh, Nssssarrrrra! And then sometimes sit down wherever she was and hold her head in her hands, overwhelmed. It was, Budur was sure, the most exciting and wonderful city on Earth.

The Travancoris had of course founded a Buddhist monastery school there, as they had in every city and town on Earth, it seemed, with all the most modern departments and laboratories, right next to the old madressa and the mosque, still operating much as they had been since the 900s. The Buddhist monks and teachers made the clerics of the madressa look very ignorant and provincial, Idelba said, but they were always courteous to Muslim practices, very unobtrusive and respectful, and over time a number of Sufi teachers and reformist clerics had eventually built laboratories of their own, and had taken classes at the monastery schools to prepare to work on questions of natural law in their own establishments. "They gave us time to swallow and digest the bitter pill of our defeat," Idelba said of these Buddhists. "The Chinese were smart to stay away and let these people be their emissaries. That way we never really see how ruthless the Chinese are. We think the Travancoris are the whole story."

But it seemed to Budur that the Chinese were not so hard as they could have been. The reparation payments were within the realm of the possible, Father admitted, or if they were not, the debts were always being forgiven, or put off. And in Firanja, at least, the Buddhist monastery schools and hospitals were the only signs of the victors of the war imposing their will—almost; that dark part, the shadow of the conquerors, opium, was becoming more and more common in Firanji cities, and Father declared angrily after reading the newspapers that as it all came from Afghanistan and Burma, its shipment to Firanja was almost certainly sanctioned by the Chinese. Even in Turi one saw the poor souls in the working district cafés downriver, stupefied by the odd-smelling smoke, and in Nsara Idelba said the drug was widespread, like any other world city in that regard, even though it was Islam's world city, the only Islamic capital not destroyed by the war: Konstantiniyye, Cairo, Moscow, Tehran, Zanzibar, Damascus, and Baghdad had been firebombed, and not yet completely rebuilt.

But Nsara had survived, and now it was the Sufis' city, the scientists' city, Idelba's city; she had gone to it after a childhood in Turi and at the family farm in the Alps; she had gone to school there, and mathematical formulations had spoken to her as if speaking aloud from the page; she understood them, she spoke that strange alchemical language. Old men explained its rules of grammar to her, and she followed them and did the work, learned more, made her mark in theoretical speculations about the nature of microscopic matter when she was only twenty years old. "Young minds are often the strongest in math," she said later, already outside the experience itself. Into the labs of Nsara, then, helping the famous Lisbi and his team to bolt a cyclic accelerator together, getting married, then getting divorced, then, apparently very quickly, rather mysteriously, Budur thought, getting remarried, which was almost unheard of in Turi; working again with her second husband, very happily, then his unexpected death; and her again mysterious return to Turi, her retreat.

Budur asked once, "Did you wear the veil there?"

"Sometimes," Idelba said. "It depended on the situation. The veil has a kind of power, in certain situations. All such signs stand for other things; they are sentences spoken in matter. The hijab can say to strangers, 'I am Islamic and in solidarity with my men, against you and all the world.' To Islamic men it can say, 'I will play this foolish game, this fantasy of yours, but only if in return you do everything I tell you to.' For some men this trade, this capitulation to love, is a kind of release from the craziness of being a man. So the veil can be like putting on a magician queen's cape." But seeing Budur's hopeful expression she added, "Or it can be like putting on a slave's collar, certainly."

"So sometimes you didn't wear one?"

"Usually I did not. In the lab it would have been silly. I wore a lab djellaba, like the men. We were there to study atoms, to study nature. That is the greatest godliness! And without gender. That simply isn't what it's about. So, the people you are working with, you see them face to face, soul to soul." Eyes shining, she quoted from some old poem: " 'Every moment an epiphany arrives, and cleaves the mountain asunder.' "

This had been the way of it for Idelba in her youth; and now she sat in her brother's little middle-class harem, "protected" by him in a way that gave her frequent attacks of hem, that in truth made her a fairly volatile person, like a Yasmina with a bent toward secrecy rather than garrulousness. Alone with Budur, pinning up laundry on the terrace, she would look at the treetops sticking over the walls and sigh. "If only I could walk again at dawn through the empty streets of the city! Blue, then pink—to deny one that is absurd. To deny one the world, on one's own terms—it's archaic! It's unacceptable."

But she did not run away. Budur did not fully understand why. Surely Aunt Idelba was capable of tramming down the hill to the train station, and taking a train to Nsara, and finding lodgings there—somewhere—and getting a job that would support her—somehow? And if not her, then whom? What woman could do it? None of good repute; not if Idelba couldn't. The only time Budur dared to ask her about it, she only shook her head brusquely and said, "There are other reasons too. I can't talk about it."

So there was something quite frightening to Budur about Idelba's presence in their home, a daily reminder that a woman's life could crash like an airplane out of the sky. The longer it went on the more disturbing Budur found it, and she noticed that Idelba too grew more agitated, wandering from room to room reading and muttering, or working over her papers with a big mathematical calculator, a net of strings holding beads of different colors. She wrote for hours on her blackboard, and the chalk squeaked and clicked and sometimes snapped off in her fingers. She talked on the phone down in the courtyard, sounding upset sometimes, pleased at others; doubting, or excited—and all about numbers, letters, the value of this and that, strengths and weaknesses, forces of microscopic things that no one would ever see. She said to Budur once, staring at her equations, "You know, Budur, there is a very great deal of energy locked into things. The Travancori Chandaala was the deepest thinker we ever have had on this Earth; you could say the Long War was a catastrophe just because of his death alone. But he left us a lot, and the energy-mass equivalence—look—a mass, that's just a measure for a certain weight, say—you multiply it by the speed of light, and square the result—multiply it by half a million li per second, think of that! then take the square of that, so—see—enormous numbers result, for even a little pinch of matter. That's the qi energy locked up in it. A strand of your hair has more energy in it than a locomotive."

"No wonder it's so hard to get a brush through it," Budur said uneasily, and Idelba laughed.

"But there's something wrong?" Budur asked.

At first Idelba did not answer. She was thinking, and lost to all around her. Then she stared at Budur.

"Something is wrong if we make it wrong. As always. Nothing in nature is wrong in itself."

Budur wasn't so sure of that. Nature made men and women, nature made flesh and blood, hearts, periods, bitter feelings . . . sometimes it all seemed wrong to Budur, as if happiness were a stale scrap of bread, and all the swans of her heart were fighting for it, starving for it.

The roof of the house was forbidden to the women; it was a place where they might be observed from the roof terraces higher up Turi's Eastern Hill. And yet the men never used it, and it was the perfect place to get above the street's treetops, and have a view of the Alps to the south of Lake Turi. So, when the men were all gone, and Ahmet asleep in his chair by the gate, Aunt Idelba and cousin Yasmina would use the laundry drying posts as the legs of a ladder, placing them in olive jars and lashing them together, so that they could climb the lashings very gingerly, with the girls below and Idelba above holding the posts. Up they would go until they were all on the roof, in the dark, under the stars, in the wind, whispering so that Ahmet would not hear them, whispering so that they would not shout at the top of their lungs. The Alps in full moonlight stood there like white cardboard cutouts at the back of a puppet stage, perfectly vertical, the very image of what mountains should look like. Yasmina brought up her candles and powders to say the magic spells that would drive her men admirers to distraction—as if they weren't already. But Yasmina had an insatiable desire for men's regard, sharpened no doubt by the lack of access to it in the harem. Her Travancori incense would swirl up into the night, sandalwood, musk, saffron, nagi, and with their exotic scents filling her head it would seem to Budur a different world, vaster, more mysteriously meaningful—things suffused with their meanings as if with a liquid, right to the limits of surface tension, everything became a symbol of itself, the moon the symbol of moon, the sky the symbol of sky, the mountains the symbol of mountains, all bathed in a dark blue sea of longing. Longing, the very essence of longing, painful and beautiful, bigger than the world itself.

But one time the full moon came, and Idelba did not organize an expedition to the roof terrace. She had spent many hours that month on the telephone, and after each conversation had been uncharacteristically subdued. She hadn't described to the girls the contents of these calls or said who she had been talking to, though from her manner of talk Budur assumed it was her nephew, as usual. But no discussion of them at all.

Perhaps it was this that made Budur sensitive and wary of some change. On the night of the full moon she scarcely slept, waking every watch to see the moving shadows on the floor, waking from dreams of anxious flight through the alleys of the old town, escaping something behind her she never quite saw. Near dawn she woke to a noise from the terrace, and looked out her little window to see Idelba carrying the laundry poles down from the terrace into the stairwell. Then the olive jars as well.

Budur slipped out into the hall and down to the window at the carrel overlooking the yard in front. Idelba was constructing their ladder against the side of the household wall, just around the corner of the house from Ahmet's locked gate. She would top the wall next to a big elm tree that stood in the alley running between the walls of their house and the al-Dins' next door, who were from Neshapur.

Without a moment's hesitation, without any thought at all, Budur ran back to her room and dressed quickly, then ran downstairs and back out into the yard, around the corner of the house, glancing around the corner to be sure Idelba had gone.

She was. The way was clear; Budur could follow without impediment.

This time she did hesitate; and it would be difficult to describe her thoughts in that crucial moment of her life. No particular train of thought occupied her mind, but rather a kind of balancing of her whole existence: the harem, her mother's moods, her father's indifference to her, Ahab's simple face always behind her like an idiot animus, Yasmina's weeping; all of Turi at once, balanced on its two hills on each side of the river Limat, and in her head; beyond all that, huge cloudy masses of feeling, like the clouds one saw boiling up over the Alps. All inside her chest; and outside her a sensation as if clusters of eyes were trained on her, the ghost audience to her life, perhaps, out there always whether she saw them or not, like the stars. Something like that. It is always thus at the moment of change, when we rise up out of the everyday and get clear of the blinders of habit, and stand naked to existence, to the moment of choice, vast, dark, windy. The world is huge in these moments, huge. Too big to bear. Visible to all the ghosts of the world. The center of the universe.

She lurched forward. She ran to the ladder, climbed swiftly; it was no different than when it was set upstairs between terrace and roof. The branches of the elm were big and solid, it was easy to climb down far enough in them to make a final jump to the ground, jarring her fully awake, after which she rolled to her feet as smoothly as if she had been in on the plan from the start.

She tiptoed to the street and looked toward the tram stop. Her heart was thumping hard now, and she was hot in the chill air. She could take the tram or walk straight down the narrow streets, so steep that in several places they were staired. She was sure Idelba was off to the train station, and if she was wrong, she could give up the chase.

Even wearing a veil it was too early for a girl from a good family to be on the tram alone; indeed, it was always too early for a respectable girl to be out alone. So she hustled over to the top of the first stair alley, and began hurrying down the weaving course, through courtyard, park, alley, the stair of the roses, the tunnel made by Japanese fire maples, down and down the familiar way to the old town and the bridge crossing the river to the train station. Onto the bridge, where she looked upstream to the patch of sky between old stone buildings, its blue arched over the pink hem of the little bit of mountains visible, an embroidery dropped into the far end of the lake.

She was losing her resolve when she saw Idelba in the station, reading the schedule for track listings. Budur ducked behind a streetlight post, ran around the building into the doors on the other side, and likewise read a schedule. The first train for Nsara was on Track 16, at the far side of the station, leaving at .5 sharp, which had to be close. She checked the clock hanging over the row of trains, under the roof of the big shed; five minutes to spare. She slipped onto the last car of the train.

The train jerked slightly and was off. Budur moved forward up the train, car to car, holding on to the seat backs, her heart knocking faster and faster. What was she going to say to Idelba? And what if Idelba was not on the train, and Budur off to Nsara on her own, with no money?

But there Idelba sat, hunched over, looking forward out the window. Budur steeled herself and burst through the compartment door and rushed to her weeping, threw herself on her, "I'm sorry, Aunt Idelba, I didn't know you were going this far, I only followed to keep you company, I hope you have money to pay for my ticket too?"

"Oh name of Allah!" Idelba was shocked; then furious; mostly at herself, Budur judged through her tears, though she took it out for a little while on Budur, saying, "This is important business I'm on, this is no girl's prank! Oh, what will happen? What will happen? I should send you right back on the next train!"

Budur only shook her head and wept some more.

The train clicked quickly over the tracks, through country that was rather bland; hill and farm, hill and farm, flat woods and pastures, all clicking by at an enormous speed—it almost made her sick to look out the window, though she had ridden in trains all her life, and had looked out before at the view without a problem.

At the end of a long day the train entered the bleak outskirts of a city, like Downbrook only bigger, li after li of apartment blocks and close-set houses behind their walls, bazaars full of people, neighborhood mosques and bigger buildings of various kinds; then really big buildings, a whole knot of them flanking the many-bridged river, right before it opened out into the estuary, now a giant harbor, protected by a jetty that was broad enough to hold a street on it, with businesses on both sides.

The train took them right to the heart of this district of tall buildings, where a station, glass roofed and grimy, let them out onto a broad tree-lined street, a two-parted street divided by huge oaks planted in a line down a center island. They were a few blocks from the docks and the jetty. It smelled fishy.

A broad esplanade ran along the riverbank, backed by a row of red-leaved trees. Idelba walked quickly down this corniche, like Turi's lake-side corniche only much grander, until she turned onto a narrow street lined with three-story apartment blocks, their first floors occupied by restaurants and shops. Up a stair into one of these buildings, then into a doorway with three doors. Idelba rang the bell for the middle one, and the door opened and they were welcomed into an apartment like an old palace fallen apart.

2 ✺ Not an old palace, it turned out, but an old museum. No room in it was very big or impressive, but there were a lot of them. False ceilings, open ceilings, and abrupt cuts in wall paintings and wainscoting patterns made it clear that bigger rooms had been divided and subdivided. Most of the rooms held little more than one bed or cot, and the huge kitchen was crowded with women making a meal or waiting to eat it. They were thin women, for the most part. It was noisy with talk and stove fans. "What is this?" Budur asked Idelba under the hubbub.

"This is a zawiyya. A kind of boardinghouse for women." Then with a bleak smile: "An antiharem." She explained that these had been traditional in the Maghrib, and now they were widespread in Firanja. The war had left many more women alive than men, despite the indiscriminate devastation of its last two decades, when more civilians than soldiers had died, and women's brigades had been common on both sides. Turi and the other Alpine emirates had kept more men at home than most countries, putting them to work in the armories, so Budur had heard of the depopulation problem, but had never seen it. As for the zawiyyas, Idelba said they were still technically illegal, as the laws against female ownership of property had never been changed; but male nominal owners and other legal dodges were used to legitimize scores of them, hundreds of them.

"Why did you not live in one of these after your husband died?" Budur asked.

Idelba frowned. "I needed to leave for a while."

They were assigned a room that had three beds, but no other occupants. The third bed would serve as desk and table. The room was dusty, and its little window looked out on other grimy windows, all facing in on an airshaft, as Idelba called it. Buildings here were so compressed together that they had to remember to leave shafts for air.

But no complaints. A bed, a kitchen, women around them: Budur was content. But Idelba was still very worried, about something having to do with her nephew Piali and his work. In their new room she stared at Budur with a dismay she couldn't conceal. "You know, I should send you back to your father. I've got enough trouble as it is."

"No. I won't go."

Idelba stared at her. "How old are you again?"

"I'm twenty-three." She would be in two months.

Idelba was surprised. "I thought you were younger."

Budur blushed and looked down.

Idelba grimaced. "Sorry. That's the effect of the harem. And no men left to marry. But look, you have to do something."

"I want to stay here."

"Well, even so, you have to inform your father where you are, and tell him that I did not kidnap you."

"He'll come here and get me."

"No. I don't think so. In any case you must tell him something. Phone him, or write him a letter."

Budur was afraid to talk to her father, even over the phone. The idea of a letter was intriguing. She could explain herself without giving away her precise location.

She wrote:

> Dear Father and Mother,
>   I followed Aunt Idelba when she left, though she did not know it. I have come to Nsara to live and to pursue a course of study. The Quran says all of Allah's creatures are equal in His eyes. I will write you and the rest of the family a weekly report

on my affairs, and will live an orderly life here in Nsara that
will not shame the family. I am living in a good zawiyya with
Aunt Idelba, and she will look after me. Lots of young women
here are doing this, and they will all help me. I will study at
the madressa. Please convey all my love to Yasmina, Rema,
Aisha, Nawah, and Fatima.

> Your loving daughter,
>
> Budur

She mailed this off, and after that stopped thinking of Turi. The letter
was helpful in making her feel less guilty. And after a while she realized,
as the weeks went on, and she did clerical work, and cleaning, and cooking, and other help of that kind in the zawiyya, and made the arrangements to start studies at the institute connected to the madressa, that
she was not going to get a letter back from her father. And Mother was illiterate; and her cousins no doubt forbidden to write, and perhaps angry
at her for abandoning them; and her brother would not be sent after her,
nor would he want to be; nor would she be arrested by the police and
sent off in a sealed train to Turi. That happened to no one. There were literally thousands of women both escaping from home, and relieving
those left behind from the burden of caring for them. What in Turi had
looked like an eternal system of law and custom that the whole world
abided by, was in reality nothing more than the antiquated habits of one
moribund segment of a single society, mountain-bound and conservative, furiously inventing pan-Islamic "traditions" even at the moment
they were all disappearing, like morning mist or (more appropriately)
battlefield smoke. She would never go back, it was that simple! And no
one was going to make her. No one even wanted to make her; that too
was a bit of a shock. Sometimes it did not feel so much that she had escaped as that she had been abandoned.

There was this fundamental fact, however, which struck her every
day when she left the zawiyya: she was no longer living in a harem. She
could go where she chose, when she chose. This alone was enough to
make her feel giddy and strange—free, solitary—almost too happy, to
the point of disorientation, or even a kind of panic: once right in the
midst of this euphoria she saw from behind a man emerging from the
train station and thought for a second it was her father, and was glad, re-

lieved; but it wasn't him; and all the rest of that day her hands shook with anger, shame, fear, longing.

Later it happened again. It happened several times, and she came to regard the experience as a kind of ghost glimpsed in the mirror, her past life haunting her: her father, her uncles, her brother, her male cousins, always in actuality the faces of various strangers, just alike enough to give her a start, make her heart jump with fear, though she loved them all. She would have been so happy to think they were proud of her, that they cared enough to come after her. But if it meant returning to the harem, she never wanted to see them again. She would never again submit to rules from anyone. Even ordinary sane rules now gave her a quick surge of anger, an instantaneous and complete NO that would fill her like a shriek in the nerves. Islam in its literal meaning meant submission: but NO! She had lost that ability. A traffic policewoman, warning her not to cross the busy harbor road outside the crosswalks: Budur cursed her. The house rules in her zawiyya: her teeth would clench. Don't leave dirty plates in the sink, help wash the sheets every Thursday; NO.

But all that anger was trivial compared to the fact of her freedom. She woke in the morning, understood where she was, leaped out of bed full of amazed energy. An hour's vigorous work in the zawiyya had her groomed and fed, and some of the communal work done, bathrooms cleaned, dishes, all the chores that had to be done over and over, all the chores that at home had been performed by the servants—but how much finer it was to do such work for an hour than to have other human beings sacrificing their whole lives to it! How clear it was that this was a model for all human labor and relations!

Those things done she was off into the fresh ocean air, like a cold salty wet drug, sometimes with a shopping list, sometimes only with her bag of books and writing materials. Wherever she was going she would go by the harbor, to see the ocean outside the jetty, and the wind whipping the flags; and one fine morning she stood at the end of the jetty with nowhere to go, and nothing to do; and no one in the world knew where she was at that moment, except for her. My God, the feel of that! The harbor crowded with ships, the brown water running out to sea on the ebb tide, the sky a pale wash of clean azure, and all of a sudden she bloomed, there were oceans of clouds in her chest, she wept for joy. Ah, Nsara! Nsssarrrrra!

But first on her list of things to do, on many mornings, was to visit the White Crescent Disabled Soldiers Home, a vast converted army barracks a good ways up the river park. This was one of those duties Idelba had pointed her toward, and Budur found it both harrowing and uplifting—like going to the mosque on Friday was supposed to be and never really had been. The larger part of this barracks and hospital was taken up by a few thousand blind soldiers, rendered sightless by gas on the eastern front. In the mornings they sat in silence, in beds or chairs or wheelchairs as the case might be, as someone read to them, usually a woman: daily newspapers on their thin inky sheets, or various texts, or in some cases the Quran and the hadith, though these were less popular. Many of the men had been wounded as well as blinded, and could not walk or move; they sat there with half a face, or without legs, aware, it seemed, of how they must appear, and staring in the direction of the readers with a hungry ashamed look, as if they would kill and eat her if they could, from unrealizable love or bitter resentment, or both all mixed together. Such naked expressions Budur had never seen in her life, and she often kept her own gaze fixed on whatever text she was reading, as though, if she were to glance up at them they would know it and recoil, or hiss with disapprobation. Her peripheral vision revealed to her an audience out of a nightmare, as if one of the rooms of hell had extruded from the underworld to reveal its inhabitants, waiting to be processed, as they had waited and been processed in life. Despite her attempts not to look, every time she read to them Budur saw more than one of them weeping, no matter what it was she read, even the weather reports from Firanja or Africa or the New World. The weather actually was one of their favorite readings.

Among the other readers there were very plain women who nevertheless had beautiful voices, low and clear, musical, women who sang their whole lives without knowing it (and knowing would have ruined the effect); when they read many in their audience sat forward in their beds and wheelchairs, rapt, in love with a woman to whom they never would have given a second glance could they have seen her. And Budur saw that some of the men leaned forward in the same way for her, though in her own ears her voice was unpleasantly high and scratchy. But it had its fans. Sometimes she read them the stories of Scheherazade, addressing them as if they were angry King Shahryar and she the wily storyteller, staying alive one more night; and one day, emerging from that antechamber of hell into the soaked sunlight of cloudy noon, she almost staggered at the realization of how completely the old story had been turned on its head, Scheherazade free to walk away, while the Shahryars were imprisoned forever in their own wrecked bodies.

3 ❀ That duty accomplished, she walked through the bazaar to the classes she was taking, in subjects suggested by Aunt Idelba. The madressa institute's classes were folded in to the Buddhist monastery and hospital, and Budur paid a fee, with money borrowed from Idelba, to take three classes: beginning statistics (which began with simple arithmetic, in fact), accounting, and the history of Islam.

This last course was taught by a woman named Kirana Fawwaz, a short dark Algerine with an intense voice hoarsened by cigarettes. She looked about forty or forty-five. In the first meeting she informed them she had served in the war hospitals and then, near the end of the Nakba (or the Catastrophe, as the war was often referred to) in the Maghribi women's brigades. She was nothing like the soldiers in the White Crescent home, however; she had come out of the Nakba with the air of one victorious, and declared in the first meeting that they would in fact have won the war, if they had not been betrayed both at home and abroad.

"Betrayed by what?" she asked in her harsh crow's voice, seeing the question on all their faces. "I will tell you: by the clerics. By our men more generally. And by Islam itself."

Her audience stared at her. Some lowered their heads uneasily, as if expecting Kirana to be arrested on the spot, if not struck down by lightning. Surely at the least she would be run down later that day by an unexpected tram. And there were several men in the class as well, one right next to Budur, in fact, wearing a patch over one eye. But none of them said anything, and the class went on as if one could say such things and get away with it.

"Islam is the last of the old desert monotheisms," Kirana told them. "It is belated in that sense, an anomaly. It followed and built on the earlier pastoral monotheisms of the Middle West, which predated Muhammad by several centuries at least: Christianity, the Essenes, the Jews, the Zoroastrians, the Mithraists, and so on. They were all strongly patriarchal, replacing earlier matriarchal polytheisms, created by the first agricultural civilizations, in which gods resided in every domesticated plant, and women were acknowledged to be crucial to the production of food and new life.

"Islam was therefore a latecomer, and as such, a corrective to the earlier monotheisms. It had the chance to be the best monotheism, and in many ways it was. But because it began in an Arabia that had been shattered by the wars of the Roman empire and the Christian states, it had to deal first with a condition of almost pure anarchy, a tribal war of all against all, in which women were at the mercy of any warring party. From those depths no new religion could leap very high.

"Muhammad thus arrived as a prophet who was both trying to do good, and trying not to be overwhelmed by war, and by his experiencing of divine voices—babbling some of the time, as the Quran will attest."

This remark drew gasps, and several women stood and walked out. All the men in the room, however, remained as if transfixed.

"Spoken to by God or babbling whatever came into his head, it did not matter; the end result was good, at first. A tremendous increase in law, in justice, in women's rights, and in a general sense of order and human purpose in history. Indeed, it was precisely this sense of justice and divine purpose that gave Islam its unique power in the first few centuries A.H., when it swept the world despite the fact that it gave no new material advantage—one of the only clear-cut demonstrations of the power of the idea alone, in all of history.

"But then came the caliphs, the sultans, the divisions, the wars, the clerics and their hadith. The hadith overgrew the Quran itself; they seized on every scrap of misogyny scattered in Muhammad's basically feminist work, and stitched them into the shroud in which they wrapped the Quran, as being too radical to enact. Generations of patriarchal clerics built up a mass of hadith that has no Quranic authority whatsoever, thus rebuilding an unjust tyranny, using frequently falsified authorities of personal transmission from male master to male student, as if a lie passed down through three or ten generations of men somehow metamorphoses into a truth. But it is not so.

"And so Islam, like Christianity and Judaism before it, stagnated and degenerated. Because its expansion was so great, it was harder to see this failure and collapse; indeed, it took up until the Nakba itself to make it clear. But this perversion of Islam lost us the war. It was women's rights, and nothing else, that gave China and Travancore and Yingzhou the victory. It was the absence of women's rights in Islam that turned half the population into nonproductive illiterate cattle, and lost us the war. The tremendous intellectual and mechanical progress that had been initiated by Islamic scientists was picked up and carried to much greater heights by the Buddhist monks of Travancore and the Japanese diaspora, and this revolution in mechanical capacity was quickly developed by China and the New World free states; by everyone, in fact, except for Dar al-Islam. Even our reliance on camels did not come to an end until midway through the Long War. Without any road wider than two camels, with every city built as a kasbah or a medina, as tightly packed as a bazaar, nothing could be done in the way of modernization. Only the war's destruction of the city cores allowed us to rebuild in a modern way, and only our desperate attempt to defend ourselves brought any industrial progress to speak of. But by then it was a case of too little and too late."

At this point the room was quite a bit emptier than it had been when Kirana Fawwaz began; and two girls had exclaimed as they stormed out that they were going to report these blasphemies to the clerics and the police. But Kirana Fawwaz only paused to light a cigarette and wave them out of the room, before continuing.

"Now," she went on, calmly, inexorably, remorselessly, "in the aftermath of the Nakba, everything has to be reconsidered, everything. Islam has to be examined root and branch and leaf, in the effort to make it well, if that is possible; in the effort to make our civilization capable of survival. But despite this obvious necessity, the regressives prattle their broken old hadith like magic charms to conjure jinns, and in states like Afghanistan or Sudan, or even in corners of Firanja itself, in the Alpine emirates and Skandistan, for instance, the hezbollah rule, and women are forced into chador and hijab and harem, and the men in power in these states try to pretend that it is the year 300 in Baghdad or Damascus, and that Haroun al-Rashid will come walking in the door to make everything right. They might as well pretend to be Christian and hope the cathedrals will spring back to life and Jesus come flying down from heaven."

4 ⚙ As Kirana spoke, Budur saw in her mind the blind men in the hospital; the walled residential streets of Turi; her father's face as he was reading to her mother; the sight of the ocean; a white tomb in the jungle;

indeed everything in her life, and many things she had never thought of before. Her mouth hung open, she was stunned, frightened—but also elated, by every single shocking word of it: it confirmed everything she had suspected in her ignorant balked furious girlhood, trapped in her father's house. She had spent her whole life thinking that something was seriously wrong with herself, or with the world, or both. Now reality seemed to have opened up under her like a trapdoor, as all her suspicions were confirmed in glorious style. She held on to her seat, even, and stared at the woman lecturing them, hypnotized as if by some great hawk circling overhead, hypnotized not just by her angry analysis of all that had gone wrong, but by the image she evoked thereby of History itself, the huge long string of events that had led to this moment, here and now in this rain-lashed western harbor city; hypnotized by the oracle of time itself, rasping on in her urgent smoky crow's voice. So much had happened already, nahdas and nakbas, time after time; what could be said after all that? One had to have courage even to try to talk about it.

But very clearly this Kirana Fawwaz did not lack for courage. Now she stopped, and looked around at the half-emptied room. "Well," she said cheerfully, acknowledging with a brief smile Budur's round-eyed look, somewhat like that of the astonished fish in the boxes at the market. "It seems we have driven out everyone who can be driven out. Left are the brave of heart to venture into this dark country, our past."

The brave of heart or the weak of limb, Budur thought, glancing around. An old one-armed soldier looked on imperturbably. The one-eyed man still sat next to her. Several women of various ages sat looking around uneasily, shifting in their seats. A few looked to Budur like women of the street, and one of these was grinning. Not what Budur had imagined when Idelba had talked about the Nsarene Madressa and Institutes of Higher Learning; the flotsam of Dar al-Islam, in fact, the sorry survivors of the Nakba, the swans in winter; women who had lost their husbands, fiancés, fathers, brothers, women who been orphaned and never since had the chance to meet a single man; and the war-wounded themselves, including a blinded veteran like the ones Budur read to, led to the class by his sister, and then the one-armed one, and the eyepatch next to her; also a Hodenosaunee mother and daughter, supremely confident and dignified, relaxed, interested, but with nothing at stake; also a longshoreman with a bad back, who seemed to be there mainly to get out of the rain for six hours a week. These were the ones that remained, lost souls of the city, looking for something indoors to occupy them, they were not sure what. But perhaps, for the moment at least, it would do to stay here and listen to Kirana Fawwaz's harsh lecture.

"What I want to do," she said then, "is to cut through all the stories, through the million stories we have constructed to defend ourselves from the reality of the Nakba, to reach explanation. To the meaning of what has happened, do you understand? This is an introduction to history, like Khaldun, only spoken among us, in conversation. I will be suggesting various projects for further research as we go along. Now let's go get a drink."

She led them out into the dusk of the long northern evening, to a café behind the docks, where they found acquaintances from other parts of her life, already there eating late meals or smoking cigarettes or puffing on communal narghiles, and drinking little cups of thick coffee. They sat and talked through the long twilight, then far into the night, the docks out the windows empty and calm, the lights from across the harbor squiggling on black water. The man with the eyepatch was a friend of Kirana's, it turned out; his name was Hasan, and he introduced himself to Budur and invited her to sit on the wall bench next to him and his group of acquaintances, including singers and actors from the institute, and the city's theaters. "My fellow student here, I venture to say," he said to the others, "was quite taken by our professor's opening remarks."

Budur nodded shyly and they cackled at her. She inquired about ordering a cup of coffee.

The talk around the dirty marble tabletops ranged widely, as was true in all such places, even back in Turi. The news in the newspapers. Interpretations of the war. Gossip about the city officials. Talk about plays and the cinema. Kirana sometimes rested and listened, sometimes talked on as if she were still in her class.

"Iran is the wine of history, they are always getting crushed."

"Some vintages are better than others—"

"—so for them all great civilizations must finally be crushed."

"This is merely al-Katalan again. It is too simple."

"A world history has to simplify," the old one-armed soldier said. His name was Naser Shah, Budur learned; his accent when speaking Firanjic marked him as Iranian. "The trick of it is to get at causes of things, to generate some sense of the overall story."

"But if there isn't one?" Kirana asked.

"There is," Naser said calmly. "All people who have ever lived on Earth have acted together to make a global history. It is one story. Certain patterns are evident in it. The collisionary theories of Ibrahim al-Lanzhou, for instance. No doubt they're just yin and yang again, but they make it seem pretty clear that much of what we call progress comes from the clash of two cultures."

"Progress by collision, what kind of progress is this, did you see those two trams the other day after the one jumped its tracks?"

Kirana said, "Al-Lanzhou's core civilizations represent the three logically possible religions, with Islam believing in one god, India in many gods, and China in no gods."

"That's why China won," said Hasan, his one eye gleaming with mischief. "They turned out to be right. Earth congealed out of cosmic dust, life appeared and evolved until a certain ape made more and more sounds, and off we went. Never any God involved, nothing supernatural, no eternal souls reincarnated time after time. Only the Chinese really faced that, leading the way with their science, honoring nothing but their ancestors, working only for their descendants. And so they dominate us all!"

"It's just that there's more of them," one of the questionable women said.

"But they can support more people on less land. This proves they are right!"

Naser said, "Each culture's strength can also be its weakness. We saw this in the war. China's lack of religion made them horribly cruel."

The Hodenosaunee women from the class appeared and joined them; they too were acquaintances of Kirana's. Kirana welcomed them, saying, "Here are our conquerors, a culture where women have power! I wonder if we could judge civilizations by how well women have done in them."

"They have built them all," proclaimed the oldest woman there, who up till now had only sat there knitting. She was at least eighty, and therefore had lived through most of the war, start to finish, childhood to old age. "No civilizations exist without the homes women build from the inside."

"Well, how much political power women have taken, then. How

comfortable their men are with the idea of women having this kind of power."

"That would be China."

"No, the Hodenosaunee."

"Not Travancore?"

No one ventured to say.

"This should be investigated!" Kirana said. "This will be one of your projects. A history of women in the other cultures of the world—their actions as political creatures, their fates. That this is missing from history as we have been given it so far, is a sign that we still live in the wreckage of patriarchy. And nowhere more so than in Islam."

5 ❈ Budur of course told Idelba all about Kirana's lecture and the after-class meeting, describing them excitedly while they washed dishes together, and then sheets. Idelba nodded and asked questions, interested; but in the end she said, "I hope you will keep working hard on your statistics class. Talk about these kinds of things can go on forever, but numbers are the only thing that will get you beyond talk."

"What do you mean?"

"Well, the world operates by number, by physical laws, expressed mathematically. If you know these, you will have a better grasp of things. And some possible job skills. Speaking of which, I think I can get you a job washing glassware in the lab. That would be good, it will give you some more money, and teach you that you need some job skills. Don't get sucked into the whirlpool of café talk."

"But talk can be good! It's teaching me so many things, not just about history, but what it all means. It sorts it out, like we used to do in the harem."

"Exactly! You can talk all you want in the harem! But it's only in institutes that you can do science. Since you've bothered to come here, you might as well take advantage of what's offered."

This gave Budur pause. Idelba saw her thinking about it, and went on:

"Even if you do want to study history, which is perfectly sensible, there is a way of doing it that goes beyond café talk, that inspects the actual artifacts and sites left from the past, and establishes what can be asserted with physical evidence to back it, as in the other sciences. Firanja is full of old places that are being investigated for the first time in a scientific manner like this, and it is very interesting. And it will take decades to investigate them all, even centuries."

She straightened up, held her lower back and rubbed it as she regarded Budur. "Come with me for a picnic on Friday. I'll take you up the coast to see the menhirs."

"The menhirs? What are they?"

"You will see on Friday."

So on Friday they took the tram as far north up the coast as it ran, then changed to a bus and rode for half a watch, looking out at the apple orchards and the occasional glimpses of the dark blue ocean. Finally Idelba led the way off at one stop, and they walked west out of a tiny village, immediately into a forest of immense standing stones, set in long lines over a slightly rolling grassy plain, interrupted here and there by huge mature oak trees. It was an uncanny sight.

"Who put these here? The Franks?"

"Before the Franks. Before the Kelts, perhaps. No one is quite sure. Their living settlements have not been found with certainty, and it's very difficult to date the time when these stones were dressed and stood on end."

"It must have taken, I don't know, centuries to put this many up!"

"It depends on how many of them there were doing it, I suppose. Maybe there were as many then as now, who can say? Only I would expect not, as we find no ruined cities, as they do in Egypt or the Middle West. No, it must have been a smaller population, taking a lot of time and effort."

"But how can a historian work with stuff like this?" Budur asked at one point, as they walked down one of the long lanes created by the rows of stones, studying the patterns of black and yellow lichen that grew on their nobbled surfaces. Most were about twice Budur's height, really massive things.

"You study things instead of stories. It's something different than history, more a scientific inquiry of material conditions that early people lived in, things they made. Archaeology. Again, it is a science begun during the first Islamic flowering, in Syria and Iraq, then not pursued again until the Nahda," this last being the rebirth of Islamic high culture in certain cities like Tehran and Cairo, in the half-century before the Long War started and wrecked everything. "Now our understanding of physics and geology is such that new methods of inquiry are being suggested all the time. And construction and reconstruction projects are digging up all kinds of new finds as well, and people are going out deliberately looking for more, and it is all coming together in a very exciting way. It is a science taking off, if you know what I mean. Most interesting. And Firanja is turning out to be one of the best places to practice it. This is an ancient place."

She gestured at the long rows of stones, like a crop seeded by great stone gods who had never come back to make a harvest. Clouds scudded by overhead, and the blue sky seemed flat and low over them. "Not just these, or the stone rings in Britain, but stone tombs, monuments, whole villages. I'll have to take you up to the Orkneys with me some time. I may be wanting to go up there soon; in any case, I'll take you along. Anyway you think about studying this kind of thing too, as a grounding for you while you listen to Madame Fawwaz and all her scheherazading."

Budur rubbed her hand over a stone dressed by a thin lichen coat of many colors. Clouds rushed by. "I will."

6 ❋ Classes, a new job cleaning Idelba's lab, walking the docks and the jetty, dreaming of a new synthesis, an Islam that included what was important in the Buddhism so prevalent in the labs: Budur's days passed in a blur of thought, everything she saw and did fed into it. Most of the women in Idelba's lab were Buddhist nuns, and many of the men there were monks. Compassion, right action, a kind of *agape*, as the ancient Greeks had called it—the Greeks, those ghosts of this place, people who had had every idea already, in a lost paradise that had included even the story of paradise lost, in the form of Plato's tales of Atlantis, which were turning out to be true, according to the latest studies of the scholars on Kreta, digging in the ruins.

Budur looked into classes in this new field, archaeology. History that was more than talk, that could be a science . . . The people working on it were an odd mix, geologists, architects, physicists, Quranic scholars, historians, all studying not just the stories, but the things left behind.

Meanwhile the talk went on, in Kirana's class and in the cafés afterward. One night in a café Budur asked Kirana what she thought of archaeology, and she replied, "Yes, archaeology is very important, sure. Although the standing stones are rather mute when it comes to telling us things. But they're discovering caves in the south, filled with wall paintings that appear to be very old, older even than the Greeks. I can give you the names of the people at Avignon involved with that."

"Thanks."

Kirana sipped her coffee and listened to the others for a while. Then she said to Budur under the hubbub, "What's interesting, I think, beyond all the theories we discuss, is what never gets written down. This is crucial for women especially, because so much of what we did never got written down. Just the ordinary, you know, daily existence. The work of raising children and feeding families and keeping a home together, as an oral culture passed along generation to generation. Uterine culture, Kang Tongbi called it. You must read her work. Anyway, uterine culture has no obvious dynasties, or wars, or new continents to discover, and so historians have never tried to account for it—for what it is, how it is transmitted, how it changes over time, according to material and social conditions. Changing with them, I mean, in a weave with them."

"In the harem it's obvious," Budur said, feeling nervous at being jammed knee to knee with this woman. Cousin Yasmina had conducted enough clandestine "practice sessions" of kissing and the like among the girls that Budur knew just what the pressure from Kirana's leg meant. Resolutely she ignored it and went on: "It's like Scheherazade, really. Telling stories to get along. Women's history would be like that, stories told one after another. And every day the whole process has to be renewed."

"Yes, Scheherazade is a good tale about dealing with men. But there must be better models for how women should pass history along, to younger women, for instance. The Greeks had a very interesting mythology, full of goddesses modeling various woman-to-woman behaviors. Demeter, Persephone . . . they have a wonderful poet for this stuff too, Sappho. You haven't heard of her? I'll give you the references."

7 ✳ This was the start of many more personal conversations over coffee, late at night in the rain-lashed cafés. Kirana lent Budur books on all kinds of topics, but especially Firanji history: the Golden Horde's sur-

vival of the plague that had killed the Christians; the continuing influence of the Horde's nomad structures on the descendant cultures of the Skandistani states; the infill of al-Andalus, Nsara, and the Keltic Islands by Maghribis; the zone of contention between the two infilling cultures in the Rhine Valley. Other volumes described the movement of Turks and Arabs through the Balkans, adding to the discord of the Firanji emirates, the little taifa states that fought for centuries, according to loyalties Sunni or Shiite, Sufi or Wahhabi, Turkic or Maghribi or Tartar; fought for dominance or survival, often desperately, creating conditions usually repressive for women, so that only in the farthest west had there been any cultural advances before the Long War, a progressiveness that Kirana associated with the ocean, and contact with other cultures by sea, and with Nsara's origins as a refuge for the heterodox and marginal, founded indeed by a woman, the fabled refugee Sultana Katima.

Budur took these books and tried reading from them aloud to her blind soldiers in the hospital. She read them the story of the Glorious Ramadan Revolution, when Turkic and Kirghizi women had led seizures of the power plants of the big reservoirs above Samarqand, and moved into the ruins of the fabled city, which had been abandoned for nearly a century because of a series of violent earthquakes; how they had formed a new republic in which the holy laws of Ramadan were extended through the year, and the life of the people made a communal act of divine worship, all humans completely equal, men and women, adult and child, so that the place had reclaimed its glorious heritage of the tenth century, and made amazing advances in culture and law, and all had been happy there, until the shah had sent his armies east from Iran and crushed them as heretics.

Her soldiers nodded as they listened. That's the way it happens, their silent faces said. The good is always crushed. Those who see the farthest have their eyes put out. Budur, seeing the way they hung on every word, like starving dogs watching people eat in sidewalk cafés, brought in more of her borrowed books to read to them. Ferdowsi's *The Book of Kings*, the huge epic poem describing Iran before Islam, was very popular. So was the Sufi lyric poet Hafiz, and of course Rumi and Khayyam. Budur herself liked to read from her heavily annotated copy of Ibn Khaldun's *Muqaddimah*.

"There is so much in Khaldun," she said to her listeners. "Everything I learn at the institute I find already here in Khaldun. One of my instructors is fond of a theory that has the world being a matter of three or four major civilizations, each a core state, surrounded by peripheral states. Listen here to Khaldun, in the section entitled 'Each dynasty has a certain amount of provinces and lands, and no more.' "

She read, " 'When the dynastic groups have spread over the border regions, their numbers are necessarily exhausted. This, then, is the time when the territory of the dynasty has reached its farthest extension, where the border regions form a belt around the center of the realm. If the dynasty then undertakes to expand beyond its holdings, its widening territory remains without military protection, and is laid open to any chance attack by enemy or neighbor. This has a detrimental result for the dynasty.' "

Budur looked up. "A very succinct description of core-periphery theory. Khaldun also addresses the lack of an Islamic core state that the others can rally around."

Her audience nodded; they knew about that; the absence of alliance coordination at the various fronts of the war had been a famous problem, with sometimes terrible results.

"Khaldun also addresses a systemic problem in Islamic economy, in its origins among Bedouin practice. He says of them, 'Places that succumb to the Bedouins are quickly ruined. The reason for this is that the Bedouins are a savage nation, fully accustomed to savagery and the things that cause it. Savagery has become their character and nature. They enjoy it, because it means freedom from authority and no subservience to leadership. Such a natural disposition is the negation and antithesis of civilization.' He goes on to say, 'It is their nature to plunder whatever other people possess. Their sustenance lies wherever the shadow of their lances falls.' And after that he gives us the labor theory of value, saying, 'Now, labor is the real basis of profit. When labor is not appreciated and is done for nothing, the hope for profit vanishes, and no productive work is done. The sedentary population disperses, and civilization decays.' Really quite amazing, how much Khaldun saw, and this back in a time when the people living here in Nsara were dying of their plague, and the rest of the world not even close to thinking historically."

The time for reading ended. Her audience settled back into their chairs and beds, hunkering down for the long empty watches of the afternoon.

Budur left with her usual combination of guilt, relief, and joy, and on this day went directly to Kirana's class.

"How can we ever progress out of our origins," she asked their teacher plaintively, "when our faith orders us not to leave them?"

Kirana replied, "Our faith said no such thing. This is just something the fundamentalists say to keep their hold on power."

Budur felt confused. "But what about the parts of the Quran that tell us Muhammad is the last prophet, and the rules in the Quran should stand forever?"

Kirana shook her head impatiently. "This is another case of taking an exception for the general rule, a very common fundamentalist tactic. In fact there are some truths in the Quran that Muhammad declared eternal—such existential realities as the fundamental equality of every person—how could that ever change? But the more worldly concerns of the Quran, involved with the building of an Arabic state, changed with circumstances, even within the Quran itself, as in its variable statements against alcohol. Thus the principle of naskh, in which later Quranic instructions supercede earlier ones. And in Muhammad's last statements, he made it clear that he wanted us to respond to changing situations, and to make Islam better—to come up with moral solutions that conform to the basic framework, but respond to new facts."

Naser asked, "I wonder if one of Muhammad's seven scribes could have inserted into the Quran ideas of his own?"

Again Kirana shook her head. "Recall the way the Quran was assembled. The mushaf, the final physical document, was the result of Osman bringing together all the surviving witnesses to Muhammad's dictation—his scribes, wives, and companions—who, together, agreed upon a single correct version of the holy book. No individual interpolations could have survived that process. No, the Quran is a single voice, Muhammad's voice, Allah's voice. And it is a message of great freedom and justice on this Earth! It is the hadith that contain the false messages, the reimposition of hierarchy and patriarchy, the exceptional cases twisted to general rules. It's the hadith that abandon the major jihad, the fight against one's own temptations, for the minor jihad, the defense of Islam against attack. No. In so many ways, the rulers and clerics have distorted the Quran to their own purposes. This has been true in all religions, of course. It is inevitable. Anything divine must come to us in worldly clothing, and so it comes to us altered. The divine is like rain striking the earth, and all our efforts at godliness are therefore muddy—all but those few seconds of complete inundation, the moments that the mystics describe, when we are nothing but rain. But those moments are always brief, as the sufis themselves admit. So we should let the occasional chalice break, if need be, to get at the truth of the water inside it."

Encouraged, Budur said, "So how do we be modern Muslims?"

"We don't," the oldest woman rasped, never pausing in her knitting. "It's an ancient desert cult that has brought ruin to countless generations, including mine and yours, I'm afraid. It's time to admit that and move on."

"On to what, though?"

"To whatever may come!" the old one cried. "To your sciences—to reality itself! Why worry about any of these ancient beliefs! They are all a matter of the strong over the weak, of men over women. But it's women who bear the children and raise them and plant the crops and harvest them and cook the meals and make the homes and care for the elderly! It's women who make the world! Men fight wars, and lord it over the rest with their laws and religions and guns. Thugs and gangsters, that's history! I don't see why we should try to accommodate any of it at all!"

There was silence in the class, and the old woman resumed her knitting as if she were stabbing every king and cleric who ever lived. They could suddenly hear the rain pouring down outside, students' voices in a courtyard, the old woman's knitting needles murderously clicking.

"But if we take that route," Naser said, "then the Chinese have truly won."

More drumming silence.

The old woman finally said, "They won for a reason. They have no God and they worship their ancestors and their descendants. Their humanism has allowed them science, progress—everything we have been denied."

Even deeper silence, so that they could hear the foghorn out on the point, bellowing in the rain.

Naser said, "You speak only of their upper classes. And their women had their feet bound into little nubbins, to cripple them, like clipping the wings of birds. That too is Chinese. They are hard bastards, you take my word for it. I saw in the war. I do not want to tell you what I saw, but I know, believe me. They have no sense of godliness, and so no rules of conduct; nothing to tell them not to be cruel, and so they are cruel. Horribly cruel. They don't think the people outside China are really human. Only the Han are human. The rest, we are hui hui, like dogs. Arrogant, cruel beyond telling—it does not seem a good thing to me that we should imitate their ways, that they should win the war so completely as that."

"But we were just as bad," Kirana said.

"Not when we behaved as true Muslims. What would be a good project for a history class, I think, would be to focus on what has been best in Islam, enduring through history, and see if that can guide us now. Every sura of the Quran reminds us by its opening words—Bismallah, in the name of God, the compassionate, the merciful. Compassion, mercy—how do we express that? These are ideas that the Chinese do not have. The Buddhists tried to introduce them there, and they were treated like beggars and thieves. But they are crucial ideas, and they are central to Islam. Ours is a vision of all people as one family, in the rule of compassion and mercy. This is what drove Muhammad, driven by Allah or by his own sense of justice, the Allah inside us. This is Islam to me! That's what I fought for in the war. These are the qualities we have to offer the world that the Chinese do not have. Love, to put it simply. Love."

"But if we don't live by these things—"

"No!" Naser said. "Don't beat us with that stick. I don't see any people on Earth living by their best beliefs anymore. This must be what Muhammad saw when he looked around him. Savagery everywhere, men like beasts. So every sura started with a call to compassion."

"You sound like a Buddhist," someone said.

The old soldier was willing to admit this. "Compassion, isn't that their guiding principle of action? I like what the Buddhists do in this world. They are having a good effect on us. They had a good effect on the Japanese, and the Hodenosaunee. I've read books that say all our progress in science comes from the Japanese diaspora, as the latest and strongest of the Buddhist diasporas. They took up the ideas from the ancient Greeks and the Samarqandis."

Kirana said, "We must find the most Buddhist parts of Islam, perhaps. Cultivate those."

"I say abandon all the past!" Click click click!

Naser shook his head. "Then there could arise a new, scientific savagery. As during the war. We have to retain the values that seem good, that foster compassion. We have to use the best of the old to make a new way, better than before."

"That seems good policy to me," Kirana said. "And it's what Muhammad told us to do, after all."

8 ❈ Thus the bitter skepticism of the old woman, the stubborn hope of the old soldier, the insistent inquiry of Kirana, an inquiry that never got to the answers she wanted, but forged on through idea after idea, testing them against her sense of things, and against thirty years of insatiable reading, and the seedy life behind the docks of Nsara. Budur, wrapping herself in her oilcloth raincoat and hunching through the drizzle home to the zawiyya, felt the invisibilities welling up all around her— the hot quick disapproval of maimed young men who passed on the street, the clouds lowering overhead, the secret worlds infolded inside everything that Aunt Idelba was working on at the lab. Her job sweeping up and restocking the empty place at night was . . . suggestive. Greater things lay in the final distillation of all this work, in the formulas scrawled on the blackboards. There were years of mathematical work behind the experiments of the physicists, centuries of work now being realized in material explorations that might bring new worlds. Budur did not feel she could ever learn the maths involved, but the labs had to run right for anything to progress, and she began to get involved in ordering supplies, keeping the kitchen and dining halls running, paying the bills (the qi bill was huge).

Meanwhile the talk between the scientists went on, endless as the chatter in the cafés. Idelba and her nephew Piali spent long sessions at the blackboards running over their ideas and proposing solutions to their mysterious mysteries, absorbed, pleased, also often worried, an edge in Idelba's voice, as if the equations were somehow revealing news she did not like or could not quite believe. Again she spent lots of time on the telephone, this time the one in its little closet in the zawiyya, and she was often gone without saying where she had been. Budur couldn't tell if all these matters were connected or not. There was a lot about Idelba's life that she didn't know. Men that she talked to outside the zawiyya, packages, calls . . . It appeared from the vertical lines etched between her eyebrows that she had her hands full, that it was a complicated existence somehow.

"Whatever is the problem with this study you are doing with Piali and the others?" Budur asked her one night as Idelba very thoroughly cleaned out her desk. They were the last ones there, and Budur felt a solid satisfaction at that; that here in Nsara they were trusted with matters; it was this that made her bold enough to interrogate her aunt.

Idelba stopped her cleaning to look at her. "We have some reason for

worry, or so it seems. You must not talk to anyone about this. But—
well—as I you told before, the world is made of atoms, tiny things with
heartknots, and around them lightning motes traveling in concentric
shells. All this at so small a scale it's hard to imagine. Each speck of dust
you sweep up is made of millions of them. There are billions of them in
the tips of your fingers."

She wiggled her grimy hands in the air. "And yet each atom stores a
lot of energy. Truly it is like trapped lightning, this qi energy, you have to
imagine that kind of blazing power. Many trillionqi in every little thing."
She gestured at the big circular mandala painted on one wall, their table
of the elementals, Arabic letters and numerals encrusted with many extra dots. "Inside the heartknot there is a force holding all that energy together, as I told you, a force very strong at very close distances, binding
the lightning power to the heart so tightly it can never be released.
Which is good, because the amounts of energy contained are really very
high. We pulse with it."

"That's how it feels," Budur said.

"Indeed. But look, it's many times beyond what we can feel. The formula proposed, as I told you, is energy equals the mass times the speed
of light squared, and light is very fast indeed. So that with only a little
matter, if any of its energy were released into the world . . ." She shook
her head. "Of course the strong force means that would never happen.
But we continue to investigate this element alactin, which the Travancori physicists call Hand of Tara. I suspect its heartknot is unstable, and
Piali is beginning to agree with me. Clearly it is very full of the jinn, both
yin and yang, in such a fashion that to me it is acting like a droplet of water held together by surface tension, but so big that the surface tension is
just barely holding it, and it stretches out like a water drop in the air, de-
forming this way and that, but held together, just, except for sometimes,
when it stretches too far for surface tension, the strong force in this case,
and then the natural repulsion between the jinn makes a heartknot split
in two, becoming atoms of lead, but releasing some of its bound power
as well, in the form of rays of invisible energy. That's what we are seeing
on the photographic plates you help with. It's quite a bit of energy, and
that's just one heartknot breaking. What we have been wondering—
what we have been forced to consider, given the nature of the phenomenon—is, if we gathered enough of these atoms together, and broke even
one heartknot apart, would the released qi break a lot more of them at

the same time, more and more again—all at the speed of light, in a space this big," holding her hands apart. "If that might not set off a short chain reaction," she said.

"Meaning . . ."

"Meaning a very big explosion!"

For a long time Idelba stared off into the space of pure mathematics, it seemed.

"Don't tell anyone about this," she said again.

"I won't."

"No one."

"All right."

Invisible worlds, full of energy and power: subatomic harems, each pulsing on the edge of a great explosion. Budur sighed as this image came to her. There was no escaping the latent violence at the heart of things. Even the stones were mortal.

9 ❂ Budur got up in the mornings at the zawiyya, helped in the kitchen and office—indeed, there was much that was the same about her work in the zawiyya and at the lab, and though the work felt quite different in each setting, it still had a basic tedium to it; her classes and her walks through the great city became the places to work on her dreams and ideas.

She walked along the harbor and the river, no longer expecting anyone from Turi to show up and take her back to her father's house. Much of the vast city remained unknown to her, but she had her routes through certain districts, and sometimes rode a tram out to its end just to see what kind of neighborhoods it went through. The ocean and river districts were her particular study, which of course gave her a lot to work on. Wan sunlight splintered through clouds galloping on the ocean on-shore wind; she sat at cafés behind the docks, or across the sea road from the strands, reading and writing, and looked up to see whitecaps dashing themselves at the foot of the great lighthouse at the end of the jetty, or up the rocky coast to the north. She walked the beaches. Pale washed blues in the sky behind the tumbling clouds, the bruised blues of the ocean, the whites of cloud and broken wave; she loved the looks of these things, loved them with all her heart. Here she was free to be her whole self. It was worth all the rain to have the air washed so clean.

In one rather shabby and storm-beaten beach district at the end of tram line number six, there was a little Buddhist temple, and one day outside it Budur saw the Hodenosaunee mother and daughter from Kirana's class. They saw her and came over. "Hello," the mother said. "You have come to visit us!"

"Actually I was just wandering around town," Budur said, surprised. "I like this neighborhood."

"I see," the mother said politely, as if she didn't believe her. "I am sorry to have presumed, but we are acquainted with your aunt Idelba, and so I thought you may have been coming here on her behalf. But you don't—well—but would you like to come in?"

"Thank you." Mystified a bit, Budur followed them into the compound, which contained a courtyard garden of shrubs and gravel, arranged around a bell next to a pond. Nuns in dark red dresses walked through on their way somewhere inside. One sat to talk with the Hodenosaunee women, whose names were Hanea and Ganagweh, mother and daughter. They all spoke in Firanjic, with a strong Nsarene accent mixed with something else. Budur listened to them talk about repairs to the roof. Then they invited her to come with them into a room containing a big wireless; Hanea sat before a microphone, and had a conversation in her language that crossed the ocean.

After that they joined a number of nuns in a meditation room, and sat chanting for a time. "So, you are Buddhists?" Budur asked the Hodenosaunee women when the session was over, and they had gone back out into the garden.

"Yes," Hanea said. "It's common among our people. We find it very similar to our old religion. And I think it must also have been true that we liked the way it put us in league with the Japanese from the west side of our country, who are like us in so many other ways. We needed their help against the people from your side."

"I see."

They stopped before a group of women and men who were sitting in a circle chipping away at sandstone blocks, making large flat bricks, it seemed, perfectly shaped and polished. Hanea pointed at them and explained: "These are devotional stones, for the top of Chomolungma. Have you heard of this project?"

"No."

"Well, you know, Chomolungma was the highest mountain in the world, but the top was destroyed by Muslim artillery during the Long War. So, now there is a project started, very slow of course, to replace the top of the mountain. Bricks like these are taken there, and then climbers who ascend Chomolungma carry one brick along with their lifegas canisters, and leave it on the summit for stonemasons to work into the new summit pyramid."

Budur stared at the dressed blocks of stone, smaller than several of the boulders decorating the courtyard garden. She was invited to pick one up, and did so; it was about as heavy as three or four books in her arms.

"It will take a lot of these?"

"Many thousands. It is a very long-term project." Hanea smiled. "A hundred years, a thousand years? It depends on how many climbers there are who want to carry one up the mountain. A considerable mass of stone was blasted away. But a good idea, yes? A symbol of a more general restoration of the world."

They were preparing a meal in the kitchen, and invited Budur to join them, but she excused herself, saying she needed to catch the next tram back.

"Of course," said Hanea. "Do give our greetings to your aunt. We look forward to meeting with her soon."

She didn't explain what she meant, and Budur was left to think it over as she walked down to the beach stop and waited for the tram into town, huddling in its little glass shelter against the stiff blast of the wind. Half-asleep, she saw an image of a line of people, carrying a whole library of stone books to the top of the world.

10 ✸ "Come with me to the Orkneys," Idelba said to her. "I could use your help, and want to show you the ruins there."

"The Orkneys? Where are they again?"

It turned out they were the northernmost of the Keltic Isles, above Scotland. Most of Britain was occupied by a population that had originated in al-Andalus, the Maghrib and west Africa; then during the Long War the Hodenosaunee had built a big naval base in a bay surrounded by the main Orkney island, and they were still there, overseeing Firanja in effect, but also protecting by their presence some remnants of the original population, Kelts who had survived the influx of both Frank and Firanji, and of course the plague. Budur had read tales of these tall, pale-skinned, red-haired, blue-eyed survivors of the great plague; and as she and Idelba sat at a window table in the gondola of their airship, watching England's green hills pass slowly underneath them, dappled by cloud shadow and cut into large squares by crops, hedgerows, and gray stone walls, she wondered what it would be like to stand before a true Kelt— whether she would be able to bear their mute accusatory gaze, stand without flinching before the sight of their albinoesque skin and eyes.

But of course it was not like that at all. They landed to find the Orkney Islands were more rolling grassy hills, with scarcely a tree to be seen, except clustered around whitewashed farmhouses with chimneys at both ends, a design ubiquitous and apparently ancient, as it was repli-cated in gray ruins in fields near the current versions. And the Orcadians were not the spavined freckled inbred half-wits Budur had been expect-ing from the tales of the white slaves of the Ottoman sultan, but burly shouting fishermen in oils, red faced and straw haired in some cases, black or brown haired in others, shouting at each other like fisherfolk in any of the villages of the Nsarene coast. They were unselfconscious in their dealings with Firanjis, as if they were the normal ones and the Fi-ranjis the exotics; which of course was true here. Clearly for them the Orkneys were all the world.

And when Budur and Idelba drove out into the country in a motor-cart to see the island's ruins, they began to see why; the world had been coming to the Orkneys for three thousand years or more. They had rea-son to feel they were at the center of things, the crossroads. Every culture that had ever lived there, and there must have been ten of them through the centuries, had built using the island's stratified sandstone, which had been split by the waves into handy plates and beams and broad flat bricks, perfect for drywall, and even stronger if set in cement. The oldest inhabitants had also used the stones to build their bedframes and kitchen shelves, so that here, in a small patch of grass overlooking the western sea, it was possible to look down into stone houses that had had the sand filling them removed, and see the domestic arrangements of people who had lived over five thousand years before, it was said, their very tools and furniture just as they had been left. The sunken rooms looked to Budur just like her own rooms in the zawiyya. Nothing essen-tial had changed in all that time.

Idelba shook her head at the great ages claimed for the settlement, and the dating methods used, and wondered aloud about certain geochronologies she had in mind that might be pursued. But after a while she fell as silent as the rest, and stood staring down into the spare and beautiful interiors of the old ones' homes. These things of ours that endure.

Back in the island's one town, Kirkwall, they walked through stone-paved streets to another little Buddhist temple complex, set behind the locals' ancient cathedral, a tiny thing compared to the big skeletons left behind on the mainland, but roofed and complete. The temple behind it was very modest, a matter of four narrow buildings surrounding a rock garden, in a style Budur thought of as Chinese.

Here Idelba was greeted by Hanea and Ganagweh. Budur was shocked to see them, and they laughed at the expression on her face. "We told you we would be seeing you again soon, didn't we?"

"Yes," Budur said. "But here?"

"This is the biggest Hodenosaunee community in Firanja," Hanea said. "We came down to Nsara from here, actually. And we return here quite often."

After they were shown the complex and sat down in a room off the courtyard for tea, Idelba and Hanea slipped away, leaving a nonplussed Budur behind with Ganagweh.

"Mother said they would need to talk for an hour or two," Ganagweh told her. "Do you know what they're talking about?"

"No," said Budur. "Do you?"

"No. I mean, I assume it has something to do with your aunt's efforts to create stronger diplomatic relations between our countries. But that's just stating the obvious."

"Yes," Budur said, extemporizing. "I know she's been interested in that. But meeting you in Kirana Fawwaz's class as I did . . ."

"Yes. And then the way you showed up at the monastery there. It seems we are fated to cross paths." She was smiling in a way Budur couldn't interpret. "Let's go for a walk, those two will talk for a long while. There's a lot to discuss, after all."

This was news to Budur, but she said nothing, and spent the day wandering Kirkwall with Ganagweh, a very high-spirited girl, tall, quick, confident; the narrow streets and burly men of the Orkneys held no fears for her. Indeed at the end of the town tram line they walked far down a deserted strand overlooking the big bay that had once been such a busy naval base, and Ganagweh stopped at some boulders and stripped off her clothes and ran screaming out into the water, bursting back out in a flurry of whitewater, shrieking, her lustrous dark skin gleaming in the sun as she dried off with her fingers, flinging the water at Budur and daring her to take the plunge. "It's good for you! It's not that cold, it will wake you up!"

It was just the kind of thing Yasmina had always insisted they do, but shyly Budur declined, finding it hard to look at the big wet beautiful animal standing next to her in the sun; and when she walked down to touch the water, she was glad she had; it was freezing. She did feel as if she had woken up, aware of the brisk salt wind and Ganagweh's wet black hair swinging side to side like a dog's, spraying her. Ganagweh laughed at her and dressed while still damp. As they walked back, they passed a group of pale-skinned children who regarded them curiously. "Let's get back and see how the old women are doing," Ganagweh said. "Funny to see such grandmothers taking the fate of the world into their own hands, isn't it?"

"Yes," Budur said, wondering what in the world was going on.

11 ✸ On the flight back to Nsara, Budur asked Idelba about it, but Idelba shook her head. She didn't want to talk about it, and was busy writing in her notebook. "Later," she said.

Back in Nsara, Budur worked and studied. At Kirana's suggestion she read about southeast Asia, and learned how the Hindu, Buddhist, and Islamic cultures had mixed there to make a vibrant new offspring, which had survived the war and was now using the great botanical and mineral riches of Burma and the Malay peninsula, and Sumatra and Java and Borneo and Mindanao, to create a group of peoples united against China's centripetal power, freeing itself from Chinese influence. They had spread into Aozhou, the big burnt island continent south of them, and even across the oceans to Inka, and in the other direction to Madagascar and south Africa: it was a kind of emerging southern world culture, with the huge cities of Pyinkayaing, Jakarta, and Kwinana on the west coast of Aozhou leading the way, trading with Travancore, and building like maniacs, erecting cities that included many steel skyscrapers more than a hundred floors tall. The war had damaged but not destroyed these cities, and now the governments of the world met in Pyinkayaing whenever they tried to work out some more durable and just postwar dispensation.

There were more meetings all the time, as the situation became more and more deranged; anything to keep war from returning, as so very little had been resolved by it. Or so the members of the defeated alliance felt. It was unclear at this point if the Chinese and their allies, or the countries of Yingzhou, who had entered the conflict so much later than the rest, had any interest in accommodating Islamic concerns. Kirana remarked casually in class one day that it was very possible Islam was in the trash bin of history without yet knowing it; and the more Budur read of her books, the less sure she could be that this was necessarily a bad thing for the world. Old religions died; and if an empire tried to conquer the world and failed, it generally then disappeared.

Kirana's own writing made that very clear. Budur took out her books from the monastery library, some published nearly twenty years before, during the war itself when Kirana had to have been quite young, and she read them with close interest, hearing Kirana's voice in her head for every sentence; it was just like a transcript of her talking, except even more long-winded. She had written on many subjects, both theoretical and practical. Whole books of her African writings were concerned with various public health and women's issues. Budur opened randomly, and found herself reading a lecture that had been given to midwives in the Sudan.

> If the parents of the girl insist, if they cannot be talked out of it, it is extremely important that only one-third of the clitoris should be cut off, and two thirds left intact. Someone who practically attacks a girl with a knife, cutting off everything, this goes against the words of the Prophet. Men and women are meant to be equal before God. But if a woman's entire clitoris is cut off it leaves her a kind of eunuch, she becomes cold, lazy, without desire, without interest, humorless, like a mud wall, a piece of cardboard, without spark, without goals, without desire, like a puddle of standing water, lifeless, her children are unhappy, her husband is unhappy, she makes nothing of her life. Those of you who must perform

circumcisions, therefore remember: cut off one third, leave two thirds! Cut off one third, leave two thirds!

Budur flipped the pages of the book, disturbed. After a while she collected herself, and read the new page that presented itself:

I was privileged to witness the return of Raiza Tarami from her trip to the New World, where she had attended the conference at Yingzhou's Long Island on women's issues, just after the end of the war. Conference members who came from throughout the world were greatly surprised to see this Nsarene woman exhibiting a full awareness of all the issues that mattered. They had been expecting a backward woman living behind the walls of the harem, ignorant and veiled. But Raiza was not like that, she stood on the same footing as her sisters from China, Burma, Yingzhou and Travancore, indeed she had been forced by conditions at home to explore theoretically far in advance of most.

So she represented us well, and when she returned to Firanja, she had come to believe that the veil was the biggest obstacle in the way of the progress of the Muslim woman, as standing for general complicity in the whole system. The veil had to fall if the reactionary system were to fall. And so, upon her arrival on the docks of Nsara, she met her companions from the women's institute, and she stood before them with her face unveiled. Her immediate companions had removed their veils as well. Around us the signs of disapproval became apparent in the crowd, shouting and jostling and the like. Then women in the crowd began to support the unveiled, by removing the veils from their own faces and throwing them to the ground. It was a beautiful moment. After that the veil started to disappear in Nsara with great speed. In just a few years unveiling had spread throughout the country, and that brick in the wall of the reactionaries had been removed. Nsara became known as the leader of Firanja because of this action. This I was lucky enough to witness with my own eyes.

Budur took a breath, marking the passage as something she would read to her blind soldiers. And as the weeks passed she read on, working her way through several volumes of Kirana's essays and lectures, an exhausting experience, for Kirana never hesitated to attack head-on and at length everything that she disliked. And yet how she had lived! Budur found herself ashamed of her cloistered childhood and youth, the fact that she was twenty-three, now almost twenty-four, and had not yet done anything; by the time Kirana Fawwaz was that age she had already spent years in Africa, fighting in the war and working in hospitals. There was so much lost time to be made up!

Budur also read in many books Kirana had not assigned, concentrating for a while on the Sino-Muslim cultures that had existed in central Asia, how they had attempted for a number of centuries to reconcile the two cultures: the books' bad old photographs showed these people, Chinese in appearance, Muslim in belief, Chinese in language, Muslim in law; it was hard to imagine such a mongrel people had ever existed. The Chinese had killed the greater part of them in the war, and dispersed the rest across the Dahai to the deserts and jungles of Yingzhou and Inka, where they worked in mines and on plantations, in effect slaves, though the Chinese claimed no longer to practice slavery, calling it a Muslim atavism. Whatever they called it, the Muslims in their northwest provinces were gone. And it could happen everywhere.

It began to seem to Budur there was no part of history she could read that was not depressing, disgusting, frightening, horrible; unless it be the New World's, where the Hodenosaunee and the Dinei had organized a civilization capable, just barely, of resisting the Chinese to their west and the Firanjis to their east. Except even there, diseases and plagues had wrought such havoc on them in the twelfth and thirteenth centuries that they had been reduced to a rather small populace, hiding in the center of their island. Nevertheless, small in number though they were, they had persevered, and adapted. They had remained somewhat open to foreign influences, tying everything they could into their leagues, becoming Buddhists, allying themselves with the Travancori League on the other side of the world, which indeed they had helped to form by their example; advancing from strength to strength, in short, even when hidden deep in their wild fastness, far from both coasts and from the Old World generally. Maybe that had helped. Taking what they could use, fighting off the rest. A place where women had always had power. And now that the Long War had shattered the Old World, they had become a sudden new giant across the seas, represented here by tall handsome people like Hanea and Ganagweh, walking the streets of Nsara in long fur or oilskin coats, butchering Firanjic with friendly dignity. Kirana had not written much about them, as far as Budur could find; but Idelba was dealing with them, in some mysterious fashion that began to involve packages, now, that Budur helped take on the tram up to Hanea and Ganagweh's temple on the north coast. Four times she did this for Idelba without asking what it was for, and Idelba did not offer much explanation. Again, as in Turi, it seemed to Budur that Idelba knew things the rest of them did not. It was a very complicated life Idelba was living. Men at the gate, some of them pining for her romantically, one pounding on the locked door shouting, "Idelbaaa, I love you, pleeease!" and drunkenly singing in a language Budur didn't recognize while punishing a guitar, Idelba meanwhile disappearing into their room and an hour later pretending nothing had occurred; then again, gone days at a time, and back, brow deeply furrowed, sometimes happy, sometimes agitated . . . a very complicated life. And yet more than half in secrecy.

12 ✺ "Yes," Kirana said once to Budur in response to a question about the Hodenosaunee, looking at a group of them passing the café they were sitting in that day, "they may be the hope of all humanity. But I don't think we understand them well enough to say for sure. When they have completed their takeover of the world, then we will learn more."

"Studying history has made you cynical," Budur noted. Kirana's knee was pressed against hers again. Budur let her do it without ever responding one way or the other. "Or, to put it more accurately, what you have seen in your travels and teaching have made you a pessimist." To be fair.

"Not at all," Kirana said, lighting a cigarette. She gestured at it and said parenthetically, "You see how they already have us enslaved to their weed. Anyway, I am not a pessimist. A realist only. Full of hope, ha ha. But you can see the odds if you dare to look." She grimaced and took a long drag on the cigarette. "Sorry—cramps. Ha. History till now has been like women's periods, a little egg of possibility, hidden in the ordinary material of life, with tiny barbarian hordes maybe charging in, trying to find it, failing, fighting each other—finally a bloody mess ends that chance, and everything has to start all over."

Budur laughed, shocked and amused. It was not a thought that had ever occurred to her.

Kirana smiled slyly, seeing this. "The red egg," she said. "Blood and life." Her knee pressed hard on Budur's. "The question is, will the hordes of sperm ever find the egg? Will one slip ahead, fructify the seed within, and the world become pregnant? Will a true civilization ever be born? Or is history doomed always to be a sterile spinster!"

They laughed together, Budur uncomfortable in several different ways. "It has to pick the right partner," she ventured.

"Yes," Kirana said with her sly emphasis, the corners of her mouth lifted just the tiniest bit. "The Martians, perhaps."

Budur recalled cousin Yasmina's "practice kissing." Women loving women; making love to women; it was common in the zawiyya, and presumably elsewhere; there were, after all, many more women than men in Nsara, as in the whole world. One saw hardly any men in their thirties or forties on the streets or in the cafés of Nsara, and the few one did see often seemed haunted or furtive, lost in an opium haze, aware they had somehow escaped a fate. No—that whole generation had been wiped out. And so one saw everywhere women in couples, hand in hand, living together in walk-ups or zawiyyas. More than once Budur had heard them in her own zawiyya, in the baths or bedrooms, or walking down the halls late at night. It was simply part of life, no matter what anyone said. And she had once or twice taken part in Yasmina's games in the harem, Yasmina would read aloud from her romance novels and listen to her wireless shows, the plaintive songs flying in from Venezia, and afterward she would walk around their courtyard singing at the moon, wishing to have a man spying on her in these moments, or leaping over the wall and taking her in his arms, but there were no men around to do it. Let's practice how it would be, she would mutter huskily in Budur's ear, so we will know what to do—she always said the same thing—and then she would kiss Budur passionately on the mouth, and press herself against her, and after Budur got over the surprise of it she felt the passion passed into her mouth by a kind of qi transference, and she kissed back thinking, Will the real thing ever make my pulse beat this hard? Could it?

And cousin Rima was even more skillful, though less passionate, than Yasmina, as like Idelba she had once been married, and later lived in a zawiyya in Roma, and she would observe them and say coolly, no, like this, straddle the leg of the man you are kissing, press your pubic bone hard against his thigh, it will drive him completely crazy, it makes a full circuit then, the qi circles around in the two of you like in a dynamo. And when they tried it they found it was true. After such a moment Yasmina would be pink cheeked, would cry unconvincingly, Oh we're bad, we're bad, and Rima would snort and say, It's like this in every harem there has ever been in the world. That's how stupid men are. That's how the world has gotten on.

Now, in the dregs of the night in this Nsarene café, Budur pressed back slightly against Kirana's knee, in a knowing manner, friendly but neutral. For now, she kept arranging always to leave with some of the other students, not meeting Kirana's eye when it counted—stringing her along, perhaps, because she was not sure what it would mean to her studies or to her life more generally, if she were to respond more positively and fall into it, whatever it might be, beyond the kissing and fondling. Sex she knew about, that would be the straightforward part; but what about the rest of it? She was not sure she wanted to get involved with this intense older woman, her teacher, still in some senses a stranger. But until you took the plunge, did not everyone remain a stranger forever?

13 ❋ They stood together, Budur and Kirana, at a garden party on a crowded patio overlooking the Liwaya River before it opened into its estuary, their upper arms just barely touching, as if by accident, as if the crush around the wealthy patron of the arts and philosopher Tahar Labid was so great that they had to do it to catch the beautiful pearls dropping from his lips; although in truth he was a terrible and obvious blowhard, a man who said your name over and over in conversation, almost every time he addressed you, so that it became very off-putting, as if he were trying to take you over, or simply to remember in his solipsism who he was talking to, never noticing that it made people want to escape him at all costs.

After a bit of this Kirana shuddered, at his self-absorption perhaps, too like hers to make her at all comfortable, and she led Budur away. She lifted Budur's hand, all bleached and cracked from her constant cleaning, and said, "You should wear rubber gloves. I should think they would make you at the lab."

"They do. I do wear them. But sometimes they make it hard to hold on to things."

"Nevertheless."

This gruff concern for the health of her hands, from the great intellectual, the teacher—suddenly surrounded by an audience of her own, asking her what she thought of certain Chinese feminists . . . Budur watched her reply immediately and at length about their origins among Muslim Chinese, particularly Kang Tongbi, who, with the encouragement of her husband the Sino-Muslim scholar Ibrahim al-Lanzhou, set out the theoretical groundwork for a feminism later elaborated in the Chinese heartland by generations of late Qing women—much of their progress contested by the imperial bureaucracy, of course—until the Long War dissolved all previous codes of conduct in the pure rationality of total war, and women's brigades and factory crews established a position in the world that could never be retracted, no matter how hard the Chinese bureacrats tried. Kirana could recite by memory the wartime list of demands made by the Chinese Women's Industrial Workers Council, and now she did just that: "Equal rights for men and women, spread of women's education and facilities for it, improvement in position of women in the home, monogamy, freedom of marriage, encouragement of careers, a ban on concubines and the buying and selling of women, and on physical mutilation, improved political position, reform of prostitution." It was a most strange-sounding song, or chant, or prayer.

"But you see, the Chinese feminists claimed women had it better in Yingzhou and Travancore, and in Travancore the feminists claimed to have learned it from the Sikhs, who learned it from the Quran. And here we focus on the Chinese. So that you see it has been a matter of pulling ourselves up by our bootstraps, each imagining that it is better in a different country, and that we should fight to equal the others . . ." On she talked, weaving the last three centuries together most brilliantly, and all the while Budur clenched her cracked white hands, thinking, She wants you, she wants your hands healthy because if she has her way, they will be touching her.

Budur wandered away on her own, disturbed, saw Hasan on another terrace and went up to join the group around him, which included Naser Shah and the ancient grandmother from Kirana's class, looking at loose ends without her knitting kit in hand. It turned out they were brother and sister, and she the hostess of this party: Zainab Shah, very curt when Budur was finally introduced; and Hasan a longtime family friend of theirs. They had all known Kirana for years, and had taken her classes before, Budur learned from Naser as the conversations swirled around them.

"What bothers me is to see how repetitive and small-minded he could be, what a lawyer—"

"That's why it works in application—"

"Works for who? He was the lawyer of the clerics."

"No writer, anyway."

"The Quran is meant to be spoken and heard, in Arabic it is like music, he is such a poet. You must hear it in the mosque."

"I will not go there. That's for people who want to be able to say, 'I am better than you, simply because I assert a belief in Allah.' I reject that. The world is my mosque."

"Religion is like a house of cards. One fingertap of fact and it all falls over."

"Clever but not true, like most of your aphorisms."

Budur left Naser and Hasan, and went to a long table containing snacks and glasses of red and white wine, eavesdropping as she walked, eating pickled herrings on crackers.

"I hear the council of ministers had to kowtow to the army to keep them out of the treasury, so it comes to the same thing in the end—"

"—the six lokas are names for the parts of the brain that perform the different kinds of mentation. The level of beasts is the cerebellum, the level of hungry ghosts the limbic archipelago, the human realm the speech lobes, the realm of the asuras is the frontal cortex, and the realm of the gods is the bridge between the two halves of the brain, which when activated gives us glimpses of a higher reality. It's impressive, really, sorting things out that clearly by pure introspection—"

"But that's only five, what about hell?"

"Hell is other people."

"—I'm sure it doesn't add up to quite as many partners as that."

"They've got control of the oceans, so they can come to us whenever they want, but we can't go to them without their permission. So—"

"So we should thank our lucky stars. We want the generals to feel as weak as possible."

"True, but nothing in excess. We may find it becomes a case of from the coffeepot to the fire."

"—it's well established that a belief in reincarnation floats around the world from one culture to the next, migrating to the cultures most stressed."

"Maybe it migrates with the few souls who are actually transmigrating, ever think of that?"

"—with student after student, it's like a kind of compulsion. A replacement for friends or something like that. Sad really, but the students are really the ones who suffer, so it's hard to feel too sorry—"

"All history would have been different, if only . . ."

"Yes, if only? Only what?"

"If only we had conquered Yingzhou when we had the chance."

"He's a true artist, it's not so easy working in scents, everyone has their own associations, but somehow he touches all the deepest ones everyone has, and as it's the sense most tied to memory, he really has an effect. That shift from vanilla to cordite to jasmine, those are just the dominant scents, of course, each waft is a mix of scores of them, I think, but what a progression, heartrending I assure you . . ."

Near the drinks table a friend of Hasan's, named Tristan, played an oud with a strange tuning, strumming simple chords over and over, and singing in one of the old Frankish languages. Budur sipped a glass of white wine and watched him play, forcing the voices talking around her from her attention. The man's music was interesting, the level tones of his voice hanging steadily in the air. His black moustache curved over his mouth. He caught Budur's eye, smiled briefly. The song came to an end and there was a patter of applause, and some of them surrounded him to ask questions. Budur moved in to hear his answers. Hasan joined them, and so Budur stood beside him. Tristan explained in clipped short phrases, as if he were shy. He didn't want to talk about his music. Budur liked the look of him. The songs were from France and Navarre, he said, and Provence. Third and fourth centuries. People asked for more, but he shrugged and put his oud in its case. He didn't explain, but Budur thought the crowd was simply too loud. Tahar was approaching the drinks table, and his group came with him.

"But I tell you, Vika, what happens is this—"

"—it all goes back to Samarqand, when there was still—"

"It would have to be beautiful and hard, make people ashamed."

"That was the day, the very hour when it all started—"

"You, Vika, are perhaps afflicted with intermittent deafness."

"But here's the thing—"

Budur slipped away from the group, and then, feeling tired of the party and its guests, she left the party as well. She read the schedule posted at the tram stop and saw that it would be almost half a watch before another came, so she took off walking on the river path. By the time she reached the city center she was enjoying walking just for itself, and she continued on out the jetty, through the fish shops and out into the wind, where the jetty became an asphalt road cracking over huge boulders that stood greenly out of the oil-slicked water slurping against their sides. She watched the clouds and the sky, and felt suddenly happy—an emotion like a child inside her, a happiness in which worry was a vague and distant thing, no more than a cloud's shadow on the dark blue surface of the sea. To think her life might have passed without her ever seeing the ocean!

14 ✸ Idelba came to her one night in the zawiyya and said, "Budur, you must remember never to tell anyone what I said to you about alactin. About what splitting it could mean."

"Of course not. But why do you mention it?"

"Well . . . we are beginning to feel that there is some kind of surveillance being placed on us. Apparently from a part of the government, some security department. It's a bit murky. But anyway, best to be very careful."

"Why don't you go to the police?"

"Well." She refrained from rolling her eyes, Budur could see it. Voice lowered to a gentleness: "The police are part of the army. That's from the war, and it never changed. So . . . we prefer not to draw any attention whatsoever to the issues involved."

Budur gestured around them. "Surely we have nothing to worry about here, though. No woman in a zawiyya would ever betray a housemate, not to the army."

Idelba stared at her to see if she was being serious. "Don't be naïve," she said finally, less gently, and with a pat on the knee got up to go to the bathroom.

This was not the only cloud to come at this time and drop its shadow on Budur's happiness. Throughout Dar al-Islam, unrest was filling the newspapers, and inflation was universal. Military takeovers of the governments in Skandistan and Moldava and al-Alemand and the Tyrol, very close to Turi, alarmed the rest of the world all out of proportion to their puny size, as seeming to indicate a resurgence of Muslim aggressivity. The whole of Islam was accused of breaking the commitments forced on them at the Shanghai Conference after the war, as if Islam were a monolithic block, a laughable concept even in the depths of the war itself. Sanctions and even embargoes were being called for in China and India and Yingzhou. The effect of the threat alone was felt immediately in Firanja: the price of rice shot up, then the price of potatoes and maple syrup, and coffee beans. Hoarding quickly followed, old wartime habits kicking in, and even as prices rose staples were cleared off the shelves of the groceries the moment they appeared. This affected everything else as well, both food and other matters. Hoarding was a very contagious phenomenon, a bad mentality, a loss of faith in the system's ability to keep everything running; and as the system had indeed broken down so disastrously at the end of the war, a lot of people were prone to hoard at the first hint of a scare. Making meals in the zawiyya became an exercise in ingenuity. They often dined on potato soup, spiced or garnished in one way or another so that it remained tasty, but it sometimes had to be watered pretty thin to get a cup of it into everyone at the table.

Café life went on as gaily as ever, at least on the surface. There was perhaps more of an edge in people's voices; eyes were brighter, the laughs harder, the binges more drunken. Opium, too, became subject to hoarding. People came in with wheelbarrows of paper money, or exhibited five trillion drachma bills from Roma, laughing as they offered them in exchange for cups of coffee and were refused. It wasn't very funny in all truth; every week things were markedly more expensive, and there didn't seem to be anything to be done about it. They laughed at their own helplessness. Budur went to the cafés less often, which saved money, and the risk of an awkward moment with Kirana. Sometimes she went with Idelba's nephew Piali to a different set of cafés, with a seedier clientele; Piali and his associates, who sometimes included Hasan and his friend Tristan, seemed to like the rougher establishments frequented by sailors and longshoremen. So through a winter of thick mists that hung in the streets like rain freed of gravity, Budur sat and listened to tales of Yingzhou and the stormy Atlantic, deadliest of all the seas.

"We exist on sufferance," Zainab Shah said bitterly as she knitted in their regular café. "We're like the Japanese after the Chinese conquered them."

"Let the occasional chalice break," Kirana murmured. Her expression in the dim light was serene, indomitable.

"They have all broken," Naser said. He sat in the corner, looking out the window at the rain. He tapped his cigarette on the ashtray. "I can't say I'm sorry."

"In Iran too they don't seem to care." Kirana appeared to be trying to cheer him up. "They are making very great strides there, leading the way in all kinds of fields. Linguistics, archaeology, the physical sciences, they have all the leading people."

Naser nodded, looking inward. Budur had gathered that his fortune had gone to fund many of these efforts, from an exile of some unexplained sort. Another complicated life.

Another downpour struck. The weather seemed to enunciate their situation, wind and rain slapping the Café Sultana's big windows and running across the plate glass wildly, pushed this way and that by gusts of wind. The old soldier watched his smoke rise, twined threads of brown and gray, oxbowing more and more as they rose. Piali had once described the dynamics of this lazy ascent, as he had the rain's deltas down the windowpanes. Storm sunlight cast a silver sheen on the wet street. Budur felt happy. The world was beautiful. She was so hungry that the milk in her coffee was like a meal inside her. The storm's light was a meal. She thought: now is beautiful. These old Persians are beautiful; their Persian accents are beautiful. Kirana's rare serenity is beautiful. Throw away the past and the future. The old Persians' Khayyam had understood this, one reason among many that the mullahs had never liked him.

> Come fill the cup and in the blaze of spring
> The winter garment of repentance fling:
> The bird of time has but a little way
> To fly—and hey! The bird is on the wing!

The others left, and Budur sat with Kirana, watching her write something down in her brown-backed notebook. She looked up, happy to see Budur watching her. She stopped for a cigarette, and they talked for a while, about Yingzhou and the Hodenosaunee. As usual, Kirana's thoughts took interesting turns. She thought the very early stage of civilization that the Hodenosaunee had been in when discovered by the Old World was what had allowed them to survive, counterintuitive though that was. They had been canny hunter-gatherers, more intelligent as individuals than the people of more developed cultures, and much more flexible than the Inka, who were shackled by a very rigid theocracy. If it weren't for their susceptibility to Old World diseases, the Hodenosaunee no doubt would have conquered the Old World already. Now they were making up for lost time.

They talked about Nsara, the army and the clerics, the madressa and the monastery. Budur's girlhood. Kirana's time in Africa.

When the café closed Budur went with her to Kirana's zawiyya, which had a little study garret with a door that was often closed, and on a couch in there they lay on each other kissing, rolling from one embrace to the next, Kirana clasping her so hard that Budur thought her ribs might break; and they were tested again when her stomach clamped down on a violent orgasm.

Afterward Kirana held her with her usual sly smile, calmer than ever.

"Your turn."

"I already came, I was rubbing myself on your shin."

"There are softer ways than that."

"No, really, I'm fine. I'm already done for." And Budur realized with a shock she could not keep out of her eyes that Kirana was not going to let her touch her.

15 ❋ After that Budur went to class feeling strange. In class and in the cafés afterward, Kirana acted toward her just as she always had, a matter of propriety no doubt; but Budur found it off-putting, also sad. In the cafés she sat on the other side of the table from Kirana, not often meeting her eye. Kirana accepted this, and joined the flow of conversation on her side of the table, discoursing in her usual manner, which now struck

Budur as a bit forced, even overbearing, although it was no more ver-
bose than ever.

Budur turned to Hasan, who was describing a trip to the Sugar Islands, between Yingzhou and Inka, where he planned to smoke opium
every day and lie on white beaches or in the turquoise water off their
shores, warm as a bath. "Wouldn't that be grand?" Hasan asked.

"In my next life," Budur suggested.

"Your next life." Hasan snorted, bloodshot eye regarding her sardon-
ically. "So pretty to think so."

"You never know," Budur said.

"Right. Maybe we should take a trip out to see Madame Sururi, and
you can see who you were in your past lives. Talk to your loved ones in
the bardo. Half the widows of Nsara are doing it, I'm sure it's quite comforting. If you could believe it." He gestured out the plate glass, where
people in black coats passed in the street, hunched under their umbrellas. "It's silly, though. Most people don't even live the one life they've
got."

One life. It was an idea Budur had trouble accepting, even though the
sciences and everything else had made it clear that one life was all you
had. When Budur was a girl her mother had said, Be good or you'll come
back as a snail. At funerals they said a prayer for the next existence of the
deceased, asking Allah to give him or her a chance to improve. Now all
that was dismissed, with all the rest of the afterlives, heaven and hell,
God himself—all that claptrap, all the supersitions of earlier generations
in their immense ignorance, concocting myths to make sense of things.
Now they lived in a material world, evolved to what it was by chance and
the laws of physics; they struggled through one life and died; that was
what the scientists had revealed by their studies, and there was nothing
Budur had ever seen or experienced that seemed to indicate otherwise.
No doubt it was true. That was reality; they had to adjust to it, or live in a
delusion. Adjust each to his or her own cosmic solitude, to Nakba, to
hunger and worry, coffee and opium, the knowledge of an end.

"Did I hear you say we should visit Madame Sururi?" Kirana asked
from across the table. "A good idea! Let's do it. It would be like a historical field trip for the class—like visiting a place where people still live as
they did for hundreds of years."

"From all I've heard she's an entertaining old charlatan."

"A friend of mine visited her and said it was great fun."

They had spent too many hours sitting there, looking at the same ashtrays and coffee rings on the tabletops, the same rain deltas on the windows. So they gathered up their coats and umbrellas, and took the number four tram upriver to a meager neighborhood of apartments abutting the older shipyards, the buildings displaying small Maghribi shops at each corner. Between a seamstress's workshop and a laundry hid a little walk-up to rooms over the shops below. The door opened to their knock, and they were invited in to an entryway, and then, farther in, to a dark room filled with couches and small tables, obviously the converted living room of a fairly large old apartment.

Eight or ten women and three old men were sitting on chairs, facing a black-haired woman who was younger than Budur had expected but not all that young, a woman who wore Zotti clothing, heavy kohl and lipstick, and a great deal of cheap glass jewelry. She had been speaking to her devotees in a low intent voice, and now she paused, and gestured to empty chairs at the back of the room without saying anything to the new arrivals.

"Each time the soul descends into a body," she resumed when they were seated, "it is like a divine soldier, entering into the battlefield of life and fighting ignorance and evil-doing. It tries to reveal its own inner divinity and establish the divine truth on Earth, according to its capacity. Then at the end of its journey in that incarnation, it returns to its own region of the bardo. I can talk to that region when conditions are right."

"How long will a soul spend there before coming back again?" one of the women in her audience asked.

"This varies depending on conditions," Madame Sururi replied. "There is no single process for the evolution of higher souls. Some began from the mineral and some from the animal kingdom. Sometimes it starts from the other end, and cosmic gods take on human form directly." She nodded as if personally familiar with this phenomenon. "There are many different ways."

"So it's true that we may have been animals in a previous reincarnation?"

"Yes, it is possible. In the evolution of our souls we have been all things, including rocks and plants. It is not possible to change too much between any two reincarnations, of course. But over many incarnations, great changes can be made. The Lord Buddha revealed that he had been a goat in a previous life, for instance. But because he had realized God, this was not important."

Kirana stifled a little snort, shifted on her chair to cover it.

Madame Sururi ignored her: "It was easy for him to see what he had been in the past. Some of us are given that kind of vision. But he knew that the past was not important. Our goal is not behind us, it is ahead of us. To a spiritual person I always say, the past is dust. I say this because the past has not given us what we want. What we want is God-realization, and contact with our loved ones, and that depends entirely on our inner cry. We must say, 'I have no past. I am beginning here and now, with God's grace and my own aspiration.' "

There was not much to object to in that, Budur thought; it cut strangely to the heart, given the source; but she could feel skepticism emanating from Kirana like heat, indeed the room seemed to be warming with it, as if a qi-burning space heater had been placed on the floor and turned on high. Perhaps it was a function of Budur's embarrassment. She reached over and squeezed Kirana's hand. It seemed to her that the seer was more interesting than Kirana's fidgets were allowing.

An elderly widow, still wearing one of the pins given to them in the middle decades of the war, said, "When a soul picks a new body to enter, does it already know what kind of life it will have?"

"It can only see possibilities. God knows everything, but He covers up the future. Even God does not use His ultimate vision all the time. Otherwise, there would be no game."

Kirana's mouth opened round as a zero, almost as if she were going to speak, and Budur elbowed her.

"Does the soul lose the details of its previous experiences, or does it remember?"

"The soul doesn't need to remember those things. It would be like remembering what you ate today, or what a disciple's cooking was like. If I know that the disciple was very kind to me, that she brought me food, then that is enough. I don't need to know the details of the meals. Just the impression of the service. This is what the soul remembers."

"Sometimes, my—my friend and I meditate by looking into each other's eyes, and when we do, sometimes we see each other's faces change. Even our hair changes color. I was wondering what this means."

"It means you are seeing past incarnations. But this is not at all advisable. Suppose you see that three or four incarnations ago you were a fierce tiger? What good would this do you? The past is dust, I tell you."

"Did any of your disciples—did any of us know each other in our past incarnations?"

"Yes. We travel in groups, we keep running into each other. There are two disciples here, for instance, who are close friends in this incarnation. When I was meditating on them, I saw that they were physical sisters in their previous incarnation, and very close to each other. And in the incarnation before that, they were mother and son. This is how it happens. Nothing can eclipse my third eye's vision. When you have established a true spiritual bond, then that feeling can never truly disappear."

"Can you tell us—can you tell us who we were before? Or who among us had this bond?"

"Outwardly I have not personally told these two, but those who are my real disciples I have told inwardly, and so they know it inside themselves already. My real disciples—those whom I have taken as my very own, and who have taken me—they are going to be fulfilled and realized in this incarnation, or in their next incarnation, or in very few incarnations. Some disciples may take twenty incarnations or more, because of their very poor start. Some who have come to me in their first or second human incarnation may take hundreds of incarnations more to reach their goal. The first or second incarnation is still a half-animal incarnation, most of the time. The animal is still there as a predominating factor, so how can they achieve God-realization? Even in the Nsara Center for Spiritual Development, right here among us, there are many disciples who have had only six or seven incarnations, and on the streets of the city I see Africans, or other people from across the sea, who are very clearly more animal than human. What can a guru do with such souls? With these people a guru can only do so much."

"Can you . . . can you put us in communication with souls who have passed over? Now? Is it time yet?"

Madame Sururi returned her questioner's gaze, level and calm. "They are speaking to you already, are they not? We cannot bring them forth in front of everyone tonight. The spirits do not like to be so exposed. And we have guests that they are not yet used to. And I am tired. You have seen how draining it is to speak aloud in this world the things they are saying in our minds. Let's retire to the dining room now, and enjoy the offerings you have brought. We will eat knowing that our loved ones speak to us in our minds."

The visitors from the café decided by glance to leave while the others were retiring to the next room, before they began to commit the crime of taking others' food without believing in their religion. They made small coin offerings to the seer, who accepted them with dignity, ignoring the tenor of Kirana's look, staring back at Kirana without guilt or complicity.

The next tram wasn't due for another half watch, and so the group walked back through the industrial district and down the riverside, reenacting choice bits of the interview and staggering with laughter. Kirana for one could not stop laughing, howling it out over the river: "My third eye sees all! But I can't tell you right now! What unbelievable crap!"

"I've already told you what you want to know with my inner voice, now let's eat!"

"Some of my disciples were sisters in previous lives, sister goats in actual fact, but you can only ask so much of the past, ah, ha ha ha ha ha ha ha!"

"Oh be quiet," Budur said sharply. "She's only making a living." To Kirana: "She tells people things and they pay her, how is that so different from what you do? She makes them feel better."

"Does she?"

"She gives them something in exchange for food. She tells them what they want to hear. You tell people what they don't want to hear for your food, is that any better?"

"Why yes," Kirana said, cackling again. "It's a pretty damned good trick, now you put it that way. Here's the deal!" she shouted over the river at the world. "I tell you what you don't want to hear, you give me food!"

Even Budur had to laugh.

They walked across the last bridge arm in arm, laughing and talking, then into the city center, trams squealing over tracks, people hurrying by. Budur looked at the passing faces curiously, remembering the worn visage of the fake guru, businesslike and hard. No doubt Kirana was right to laugh. All the old myths were just stories. The only reincarnation you got was the next day's waking. No one else was you, not the you that existed a year before, not the you that might exist ten years from now, or even the next day. It was a matter of the moment, some unimaginable minim of time, always already gone. Memory was partial, a dim tawdry room in a beat-up neighborhood, illuminated by flashes of distant lightning. Once she had been a girl in a good merchant's harem, but what did that matter now? Now she was a free woman in Nsara, crossing the city at night with a group of laughing intellectuals—that was all there was. It made her laugh too, a painful wild shout of a laugh, full of a joy akin to ferocity. That was what Kirana really gave in exchange for her food.

16 ✹ Three new women showed up in Budur's zawiyya, quiet women who had arrived with typical stories, and mostly kept to themselves. They started work in the kitchen, as usual. Budur felt uncomfortable with the way they glanced at her, and did not look at each other. She still could not quite believe that young women like these would betray a young woman like her, and two of the three were actually very nice. She was stiffer with them than she would have wanted to be, without actually being hostile, which Idelba had warned might give away her suspicions. It was a fine line in a game Budur was completely unused to playing—or not completely—it reminded her of the various fronts she had put on for her father and mother, a very unpleasant memory. She wanted everything to be new now, she wanted to be herself straight up to everybody, chest to chest as the Iranians said. But it seemed life entailed putting on masks for much of the time. She must be casual in Kirana's classes, and indifferent to Kirana in the cafés, even when they were leg to leg; and she must be civil to these spies.

Meanwhile, across the plaza in the lab, Idelba and Piali were hard at work, staying late into the night almost every night; and Idelba became more and more serious about it, trying, Budur thought, to hide her worries behind an unconvincing dismissiveness. "Just physics," she would say when asked. "Trying to figure something out. You know how interesting theories can be, but they're just theories. Not like real problems." It seemed everyone put on a mask to the world, even Idelba, who was not good at it, even though she seemed to have a frequent need for masks. Budur could see very plainly now that she thought the stakes were somehow high.

"Is it a bomb?" Budur asked once in a low voice, one night as they were closing up the emptied building.

Idelba hesitated only a moment. "Possibly," she whispered, looking around them. "The possibility is there. So, please—never speak of it again."

During these months Idelba worked such long hours, and, like everyone else in the zawiyya, ate so little, that she fell sick, and had to rest in her bed. This was very frustrating to her, and along with the misery of illness, she struggled to get up before she was ready, and even tried to work on papers in her bed, pencil and logarithmic abacus scritching and clacking all the time she was awake.

Then one day she got a phone call while Budur was there, and she dragged herself down the hall to take it, clutching her night robe to her. When she got off the phone she hurried to the kitchen and asked Budur to join her in her room.

Budur followed her, surprised to see her moving so quickly. In her room Idelba shut the door and began to pile a mass of her papers and notebooks into a cloth book bag. "Hide this for me," she said urgently. "I don't think you can leave, though, they'll stop you and search you. It has to be in the zawiyya someplace, not in your room or mine, they'll search them both. They may search everywhere, I'm not sure where to suggest." Her voice was low but the tone frantic; Budur had never heard her like that.

"Who is it?"

"It doesn't matter, hurry! It's the police. They're on their way, go."

The doorbell rang, and rang again.

"Don't worry," Budur said, and ran down the hall to her room. She looked around: a room search, perhaps a house search; and the bag of papers was big. She looked around, thinking over the zawiyya in her mind, wondering if Idelba would mind if she somehow managed to destroy the bag entirely—not that she had any method in mind, but she wasn't sure how crucial the papers were—but possibly they could be shredded and flushed down a toilet.

There were people in the hall, women's voices. Apparently the police who had entered were women officers, so they were not breaking the house rule against men. A sign perhaps; but men's voices came from out in the street, arguing with the zawiyya elders; women were in the hall; a big knock on her door, they had come to hers first, no doubt along with Idelba's. She put the bag around her neck, climbed onto her bed, then the iron headboard, and pulled herself up the wall and shoved up a panel of the false ceiling, and with a push off like a dance step, knee in the meeting of the two walls, got under the panel and onto the wall's dusty top, which was about two feet wide. She sat on it and put the panel back down into place, very quietly.

The old museum had had very high ceilings, with some glass sky-lights that were now almost perfectly opaque with dust. In the dimness she could see over the ceilings of several rows of rooms, and the open tops of the hallways, and the true walls, far away in every direction. It was not a good hiding place at all, if they only thought to look up here, from anywhere.

The top of the walls consisted of warped wood beams, nailed to the top of the framing and over the drywall like coping. To each wall there were two sheets of drywall, notoriously transparent to sound, nailed onto each side of the framing; so there would be gaps between the two sheets of drywall, if she could get a beam off the top somewhere.

She moved onto her hands and knees and swung the bag onto her back, and began crawling over the dusty beams, looking for a hole while staying well away from the hallways, where a glance up could reveal her. From here the whole arrangement looked ramshackle, cobbled together in a hurry, and soon enough she found a cap where three walls met and a beam had been cut short. It wasn't big enough to fit the whole bag, but she could stuff papers in there, and she did so quickly, until the bag was empty, and the bag dropped in last. It wasn't a perfect hiding place if they wanted to be comprehensive, but it was the best she could think of, and she was pretty pleased with it, actually; but if they found her up on the beams, all would be lost. She crawled on as quietly as she could, hearing voices back in the direction of her room. They would only have to stand on her bed's headboard and push up a panel for a look to see her. The far bathroom did not sound as though it had anyone in it, so she crawled in that direction, ripping the skin over one knee on a nailhead, and pulled up a panel an inch and peered in—empty—she pulled it aside, hung from the beam, dropped, hit the tiled floor hard. The wall was smeared with dust and blood; her knees and the tops of her feet were filthy with dust, and the palms of her hands marked everything like the hand of Cain. She washed in a sink, tore off her djebella and put it in the laundry, pulled clean towels from the cabinet and wetted one to clean the wall off. The panel above was still pulled aside, and there were no chairs in the bathroom; she couldn't get up there to move it back in place. Glancing out in the hall—loud voices arguing, Idelba's among them, protesting, no one in sight—she dashed across the hall to a bedroom and took a chair and ran back into the bathroom and put the chair against the wall, stepped up onto it, stepped gently on the chair back, reached up and yanked the panel back into place, smashing her fingers between two panels. Yank them free, push the panel into position, down again, the chair slipping across the tile with her movement. Clatter, bang, catch herself, another glance out, more arguing, coming closer; she put the chair back, went back in the bathroom, went to the showers and got in, soaping her knees and feeling the sting in the cut. She soaped and soaped, heard voices outside the bathroom. She washed off the soap as quickly as possible, and was dried and wrapped in a big towel when women came into the room, including two in army uniforms, looking like soldiers from the war whom Budur had seen long ago, in the Turi train station. She looked as startled as she could, held the towel to herself.

"Are you Budur Radwan?" one of the policewomen demanded.

"Yes! What do you want?"

"We want to talk to you! Where have you been?"

"What do you mean, where have I been? You can see very well where I've been! What is this all about, why do you want me? What could have brought you in here?"

"We want to talk to you."

"Well, let me go get dressed and I will talk to you. I have done nothing wrong, I assume? I can get dressed before talking to my own country-women, I assume?"

"This is Nsara," one of them said. "You're from Turi, right?"

"True, but we are all Firanjis here, all good Muslim women in a za-wiyya, unless I am mistaken?"

"Come on, get dressed," the other one said. "We have some questions to ask about affairs here, security threats that may be centered here. So come. Where are your clothes?"

"In my room, of course!" And Budur swept past them to her room, considering which djebella would best hide her knees and any blood that might be seeping down her leg. Her blood was hot, but her breathing calm; she felt solid; and there was an anger growing in her, like a boulder from the jetty, anchoring her from the inside.

17 ✸ Though they made a fairly thorough search, they did not find Idelba's papers, nor did they get anything but bewilderment and indignation from their questionings. The zawiyya filed suit with the courts against the police, for invasion of privacy without proper authorization, and only the invocation of wartime secrecy laws kept it from being a scandal in the newspapers. The courts backed the search but also the zawiyya's future right to privacy, and after that it was back to normal, or sort of; Idelba never talked about her work anymore, no longer worked in certain labs she had before, and she no longer spent any time with Piali.

Budur continued in her routine, making her rounds from home, to work, to the Café Sultana. There she sat behind the big plate-glass windows and looked out at the docks, and the forests of masts and steel superstructures, and the top of the lighthouse at the end of the jetty, while the talk swirled around her. At their tables too, very often, were Hasan and Tristan, sitting like limpets in their pool with the tide gone out, exposing them wetly to the moon. Hasan's polemics and poetry made him a force to be reckoned with, a truth that all the city's avant-garde acknowledged, either enthusiastically or reluctantly. Hasan himself spoke of his reputation with a smirk meant to be self-deprecating, wickedly smiling as he briefly exposed his power to view. Budur liked him although she knew perfectly well he was in some senses a disagreeable person. She was more interested in Tristan and his music, which included not only songs like those he had sung at the garden party, but also vast long works for bands of up to two hundred musicians, sometimes featuring him on the kundun, an Anatolian stringed box with metal tabs to the side that slightly changed the tones of the strings, a fiendishly difficult instrument to play. He wrote out the parts for each instrument in these pieces, down to every chord and change, and even every note. As in his songs, these longer compositions showed his interest in adapting the primitive tonalities of the lost Christians, for the most part simple harmonic chords, but containing within them the possibility of various more sophisticated tonalities, which could at strategic moments return to the Pythagorean basics favored in the chorales and chants of the lost ones. Writing down every note and demanding that the musicians in the ensemble play only and exactly the written notes was an act that everyone regarded as megalomaniacal to the point of impossibility; ensemble music, though very highly structured in a way that went back ultimately to Indian classical ragas, nevertheless allowed for individual improvisation of the details of the variations, spontaneous creations that indeed provided much of the interest of the music, as the musician played within and against the raga forms. No one would have stood for Tristan's insane strictures if it were not that the results were, one could not deny it, superb and beautiful. And Tristan insisted that the procedure was not his idea, but merely the way that the lost civilization had gone about it; that he was following the lost ways, even doing his best to channel the hungry ghosts of the old ones in his dreams and in his musical reveries. The old Frankish pieces he hoped to invoke were all religious music, devotionals, and had to be understood and utilized as such, as sacred music. Although it was true that in this hyperaesthetic circle of the avant-garde it was music itself that was sacred, like all the arts, so that the description was redundant.

It was also true that treating art as sacred often meant smoking opium or drinking laudanum to prepare for the experience; some even used the stronger distillates of opium developed during the war, smoking or even injecting them. The resulting dream states made Tristan's music mesmerizing, the practitioners said, even those who were not fond of the lost civilization's simplistic tootles; opium induced a deep absorption in the sensuous surface of musical sound, in the plainsong harmonies, vibrating between a drugged band and a drugged audience. If the performance was combined with the fanned aromas of a scent artist, the results could be truly mystical. Some were skeptical of all this: Kirana said once, "As high as they all get, they could simply sing a single note for the whole hour, and smell their armpits, and all would be as happy as birds."

Tristan himself often led the opium ceremonies before leading the music, so these evenings had a somewhat cultic air to them, as if Tristan were some kind of mystic Sufi master, or one of the Hosain actors in the plays about Hosain's martyrdom, which the opium crowd also attended after crossing into dreamland, to watch Hosain putting on his own shroud before his murder by Shemr, the audience groaning, not at the murder onstage, but at this choice of martyrdom. In some of the Shiite countries the person playing Shemr had to run for his life after the performance, and more than one unlucky actor had been killed by the crowd. Tristan thoroughly approved; this was the kind of immersion in the art that he wanted his musical audiences to achieve.

But only in the secular world; it was all for music, not for God; Tristan was more Persian than Iranian, as he put it sometimes, much more an Omarian than any kind of mullah, or a mystic of Zoroastrian bent, concocting rituals in honor of Ahura-Mazda, a kind of sun worship that in foggy Nsara could come straight from the heart. Channeling Christians, smoking opium, worshiping the sun; he did all kinds of crazy things for his music, including working for many hours every day to get every note right on the page; and though none of it would have mattered if the music had not been good, it was good, it was more than that; it was the music of their lives, of Nsara in its time.

He spoke of all the theory behind it, however, in cryptic little phrases and aphorisms that then made the rounds, as "Tristan's latest"; and often it was just a shrug and a smile and an offered opium pipe, and, most of all, his music. He composed what he composed, and the intellectuals of the city could listen and then talk about what it all meant, and they often did all through the night. Tahar Labid would go on endlessly about it, and then say to Tristan, with almost mock aggressiveness, That's right, isn't it Tristan Ahura, then go on without pausing for an answer, as if Tristan were to be laughed at as an idiot savant for never deigning to reply one way or the other; as if he didn't really know what his music meant. But Tristan only smiled at Tahar, sphinxlike and enigmatic under his moustache, relaxed as if poured into his window seat, looking out at the wet black cobbles or spearing Tahar with an amused glance.

"Why don't you ever answer me!" Tahar exclaimed once.

Tristan pursed his lips and whistled a response at him.

"Oh come on," Tahar said, reddening. "Say something to make us think you have a single idea in your head."

Tristan drew himself up. "Don't be rude! Of course there are no ideas in my head, what do you think I am!"

So Budur sat next to him. She joined him when, with a tilt of the chin and pursing of the lips, he invited her into one of the back rooms of the café where the opium smokers gathered. She had decided ahead of time to join them if the opportunity was offered, to see what hearing Tristan's music under the influence would be like; to see what the drug felt like, using the music as the ceremony that allowed her to overcome her Turic fear of the smoke.

The room was small and dark. The huqqah, bigger than a narghile, sat on a low table in the middle of floor pillows, and Tristan cut a chunk from a black plug of opium and put it in the bowl, lit it with a silver cigarette lighter as one of the others inhaled. As the single mouthpiece was passed around the smokers sucked on it, and each in turn began immediately to cough. The black plug in the bowl bubbled to tar as it burned; the smoke was thick and white, and smelled like sugar. Budur decided to take in so little that she wouldn't cough, but when the mouthpiece came to her and she inhaled gently through it, the first taste of the smoke caused her to hack like a demon. It seemed impossible she could be so affected by anything that had been in her so briefly.

Then it struck deeper. She felt her blood filling her skin, then all of her. Blood filled her like a balloon, it would spurt out if her hot skin didn't hold it in. She pulsed with her pulse, and the world pulsed with her. Everything jumped forward into itself somehow, in time with her heart. The dim walls pulsed. More color revealed itself with every beat of her heart. The surfaces of things swirled with coiled pressure and tension, they looked like what Idelba said they really were, bundles of bundled energy. Budur pulled herself to her feet with the others, walked, balancing carefully, through the streets to the concert hall in the old palace, into a space long and tall like a deck of cards set on its side. The musicians filed in and sat, their instruments like strange weapons. Following Tristan's lead, conveyed by hand and eye, they began to play. The singers chanted in the ancient Pythagorean tonality, pure and sugary, a single voice wandering above in descant. Then Tristan on his oud, and the other string players, bass to treble, sneaked in underneath, wrecking the simple harmonies, bringing in a whole other world, an Asia of sound, so much more complex and dark—reality—seeping in, and, over the course of a long struggle, overwhelming the old west's plainchant. This was the story of Firanja that Tristan was singing, Budur thought suddenly, a musical expression of the history of this place they lived in, late arrivals that they were. Firanjis, Franks, Kelts, the oldest ones back in the murk of time . . . Each people overrun in its turn. It was not a scent performance, but there was incense burning before the musicians, and as their songs wove together the thick smells of sandalwood and jasmine choked the room, they came in on Budur's breath and sang inside her, playing a complex rondelay with her pulse, just as in the music itself, which was so clearly another speech of the body, a language she felt she could understand in the moment it happened, without ever being able to articulate or remember it.

Sex too was a language like that; as she found later that night, when she went home with Tristan to his grubby apartment, and to bed with him. His apartment was across the river in the south wharf district, a cold and damp garret, an artistic cliché, and uncleaned, it appeared, since his wife had died near the end of the war—some factory accident, Budur had gathered from others, a chance of bad timing and broken machinery—but the bed was there, and the sheets clean, which made Budur suspicious; but after all she had been showing interest in Tristan, so perhaps it was only a matter of politeness, or self-respect of some heartening kind. He was a dreamy lover and played her like an oud, languorous and faintly teasing, so that there was an edge to her passion, of resistance and struggle, all adding somehow to the sexiness of the experience, so that it nagged at her afterward, as if set into her with hooks— nothing like the blazing directness of Kirana—and Budur wondered what Tristan intended by it, but realized also in that very first night that she was not going to learn from Tristan's words, as he was as reticent with her as he was with Tahar, almost; so that she would have to know him by what could be intuited from his music and his looks. Which were indeed very revealing of his moods and their swings, and so of his character (perhaps); which she liked. So for a while she went home with him fairly often, arranging for prophylactics with the zawiyya clinic, going out at night to the cafés and taking the opportunity when it came.

After a time, however, it became annoying to try to have conversation with a man who only sang melodies—like trying to live with a bird. It echoed painfully that distance in her father, and the mute quality of her attempts to study the remote past, which were equally speechless. And as things in town got tighter, and each week added another zero to the numbers on the paper money, it got harder and harder to gather the large ensembles that Tristan's current compositions required. When the district panchayat that ran the old palace chose not to lend a concert room, or the musicians were occupied with their real jobs, in class or on the docks or in the shops selling hats and raincoats, then Tristan could only strum his oud, and finger his pencils and take endless notes, in an Indian musical notation that was said to be older than Sanskrit, although Tristan confessed to Budur that he had forgotten the system during the war, and now used one of his own devising that he had had to teach to his players. His melodies became more morose, she thought, tunes from a heavy heart, mourning the losses of the war, and the ones that had happened since, and were still occuring now, in the moment of listening itself. Budur understood them, and kept joining Tristan from time to time, watching the twitches under his moustache for clues as to what amused him when she or others spoke, watching his yellowed fingers as they felt their tunes forward, or noted down one quicksilver lament after another. She heard a singer she thought he would like, and took him to hear her, and he did like her, he hummed on the way home, looking out the tram window at the dark city streets, where people hurried from streetlight to streetlight over gleaming cobblestones, hunched under umbrellas or serapes.

"It's like in the forest," Tristan said with a lift of the moustache. "Up in your mountains, you know, you see places where avalanches have bent all the trees down sideways, and then after the snow melts, the trees there all stay bent sideways together." He gestured at the crowd waiting at a tram stop. "That's what we're like now."

18 ❀ As the days and the weeks passed Budur continued to read voraciously, in the zawiyya, the institute, the parks, at the jetty's end, in the hospital for the blind soldiers. Meanwhile there were ten-trillion piastre bills arriving with immigrants from the Middle West, and they were at ten-billion drachma bills themselves; recently a man had stuffed his house from floor to ceiling with money, and traded the whole establishment for a pig. At the zawiyya it was harder and harder to put together meals big enough to feed them all. They grew vegetables in crops on the roof, cursing the clouds, and lived on their goats' milk, their chickens' eggs, cucumbers in great vats of vinegar, pumpkins cooked in every conceivable fashion, and potato soup, watered to a thinness thinner than milk.

One day Idelba found the three spies going through the little cabinet above her bed, and she had them kicked out of the house as common thieves, calling in the neighborhood police and bypassing the issue of spying, without, however, getting into the tricky issue of what else besides her ideas she had that would be worth stealing.

"They'll be in trouble," Budur observed after the three girls were taken away. "Even if they're plucked out of jail by their employers."

"Yes," Idelba agreed. "I was going to leave them here, as you saw. But once they were caught, we had to act as if we didn't know who they were.

And the truth is we can't afford to feed them. So they can go back to who sent them. Hopefully." A grim expression; she didn't want to think about it—about what she might have condemned them to. That was their problem. She had hardened in just the two years since she had brought Budur to Nsara, or so it seemed to Budur. "It's not just my work," she explained, seeing Budur's expression. "That remains latent. It's the problems we have right now. Things won't need blowing up if we all starve first. The war ended badly, that's all there is to it. I mean not just for us, as the defeated, but for everyone. Things are so out of balance, it could bring everything down. So everyone needs to pull together. And if some people don't, then I don't know . . ."

"All that time you spend working in the music of the Franks," Budur said to Tristan, one evening in the café, "do you ever think about what they were like?"

"Why yes," he said, pleased at the question. "All the time. I think they were just like us. They fought a lot. They had monasteries and madressas, and water-powered machinery. Their ships were small, but they could sail into the wind. They might have taken control of the seas before anyone else."

"Not a chance," said Tahar. "Compared to Chinese ships they were no more than dhows. Come now, Tristan, you know that."

Tristan shrugged.

"They had ten or fifteen languages, thirty or forty principalities, isn't that right?" said Naser. "They were too fractured to conquer anyone else."

"They fought together to capture Jerusalem," Tristan pointed out. "The infighting gave them practice. They thought they were God's chosen people."

"Primitives often think that."

"Indeed." Tristan smiled, leaning sideways to peer through the window toward the neighborhood mosque. "As I say, they were just like us. If they had lived, there would be more people like us."

"There's no one like us," Naser said sadly. "I think the Franks must have been very different."

Tristan shrugged again. "You can say anything you like about them, it doesn't matter. You can say they would have been enslaved like the

Africans, or made slaves of the rest of us, or brought a golden age, or waged wars worse than the Long War . . ."

People shook their heads at all these impossibilities.

". . . but it doesn't matter. We'll never know, so you can say whatever you like. They are our jinn."

"It's funny how we look down on them," Kirana observed, "just because they died. At an unconscious level it seems like it must have been their fault. A physical weakness, or a moral failing, or a bad habit."

"They affronted God with their pride."

"They were pale because they were weak, or vice versa. Muzaffar has showed it, how the darker the skin, the stronger the persons. The blackest Africans are strongest of all, the palest of the Golden Horde are weakest. He did tests. The Franks were hereditarily incompetent, that was his conclusion. Losers in the evolutionary game of survival of the fittest."

Kirana shook her head. "It was probably just a mutation of the plague, so strong it killed off all its hosts, and therefore died itself. It could have happened to any of us. The Chinese, or us."

"But there's a kind of anemia common around the Mediterranean, that might have made them more susceptible . . ."

"No. It could have been us."

"That might have been good," Tristan said. "They believed in a god of mercy, their Christ was all love and mercy."

"Hard to tell that by what they did in Syria."

"Or al-Andalus—"

"It was latent in them, ready to spring forth. While for us what is latent is jihad."

"They were the same as us, you said."

Tristan smiled under his moustache. "Maybe. They're the blank on the map, the ruins underfoot, the empty mirror. The clouds in the sky that look like tigers."

"It's such a useless exercise," Kirana reflected. "What if this had happened, what if that had happened, what if the Golden Horde had forced the Gansu Corridor at the start of the Long War, what if the Japanese had attacked China after retaking Japan, what if the Ming had kept their treasure fleet, what if we had discovered and conquered Yingzhou, what if Alexander the Great had not died young, on and on, and they all would have made enormous differences and yet it's always entirely useless. These historians who talk about employing counterfactuals to bolster their theories, they're ridiculous. Because no one knows why things happen, you see? Anything could follow from anything. Even real history tells us nothing at all. Because we don't know if history is sensitive, and for want of a nail a civilization was lost, or if our mightiest acts are as petals on a flood, or something in between, or both at once. We just don't know, and the what-ifs don't help us figure it out."

"Why do people like them so much, then?"

Kirana shrugged, took a drag on her cigarette. "More stories."

And indeed more of them were immediately proposed, for despite their uselessness in Kirana's eyes, people enjoyed contemplating the what-might-have-been: what if the Moroccan lost fleet of 924 had been blown to the Sugar Islands and then made it back; what if the Kerala of Travancore had not conquered much of Asia and set out his railways and legal system; what if there had been no New World islands there at all; what if Burma had lost its war with Siam . . .

Kirana only shook her head. "Perhaps it would be better just to focus on the future."

"You, a historian, say this? But the future can't be known at all!"

"Well, but it exists for us now as a project to be enacted. Ever since the Travancori enlightenment we have had a sense of the future as something we make. This new awareness of time to come is very important. It makes us a thread in a tapestry that has unrolled for centuries before us, and will unroll for centuries after us. We're midway through the loom, that's the present, and what we do casts the thread in a particular direction, and the picture in the tapestry changes accordingly. When we begin to try to make a picture pleasing to us and to those who come after, then perhaps you can say that we have seized history."

19 ✳ But one could sit with people like that, have conversations like that, and still walk outside into watery sunlight with nothing to eat and no money worth anything. Budur worked hard at the zawiyya, and set up classes in Persian and Firanjic for the hungry girls moving in who only spoke Berber or Arabic or Andalusi or Skandistani or Turkish. At night she continued as a habitué of the cafés and coffeehouses, and sometimes the opium dens. She got work with one of the government agencies as a translator of documents, and continued to study archaeology. She was worried when Idelba fell ill again, and spent a lot of time caring for her. The doctors said that Idelba was suffering from "nervous exhaustion," something like the battle fatigue of the war; but to Budur she seemed very obviously physically weaker, harmed by something the doctors could not identify. Illness without cause; Budur found this too frightening to think about. Probably it was a hidden cause, but that too was frightening.

She got more involved with the running of the zawiyya, taking over some of what Idelba had done before. There was less time to read. Besides, she wanted to do more than read, or even write reports: she felt too anxious to read, and merely perusing a number of texts and then boiling them down into a new text struck her as an odd activity; it was like being a still, distilling ideas. History as a brandy; but she wanted something more substantial.

Meanwhile, many a night she still went out and enjoyed the midnight scene at the coffee and opium cafés, listening to Tristan's oud (they were friends only now), sometimes in a opiated dream that allowed her to wander the fogged halls of her thoughts without actually entering any rooms. She was deep in a reverie concerning the Ibrahamic collisional nature of progress in history, something like the continents themselves, if the geologists were right, creating new fusions, as in Samarqand, or Mughal India, or the Hodenosaunee dealing with China to the west and Islam to the east, or Burma, yes—all this was coming clear, like random bits of colored rock on the ground swirling into one of Hagia Sophia's elaborate self-replicating arabesques, a common opium effect to be sure, but then that was what history always was, a hallucinated pattern onto random events, so there was no cause to disbelieve the illumination just because of that. History as an opium dream—

Halali from the zawiyya burst into the café's back room looking around; spotting her Budur knew immediately that something was wrong with Idelba. Halali came over, her face holding a serious expression. "She's taken a turn for the worse."

Budur followed her out, stumbling under the weight of the opium, trying to banish all its effects immediately with her panic, but that only cast her further out into visual distortions of all kinds, and never had Nsara looked uglier than on that night, rain bouncing hard on the streets, squiggles of light cobbling underfoot, shapes of people like rats swimming . . .

Idelba was gone from the zawiyya, she had been taken to the nearest hospital, a huge rambling wartime structure on the hill north of the harbor. Slogging up there, inside the rain cloud itself; then the sound of rain pounding on the cheap tin roof. The light was an intense throbbing yellow-white in which everyone looked blank and dead, like walking meat as they had said during the war of men sent to the front.

Idelba was no worse-looking than the rest, but Budur rushed to her side. "She's having trouble breathing," a nurse said, looking up from her chair. Budur thought: these people work in hell. She was very frightened.

"Listen," Idelba said calmly. She said to the nurse, "Please leave us alone for ten minutes." When the nurse was gone, she said in a low voice to Budur, "Listen, if I die, then you need to help Piali."

"But Aunt Idelba! You aren't going to die."

"Be quiet. I can't risk writing this down, and I can't risk telling only one person, in case something happens to them too. You need to get Piali to go to Isfahan, to describe our results to Abdol Zoroush. Also to Ananda, in Travancore. And Chen, in China. They all have tremendous influence within their respective governments. Hanea will handle her end of things. Remind Piali of what we decided was best. Soon, you see, all atomic physicists will understand the theoretical possibilities of the way alactin splits. The possible application. If they all know the possibility exists, then there will be reason for them to press to make peace permanent. The scientists can pressure their respective governments, by making clear the situation, and taking control of the direction of the relevant fields of science. They must keep the peace, or there will be a rush to destruction. Given the choice, they must choose peace."

"Yes," Budur said, wondering if it would be so. Her mind was reeling at the prospect of such a burden being placed on her to carry. She did not like Piali very much. "Please, Aunt Idelba, please. Don't distress yourself. It will be all right."

Idelba nodded. "Very possibly."

She rallied late that night, just before dawn, just as Budur was beginning to come down from her opium delirium, unable to remember much of the night that had taken so many eons to pass. But she still knew what Idelba wanted her to try to do. Dawn came as dark as if an eclipse had come and stayed.

It was the following year before Idelba died.

The funeral was attended by many people, hundreds of them, from zawiyya and madressa and institute, and the Buddhist monastery, and the Hodenosaunee embassy, and the district panchayat and the state council, and many other places all over Nsara. But not a single person from Turi. Budur stood numbly in a reception line with a few of the senior women from the zawiyya, and shook hand after hand. Afterward, during the unhappy wake, Hanea came up to her again. "We loved her too," she said with a flinty smile. "We will make sure to keep the promises we made to her."

A couple of days later Budur kept her usual appointment to read to her blind soldiers. She went in their ward and sat there staring at them in their chairs and beds, and thought, This is probably a mistake. I may feel blank but I'm probably not. She told them of her aunt's death, then, and tried to read to them from Idelba's work, but it was not like Kirana's; even the abstracts were incomprehensible, and the texts themselves, scientific papers on the behavior of invisible things, were composed largely of tables of numbers. She quit trying with those, and picked up another book. "This is one of my aunt's favorite books, a collection of the autobiographical writings found in the works of Abu Ali Ibn Sina, the early scientist and philosopher who was a great hero to her. From what I have read of him, Ibn Sina and my aunt were alike in many ways. They both had a great curiosity about the world. Ibn Sina first mastered Euclid's geometry, then set out to understand everything else. Idelba did that very same thing. When Ibn Sina was still young he fell into a sort of fever of inquiry, which gripped him for almost two years. Here, I will read to you what he himself says about that period."

> During this time I did not sleep completely through a single night, or devote myself to anything else but study by day. I compiled a set of files for myself, and for each proof that I examined, I entered into the files its syllogistic premises, their classification, and what might follow from them. I pondered over the conditions that might apply to their premises, until I had verified this question for myself in each case. Whenever sleep overcame me or I became conscious of weakening, I would turn aside to drink a cup of wine, so that my strength would return to me. And whenever sleep seized

me I would see those very problems in my dreams; and many questions became clear to me in my sleep. I continued in this until all of the sciences were deeply rooted within me and I understood them as far as is humanly possible. Everything which I knew at that time is just as I know it now; I have not added anything much to it to this day.

"That's the kind of person my aunt was," Budur said. She put down that book and picked up another one, thinking that it would be better to stop reading things inspired by Idelba. It wasn't making her feel any better. The book she chose out of her bag was called *Nsarene Sailor's Tales,* true stories about the local seamen and fisherfolk, rousing adventures full of fish and danger and death but also of the sea air, the waves and the wind. The soldiers had enjoyed chapters of the book she had read to them before.

But this time she read one called "The Windy Ramadan," and it turned out to be about a time long before, in the age of sail, when contrary winds had held the grain fleet out of the harbor, so that they had had to anchor offshore in the roads as darkness fell, and then in the night the wind shifted around and a great storm came roaring in from the Atlantic, and there was no way for those out on the ships to get safely to shore, and nothing those on shore could do but walk the shore through the night. The author of the account had a wife who was taking care of three motherless children whose father was one of the sea captains out in the fleet, and, unable to watch the children at their nervous play, the author had gone out to walk the strand with the rest, braving the howling winds of the tempest. At dawn they had all seen the fringe of soaked grain lining the high-water mark, and knew the worst had come. "Not a single ship survived the gale, and all up and down the beach the bodies washed ashore. And as it had dawned a Friday, at the appointed hour the muezzin went to the minaret to ascend and make the call for prayer, and the town idiot in a rage detained him, crying, 'Who in such an hour can praise the Lord?' "

Budur stopped reading. A deep silence filled the room. Some of the men nodded their heads, as if to say, Yes, that's the way it happens; I've had that very thought for years; still others reached out as if to snatch the book from her hands, or gestured as if waving her away, telling her to leave. If they had had their sight they would have walked her to the door, or done something; but as it was no one knew what to do.

She said something and got up and left, and walked downriver through the city, out onto the docks, then out the big jetty, out to its end. The beautiful blue sea sloshed against the boulders, hissing its clean salt mist into the air. Budur sat on the last sun-warmed rock and watched the clouds fly in over Nsara. She was as full of grief as the ocean was of water, but still, something in the sight of the noisy city was heartening to her; she thought, Nsara, now you are my only living relative. Now you will be my aunt Nsara.

20 ✸ And now she had to get to know Piali.

He was a small, self-absorbed man, dreamy and uncommunicative, seemingly full of himself. Budur had thought that his abilities in physics were compensated for by an exceptional lack of gracefulness.

But now she was impressed by the depth of his grief at Idelba's death. In life he had treated her, Budur often thought, as an embarrassing appurtenance, a needed but unwanted collaborator in his work. Now that she was gone, he sat on a jetty fishermen's bench where they had occasionally sat with Idelba when the weather was good, and sighed, saying, "She was such a joy to talk things over with, wasn't she? Our Idelba was a truly brilliant physicist, let me tell you. If she had been born a man, there would have been no end to it—she would have changed the world. Of course there were things she wasn't so good at, but she had such insight into the way things might work. And when we got stuck, Idelba would keep hammering away forever at the problem, forehead pounding the brick wall, you know, and I would stop, but she was persistent, and so clever at finding new ways to come at the thing, turning the flank if the wall wouldn't give. Lovely. She was a most lovely person." He was deadly serious now, and emphasizing "person" rather than "woman," as if Idelba had taught him some things about what women might be that he was not so stupid as to have missed. Nor would he fall into the error of exceptionalism, no physicist tended to think of exceptions as a valid category; and so now he spoke to Budur almost as he would have to Idelba or his male colleagues, only more intently, concentrating to achieve some semblance of normal humanity, perhaps—and yet achieving it. Almost. He was still a very distracted and graceless man. But Budur began to like him better.

This was a good thing, as Piali took an interest in her too, and over the next several months, courted her in his peculiar way; he came by the zawiyya, and got to know her house family there, and listened to her describe her problems with her studies in history, while also going on at nearly intolerable length about his problems in physics and at the institute. He shared with her a propensity for the café life as well, and did not seem to care about the assorted indiscretions she had committed since her arrival in Nsara; he ignored all that, and concentrated on things of the mind, even when sitting in a café sipping a brandy, and writing all over his napkins, one of his peculiar habits. They talked about the nature of history for hours, and it was under the impact of his deep skepticism, or materialism, that she finally completed the shift in the emphasis of her study from history to archaeology, from texts to things—convinced, in part, by his argument that texts were always just people's impressions, while objects had a certain unchangeable reality to them. Of course, the objects led directly to more impressions, and meshed with them in the web of proofs that any student of the past had to present in order to make a case; but to start with the tools and buildings rather than the words of the past was indeed a comfort to Budur. She was tired of distilling brandy. She began consciously to take on some of the inquisitiveness about the real world that Idelba had always exhibited, as a way of honoring her memory. She missed Idelba so much that she could not think of it directly, but had to parry it by homages such as these, invoking Idelba's presence by her habits, as if becoming a kind of Madame Sururi. It occurred to her more than once that there were ways in which we know the dead better than the living, because the actual person is no longer there to distract our thinking about them.

Following these various trains of thought, Budur also began to come up with a great number of questions that connected her work with Idelba's as she understood it, as she considered physical changes in the materials used in the past: chemical or physical or qi or qileak changes, which might be used as clocks, buried in the texture of the materials used. She asked Piali about this, and he quickly mentioned the shift over time in the types of particulates in the heartknots and shells, so that, for instance, lifering fourteens within a body would, after the death of an organism, begin slowly to fall back to lifering twelves, beginning about fifty years after the death of an organism and continuing for about a hundred thousand years, until all the lifering in the material was back to twelves, and the clock would stop functioning.

This would be long enough to date most human activities, Budur thought. She and Piali began to work on the method together, enlisting the help of other scientists at the institute. The idea was taken up and extended by a team of Nsarene scientists that grew by the month, and the effort quickly became global as well, in the usual way of science. Budur had never studied harder.

Thus it was that over time she became an archaeologist, working among other things on dating methods, with the help of Piali. In effect she had replaced Idelba as Piali's partner, and he had therefore moved part of his work to a different field, to accommodate what she was doing. His method of relating to someone was to work with them; so even though she was younger, and in a different field, he simply adjusted and continued in his habitual way. He also continued to pursue his studies in atomic physics, of course, collaborating with many colleagues at the laboratories of the institute, and some of the scientists at the wireless factory on the outskirts of the city, whose lab was now beginning to match the madressa and the institute as a center of research in pure physics.

The military of Nsara were getting involved as well. Piali's physics research continued along the lines set by Idelba, and though there was nothing more published about the possibility of creating a chain-reaction splitting of alactin, there was certainly a small crowd of Muslim physicists, in Skandistan and Tuscany and Iran, who had discussed the possibility among themselves; and they suspected that similar discussions were taking place in Chinese and Travancori and New World labs. Internationally published papers on this aspect of physics were now analyzed in Nsara to see what they might have left out, to see if new developments one might expect to see were appearing or if sudden silences might mark government classification of these matters. So far no unequivocal signs of censorship or self-silencing had appeared, but Piali seemed to feel it was only a matter of time, and was probably happening in other countries as it was among them, semiconsciously and without a plan. As soon as there was another global political crisis, he said, before hostilities came to a head, one could expect the field to disappear entirely into classified military labs, and along with it a significant number of that generation of physicists, all cut off from contact with colleagues anywhere else in the world.

And of course trouble could come at any time. China, though victorious in the war, had been wrecked almost as thoroughly as the defeated coalition, and it appeared to be falling into anarchy and civil war. Apparently it was near the end for the wartime leadership that had replaced the Qing dynasty.

"That's good," Piali told Budur, "because only a military bureaucracy would have tried to build a bomb so dangerous. But it's bad because military governments don't like to go down without a fight."

"No government does," said Budur. "Remember what Idelba said. The best defense against government seizure of these ideas would be to spread the knowledge among all the physicists of the world, as quickly as possible. If all know that all could construct such a weapon, then no one would try."

"Maybe not at first," Piali said, "but in years to come it might happen."

"Nevertheless," Budur said. And she continued to pester Piali to pursue Idelba's suggested course of action. He did not renounce it, nor did he make any move to enact it. Indeed, Budur had to agree with him that it was difficult to see exactly what to do about it. They sat on the secret like pigeons on a cuckoo egg.

Meanwhile the situation in Nsara continued to deteriorate. A good summer had followed several bad ones, taking the sharpest edge off the possibility of famine, but nevertheless the newspapers were full of bread riots, and strikes in the factories on the Rhine and the Ruhr and the Rhône, and even a "revolt against reparations" in the Little Atlas Mountains, a revolt that could not easily be put down. The army appeared to have within it elements who were encouraging rather than suppressing these signs of unrest, perhaps out of sympathy, perhaps to destabilize things further and justify a complete military takeover. Rumors of a coup were widespread.

All this was depressingly similar to the endgame of the Long War, and hoarding increased. Budur found it hard to concentrate on her reading, and was often oppressed by grief for Idelba. She was surprised therefore, and pleased, when Piali brought news of a conference in Isfahan, an international gathering of atomic physicists to discuss all the latest results in their field, "including," he said, "the alactin problem." Not only that, but the conference was linked to the fourth convocation of a large biannual meeting of scientists, the first of which had occurred outside Ganono, the great harbor city of the Hodenosaunee, so that they were now called the Long Island Conferences. The second one had taken place in Pyinkayaing, and the third in Beijing. The Isfahan conference was therefore the first one to take place in the Dar, and it was going to include a track of meetings on archaeology; and Piali had already gotten Budur funding from the institute to attend with him, as coauthor of papers they had written with Idelba on lifering dating methods. "It looks to me like a good place to talk privately about your aunt's ideas. There'll be a session devoted to her work, organized by Zoroush, and Chen and quite a few others of her correspondents will be there. You'll come?"

"Of course."

21 ⚘ The direct trains to Iran all ran through Budur's hometown Turi, and whether it was for this reason or another, Piali arranged for them to fly from Nsara to Isfahan. The airship was similar to the one Budur had taken with Idelba to the Orkneys, and she sat in the window seats of the gondola looking down at Firanja: the Alps, Roma, Greece and the brown islands of the Aegean; then Anatolia and the Midwestern states. It was, Budur thought to herself as the long floating hours passed, a big world.

Then they were flying over the snowy Zagros Mountains to Isfahan, situated in the upper reaches of the Zayandeh Rud, a high valley with a swift river, overlooking salt flats to the east. As they approached the city's airport they saw a vast expanse of ruins around the new town. Isfahan had lain on the Silk Road, and successive cities had been demolished in their turn by Chinggis Khan, Temur the Lame, the Afghans in the eleventh century, and lastly by the Travancoris, in the late war.

Nevertheless the latest incarnation of the city was a bustling place, with new construction going on everywhere, so that as they trammed into the downtown it looked as if they were passing through a forest of construction cranes, each canted at a different angle over some new hive of steel and concrete. At a big madressa in the new center of the city, Abdol Zoroush and the other Iranian scientists greeted the contingent from Nsara, and took them to rooms in their Institute for Scientific Research's big guest quarters, and then into the city center surrounding it for a meal.

The Zagros Mountains overlooked the city, and the river ran through it just south of the downtown, which was being built over the ruins of the oldest city center. The institute's archaeological collection, the locals informed them, was filling with newly recovered antiquities and artifacts from previous eras of the city. The new town had been designed with broad tree-lined streets, raying north away from the river. Set at a high altitude, under even higher mountains, it would be a very beautiful city when the new trees grew to their full heights. Even now it was impressive.

The Isfaharis were obviously proud of both the city and their institute, and of Iran more generally. Crushed repeatedly in the war, the whole country was now being rebuilt, and in a new spirit, they said, a kind of Persian worldliness, with their own Shiite ultraconservatives awash in a more tolerant influx of polyglot refugees and immigrants, and local intellectuals who called themselves Cyruses, after the supposed first king of Iran. This new kind of Iranian patriotism was very interesting to the Nsarenes, as it seemed to be a way of asserting some independence from Islam without renouncing it. The Cyruses at the table informed them cheerfully that they now spoke of the year as being not A.H. 1423, but 2561 of "the era of the king of kings," and one of them stood to offer a toast by reciting an anonymous poem that had been discovered painted on the walls of the new madressa.

> Ancient Iran, Eternal Persia,
> Caught in the press of time and the world,
> Giving up to it beautiful Persian,
> Language of Hafiz, Ferdowski and Khayyam,
> Speech of my heart, home of my soul,
> It's you I love if I love anything.
> Once more, great Iran, sing us that love.

And the locals among them cheered and drank, although many of them were clearly students from Africa or the New World or Aozhou.

"This is how all the world will look, as people become more mobile," Abdol Zoroush said to Budur and Piali afterward, as he showed them around the institute's grounds, very extensive, and then the riverside district just south of it. There was a promenade overlooking the river being built, with cafés backing it and a view of the mountains upstream, which Zoroush said had been designed with the estuary corniche of Nsara in mind. "We wanted to have something like your great city, landlocked though we are. We want a little of that sense of openness."

The conference began the next day, and for the next week Budur did little else but attend sessions on various topics related to what many there were calling the new archaeology, a science rather than just a hobby of antiquarians, or the misty starting point of the historians. Piali meanwhile disappeared into the physical sciences buildings for meetings on physics. The two of them then met again for supper in big groups of scientists, seldom getting the chance to talk in private.

For Budur the archaeological presentations, coming from all over the world, were a very exciting education all by themselves, making clear to her and everyone else that in the postwar reconstruction, with the new discoveries and the development of new methodologies, and a provisional framework of early world history, a new science and a new understanding of their deep past was coming into being right before their eyes. The sessions were overbooked, and went long into the evenings. Many presentations were made in the hallways, with the presenters standing by posters or chalkboards, talking and gesturing and answering questions. There were more that Budur wanted to attend than was possible, and she quickly developed the habit of positioning herself at the back of the rooms or the crowds in the halls, taking in the crux of a presentation while perusing the schedule, and planning her next hour's wandering.

In one room she stopped to listen to an old man from western Yingzhou, Japanese or Chinese in ancestry, it appeared, speaking in an awkward Persian about the cultures that existed in the New World when it had been discovered by the Old. It was her acquaintance with Hanea and Ganagweh that made her interested.

"Although in terms of machinery, architecture, and so forth, the inhabitants of the New World still existed in the oldest days, without domesticated animals in Yingzhou, and none but guinea pigs and llamas in Inka, the culture of the Inkas and Aztecs somewhat resembled what we are learning of ancient Egypt. Thus the Yingzhou tribes lived as people in the Old World did before the first cities, say around eight thousand years ago, while the southern empires of Inka resembled the Old World of about four thousand years ago: a distinct difference, which it would be interesting to explain, if you could. Perhaps Inka had some topographical or resource advantages, such as the llama, a beast of burden which, though slight by Old World standards, was more than Yingzhou had. This put more power at their disposal, and as our host Master Zoroush has made clear, in the energy equations used to judge a culture, the power they can bring to bear against the natural world is a crucial factor in their development.

"In any case, the great degree of primitivity in Yingzhou actually gives us a view into social structures that might be like the Old World's pre-agricultural societies. They are curiously modern in certain respects. Because they had the basics of agriculture—squash, corn, beans, and so on—and had a small population to support in a forest that provided enormous numbers of game animals and nut-bearing trees, they lived in a prescarcity economy, just as we now glimpse a technologically created postscarcity state in its theoretical possibility. In both, the individual receives more recognition as a value bearer him- or herself, than does the individual in a scarcity economy. And there is less domination of one caste by another. In these conditions of material ease and plenty, we find the great egalitarianism of the Hodenosaunee, the power wielded by women in their culture, and the absence of slavery—rather, the rapid incorporation of defeated tribes into the full texture of the state.

"By the time of the First Great Empires, four thousand years later, all this was gone, replaced by an extreme vertical scale, with god-kings, a priest caste with ultimate power, permanent military control, and slavery of defeated nations. These early developments, or one should say pathologies, of civilization (for the gathering into cities greatly speeded this process) are only now being dealt with, some four thousand years later still, in the most progressive societies of the world.

"In the meantime, of course, both these archaic cultures have almost entirely disappeared from this world, mostly due to the impact of Old World diseases on populations that apparently had never been exposed to them. Interestingly, it was the southern empires that collapsed most quickly and completely, conquered almost incidentally by the Chinese gold armies, and then quickly devastated by disease and famine, as if the body without its head must die instantly. Whereas in the north it was completely different, first because the Hodenosaunee were able to defend themselves in the depths of the great eastern forest, never fully succumbing to either the Chinese or to the Islamic incursion from across the Atlantic, and second because they were much less susceptible to Old World diseases, possibly because of early exposure to them from wandering Japanese monks, traders, trappers, and prospectors, who ended up infecting the local populace in small numbers, thus serving in effect as human inoculants, immunizing or at least preparing the population of Yingzhou for a fuller incursion of Asians, who did not have quite as devastating an effect, although of course many people and tribes did die."

Budur moved on, thinking about the notion of a postscarcity society, which in hungry Nsara she had never heard of at all. But it was time for another session, a plenary affair that Budur did not want to miss, and which turned out to be one of the most heavily attended. It concerned the question of the lost Franks, and why the plague had hit them so hard.

Much work had been done in this area by the Zott scholar Istvan Romani, who had done his research around the periphery of the plague zone, in Magyaristan and Moldava; and the plague itself had been studied intensively during the Long War, when it seemed possible that one side or another would unleash it as a weapon. It was understood now that it had been conveyed in the first centuries by fleas living on gray rats, traveling on ships and in caravans. A town called Issyk Kul, south of Lake Balkhash in Turkestan, had been studied by Romani and a Chinese scholar named Jiang, and they had found evidence in the cemetery of the town's Nestorians of a heavy die-off from the plague around the year 700. This had apparently been the start of the epidemic that had moved west on the Silk Roads to Sarai, capital at that time of the Golden Horde khanate. One of their khans, Yanibeg, had besieged the Genoese port of Kaffa in the Crimea by catapulting the bodies of plague victims over the town walls. The Genoese had thrown the bodies in the sea, but this had not stopped the plague from infecting the entire Genoese network of trading ports, including, eventually, the whole of the Mediterranean. The plaque moved from port to port, took a respite during the winters, then a renewal in the hinterlands the following spring; this pattern continued for over twenty years. All the westernmost peninsulas of the Old World were devastated, moving north from the Mediterranean and back to the east as far as Moscow, Novgorod, Kopenhagen and the Baltic ports. At the end of this time the population in Firanja was perhaps thirty percent of what it had been before the onset of the epidemic. Then in the years around 777, a date considered significant at the time by some mullahs and Sufi mystics, a second wave of the plague—if it was the plague—had killed off almost all the survivors of the first wave, so that sailors at the start of the eighth century reported witnessing, usually from offshore, a completely emptied land.

Now there were scholars giving presentations who believed that the second plague had actually been anthrax, following on the bubonic plague; there were others who held the reverse position, arguing that contemporary accounts of the first sickness matched the freckling of anthrax more often than the buboes of bubonic plague, while the final blow had been the plague. It was explained in this session that the plague itself had bubonic, septic, and pneumonic forms, and that the pneumonia caused by the pneumonic form was contagious, and very fast and lethal; the septic form even more lethal. Indeed, much had been clarified about all these diseases by the unfortunate experiences of the Long War.

But why had the disease, whichever one it had been, or in whatever combinations, been so lethal in Firanja and not elsewhere? The meeting offered presentation after presentation by scholars advancing one theory after another. From her notes Budur described them all for Piali at the end of the day, over supper, and he quickly jotted them down on a napkin.

- Plague animalcules mutated in the 770s to take on forms and virulence similar to tuberculosis or typhoid
- Cities of Tuscany had reached enormous numbers by the eighth century, say two million people, and hygienic systems broke down and plague vectors ran wild
- Depopulation of the first plague followed by a series of disastrous floods that wrecked agriculture leading to starvation
- Supercontagious form of the animalcule mutated in northern France at the end of the first epidemic

- Pale skin of the Franks and Kelts lacked pigments that helped resist the disease, accounting for the freckling
- Sunspot cycle disrupted weather and caused epidemics every eleven years, effect worse every time—

"Sunspots?" Piali interjected.

"That's what he said." Budur shrugged.

"So," Piali said, looking over the napkin, "it was either the plague animalcules, or some other animalcules, or some quality of the people, or their habits, or their land, or the weather, or sunspots." He grinned. "That pretty much covers it, I should think. Perhaps cosmic rays ought to be included. Wasn't there a big supernova spotted about that time?"

Budur could only laugh. "I think it was earlier. Anyway, you must admit, it does merit explaining."

"Many things do, but it looks as though we have a way to go on this one."

The presentations continued, ranging from the recording of the world that had existed just before the Long War, all the way back through time to the earliest human remains. This work on the first humans forced everyone to the contemplation of one of the larger arguments shaping up in the field, concerning human beginnings.

Archaeology as a discipline had its origins for the most part in the Chinese bureaucracy, but it had been picked up quickly by the Dinei people, who studied with the Chinese and went back to Yingzhou intending to learn what they could about the people they called the Anasazi, who had preceded them in the dry west of Yingzhou. The Dinei scholar Anan and his colleagues had offered the first explanations of human migration and history, asserting that tribes on Yingzhou had mined the tin on Yellow Island in the biggest of the great lakes, Manitoba, and shipped this tin across the oceans to all the bronze-era cultures in Africa and Asia. Anan's group contended that civilization had begun in the New World with the Inka and Aztecs and the Yingzhou tribes, in particular the old ones who preceded their Anasazi in the western deserts. Their great and ancient empires had sent out reed and balsam rafts, trading tin for spices and various plant stocks with Asian ancestry, and these Yingzhou traders had established the Mediterranean civilizations predating Greece, especially the ancient Egyptians and Midwestern empires, the Assyrians and Sumerians.

So the Dinei archaeologists had claimed, anyway, in a very fully articulated case, with all sorts of objects from all over the world to support it. But now a great deal of evidence was appearing in Asia and Firanja and Africa that indicated this story was all wrong. The oldest lifering dates for human settlement in the New World were about twenty thousand years before the present, and everyone had agreed at first that this was extremely old, and predated by a good deal the earliest civilizations known to Old World history, the Chinese and the Midwestern and Egyptian; so at that point it had all seemed plausible. But now that the war was over, scientists were beginning to investigate the Old World in a way that hadn't been possible since a time predating modern archaeology itself. And what they were finding was a great quantity of signs of a human past far older than any yet known. Caves in the Nsaran south containing superb drawings of animals were now reliably dated at forty thousand years. Skeletons in the Midwest appeared to be a hundred thousand years old. And there were scholars from Ingali in South Africa saying they had found remains of humans, or evolutionarily ancestral prehumans, that appeared to be several hundred thousand years old. They could not use lifering dating for these finds, but had different dating methods they thought were just as good as the lifering method.

Nowhere else on Earth were people making a claim like this one from the Africans, and there was a great deal of skepticism about it; some queried the dating methods, other simply dismissed the claim out of hand, as a manifestation of some kind of continental or racial patriotism. Naturally the African scholars were upset by this response, and the meeting that afternoon took on a volatile aspect that could not help but remind people of the late war. It was important to keep the discourse on a scientific basis, as an investigation into facts uncontaminated by religion or politics or race.

"I suppose there can be patriotism in anything," Budur said to Piali that night. "Archaeological patriotism is absurd, but it's beginning to look that's how it started in Yingzhou. An unconscious bias, no doubt, toward one's own region. And until we sort out the dating of things, it's an open question what model will replace theirs."

"Certainly the dating methods will improve," Piali said.

"True. But meanwhile all is confusion."

"That's true of everything."

The days shot by in a blur of meetings. Every day Budur got up at dawn, went to the madressa's dining commons to have a small breakfast, and then attended talks and sessions and poster explanations from then until supper, and after that far into the evenings. One morning she was startled to hear a young woman describing her discovery of what appeared to be a lost feminist branch of early Islam, a branch which had fueled the renaissance of Samarqand, and was then destroyed and the memory of it erased. Apparently a group of women in Qom had taken against a ruling by the mullahs, and led their families east and north to the walled town of Derbent, in Bactria, a place that had been conquered by Alexander the Great and was still living a Greek life in Transoxianic bliss a thousand years later, when the Muslim women rebels and their families arrived. Together they created a way of life in which all living beings were equal before Allah and among themselves, something like what Alexander would have made, for he was a disciple of the queens of Kreta. Then all the people of Derbent lived happily for many years, and though they kept to themselves and did not try to impose themselves on all the world, they did tell some of what they had learned to the people they traded with in nearby Samarqand; and in Samarqand they took that knowledge, and made of it the start of the rebirth of the world. You can read all this in the ruins, the young researcher insisted.

Budur wrote down the references, realizing as she did that archaeology too could be a kind of wish, or even a statement about the future. She went back into the halls, shaking her head. She would have to ask Kirana about it. She would have to look into it herself. Who knew, really, what people had done in the past? Many things had happened and never been written about and after a time had been utterly forgotten. Almost anything might have happened, anything. And there was that phenomenon Kirana had mentioned once in passing, of people imagining that things were better in another land, which then gave them the courage to try to enact some progress in their own country. Thus women had everywhere imagined that women elsewhere had it better than they did, and thus they had had the courage to press for changes. And no doubt there were other examples of the tendency, people imagining the good in advance of its reality, as in the stories of the good place discovered and then lost, what the Chinese called "Source of the Peach Blossom Stream" stories. History, fable, prophecy; no way to distinguish, until perhaps centuries had passed, and they had made the stories one thing or the other.

She dropped in on many more sessions, and this impression of people's endless struggle and effort, endless experimentation, of humans thrashing about trying to find a way to live together, only deepened in her. An imitation Potala built outside Beijing at two-thirds full size; an ancient temple complex, perhaps Greek in origin, lost in the jungles of Amazonia; another in the jungles of Siam; an Inka capital set high in the mountains; skeletons of people in Firanja who were not quite like modern humans in their skull shape; roundhouses made of mammoth bones; the calendrical purposes of the stone rings of Britain; the intact tomb of an Egyptian pharaoh; the nearly untouched remains of a French medieval village; a shipwreck on the peninsula of Ta Shu, the ice continent surrounding the south pole; early Inkan pottery painted with patterns from the south of Japan; Mayan legends of a "great arrival" from the west by a god Itzamna, which was the name of the Shinto mother goddess of the same era; megalithic monuments in Inka's great river basin that resembled megaliths in the Maghrib; old Greek ruins in Anatolia that seemed to be the Troy of Homer's epic poem The Iliad; huge lined figures on the Inkan plains that could only be seen properly from the sky; the beach village in the Orkneys that Budur had visited with Idelba; a very complete Greek and Roman city at Ephesus, on the Anatolian coast; these and many, many more such finds were described. Each day was a rush of talk, Budur all the while scribbling notes in her notebook, and asking for reprints of articles, if they were in Arabic or Persian. She took a particular interest in the sessions on dating methods, and the scientists working on this matter often told her how much they owed to her aunt's pioneering work. They were now investigating other methods of dating, such as the matching up of successive tree rings to create a "dendrochronology," proceeding fairly well, and also the measurement of a particular kind of qileak luminescence that was fixed into pottery that had been fired at high enough temperatures. But there was much work to be done on these methods, and no one was happy with the current state of their abilities to date what they found of the past in the earth.

One day a group of the archaeologists who had used Idelba's work on dating joined Budur, and they crossed the campus of the madressa to attend a memorial session for Idelba put on by the physicists who had known her. This session was to consist of a number of eulogies, a presentation on the various aspects of her work, some presentations of recent work that referred back to hers, and then a short party or wake in celebration of her life.

Budur wandered the rooms of this memorial session accepting praise for her aunt, and condolences of her passing. The men in the room (for they were mostly men) were very solicitous of her and, for the most part, quite cheerful. Even the memory of Idelba brought smiles to their faces. Budur was filled with amazement and pride by this outpouring of affection, though often it made her ache as well; they had lost a valued colleague, but she had lost the only family that mattered to her, and could not always keep her focus on her aunt's work alone.

At one point she was asked to speak to the assemblage and so she struggled to pull herself together as she went up to the lectern, thinking as she walked of her blind soldiers, who existed in her mind as a kind of bulwark or anchor, a benchmark of what was truly sad. In contrast to that this was indeed a celebration, and she smiled to see all these people congregated to honor her aunt. It only remained to figure out what to say, and as she went up the stairs it occurred to her that she only needed to try to imagine what Idelba herself would say, and then paraphrase that. That was reincarnation in a sense she could believe in.

So she looked down at the crowd of physicists, feeling calm and anchored inside, and thanked them for coming, and added, "You all know how concerned Idelba was for the work that you are doing in atomic physics at this time. That it should be used for the good of humanity and not for anything else. I think the best memorial you could make to her would be some kind of organization of scientists devoted to the proper dissemination and use of your knowledge. Perhaps we can talk about that later. It would be very appropriate if such an organization came to be as a result of thinking about her wishes, because of a belief she held, as you know, that scientists, among all people, could be counted on to do what was right, because it would be the scientific thing to do."

She felt a stilling in the audience. The looks on their faces were all of a sudden very much like those on the faces of her blind soldiers: pain, longing, desperate hope; regret and resolve. Many of the people in this room had no doubt been involved in the war effort of their respective countries—at the end, too, when the race in military technologies had speeded up, and things had gotten particularly ferocious and dire. The inventors of the gas shells that had blinded her soldiers could very well be in this room.

"Now," Budur continued cautiously, "obviously this has not always been the case, so far. Scientists have not always done the right thing. But Idelba's vision of science had it as being progressively improvable, just as a matter of making it more scientific. That aspect is one of the ways you define science, as against many other human activities or institutions. So to me this makes it a kind of prayer, or worship of the world. It is a devotional labor. This aspect should be kept in mind, whenever we remember Idelba, and whenever we consider the uses of our work. Thank you."

After that more people than ever came up to her to speak their thanks and appreciation, displaced though it was from its absent object. And then, as the memorial hour wound down, some of them moved on to a meal in a nearby restaurant, and when it was over, an even smaller group of them lingered afterward over coffee and baklava. It was as if they were in one of the rain-lashed cafés of Nsara.

And finally, very late in the night, when no more than a dozen of them remained, and the waiters of the restaurant looked like they wanted to close down, Piali looked around the room, and got a nod from Abdol Zoroush, and said to Budur, "Doctor Chen here," indicating a white-haired Chinese man at the far end of the table, who nodded, "has brought work from his team on the matter of alactin. This was one of the things Idelba was working on, as you know. He wanted to share this work with all of us here. They have made the same determinations we have, concerning the splitting of the alactin atoms, and how this might be exploited to make an explosive. But they have done further calculations, which the rest of us have checked during the conference, including Master Ananda here," and another old man seated next to Chen nodded, "that make it clear that the particular form of alactin that would be necessary for any explosive chain reaction is so rare in nature that it could not be gathered in sufficient quantities. A natural form would have to be gathered first, and then processed in factories, in a procedure that right now is hypothetical only; and even if made practicable, it would be so difficult that it would take the entire industrial capacity of a state to produce enough material to make even a single bomb."

"Really?" Budur said.

They all nodded, looking quietly relieved, even happy. Doctor Chen's translator spoke to him in Chinese and he nodded and said something back.

The translator said in Persian, "Doctor Chen would like to add that from his observations, it seems very unlikely any country will be able to create these materials for many years, even if they should want to. So we are safe. Safe from that, anyway."

"I see," Budur said, and nodded at the elderly Chinese. "As you know, Idelba would be very pleased to have heard these results! She was quite worried, as no doubt you know. But she would also press again for some kind of international scientific organization, of atomic physicists perhaps. Or a more general scientific group, that would take steps to make sure humanity is never threatened by these possibilities. After what the world has just been through in the war, I don't think it could take the introduction of some superbomb. It would lead to madness."

"Indeed," Piali said, and when her words were translated, Doctor Chen spoke again.

His translator said, "The esteemed professor says that he thinks scientific committees to augment, or, or advise—"

Doctor Chen intervened with a comment.

"To guide the world's governments, he says, by telling them what is possible, what is advisable . . . He says he thinks this could be done unobtrusively, in the postwar . . . exhaustion. He says he thinks governments will agree to the existence of such committees, because at first they will not be aware of what it means . . . and by the time they learn what it means, they will be unable to . . . to dismantle them. And so scientists could take a . . . a larger role in political affairs. This is what he said."

The others around the table were nodding thoughtfully, some cautious, others worried; no doubt most of the men there were funded by their governments.

Piali said, "We can at least try. It would be a very good way to remember Idelba. And it may work. It seems it would help, at the very least."

Everyone nodded again, and after translation, Doctor Chen nodded too.

Budur ventured to say, "It might be introduced simply as a matter of scientists doing science, coordinating their efforts, you know, as part of doing better science. At first simple things that look completely innocuous, like uniform weights and measures, rationalized mathematically. Or a solar calendar that is accurate to the Earth's actual movement around the sun. Right now we don't even agree on the date. We all come here in different years, as you know, and now our hosts have resuscitated yet another system. Right now there must be constant multiple listings of dates. We don't even agree on the length of the year. In effect we are still living in different histories, even though it is just one world, as the war taught us. You scientists should perhaps gather your mathematicians and astronomers, and establish a scientifically accurate calendar, and start using it for all scientific work. That might lead to some larger sense of world community."

"How would we start it?" someone asked.

Budur shrugged; she hadn't thought about that part of it. What would Idelba say? "What about just starting now? Call this meeting the zero date. It's spring, after all. Start the year on the spring equinox, perhaps, as most years already do, and then simply number the days of every year, avoiding the various ways of calculating months and the like, the seven-day weeks, the ten-day weeks, all that. Or something else simple, something beyond culture, unarguable because it is physical in origin. Day two fifty-seven of Year One. Forward and backward from that zero date, three hundred and sixty-five days, leap days added, whatever it takes to be accurate to nature. Then as these kinds of matters are all universalized, or made standard all over the world, when the time comes that governments begin to put pressure on their scientists to work for just one part of humanity, they can say, I'm sorry, science doesn't work that way. We are a system for all peoples. We only work to make things so that they will be all right."

The translator was saying all this in Chinese to Doctor Chen, who watched Budur closely as she spoke. When she was done, he nodded and said something.

The interpreter said, "He says, Those are good ideas. He says, Let's try them and see."

———

After that evening, Budur continued to attend the sessions, and take her notes, but she was distracted by thoughts of the private discussions she knew were taking place among the physicists on the other side of the madressa: the plans being made. Piali told her all about them. Her notes tended to become lists of things to do. In sunny Isfahan, a city that was old but entirely new, like a garden just planted in a vast set of ruins, it was easy to forget how hungry they were in Firanja, in China and Africa and indeed over most of the world. On paper it seemed as if they could save everything.

One morning, however, she passed a poster presentation that caught her attention, called "A Tibetan Village Found Intact." It looked just the same as a hundred other hallway exhibits, but something about it caught her. Like most of them, it had its principal text in Persian, with smaller translated texts in Chinese, Tamil, Arabic, and Algonquin, the "big five" languages of the conference. The presenter and author of the poster was a big flat-faced young woman, nervously answering questions from a small group, no more than a half-dozen people, who had gathered to hear her formal presentation. She was Tibetan herself, apparently, and was using one of the Iranian translators to answer any questions she got. Budur wasn't sure if she was speaking in Tibetan or Chinese.

In any case, as she was explaining to someone else, an avalanche and landslide had covered a high mountain village in Tibet, and preserved everything within as if in a giant rocky refrigerator, so that bodies had stayed frozen, and everything been preserved—furniture, clothing, food, even the last messages that two or three literate villagers had written down, before the lack of air had killed them.

The tiny photos of the excavated village made Budur feel very odd. Ticklish just behind her nose, or above the roof of her mouth, until she thought she might sneeze, or retch, or cry. There was something awful about the corpses, almost unchanged through all the centuries; surprised by death, but forced to wait for it. Some of them had even written down good-bye messages. She looked at the photos of the messages, crammed into a margin of a religious book; the handwriting was clear, and looked like Sanskrit. The Arabic translation underneath one had a homely sound:

We have been buried by a big avalanche, and cannot get out. Kenpo is still trying, but it is not going to work. The air is getting bad. We do not have much time. In this house we are Kenpo, Iwang, Sidpa, Zasep, Dagyab, Tenga and Baram. Puntsok left just before the avalanche hit, we don't know what happened to him. "All existence is like a reflection in the mirror, without substance, a phantom of the mind. We will take form again in another place." All praise to Buddha the Compassionate.

The photos looked somewhat like those Budur had seen of certain wartime disasters, death impinging without much of a mark on daily life, except that everything was changed forever. Looking at them Budur felt dizzy all of a sudden, and in the hall of the conference chamber she could almost feel the shock of snow and rock falling on her roof, trapping her. And all her family and friends. But this was how it had happened. This was how it happened.

She was still under the spell of this poster, when Piali came hurrying up. "I'm afraid we should get back home as fast as possible. The army command has suspended the government, and is trying to take over Nsara."

22 ✸ They flew back the next day, Piali fretting at the slowness of the airship, wishing that the military airplanes had been adapted more generally for civilian passenger use, also wondering if they would be arrested on their arrival, as intellectuals visiting a foreign power during a time of national emergency, or some such thing.

But when their airship landed at the airfield outside Nsara, not only were they not arrested, but in fact, looking out the windows of the tram as it rolled into the city, they could not tell that anything at all had changed.

It was only when they got out of the tram and walked over to the madressa district that a difference became apparent. The docks were quieter. The longshoremen had closed down the docks to protest the coup. Now soldiers stood guard over the cranes and gantries, and groups of men and women stood on the street corners watching them.

Piali and Budur went into the offices of the physics building, and heard all the latest from Piali's colleagues. The army command had dissolved the Nsarene state council and the district panchayats, and declared martial law over all. They were calling it sharia, and they had a few mullahs going along with it to provide some religious legitimacy, though it was very slight; the mullahs involved were hard-line reactionaries out of step with everything that had happened in Nsara since the war, part of the "we won" crowd, or, as Hasan had always called them, the "we would have won if it weren't for the Armenians, Sikhs, Jews, Zott, and whoever else we dislike" crowd, the "we would have won if the rest of the world hadn't beaten the shit out of us" crowd. To be among like-minded people they should have moved to the Alpine emirates or Afghanistan long before.

So no one was fooled by the façade of the coup. And as things had recently been getting a bit better, the timing of the coup was not particularly good. It made no sense; apparently it had only happened because the officers had been living on fixed incomes during the period of hyperinflation, and thought everyone else was as desperate as they were. But many, many people were still sick of the army, and supportive of their district panchayats if not of the state council. So it seemed to Budur that the chances for successful resistance were good.

Kirana was much more pessimistic. She was in the hospital now, as it turned out; Budur went running to it the moment she found out, feeling raw and frightened. For tests only, Kirana informed her brusquely, though she did not identify them; something to do with her blood or her lungs, Budur gathered. Nevertheless, from her hospital bed she was calling every zawiyya in the city, organizing things. "They've got the guns so they may win, but we're not going to make it easy."

Many of the madressa and institute's students were already out in crowds on the central plaza, and the corniche and docks, and the grand mosque's courtyards, shouting, chanting, singing, and sometimes throwing stones. Kirana was not satisfied with these efforts, but spent all her time on the phone trying to schedule a rally: "They'll have you back behind the veil, they'll try to turn back the clock until you are all domestic animals again, you have to get out in the streets in great numbers, this is the only thing that scares coup leaders"—always "you" and not "we," Budur noticed, excluding herself as if speaking posthumously, although she was clearly pleased to be involved in all the activities. And pleased also that Budur was visiting her in the hospital.

"They mistimed it," she said to Budur with a kind of mordant glee. Not only were the food shortages becoming less frequent and severe, but it was spring, and as sometimes happened in Nsara, the endlessly cloudy skies had abruptly cleared and the sun was shining day after day, illuminating new greens that welled up everywhere in the gardens and the cracks in the pavement. The sky was washed clear and gleaming like lapis overhead, and when twenty thousand people gathered on the commercial docks and marched down Sultana Katima Boulevard to the Mosque of the Fishermen, many thousands more came to watch, and joined the crowd marching, until when the army ringing the district shot pepper-gas canisters into the crowd, people poured in every direction out the big transverse streets, cutting through the medinas flanking the Lawiyya River, causing it to appear that the whole city had rioted. After those hurt by the gas were cared for, the crowd returned bigger than it had been before the attack.

This happened two or three times in a single day, until the huge square before the city's great mosque and the old palace was completely filled with people, facing the barbed wire fronting the old palace and singing songs, listening to speeches, and chanting slogans and various suras of the Quran that supported the rights of the people against the ruler. The square never emptied, nor even grew uncrowded; people went home for meals and other necessities, leaving the young to carouse through the nights, but they refilled the square during the beautiful lengthening days to bear witness. The whole city was in effect shut down for all of the first month of spring, like an extreme Ramadan.

One day Kirana was wheeled to the palace square in a wheelchair by her students, and she grinned at the sight. "Now this is what works," she said. "Sheer numbers!"

They brought her through the crowd to the rough podium they were constructing daily, made of dock pallets, and got her up there to make a speech, which she did with gusto, in her usual style, despite her physical weakness. She grabbed the microphone of the amplifier and said to them, "What Muhammad began was the idea that all humans had rights that could not be taken away from them without insulting their Creator. Allah made all humans equally His creatures, and none are to serve others. This message came into a time very far from these practices, and the course of progress in history has been the story of the clarification of these principles of Islam, and the establishment of true justice. Now we are here to continue that work!

"In particular women have had to struggle against misinterpretation of the Quran, jailed in their homes and their veils and their illiteracy, until Islam itself foundered under the general ignorance of all—for how can men be wise and prosper when they spend their first years taught by people who don't know anything?

"Thus we fought the Long War and lost it, for us it was the Nakba. Not the Armenians or the Burmese or the Jews or the Hodenosaunee or the Africans were responsible for our defeat, nor any problem with Islam itself fundamentally, as it is the voice of the love of God and the wholeness of humanity, but only the historical miscarriage of Islam, distorted as it has been.

"Now, we have been facing that reality in Nsara ever since the war ended, and we have made great strides. We have all witnessed and taken part in the burst of good work done here, despite physical privations of every sort and underneath the constant rain.

"Now the generals think they can stop all this and turn the clock back, as if they did not lose the war and cast us into this necessity of creation that we have used so well. As if time could ever run backward! Nothing like that can ever happen! We have made a new world here on old ground, and Allah protects it, through the actions of all the people who truly love Islam and its chances to survive in the world to come.

"So we have gathered here to join the long struggle against oppression, to join all the revolts, rebellions, and revolutions, all the efforts to take power away from the armies, the police, the mullahs, and give it back to the people. Every victory has been incremental, a matter of two steps forward one step back, a struggle forever. But each time we progress a little further, and no one is going to push us backward! If they expect to succeed in such a project, the government will have to dismiss the people and appoint another one! But I don't think that's how it happens."

This was well received, and the crowd kept growing, and Budur was pleased to see how many of them were women, working women from the kitchens and the canning factories, women for whom the veil or the harem had never been an issue, but who had suffered as they all had with the war and the crash; indeed they formed the raggedest, hungriest-looking mob possible, with a tendency merely to stand there as if asleep on their feet; and yet there they were, filling the squares, refusing to work;

and on Friday they faced Mecca only when one of the revolutionary clerics stood among them, not a policeman in a pulpit, but a man among neighbors, as Muhammad had been in his life. As it was Friday, this particular cleric said the first chapter of the Quran, the Fatiha, known to everyone, even the large group of Buddhists and Hodenosaunee always standing there among them, so that the whole crowd could recite it together, over and over many times:

> Praise be to God, Lord of the Worlds!
> The compassionate, the merciful!
> King on the day of reckoning!
> Thee only do we worship, and to Thee do we cry for help.
> Guide us on the straight path,
> The path of those to whom Thou has been gracious;
> With whom Thou are not angry, and who go not astray!

The next morning this same cleric got up on the dais and started the day by reciting into the microphone a poem by Ghaleb, waking people up and calling them out to the square again:

> Soon I will be only a story
> But the same is true of you.
> I hope the bardo will not be empty
> But people do not yet know where they live.
> Past and future all mixed together,
> Let those trapped birds out the window!
> What then remains? The stories you no longer
> Believe. You had better believe them.
> While you live they carry the meaning.
> When you die they carry the meaning.
> To those who come after they carry the meaning.
> You had better believe in them.
> In Rumi's story he saw all the worlds
> As one, and that one, Love, he called to and knew,
> Not Muslim or Jew or Hindu or Buddhist,
> Only a Friend, a breath breathing human,
> Telling his boddhisatva story. The bardo
> Waits for us to make it real.

Budur on that morning was awakened in the zawiyya by someone bringing news to her of a phone message: it was from one of her blind soldiers. They wanted to talk to her.

She took the tram and then walked into the hospital, feeling apprehensive. Were they angry at her for not coming recently? Were they worried about the way she had left after her last visit?

No. The oldest ones spoke for them, or for some part of them, anyway; they wanted to march in the demonstration against the army takeover, and they wanted her to lead them. About two-thirds of the ward said they wanted to do it.

It wasn't the kind of request one could refuse. Budur agreed, and feeling shaky and uncertain, led them out the gate of the hospital. There were too many of them for the trams, so they walked down the riverfront road, and then the corniche, hands on the shoulders before them, like a parade of elephants. Back in the ward Budur had gotten used to the look of them, but out here in the brilliant sunshine and the open air they were a shocking sight once again, maimed and awful. Three hundred and twenty-seven of them, walking down the corniche; they had taken a head count when leaving the ward.

Naturally they drew a crowd, and some people began following them down the corniche, and in the big plaza there was already a crowd, a crowd that quickly made room for the veterans at the front of the protest, facing the old palace. They arranged themselves into ranks by feel, and counted off in undertones, with a little aid from Budur. Then they stood silently, right hands on the shoulders to their left, listening to the speakers at the microphone. The crowd behind them grew bigger and bigger.

Army airships floated low over the city, and amplified voices from them ordered everyone to leave the streets and plazas. A full curfew had been declared, the mechanical voices informed them.

This decision had no doubt been made in ignorance of the blind soldiers' presence in the palace square. They stood there without moving, and the crowd stood with them. One of the blind soldiers shouted, "What are they going to do, gas us?"

In fact this was all too possible, as pepper gas had been deployed already, at the State Council Chambers and the police barracks, and down on the docks. And later it was said by many that the blind soldiers were in fact tear-gassed during that tense week, and that they just stood there and took it, for they had no tears left to shed; that they stood in their square with their hands on each others' shoulders and chanted the Fatiha, and the bismallah that starts every sura:

> In the name of Allah, the compassionate, the merciful!
> In the name of Allah, the compassionate, the merciful!

Budur herself never saw any pepper gas dropped in the palace square, although she heard her soldiers chanting the bismallah for hours at a time. But she was not there in the square every hour of that week, and hers was not the only group of blind soldiers to have left their hospitals and joined the protests either. So possibly something of the sort occurred. Certainly in the time afterward everyone believed it had.

In any case, during that long week people passed the time by reciting long passages from Rumi Balkhi, and Ferdowski, and the joker mullah Nusreddin, and the epic poet of Firanja, Ali, and from their own Sufi poet of Nsara, young Ghaleb, who had been killed on the very last day of the war. Budur made frequent visits to the women's hospital where Kirana was staying, to tell her what was happening on the plaza and elsewhere in the great city, now pulsing everywhere with its people. They had taken to the streets and were not leaving them. Even when the rain returned they stayed out there. Kirana ate up every word of news, hungry to be out herself, supremely irritated that she was confined at this time. Obviously she was seriously ill or she wouldn't have suffered it, but she was emaciated and sallow, dark rings under her eyes like a raccoon from Yingzhou, "stuck," as she put it, "just when things are getting interesting," just when her long-winded acid-tongued facility for speech could have been put to use, could have made history as well as commented on it. But it was not to be; she could only lie there fighting her illness. The one time Budur ventured to ask how she was feeling, she grimaced and said only, "The termites have got me."

But even so she stayed close to the center of the action. A delegation of opposition leaders, including a contingent of women from the zawiyyas of the city, were meeting with adjutants of the generals to make their protests and negotiate if they could, and these people visited Kirana often to talk over strategy. On the streets the rumor was that a deal was being hammered out, but Kirana lay there, eyes burning, and shook her head at Budur's hopefulness. "Don't be naïve." Her sardonic grin wrinkled her wasted features. "They're just playing for time. They think that if they hold on long enough the protests will die down, and they can get on with their business. They're probably right. They've got the guns after all."

But then a Hodenosaunee fleet steamed into the harbor roads and anchored. Hanea! Budur thought when she saw them: forty giant steel battleships, bristling with guns that could fire a hundred li inland. They called in on a wireless frequency used by a popular music station, and though the government had seized the station, they could do nothing to stop this message from reaching all the wireless receptors in the city, and many heard the message and passed it along: the Hodenosaunee wanted to speak to the legitimate government, the one they had been dealing with before. They refused to speak to the generals, who were breaking the Shanghai Convention by usurping the constitutionally required government, a very serious breach; they declared they would not move from Nsara's harbor until the council established by the postwar settlement was reconvened; and they would not trade with any government led by the generals. As the grain that had saved Nsara from starvation in the previous winter had mostly come from Hodenosaunee ships, this was a serious challenge indeed.

The matter hung for three days, during which rumors flew like bats at dusk: that negotiations were going on between the fleet and the junta, that mines were being laid, that amphibious troops were being readied, that negotiations were breaking down . . .

On the fourth day the leaders of the coup were suddenly nowhere to be found. The Yingzhou fleet was a few ships smaller in size. The generals had been spirited off, everyone said, to asylums in the Sugar Islands or the Maldives, in exchange for quitting without a fight. The ranking officers left behind led the deployed units of the army back to their barracks and stood down, waiting for further instructions from the legitimate state council. The coup was canceled.

The people in the streets cheered, shouted, sang, embraced total strangers, went crazy for joy. Budur did all these things, and led her soldiers back to their ward, and then rushed to Kirana's hospital to tell Kirana everything she had seen, feeling a pang to see her so sick in the midst of this triumph. Kirana nodded at the news, saying, "We were lucky to get help like that. The whole world saw that; it will have a good effect, you'll see. Although now we're in for it! We'll see what it's like to be part of a league, we'll see what kind of people they really are."

Other friends wanted to wheel her out to give another speech, but she wouldn't do it, she said, "Just go tell people to get back to work, tell them we need to get the bakeries baking again."

i ✹ Darkness. Silence. Then a voice in the void: Kirana? Are you there? Kuo? Kyu? Kenpo?

What.

Are you there?

I'm here.

We're back in the bardo.

There is no such thing.

Yes there is. Here we are. You can't deny it. We keep coming back.

(Blackness, silence. A refusal of speech.)

Come on, you can't deny it. We keep coming back. We keep going out again. Everybody does. That's dharma. We keep trying. We keep making progress.

A noise like a tiger's growl.

But we do! Here's Idelba, and Piali, and even Madame Sururi.

So she was right.

Yes.

Ridiculous.

Nevertheless. Here we are. Here to be sent back again, sent back together, our little jati. I don't know what I would do without all of you. I think the solitude would kill me.

You're killed anyway.

Yes, but it's less lonely this way. And we're making a difference. No, we are! Look at what has happened! You can't deny it!

Things were done. It's not very much.

Of course. You said it yourself, we have thousands of lifetimes of work to do. But it's working.

Don't generalize. It could all slip away.

Of course. But back we go, to try again. Each generation makes its fight. A few more turns of the wheel. Come on—back with a will. Back into the fray!

As if one could refuse.

Oh come on. You wouldn't even if you could. You're always the one leading the way down there, you're always up for a fight.

. . . I'm tired. I don't know how you persist the way you do. You tire me too. All that hope in the face of calamity. Sometimes I think you should be more marked by it. Sometimes I think I have to take it all on myself.

Come on. You'll be your old self once things get going again. Idelba, Piali, Madame Sururi, are you ready?

We're ready.

Kirana?

. . . All right then. One more turn.

BOOK 10

❋ THE FIRST YEARS ❋

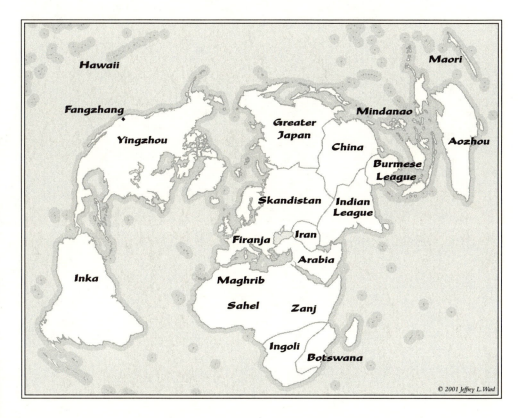

Hawaii

Maori

Fangzhang

Mindanao

Greater
Japan

Yingzhou

China

Aozhou

Burmese
League

Skandistan

Indian
League

Firanja

Iran

Inka

Arabia

Maghrib

Sahel

Zanj

Ingoli

Botswana

© 2001 Jeffrey L. Ward

1

Always China

Bao Xinhua was fourteen years old when he first met Kung Jianguo, in his work unit near the southern edge of Beijing, just outside the Dahongmen, the Big Red Gate. Kung was only a few years older, but he was already head of the revolutionary cell in his work unit next door, quite an accomplishment given that he had been one of the sanwu, the "three withouts"—without family, without work unit, without identity card—when he showed up as a boy at the gate of the police station of the Zhejiang district, just outside the Dahongmen. The police had placed him in his current work unit, but he always remained an outsider there, often called "an individualist," which is a very deep criticism in China even now, when so much has changed. "He persisted in his own ways, no matter what others said." "He clung obstinately to his own course." "He was so lonely he didn't even have a shadow." This is what they said about him in his work unit, and so naturally he looked outside the unit to the neighborhood and the city at large, and was a street boy for no one knew how long, not even him. And he was good at it. Then at a young age he became a firebrand in Beijing underground politics, and it was in this capacity that he visited Bao Xinhua's work unit.

"The work unit is the modern equivalent of the Chinese clan compound," he said to those of them who gathered to listen. "It is a spiritual and social unit as much as an economic one, trying its best to continue the old ways in the new world. No one really wants to change it, because everyone wants to have a place to come to when they die. Everyone needs a place. But these big walled factories are not like the old family compounds that they imitate. They are prisons, first built to organize our labor for the Long War. Now the Long War has been over for fifty years and yet we slave all our lives for it still, as if we worked for China, when really it is only for corrupt military governors. Not even for the emperor, who disappeared long ago, but for the generals and warlords, who hope we will work and work and never notice how the world has changed.

"We say, 'We are of one work unit' as if we were saying, 'We are of the same family,' or 'We are brother and sister,' and this is good. But we never see over the wall of our unit, to the world at large."

Many in his audience nodded. Their work unit was a poor one, made up mostly of immigrants from the south, and they often went hungry. The postwar years in Beijing had seen a lot of changes, and now in the Year 29, as the revolutionaries liked to call it, in conformity with the practice of scientific organizations, things were beginning to fall apart. The Qing dynasty had been overthrown in the middle years of the war, when things had gone so badly; the emperor himself, aged six or seven at the time, had disappeared, and now most assumed he was dead. The Fifth Assemblage of Military Talent was still in control of the Confucian bureaucracy, its hand still on the wheel of their destiny; but it was a senile old hand, the dead hand of the past, and all over China revolts were breaking out. They were of all sorts: some in the service of foreign ideologies, but most internal insurgencies, organized by Han Chinese hoping to rid themselves once and for all of the Qing and the generals and warlords. Thus the White Lotus, the Monkey Insurgents, the Shanghai Revolutionary Movement, and so on. Joining these were regional revolts by the various nationalities and ethnic groups in the west and south— the Tibetans, Mongolians, Xinzing, and so on, all intent on freeing themselves from the heavy hand of Beijing. There was no question that despite the big army that Beijing could in theory bring to bear, an army still much admired and honored by the populace for its sacrifices in the Long War, the military command itself was in trouble, and soon to fall. The Great Enterprise had returned again to China; dynastic succession; and the question was, who was going to succeed? And could anyone succeed in bringing China back together again?

Kung spoke to Bao's work unit in favor of the League of All Peoples

School of Revolutionary Change, which had been founded during the last years of the Long War by Zhu Tuanjie-kexue ("Unite for Science"), a half-Japanese whose birth name had been Isao. Zhu Isao, as he was usually called, had been a Chinese governor of one of the Japanese provinces before their revolution, and when that revolution came he had negotiated a settlement with the Japanese independence forces. He had ordered the Chinese army occupying Kyushu back to China without loss of life on either side, landing with them in Manchuria and declaring the port city of Tangshan to be an international city of peace, right there in the homeland of the Qing rulers, and in the midst of the Long War. The official Beijing position was that Zhu was a Japanese and a traitor, and that when the appropriate time came his insurgency would be crushed by the Chinese armies he had betrayed. As it turned out, when the war ended and the postwar years marched by in their dreary hungry round, the city of Tangshan was never conquered; on the contrary, similar revolts occurred in many other Chinese cities, particularly the big ports on the coast, all the way down to Canton, and Zhu Isao published an unending stream of theoretical materials defending his movement's actions, and explaining the novel organization of the city of Tangshan, which was run as a communal enterprise belonging equally to all the people who lived within its embattled borders.

Kung talked about these matters with Bao's work unit, describing Zhu's theory of communal creation of value, and what it meant for ordinary Chinese, who had for so long had the fruits of their labor stolen from them. "Zhu looked at what really happens, and described our economy, politics, and methods of power and accumulation in scientific detail. After that he proposed a new organization of society, which took this knowledge of how things work and applied it to serve all the people in a community and in all China, or any other country."

During a break for a meal, Kung paused to speak to Bao, and asked his name. Bao's given name was Xinhua, "New China"; Kung's was Jianguo, "Construct the Nation." They knew therefore that they were children of the Fifth Assemblage, who had encouraged patriotic naming to counteract their own moral bankruptcy and the superhuman sacrifices of the people during the postwar famines. Everyone born around twenty years before had names like "Oppose Islam" (Huidi) or "Do Battle" (Zhandou) even though at that point the war had been over for thirty years. Girls' names had suffered especially during this fad, as parents at-

tempted to keep some traditional elements of female names incorporated into the whipped-up patriotric fervor, so that there were girls their
age named "Fragrant Soldier" or "Graceful Army" or "Public Fragrance"
or "Nation-loving Orchid" and the like.

Kung and Bao laughed together over some of these examples, and
spoke of Bao's parents, and Kung's lack of parents; and Kung fixed Bao
with his gaze, and said, "Yet Bao itself is a very important word or concept, you know. Repayment, retribution, honoring parents and ancestors—holding, and holding on. It's a good name."

Bao nodded, captured already by the attention of this dark-eyed person, so intense and cheerful, so interested in things. There was something about him that drew Bao, drew him so strongly that it seemed to
Bao that this meeting was a matter of yuanfen, a "predestined relation,"
a thing always meant to be, part of his yuan or "fate." Saving him perhaps from a nieyuan, a "bad fate," for his work unit struck him as small-
minded, oppressive, stultifying, a kind of death to the soul, a prison from
which he could not escape, in which he was already entombed. Whereas
he already felt like he had known Kung forever.

So he followed Kung around Beijing like a younger brother, and because of him became a sort of truant from his work unit, or in other
words, a revolutionary. Kung took him to meetings of the revolutionary
cells he was part of, and gave him books and pamphlets of Zhu Isao's to
read; took charge of his education, in effect, as he had for so many others; and there was nothing Bao's parents or his work unit could do about
it. He had a new work unit now, spread out across Beijing and China and
all the world—the work unit of those who were going to make things
right.

Beijing at the time was a place of most severe deprivations. There
were millions who had moved there during the war, who still lived in improvised shantytowns outside the gates. The wartime work units had expanded far to the west, and these still stood like a succession of gray
fortresses, looking down on the wide new streets. Every tree in the city
had been cut down during the Twelve Hard Years, and even now the city
was bare of almost all vegetation; the new trees had been planted with
spiked fences protecting them, and watchmen to guard them at night,
which did not always work; the poor old guards would wake in the
mornings to find the fence there but the tree gone, cut at the ground for

firewood or pulled out by the roots for sale somewhere else, and for these lost saplings they would weep inconsolably, or even commit suicide. The bitter winters would sweep down on the city in the fall, rains full of yellow mud from the dust torn out of the loess to the west, and drizzle down onto a concrete city without a single leaf to fall to the ground. Rooms were kept warm by space heaters, but the qi system often shut down, in blackouts that lasted for weeks, and then everyone suffered, except for the government bureaucrats, whose compounds had their own generating systems. Most people stayed warm then by stuffing their coats with newspaper, so that it was a bulky populace that moved around in their thick brown coats, doing what work they could find, looking like they were all fat with prosperity; but it wasn't so.

Thus many people were ripe for change. Kung was as lean and hungry as any of them, but full of energy, he didn't seem to need much food or sleep: all he ever did was read and talk, talk and read, and ride his bike from meeting to meeting and exhort groups to unify to join the revolutionary movement spearheaded by Zhu Isao, and change China.

"Listen," he would say to his audiences urgently, "it's China we can change, because we are Chinese, and if we change China, then we change the world. Because it always comes back to China, do you understand? There are more of us than all the rest of the people of the Earth combined. And because of the colonialist-imperialist years of the Qing, all the wealth of the world has come to us over the years, in particular all the gold and silver. For many dynasties we brought in gold by trade, and then when we conquered the New World we took their gold and silver from them, and all that came back to China too. And none of it has ever left! We are poor not for any material reason, but because of the way we are organized, do you see? We suffered in the Long War the way every nation suffered in the Long War, but the rest of the world is recovering and we are not, even though we won, because of the way we are organized! The gold and silver is hidden in the treasure chests of the corrupt bureaucrats, and people freeze and starve while the bureaucrats hide in their holes, warm and full. And that will never change unless we change it!"

He would go on to explain Zhu's theories of society, how for many long dynasties a system of extortion had ruled China and most of the world, and because the land was fecund and the farmers' taxes supportable, the system had endured. Eventually, however, a crisis had come to this system, wherein the rulers had grown so numerous, and the land so depleted, that the taxes they required could not be grown by the farmers; and when it was a choice of starvation or revolt, the farmers had revolted, as they had often before the Long War. "They did it for their children's sake. We were taught to honor our ancestors, but the tapestry of the generations runs in both directions, and it was the genius of the people to begin to fight for the generations to come—to give up their lives for their children and their children's children. This is the true way to honor your family! And so we had the revolts of the Ming and the early Qing, and similar uprisings were happening all over the world, and eventually things fell apart, and all fought all. And even China, the richest nation on Earth, was devastated. But the necessary work went on. We have to continue that work, and end the tyranny of the rulers, and establish a new world based on the sharing of the world's wealth among all equally. The gold and silver come from the Earth, and the Earth belongs to all of us, just like the air and the water belong to all of us. There can no longer be hierarchies like those that have oppressed us for so long. The fight has to be carried on, and each defeat is simply a necessary defeat in the long march toward our goal."

Naturally anyone who spent every hour of every day making such speeches, as Kung did, was quickly going to get in serious trouble with the authorities. Beijing, as the capital and biggest manufacturing city, undamaged in the Long War compared to many other cities, was assigned many divisions of the army police, and the walls of the city made it possible for them to close the gates and conduct quarter-by-quarter searches. It was, after all, the heart of the empire. They could order an entire quarter razed if they wanted to, and more than once they did; shantytowns and even legally allowed districts were bulldozed flat and rebuilt to the standard work-unit compound plan, in the effort to rid the city of malcontents. A firebrand like Kung was marked for trouble. And so in the Year 31, when he was around seventeen, and Bao fifteen, he left Beijing for the southern provinces, to take the message to the masses, as Zhu Isao had urged him and all the cadres like him to do.

Bao followed along with him. At the time of his departure he took with him a bag containing a pair of silk socks, a pair of blue wool shoes with leather bottoms, a wadded jacket, an old lined jacket, a pair of lined trousers, a pair of unlined trousers, a hand towel, a pair of bamboo chopsticks, an enamel bowl, a toothbrush, and a copy of Zhu's *Analysis of Chinese Colonialism.*

The next years flew by, and Bao learned a great deal about life and people, and about his friend Kung Jianguo. The riots of Year 33 evolved into a full revolt against the Fifth Military Assemblage, which became a general civil war. The army attempted to keep control of the cities, the revolutionaries scattered into the villages and fields. There they lived by a series of protocols that made them the favorite of the farmers, taking great pains to protect them and their crops and animals, never expropriating their possessions or their food, preferring starvation to theft from the very people they had pledged themselves to liberate.

Every battle in this strange diffuse war had a macabre quality; it seemed like an endless string of murders of civilians in their own clothes, no uniforms or big formal battles about it; men, women, and children, farmers in the field, shopkeepers in their doorways, animals; the army was merciless. And yet it went on.

Kung became a prominent leader at the revolutionary military college in Annan, a college headquartered deep in the gorge of the Brahmaputra, but also spread through every unit of the revolutionary forces, the professors or advisors doing their best to make every encounter with the enemy a kind of education in the field. Soon Kung headed this effort, particularly when it came to the struggle for the urban and coastal work units; he was an endless source of ideas and energy.

The Fifth Military Assemblage eventually abandoned the central government, and fell away into a scattering of warlords. This was a victory, but now each warlord and his little army had to be defeated in turn. The struggle moved unevenly from province to province, an ambush here, a bridge blown up there. Often Kung was the target of assassination attempts, and naturally Bao, as his comrade and assistant, was also endangered by these attacks. Bao tended to want vengeance against the attempted assassins, but Kung was imperturbable. "It doesn't matter," he would say. "We all die anyway." He was much more cheerful about this fact than anyone else Bao ever met.

Only once did Bao see Kung seriously angry, and even that was in a strangely cheerful way, considering the situation. It happened when one of their own officers, one Shi Fandi ("Oppose Imperialism"), was convicted by eyewitnesses of raping and killing a female prisoner in his keeping.

Shi emerged from the jail they had kept him in shouting, "Don't kill me! I've done nothing wrong! My men know I tried to protect them, the bandit that died was one of the most brutal in Sechuan! This judgment is wrong!"

Kung appeared from the storeroom where he had slept that night.

Shi said, "Commander, have mercy. Don't kill me!"

Kung said, "Shi Fandi, don't say anything more. When a man does something as wrong as you have, and it's time for him to die, he should shut up and put a good face on it. That's all he can do to prepare himself for his next time around. You raped and killed a prisoner, three eyewitnesses testified to it, and that's one of the worst crimes there is. And there are reports it wasn't the first time. To let you live and do more such things will only make people hate you and our cause, so it would be wrong. Let's have no more talk. I'll make sure your family is taken care of. You be a man of more courage."

Shi said bitterly, "More than once I've been offered ten thousand taels to kill you, and I always turned them down."

Kung waved this away. "That was only your duty, but you think it makes you special. As if you had to resist your character to do the right thing. But your character is no excuse! I'm sick of your character! I too have an angry soul, but this is China we're fighting for! For humanity! You have to ignore your character, and do what is right!"

And he turned away as Shi Fandi was led off.

Afterward Kung was in a dark mood, not remorseful about the condemnation of Shi, but depressed. "It had to be done but it did nothing. Such men as he often come out on top. Presumably they will never die out. And so perhaps China will never escape her fate." He quoted from Zhu: " 'Vast territories, abundant resources, a great population—from such an excellent base, will we only ever go in circles, trapped on the wheel of birth and death?' "

Bao did not know how to reply; he had never heard his friend speak so pessimistically. Although now it seemed familiar enough. Kung had many moods. But in the end, one mood dominated; he sighed, leaped to his feet: "On with it, anyway! Go on, go on! We can only try. We have to occupy the time of this life somehow, we might as well fight for the good."

It was the farmers' associations that made the difference in the end. Kung and Bao attended nightly meetings in hundreds of villages and towns, and thousands of revolutionary soldiers like them were conveying Zhu's analysis and plan to the people, who in the country were still for the most part illiterate, so that the information had to be conveyed by word of mouth. But there is no form of communication faster and more certain, once it reaches a certain critical point of accumulation.

Bao learned every detail of farming existence during that time. He learned that the Long War had stripped away most of the men who had been alive, and many of the younger women. There were only a few old men around no matter where you went, and the total population was still less than it had been before the war. Some villages were abandoned, others were occupied by skeleton crews. This made planting and harvesting crops difficult, and the young people alive were always at work ensuring that the season's food and tax crops would be grown. The old women worked as hard as anyone, doing what they could at their age to help, maintaining at all times the imperial demeanor of the ordinary Chinese farmwife. Usually the ones in the village who could read and do accounts were the grandmothers, who as girls had lived in more prosperous families; now they taught the younger folk how to run the looms, and to deal with the government in Beijing, and to read. Because of this they were often the first ones cut down when a warlord army invaded their region, along with the young men who might join the fight.

In the Confucian system the farmers were the second most highly regarded class, just below the scholar bureaucrats who invented the system, but above the artisans and merchants. Now Zhu's intellectuals were organizing the farmers in the backcountry, and the artisans and merchants in the cities mostly waited to see what would happen. So it seemed Confucius himself had identified the revolutionary classes. Certainly there were many more farmers than city dwellers. So when the farmer armies began to organize and march, there was little the old Long War remnants could do about it; they had been decimated themselves, and had neither the means nor the will to kill millions of their countrymen. For the most part they retreated to the biggest cities, and prepared to defend them as if against Muslims.

In this uneasy standoff, Kung argued against any all-out assaults, advocating more subtle methods for defeating the city-based warlords that remained. Certain cities had their supply lines cut off, their airports destroyed, their ports blockaded; siege tactics of the oldest kind, updated to the new weapons of the Long War. Indeed another long war, this time a civil war, seemed to be brewing, though there was no one in China who wanted such a thing. Even the youngest child lived in the wreckage and shadow of the Long War, and knew another one would be a catastrophe.

Kung met with White Lotus and other revolutionary groups in the cities controlled by the warlords. Almost every work unit had within it workers sympathetic to the revolution, and many of them were joining Zhu's movement. In reality there was almost no one who actively and enthusiastically supported the old regime; how could there be? Too much bad had happened. So it was a matter of getting all the disaffected to back the same resistance, and the same strategy for change. Kung proved to be the most influential leader in this effort. "In times like these," he would say, "everyone becomes a sort of intellectual, as matters so dire demand to be thought through. That's the glory of these times. They have woken us up."

Some of these talks and organizational meetings were dangerous visits to enemy ground. Kung had risen too far in the New China movement to be safe making such missions; he was too famous now, and had a price on his head.

But once, in the thirty-second week of Year 35, he and Bao made a clandestine visit to their old neighborhood in Beijing, hiding in a delivery truck full of cabbage heads, and emerging near the Big Red Gate.

At first it seemed everything had changed. Certainly the immediate neighborhood outside the gate had been razed, and new streets laid out, so that there was no way they could find their old haunts by the gate, as they were gone. In their place stood a big police station and a number of work-unit compounds, lined up parallel to the old stretch of city wall that still existed for a short distance on each side of the gate. Fairly big trees had been transplanted to the new street corners, protected by thick wrought-iron fences with spikes on top: the greenery looked very fine. The work-unit compounds had dorm windows looking outward, another welcome new feature; in the old days they were always built with blank walls facing the outside world, and only in their inner courtyards were there any signs of life. Now the streets themselves were crowded with vendor carts and rolling bookstalls.

"It looks good," Bao had to admit.

Kung grinned. "I liked the old place better. Let's get going and see what we can find."

Their appointment was in an old work unit, occupying several smaller buildings just to the south of the new quarter. Down there the alleys were as tight as ever, all brick and dust and muddy lanes, not a tree to be seen. They wandered freely here, wearing sunglasses and aviator's caps like half the other young men. No one paid them the slightest attention, and they were able to buy paper bowls of noodles and eat standing on a street corner among the crowds and traffic, observing the familiar scene, which did not seem to have changed a bit since their departure a few packed years before.

Bao said, "I miss this place."

Kung agreed. "It won't be long before we can move back here if we want. Enjoy Beijing again, center of the world."

But first, a revolution to finish. They slipped into one of the shops of the work unit and met with a group of unit supervisors, most of them old women. They were not inclined to be impressed by any boy advocating enormous change, but by this time Kung was famous, and they listened carefully to him, and asked a lot of detailed questions, and when he was done they nodded and patted him on the shoulder and sent him back out onto the street, telling him he was a good boy and that he should get out of the city before he got himself arrested, and that they would back him when the time came. That was the way it was with Kung: everyone felt the fire in him, and responded in the human way. If he could win over the old women of the Long War in a single meeting, then nothing was impossible. Many a village and work unit was staffed entirely by these women, as were the Buddhist hospitals and colleges. Kung knew all about them by now, "the gangs of widows and grandmothers," he called them; "very frightening minds, they are beyond the world but know every tael of it, so they can be very hard, very unsentimental. Good scientists frequent among them. Politicians of great cunning. It's best not to cross them." And he never did, but learned from them, and honored them; Kung knew where the power lay in any given situation. "If the old women and the young men ever get together, it will be all over!"

Kung also traveled to Tangshan to meet with Zhu Isao himself, and discuss with the old philosopher the campaign for China. Under Zhu's aegis he flew to Yingzhou and spoke with the Japanese and Chinese representatives of the Yingzhou League, meeting also Travancoris and others in Fangzhang, and when he returned, he came with promises of support from all the progressive governments of the new world.

Soon after that, one of the great Hodenosaunee fleets arrived in Tangshan, and unloaded huge quantities of food and weapons, and similar fleets appeared off all the port cities not under revolutionary control already, blockading them in effect if not in word, and the New China forces were able over the next couple of years to win victories in Shanghai, Canton, Hangzhou, Nanjing, and inland all over China. The final assault on Beijing became more of a triumphal entry than anything else; the soldiers of the old army disappeared into the vast city, or out to their last stronghold in Gansu, and Kung was with Zhu in the first trucks of a giant motorcade that entered the capital uncontested, indeed hugely celebrated, on the spring equinox marking the Year 36, though the Big Red Gate.

It was later in that week that they opened up the Forbidden City to the people, who had only been in there a few times before, after the disappearance of the last emperor, when for a few years of the war it had been a public park and army barracks. For the past forty years it had been closed again to the people, and now they streamed in to hear Zhu and his inner circle speak to China and the world. Bao was in the crowd accompanying them, and as they passed under the Gate of Great Harmony he saw Kung look around, as if surprised. Kung shook his head, an odd expression on his face; and it was still there when he went up to the podium to stand by Zhu and speak to the ecstatic masses filling the square.

Zhu was still speaking when the shots rang out. Zhu fell, Kung fell; all was chaos. Bao fought his way through the screaming crowd and got to the ring of people around the wounded on the temporary wooden stage, and most of those people were men and women he knew, trying to establish order and get medical assistance and a route out of the palace grounds to a hospital. One who recognized him let Bao through, and he rushed and stumbled to Kung's side. The assassin had used the big soft-tipped bullets that had been developed during the war, and there was blood all over the wood of the stage, shocking in its copious gleaming redness. Zhu had been struck in the arm and leg; Kung in the chest. There was a big hole in his back and his face was gray. He was dying. Bao knelt beside him and took up his splayed right hand, calling out his name. Kung looked through him; Bao couldn't be sure he was seeing anything. "Kung Jianguo!" Bao cried, the words torn out of him like no others had ever been.

"Bao Xinhua," Kung mouthed. "Go on."

Those were his last words. He died before they even got him off the stage.

2

This Square Fathom

All that happened when Bao was young.

After Kung's assassination he wasn't much good for a time. He attended the funeral and never shed a tear; he thought he was beyond such things, that he was a realist, that the cause was what mattered and that the cause would go on. He was numb to his grief, he felt he didn't really care. That seemed odd to him, but there it was. It wasn't all that real, it couldn't be. He had gotten over it.

He kept his nose in books, and read all the time. He attended the college in Beijing and read history and political science, and accepted diplomatic posts for the new government, first in Japan, then Yingzhou, then Nsara, then Burma. The New China program progressed, but slowly, so slowly. Things were better but not in any rapid marked way. Different but in some ways the same. People still fought, corruption infected the new institutions, it was always a struggle. Everything took much longer than anyone had anticipated, and yet every few years everything was also somehow entirely different. The pulse of history's long duration was much slower than an individual's time.

One day, after some years had passed, he met a woman named Pan Xichun, a diplomat from Yingzhou, in Beijing on assignment to the embassy there. They were assigned together to work on the Dahai League, the association of states encircling the Great Ocean, and as part of that work they were both sent by their governments to a conference in Hawaii, in the middle of the Dahai. There on the beaches of the big island they spent a great deal of time together, and when they returned to Beijing they were a couple. Her ancestry was both Chinese and Japanese, and all her great-grandparents had lived in Yingzhou, in Fangzhang and the valley behind it. When Pan Xichun's assignment in Beijing ended and she went back home, Bao made arrangements to join the Chinese embassy in Fangzhang, and flew across the Dahai to the dramatic green coastline and golden hills of Yingzhou.

There he and Pan Xichun married and lived for twenty years, raising two children, a son, Zhao, and a daughter, Anzi. Pan Xichun took on one of the ministries of the Yingzhou government, which meant she traveled fairly often to Long Island, to Qito, and around the Dahai Rim countries. Bao stayed home and worked for the Chinese embassy, saw after the children, and wrote and taught history at the city college. It was a good life in Fangzhang, that most beautiful and dramatic of all cities, and sometimes it would seem to him that his youth in revolutionary China was a kind of vivid intense dream he had once had. Scholars came over to talk to him sometimes, and he would reminisce about those years, and once or twice he even wrote about parts of it himself; but it was all at a great distance.

Then one day he felt a bump on the side of Pan Xichun's right breast; cancer; and a year later, after much suffering, she died. In her usual way she had gone on before.

Bao, desolate, was left to raise their children. His son Zhao was already almost grown, and soon took a job in Aozhou, across the sea, so that Bao rarely saw him in person. His daughter Anzi was younger, and he did what he could, hiring women to live in and help him, but somehow he tried too hard, he cared too much; Anzi got angry with him often, moved out when she could, got married, and seldom came to see him after that. Somehow he had botched that and he didn't even know how.

He was offered a post in Beijing, and he returned, but it was too strange; he felt like a preta, wandering the scenes of some past life. He stayed in the western quarters of the city, new neighborhoods that bore no particular resemblance to the ones he had known. The Forbidden City he forbade to himself. He tried reading and writing, thinking that if only he could write everything down, then it would never come back again.

After not too many years of that he took a post in Pyinkayaing, the capital of Burma, joining the League of All Peoples Agency for Harmony With Nature, as a Chinese representative and diplomat at large.

3

Writing Burmese History

Pyinkayaing was located on the westernmost channel of the mouths of the Irrawaddy, that great river road of Burmese life, which was by now urbanized all across the mouths in one enormous seafront city, or congeries of cities, all the way up each branch of the delta to Henzada, and indeed from there up the river all the way to Mandalay. But it was Pyinkayaing where the supercity could be seen at its most huge, the river channels running out into the sea like grand avenues, between stupendous bunched skyscrapers that made of the rivers deep gorges, bridged by innumerable streets and alleyways, alternating with the many more numerous canals, all crisscrossing each other in hundreds of overlapping grids, and all dominated by the deep canyons formed by the myriad tall buildings.

Bao was given an apartment on the hundred and sixtieth floor of one of the skyscrapers set on the main channel of the Irrawaddy, near the seafront. Walking out onto his balcony for the first time he was amazed at the view, and spent most of an afternoon looking around: south to sea, west to Pagoda Rock, east along the other mouths of the Irrawaddy, and upstream, looking down onto the rooftops of the supercity, into the million windows of the other skyscrapers lining the riverbanks and crowding the rest of the delta. All the buildings had been sunk deep through the alluvial soil of the delta to bedrock, and a famous system of dams and locks and offshore breakwaters had secured the city against floods from upstream, high tides from the Indian Ocean, typhoons—even the rise in sea level that was now beginning did not fundamentally threaten the city, which was in truth a kind of collection of ships anchored permanently in the bedrock, so that if eventually they had to abandon the "ground floors" and move up it would be just one more engineering challenge, something to keep the local construction industry occupied in years to come. The Burmese were not afraid of anything.

Looking down at the little junks and water taxis brushing their delicate white calligraphy over the blue-brown water, Bao seemed to read a kind of message in them, just outside the edge of his conscious comprehension. He understood now why the Burmese wrote "Burmese history"; because maybe it was true—maybe all that had ever happened, had happened so that it could collide here, and make something greater than any of its elements. As when the wakes from several different water taxis struck all together, shooting a bolt of white water higher than any individual wave ever would have gotten.

This monumental city, Pyinkayaing, was then Bao's home for the next seven years. He took a cable car high across the river to the league offices on the other bank, and worked on the balance-with-nature problems beginning to plague the world, wreaking such damage that even Burma itself might someday suffer from it, unless they were to remove Pyinkayaing to the moon, which did not seem completely impossible given their enormous energy and confidence.

But they had not been a power long enough to have seen the way the wheel turns. Over the years Bao visited a hundred lands as part of his job, and many reminded him that in the long run of time, civilizations rose, then fell; and most, upon falling, never really rose again. The locus of power wandered the face of the Earth like some poor restless immortal, following the sun. Presumably Burma would not be immune to that fate.

Bao now flew in the latest spaceplanes, popping out of the atmosphere like the artillery shells of the Long War, and landing on the other side of the globe three hours later; he also flew in the giant airships that still conveyed the bulk of traffic and cargo around the world, their slowness more than compensated for by their capacity, humming around like great ships in the sea of air, for the most part unsinkable. He conferred with officials in most of the countries of the Earth, and came to understand that their balance-with-nature problems were partly a matter of pure numbers, the human population of the planet rebounding so strongly from the Long War that it was now approaching eight billion people; and this might be more people than the planet could sustain, or so many scientists speculated, especially the more conservative ones, those of a kind of Daoist temperament, found in great numbers in China and Yingzhou especially.

But also, beyond the sheer number of people, there was the accumulation of things, and the uneven distribution of wealth, so that people in Pyinkayaing thought nothing of throwing a party in Ingali or Fangzhang, spending ten years of a Maghribi's life earnings on a weekend of pleasure; while people in Firanja and Inka still frequently suffered from malnutrition. This discrepancy existed despite the efforts of the League of All Peoples and the egalitarian movements in China, Firanja, Travancore and Yingzhou. In China the egalitarian movement came not just from Zhu's vision, but also the Daoist ideas of balance, as Zhu would always point out. In Travancore it rose out of the Buddhist idea of compassion, in Yingzhou from the Hodenosaunee idea of the equality of all, in Firanja from the idea of justice before God. Everywhere the idea existed, but the world still belonged to a tiny minority of rich; wealth had been accumulating for centuries in a few hands, and the people lucky enough to be born into this old aristocracy lived in the old manner, with the rights of kings now spread among the wealthy of the Earth. Money had replaced land as the basis of power, and money flowed according to its own gravity, its laws of accumulation, which though divorced from nature, were nevertheless the laws ruling most countries on Earth, no matter their religious or philosophical ideas of love, compassion, charity, equality, goodness, and the like. Old Zhu had been right: humanity's behavior was still based on old laws, which determined how food and land and water and surplus wealth were owned, how the labor of the eight billions was owned. If these laws did not change, the living shell of the Earth might well be wrecked, and inherited by seagulls and ants and cockroaches.

So Bao traveled, and talked, and wrote, and traveled again. For most of his career he worked for the league's Agency for Harmony with Nature, trying for several years to coordinate efforts in the Old World and the New to keep some of the greater mammals alive; many of them were going extinct, and without action they would lose most of them, in an anthropogenic extinction event to rival even the global crashes now being found in the fossil record.

He came back from these diplomatic missions to Pyinkayaing, after traveling in the big new airships that were a combination of blimp and flier, hovercraft and catamaran, skating over the water or in the air depending on weather conditions and freight loads. He looked down on the world from his apartment, and saw the human relationship to nature drawn in the calligraphy of the water taxis' wakes, the airships' contrails, the great canyons formed by the city's skyscrapers. This was his world, changing every year; and when he visited Beijing and tried to remember his youth, or went to Kwinana in Aozhou, to see his son Zhao and family there, or when he tried to remember Pan Xichun—even when he visited Fangzhang once, the actual site of those years—he could scarcely call them to mind. Or, to be more precise—for he could remember a great many things that had happened—it was the feeling for these things that was gone away, leached out by the years. They were as if they had happened to someone else. As if they had been previous incarnations.

It was someone else in the league offices who thought to invite Zhu Isao himself to Pyinkayaing, and teach a set of classes to the league workers and anyone else who cared to attend. Bao was surprised when he saw this notice; he had assumed that somewhere along the way Zhu must have died, it had been so long since they had all changed China together; and Zhu had been ancient then. But that turned out to have been a youthful mistake on Bao's part; Zhu was about ninety now, Bao was informed, meaning he had been only about seventy years old at that time. Bao had to laugh at his youthful miscalculation, so characteristic of the young. He signed up for the course with great anticipation.

Zhu Isao turned out to be a sprightly white-haired old man, small but no smaller than he had been all those years before, with a lively curious look in his eye. He shook Bao's hand when Bao went up before the introductory lecture, and smiled a slight but friendly smile: "I remember you," he said. "One of Kung Jianguo's officers, isn't that right?" And Bao gripped his hand hard, ducking his head in assent. He sat down feeling warm. The old man still walked with the ghost of a limp from that terrible day. But he had been happy to see Bao.

In his first lecture he outlined his plan for the course, which he hoped would be a series of conversations on history, discussing how it was constructed, and what it meant, and how they might use it to help them plot their course forward through the next difficult decades, "when we have to learn at last how to inhabit the Earth."

Bao kept notes as he listened to the old man, tapping at his little hand lectern, as did many others in the class. Zhu explained that he hoped first to describe and discuss the various theories of history that had been proposed through the centuries, and then to analyze those theories, not only by testing them in the description of actual events, "difficult since events as such are remembered for how well they prop up the various theories," but also for how the theories themselves were structured, and what sort of futures they implied, "this being their chief use to us. I take it that what matters in a history is what there is in it we can put to use."

So, over the next few months a pattern was set, and every third day the group would meet in a room high in one of the league buildings overlooking the Irrawaddy: a few score diplomats, local students, and younger historians from everywhere, many of whom had come to Pyinkayaing specifically for this class. All sat and listened to Zhu talk, and though Zhu kept encouraging them to enter the discussion and make of it a large conversation, they were mostly content to listen to him think aloud, only egging him on with their questions. "Well, but I am here to listen too," he would object, and then, when pressed to continue, would relent. "I must be like Pao Ssu, I suppose, who used to say, 'I am a good listener, I listen by talking.' "

So they made their way through discussions of the four civilizations theory, made famous by al-Katalan; and al-Lanzhou's collision of cultures theory, of progress by conflict ("clearly accurate in some sense, as there has been much conflict and much progress"); the somewhat similar conjunction theories, by which unnoticed conjunctions of developments, often in unrelated fields of endeavor, had great consequences. Zhu's many examples of this included one he presented with a small smile: the introduction of coffee and printing presses at around the same time in caliphate Iran, causing a great outpouring of literature.

They discussed the theory of the eternal return, which combined Hindu cosmologies with the latest in physics to suggest that the universe was so vast and ancient that everything possible had not only happened, but had happened an infinite number of times ("limited usefulness to that one, except to explain the feeling you get that things have happened before"); and the other cyclical theories, often based on the cycle of the seasons, or the life of the body.

Then he mentioned "dharma history" or "Burmese history," meaning any history that believed there was progress toward some goal making itself manifest in the world, or in plans for the future; also "Bodhisattva history," which suggested that there were enlightened cultures that had sprung ahead somehow, and then gone back to the rest and worked to bring them forward—early China, Travancore, the Hodenosaunee, the Japanese diaspora, Iran—all these cultures had been proposed as possible examples of this pattern, "though it seems to be a matter of individual or cultural judgment, which is less than useful to historians seeking a global pattern. Although it is a weak criticism to call them tautological, for the truth is, every theory is tautological. Our reality itself is a tautology."

Someone brought up the old question of whether the "great man" or "mass movements" were the principle force for change, but Zhu immediately dismissed this as a false problem. "We are all great men, yes?"

"Maybe you are," muttered the person sitting next to Bao.

". . . what has mattered are the moments of exposure in every life, when habit is no longer enough, and choices have to be made. That's when everyone becomes the great man, for a moment; and the choices made in these moments, which come all too frequently, then combine to make history. In that sense I suppose I come down on the side of the masses, in that it has been a collective process, whatever else it is.

"Also, this formulation 'the great man' of course should bring up the question of women; are they included in this description? Or should we describe history as being the story of women wresting back the political power that they lost with the introduction of agriculture and the creation of surplus wealth? Would the gradual and unfinished defeat of patriarchy be the larger story of history? Along with, perhaps, the gradual and uncertain defeat of infectious disease? So that we have been battling microparasites and macroparasites, eh? The bugs and the patriarchs?"

He smiled at this, and went on to discuss the struggle against the

Four Great Inequalities, and other concepts grown out of the work of Kang and al-Lanzhou.

After that, Zhu took a few sessions to describe various "phase change moments" in global history that he thought significant—the Japanese diaspora, the independence of the Hodenosaunee, the shift of trade from land to sea, the Samarqand Flowering, and so forth. He also spent quite a few sessions discussing the latest movement among historians and social scientists, which he called "animal history," the study of humanity in biological terms, so that it became not a matter of religions and philosophies, but more a study of primates struggling for food and territory.

It was many weeks into the course when he said, "Now we are ready to come to what interests me extremely these days, which is not history's content, but its form.

"For we see immediately that what we call history has at least two meanings to it: first, simply what happened in the past, which no one can know, as it disappears in time, and then second, all the stories we tell about what happened.

"These stories are of different kinds, of course, and people like Rabindra and Scholar White have categorized them. First come eyewitness accounts and chronicles of events made soon after things happened, also documents and records—these are history as wheat still in the field, as yet unharvested or baked, thus given beginnings or ends or causes. Only later come these baked histories that attempt to coordinate and reconcile source materials, that not only describe but explain.

"Later still come the works that eat and digest these baked accounts, and attempt to reveal what they are doing, what their relationship to reality is, how we use them, that kind of thing—philosophies of history, epistemologies, what have you. Many digestions use methods pioneered by Ibrahim al-Lanzhou, even when they denounce his results. Certainly there is great sustenance in going back to al-Lanzhou's texts and seeing what he had to say. In one useful passage, for instance, he points out that we can differentiate between explicit arguments, and more deeply hidden unconscious ideological biases. These latter can be teased out by identifying the mode of emplotment chosen to tell the tale. The emplotment scheme al-Lanzhou used comes from Rabindra's typology of story types, a rather simplistic scheme, but fortunately, as al-Lanzhou pointed out, historians are often fairly naive storytellers, and use one or another of Rabindra's basic types of emplotment rather schematically, compared to the great novelists like Cao Xueqin or Murasaki, who constantly mix them. Thus a history like Than Oo's is what some call 'Burmese history,' rather literally in this case, but that I would prefer to call 'dharma history,' being a romance in which humanity struggles to work out its dharma, to better itself, and so generation by generation to make progress, fighting for justice, and an end to want, with the strong implication that we will eventually work our way up to the source of the peach blossom stream, and the age of great peace will come into being. It is a secular version of the Hindu and Buddhist tale of nirvana successfully achieved. Thus Burmese history, or Shambala tales, or any teleological history that asserts we are all progressing in some way, is dharma history.

"The opposite of this mode is the ironic or satiric mode, which I call entropic history, from the physical sciences, or nihilism, or, in the usage of certain old legends, the story of the fall. In this mode, everything that humanity tries to do fails, or rebounds against it, and the combination of biological reality and moral weakness, of death and evil, means that nothing in human affairs can succeed. Taken to its extreme this leads to the Five Great Pessimisms, or the nihilism of Shu Shen, or the anti-dharma of Buddha's rival Purana Kassapa, people who say it is all a chaos without causes, and that taken all in all, it would have been better never to have been born.

"These two modes of emplotment represent end-point extremes, in that one says we are masters of the world and can defeat death, while the other says that we are captives of the world, and can never win against death. It might be thought these then represent the only two possible modes, but inside these extremes Rabindra identified two other modes of emplotment, which he called tragedy and comedy. These two are mixed and partial modes compared to their absolutist outliers, and Rabindra suggested they both have to do with reconciliation. In comedy the reconciliation is of people with other people, and with society at large. The weave of family with family, tribe with clan—this is how comedies end, this is what makes them comedy: the marriage with someone from a different clan, and the return of spring.

"Tragedies make a darker reconciliation. Scholar White said of them, they tell the story of humanity face-to-face with reality itself, therefore facing death and dissolution and defeat. Tragic heroes are destroyed, but for those who survive to tell their tale, there is a rise in consciousness, in awareness of reality, and this is valuable in and of itself, dark though that knowledge may be."

At this point in his lecture Zhu Isao paused, and looked around the room until he had located Bao, and nodded at him; and though it seemed they had only been speaking of abstract things, of the shapes stories took, Bao felt his heart clench within him.

Zhu proceeded: "Now, I suggest that as historians, it is best not to get trapped in one mode or another, as so many do; it is too simple a solution, and does not match well with events as experienced. Instead we should weave a story that holds in its pattern as much as possible. It should be like the Daoists' yin-yang symbol, with eyes of tragedy and comedy dotting the larger fields of dharma and nihilism. That old figure is the perfect image of all our stories put together, with the dark spot of our comedies marring the brilliance of dharma, and the blaze of tragic knowledge emerging from black nothingness.

"The ironic history by itself, we can reject out of hand. Of course we are bad; of course things go wrong. But why dwell on it? Why pretend this is the whole story? Irony is merely death walking among us. It doesn't take up the challenge, it isn't life speaking.

"But I suppose we also have to reject the purest version of dharma history, the transcending of this world and this life, the perfection of our way of being. It may happen in the bardo, if there is a bardo, but in this world, all is mixed. We are animals, death is our fate. So at best we could say the history of the species has to be made as much like dharma as possible, by a collective act of the will.

"This leaves the middle modes, comedy and tragedy." Zhu stopped, held up his hands, perplexed. "Surely we have a great deal of both of these. Perhaps the way to construct a proper history is to inscribe the whole figure, and say that for the individual, ultimately, it is a tragedy; for the society, comedy. If we can make it so."

Zhu Isao's own predilection was clearly for comedy. He was a social creature. He was always inviting Bao and some others from the class, including the league's Minister for Health of the Natural World, to the rooms provided for him during his stay, and these small gatherings were sparked by his laughter and curiosity about things. Even his research amused him. He had had a great many books shipped down from Beijing, so that every room of his apartment was filled like a warehouse. Because of his growing conviction that history should be the story of everyone who had ever lived, he was now studying anthologies of biography as a genre, and he had many examples of the form in his apartment. This explained the tremendous number of volumes standing everywhere, in tall unsteady stacks. Zhu picked up one huge tome, almost too heavy for him to lift: "This is a first volume," he said with a grin, "but I've never found the rest of the series. A book like this is only the antechamber to an entire unwritten library."

The collection-of-lives genre seemed to have begun, he said as he tapped the piles affectionately, in religious literatures: collections of the lives of Christian saints and Islamic martyrs, also Buddhist texts that described lives through long sequences of reincarnations, a speculative exercise that Zhu clearly enjoyed very much: "Dharma history at its purest, a kind of protopolitics. Plus they can be so funny. You see a literalist like Dhu Hsien trying to match up his subjects' death and birth dates exactly, so that he creates strings of prominent historical actors through several reincarnations, asserting that he can tell they have always been one soul by what they do, but the difficulties of getting the dates to match up cause him in the end to select some odd additions to his sequences to make them all match life to life. Finally he has to theorize a 'work hard then relax' pattern in these immortals, to justify those who alternate lives as geniuses and generals with careers as minor portrait artists or cobblers. But the dates always match up!" Zhu grinned delightedly.

He tapped other tall piles that were examples of the genre he was studying: Ganghadara's *Forty-six Transmigrations*, the Tibetan text *Twelve Manifestations of Padmasambhava*, the guru who established Buddhism in Tibet; also the *Biography of the Gyatso Rimpoche, Lives One Through Nineteen*, which brought the Dalai Lama up to the present; Bao had once met this man, and had not realized then that his full biography would take up so many volumes.

Zhu Isao also had in his apartment copies of Plutarch's *Lives*, and Liu Xiang's *Biographies of Exemplary Women*, from about the same time as the Plutarch; but he admitted that he was finding these texts not as interesting as the reincarnation chronicles, which in certain cases spent as much time on their subjects' time in the bardo and the other five lokas as they did on their time as humans. He also liked the *Autobiography of the Wandering Jew,* and the *Testaments of the Trivicum Jati,* and a beautiful volume, *Two Hundred and Fifty-three Travelers,* as well as a scurrilous-looking collection, possibly pornographic, called *Tantric Thief Across Five Centuries.* All of these Zhu described to his visitors with great enthusiasm. They seemed to him to hold some kind of key to the human story, assuming there could be any such thing: history as a simple accumulation of lives. "After all, in the end all the great moments of history have taken place inside people's heads. The moments of change, or the clinamen as the Greeks called it."

This moment, Zhu said, had become the organizing principle and perhaps the obsession of the Samarqandi anthologist Old Red Ink, who had collected the lives in his reincarnation compendium using something like the clinamen moment to choose his exemplars, as each entry in his collection contained a moment when the subjects, always reincarnated with names that began with the same letters, came to crossroads in their lives and made a swerve away from what they might have been expected to do.

"I like the naming device," Bao remarked, leafing through one volume of this collection.

"Well, Old Red Ink explains in one marginalia that it is merely a mnemonic for the ease of the reader, and that of course in reality every soul comes back with every physical particular changed. No telltale rings, no birthmarks, no same names—he would not have you think his method was anything like the old folk tales, oh no."

The Minister for Natural Health asked about a stack of extremely slender volumes, and Zhu smiled happily. As a reaction against these endless compendiums, he explained, he had gotten into the habit of buying any books he came across that seemed required by their subject matter to be short, often so short that their titles would scarcely fit on their spines. Thus *Secrets to Successful Marriage,* or *Good Reasons to Have Hope for the Future,* or *Stories About Not Being Afraid of Ghosts.*

"But I have not read them, I must admit. They exist only for their titles, which say it all. They could be blank inside."

Later, outside on his balcony, Bao sat next to Zhu watching the city flow beneath them. They drank cup after cup of green tea, talking about many different things, and as the night grew late, and Zhu feeling pensive, it seemed, Bao said to him, "Do you ever think of Kung Jianguo? Do you ever think of those times anymore?"

"No, not very often," Zhu admitted, looking at him directly. "Do you?"

Bao shook his head. "I don't know why. It's not like it's so very painful to recall. But it seems so long ago."

"Yes. Very long."

"I see you still have a bit of a limp from that day."

"Yes, I do. I don't like it. I walk slower and it's not so bad. But it is still there. I set off metal detectors in the high-security zones." He laughed. "But it is a long time ago. So many lives ago—I get them all confused, don't you?" And he smiled.

One of Zhu Isao's last sessions was a discussion of what purpose the study of history might have, and how it might help them now in their current predicament.

Zhu was tentative in this matter. "It may be no help at all," he said. "Even if we gained a complete understanding of what happened in the past, it might not help us. We are still constrained in our actions in the present. In a way we can say that the past has mortgaged the future, or bought it, or tied it up, in laws and institutions and habits. But perhaps it helps to know as much as we can, just to suggest ways forward. You know, this matter of residual and emergent that we discussed—that each period in history is composed of residual elements of past cultures, and emergent elements that later on will come more fully into being— this is a powerful lens. And only the study of history allows one to make this distinction, if it is possible at all. Thus we can look at the world we live in, and say, these things are residual laws from the age of the Four Great Inequalities, still binding us. They must go. On the other hand we can look at more unfamiliar elements of our time, like China's commu- nal ownership of land, and say, perhaps these are emergent qualities that will be more prominent in the future; they look helpful; I will sup- port these. Then again, there may be residual elements that have always helped us, and need to be retained. So it is not as simple a matter as 'new is good, old is bad.' Distinctions need to be made. But the more we un- derstand, the finer we can make the distinctions.

"I begin to think that this matter of 'late emergent properties' that the physicists talk about when they discuss complexity and cascading sensititivities is an important concept for historians. Justice may be a late emergent property. And maybe we can glimpse the beginnings of it emerging; or maybe it emerged long ago, among the primates and pro-tohumans, and is only now gaining leverage in the world, aided by the material possibility of postscarcity. It is hard to say."

He smiled again his little smile. "Good words to end this session."

His final meeting was called "What Remains to Be Explained," and con-sisted of questions that he was still mulling over after all his years of study and contemplation. He made comments on his list of questions, but not many, and Bao had to write as fast as he could to get the ques-tions themselves recorded:

What Remains to Be Explained

Why has there been inequality in accumulation of goods since the earliest recorded history? What causes the ice ages to come and go? Could Japan have won its war of indepen-dence without the fortuitous combination of the Long War and the earthquake and fire striking Edo? Where did all the Roman gold end up? Why does power corrupt? Was there any way that the native peoples of the New World could have been saved from the devastation of Old World diseases? When did people first arrive in the New World? Why were the civilizations on Yingzhou and Inka at such different stages of development? Why can't gravity be reconciled mathemati-cally with pulse microprobability? Would Travancore have initiated the modern period and dominated the Old World, if the Kerala had never lived? Is there life after death, or trans-migration of souls? Did the polar expedition of the fifty-second year of the Long War reach the south pole? What causes well-fed and secure people to work for the subju-gation and immiseration of starving insecure people? If al-Alemand had conquered Skandistan, would the Sami people have survived? If the Shanghai Conference had not arranged such punitive reparations, would the postwar world have been more peaceful? How many people can the Earth sup-port? Why is there evil? How did the Hodenosaunee invent their form of government? Which disease or combination of diseases killed the Christians of Firanja? Does technology drive history? Would things have turned out differently if the birth of science in Samarqand had not been delayed in its dispersal by the plague? Did the Phoenicians cross the Atlantic to the New World? Will any mammals larger than a fox survive the next century? Is the Sphinx thousands of years older than the Pyramids? Do gods exist? How can we return the animals to the earth? How can we make a decent existence? How can we give to our children and the generations following a world restored to health?

Soon after that final session, and a big party, Zhu Isao returned to Beijing, and Bao never saw him again.

They worked hard in the years after Zhu's visit to enact programs that helped to frame some answers to his final questions. Just as the geologists had been greatly helped in their labors by the construction of a framework of understanding based on the movement of the broken eggshell plates of the crust, so the bureaucrats and technocrats and scientists and diplomats at the League of All Peoples were helped in their labors by Zhu's theoretical considerations. It helps to have a plan! as Zhu had often remarked.

And so Bao crisscrossed the world, meeting and talking to people, helping to put certain strands into place, thickening the warp and weft of treaties and agreements by which all the peoples on the planet were tied together. He worked variously on land tenure reform, forest management, animal protection, water resources, panchayat support, and divestiture of accumulated wealth, chipping away at the obdurate blocks of privilege left in the wake of the Long War and all that had happened in the centuries before it. Everything went very slowly, and progress came always in small increments, but what Bao noticed from time to time was that improvements in one part of the world situation often helped elsewhere, so that, for instance, the institution of panchayat governments at the local level in China and the Islamic states led to increased power for more and more people, especially where they adopted the Tranvacori law of requiring at least two of every five panchayat members to be women; and this in turn mitigated many land problems. Indeed, as many of the world's problems stemmed from too many people competing for too few resources, using too crude technologies, another happy result of the panchayat empowerment of localities and of women was that birthrates dropped rapidly and dramatically. The replacement rate for a population was 2.1 births per woman, and before the Long War the world rate had been more like five; in the poorest countries, more like seven or eight. Now, in every country where women exerted the full range of rights advocated by the League of All Peoples, the replacement rate had fallen to less than three, and often less than two; this, combined with improvements in agriculture and other technologies, boded well for the future. It was the ultimately hopeful expression of the warp and the weft, of the principle of late emergent properties. It seemed, though everything went very slowly, that they might be able to concoct some kind of dharmic history after all. Perhaps; it was not yet clear; but some work got done.

So when Bao read of Zhu Isao's death, some years later, he groaned and threw the paper to the floor. He spent the day out on his balcony, feeling unaccountably bereft. Really there was nothing to mourn, everything to celebrate: the great one had lived a hundred years, had helped to change China and then all the world; late in life he had appeared to be thoroughly enjoying himself, going around and listening by talking. He had given the impression of someone who knew his place in the world.

But Bao did not know his place. Contemplating the immense city below him, looking up the great watery canyons, he realized that he had been living in this place for over ten years, and he still didn't know a thing about it. He was always leaving or coming back, always looking down on things from a balcony, eating in the same little hole-in-the-wall, talking to colleagues from the league offices, spending most of his mornings and evenings reading. He was almost sixty now, and he didn't know what he was doing or how he was supposed to live. The huge city was like a machine, or a ship half-sunk in the shallows. It was no help to him. He had worked every day trying to extend Kung and Zhu's work, to understand history and work on it in the moment of change, also to explain it to others, reading and writing, reading and writing, thinking that if he could only explain it then it wouldn't oppress him quite so much. It did not seem to have worked. He had the feeling that everyone who had ever meant something to him had already died.

When he went back inside his apartment, he found a message on the screen of his lectern from his daughter Anzi, the first he had gotten from her in a long time. She had given birth to a daughter of her own, and wondered if Bao wanted to visit and meet his new grandchild. He typed an affirmative reply and packed his bag.

Anzi and her husband Deng lived above Shark Point, in one of the crowded hilly neighborhoods on the bay side of Fangzhang. Their baby girl was named Fengyun, and Bao enjoyed very much taking her out on the tram and walking her in a stroller around the park at the south end of town, overlooking the Gold Gate. There was something about her look that re- minded him very strongly of Pan Xichun—a curve of the cheek, a stubborn look in her eye. These traits we pass on. He watched her sleep, and the fog roll in the gate, under and over the sweep of the new bridge, listening to a feng shui guru lecture a small class sitting at his feet. "You can see that this is the most physically beautiful setting of any city on Earth," which seemed true enough to Bao. Even Pyinkayaing had no prospect compared to this, the glories of the Burmese capital were all artifactual, and without those it was just like any other delta mouth, unlike this sublime place he had loved so in a previous existence, "Oh no, I don't think so, only geomantic imbe- ciles would have located the city on the other side of the strait, aside from practical considerations of street platting, there is the intrinsic qi of place, its dragon arteries are too exposed to the wind and fog, it is best to leave it as a park." Certainly the opposing peninsula made a beautiful park, green and hilly across the water, sunlight streaming down on it through cloud, the whole scene so vibrant and gorgeous that Bao lifted the babe up out of her stroller to show it all to her; he pointed her in the four directions; and the scene blurred before his eyes as if he too were a babe. Everything became a flow of shapes, cloudy masses of brilliant color swimming about, vivid and glowing, stripped of their meanings as known things, blue and white above, yellow below . . . He shivered, feeling very strange. It was as if he had been looking through the babe's eyes; and the child seemed fretful. So he took her back home, and Anzi reproached him for letting her get cold. "And her diaper needs changing!"

"I know that! I'll do it."

"No I'll do it, you don't know how."

"I most certainly do too, I changed your diapers often enough in my time."

She sniffed disapprovingly, as if he had been rude to do so, invading her privacy perhaps. He grabbed up the book he was reading and went out for a walk, upset. Somehow things were still awkward between them.

The great city hummed, the islands in the bay with their skyscrapers looking like the vertical mountains of south China, the slopes of Mount Tamalpi equally crowded with huge buildings; but the bulk of the city hugged its hills tightly, most of it still human scale, buildings two and three stories tall, with upturned corners on all the roofs in the old-fashioned way, like a city of pagodas. This was the city he had loved, the city he had lived in during the years of his marriage.

And so he was a preta here. Like any other hungry ghost, he walked over the hill to the ocean side, and soon he found himself in the neighborhood where they had lived when Pan was alive. He walked through the streets without even thinking about navigating his way, and there he was: the old home.

He stood before the building, an ordinary apartment block, now painted a pale yellow. They had lived in an apartment upstairs, always in the wind, just as it was now. He stared at the building. He felt nothing. He tested it, he tried to feel something: no. The main thing he felt was wonder that he could feel so little; a rather pale and unsatisfactory feeling to have at such a momentous confrontation with his past, but there it was. The kids each had had a bedroom to themselves up there, and Bao and Pan had slept on an unrolled futon in the living room, the stove of the kitchenette right at their feet; it had been a cricket box of a place, really, but there they had lived, and for a time it had seemed it would always be just like that, husband, wife, son, daughter, clothed in a tiny apartment in Fangzhang, and every day the same, every week the same, in a round that would last forever. Thus the power of thoughtlessness, the power people had to forget what time was always doing.

He took off walking again, south toward the gate, on the busy promenade high over the ocean, the trams squealing by. When he reached the park overlooking the strait he returned to the spot where he had been just hours before with his granddaughter, and looked around again. Everything remained the same this time, retaining their shapes and their meanings; no flow into colors, no yellow ocean. That had been an odd experience, and he shuddered again remembering it.

He sat on the low wall overlooking the water, and took his book from his jacket pocket, a book of poems translated from the ancient Sanskrit.

He opened it at random, and read, "this verse from Kalidasa's Sakuntala is considered by many scholars of Sanskrit to be the most beautiful in the language":

> ramyani viksya madhurans ca nisamya sabdan
> paryutsuki bhavati yat sukhito pi jantuh
> tac cetasa smarati nunam abodhapurvam
> bhavasthirani jananantarasauhrdani

> Even the man who is happy glimpses something
> Or a thread of sound touches him

> And his heart overflows with a longing
> he does not recognize

> Then it must be that he is remembering
> a place out of reach people he loved

> In a life before this their pattern
> Still there in him waiting

He looked up, looked around. An awesome place, this great gate to the sea. He thought, Maybe I should stay here. Maybe this day is telling me something. Maybe this is my home, hungry ghost or not. Maybe we cannot avoid becoming hungry ghosts, no matter where we live; so this might as well be home.

He walked back to his daughter's. A letter had arrived on his lectern from an acquaintance of his, living at the farm station of Fangzhang's college, inland from the city a hundred li, in the big central valley. This acquaintance from his Beijing years had heard he was visiting the area, and wondered if he would like to come out and teach a class or two—a history of the Chinese revolution, perhaps—foreign relations, league work, whatever he liked. Because of his association with Kung, among other things, he would be viewed by the students as a living piece of world history. "A living fossil, you mean," he snorted. Like that fish whose species was four hundred million years old, dragged up recently in a net off Madagascar. Old Dragonfish. He wrote back to his acquaintance and accepted the invitation, then wrote to Pyinkayaing and put in for a more extended leave of absence.

4

The Red Egg

The farm extension of the college, now a little college itself, was clustered at the west end of a town called Putatoi, west of the North Lung River, on the banks of Puta Creek, a lively brook pouring out of the coastal range and creating a riverine gallery of oaks and brush on an alluvial berm just a few hands higher than the rest of the valley. The valley otherwise was given over entirely to rice cultivation; the big rivers flowing into it out of the mountains on both sides had been diverted into an elaborate irrigation system, and the already flat valley floor had been shaved even flatter, into a stepwise system of broad flooded terraces, each terrace just a few fingers higher than the one below it. All the dikes in this system curved, as part of some kind of erosion resistance strategy, and so the landscape looked somewhat like Annam or Kampuchea, or anywhere in tropical Asia really, except that wherever the land was not flooded, it was shockingly dry. Straw-colored hills rose to the west, in the first of the coastal ranges between the valley and the bay; then to the east the grand snow-topped peaks of the Gold Mountains stood like a distant Himalaya.

Putatoi was tucked into a nest of trees in this broad expanse of green and gold. It was a village in the Japanese style, with shops and apartments clustered by the stream, and small groupings of cottages ringing the town center north of the stream. After Pyinkayaing it seemed tiny, dowdy, sleepy, green, dull. Bao liked it.

The students at the college mostly came from farms in the valley, and they were mostly studying to be rice farmers or orchard managers. Their questions in the Chinese history class that Bao taught were amazingly ignorant, but they were fresh-faced and cheerful youths; they didn't care in the slightest who Bao was, or what he had done in the postwar period so long ago. He liked that too.

His little seminar of older students, who were studying history specifically, were more intrigued by his presence among them. They asked him about Zhu Isao, of course, and even about Kung Jianguo, and about the Chinese revolution. Bao answered as if it were a period of history that he had studied extensively, and perhaps written a book or two about. He did not offer them personal reminiscences, and most of the time felt that he had none to offer. They watched him very closely as he spoke.

"What you have to understand," he told them, "is that no one won the Long War. Everyone lost, and we have not yet recovered from it even now.

"Remember what you have been taught about it. It lasted sixty-seven years, two-thirds of a century, and it's estimated now that almost a billion people died in it. Think of it this way: I've been talking to a biologist here who works on population issues, and he has tried to estimate how many humans have lived in all of history, from the start of the species until now."

Some in the class laughed at such an idea.

"You haven't heard of this? He estimates that there have been about forty billion humans to have lived since the species came into being—although of course that was no determinate moment, so this is just a game we play. But it means that if there have been forty billion humans in all history, then one in forty of all the people ever to have lived, were killed in the Long War. That's a big percentage!

"So. The whole world fell into disarray, and now we've lived in the war's shadow for so long we don't know what full sunlight would look like. Science keeps making advances, but many of them rebound on us. The natural world is being poisoned by our great numbers and our crude industries. And if we quarrel again, all could be lost. You are probably aware, certainly most governments are, that science could provide us very quickly with extremely powerful bombs, they say one bomb per city, and so that threat hangs over us too. If any country tries for such a bomb, all may follow.

"So, all these dangers inspired the creation of the League of All Peoples, in the hope of making a global system that could cope with our global problems. That came on the heels of the Year One effort, standardized measurements, and all the rest, to form what has been called the scientizing of the world, or the modernization, or the Hodenosaunee program, among other names for it. Our time, in effect."

"In Islam they don't like all that," one student pointed out.

"Yes, this has been a problem for them, how to reconcile their beliefs with the scientizing movement. But we have seen changes in Nsara spread through most of Firanja, and what a united Firanja implies is that they have agreed there is more than one way to be a good Muslim. If your Islam is a form of Sufism that is Buddhist in all but name, and you say it is all right, then it is hard to condemn the Buddhists in the next valley. And this is happening in many places. All the strands are beginning to weave together, you see. We have had to do it to survive."

At the end of that first set of classes, the history teachers invited Bao to stay on and do it on a regular basis; and after some thought, he accepted their invitation. He liked these people, and the work that came from them. The bulk of the college's efforts had to do with growing more food, with fitting people into the natural systems of the earth less clumsily. History was part of this, and the history teachers were friendly. Also a single woman his age, a lecturer in linguistics, had been particularly friendly through the time of his stay. They had eaten quite a few meals together, and gotten into the habit of meeting for lunch. Her name was Gao Qingnian.

Bao moved into the small group of cottages where Gao lived, renting one next to hers that had come open at just the right time. The cottages were Japanese in style, with thin walls and big windows, all clustered around a common garden. It was a nice little neighborhood.

In the mornings Bao started to hoe and plant vegetables in one corner of that central garden. Through a gap between the cottages he could see the great valley oaks in their streamside gallery; beyond them the green rice paddies, and the isolated peak of Mount Miwok, over a hundred li away, south of the great delta. To the east and north, more rice paddies, curving green on green. The coastal range lay to the west, the Gold Mountains to the east. He rode an old bicycle to the college for classes, and taught his smaller seminars at a set of picnic tables by the side of the stream, under a stand of enormous valley oaks. Every once in a while he would rent a little airboat from the airport just west of town, and pilot it down the delta to Fangzhang, to visit Anzi and her family. Though Bao and Anzi remained stiff and fractious with each other, the repetition of these visits eventually made them seem normal, a pleasant ritual in most respects. They did not seem connected to his memories of the past, but an event of their own. Well, Bao would say to Gao, I'm going to go down to Fangzhang and bicker with my daughter.

Have fun, Gao would say.

Mostly he stayed in Putatoi, and taught classes. He liked the young people and their fresh faces. He liked the people who lived in the cluster of cottages around the garden. They worked in agriculture, mostly, either in the college's agronomy labs and experimental fields, or out in the paddies and orchards themselves. That was what people did in this valley. The neighbors all gave him advice on how best to cultivate his little garden, and very often it was conflicting advice, which was no very reassuring thing given that they were among the world's experts on the topic, and that there might be more people than there was food in the world to feed them. But that too was a lesson, and though it worried him, it also made him laugh. And he liked the labor, the sitting in the dirt, weeding and looking at vegetables grow. Staring across rice terraces at Mount Miwok. He baby-sat for some of the younger couples in the cottages, and talked with them about the events of the town, and spent the evenings out lawn bowling with a group who liked to do that.

Before long the routines of this life became as if they were the only ones he had ever known. One morning, baby-sitting for a little girl who had caught the chicken pox, sitting by her as she lay thoughtlessly in a lukewarm oatmeal bath, stoically flicking the water with her finger and occasionally moaning like a small animal, he felt a sudden gust of happiness sweep through him, simply because he was the old widower of the neighborhood, and people used him as a baby-sitter. Old Dragonfish. There had been just such a man back in Beijing, living in a hole in the wall by the Big Red Gate, repairing shoes and watching the kids in the street.

The deep sense of solitude that had afflicted Bao since Pan's death began to slip away. Although the people he lived among now were not Kung, nor Pan, nor Zhu Isao—not the companions of his fate, just people he had fallen in with by accident—nevertheless, they were now his community. Maybe this was the way it had always happened, with no fate ever involved; you simply fell in with the people around you, and no matter what else happened in history or the great world, for the individual it was always a matter of local acquaintances—the village, the platoon, the work unit, the monastery or madressa, the zawiyya or farm or apartment block, or ship, or neighborhood—these formed the true circumference of one's world, some twenty or so speaking parts, as if they were in a play together. And no doubt each cast included the same character types, as in Noh drama or a puppet play. And so now he was the old widower, the baby-sitter, the broken-down old bureaucrat-poet, drinking wine by the stream and singing nostalgically at the moon, scratching with a hoe in his unproductive garden. It made him smile; it gave him pleasure. He liked having neighbors, and he liked his role among them.

Time passed. He continued to teach a few classes, arranging for his seminars to meet out under the valley oaks.

"History!" he would say to them. "It's a hard thing to get at. There is no easy way to imagine it. The Earth rolls around the sun, three hundred and sixty-five and a quarter days a year, for year after year. Thousands of these years have passed. Meanwhile a kind of monkey kept on doing more things, increasing in number, taking over the planet by means of meanings. Eventually much of the matter and life on the planet was entrained to their use, and then they had to figure out what they wanted to do, beyond merely staying alive. Then they told each other stories of how they had gotten where they were, what had happened, and what it meant."

Bao sighed. His students watched him.

"The way Zhu told the story, it is a matter of tragedy for the individual, comedy for the society. Over the long pulses of historical time, reconciliations can be achieved, that's the comedy; but every individual meets a tragic end. We have to admit here that no matter what else we say, for the individual death is always an end and a catastrophe."

His students regarded him steadily, perfectly willing to admit this, for they were about twenty-five, while he was near seventy, and so they felt immortal. This was perhaps the evolutionary usefulness of the elderly, Bao had concluded: to give the young some kind of psychic shield from reality, putting them under a description that allowed them to ignore the fact that age and death would come to them too, and could come early and out of sequence. A very useful function! And it gave the old some amusement as well, in addition to an extra pinch from their own mortality to remind them to appreciate life.

So he smiled at their unfounded equanimity, and said, "But all right, we admit that catastrophe, and the people who live go on. Go on! They knit things together as best they can. So, what Zhu Isao used to say, what my old comrade Kung Jianguo used to say, was that each time a generation pulls itself together, and revolts against the established order of things in an attempt to make them more just, it is doomed to fail in some respects; but it succeeds in others; and in any case it gives something to posterity, even if it be only knowledge of how hard things are. Which makes it retroactively a kind of success. And so people go on."

A young Aozhani woman, come here like so many others did from all around the world, to study agriculture with the old adepts at the college, said, "But since we are all reincarnated anyway, is death really such a catastrophe?"

Bao felt himself take a long breath. Like most scientifically educated people, he did not believe in reincarnation. It was clearly just a story, something out of the old religions. But still—how to account for his feeling of cosmic solitude, the feeling that he had lost his eternal companions? How to account for that experience at the Gold Gate, holding his granddaughter aloft?

He thought about it for so long that the students began to look at each other. Then he said carefully to the young woman, "Well, let us try something. Think that there might be no bardo. No heavens or hells; no afterlife at all. No continuation of your consciousness, or even your soul. Imagine all you are is an expression of your body, and when it finally succumbs to some disorder and dies, you are gone for good. Gone utterly."

The girl and the others stared at him.

He nodded. "Then indeed you have to think again what reincarnation might mean. For we need it. We all need it. And there might be some way to reconceptualize it so it still has meaning, even if you admit that the death of the self is real."

"But how?" the young woman said.

"Well, first, of course, there are the children. We are literally reincarnated in new beings, though they are the mix of two previous beings— two beings who will live on in the twisting ladders that detach and recombine, passed on to subsequent generations."

"But that's not our consciousness."

"No. But consciousness gets reincarnated another way, when the people of the future remember us, and use our language, and unconsciously model their lives on ours, living out some recombination of our values and habits. We live on in the way future people think and talk. Even if things change so much that only the biological habits are the same, they are real for all that—perhaps more real than consciousness, more rooted in reality. Remember, reincarnation means 'return to a new body.' "

"Some of our atoms may do that literally," one young man offered.

"Indeed. In the endlessness of eternity, the atoms that were part of our bodies for a time will move on, and be incorporated in other life on this earth, and perhaps on other planets in subsequent galaxies. So we are diffusely reincarnate through the universe."

"But that's not our consciousness," the young woman said stubbornly.

"Not consciousness, nor the self. The ego, the string of thoughts, the flow of consciousness, which no text or image has ever managed to convey—no."

"But I don't want that to end," she said.

"No. And yet it does. This is the reality we were born into. We can't change it by desire."

The young man said, "The Buddha says we should give up our desires."

"But that too is a desire!" the young woman exclaimed.

"So we never really give it up," Bao agreed. "What the Buddha was suggesting is impossible. Desire is life trying to continue to be life. All living things desire, bacteria feel desire. Life is wanting."

The young students thought it over. There is an age, Bao thought, remembering, there is that time in your life, when you are young and everything seems possible, and you want it all; you are simply bursting with desire. You make love all night because you want things so much.

He said, "Another way of rescuing the concept of reincarnation is simply to think of the species as the organism. The organism survives, and has a collective consciousness of itself—that's history, or language, or the twisting ladder structuring our brains—and it doesn't really matter what happens to any one cell of this body. In fact their deaths are necessary for the body to stay healthy and go on, it's a matter of making room for new cells. And if we think of it that way, then it might increase feelings of solidarity and obligation to others. It makes it clearer that if there is part of the body that is suffering, and if at the same time another part commandeers the mouth and laughs and proclaims that everything is really fine, dancing a jig like the lost Christians as their flesh fell off— then we understand more clearly that this creature-species or species-creature is insane, and cannot face its own sickness-unto-death. Seen in that sense, more people might understand that the organism must try to keep itself healthy throughout its whole body."

The young woman was shaking her head. "But that's not reincarnation either. That's not what it means."

Bao shrugged, gave up. "I know. I know what you mean, I think; it seems there should be something that endures of us. And I myself have sometimes felt things. One time, down at Gold Gate . . ." He shook his head. "But there is no way to know. Reincarnation is a story we tell; then in the end it's the story itself that is the reincarnation."

Over time Bao came to understand that teaching too was a kind of reincarnation, in that years passed, and students came and went, new young people all the time, but always the same age, taking the same class; the class under the oak trees, reincarnated. He began to enjoy that aspect of it. He would start the first class by saying, "Look, here we are again." They never knew what to make of it; same response, every time.

He learned, among other things, that teaching was the most rigorous form of learning. He learned to learn more from his students than they did from him; like so many other things, it was the reverse of what it seemed to be, and colleges existed to bring together groups of young people to teach some chosen few of their elders the things that they knew about life, that the old teachers had been in danger of forgetting.

So Bao loved his students, and studied them assiduously. Most of them, he found, believed in reincarnation; it was what they had been taught at home, even when they hadn't been given explicit religious instruction. It was part of the culture, an idea that kept coming back. So they brought it up, and he talked about it with them, in a conversation reincarnated many times. Over time the students added to his growing internal list of ways reincarnation was true: that you might really come back as another life; that the various periods of one's life were karmic reincarnations; that every morning you reawakened to consciousness newly, and thus are reincarnated every day to a new life.

Bao liked all of these. The last one he tried to live in his daily existence, paying attention to his morning garden as if he had never seen it before, marveling at the strangeness and beauty of it. In his classes he tried to talk about history newly, thinking things through yet again, not allowing himself to say anything that he had ever said before; this was hard, but interesting. One day in one of the ordinary classrooms (it was winter, and raining), he said, "What's hardest to catch is daily life. This is what I think rarely gets written down, or even remembered by those who did it—what you did on the days when you did the ordinary things, how it felt doing it, the small variations time and again, until years have passed. A matter of repetitions, or almost-repetitions. Nothing, in other words, that could be easily encoded into the usual forms of emplotment, not dharma or chaos, or even tragedy or comedy. Just . . . habit."

One intense young man with thick black eyebrows replied, as if contradicting him, "Everything happens only once!"

And that too he had to remember. There was no doubt at all that it was true. Everything happens only once!

And so, eventually, one particular day came: first day of spring, Day One of Year 87, a festival day, first morning of this life, first year of this world; and Bao got up early with Gao and went out with some others, to hide colored eggs and wrapped candy in the grass of the lawn and meadow, and on the streambank. This was the ritual in their ring of cottages; every New Year's Day the adults would go out and hide eggs that had been colored the day before, and candy wrapped in vibrantly colored metallic wrapping, and at the appointed hour of the morning all the children of the neighborhood would be unleashed on their hunt, baskets in hand, the older ones racing forward pouncing on finds to pile in their baskets, the youngest ones staggering dreamily from one great discovery to the next. Bao had learned to love this morning, especially that last walk downstream to the meeting point, after all the eggs and candy had been hidden: he strolled through the high wet grass with his spectacles taken off, sometimes, so that the real flowers and their pure colors were mixed in with the artificial colors of the eggs and the candy wrappers, and the meadow and streambank became like a painting or a dream, a hallucinated meadow and streambank, with more colors, and stranger colors, than any nature had ever made on her own, all dotting the omnipresent and surging vivid green.

So he made this walk again, as he had for so many years now, the sky a perfect blue above, like another colored egg over them. The air was cool, the dew heavy on the grass. His feet were wet. The glimpsed candy wrappers broke in his peripheral vision, cyanic and fuschia and lime and copper, sparkier even than in previous years, he thought. Puta Creek was running high, purling over the salmon weirs. A doe and fawn stood in one brake like statues of themselves, watching him pass.

He came to the gathering place and sat to watch the kids race about in their egghunt, shouting and squealing. He thought, If you can see that all the kids are happy, then maybe things are going to be all right after all.

In any case, this hour of pleasure. The adults stood around drinking green tea and coffee, eating cakes and hard-boiled eggs, shaking hands or embracing. "Happy new year! Happy new year!" Bao sat down in a low chair to watch their faces.

One of the three-year-olds he sometimes baby-sat came wandering by, distracted by the contents of her wicker basket. "Look!" she said when she saw him. "Egg!"

She plucked a red egg from her basket and shoved it in his face. He pulled back his head warily; like many of the children in the neighborhood, this one had come into the world in the avatar of a complete maniac, and it would not be unlike her to whack him on the forehead with the egg just to see what would happen.

But this morning she was serene; she merely held the egg out between them for their mutual inspection, both rapt in contemplation of it. It had been steeped in the vinegar-and-dye solution for a long time, and was as vividly red as the sky was blue. Red curve in a blue curve, red and blue together—

"Very nice!" Bao said, pulling his head back to see it better. "A red egg, that means happiness."

"Egg!"

"Yes, that too. Red egg!"

"You can have it," she said to him, and put the egg in his hand.

"Thank you!"

She wandered on. Bao looked at the egg; it was redder than he could remember the dye being, mottled in the way eggshells got when dyed, but everywhere deeply red.

The breakfast party was coming to a close, the kids sitting around busily chewing some of their treasure, the adults taking the paper plates inside. All at peace. Bao wished for a second that Kung had lived to see this scene. He had fought for something like this little age of peace, fought so full of anger and hilarity; it seemed only fair that he should have gotten to see it. But—fair. No. No, there would be another Kung in the village someday, perhaps that little girl, suddenly so intent and serious. Certainly they were all repeated again and again, the whole cast: in every group a Ka and a Ba, as in Old Red Ink's anthology, Ka always complaining with the kaw of the crow, the cough of the cat, the cry of coyote, kaw, kaw, that fundamental protest; and then Ba always Ba, the banal baa of the water buffalo, the sound of the plow bound to the earth, the bleat of hope and fear, the bone inside. The one who missed the missing Ka, and felt the loss keenly, if intermittently, distracted by life; but also the one who had to do whatever possible to keep things going in that absence. Go on! The world was changed by the Kungs, but then the Baos had to try to hold it together, baaing their way along. All of them together playing their parts, performing their tasks in some dharma they never quite understood.

Right now his task was to teach. Third meeting of this particular class, when they began to get into things. He was looking forward to it.

He took the red egg back with him to his cottage, put it on his desk. He put his papers in his shoulder bag, said good-bye to Gao, got on his old bike and pedaled down the path to the college. The bike path followed Puta Creek, and the new leaves on the trees shaded the path, so that its asphalt was still wet with dew. The flowers in the grass looked like colored eggs and candy wrappers, everything stuffed with its own color, the sky overhead unusually clear and dark for the valley, almost cobalt. The opaque water in the stream was the color of apple jade. Valley oaks as big as villages overhung its banks.

He parked his bike, and seeing a gang of snow monkeys in the tree overhead, locked it to a stand. These monkeys enjoyed rolling bikes down the bank into the stream, two or three cooperating to launch them upright on their course. It had happened to Bao's bike more than once, before he purchased a lock and chain.

He walked on, downstream to the round picnic table where he always instructed his spring classes to meet him. Never had the greens of grass and leaf been so green before, they made him a bit unsteady on his feet. He recalled the little girl and her egg, the peace of the little celebration, everyone doing what they always did on this first day. His class would be the same as well. It always came down to this. There they were under the giant oak tree, gathering around the round table, and he would sit down with them and tell them as much as he could of what he had learned, trying to get it across to them, giving them what little portion of his experience he could. He would say to them, "Come here, sit down, I have some stories to tell, about how people go on."

But he was there to learn too. And this time, under the jade and emerald leaves, he saw that there was a striking young woman who had joined them, a Travancori student he had not seen before, dark skinned, black haired, thick eyebrowed, eyes flashing as she glanced briefly up at him from across the picnic table. A sharp glance, suffused with a profound skepticism; by that look alone he could tell that she did not believe in teachers, that she did not trust them, that she was not prepared to believe a single thing he said. He would have a lot to learn from her.

He smiled and sat down, waited for them to grow still. "I see we have someone new joining us," he said, indicating the young woman with a polite nod. The other students looked at her curiously. "Why don't you introduce yourself?"

"Hello," the young woman said. "My name is Kali."